THE
OPENED
TOMB

A Novel

JULIANNA MECHOWSKA

Cover artwork, interior design, and formatting generated using AI via OpenAI's ChatGPT and designed and customized by Julianna Mechowska

V1, First Paperback edition: July 2025

Paperback ISBN: 979-8-9992810-0-5
Printed by Amazon KDP in the USA
eBook ISBN: 979-8-9992810-1-2

Inspired by *Dracula* by Bram Stoker (1897). This text is in the public domain and may be freely used, shared, adapted, or reproduced in any form by any person without permission or restriction. No rights are reserved.

In affiliation with

ESTD Asterid 2025
AN IMPRINT OF BLUE DANDELION PRESS, LLC

Blue Dandelion Press, LLC
https://www.bluedandelionpress.com/

This work contains sensitive material that may be distressing to some readers, including **suicide, suicidal ideation, infant harm, attempted sexual assault, occult themes, death,** and **graphic bodily harm**. Reader discretion is advised.

+   J   M   J   +

CONTENTS

PART I

Semblance of a Man

If a man walks in the day, he doesn't stumble,
because he sees the light of the world.
But if a man walks in the night, he stumbles,
because the light isn't in him.

John 11:9-10

Prologue

ENIGMA

Diary of Isadora L. Kane

22 January

Well, all has been decided. On 29 April, I will leave for Romania on my first official teaching assignment abroad. I admit that I am worried about what I will find there as it seems more trouble than it's worth.

When I applied for this job, I wasn't quite expecting that my first assignment would be a special request. My recruiter even commented saying how uncommon it was. I will be teaching a grown, middle-aged man who calls himself Count Vladislav Negrescu. My student is a rather particular individual. He wishes to practice his English in depth for the purpose of better understanding business and marketing in Western countries. It seems a big waste of time that he would be willing to pay such a substantial sum for me to fly all the way to his home in the Carpathian Mountains, no less, to teach him. Perhaps he is eccentric though I wonder how genuine his interests are.

Another thing that confuses me is his title of 'Count'. As I understand it, Romania has not had a monarchy for decades, so how does he have this title? With the communist regime that followed, and onto the current republic, would they have permitted his family to keep that title? I doubt it.

I have expressed my concerns about this assignment to my superiors and they only brushed me off. One even told me that the Count is a trustworthy man and has interests are in more areas of study than just business. That's fair enough, but it doesn't satisfy or comfort me as to why I was chosen. There is so little known about him but he passed all background checks and other extensive interviews with flying colors. Maybe I'm just paranoid about this because I'll be traveling so far away for a year to teach a man I know nothing about and for reasons I find questionable. Just in case, I have vowed to myself to write frequently about my stay with him. I will make every effort to keep this record true.

There are only three months left to prepare myself and learn what I can about Romania and its customs. I sure have my work cut out for me. The next I write here will be upon my arrival there. I pray that I'm making the right decision and that I won't come to regret this by the time it's too late.

Chapter One
THE DRAGON

30 April

Morning…

After many hours of flying with little sleep, I have finally arrived in Romania. Needless to say, after 12 hours of being packed into an airplane, surrounded by strangers, I was in a grumpy mood when we landed. It was morning, and although I was exhausted, I willed myself into action to fetch my baggage and try to navigate my way through the Henri Coandă airport. With my limited Romanian, I somehow managed to find the appropriate departure area.

Despite the earliness of the morning, the number of people waiting to find their contacts surprised me. I searched the signs to find my name, but couldn't find it in the lineup. I panicked at the thought that they had forgotten my arrival date.

I was getting discouraged when, from right behind me, I heard, "*Domnişoară* Kane?"

The closeness of the voice made me jump, and I turned to face it. Inches in front of me was a man who appeared to be around my age, perhaps a bit older, with light brown hair and a fair complexion. Although dawn had just broken, he wore dark sunglasses along with a formal driver's suit.

I felt slightly flustered to be called "Miss" in Romanian, but I composed myself and confirmed with him who I am.

"I am Dumitru," he spoke slowly to articulate his words through his accent. "Count Negrescu's driver. He instructs me to have you breakfast, then we will go to his home."

Something in me hesitated as he gestured to the road lined with vehicles. Thanking him, I forced myself to go with the flow and agreed to his offer of breakfast. Once we had gotten to the car, which appeared to be a well-armored vehicle with heavy tinted windows, I settled into the back seat. Little light pierced through the dark tint, and to my surprise, I was served breakfast right then. On fine china, I was presented with a diverse meal of traditional Romanian breakfast foods, all at the appropriate temperatures. The tea was piping hot, the fruit cool and refreshing in comparison to the terrible food that I had on the flight. It was all so elegantly laid out on the service table that was built into the vehicle's seat.

When we had left the airport, I asked this Dumitru how long it was until we would reach the Count's residence, and he grimly mentioned that it was about a three-hour drive. So, I sit here, sipping spiced tea alone in dead silence with a strange man who wears sunglasses when there is no sun. I shouldn't sleep, but I am exhausted.

Later…

Despite my resolve to stay awake, I did eventually fall asleep. It must have been two hours before I awoke again, startled by the realization that I had indeed fallen unconscious. Discreetly as I could, I frantically reevaluated my surroundings. The driver was still in his place, cruising steadily along. I breathed a short sigh of relief.

The scene outside, however, caught my attention. We are in the middle of nowhere, literally. On either side of the road, dense forest crowded up to the pavement, nearly overtaking it. Peering between the thinly trunked trees, I can hardly see with as little sunlight as there is. Another thing that disturbs me is that we are the only car on this road, which seemed to stretch for miles along winding mountain and valley passes. I am becoming more and more anxious since it is most evident that we are isolated.

"*Domnișoară*," Dumitru's voice suddenly broke that dead silence, making me jump again. "Did you sleep well?"

I had to search for an answer. "Uh, yes, well enough."

"We are only an hour away from the Count's residence." I saw him eyeing me from beneath his sunglasses in the rear-view mirror. He must have been watching me the entire time, as the mirror had been directly trained on me and not on the road behind us. "It won't be long now."

My apprehension about my situation resurfaces at the thought that I am only an *hour* away. Before I came out to this place, I tried looking up my student on the web to find only some obscure explanation about the Count's royal lineage, which stretches back hundreds of years. There was nothing about him specifically that I could find, especially no photo. On paper, at least, he seems to be a kind and genuine man. Logically, one would say he lives out in the middle of nowhere because this is his ancestral home. But still, my paranoia leaves me on edge. So far from home, all alone yet not alone.

I hope my work will drown out that paranoia and that my fears are only the results of my imagination. I'm assigned to be here for a year, so perhaps it won't be as dreadful as I'm feeling that it may be. I just have to keep reminding myself to keep reason at the forefront and to remain kind, understanding, open-minded, and respectful. This is my first international assignment from my prestigious organization, and I have to show that I can do all that is expected of me.

Afternoon…

What a day. After another hour of that silent, awkward drive, we finally reached the Count's residence. Passing through high mountain paths, I watched my surroundings intently, looking for any sign of civilization. I found none. On either side of the road was nothing but gnarled trees and rocks, and a terrifying mist that remained low against the ground, giving the place an eerie feeling. A few times, I could have sworn that I had seen something dart out between the trees in the distance, only to be concealed again by the time my eyes got a chance to catch it.

Eventually, we reached an open pass, and to my awe, there stood a tall castle, erected alone against the cloudy sky. It was an ancient fortress, with three sides etched into a cliff that dropped down into a deep river valley. It is truly impregnable, with thick stone walls and old battlements at the ready.

We entered the gates and came around to the front. The driver promptly opened the door for me after we had parked, and I stepped out into the fresh mountain air. Under a compulsion of pure curiosity, I stared up in wonder at the monstrous structure, worn with age and disuse. My creative mind was whirling when Dumitru passed me with my luggage in hand, adding a stern order for me to follow him.

He went up to the massive doors, and opening a smaller one to the side, stepped aside for me to enter first. "Enter the house of your own accord, *Domnișoară*."

The way he said it unnerved me, but I thanked him and entered. The scene before me was shocking, being heavily layered with dust. If the Count is such a wealthy man, where were the maids and butlers? The house staff should have been there to greet me, even the master of the house himself, but there was no one. It felt so void of life. I was uneasy and flinched when the door closed heavily behind me, and the bolt was latched.

"Where is the Count?" I asked timidly.

"His Excellency is out on business and will return at evening time. Until then, you are to rest and settle into your rooms. Lunch will be served in three hours." Dumitru rambled off quickly as he ascended the steps with me close on his heels.

Before I knew it, he had brought me to a wooden door on the second floor and opened it, leading me inside. I poked my head in sheepishly, surprised to find these rooms in a much more livable condition. There was no dust, and the whole space looked to be bright and fresh compared to the other parts of this castle. The exquisite woodwork, obviously ancient, gleamed with a recent thorough polish.

The sitting room, which is what I take it to be, was cheerful and airy. Beyond it is another door that leads to a strange octagonal-shaped room, and then onto my bedroom with a small fireplace and a private bath attached to it. I am surprised that there is a private bath, equipped with a Western toilet, bathtub, and sink. Not to mention that between these two rooms, electric lights were everywhere. Lamps rest on tables as well as overhead artificial lighting. I was in the lap of modern luxury and also in Romania's medieval age.

"Lunch will be served here in your sitting room." My driver explained. "You must not leave your rooms until you see the Count, as he will give you the proper rules for living in his house. When he comes, although it may seem strange to you Americans, you will bow and refer to him as 'my lord'. After that address, 'sir' or 'Count'. This is the way it is done here. He is a hospitable man, but do not overstep yourself. Be warned, or you will deal with me."

The threat of his last sentence made me uneasy, but wishing to be polite, I said I understood and thanked him for everything. After a curt nod, adding that if I needed anything that there is a servant's bell pull in the corner of the room, he left.

I decided not to sleep even though my jetlag begged me to, and tried to keep myself busy organizing my things before I explored my new surroundings. Although foreign, I think I can easily get used to them. Eventually, I settled into a comfy chair in front of the fire in my sitting room with my computer. I guess time flew by, for to my surprise, there was a knock at the door and Dumitru entered with a pushcart. I was baffled that the driver should be serving me a meal, but didn't ask questions, and thanked him. He only responded as a forced courtesy. Before he left, I asked him what time he would be leaving to get the Count from his business, so I would know when he wouldn't be available if I needed something. He stammered out some answer about after dinner, then left immediately. I am left perplexed since I have no idea when dinner is.

Luckily, however, lunch consists of a variety of small sandwiches, fruits, and a carafe of ice water. The carafe and drinking glasses are crystal, the plates are fine hand-painted china, and the utensils are gold. The display was quite pleasant, and I wondered if I could speak to the chef to thank him for making me such a wonderful meal. But of course, I'm not allowed to leave my rooms…not that I would even dare to roam those eerie halls without a guide.

Evening…

For the next hour I felt restless, having nothing to do but sit and twiddle my thumbs like an idiot. I tried to work on my lesson plans, but I was so tired that I was seeing double. I took a 30-minute nap, but still awoke tired and wearier. After Dumitru brought tea, about 3 pm, I settled myself to take a bath and prepare for my first meeting with the Count.

Sadly, there was no shower-bath combination, so I had to run a bath to wash, and then wash my hair separately. Anyway, I dressed and reapplied my makeup and redid my hair. First impressions are more important than anything in this case.

Dinner was at 6 pm, and I was given another superb meal. I can only guess that Dumitru left after serving me dinner to retrieve the Count, since he didn't return afterward to pick up the finished plates until much later. By that time, the sun was setting, so I went to one of the deep inset windows in the sitting room and looked out into the precipice. The sunlight shone pink against the surrounding mountain range, and the clouds were distinct hues of orange and purple. It was a beautiful sight, and I was transfixed by it until I was jolted back into reality by the distant howling of wolves. The hair on the back of my neck stood up and a shiver wracked my spine.

Despite the howling, which continued sporadically, I remained at the window to watch the sunlight die away and the night encroach. Once the sun was gone, the stars and moon were finally visible, casting a pale white over the mountains. The contrasting shadows appeared ominously black, sending the scene into a colorless scape. Frustrated, I checked the time, which was nearly 8 pm, and wondered when the Count would come to see me. Just then, as if on cue, there was a knock at the door.

I sprang up and went to my chair before managing to stutter out. "E-Enter."

I watched the door float open, and a man entered from the shadows beyond the threshold. I was taken aback by him. I had imagined an older man with gray hair and a dated fashion sense. Instead, he appears to be in his early 40s, with wavy, rich brown hair that goes to his shoulders. He wore normal clothes, just a black dress shirt, blazer, and pants, with eyes a most piercing brown-red I have ever seen. And when those eyes set upon me, they saw through my very being, making the air in my chest hang up in my throat.

The man smiled widely, his white teeth gleaming in the firelight, and all at once greeted me with the warmest affection. "My dear Miss Kane!" He came forward in only a few steps, grasping my limp hands and shaking them. "I am Count Vladislav Negrescu. I am so pleased to make your acquaintance. I hope your journey went well and that you have rested."

He radiated with excitement, although I noticed immediately his hands, though large and strong, were fearfully cold. Gathering my wits, I bowed my head. "Thank you, my lord. It's a pleasure to meet you as well."

"Please, just call me Count." He waved my formality away. "I know titles may seem odd to you, but I hope you will oblige me."

I told him I understood perfectly, and his eyes smiled with mirth. His energy, his charisma were intoxicating. "Good, good! Please, let us sit and talk. I shall not keep you long, as I know you must be tired still."

After both of us took our seats in the two chairs that faced the fireplace, he barraged me with so many questions that I can hardly remember what they were. It was mostly a long series of small talk that lasted an hour and a half. He mostly asked questions about me, and of course, I forgot every single aspect of my life. I told him of my home and educational experience. Of course, my story paled in comparison to his. The Count explained some about his castle's history, family line, but only bits and pieces about himself. I was fascinated by it all and hung on his every word. His English, I observed as I listened to him, is perfect as he speaks without any error in grammar or intonation. His accent is peculiar and sounds like a mix of Received Pronunciation with the slightest hint of Romanian. If I didn't know any better, I would think him to be a native English speaker.

When a clock sweetly chimed 9:30 pm, he changed the conversation. "Ah, it is getting quite late. I can see you are barely awake. No problem, you have been through much today. Sleep for as long as you wish tomorrow, no need for an early rise. My duties usually keep me away during the day, so in the evenings we will begin the lessons. If you need anything at all, Dumitru will be here to await your every need. Before I go, however, there are certain things I must explain."

When I asked what he meant, he stood and meandered closer to the fire. "This house is very old, and there are many old memories in it. You are allowed to go anywhere you wish within this house, except for where the doors are locked. When you are about the house, do not accidentally fall asleep in some 'nook' or 'cranny'; only sleep in your rooms. This house is a maze, so I ask you this for your own good. Down the hall, there is a library that is at your disposal, and it is there you will conduct my lessons."

"I will do as you ask, Count. Thank you for explaining." I said as I watched him from behind. I hadn't noticed it before since we were sitting down, but he is quite pleasing to the eye, especially with his back turned.

"One more thing," he added, turning to me. "I also ask that you never leave this castle at night. I doubt that you could, as everything will be locked, and this place is a fortress, but there are creatures of the night out there that would find you a tasty treat, my dear."

His humor on such a subject was unsettling to me, especially with those wolves, but I smiled and nodded. "Trust me, sir, I wouldn't go out there even if my life depended on it."

The Count grinned widely. Coming to me, he took my hand and kissed it. "It relieves me to hear that. Goodnight and pleasant dreams, my new friend and teacher."

And with that, he left, closing the door behind him. I heard a click and knew it was the lock bolting shut. The sound made me quiver for some reason, but I rationalized it as he didn't want me wandering around at night. It is his house, so I shook it off. I guess I will have to trust him implicitly since he holds me in the palm of his hand. I don't particularly like the idea of having him and *only* him as the ultimate authority to rely upon, but I will have to grin and bear it for now. I may say a rosary for thanks for my safe arrival here, and that those things lurking outside don't find their way in.

1 May
Name Day
Afternoon…

I slept for nearly 12 hours and woke quite refreshed. Dressing and readying myself quickly, I went to ring for Dumitru to bring me brunch but found a disassembled breakfast on the table in my sitting room waiting for me. Nestled on ice were corked carafes of milk and juice, and on a small heater, warm coffee. There was another arrangement of a variety of oatmeal and fruit. I was relieved that it had been waiting for me, so I sat down and ate. I tried to decide what to do for the whole day while the Count was away, and guessed I could venture to go to the library and explore there. I was hesitant to leave the safe confines of my room, but I knew I shouldn't be afraid since the Count had permitted me to explore at my leisure.

I rang for Dumitru after I was finished with brunch and waited for him to come to pick up the dishes. Not too long after, there was a knock and he entered, a scowl on his face. "Yes, *Domnișoară?*"

"Good morning, Dumitru," I smiled, ignoring his foul mood. "I am finished with the dishes —"

"Very well." He snapped back and came to place all the fine utensils on the cart.

I frowned but was resolute to make friends with him nonetheless. "Is it alright if I use the library until the Count returns?"

"If my Master says you may, you may." Dumitru didn't bother to look in my direction and only focused on his work.

I was put off by his shortness, but pressed further. "Is the chef in the kitchen today? I would love to —"

"No." He eyed me sharply.

The forcefulness of his answer made me wince, and my brows furrowed as he began to wheel the cart out of the room. "Forgive me if I have insulted you in some way. Please tell me what I did so that I may apologize."

Just as he reached the door, he stopped and turned back to me. Again, those eyes of his, which are a stunning gray, narrowed as he spoke. "You have done nothing to offend me. I know you *Westerners* don't know *our* ways. Don't interfere, or you will find yourself in a bad place."

"What's that supposed to mean?"

"You'll know when you get there." And without another word, he closed the door behind him.

Later...

After gathering my work, I went down the dim hall to the library. I was utterly dumbfounded at the sheer size of the room and the quantity of books. Setting my things on the table, I was drawn to the stacks. The books are from all different times and in all different languages. Of course, the majority are in Romanian, but I saw others in English, German, Latin, Greek, Russian, and other Slavic languages. I dared not touch the more ancient books bound in leather, and the ones I did take out to examine, I did so as gently as I could. As I went through the rows, I noticed a large variety of subjects: chemistry, botany, geology, mathematics, history, language, geography, business, law, and so many, many more. All of the books are in pristine condition for their age, although covered in a layer of dust.

After exploring the stacks, I went around the room to look at the portraits hanging on the walls. They were all relatives of the Count, I could tell due to their resemblance to him in one way or another. There is one, definitely hundreds of years old, that looks like it could be his twin brother. How nice it must be to know one's family stretching back centuries. From last night, I know he is very proud of his heritage, and I feel a bit envious of it. He displays the portraits of his ancestors with such honor, meanwhile, I don't even have a picture of my parents with me.

Well, I ought to prepare thoroughly for our first lecture tonight.

Evening...

I went over the lecture many times in my head before Dumitru served dinner at 6 pm, when he informed me that the Count would be arriving within the hour. This evening, the dying light that filtered in through the high windows bathed the entire library in an intense shade of blood-orange. Then, as what seems to be the proper time, those damned wolves began howling again. It was much quieter there than in my rooms, but still, the eeriness of the lonely sound made me uneasy.

A knock at the door made me cry out and jump, but it was just Dumitru, coming in to light the gas lamps. He didn't even bother to acknowledge me, but completed his work in silence, just as the

Count strode in through the open door. As yesterday, his face beamed as he came to me, grasping my hands, all the meanwhile saying, "Oh Miss Kane, how are you today? I trust you had a good rest? Please, tell me of your day before we begin."

I told him I was very well, and that all day I had been captivated by his collection of books and wonderful portraits of his family.

He was pleased that I was getting along so well. "I hope in time you can come to see my home as your home, Miss Kane."

I thanked him, and soon after, we began our work. After explaining my plan for the 'semester', my expectations, and what would be required of him, he was content enough with the workload, which honestly, isn't much at all.

The lesson itself lasted a little over an hour, just as any college lecture on such a specific topic would. He is a very astute student, as I expected him to be, with a genius that I guess runs in his family. He absorbed concepts like a sponge, and I have to say I was very impressed.

By the time everything was over, I was quite exhausted. After asking if he had any questions about his assignment, to which he replied he didn't, I began to pack my things.

"You are leaving already?" He frowned.

I half-lied to him. "I assume you'd be tired after a full day's work."

"Trust me, I am far from tired," he crossed his arms and sat back in the chair. "And I insist on your staying for a cup of tea with me. All day I have been looking forward to having a conversation with you since, around here, foreigners are 'few and far between', as is your expression."

I could hardly say no, and although I wanted to go back to my room to sleep, I returned to my seat and accepted his offer.

"Wonderful!" He stood abruptly and went to the cord near the doorway and pulled it. "I have this exquisite Earl Grey that I know you will love."

In no time at all, Dumitru opened the door, and the Count ordered a pot of tea with sweet cakes. We were left alone in the library yet again, and I shrank back into my chair. He returned to his seat, and we chatted about Romania more until tea came. Before I could even examine the lovely display, the Count poured me a cup, as a good host would. I wasn't exactly in any mood for it, but I accepted the cup graciously along with one of the small pastries.

Afterward, the conversation turned to tea and then to England. I asked if he had ever been there, but he replied that he had some time ago, but that it hadn't been a pleasant experience. The Count didn't seem to want to go into the details, so I didn't press further. Instead, we dove deeply into a conversation about English history. We spoke on it for some time until something bewildering happened.

As we conversed, I had reached across the table for a sweet cake when I heard this low hiss come from the Count. I tensed and looked at him, puzzled. The sight of him was fearsome, and his eyes were redder as they squinted at me. The Count had almost recoiled back into his seat, his jaw clenching, as he stared openly at my chest. Looking down, I saw nothing. Perplexed, I blinked. "What…what is it?"

He didn't respond, but then realizing I had said something, he visibly relaxed and composed himself. Clearing his throat, he straightened. "Forgive me, Miss Kane, for my rude reaction. I have no love for talismans, especially ones of *that* nature. If you would not mind, please put it away."

"Talisman?" I looked at myself again, seeing nothing. "Forgive me, I don't understand what you're talking about."

The Count's mouth flattened into a thin line before he muttered. "The symbol of your…'faith'…"

Blinking, I reached for my cross that had fallen out of my shirt. I paused, wondering why it would offend him so, but still I stuffed it away behind my collar. "I'm sorry it upset you, Count."

"You should not put faith in such…" He added, his expression visibly calmed as the cross disappeared.

I furrowed my brow, offended. Biting my lip, I said nothing to him, not wishing to fuel the flames of the sensitive subject. I would let him have his opinion and keep my own to myself. I plucked the little cake off the platter and set it on my plate and chose not to respond.

After a bit of silence, he grinned at me. "You hide your offense well, Miss Kane."

"Count, you have every right to your beliefs and opinions, just as I have every right to mine." I smiled and then took a bite of the pastry.

The Count's grin widened. "You are right. Since you are dear to me, my friend, I will allow it within my house."

Swallowing, I put up another smile. "I appreciate that very much. I will try my best not to offend you again."

He thanked me cordially for my efforts, but continued. "Let us not depart in tension, my friend. I did not tell you of my personal beliefs before you entered my house, so let this stress of our miscommunication pass. Agreed?"

He gave me his hand to shake.

The Count sounded to me very sincere in his wish, and so I nodded and shook his hand. It was foolish to have tension over a difference in religious views when our teacher-student relationship has nothing to do with religion at all. I guess I was touched by his gesture of peace. "Agreed. Well said, sir."

Rising from his chair, his hand still in mine, he kissed it gently before letting it go. A chill ran up my arm. "I will bid you goodnight, for I can see you are tired. Have a pleasant rest, Miss Kane."

I hadn't realized how tense I was, as my body seemed to melt back into its normal, relaxed shape when he left. The clock chimed 9:30 pm, and my heavy eyes reminded me it was time for bed. However, I noticed as I gathered my things that his tea had remained untouched for the entire time, and not a single pastry had been eaten. What a waste.

Chapter Two
BARRIERS

6 May

Morning...

I haven't written in a few days since things have been quite repetitious...almost *too* repetitious. Each morning I awake around 8 or 9 am, dress, go to the library, and work until the Count arrives in the late evening. The only diverse aspects have been the meals and a different lecture covering a different topic. There has been nothing new. Dumitru still treats me with disdain and hardly ever speaks to me, only to say something mildly rude or offensive. My only reprieve from the grueling days has been the conversations with the Count after my lectures.

Things around here seem too perfectly timed. Everything is regulated from the meal times, to when Dumitru lights the lamps in the library, the howling of the wolves at dusk, which always seems to be a little after 7 pm. After that, their echoed calls in the night are sporadic and random. However, oddly enough, I've gotten used to their regimented howl, and it reminds me that the Count will soon appear for his lesson if I lose track of time.

Concerning the Count, he seems to have gone past any offense that I had done him after the incident with my cross. He is his usual cheerful self, always eager to learn and converse, and we talk about a variety of subjects that are quite nonsense compared to the grand scheme of things. The more I speak to him, the more I see how out-of-touch he is with the world. I guess being so isolated like he is, reaching out past the boundaries of his native land is a big deal.

There was one morning a few days ago that I couldn't sleep and sat at the window in my room which overlooks the courtyard. I wanted to watch and see when the Count left in the morning. I began my watch at about 5 am, but nothing happened. I wonder if perhaps he left earlier than 5 am and what his business is that occupies his entire day. His mysteriousness makes me question many things. But, I digress…

Since it's Saturday, there will be no lesson tonight. I feel a bit sad about it, since I've started to look forward to them. I don't know what I will do with the extra time. I wish I could contact my family and friends to let them know I'm doing well. But, with no access to a telephone, cell service, or even Wi-Fi, I am left with only letters. Perhaps I could ask the Count for envelopes and stamps?

God, it feels like these walls are closing in around me. I have to keep cool. It's only been six days…

Later…

When Dumitru came for my dishes, I asked him about posting letters to my family, and if it would be possible for him to send them. I assured him, if he wished, I would pay him for his service. He only put his nose up in the air and spoke. "Ask the Count."

"Surely the Count doesn't need to be bothered with such things." I tried to reason with him. "All I need are envelopes and stamps."

"Ask the Count." Dumitru repeated, stacking more dishes on the cart.

I bit my tongue, wanting to snap at him for his lack of empathy. Swallowing hard, I let out a breath. "And when will I see the Count? Monday?"

"He will come to you in your sitting room at the usual time after you have dinner." He explained plainly. "Ask him then. Don't ask me for any favors, *Domnișoară.*"

I slouched, defeated.

And, as usual, he didn't say a word and left.

There is simply no getting through to that man. He is just a brick wall that I have been trying to talk to. A part of me wishes I could wring his neck for it. I know I shouldn't say it, but he's such a pain. I guess I'll compile a list of things to ask the Count and then sit on my hands until sometime after 7 pm!

…

After tea I went to the library for a change of scenery and to compose a list of requests and questions for the Count. I tried to keep it short but I found myself listing a page and a half of things. So, I weeded out the least important ones. After I was finished, I was just leaving the library when a spark of curiosity overtook me, and I stopped, looking towards the stairs. Instantly my heart raced in apprehension at the thought of exploring the castle further. There was a chance of getting lost, but my feet walked to the landing and looked down.

There was little light in the winding staircase and I gulped, fearing to take a step. Just as I thought my feet would move, I heard the rapid clicking of footsteps ascending the stairwell. They were coming fast, and I panicked. Turning quickly to run to my room, I ran into something hard. It really felt like a wall and I cried out in shock, which really was a scream. Something grabbed my arms and I tried instinctively to wrench away, but I was held firmly in place. I looked up, and to my genuine surprise, the Count stood before me, grasping my arms to keep me from falling backward.

"Count!" I exclaimed.

The surprise on my face must have been amusing, for he chuckled as he released me. "Forgive me, Miss Kane, I thought I had made my presence known."

I was just about to say something when the hurried steps behind me reached the landing, and Dumitru, pale with alarm, asked in Romanian what had happened. The look on his face was something I found amusing. He must have come running when he heard me scream, as he was panting hard.

"Everything is alright, Dumitru." The Count smiled, showing his teeth. "Miss Kane simply had a fright."

Looking at the Count, then back at me, he nodded. "If you say so, Master."

"Are you well?" The Count turned his attention back to me once Dumitru had left.

"Yes, you just scared me." I took in a deep breath and placed my hand over my erratic heart. "I didn't see you."

"Forgive me again." He repeated with a slight bow of his head.

I had to reassure him multiple times that I was fine, and once he seemed satisfied with that, I nervously changed the subject. "What are you doing here? I thought you were on business?"

"I came back early," he said, eyeing the crumpled piece of paper in my hand. "Working on something?"

"No," I pursed my lips. "They are just some questions I have for you."

His eyebrow arched in interest. "What kind of questions?"

"Oh," my voice shook as I stuffed the paper into my pocket. "That can wait until later. Uh, please, don't let me detain you. Dumitru said you will see me after dinner. It can all wait until then."

He hummed. "If you insist."

With a quick goodbye, I slipped back to my room and shut the door gently behind me. Coming to my senses, I could feel the resonating pain on my upper arms from where he held me in a death grip. What a fool I was for not watching where I was going. I must have looked like a complete idiot to him.

I sat there for quite a while thinking of the series of events, wondering where he may have come from. When I exited the library, one would think I would have seen him coming since the hall was well lit. Had I been that careless in what I was doing? The only thing I could think of was that he had materialized out of thin air, which is impossible.

Late evening…

When Dumitru came with my supper, he didn't acknowledge me at all. He came and went without a word, and although I didn't have much of an appetite, I forced down some of the food. I found myself wishing I had asked him if they had any brandy, anything to make the chill of the incident from earlier go away.

I just finished all that I could when he returned to take the plates. At first, he didn't say a word, but noticing that not all my food was gone, his brow furrowed. "The food displeased you?"

I shook my head and answered flatly. "No, it was lovely. I'm just…not very hungry."

To my surprise, he asked quite gently. "Are you ill?"

I told him that I wasn't and thanked him for asking. Silence crept in as I watched him work before I finally dared to pipe up and inquire. "I know you said don't ask you for favors, but do you have any brandy?"

"No." Dumitru snapped, his tone was unusually more vicious that it made me wince, and then he added. "The Master does not drink."

I sighed, rolling my eyes. "Right…sorry I asked."

I didn't care to watch him go this time. It's odd how he puts forth this air of indifference, but cares all too much underneath; that is, if what I saw on his face was concern. And men say women are hard to read…

I went to the window and climbed up on the sill to watch the colors of the sunset. I waited, expecting the howling of the wolves, but it never came, even when the colors faded, and dusk was giving way to night. I was bewildered by this, though I'm grateful that there was no chorus to frighten me tonight, not that I needed it.

A knock came from the door, and I called for the Count to enter. When we made eye contact, I forced a smile and greeted him.

"Good evening, Miss Kane," he came toward me, and I noticed how his steps were quite silent. "Were you watching the sunset?"

"Ah, yes, I was," I turned back to the window. "Your mountains are wonderful canvases."

"I am glad they please you." He went to the window to look out at them. "Would you prefer to sit by the window?"

"Would you mind it?"

"Of course not, it is a lovely view, especially at night." The Count pulled up two chairs and placed them next to the window, and we sat together before he spoke again. "Forgive me for saying so, Miss Kane, but Dumitru mentioned to me that you wished for alcohol. That is one thing I will not permit in my house. I am sorry."

One thing off my list to ask, but I only replied that I understood.

"And I regret that I frightened you so this afternoon." He leaned forward, those red-brown eyes capturing the firelight. "Please do forgive me."

"No apology needed," I forced another cheerful smile. "It was my fault for not looking where I was going."

The Count shifted in his chair, crossing his legs. "You said you had questions for me?"

"Right…" I bit my lip, now wondering if I should have even bothered to mention them at all. "They are more like requests…I hope it's not too much to ask them."

"Ask."

To the request of sending letters, he replied that he would supply me with the appropriate materials and would instruct Dumitru to send them. I am relieved by this. I asked him if I would be allowed to take walks in the courtyard some afternoons for exercise, and he agreed to that as long as I didn't leave the confines of the walls and that Dumitru was with me at all times. I know Dumitru won't like that at all and will surely put up a fuss when the Count isn't around. I can't wait for that confrontation…

I also asked that, someday soon, the Count give me a tour of his house so that I would know where I was not allowed. With that request, he mulled it over for a few seconds before agreeing. I didn't think it was so unreasonable since it would prevent me from getting into trouble.

Then I approached the more sensitive topic that I had been thinking of and asked if I might be allowed to help with some upkeep of the house. I explained I knew it wasn't my official role, but it would give me something manual to do. I could tell by the look on his face that he didn't like the idea, which I expected from him.

Even after a lengthy essay as to why I should be able, he only replied. "Absolutely not." Then went off in a stern rant, giving his reasons why; something about the propriety of a lady is equivalent to her station.

Eventually, I drowned it out and apologized if I had offended him again.

"You have not." He leaned forward in his chair again to chide me. "You simply do not understand the way it is here. If I allowed you to do such physical work, I would disgrace this house, as you are an honored guest."

"I understand."

The Count smiled warmly at me and appeared to be pleased with me. "Do you have any more requests?"

I decided that was enough prodding for one night, so I answered that I did not.

I felt a bit hopeless at that moment, but the Count drew me out of it. "I have a question for you as well."

A sense of foreboding came over me. "Yes?"

"It has been about a week since you have been in my house…" I saw him eyeing me carefully to read my expression. "Are you comfortable here?"

"Yes, I'd say so. You know I love my rooms, the library, and teaching you has been a joy. Even after such a short time, I am starting to see this place as my home away from home." That was true.

The Count seemed quite pleased by that, for he beamed. "Then you can affirm you will stay for the entire year?"

My throat constricted. "I would love to stay if you will have me."

"Excellent," he radiated with delight. "I am so very pleased."

I feel like I was intentionally placing myself in a gilded cage to please this man. But how can I not? Out here, so isolated, I am at his mercy. I must smile and nod to agree with and do everything he says to make this painless. I shouldn't be complaining about it since I feel like I'm making it sound worse than it is. But at the same time, he gives me a foot of rein, just to pull me back an inch. He's giving me just enough of what I want to appease me, but also keep me dependent on him. The Count may think I don't know what he's doing, and by God, I want to keep it that way. For now, I must focus on my work and revel in the small victories he gave me tonight.

We continued to talk on until nearly 9 pm, then the Count sent me to bed. He tells me he will see me tomorrow evening for a tour and then a walk in the courtyard. I thanked him. Now that I have something to look forward to.

7 May

Morning, 4 am...

I cannot return to sleep in spite of my exhaustion. I will try my best to write down everything I remember.

After the Count left, and I had written the account of the conversation, I went and took my hot bath. It helped a lot to relax my sore muscles. After, however, the water was too calming, and my body felt so heavy I could hardly make it out of the tub. I went to bed, though in my fatigue, I must have taken my rosary and wrapped it around my wrist. I don't know why I did that, but I guess it was my tiredness that had decided that it needed to be kept near me.

My room, I soon noticed, was rather stuffy and oppressive. I needed some cool air, so I opened the window that looked out into the dark void beneath. This window is the only one that opens in my bedroom and sadly has bars on it. I assume that is to keep someone from falling. A soft, cool breeze immediately began to whirl into the room, bringing the sweet mountain air inside along with it. I set the stopper open only a quarter of the way, then returned to bed.

The breeze must have lulled me to sleep within minutes, for I remember nothing else. In the night, however, something terribly strange happened. It must have been a dream since there is no way in logic's name, even God's name, that what happened could have been reality.

I was lying in bed when I suddenly became aware that I was awake, or at least I was still in a semi-waking state. Opening my eyes until I could just see under the lashes, I saw this white mist coming in through the open window. I had never seen a mist so thick before, but for some reason, I didn't think to get up and close the window. I just lay there, dozing in and out of consciousness. I didn't feel threatened, although a small voice somewhere in the back of my mind said I should get up to close the window *now*, but I didn't seem to care enough. I watched as it filtered into the room like smoke and, gradually, it transformed into the shape of a man. Again, I felt no distress but remained calm since I was still half asleep, and my body didn't think it wise to move, like an unnatural calm kept me in my place.

To my horror, the shape of the man metamorphosed into the Count. At that moment, I remember thinking why was he in my room? How did he just appear out of nowhere? First, he crept over to me, his feet making no sound on the floorboards. He stared at me intently, and in the faint nightlight, his eyes were glowing red. By then, the Count's face was so close to my own I could feel his stubble against my cheek, and then, to my disgust, I heard him inhale deeply as if to smell me. I was screaming in my head, but remained paralyzed. With his mouth close to my ear, I heard him whisper. "My very own…"

It was so unsettling to feel him that close to me. The Count's hands went to the sheets and, almost tenderly, pulled them up over my shoulders. I felt his knuckles brush my hands, which were nestled against my chest, when suddenly he was across the room, a sharp hiss tore the air in half as he cradled his hand against him. Just then, I heard a low rumble of thunder in the distance, and my body seemed freer. Struggling, I began to stir, trying to raise my head as I moaned against sleep.

I know he watched me closely for a few moments, still holding his hand, and grinned at me with this knowing expression on his face. When his red eyes widened, a storm was suddenly upon us. A clap of thunder and lightning made me gasp and sit up in bed, ready to face the Count. Yet, when I looked over to the corner where he stood, no one was there. There was no one in the room, not even the mist; there was only me. Another burst of lightning came from the heavens, accompanied by an exploding thunder so loud it shook the room.

Struggling out of bed, I ran to the window, locked it, then pulled all the curtains shut. I was shaking as the sky opened up and a heavy rain pounded the castle. I ran back to bed to hide under the covers. I wanted to cry. I was so frightened and wished someone was there to tell me it was just a dream. I quivered in fear, grasping the rosary still wound around my hand.

I tried to wrap my head around what had happened, but it has been hard to focus on my thoughts. It had to have been a dream. There can't be any other explanation for something so fantastic, so surreal, so bizarre. This has to have been a result of my encounter with him yesterday afternoon. Am I still so frightened? How can I face him tomorrow evening after dreaming about him like this?

I can hardly bear it. Lord, give me strength this night! The dawn will be here in a few hours, and I will be safe from the dark. Christ, I beg you, let it come soon.

. . .

Eventually, I did fall asleep. When I woke, it was 11 am and the sun was shining through the drawn curtains. When I opened them, the brilliant light almost blinded me, and I had to dart into the shadows. Eventually, my eyes adjusted, and to my surprise, this early morning's storm had left no trace of itself. Had I dreamt that too? Gathering my wits, something that I seem to be doing more often now, I got ready and went into the sitting room.

I was caught off guard by Dumitru, who was sitting at the table waiting for me. I blinked, barely registering that he was there. Once we made eye contact, I spoke, my voice raspier than I had expected. "What are you doing here?"

"Waiting," he retorted, looking at his watch. "For three hours."

I rolled my eyes, thinking of quite a few good counters, but instead looked down at my breakfast. I was very hungry and began eating the scrambled eggs and bacon. "So why are you here?"

"The Master regrets to say that he cannot see you tonight. There is unexpected and urgent business that draws him away, and he won't be back until Monday evening." He paused before stating further. "In time for your lesson, of course."

Honestly, I wasn't disappointed whatsoever. I didn't want to see the Count anytime soon after what happened last night, and I breathed out a relieved sigh. "I'm sorry to hear that. I hope it's nothing serious?"

"It's not my business to know." Dumitru checked his watch again as though I were wasting his precious time. "The Master instructed that I am to give you the tour and then to take you outside for 'exercise'."

From the look on his face, I could tell he was dreading spending so much time with me. I tried to withhold a satisfied grin and said nothing. Quickly finishing my breakfast, I followed Dumitru out of my rooms.

It wasn't much of a tour. He pretty much just took me from room to room in some areas of the castle and pointed out what they are. He gave no history or explanation about the castle's background, which I'm sure he knows well but doesn't want to take the time to tell me. He began at the entrance, then went to the kitchens, where I noticed there was no cook, and up to the floor below mine, where the Count's rooms are located. He passed many rooms that I could only assume were locked, because he did not explain whatsoever what was in them, or where they lead. I had barely gained much by observing what I did of the castle, but I did affirm my suspicions that there are no other servants. We three are completely isolated here.

There also seems to be no access to electricity anywhere else in the castle. I made a point to take note of this.

When he had finished showing me around only a few of the rooms, Dumitru took me back down to the foyer and unbolted the smaller door. My heart fluttered as he stood aside to let me pass. It had been a whole week since I could stand outside in the sun, and instantly I felt so much lighter. When I descended the massive stone stairs and into the courtyard, I asked. "Would you like to walk with me?"

Dumitru, who was a few steps behind me, put his nose up in the air. "No."

I crossed my arms, turning on my heels to face him. "You know, I wish you treated me with a bit more respect. Your Master does, I don't know why you can't."

The stoic jack-of-all-trades said nothing, but sat down on the steps, and waved me away like a stray dog. Huffing, very offended by his rude gesture, I did an abrupt about-face and stomped off to explore my new terrain. The state of the courtyard was similar to that of the castle: in disrepair and need of a good tidying up, also maybe a few flowers. Other than a few stray stone blocks and other odds and ends, there was nothing uniquely interesting about the yard. Taking my opportunity, I examined the wall and the gate fortifications for any weaknesses my untrained eye could spot. In some places, it seems as though one *could* scale the wall, but what lives beyond it worries me more than what lives within.

I came to one side of the yard where the thick wall had fallen away a bit, and I peered out over the edge. Below me was the encroaching void, and the sudden drop made me feel a bit dizzy.

"No!" I heard Dumitru snap warningly from the stairs.

Shooing him away, I ignored him and continued to look straight down to the bottom of the massive valley, where a river flowed hundreds of feet below. What a terrible drop it was. A person would have time to contemplate their existence by the time they reached the bottom.

"No." Dumitru was suddenly behind me, taking my arm and pulling me back from the wall. Once he jerked me away, he let go, and I landed hard on my backside. "Do *not* go near the wall!"

"Would you cool it?" I glared up at him, my anger boiling. I stood, brushing the dust from my clothes. "It wasn't like I was going to jump."

Again, Dumitru grabbed my arm, invading my space. "We're going inside. Now."

Even as I protested, he lugged me back into the castle and bolted the small door shut. I was stunned that he would react in such a way and snapped at him that it was unnecessary and excessive. I had lost my temper because I don't remember what I said.

When he turned, he fixed his intense gray eyes on me. Dumitru's tone was cold and dismissive. "You do not understand, *Domnișoară*. Now, return to your rooms."

It was not a request.

I wanted to retort something to get back at him, but despite my anger, I remembered how I am not in the position to step on Dumitru's toes. In my delicate situation I don't yet fully understand, I couldn't afford to fight a useless battle of words. I swallowed my pride and thanked him for the tour, then simply turned and went back upstairs.

FLAME OF WOE

8 May

I've thought a lot about everything that has happened since I came here. The scare the Count gave me, my dream of him, and then the little things that all seem to add up to a big picture that I can't see. I have never felt so anxious, sad, and frustrated in my life. God in Heaven, I feel this is the ultimate test of my strength. Why test me now?

When Dumitru came to bring me dinner, I heard him knock on the sitting room door. I was in my bedroom and couldn't bring myself to go out there to face him. When he left, I went out to the food that he had brought, but found I couldn't will myself to eat any of it. My tears and anxiety made my stomach turn, so I had one or two bites and left the rest. About an hour later, I heard him come back in, and instead of the sound of the prompt stacking of dishes, there was silence for quite a while. Soon enough, however, I heard the distinctive clinking of the tableware, and then he left.

I went to bed early and slept hard and dreamlessly. The next thing I knew it was morning, around 7 am, and I was starving. The last thing I wanted was to call for Dumitru, so I just dealt with my hunger. I took a cool bath and then went and sat at the barred window with it open. The morning breeze feels so refreshing as I sit here and write.

Later...

I heard him come in at 8:30 am with my meal, and when I opened my bedroom door he froze for a moment, looking at me, his expression softening. Then, as if remembering himself, he went back to organizing the dishes and utensils into their proper place.

I bade him a good morning, which he answered the same in a whisper with a tensed jaw. I got the same kind of response again when I asked him how he was, as he replied curtly that he was fine.

He didn't repay me with the same courtesy of asking how I was, but I still pressed him. "Did you speak with the Count about what happened yesterday?"

Straightening, he looked me in the eye. "I have not spoken to him today. He is still out."

Since he is taller than I am, I craned my neck up instinctively to make myself look taller. "Do you intend to speak to him about it?"

The side of his mouth twitched before he spoke. "No."

His answer caught me off guard. "Why not?"

"I have my reasons," he abruptly turned to the cart. "You do as you will."

I stood there for a moment when he departed. I would have thought he'd use any ploy to oust me from the castle. Everything this young man does only makes me scratch my head. One minute he is approachable, but in a second, he blocks everyone out. I wish I knew why he is the way he is.

Evening...

I spent the rest of the afternoon in the library, taking lunch, tea, and dinner there. Dumitru didn't say a word to me each time he came to bring food or take it away. Although against my better judgment, I decided I would tell the Count about what had occurred.

I worried when he was to come. I watched the hours pass by as the sun sank deeper and deeper into the western horizon. My palms became sweaty, something they don't usually do. A part of me thought it was foolish to fear something I'm sure I imagined, but the other part couldn't shake the thought of those red eyes.

I had to keep telling myself that it was a dream, no matter how real it felt.

And, when the time of reckoning came with the howl of the wolves, the Count appeared smiling so gleefully. "Miss Kane, please forgive me for not seeing you yesterday. Some dreadful business came up and I was called away."

I found it hard to answer him directly. "It's alright, Count. Business before pleasure. I hope everything has been taken care of?"

"Oh yes, all is well." He sat, and I did as well. "I trust Dumitru gave you a pleasant tour, and you enjoyed your exercise outside?"

My brief hesitation roused his suspicion, but I still answered. "The tour was all well enough, Count. However…" I bit my lip, trying to come up with the words I had rehearsed.

His tone became utterly serious, almost chilling. "Be frank with me, Miss Kane."

I swallowed hard, struggling to find the appropriate words, and with short and choppy sentences, I replayed to him how rough Dumitru had been with me. Eventually, I ended with: "It's not that I'm upset that he tried to warn me that the wall is dangerous, but that he was rather crass."

The Count peered at me through a hooded gaze, listening quietly all the meanwhile with a frozen poker face. By the end, I could not tell if he was displeased or didn't care at all. I waited in silence for him to say anything. Yet he remained, his mouth formed into a perfect line.

I wasn't sure if I should say anything, but sheepishly squeaked out. "Count?"

Suddenly, he stood, holding his hand out to me. "Come, I wish to show you something."

I hesitated again but forced my hand to take his. Then, putting his arm in mine, he led me from the library. We walked in silence down the stairwell to his floor, my heart racing like a jackrabbit as we did. We went down the hall a ways and then stopped at an old door. Letting me go, he reached for the aged handle. Strangely, I could have sworn that I heard it unlock before he even grasped it. It groaned open, a groan that echoed in agony throughout the castle.

There were lamps lit in the old, musty room. Cobwebs and a fine layer of dust were the main décor, save for a few old pieces of furniture that were scattered about. The walls were bare except for one painting of a woman dressed in traditional finery. It captivated me, but my attention was drawn away by the Count sighing and asking rhetorically. "You ask why Dumitru acted as he did?" He paused, contemplating something before continuing. "Many years ago, in a different time than this one, there were unfortunate events that led to my wife, may she rest in peace, to fall of her own accord to the river below. It caused me much sorrow, much pain. Dumitru knows this story and the change it brought upon this house."

I stared at him in awe, my heart tearing in two. Suddenly, Dumitru's reasoning made every sense in the world, and a great sadness entered me. "I am so, so sorry. That's her?"

"Yes..." I saw his eyes drift away from the portrait as though he couldn't bear to look at his wife's face. His expression tried to withhold all the emotion he was feeling, but I saw through it.

Curious, I took a few steps further to have a better look in the dim light. The woman was extraordinarily beautiful, with long brown hair which was partially concealed by a veil, intense hazel eyes, and fair skin. She was a true vision of beauty, especially when adorned in her medieval splendor. Oddly, the portrait looked centuries old. Perhaps it was just the lighting and the dress she wore that gave it the illusion of being so?

"What was her name?"

"Ioana..." he whispered almost inaudibly to me. "It means 'God is gracious'."

"A fitting name for so lovely a lady." I admired her a second more before turning back to him and asking. "During her life, was God ever gracious to her?"

His brow creased deeply. "No. Despite her piety, He failed her in the end."

Frowning, I had to lower my eyes from him. The Count's bitterness for religion, from what I gathered, was caused by his wife's self-inflicted death. "Surely she is in a better place."

Instantly his face hardened as if I had angered him, and he moved to the door. "Let us return to the library. We are late for the lesson."

I couldn't help but want to reach out to him, to tell him I under-stood his feelings, but I feared him. Surges of pity filled my heart, and I felt an oppressive sadness weigh me down as I followed him from the chamber.

Seeing my distraught expression, the Count laid a heavy hand on my shoulder. "What troubles you?"

My heart was desperate to tell him my feelings, but my voice could not bring itself to utter them. "The whole thing, it's so terrible. I am so sorry for you, Count...oh so very sorry."

He took my arm in his again. When he spoke, his voice was so soft, almost like warm velvet against my ear. "Come, my friend."

The Count led me back to the library, and after taking a few minutes to compose myself, I began to teach. I noticed he was distant today and not so engrossed as he usually is. I knew why, but kept teaching even if he wasn't listening at all. Afterward, he didn't stay for a conversation but said he had to check on some papers that would, unfortunately, take him a few hours. I don't think he really had anything to do, but nonetheless, I took his hands in mine to tell him of my sympathies. I happened to look at his hands for just a second as I held them, noting how large they are compared to my own, and so cold. Then, to my disbelief, I noticed on his right knuckles were specks of burned flesh, evenly spaced and perfectly round, like the impressions of rosary beads.

Something clicked in my head, and a grim realization dawned on me as I observed those marks. The world fell away as that nightmare replayed in my brain. I had been conscious enough to know that my imagined Count Negrescu had grazed his hand against mine as he had pulled the covers over me. The hand that held my rosary was the one he had inadvertently touched, and it was only after then that he had cried out in pain. I saw with my eyes my nightmare manifest itself into reality.

What could have caused the rosary to burn him? I cannot guess it. I was so dumbfounded that my blood drained from my face.

Time turned to ash before me, and I could not speak.

"Miss Kane?" The Count asked again in a sweet voice, breaking my stupor.

Instantly I began to shake, but I somehow forced down what I really wanted to say and said something else. "If...If you ever need anything, please don't hesitate to ask me. I am just a small fish in a big pond, but I will do my best. I wish you a good night, Count."

I let go of his hands, gathered my things, and left. He hadn't moved or said a word, and I wondered if he had realized that I knew my nightmare had not been something I imagined. It has been a long while since I have had time to think rationally. I cannot believe any of what I dare to think could be true.

I am a mess. I must sleep.

9 May

Afternoon...

Right now I'm sitting in the library. For my sanity, I have to write down all of my suspicions.

The first thing I'd like to address is his late wife and his attitude against anything relating to faith. Of course, I don't know the story behind him and his wife, not that it's any of my business, but I truly believe it must have played a role in his current attitude towards the Faith. Of course, he puts up a mask to hide his true anguish beneath his rough exterior. As the Count said himself, Ioana's death had a lasting effect on his house, and Dumitru knew of it, which is why he pulled me away from accidentally falling to my death.

Ioana was a pious woman, and the Count must blame the Almighty for forsaking her at the hour she needed Him the most. My pity for the Count, despite his unwelcomed visit, grows and grows when I think about all of this. If only we had a close relationship so that I could be frank with him about it. He wouldn't like it, obviously, but my words cannot hurt him more than he has already been hurt.

I have a strange feeling that there is more to this story than he lets on. I can see it on his face and hear it in his voice. His aversion comes from more areas than just his wife's death. What could have possibly happened in this man's life to have him be so physically repulsed by seeing a cross and be burned by a rosary? I cannot fathom it.

Secondly, those burn marks on his right hand that I had seen last night. I am frightened to no end by this revelation. There have been too many things that I have seen during my short stay here that have led me to come to the most ridiculous and illogical of conclusions.

But...didn't he think I would figure it out eventually? I mean, no matter how much he tries, he cannot deny the things he has said and done in my presence that would lead me to conclude such a thing. I have played a 'connect the dots' since I got here, and I know the proof is staring me in the face. Yet there is no 'smoking gun', no neon sign, that is obvious enough for me to conclude what I think he is. I am at a loss, but at the same time, know what I must do now.

If I'm correct, there is no way I could ever defend myself against him on my own. I must continue to keep my resistance to him clouded in kindness and compassion. The Count must not know that I know. I must not show fear but trust in God that His mercy will be on me if I can last a year in this fool's paradise. I do feel pity for him, but I fear him more.

I see now I am being tested too, by God and by the Count. There must be something bigger going on here. How can there not be? It can't be a coincidence that I have been placed on this assignment. Maybe I'm blowing this far out of proportion? Or it could be the exact opposite.

Lord, do not abandon me here in this place.

...

Dumitru walked in with lunch just as I had finished writing, frightening me half to death. Inconspicuously as I could, I closed this record and put it away. A thought flashed through my brain in that I wondered if he knew what I believe the Count to be. Wait, is he one like the Count? No, he cannot be. Dumitru is strange, but he is like me. I hadn't thought of it before, and although I wanted to ask him discreetly about my suspicions, I know I cannot. He isn't on my side, flesh and blood or not.

When he started setting out my meal, I took the opportunity instead to apologize to him for my behavior yesterday and admitted I should have listened to him.

Dumitru tried to hide his shock, but I could see that his rigid features had softened, and he accepted my apology with a quiet, "You are forgiven."

15 May

Afternoon…

It's been about a week since I wrote last, and to my surprise, life has gone on as normal. That same regulated schedule from last week continues to this week, but I still find myself looking over my shoulder at every sound. Even in my constant paranoid state, I have found an odd sense of peace in the monotony of the endless days. Dumitru and I have grown closer over the week, too. Although he is still curt and indifferent, he shows his thoughtfulness through small gestures. His change in attitude has made life here less stressful and almost enjoyable.

The Count has changed his behavior toward me, though I don't know if it's completely voluntary. Before, he was always cheery but serious, and now he lulls me with a smooth and tempting voice. Sometimes, while I am teaching, I see him watching me rather than the lecture slides. The Count's eyes wander, but once he knows I'm looking, he seamlessly redirects his attention to the lesson. I know it's not my imagination. There are times I can feel his eyes drifting to places I dare not mention.

This morning I wrote letters to my parents and to my employer. Since the envelopes the Count gave me have no sealant on them, I had to give them to him open. Luckily, I had spotted that before I wrote them, and added nothing regarding my suspicions about the Count. I only wrote the pleasantries, and perhaps sounded a bit too formal in my personal letter to my family.

May they find their destinations safely. That's all I can wish for now.

Evening…

This evening, something so strange happened at my lesson that I think I should report it here. After the predicted howling of the wolves, the Count entered in his usual fashion. But when he drew near, his face suddenly grimaced, his nostrils flaring, like he smelled something awful. I was perplexed by this, and since I had smelled nothing, I asked him if something was wrong. Instantly he clamped his hand over his mouth and turned his face away from me.

The Count didn't answer me but was so still he could have been a statue.

Hesitantly, I touched his arm and I asked him again. "What's the matter, Count?"

He yanked his arm away with such ferocity, and gritting his teeth, he hissed out. "Forgive me, Miss Kane. I am feeling suddenly unwell. We will have no lesson tonight."

Then he turned and fled from the room.

I stood there in shock. My hands were shaking from his outburst as I gathered my things and returned to my rooms. What did he smell that made him feel so sick? Was it me? I can't see how. But yet —

Never mind.

. . .

I believe I have found the culprit, and the whole thing is now even more disturbing than I initially thought. I have discovered, although at this point I'm not even surprised, that I have begun my monthly time. Do I dare to write down that I believe he smelled my blood? Saying it sounds insane…it *is* insane. His sense of smell cannot be that good. I have to be crazy to even think something like this. Am I even thinking rationally? I have to be going mad.

Dumitru just came and told me that the Count is ill and won't be to his lessons for a few days. As of now, I have the time off. When I asked how the Count was ill, Dumitru became quite uncomfortable and gave another cryptic answer that it was his stomach.

His 'stomach'…right.

Chapter Four
STRIKING THE IRON

17 May

Morning…

There has been no word from the Count. From what I have been able to glean from Dumitru, he has been quite ill and has shut himself away in his room. I've spent hours contemplating the Count's preternatural behavior that I've been the unfortunate witness to. The way he appears from nowhere, is revolted and injured by holy devices, the unnatural glow in his eyes, and most of all, his teeth when he smiles. And, not to mention, how he had formed himself from smoky mist into the figure of a man—or semblance of one. It is like he can craft the laws of physics and make them malleable to his will. The Count can somehow seduce my will with just a glance, he can see deeply into me, and I am none the wiser until he has left me.

I do believe in the presence of Evil in the world and that it can present itself in any form. It will act as a friend as it holds the damning axe over your head. I hate to think that *that* is what is happening to me. Am I being pulled by something evil into an abyss, the bottom of which I cannot see? My mind is never completely clear these days, and it's hard for me to see the bigger picture. I know I must *act* or be damned. I must destroy the evil before it can destroy me.

Afternoon…

Despite the gloominess of my thoughts, the day was positively lovely. The sun was shining, and the big, puffy cumulus clouds were so close that one could almost touch them. Being so high up in the mountains, there is a constant freshness and vitality to the air that permeates every living thing. I wish I were able to go beyond the wall and see the mountains in their natural beauty during this time of year. I can almost imagine the wildflowers, nestled in groves, bringing vibrant color to otherwise colorless rock. The wildlife must be enjoying the day, as I could hear the distant song of birds and the chattering of other small mammals. Beyond the wall, the otherwise quiet forests buzzed with their pleasant ballads. Not being able to see them made me feel so downcast.

Today, Dumitru noticed my silence as I sat next to him. "Are you unwell, *Domnișoară*?"

"Yeah…" I admitted after a while, taking a stray rock in my hand.

Out of the corner of my eye, he looked at me, although I couldn't read his expression. "Is it of the body or of the mind?"

Sighing, I threw the small rock. "A bit of both, I guess."

"Are you homesick?"

I fell silent. I hadn't really thought of home because all my thoughts have been so focused on surviving here. Of course, I miss home, who wouldn't? The fact that I haven't been thinking about home these past three weeks alarms me. I guess when I didn't answer, he took that to be the case for my forlorn behavior, for suddenly his arm was around my shoulders. I tensed, shocked by his comforting gesture that was so out of character.

"I have not seen my home in many years." He spoke so softly, yet longingly. "I know you are only staying for a year, but the memories will pass behind you."

Perhaps it was the sincerity of his voice, but for some reason, I leaned into him. "Where were you from before?"

I could feel his reluctance to answer me, but for some reason, he did. "A small village far away from here."

Glancing over at him, I was surprised at how close our faces were. An unfamiliar heat rose to my cheeks. "Do you have any family?"

His gray eyes darted to mine, then away, as he stuttered. "N-Not anymore…"

"Oh…I'm sorry." I breathed out. Feeling the awkwardness of the conversation deepen, I cleared my throat and stood. Limply, his arm fell away from my shoulders. "Hey, since I won't be seeing the Count this evening, why don't you and I have dinner together? What do you say?"

At first, he didn't respond, but then whispered. "No."

"Why not?"

"I just can't." Dumitru snapped, standing. All at once, he turned and headed back inside. "Enough sun for the day."

I frowned, letting out another long sigh before following him back in. Just when I was getting somewhere with him, he gets defensive and runs away. I was hoping to be able to speak to Dumitru privately to learn more about the Count, but I guess I had scratched too deeply into his shell. Next time, I'll be more sensitive.

Evening…

At dinnertime, Dumitru said he had told the Count of my feeling of melancholy, and he has permitted us to go to town. That is, go to Bucharest and go shopping for groceries and any supplies we need! I was stunned at the sudden opportunity that was laid before me, and I hugged Dumitru, whose face got so red. We will go this Saturday early in the morning and be back by late evening.

I have been pondering whether I should take advantage of this situation. I will be far from the Count's clutches and have enough money to steal away. I could easily make a break from Dumitru in such a busy city, get to the airport, and book passage home. I would be leaving all I have behind, even my position. No one would believe the things I've seen in this castle. Perhaps I would return in disgrace, but I would be returning with my life. But at the same time, I have this sickening feeling in the pit of my stomach that this is a test. The Count could be giving me a chance to run to see if I would dare take it. Could I do it if given the opportunity? I know Dumitru could catch me and haul me back here with ease. He had no problem tossing me around before.

I guess the real question for me is, should I abandon my post or return with enough force to face the Count? Am I willing to run and leave my good reputation behind, just to save myself from what I believe he is? In a way, my employment ties my hands. I am damned if I stay and damned if I leave. If this is a test, I must return or I will face some unknown consequence; maybe that 'bad place' that Dumitru once spoke of. Yet…if I come back with a card up my sleeve? I might have an idea…

I hear the wolves again.

20 May

I got up at 4 am, wide awake and ready for the day. After much debate, I settled on some plain and inconspicuous clothes. When I went out to the sitting room, I saw Dumitru come in with my light breakfast, and I greeted him with a cheerful good morning. He didn't say much to me at the beginning, but as I began to eat my meal, he muttered off a quick list of rules that I had to follow while we were on this trip. He said that I couldn't leave his sight, to leave the talking to him, and that I had to obey anything he told me to do. Those were the terms and conditions of my trip. They would complicate things, but I had to agree to them.

We left soon afterward for the long journey to Bucharest. I had all that time to run over my plan and steel myself for what was to come.

…

After the long drive, we finally made it to Bucharest at about 9 am. First, I got my essential and some non-essential shopping done. All the meanwhile, Dumitru followed me like my own shadow. I knew he hated going into ladies' shops, for he couldn't conceal the blush on his face. I soon noticed he was often looking over his shoulder, like he expected someone to jump out at us. It got quite annoying after a while.

After lunch, we did his grocery shopping. Dumitru took hours and hours going among the open-air and farmers markets. He haggled like a professional and always got the most food for a surprisingly small amount of money. Honestly, I was impressed by his skills, except when I was left holding a majority of the bags, which got heavier and heavier as the day went on. I didn't mind helping him because it offered me a chance to see local life. Everything was so refreshing.

I was so relieved when we got back to the car and unloaded all the foodstuffs. We had a few hours to spare before we had to go, and after much pleading, we walked around the area to take in the sights and sounds. I was feeling quite bold in my freedom, and I wanted to see more of Bucharest before we were scheduled to return. I begged him to let me see just a small part of the older districts of the city, and begrudgingly, Dumitru accepted.

It was lovely to see the charming architecture, so picturesque and full of history. I wished I had the time to explore more, but I had something else in mind. I searched between the buildings as Dumitru muttered off to me what structures he knew. I half-listened until we finally came upon what I had been searching for. As we approached the church, I pretended not to take much interest in it. I casually asked Dumitru about another building across the way. That distracted my guide just enough that I could back track a few steps and slip into the open door unnoticed.

The large stone structure enclosed around me with protective arms, and for once in weeks, I felt safe. There were a few other church-goers inside, and I entered unnoticed by them as well. With Dumitru screaming for me somewhere outside, the quiet worshippers turned their heads to the ruckus. I pretended to be shocked as well, but I knew I had no time to dawdle. I was there for a reason. Quickly chugging the rest of the water in my bottle, I submerged it in the font of holy water and filled it to the brim. Once I had replaced the cap, I concealed it in my bag.

All in all, the whole operation took under 15 seconds at the most. Then it was my chance to make a run for it. When I moved to conceal myself behind a marble pillar, a firm hand latched onto my arm. I accidentally shrieked and it echoed throughout the quiet church. Before everyone could swing back around to look at me again, Dumitru had tossed me outside.

"What the hell, Dumitru!" I cried, attempting to fight against his strength. "Let me go!"

He was beyond furious and glared at me as he wrenched me closer. "Where the hell did you think you were going? Do you understand how dangerous this city can be?"

"It's a *church*," I emphasized and made up a quick lie. "I just wanted to see the inside."

"And you didn't think to just ask me?" He snapped at me viciously. "Away from the castle, you are my responsibility. The Count will have our heads if he finds this out."

A new apprehension entered me, and I bit my lip.

Dumitru's face softened when he saw my fearful reaction to his words. With a frustrated sigh, his grip lessened in its intensity. "Look, *Domnişoară*, I warn you. Whatever you think you're doing, don't do it."

My throat constricted in fear that he suspected that I was going to attempt an escape. "Y-You don't know what I —"

"I can only protect you if you allow yourself to actually be protected." He cut me off and began to drag me behind him back in the direction where the car was parked. "Believe me, you're safer with me than out there."

I was struck by the seriousness of his tone. "Are...are you going to tell him?"

He glanced over his shoulder and eyed me. "Like I said, he'd have my head."

I looked down as I was hauled away. A new understanding came between Dumitru and me: he wouldn't tell the Count if I didn't. "This never happened."

Dumitru only nodded.

We headed back to the castle early. I hate lying, but Dumitru wouldn't have allowed me to go into the church if I told him what I was after...or why I was after it. In all of this, I have no luxury of being honest about my fears and theories. I have no idea what is fact and what is fiction, so I must accumulate every defense I know of and that I can obtain.

Evening...

We returned to the castle about 7:30 pm, both of us tired from the ordeal of the day. Dumitru opened the car door for me and started unloading the numerous amounts of groceries.

I grabbed as many as I could before he could say anything and jogged up the stairs. Just as I got to the landing, the door opened before me, and the Count stood on the other side, a gentle, welcoming smile on his face.

His sudden appearance startled me. "Oh, Count!"

"Good evening, Miss Kane." He moved aside for me to enter, eyeing the bags in my hands. "Did you have a good time?"

"Oh y-yes," I stammered. "You are feeling better?"

"Immensely." He smiled widely when he took in a deep breath, those long teeth of his glinting unnaturally. He did appear to be more reinvigorated than when I had last seen him. Maybe he had been feeling legitimately ill before, and I hadn't been the cause of his sickness.

"I am glad to hear it." I smiled back, and before he could stop me, I trotted off to the kitchen.

Dumitru came in behind me and told me sternly. "Go to your room, His Excellency summons you there."

In the semi-darkness of the kitchen, I pursed my lips, seeing the intense seriousness on his face. His tone made me fear that the Count had chastised him for letting me take in some of the bags.

Just as he was about to turn away, I thanked him for taking me to Bucharest. Quickly, I departed and made my way up to my rooms.

When I reached the second floor, the door to my room was open and the light was on. I knew the Count was in there, waiting for me. I steeled myself, clutching my purse with the holy water sloshing within. The room was warm when I finally entered, and the Count was sitting in his chair in front of the fire. He stood at the sight of me. "Miss Kane, please sit and let us talk. It has been quite a long time."

"It has indeed," I went to my chair, and just as I sat, he did as well. "I'm so glad you're feeling better. When you got ill, I was worried I had done something to cause it."

"Oh, it was not you, my dear." He reassured me smoothly. "I guess it would have seemed like that. I had been feeling unwell all that evening, and unfortunately, it was poor timing on my stomach's part. Please do not think it was your doing. Far from it."

The Count said his spiel so effortlessly that it sounded like the truth. My jaw tensed unconsciously, and I forced a soft smile. "That is a relief. I was very worried about you."

Reaching out his hand, he touched mine gently, his fingertips grazed over my knuckles in an almost sensual manner. "I am flattered you were, my dear friend. But now you must tell me about your journey to București. I am eager to hear every detail."

I didn't want to tell him anything about anything, but I knew he wouldn't settle for anything less than a lengthy description. I told him as much as I dared and highlighted the most important parts of the trek. By the end, he seemed content enough and regretted he couldn't have joined us. Of course, I didn't regret it. By then, Dumitru had come with all the things I had bought. Just as I was about to tell the Count I would retire for the evening, he ordered Dumitru to bring me dinner. With my stomach in knots, I was far from hungry, but this was the Count's way of passively saying that he wasn't through speaking with me yet.

I had to suffer through another two hours of conversation with him, all the meanwhile keeping up my delighted pretense. Finally, and I mean finally, he let me go to bed. But of course, not before a kiss on the hand that made my entire being quiver. Once he left, a weight came off my chest. I'm leaving all my things in the sitting room for tomorrow, but have safely hidden the holy water. Now I must wait for the right time.

Chapter Five

BEHIND THE
MASK

1 June

Afternoon…

It's officially been one month since I've come to Castle Negrescu, so I thought I'd write to commemorate the day. Time has gone by so quickly, yet so slowly. The days run together like one continuous string of evenings and nights, and I find it difficult to remember the daytime. Dumitru still takes me outside and allows me to walk around, but I've become so used to the space that it's become just another part of the castle to me. I try to make the best of it while staying active and keeping my wits about me, but some days I find it hard.

The beginnings of summer are making themselves felt with each passing day. Those distant mountains and the valley below have come into full bloom. They are a sea of color and life around the castle, which remains perpetually drab. It resembles a scar across the land, where nothing grows or thrives. Even those few weeds that were growing along the wall have died off where they should have flourished. Although the sun is warmer, the days are longer, and there is a periodic gentle rain, nothing grows within these walls. Nothing lives.

I see things clearer now that I understand what is happening to me, and so I sit, I watch, and I wait. I continue to keep up the façade with a smile on my face, and life goes on as usual. During the past month, I've become a master at deceiving those around me, even myself. I almost like playing the game and passing the tests that have been laid out for me: those small tests, which by themselves look insignificant, are definers of my fate.

One thing I've noticed in myself is that I'm becoming increasingly lonely. Yes, Dumitru and the Count steadily occupy my days and evenings, but there is that key component of companionship that I lack. Since our excursion, Dumitru has grown to be like a friend, but he continues to put up barriers of class and sex between us. He doesn't dare get close to me like he did that one day he spoke of his family. The ocean he has dug between us has made me feel like this place really is a desert island. Let me be clear, I don't want to be close to him because he's the only man near my age for miles, but because he's kind in his own way, and needs a friend more than he knows.

The only satisfying relationship has been with the Count, of all people in this place. He engages me, challenges me, and most of all, offers a small feeling of fellowship. He has placed no true barrier between us, only that which I have placed as well: the relationship between teacher and student. Recently, I've observed that relationship degrading, and I can't figure out which of us was the one to break it. For the last few consecutive evenings, once the lesson was over, we'd get on topics that dove into subjects I could never imagine would pass between us a month ago.

And somehow, without fail, we would end up close to each other. Once he ended up showing me how to waltz, and other such foolish things that shouldn't have happened. I've become, to my dismay, to greatly look forward to seeing the Count. It's become as if I only live for the evenings, only to see him. It wracks my heart with such distress in the morning that I lose myself so easily. I should be keeping emotionally distant, be terrified of him for the things I've witnessed, but I can't help but still feel that need to show him human companionship. I know I'm leading myself into the void, but I can't stop.

I've been trying to occupy myself today by reading the small Bible that I brought with me. If the Count knew I had this, he would be positively furious. As far as he knows, I only have my cross and rosary, but not a Bible or holy water. I've wondered if I should try to press him once again on religion, but I fear to overstep a line in the sand I can't see. Maybe tonight, when I know he'll be in a good mood, I should inquire on a philosophical matter and see where it takes us. What harm would it be to ask him his opinion? Being a well-traveled man, at least twice my age, he should have some advice to give me. Besides, he has never a lack of words when expressing his opinion.

I just hope I can keep my head from floating to the stars tonight.

Evening...

After our lesson, the Count entreated me to sit and talk with him as usual. Tonight, saw him staring at my hair, which I had straightened to its full length out of boredom this afternoon. Small parts of me liked that he stared, while others were repulsed, and I couldn't figure out which one was right or wrong. I sat next to him, debating with myself whether I should start to test him.

The Count saw my discomfort, and he drew nearer to me. "Dear friend, you seem troubled tonight. Tell me what bothers you."

He spoke to me so damn sweetly I had almost forgotten what I was thinking about. Clearing my throat, I stood and walked a bit away from him, towards that portrait of his look-alike that was fixed to the wall above us. "What do you say we switch roles for tonight? You be the teacher, and I, the student."

"An intriguing prospect," he mused thoughtfully. "But are there things *I* could teach you?"

I faced him again, carefully choosing my words. "Of course there are. You have more life experience. I think you could teach me many things."

He raised an eyebrow, very interested in this new game. "Then, pray tell, what is it you wish to be taught?"

"Philosophy." I paused, thinking for a moment, and took in a deep breath. "Do you think forgiveness should be given to someone who has hurt another?"

His eyes narrowed slightly at my question. I'm sure he was thinking of something completely different. "Have you done something that would warrant my forgiveness?"

"No, Count," I assured him. "I'm just asking what you think about it."

"Someone has hurt you, then?" He concluded like he didn't even hear what I said.

"No, Count," I repeated. "Let's just say, for example, someone hurt you beyond belief. Be it words or actions that were passed between you two. Could you find it in you to forgive them?"

The Count's suspicion was sparked by this, and he straightened in his chair. "Why do you ask me such a thing?"

"Because you are the teacher and I am the student."

He was silent for a while as I moved back to the chair next to him and waited. I was very eager to hear what he thought, but as the seconds went by and he didn't answer, my brow furrowed. His jaw was set firmly, and a vein in his forehead pulsed until he finally broke the silence. "I fear to answer you with my opinion on the matter."

"I will respect your opinion, no matter what it is." I reassured him and then waited.

The Count let out an annoyed sigh. "If someone hurt me beyond belief, I would not hesitate to shut them out of my life. Any wrongs done by a person cannot be undone. Things said or performed by someone against another, be it purposeful or not...there is no going back to the way it was before. Especially if the thing done has permanence, such as murder."

I sat back in my chair, thinking of his words. In a way, he was not wrong by them: after a thing is done, it *is* done. But, I asked hypothetically. "Then there should be no room for forgiveness?"

"Forgiveness is the release chosen by those who can no longer bear the weight of what was done. It is not an act of forgetting, but freeing oneself from the burden of remembrance." He explained.

"What if you loved this person?" I gazed up at him. "And they loved you?"

He peered down at me, sparks flying in his eyes. "Then the hurt is dealt a hundred-fold."

Yet still, I pressed on. "But if you love someone, truly and unconditionally, shouldn't that love help you pardon them for the wrong they committed?"

"It depends on whether the act was malicious." He pressed back. "If a boy breaks a priceless vase, his parents will chastise him, but forgive him since he is young and foolish. But if the boy commits matricide in revenge against the father, should the father truly forgive the son who has robbed him of his beloved wife? In a perfect world, he would. But you and I do not live in that perfect world."

I was silent for a moment, thinking of the moral dilemmas that he had presented me. "May I ask, Count, what is your definition of love?"

He held my gaze, reading me thoroughly through my calm exterior. "Love is the quiet surrender of the self, offered without expectation. It is a sacred tether that binds souls beyond time or condition."

His answer impressed me greatly, but at the same time confused me. "Is it so unbreakable? Yet faced with a terrible incident, one party should be shunned by the other?"

"Like I said," his voice strained as he closed his textbook. "It depends on the situation."

From his hardening features, something weighed heavily on his mind as he grew quiet. Before he went too deep into thought, I inquired. "Please, could you give me an example?"

Still, he remained silent, his eyes drifting down to his hands. I wondered if I had stepped over an invisible line as a faint red manifested itself in his eyes, and it unnerved me. In a low, grave tone, almost like a growl, he explained. "When I was young, my father and my brother, who were much hated by some of the other noblemen of this region at the time, were murdered. My father's assassination was swift, but my elder brother's was not. They blinded him, burned him alive, and even when he was still living after all of that, they buried him alive." When his eyes shot to mine, they were the brightest crimson. "Should the men responsible for that be forgiven? Never, and I made sure of that."

I was paralyzed by those eyes that glowed with such ferocity, the same as those I had seen staring at me in the dark. I hadn't expected him to tell me something so personal, so close to home, especially something so traumatizing. How much suffering has this man endured in his years? I felt truly disturbed by what he had said, but also absolutely terrible for having asked him anything at all. I stuttered out an apology, but he cut me off.

"Now let us reverse these roles," the Count fired back without missing a beat, and a shiver ran through me. "If someone hurt you beyond belief, would you forgive them?"

My heart hammered wildly, and I stuttered out. "I…I think I would forgive them, no matter the deed."

"No matter the deed?" He laughed and scoffed. "You are too innocent, Miss Kane."

I breathed in deeply, and with both my hands, I took his own closest to me. "Forgiveness doesn't mean I forget what the person has done to me. Forgiveness is acknowledging the wrongs committed but choosing not to let those wrongs have power over you. To say to someone, 'I forgive you for murdering my brother' doesn't mean I disregard what has happened to him and me. I'm moving past that hurt, grief, anger, or whatever it is. I decide to forgive, but not forget."

After a moment's thought, his hand squeezed mine and held it there. He rubbed his chin with his other hand, pondering his next counter. "If you know what forgiveness means, Miss Kane, then why do you ask me? I warned you beforehand that you would not be pleased."

I nodded in acknowledgment. "I may have my own opinion, Count, but I'd like to know more about yours. Even if I don't agree with them, I can always learn something from them anyway. I do believe you are correct that actions committed cannot be undone. I just think that everyone deserves second chances to right those wrongs and be forgiven for them, no matter how terrible."

"That is easier said than done."

"No one said forgiveness is easy." I let go of his hands and stood as I gathered my things. "If you'll excuse me, Count, I am very tired. But, you have left me with much to think about, and I thank you for that. I hope I didn't offend you by anything I said."

"You did not." He grumbled.

It was so obvious that I had, so I touched his shoulder. "Even if I did, I'd hope you'd forgive me. Have a pleasant rest of your night, Count."

When I returned to my sanctuary, I barely got to a chair before I collapsed into it. My legs were like Jell-O, and my face was hot. I had been in debates before, but none such as that. Again, the Count showed me pieces of his inner thoughts and inner war. This is his game he plays… I don't know who won the game here.

My thoughts then turned to what the Count mentioned about his father and brother, and how he had 'dealt' with those responsible for their murders. I could never imagine my relatives dying so tragically, so prematurely, for whatever reason. The manner in which his brother's life was ended resonates with me, and I cannot fathom how he must feel about it. His wife, his father, his brother, all their lives ended so tragically…I cannot blame him for feeling as he does.

In the distance, I can feel a static in the air from an approaching storm, and there is a thick fog encircling the castle. I am beyond exhausted and must sleep.

4 June
Pentecost
Afternoon…

I had been hesitant to tell Dumitru of the Count's behavior the other night. I wanted to ask him again about what he knew of the Count's past, especially of his father and elder brother, who were so savagely put to death. Yet, I was afraid to press the topic. What if Dumitru told the Master that I was asking questions too intrusive or too sensitive, and the Count would be wrathful? But this morning, when Dumitru brought my breakfast, I had to say something.

I began carefully, simply saying. "May I ask you a question?"

Dumitru only hummed a comply.

"What happened to the Count's family?" There was an immediate tension in the air, but I continued. "He told me about how his wife committed suicide, how his father and brother were brutally murdered…"

"To my knowledge, these are true." He said plainly to end the conversation there.

"Did you know them?" I urged further. "What were they like?"

He was quite uncomfortable and shifted uneasily. "No, they died long before I came into the Count's service."

I frowned at that. "Do you know the names of his father —?"

"*Domnişoară,*" Dumitru snapped at me. "You cannot ask me questions that I cannot answer. Do not ask the Count these things either. You will overstep yourself and will be in that bad place. I warn you."

After that outburst, he promptly left the room.

Despite being stunned by his anger, I am even more intrigued than I was before. I hate to let sleeping dogs lie, but perhaps for now, it is better to let the subject rest. The Count was angered enough by me for asking him questions, but I will figure out his past one way or another. Then, with this discovery, I know I will determine what he is. There are so many things that are hidden in plain sight, just waiting to be uncovered. Surely his past is the key to everything.

Evening, 11:30 pm...

In the name of the angels and ministers of grace! As I write, I can hardly believe the things I have seen. My entire body is shaking, and I fear I may pass out from shock. I'll try to recount every detail, no matter how terrible to remember.

I was having a hard time sleeping because I was so preoccupied with the Count's traumatic past. I needed air, so I opened the barred window and sat on the low stone sill. The night air was so calm, with only a slight breeze that was barely enough to ruffle the curtains. The atmosphere was all I needed to unwind from the past few days, especially with the dim moonlight casting the entire landscape into a pale white gleam. I was thinking that this place is so beautiful, but so terrifying at night when I heard a noise below me. Puzzled, I looked down and saw the window beneath mine open. The Count, whom I recognized immediately from his hair, poked his head out and looked around. I withdrew a little, yet continued to watch.

To my horror, the Count hoisted himself out of the window so that he stood on the ledge, looking down into the abyss. My heart surged into my mouth, thinking that he was going to jump. I had just begun to inhale to scream for him to stop, but my inhale was morphed into a grotesque gasp, as I saw the Count grab onto the stone wall and crawl on all fours face-first down into the darkness.

I was so stunned my vision tunneled and I fell back from the window, scrambling to the other side of the room. I sat there in the darkness, with only the light from the barred window illuminating the room. The images of whatever I just saw will be burned into my eyes for the rest of my life. The motion in which he walked reminded me of that which one sees of a demon walk up a wall, like the scurrying of a rat, lizard, or spider. That was what disturbed me the most, next to the mere sight of him suspended on the wall as if gravity were nonexistent. It was all something so unnatural, and no trick of light or shadow. I cannot deny anything now, especially since I have seen it before my very eyes. Even though it seems so unreal, this is no dream, no fantasy, or fairytale to scare children. This is reality, *my* reality. Oh God in Heaven, why was I brought here? What did I ever do in my short life to be thrust into this Hell with this devil? How will I ever survive this? If anything, don't forsake me now…not now.

I must wait for him to return to be certain that he is what I dare to think he is.

GRIM REALITY

5 June

Morning…

For the life of me, I could not close my eyes. Each time I would see him crawling down the wall, the jerking motions of his body revolting me into wakefulness. So, I remained awake and alert.

Eventually, I found the courage in me to return to the window and look out. Of course, the Count was nowhere to be found, still, something compelled me to sit and watch, no matter the mortal danger. I was in a state of denial, but I could not deny what I saw. I had to watch and wait for him so that I could see what he was up to. Every fiber of me had to know, as my life depended on it.

So, I lay low enough that my eyes were just able to peek over the ledge, past the bars, and into the void. I don't know how long I must have sat there, not moving, and barely breathing. I sat like a predator waiting for my prey with perfect patience, though if I were caught, I'd be the prey. I don't believe I have ever been so focused on anything in my life. My eyes strained in the dark for any slight movements, and my ears were acute to every sound.

More hours passed, and although I was sure it was becoming dawn, no sign of the sun came. I was freezing, but I didn't dare move from the window to get a blanket. My eyes and body were feeling my efforts by this time, and everything felt so heavy, so exhausted. I found myself dozing, my eyes drifting to look at the mountains, still so beautiful in this horror. I thought I'd just close my eyes and listen for him. Yet, as expected, I fell asleep at the open window.

Not long after that, I became conscious again, my eyes struggling to flit open just enough to see through my lashes. At first, I had no idea where I was. Everything around me was in a fog, a literal one, for surrounding me swirled a thick mist that was pouring in from the window. I knew who, not what, it was.

My body wanted to spring into action, but again found itself paralyzed by half-sleep. No will of my own could bring me to move. I had to sit there helplessly against the sill, watching from my lashes as, to my utter terror, the form of the Count rematerialized next to me. He chuckled to himself as he knelt, daintily moving fallen hair away from my face and neck. "Silly girl, you will catch your death."

His voice lulled me in its sweet nectar and lured me to not resist him. The Count leaned in and slipped his arms beneath my back and knees, lifting me as easily as a rag doll. I lay against him, completely limp. One thing that struck me at that moment was his strength that I could feel through our clothes. It reminded me of the rippling muscles of a bull; an odd association, but the most accurate. Being in his arms suffocated me and reduced me to a state of dizzying helplessness, like I had no ounce of will within me to resist him. There was no means to defend myself. I wanted to cry, but there was a small voice in the back of my brain that liked this feeling. It wanted to be at his mercy, and with all my might, I could not crush it.

The Count laid me on my bed and covered me with the sheets. I had been so cold that the instant warmth made me sigh softly with relief. I saw him smile gently, revealing his teeth. They were terrifying to look upon, with canines that were long and sharp as a wolf's, deadly and menacing. A shiver of shock echoed through me, and everything that I had speculated was plain before my eyes. In my state of hopelessness, tears involuntarily fell from my eyes.

All at once, the Count's smile faded, and he wiped the tears away with his finger. Then, with the same finger, he traced down my cheek to my jaw, and finally to my collarbone. There was a vibration that pulsed in the air, almost like a purr of a mountain lion, and I felt him get closer and closer so that his face was just inches away from my neck. The closeness to such a sensitive area made my physical body shudder against him, and I realized he was pinning me against the bed. That sick whisper in my head grew louder, drowning out my reason. I knew this feeling: it was temptation in its rawest form, beckoning me to give in. My blood was on fire, my skin now ablaze. I wanted to writhe against him, yet I was immobile. A noise escaped my throat, something I had never heard myself make in my life. It was a whimper, so needy and base.

With his face still in my neck, his hands moved to my shoulders, gripping them with a subduing force. Yet, he just remained there, as if uncertain what to do. He moved his mouth to my ear and softly whispered. "No. Sleep for now, my sweet one."

I felt my world fall away again, and I drifted into a deep sleep. The next thing I knew, it was morning and the sun was blazing in through the window. I struggled to remember what had happened. If all I saw was a dream, how did I end up in bed in the same position in which the Count had left me? Why was the window fastened closed, and no sign of my late-night fright anywhere to be found? I sat there, by and by rubbing the remnants of crusted tears from around my eyes. For the longest time, I felt nothing as I replayed the entire night over and over again in my head. I analyzed everything I could remember, hoping in some way it was just one very, very long nightmare. But I knew I was only fooling myself. I had been awake, I had been conscious, and had been of sound mind for the parts of the night I could account for.

There can be no denying it now. I know I have been half-accepting and half-denying it all this time. If I continue to delude myself into a lie, I would not be helping anyone. I cannot keep turning a blind eye to the facts that have been piling up for over a month. All my life, I have lived as an academic, demanding the facts before I make an educated decision. This is no different from that. My Count

Negrescu is a child of the Devil, a spawn of Satan incarnated. He is a creature of fables, a legend passed down through generations, and I am his willing prisoner.

...

I have been unable to do much of anything all day but think. I had completely forgotten about breakfast and almost lunch if Dumitru hadn't knocked on the door to remind me. When I came to the door, his face grew grave with concern, but he only asked if I was alright. Of course, I am very much not alright. And, of course, I lied and told him I had a bad night and then realized I had a lot of work to do. I don't think he bought it, and I hope he doesn't tell the Count that I'm acting strangely. The very last thing I need is for either of them to find out that I know.

After I dressed, I only picked at my lunch. My stomach felt so empty, but I had no will to eat, no will to exist. I want to fade away from this place and not exist, but that would be too easy. I feel so disgusting, so dirty, for the way I acted last night, that I don't want to give him any satisfaction from that. Even if I must die, I will not give in to temptation. I must promise myself that.

For hours, I neglected my lesson work and sat in my sitting room just contemplating what I should do next. There are multiple options open to me. Some wise, others not so much. I know for certain I cannot call him out with all I have learned; that would result in something terrible. I cannot even tell Dumitru, lest he tell the Count, and I am sunk. After much debate within myself, my only thought is to continue as if nothing has happened. Absolutely nothing. My life and sanity depend on it. I must act normal, natural, and treat him no differently than when I first met him.

At all times, I must be in control of my faculties, no matter what situation I find myself. To swallow my fear, push away my anger, all to move forward. I must show no human weakness in his eyes, but only the strength that has kept me going to this day. Surely some heavenly power will be by my side when I face the beast because it is from there that I draw all my consolation and courage.

Last night I was at his mercy, my body willing, but he said no. For some unknown reason, he could resist the urges I know we both felt. As much as it would be hard for some to accept, there is goodness in him somewhere. There has to be. Despite all the terrible things he said and did, he shows me unwavering kindness and respect. He has never shown me anything but civility, politeness, and most of all courtesy, even when angered.

I hate saying this since I should hate him, curse him, and damn him back to Hell, but all I still feel in my heart is pity. Why do I feel that for a man who is most certainly a monster? Am I blinded by something that is keeping me from seeing a truth that is so blatant before my eyes? After this long night, I have no idea anymore. I am at my wits' end, yet I have to continue. I cannot run or hide from this place or its Master. God, defend me this evening when I face him with the full knowledge of all I have learned.

I must now go to the library to prepare. Never before has the place felt like a lion's den.

Evening…

My heart wasn't in the lecture as it should have been, but with my lack of sleep and worn nerves, I tried as hard as I could. When the Count had come in, I greeted him as I always have, and we exchanged pleasantries as was normal for us before we began. All the meanwhile my heart raced, and nothing I could do would calm it. There were times I thought I'd pass out, but I forced myself with every shred of sanity I had to have the show go on. I have no doubt he saw past my charade because I know he sees everything I do.

Once the lesson was over, I knew I had only just begun my night with him, so I steeled myself to face whatever conversation he wished to pursue. I could only pray he wouldn't mention my odd behavior, but of course, he did anyway. "Are you alright, Miss Kane? You seem quite distressed."

"Distressed?" I repeated, shrugging off his question. "I am fine, I assure you."

The Count smirked with a hint of something sinister. "Are you sure? If you ever need to speak of something that is bothering you, you know you can always tell me."

"I appreciate that, Count," I faked a smile. "But I am fine. I just didn't sleep well last night."

"Do you mind if I ask about it?" His inquiry to an outsider would have looked so innocent.

I knew better, and I kept myself steady. "I was only restless, that's all."

"What made you restless?" He rested his elbows on the table, leaning closer to me.

"You."

Of course, this sparked his keen interest as he chimed back. "Me?"

"Yes," I nonchalantly passed his recent assignment over to him. "You got one wrong. That's very unlike you."

The look on his face was priceless, one of shock and confusion with a twinge of anger. Blinking, he ripped the paper from my hands to examine his work. It was quite a bit before he could bring himself to speak again. "It appears...I did."

"I'm sure it's nothing to worry about," I reassured him, content that I had thrown him off guard. "You're only human, and your other work must be quite stressful. Would you prefer we lessen the difficulty of your assignments?"

"No." He snapped, handing the paper back to me. "There is no need."

"If you insist, Count," I filed the paper away in a folder and stuck it in my bag. "But always know I am flexible when it comes to this."

The Count forced a smile. "You are quite fair, I know."

My swift kick to his ego was crippling indeed, for he crossed his arms and began to sulk. Playing on his emotions was rather satisfying. "Oh, come now, Count, you mustn't be so hard on yourself. It's not the end of the world."

He glared at me. "I am unaccustomed to such."

I raised my eyebrows. "Just one minor mistake is nothing to worry about, I'm sure. Besides, your work here has been exemplary."

The Count squinted and turned away after muttering. "Thank you."

"You're welcome." I smiled to myself, satisfied that I had successfully taken him down a few notches. But when I turned to him, I was shaken to see that he had been staring at me with such intensity. I suddenly felt self-conscious.

"Miss Kane, my friend, may I ask you a question?" He leaned in closer to me, those eyes of his studying my every move.

The Opened Tomb

My anxiety spiked, but I asked him what was on his mind. "Are you frightened by me?"

Pressure began to build inside my stomach, and I tried not to panic. I could not lie. He would know immediately if I did, so I stared right back at him. "I admit that I am intimidated by you, but it is out of respect for you and your position."

The side of his mouth curved into the smallest smile. He was satisfied with my answer, that much was evident, and hummed and leaned back into his chair. "Very well, as you say."

Relief entered me like a flood, and the tension of that question dissipated. As I began to pack my things, I asked. "And you? Are you frightened by me?"

The Count laughed once and was about to answer when we were interrupted by a knock at the door. Dumitru entered, appearing flustered, and spoke to his Master in Romanian. This had never happened before, and I found it rather curious. The fact that Dumitru had intruded on our lesson for this reason was enough to cause me alarm.

The Count stood immediately and apologized, adding that since he was to be occupied, I should retire. It wasn't a bad idea since I was exhausted, and once he assured me all was well, he quickly followed after Dumitru. So, I gathered my things and went back to my room.

It's raining quite hard outside now, and another thick fog is settling in around the castle. Remembering last night, I dared not look too long, so I have drawn all the curtains and made sure all the windows are locked.

What a day this has been. I hope I can sleep.

61

Chapter Seven

DISCORD

16 June

L ife has returned to a sense of normalcy. Since I last wrote, I have strangely become more accustomed to what I know the Count is, and thereby more accustomed to him. Since that night I have witnessed his demonic nature, he has acted quite human and has revealed no other special abilities. No doubt there is more to him than what meets the eye, but he hasn't yet shown to me his true face. He has remained a proper gentleman toward me. And most of all, there have been no midnight visits and no displays to frighten me.

In the meantime, the weather is getting warmer by the day, and summer is so close to taking full hold of the landscape. Now the mountains are lush green, as well as the surrounding valley and forests. In the distance, if I look closely enough from my sitting room windows, I can sometimes glimpse the wildlife going about their day. I wish a bird would come close, but everything seems to keep its distance from this place…even the bugs.

Dumitru has mellowed out considerably with the weather. I never realized how tense he was before, but there has been a change in him. When we go outside, the sun warms us, and the mountain breeze refreshes us. It is a perfect combination that relaxes his features and lets him breathe easy.

Even though our employer is a hellish creature, a kind of beast whose name I still dare not write down, we go on living as normal. There is a comforting monotony to this life, but all this doesn't make me less wary of my delicate position. Something has to happen to turn everything inside out. I feel it coming.

Evening…

Oh, the irony! Why does fate torment me?

It was obvious all during our lesson tonight that the Count was agitated. His uncharacteristic silence set me on edge, and that looming sense of foreboding I had was suddenly over my head like Madame Guillotine.

I was in the middle of speaking when the Count stood abruptly and cut me off. "Miss Kane, we are done for today. Please, pack your things and return to your room."

I was stunned by his urgency, and I opened my mouth to speak, but he had already begun closing open books and putting them in my bag.

"But —"

"Do as I say. Please"

I had never heard the Count's voice raised before, and it was frightening to hear. His face conveyed such frustration, but I couldn't imagine what had brought all this on.

"We will continue tomorrow —"

Just as he was halfway through his sentence, we heard Dumitru yelling and running up the hallway. Then, without any warning, the double doors to the library burst open, and a man I didn't recognize stepped in. Spontaneously, he exclaimed in a shrill voice. "Vlady!"

Instantly, he leapt over to the Count and embraced him, kissing him twice on both cheeks as he spoke in Greek...very flamboyant and highly intonated Greek. He did appear to be Greek with his ashen olive colored skin and deep brown hair. I was struck by his unusual beauty, and my face got hot. I wanted to look away from him, but I was transfixed.

"Ah!" The man made an exaggerated gasp as he suddenly took notice of me. Forgetting all about the Count, he turned his direct attention to me and, in Romanian, asked me who I was. I could only blink at his deep brown eyes.

"Petros, this is my teacher and my honored guest, Miss Isadora Kane." The Count butted in with an introduction in English when I gave no reply.

"Oh, yes!" This Petros took my hand from my side and kissed it. His touch was cold, like that of the Count's. A small voice in the back of my mind said that something wasn't right about this man, but the forefront of my mind was focused on his alluring smile. Both of his hands encompassed mine as he greeted me. "What a pleasure it is to meet you, Miss Isadora. How wonderful it is to see new blood in his old man's house."

His use of words confused me, but still, I forced a smile. "It's a pleasure to meet you, too, Mister...?"

"Oh, just call me Petros. I simply detest formality." He smiled devilishly as his eyes drifted over me. The act made me feel like I was being undressed by them. Then, Petros took my chin and moved it side to side. "What a lovely little thing you are, indeed! Vlady, you have chosen quite well!"

Immediately, the Count snapped in a low and threatening tone. "You insult me, Petros."

"Insult? It was a compliment." Petros waved the Count away. "I'm only admiring her. It's not every day you see such a specimen."

I was shocked by his insulting use of the word and echoed. *"Specimen?"*

"Darling Miss Isadora, you must tell me all about you." Petros changed the subject and tightened his grip on my hand. "I'm just dying to know every detail! You have no idea how long it has been since my old friend has —"

"It is late for Miss Kane." The Count swiftly stepped between us, which forced our hands to part. "She was just about to retire before you so rudely interrupted us."

Petros scoffed. "The night has just begun! Let's all catch up —"

The Count stuck his index finger up to silence his guest. "I think not tonight, as you have disrupted too much already."

In the blink of an eye, Petros was beside me, his arm wrapping around my shoulders. I jumped, but just then I felt Petros put his lips close to my ear. A familiar sensation of weak dizziness covered my senses like a shroud as I heard him say. "What say you, Isadora? Shall we put away the books for the evening? Why don't you join Vlady and me in some *lively* conversation?"

My mouth spoke words on its own, but I had no recollection of ever *thinking* about saying them. They just manifested themselves out of thin air. "It's alright, Count, we can continue Monday. There's no problem."

And just like that, the dizzying weakness was gone, and I struggled to comprehend what had just happened. In my confusion, I looked up to the Count, but somehow his face didn't look right to me. It was strangely angular, on the cusp of being beast-like. I had to blink a few times for the haze to fully dissipate from my brain and eyes.

"See!" Petros' voice pierced into my ears. "Join us when you're ready, Miss Kane."

Then he was off of me and took the Count's arm to drag him out of the room as he chatted to him in quick Romanian. I watched them as they disappeared passed the doorway and into the shadow of the hall. As soon as they were out of sight, my head instantly cleared, and I remembered that familiar weakness and where I had last felt it. That night, not so long ago, when I had been visited by the Count during what I thought was a dream but was, in reality, no illusion. When he had lulled me into a kind of paralysis and then sleep against my will. I had been conscious yet unconscious of it. Petros had hypnotized me, entranced me, and used me to agree with him. In shock, I half-collapsed back into the chair, and my head swam.

Petros is the same kind of beast as the Count. I felt sick.

In my despair, I almost didn't notice Dumitru come up to me, and between heavy breaths, asked me if I was alright. His voice and face told me that he was very concerned. He must know. He has to know.

There was an urge that welled up inside me to tell him outright, there and then that I knew, but I swallowed it. Sitting there for a minute, it took me a while to know how to answer. "I'm fine. I'm just...lightheaded all of a sudden. But, who was that?"

"Petros is..." he cringed. "An old friend of the Count's. You must be careful of him. Promise me that you will stay away from him."

I had to hide my fear, so I looked away from him. Surely, Petros, since he had somehow hypnotized me to say things that I didn't mean, could make me do other things that I didn't want to do. The Count has done the same to me in some way as well. God knows what tricks of the mind they could play on me.

"Promise me," Dumitru stressed.

"I promise..."

I didn't think my answer satisfied him. Usually, Dumitru can hide his emotions rather well, but he was visibly shaken. Worry was etched on his face, and if that was so plain for me to see, I know I should be worried too.

Reluctantly, he told me. "Put your things away and I'll take you to the Master's private reception room."

"Right now?" My stomach twisted. "Must I?"

Dumitru was conflicted as to how to answer, and after hesitation, he stuttered out. "It's...it's not my place to say. Though it would appease Petros for tonight. Tomorrow you can say you are sick."

I hated hearing that answer. Begrudgingly, I set my things in my room and followed Dumitru down to the floor below mine, where the Count's private quarters are. Once I was announced, and I was allowed to enter through a magnificently carved wooden door, I was in wonder at the extravagance of the room. The décor hasn't been changed in centuries, and I thought I had just stepped back in time to Romania's medieval past, or a museum exhibit. The Negrescu family crest rested over the great fireplace, flanked by two fearsome-looking dragons. I was in such awe of the vibrancy and intricacies of the colors around me, not to mention the history, that I had forgotten why I was there in the first place. Of course, Petros' shrill voice reminded me immediately.

"Miss Isadora!" Petros was suddenly at my side, kissing both my cheeks, which instantly reddened. "I'm so delighted you joined us! Please, sit by me."

Heat radiated throughout my face and neck. By God, I did not want to sit by him, but Petros promptly dragged me over to sit on the settee. Of course, he sat so close to me that our hips touched. I was mortified and hyperaware of his extremely intimate proximity.

"You know, I had no idea that Vlady was taking lessons again." Petros noted with a sly smile as he leaned into me. "Vlady and I have been friends for what, centuries? I should be offended that he hasn't kept me updated."

The Count shifted in his seat across from us. "You exaggerate, Petros."

If I had no prior understanding, I would have taken Petros' emphasis on 'centuries' as hyperbole. My stomach turned over that I know otherwise, and I desperately tried to suppress the sick feeling rising from it.

"To the contrary," Petros spoke to me. "I can see why he is so adamant to learn your lessons. If only *I* had a teacher so lovely."

I swallowed hard and averted my eyes from his intense gaze.

"I do it for business, you know this." From my peripherals, I saw the Count cross his arms. His buttons were being pushed; I could tell from his stiff body language.

Yet Petros completely ignored him and continued to focus his attention on me. He asked me how long I have been a resident here, where I am from, and other frivolous questions. I did not want to reveal more than I had to, so I gave him brief answers. Petros listened intently and did not interrupt me once, not like he had done so rudely to his old friend. Meanwhile, the Count sat silently, listening to our conversation with narrowed eyes.

Petros began to turn the conversation to speak about himself, saying he was born in Greece, but he has traveled much around Europe, parts of the Middle East, and North Africa. He was very willing to talk about himself and went into great detail about his experiences.

"Where did you two meet?" I asked daringly.

"Oh, Vienna!" Petros beamed as he gestured to his friend. "You remember, Vlady?"

"I remember." He mumbled.

Petros chuckled to himself. "You see, Miss Isadora, in our younger years, we were, shall I say, avid patrons of houses of ill repute and —"

"Petros!" the Count hissed so viciously that it frightened me. "If you choose to have no sense of tact in the presence of my guest, then you will end this conversation here."

Instead of heeding his friend's warning, Petros laughed him off. "Don't be so prudish, Vlady. We are all adults here, aren't we?"

"Miss Kane, you seem very tired. You may retire." The Count announced and gestured that I should leave.

Petros groaned annoyedly and rolled his eyes while muttering some obscenity under his breath.

Out of fear of the Count and my wish to escape from Petros, I obeyed. Wishing them both a goodnight, I slipped from Petros' grasp and stole out of the room. Instantly, I felt freer when that door closed behind me, and I could breathe again.

Dumitru was waiting for me in the hallway, and without saying much at all, he promptly escorted me back up to my quarters. Just before he left, he warned me not to leave my rooms tonight, as it was the Count's orders. I could only stutter out that I understood before Dumitru closed my door.

The instant loneliness was a reprieve, but also terrifying. I had a hard time gathering my thoughts together and calming my erratic heart. There has been so much said and done to analyze and comprehend. I knew the only way to get it all down and plain before my face was to write.

My hand is cramping from writing for nearly two hours, and I am exhausted, but I cannot dream of sleeping now. I know too much. They are both the same thing. They have to know that I suspect something, especially the Count. He has known me too long and can see right through me. With such a dreadful secret as this, surely I am a dead man.

...

There was just a knock at the door that made me jump out of my skin, so much so that I was too petrified to ask who was there.

"Miss Kane? May I enter?" The Count called from the other side of the door.

I hesitated for a second as I hastily shoved this account behind the pillow of the chair I was sitting in. Stuttering, I called for him to come in.

He entered my sitting room alone, thank God, and I stood to greet him when he approached.

I am no actress, but I put on my most superficially calm face I could make to shield my anxiety. In the dim light, I saw the perturbed and agitated expression on his face, but there was also remorse muddled in the mix. "Is there something wrong?"

"No," the Count whispered. "My friend, I wish to…apologize."

I was surprised. "But there's nothing —"

"Please," he held up his hand for silence. "I apologize for Petros' ill manners tonight. He and I are old acquaintances, and because of that, he believes he can act crudely. I have warned him of the consequences if he should continue." After a pause, the Count promised. "He will not stay long, I assure you of this, my friend."

I swallowed hard as I mulled over what he said. "It is not you who should be apologizing, but all the same, thank you. I appreciate it."

The Count was quiet for a short while, but slowly, he extended his hand out for me to take it. "You are correct, but you are my honored guest. Any shame he brings upon himself under my roof is my shame as well."

I was struck by the sincerity of his words, and with a sad smile, I did give him my hand. His touch was very gentle, I admit, but my hand still trembled in his grip. "Then, for your sake, Count, all is forgiven."

The look he gave me was unreadable. With those eyes that reflected the dancing flames of the fireplace, he stared straight into me and through me. Then, with a courteous bow of his head, the Count wished me a goodnight. I heard the lock bolt shut from the outside when he closed the door. I am trapped.

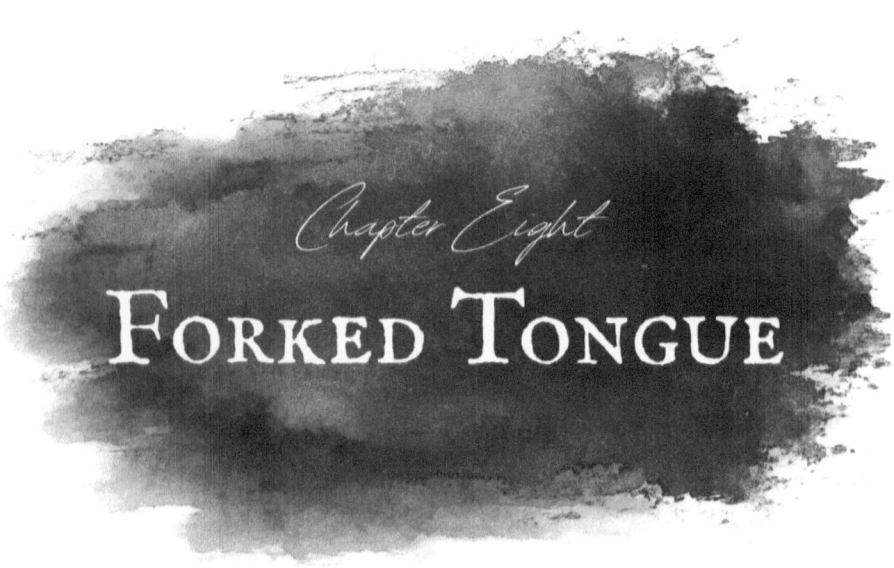

Chapter Eight

FORKED TONGUE

17 June

L ong and hard I have sat alone in my bedroom, my door locked and curtains drawn open to let the sunlight in, reflecting on everything I have learned. At my desk, I have been writing out the facts I know to be true and ones I wonder are real. I sincerely wish I had access to the internet so that I could do research, since I am ignorant concerning the supernatural. I am at my wits' end. I say that so often now…

As much as I hate to think it, I wish I could confide in Dumitru my suspicions. He is the only one I know to be alive and human, but God forbid I tell him. I know that he *knows* what the Count and Petros are. He is the Count's servant, first and foremost, and it's his job to tell his Master everything that I do. I will have to be cautious of him as well in case he learns that I know.

When I think about it, I have little hope for my future. Surely my true purpose here is not to teach the Count or be his 'friend', as he calls it. I don't have a clue as to the Count's plans for me, but I can only assume the worst in the end. I think back to that night when he had visited me and told me that I am, as he stated, "My very own." It makes me sick to consider what he has in store for me, or what Petros could do to me first.

...

I have been praying for liberation from this hell, but it was long enough that I noticed that the sun had dipped low in the sky. When I shakily got to my feet and put my rosary away, there was a knock at my door. Luckily, it was only Dumitru with my evening meal.

At the sight of me, he got this confused, almost funny, look on his face. He asked me if I was alright, to which, of course, I replied that I am feeling unwell and that I will not see the Count or Petros tonight. He tried to ask if there was anything he could bring me to make me feel more comfortable, but I told him there was nothing he could do.

My friend nodded knowingly after that. He only added that he would inform his Master that I was indisposed before he left.

At least for tonight, I am safe. Tomorrow night, however, I can't say for sure.

Later…

The sun has just set, and the familiar howl of the wolves has heralded in the coming of *those* two. I was in my bedroom preparing for a dreadful night. All my curtains are drawn tightly closed, and I made sure the barred window was locked. I intend to go to bed early in case my night is interrupted and I lose sleep.

I was about to get into bed when there was a knock at my bedroom door, and the Count's voice called from the other side. "Good evening, Miss Kane."

I hadn't expected him to come to see me, and panic set in. Shakily, I called back. "Good evening, Count. I'd open the door, but I am not decent."

"Worry not, my friend," he told me. "Dumitru tells me you are unwell. Is there anything I can do?"

I admit, I was touched that he would come and see me.

"It's just a migraine, that's all." I fabricated out of thin air and added that all I needed was a good night's rest.

There was a momentary pause from the other side of the door. "Then, my dear friend, you shall have one. Sleep well."

I took a big sigh of relief when I heard his footfalls disappear. Tonight, I hope I will enjoy my respite and wake with a clear head.

18 June

...

Just as the Count had promised, my sleep had been undisturbed. Internally, however, was another question. I tossed and turned and found it hard to become comfortable. My mind wouldn't shut itself off, and it would jump from one subject to another. Eventually, somehow, my head shut up and I slept deeply for at least six hours, and then on and off for another two.

When I got up and had eaten a good breakfast, I felt a bit better but no less anxious. I know I'll have to return to the library to resume my work, despite it being Sunday, since our last lesson was cut short. I have much more space to work there than in my sitting room, so I am determined not to shut myself away simply because there are dangers outside the walls of my rooms. I also told myself deep down that I would not allow myself to be intimidated any further by Petros, though he has the upper hand. Besides, it's unlikely either of them will be out during the day since they only crawl out of the woodwork at night...like cockroaches.

I should be safe while the sun is up.

10 pm...

Around noontime, I was able to settle my paranoia enough to leave my quarters and go to the library. For the first hour or so, I was very jumpy and looked over my shoulder at every sound. Once I became engrossed in my studies, I ultimately forgot about my anxiety and actually got a lot more done than I had anticipated.

Dumitru came and went with my tea as he usually did during the week, but this time he brought me a few honey pastries too, along with the standard bread and jam with finger sandwiches. It was a sweet gesture.

Of course, my taste of normalcy soon faded.

After tea and all the dishes had been cleared, I began typing out some extra notes on my computer. I was not particularly absorbed in my work; in fact, I was feeling a bit bored. I recall yawning deeply and rubbing my sore shoulder, which was sore from my uncomfortable night's sleep.

"Rough night?"

I must have jumped a foot out of my chair. My eyes burst open from my lazy yawn, and I saw Petros sitting cross-legged on the table in front of me. All my fears rushed upon me, and my palms began to sweat. I was utterly dumbfounded by his unexpected appearance, and I lost all ability to speak. My head rushed with panic, and my stomach rolled over. I felt like I was going to be sick.

"Did I startle you?" Petros grinned and chuckled to himself. "You've gone terribly pale."

"Yes…you did…" I muttered quietly. Discreetly, I turned off my computer screen as I pretended to reach for a nearby textbook. "Is there something I can help you with?"

"Maybe there is…" Petros hummed as he picked up some of the Count's assignments and examined them. After taking a moment, he commented. "Vlady tells me that last night you were sick with a migraine. I admit it was terribly boring without your company."

I averted his gaze entirely and acted like I was rifling through the textbook. "Is that so…"

"In your absence, Vlady told me a lot about you." He said it in a way so that my interest would be piqued.

"That's nice," I answered disinterestedly.

"Did you know that you have made quite an impression on him?" Petros leaned over closer to me. "All he could talk about was, 'Miss Kane this, Miss Kane that'. It was positively adorable, you know."

My brow furrowed in disgust at his gossipy tone. "Right…"

He huffed and rolled his eyes. "You don't believe me?"

I only shrugged my shoulders.

Hopping off the table, Petros haphazardly let the papers fall to the ground. "I'd like to apologize if I began our relationship on the wrong foot. Any friend of Vlady's is a friend of mine. Let's start again, hmm?"

I didn't say anything. Honestly, I don't think that I was breathing.

He came to stand next to me and leaned down, almost hunching to my level, as he languidly swept strands of hair behind my ear. I tensed, expecting the worst, but he only smiled and whispered. "What do you say, Isadora?"

His words echoed in my ear, and a volt of electricity shot down my spine. A chill followed as I stared ahead of me, wide-eyed. My laptop screen, which I had left open, showed only my reflection. Petros was right next to me, but his image was missing. Time slowed for me as all of my fears came bubbling to the surface again.

This only reaffirmed everything I suspected was true. They are undead. Both of them are.

I was lost in the horror of them moment when the sensation of his lips drawing closer to my ear threw me back into reality. Reaching forward, I slammed my computer shut with such force. I'm not sure what possessed me, but I whirled around to face him. He was inches from me, so close that I could smell his breath and see every fleck of burning color in his eyes.

Petros' sneer, which revealed hints of glinting teeth, relayed that he knew that I know what he is. He snickered and opened his mouth to speak when suddenly he was gone. I blinked, stunned.

"Vlady!" I heard Petros cry from the seat next to me. "You join us early tonight, what a surprise."

I blinked again, my eyes darting from him to the doorway where the Count stood. A wave of frozen air stung my flushed cheeks. A shadow loomed over the Count, and he glared at Petros. If looks could kill, he would have sliced Petros in two.

I don't remember what the Count said to Petros, something about wishing him to join him this evening for an early dinner. Petros protested, of course, saying he wanted to join us. I suppose the Count convinced him that this 'dinner' would be more eventful. Petros left the room begrudgingly, and we were left alone.

The Count approached me and, upon seeing how shaken I was, apologized and told me to return to my rooms for the rest of the night. He didn't have to tell me twice. Once he left, I packed my things and fled to my room. My hands shaking, I clenched my rosary and hid like a child under the covers of my bed.

20 June

Evening...

Today is the Summer Solstice, and it couldn't have come at a better time. The days are getting steamy, but the nights, for their reasons, are completely unbearable. Petros' continuous stay in the castle has been nearly intolerable. I truly do not understand how the Count deals with him, and I am close to ripping out my hair. For the past two nights, his behavior has persisted. I have come to realize that since I am something new to him, and I openly resist his advances, he is eager to woo me.

On Monday, Petros sat in on our lesson. I knew it was going to be trouble from the start, but thank God he got bored within ten minutes and left to go do something else. Luckily, it was then that I was able to ask the Count how long he'd be staying.

The Count's only reply was, "Until he gets bored."

On Tuesday, the same pattern continued. Petros left after five minutes this time; however, later that evening, something else exasperated me so that I must write it down. I know I shouldn't be giving Petros the time of day in my records, but this was too odd to just ignore.

We were in the Count's reception room, chatting about mundane things. This night, the Count's Greek friend was much quieter, as if lost in thought. He seemed distant and was obviously not listening to the conversation between the Count and me. Oddly, about an hour into our discussion, Dumitru entered and spoke to the Count in Romanian, and spoke so quickly I didn't catch what he said. The Count was shocked by whatever he said, and reluctantly, went to the other side of the room to speak to him in hushed tones.

"What's going on?" I asked Petros, who didn't seem to care about the sudden change.

"There is a message from one of the Gypsies who work for him." He muttered absentmindedly, checking his watch for the time.

I was perturbed by whatever was going on. Never before had anyone called upon the Master of this castle so late at night, in fact, no one has ever called on him. Tensing, I turned to the Count just as he announced to us. "I must attend to a matter, please forgive me. Dumitru, you will stay with them."

Dumitru nodded curtly. "Yes, Master."

"Don't be gone long, Vlady!" Petros called, yet his voice didn't sound as convincing. The Count, as I had expected, caught onto his friend's sarcasm and watched with eyes trained on him as he exited the room. Something was wrong; I could feel that subtle shift in the air, and a chill shot down my spine. I swallowed hard and watched as Dumitru came over to us and sat in the Count's place, and he watched Petros intently.

"Are you just going to stare at me, *boy?*" Petros' tone was biting, almost bitter.

Dumitru remained calm as he glared back at him. "The Master said to wait with you, so I am."

Petros sighed exasperatedly with a dramatic roll of his eyes. "Go make yourself useful and make us some tea, would you?"

Without missing a beat, as if he were completely undeterred by Petros' prodding, Dumitru shot back. "I will wait here until the Master returns."

Eyes flashing a crimson, similar to that of the Count's, his temper shot to a new high. "The Master will flay you alive for disobeying *me.*"

"Petros, please," I spoke up in my meager attempt to intercede on Dumitru's behalf. "He's only following the Count's wishes."

"And yet I wish for tea." He laid his hand on his chest.

I sighed openly, and as much as I wanted to simply appease him, I knew I could not be alone with Petros. "Dumitru, please make us some tea."

"I am sorry, *Domnișoară.*" He shook his head once.

"I wish to speak with Miss Isadora privately, *boy,*" Petros' voice strained through clenched teeth that had seemed to sharpen. "If you must remain here, go to the other side of the room."

Dumitru was hesitant to move from his seat, but when I nodded, he stood and went to the windows on the far side of the room. He was just close enough to be near us but far enough to pacify Petros' ire. I could see he was still watching us, although it looked like he was gazing out of the window.

"Miss Isadora," Petros cooed after Dumitru was out of earshot, his rage suddenly dissipating into nothingness. The swing in the mood between us was dizzying, yet he acted as though nothing had happened. "May I ask you something?"

I gulped. "Yes?"

He took my hand in his and interwove our fingers together. "You are single, yes?"

By my shocked reaction, he took that as a yes.

"Have you ever felt such passion for another that you craved to have them?" Petros examined our hands most carefully.

I could only blink. "I'm not sure what you mean."

"Don't play coy." He leaned in so his nose traced my cheekbone. "I've seen the way you look at me, and I know women your age crave a certain amount of…satisfaction."

I didn't need a map to know exactly where he was going, but I didn't want to go there at all. I didn't rely

"Playing hard to get?" He went as if to whisper something in my ear, but instead, he bit it playfully. The sensation made me gasp, and I wanted to get away, but his teeth were so sharp that I thought my ear would be torn away. A ripple of dizziness rushed over me, and I knew what was coming. I looked at Dumitru, but from his angle, it only looked as if Petros were whispering to me. "I know what you want, sweet flower. Why do you resist the joys I could give you?"

He nibbled more on my ear, then kissed around my jaw so slowly. I was so horrified I couldn't move or speak. This man, so handsome and otherworldly, was reeling me in against my will. My heart surged in terror and sick delight.

I heard him chuckle. "Don't tell me you're frightened? Could it be you've never —"

"Stop this…" I whispered desperately, my voice cracking.

"Your words say one thing," he twirled a lock of my hair around his finger. "Your voice says another."

"Please…"

His hand wrapped around my inner thigh, which of course, was out of Dumitru's line of sight. "I will please you more than he ever could. All you need to say is when and where."

Then, as if he were never there, he had made distance between us again as the door opened and the Count came in. I looked to him, then back to Petros, who held up his finger to shush me. "It's a secret."

My head swam as the Count approached and apologized for being called away. I didn't hear the rest of the conversation, but left my eyes downcast and kept replaying his words over in my mind. I couldn't make sense of them. I felt like I was out of my body, that my eyes were open but I could see nothing. I wanted to scream to the Count that Petros had touched me most inappropriately, but what proof did I have? Dumitru was in the room, and he had seen nothing. It was my word against Petros', and if I said anything, surely he would seek me out with a vengeance. I felt like an emotional wreck, but somehow retained my outward composure. I don't know how long I stayed like that until I felt Petros' hand on mine. I jumped, blinking back into reality.

"Miss Kane, are you alright?" The Count looked down at me with a worry etched on his brow.

"Uh, I'm so sorry," I touched my cheek, searching for some reasonable answer. "I must have dozed off."

"You look unwell," Petros placed his cool hand upon my forehead. I wanted to move away from him, but I had no power. "You're burning up."

"I am?" I knew I wasn't hot, but actually very cold.

"Dumitru," Petros called to him with a few rude snaps of his fingers. "Miss Isadora is unwell, please take her to her room."

Suddenly, Dumitru was beside me, taking my arm for me to stand. I had almost lost my balance, but he steadied me. "Well, goodnight, gentlemen."

They replied with their goodnight wishes as I was led from the room. Before he could even close the door, Dumitru whispered. "What did he say to you?"

I couldn't look at my friend. "Nothing. I just need air."

"Don't lie to me."

"Dumitru, please, don't ask me. Don't make me say it. Not now." I leaned heavily on him, my vision distorting like a slinky. This must be something they are able to do to immobilize their prey so that they are helpless. I had experienced this too many times before from the Count to not know what this was. When I was under the Count's spell, I felt more willing to comply with his wishes, but with Petros, I am an innocent bystander screaming and suffocating as he encroaches.

Dumitru didn't pressure me again to answer him about what Petros had said to me. Honestly, I can barely acknowledge them as fact, although they are so unmistakably true. He wanted to get me some kind of local medicinal concoction to help me sleep, but I refused. If *he* was coming for me, I had to be as alert as possible. I will sleep for the next few hours until around midnight, and then remain awake until dawn. I can sleep until the afternoon when I know both of them will be out of the castle. But for now, I must be on my guard.

I cannot tell the Count or Dumitru about this because, in doing so, I risk both Petros' wrath and the Count discovering I know their secret. I know what both of them are, and I must use all the knowledge I have to defend myself.

21 June

Morning, 1:30 am...
I'm writing by the light of the small fireplace in my room so that no one knows I'm up. I don't dare draw the curtains to let the moonlight in unless Petros can walk on walls and peek in like the Count. So, I sit in my chair in the corner next to my desk, listening for any sound from outside my door or windows. I have readied myself with the holy water, Bible, and rosary, just in case.

I've been sitting here for about an hour, thinking of ways I could cleverly use my few 'tools' to the most advantage they can give me, and I think I have figured out one that's most capable of doing severe damage if the need arises.

However, the main downfall of this strategy is that I will have no idea if it works until a certain time. I don't dare reveal it here unless this record is discovered before I have a chance to use it. And, of course, I can only use it once before it's found out. The other major failure of it is that it will take time to take effect. I may not have the luxury of such time, so I must perceive any potential threat as a real threat and put it into motion before it's too late.

Later, 6 am…

The sun is rising, and there has been no attack. I wonder if I was a fool to stay up all night waiting, but who can say for certain? During this night, I also brushed up on some Latin phrases that may be of use, but now I am exhausted. I will hopefully write later.

Afternoon, 4 pm…

I have gotten just under seven hours of sleep, which is plenty for me. When I awoke, it was just lunchtime, so I had two meals to eat. Again, Dumitru asked me what Petros had told me since he has denied saying anything upsetting. The Count knows he's lying and insists I relay the truth to Dumitru. I couldn't bring myself to tell him, but I told him I would tell the Count when we are alone at our lesson tonight. He seemed content enough with that.

As much as I don't dare leave my rooms, I know I must prepare for the lesson. Duty before the self? I'll keep telling myself that. All day and night, I've been psyching myself into preparing for something to happen tonight. But I know as long as Dumitru and the Count are there, I am safe to a point.

I have my tools and my wit, and with God's unceasing grace and mercy, I will prevail against whatever I face. St. Michael, pray for me, I am at the mercy of the Devil and his minions. This may be my last entry, but I am ready.

Chapter Nine
VENENUM DRACONIS

25 June

Afternoon...

It has been only a few days since I wrote last, and I feel decades behind. I write with much effort, much pain, but I am determined to compile in order all that transpired between the evenings of 21 June to today. So much, so very much, has happened. I feel perpetually changed by it all, not only physically, but especially emotionally.

So, I will return to 21 June, that terrible evening, and tell the story the best I can remember it after so long. I will be as faithful as I can to the account, no matter how long it takes to write it down.

*21 June

Evening...

That morning, I had begun my monthly time, which complicated things so much more. If the Count was still so repulsed as he was before, then surely it would draw Petros in. There was nothing I could do to mask whatever scent I was emanating, for surely it would be picked up by their keen noses. I was determined not to let it be my crutch, though I still kept looking over my shoulder, expecting something to happen. As I recall, I was quite nervous when I got to the library and set my things out to prepare for the lesson. Promptly, I placed the holy water, concealed in a normal plastic water bottle, nonchalantly on the table. The rosary was secure in my pocket, ready to be pulled out at a moment's notice. I was ready, in body and soul, for anything.

To my great relief, the hours ticked by in silence, and I waited in anticipation for the hour of the howling of the wolves. As time got closer and closer to the approaching moment, I kept telling myself to have faith in God and my abilities. I could do anything if I only believed.

It was only about 15 minutes before the howling when a figure, seemingly from the shadows of the hall, emerged in the doorway. As I heard his voice, my blood ran cold. "Miss Isadora."

My eyes darted to where Petros stood, his shirt casually unbuttoned, exposing some of his chest, like he just rolled out of bed. I felt my throat tighten at the sight of him, and it caught me off guard. "Mr. Petros, you're here early."

I calmly reached for my water bottle and managed to chug just under a quarter of the sacred water.

"I thought I'd come to see you." He entered the library and came to stand near me. "We never finished our conversation from yesterday evening."

Deeply inhaling, I let out a long exhale as I closed my computer and secured it in my bag. "Our conversation? What about it?"

He bent down and used his elbows to rest on the table. "You never gave me an answer."

"Perhaps I will never give you an answer." I snapped. I had to do anything to prolong his intended actions until either Dumitru or the Count could show up.

"You can deny me all you want." With one finger, he touched my lips, and of course, I jolted away. "But that need of yours can't."

I shivered at his soft touch and sweet words, and a sickening feeling pitted itself deep in my stomach. "I won't give in to sexual harassment."

"You and your modern terms," he sighed in his usual exasperation and leaned in closer. "In my day, we called this seduction."

I winced and clenched my jaw at his erroneous definition. "To me, it's coercion to do something I do not want."

"Really?" He asked with a high intonation, then sniffed the air. "I can smell otherwise."

I was absolutely appalled. What the hell was that supposed to mean anyway? Again, my shock caused me not to answer.

"My nose does not lie." He swooped in beside me so that he was inches from my face. "I arouse you, don't I?"

I could feel the wooziness of the first effects of his ability, and I stood, making distance between us. "Not in the slightest."

"Hmm," he whined like a child and came around to me again. "You love to play this game, don't you? But I can tell you that you won't win."

"Do not underestimate me," I warned him quite plainly. "And I'm playing no game."

"You are. I can smell it." He was suddenly in my face again, and a wave of dizziness came over me, but I backed away as fast as I could. "Tell me, Miss Isadora, when was the last time a man treated you like a woman?"

I didn't answer and just kept retreating, something I knew I could only do for so long.

"You have been in Vlady's house for a while now," he kept steadily on my trail. "Why does he wait?"

I squinted in sheer confusion at him. "Wait for what?"

"To take you to his bed, of course." Petros came in on the other side of me, his nose right on my throat. "Among other things…"

"Ridiculous," I jumped away, moving towards the book stacks, my hands trembling. "The Count has no feelings for me. Only respect as his teacher."

Petros scoffed and laughed once. "That's what he'd like you to think, little flower. Have you not seen the way he looks at you? Perhaps you are not used to seeing what it looks like when a man is in pursuit of a woman. The things they do are, at times, irrational, erratic."

"Maybe you're blind to the truth." I tried to stand my ground, feeble as my opposing argument was. "The Count has been protecting me from you. He told me he has warned you of the consequences if you touch me."

He laughed at that. "Do you think I am afraid of him? He is weak and has been for some time. You may not understand his actions, but he has claimed you as his."

"You *should* be afraid of him." I tried to stare him down, but it was no use since I kept moving back and back. "And how absurd, don't lie to me about things which are so obviously untrue."

"Vlady is very particular about his women." Petros was suddenly behind me, his fingers rubbing into my shoulders. "You should feel honored."

"Don't touch me!" I hissed and pushed him away, shaken by his unnatural quickness. "You'll regret this when Dumitru gets here. Do you think he will take so kindly to this?"

"That *boy*?" Petros grimaced at the sound of his name as if it left a bad taste in his mouth. "How can he save you? He's dead. I should know since I had the pleasure of dispensing with him."

My world began to spiral, and I faltered. The idea of Dumitru being dead was so inconceivable to me that I knew it couldn't be true, yet at the same time, I knew Petros would do something like that to make sure I was completely alone. I had to keep my bluff. "You can't trick me, Petros."

"Why would I want to trick you, dear? You'll find him on the kitchen floor with his head bashed in." Like a panther crouching low to strike, he poised, ready to launch at me. An instinct was struck within my primitive brain that told me that I stood no chance against him and that I should run. Petros chuckled at the horrified expression on my face. "For you, though, I have other plans."

His face morphed into this hideous, feral beast, something that drives horror into my very soul just thinking about it. Petros' handsome features had all at once vanished, and all that surfaced was the true demon that lies within. Before me was manifest a devil, so real and tangible. I knew there was evil in the world, but never before did I think I would see it firsthand, not like this. All my fears about my situation appeared in front of me and stared me right in the face. I wanted to scream, but another instinct came upon me, and I grabbed the rosary from my pocket just in time. The crucifix in hand and the chain around my wrist, I held it before the demon that was called Petros, screaming at the top of my lungs. *"Vade retro, Satana!"*

At the sight of the crucifix, the creature hissed and withdrew, angered rather than subdued by my first attack. He bared his teeth, revealing his sharpened canines as he eyed me with such hatred as I had never seen in the eyes of any creature.

"Nunquam suade mihi vana! Sunt mala quae libas!" I jumped forward, the crucifix held firmly in my hand, desperate to show my dominance over him.

He only took a step back and laughed mockingly at my attempts. "You think something so pitiful can stop me?"

"You have no power over me!" I shouted, and yet to my dismay, my cries seemed to only make him angry, as if I were shooting a bear with a revolver. I gritted my teeth, this time being forced to retreat to my chair, where my other tools were waiting.

"No *power?*" Petros sneered, the maddened bloodlust in his eyes sparking. "You are an ensnared fly, struggling to free yourself from the web I have spun. In your case, this is nothing personal, but I will devour your 'Count' as well as you. For once, he will be the one prostrate before me after I have taken his house as my house, his wealth as my wealth, and you, his prize as my prize."

All of this, killing Dumitru and attacking me, was just to show his superiority over the Count? I dared to ask him. "In God's name, why?"

"What prestige it is to depose a king?" He responded to my question with a question. "To take his spoils? Supersede his glory? Not to mention the women…and the men."

"*He's* your friend!" Appalled as I was, I could see Petros committing such a betrayal against his own brother. He was vain enough to covet all his neighbor has, just to satisfy his ego. "*You're* his friend!"

He only shrugged. "Here today, gone tomorrow. When you have only lived one life, I don't expect you to understand, darling."

I could no longer listen to the things he said, knowing the lies or tricks that he was spouting to distract me. There was no more reason to converse with him. He was bound and determined to end this, and so was I. Crying out again, I resumed. *"Vade retro, Satana!"*

He suddenly grabbed my wrist that had the rosary tied tightly around it. A burning smell flooded the air, and as I desperately ripped my arm away, the chain broke and the beads scattered on the floor. A terror entered my heart, and he slinked forward to me. "I've grown tired of this."

Turning, I dove for the water bottle, but he grabbed me and hauled me back. Somehow, the small crucifix was dislodged from my hand and thrown a distance away. I fought as hard as I could against him. With all my strength my body had, I punched, scratched, and kicked, but it all did nothing. Petros only laughed.

Taking me by my waist, Petros set me on the side of the table and grabbed my cross necklace and shirt, tearing the fabric on my shoulder away. At my proximity to him, I could feel that false sense of calm and acceptance come over me. I knew it was a lie, but I still fought him with my words. *"Vade retro, Satana.* I rebuke you…"

A dark laugh came from Petros now that I was in his clutches, his eyes burning for blood. Taking my hair, he wound it around his fist and yanked it back, exposing my throat to him. I cried out, trying to push him away, but he remained solidly in place.

The next thing I remember, four hot needles sank deep into the left side of my neck, and all strength left my limbs. All at once, my vision went dark, and the world was drowned out by a cold that was seeping into my being. My heart struggled to beat, my lungs to breathe, and I knew death was close. I felt my body slump, and I hit the ground hard. My eyes flashed open, and I saw Petros quivering above me as he coughed up blood, my blood, almost choking on it. The blue veins in his neck swelled as he looked at me, a deranged craze in his eyes. "What have you done?!"

I was just about to respond when a chorus of howls echoed in the distance, and a great wave of relief rushed over me. I could only laugh.

Fury ripped through him, and he was about to stomp my head in when he stopped, looking far off into the distance. Petros' breathing grew hoarser, and his body shook so violently that he stumbled back from me. Muttering obscenities, he had turned abruptly and taken off running the way he came. I was left alone and again felt that cold making its way under my skin. All I knew was that I had to get up, but there was no strength left in me, and I collapsed back onto the floor.

I must have passed out, for the next thing I knew, someone was calling my name. I thought I had died if the pain in my neck wasn't still there. Eventually, I opened my eyes, and the Count was kneeling over me. His eyes were wide with a mix of wrath and fear, his nostrils flared, his chest heaving. My eyes immediately blurred, and my entire being relaxed knowing I was safe. I tried to call out to him, but my voice was hoarse and broken.

"Isadora," he was holding my head steady in his hands. I had never heard him call me by just my name before. "Do not move, do not speak."

"He killed Dumitru," was the only thing I thought to say. "He's in the kitchen. You…you have to help him."

The Count's face froze, a new expression coming over him. Ripping his shirt over his head, he bunched it gently beneath my neck to support it. As he did, his face came close to mine as he spoke firmly. "Listen to me, you must stay here. Promise me you will stay here. I will return for you."

Before I could say anything, he had departed. Again, I was left alone. However, no matter what the Count told me, I was determined to find Dumitru. Using whatever power I had left within me, from where it came from I know not, I rolled over and forced myself to my hands and knees. I cried out, feeling the torn ligaments in my neck strain under the weight of my head. But still, I pressed forward, grabbing the edge of the table to hoist myself to my feet. Nausea and dizziness followed, and I was certain I was already in shock.

My neck burned, so I used the Count's shirt to help slow the bleeding. I knew I couldn't focus on it now, and somehow, I managed to gain enough balance to stagger out of the library. I pushed hard, falling against the wall, but I steadily got to the stairs. By some miracle, of which I don't remember, I got down the two flights of steps before the main floor opened out in front of me. The door was open, and the warm air of evening was sweeping inside.

Howls, this time louder and clearer than before, let loose nearby. They sounded ferocious and were accompanied by short bursts of frenzied yelping to signal the kill was afoot. A sharp fear pierced my heart, and I worried about the Count's safety. I pleaded to God not to let it end this way.

I trudged on and somehow made it down into the kitchen. I screamed for Dumitru, but when there was no answer, I began to panic. Finally, I found him lying in the corner, face down, not moving. I staggered to him, falling from my lack of balance. "Dumitru?"

I grabbed him by his clothes and pulled him over. I had expected the scene to be much worse, but he only seemed to have been knocked unconscious. However, a deep blow to his head was bleeding profusely on the stone floor, creating a red pool beneath him. I placed myself at his head and rested it gently in my hands to keep it steady. The Count's shirt began to soak up his blood, too.

I felt for his pulse with my freezing, shaking fingers. He was still alive, but barely. If he didn't get help soon, he'd surely die. But, there was nothing I could do for him but hold his head as steady as my trembling hands could manage, and periodically check his pulse. I don't know if it was to comfort myself or to comfort him if he could hear me, but I began to talk to him. "Dumitru, listen to me, you need to fight this. You can't leave me, you can't leave the Count."

I was spouting whatever came to mind, whatever words I could tell him to make him not slip away into the next world. "Please, don't go."

Of course, his face remained stoic even when unconscious, and he didn't move; he barely drew any breath. My tears let loose as I could feel him beginning to fade as his color was changing to a pale gray, and his features seemed to sink into his face. I cried out to God to have some mercy on him, when suddenly, quick footsteps were coming closer.

If it were Petros coming to finish both of us off, I think I would dive into that wild animal that I had vowed to repress. For the first time in my life, I wanted to kill and bare my teeth in the most furious rage. But when I looked up at the threshold, it was not Petros who stood there.

My eyes widened in awe and horror at the sight before me. The Count, shirtless, stood atop the landing looking down at us. Blood that was not his own was splattered on his chest and torso and dripped from his mouth down to his neck. From his fingertips, stringy blood and other fluids flowed in thin cords to the floor. There was the faintest scent that something was burning, and light smoke-like wisps evaporated off his bloodied frame. He reminded me of some ancient warrior who had painted himself with the blood of his enemies. The Count's hair was matted at the ends with blood, and his eyes shone like red rubies in the fading light. The sight struck me with such wonder and dread that I had almost forgotten all about Dumitru.

He came down the steps slowly, examining both of us in our broken states. As he came closer, I saw the white of his fangs protrude from his lips, so sharp, so deadly. I was in frightened awe.

His eyes settled directly on me. "Now, you know."

"I have known for some time." My voice sounded unusually flat and emotionless, and I quickly moved the subject to more important things. "He won't last long. Can you do anything for him?"

He cocked his head to the side at Dumitru as he approached. I wanted to move away in fear of the Count, but I could not leave Dumitru's side. Taking only a second to examine him, he bit his wrist and placed it to Dumitru's mouth, forcing his blood into it. "This will help him if he does not die before then."

The action made my stomach turn over, but I said nothing nor showed my disgust. "We should get him to his room."

The Count nodded and lifted the young man in his arms with ease. Then, with much care, the Count and I left the kitchen for his room. I had never known where Dumitru slept before, but he is situated off of the main level, down in the servants' quarters. When the Count indicated which room, I opened the door and we went inside. It was barely furnished, with only a wide bed, a chair, a wood stove, and a nightstand. It reminded me of a prison cell more than a bedroom.

The Count laid him on his bed and told me to stay with him while he fetched some bandages. I did try to keep the blood off his pillow with little success. By this time, I started to feel increasingly dizzy and lightheaded, my vision blurring in and out. I wanted to shake my head, but my wound left me with a limited range of motion. I could only force my eyes to stay open and told myself not to fall asleep. Luckily, the Count returned quickly, and I helped him bandage the poor boy's head as I held his neck stable.

Suddenly, the Count spoke with a calm tone. "What did you do to Petros?"

I swallowed hard. Even though he didn't sound angry, I was unwilling to answer and let my secret out, so I looked away from him.

He continued to wrap his servant's head. "Whatever it was, it was most effective. I was able to make quick work of him. However, I think I should have let him burn from the inside out, as you had apparently intended. I would not think you were capable of something so…brutal."

I said nothing, my jaw clenching hard against my upper teeth. I could feel the throbbing in my neck grow worse from having to hold up my head, my arms, and Dumitru's head. There was simply no strength left in my upper body to sustain the strain.

"Just a moment longer, I am almost finished." He said calmly as he fastened the bandages and told me to let go.

With great relief, I did, immediately grabbing my wound with my left hand, and hunching over against the bed. My hands were still shaking, and I could feel the coagulated blood mush against my already bloodied fingers. The pain was spreading into my head and shoulders, and my breathing sounded more like low growls at every exhale.

"Isadora?" I felt a hand on my back, and I flinched away, yet the Count didn't let me escape. Grabbing my shoulders, he helped me straighten. "Let me help you."

"I'm fine." I snapped through my teeth.

"You know you are not." He spoke soothingly, and that calm eased my mind. "I can help you. Let me."

I looked at him questioningly, wondering if I could really trust him. The thing is, I knew I could do so completely, but suddenly there was this new wariness of him that I knew stemmed from his appearance. He was still bloodied, and he had admitted to me what he is. If he wanted to kill me, he could have done it at any time. There was no use in fighting him, although I still had the advantage of having purified blood. So, I sat on the foot of the bed and allowed him to treat my wound as he saw fit.

"Do you want to tell me what he said?" The Count asked as he worked.

I thought for a moment, staring off into space, before speaking. "He told me he wanted…" My voice broke, but I forced out the words hoarsely. "He wanted to take what is yours and me as some sort of prize. Something about making you bow before him. He told me all these lies about you, at least I know they're lies since I can't imagine they're true."

He only listened to my words and replied with little emotion. "What did he say?"

"Lies…" I repeated, wincing at a sharp pain.

He wasn't forceful in his demand for information, but stern. "Tell me his lies."

My lips pursed, and I recalled the things Petros had said to me. I was so unwilling to tell the Count anything about it since it involved not just him, but me too. "They were about us. He insisted you have some romantic affection for me."

"And you believe that is a lie?" The Count carefully smoothed out the edges of the large sticky bandage against my skin.

I looked at him, his eyes were soft and back to a warm brown. I recalled the night that seems so long ago when we had been so close to passion. I wanted to say, 'it should be' but I couldn't bring myself to say it, instead I deflected. "I don't know what to think anymore."

The Count was silent for a moment before changing the subject. "Stay with Dumitru while I clean up. Then, I will be back."

I nodded, still not looking at him, and I didn't watch him go. I just sat on the edge of the bed, staring at nothing. The Count's words came to me of how Petros was 'burning from the inside out', and I shuddered. Although I had not given the *coup de grâce*, I had been a key instrument in the process. I had willingly inflicted pain on another being with the intent to kill. I looked down at my hands, and although within me was a storm of emotions, on the outside, I could feel nothing. Petros might as well have died by my hand, and for some reason, I was glad about that. I guess he was right: women my age *do* crave a certain 'satisfaction', something he promised to give me.

The Count returned a bit later carrying a load of different things from linens, medicinal herbs, and even food. Among the various linen towels was my nightgown, which he told me to change into. He explained that since Dumitru could not move, I would be staying in his room so that he could monitor us. It was a logical decision, for the Count could not be in two places at once with two very injured people on his hands.

I was a bit wary, but in privacy, I did change out of my ruined and bloodied clothes. The sight of them shocked me when I saw the large blots of red with splatters crisscrossed in different patterns. The shoulder of my blouse was destroyed, and there were other tears that I hadn't noticed. When I turned my attention to my body, I was even more shocked. Bruises were already forming on my legs, and my wrist that had held the rosary was cut from when the chain had broken. It was bruising as well from where he held me and I had ripped away. I hadn't felt any of these injuries.

After wiping myself down with a wet cloth and putting on my gown, I returned to the sad scene. The Count was staring pensively into the fire he had just made, and he gazed over at me and asked me how I was. I know he was asking about more than just the physical, but I only said that I thought my wrist had a minor sprain. Like a mother hen, he insisted that it be wrapped, even though I said it wasn't that bad. Yet, as he was wrapping it, I couldn't help but feel the gentle nature in which he bound it; those same hands that before had been stained with the blood of his friend, who had betrayed him.

I could not imagine what he was feeling. What inner turmoil he must have been experiencing that he kept bottled in. The Count promptly told me to go to sleep and that he would wake me if he needed me to assist him with Dumitru. I had no choice but to comply, and I lay next to Dumitru, careful not to disturb him too much. The Count's back was turned to us as he sat in the chair and continued to stare into the dancing flames. So, under the sheets, I took Dumitru's hand to hold it and to let him know he wasn't alone, then I drifted to sleep.

KISMET

*22 June

Pain in my neck woke me sometime in the early morning, and when I came to, the scene had not changed. Dumitru was still unconscious but was breathing regularly. I was checking his temperature with my hand when the Count spoke. "He is improving."

"I'm relieved." My voice was so raspy, and I let a deep sigh escape me. "How long have I been asleep?"

"Only five hours." He commented flatly, still not turning to acknowledge me.

From his distancing and cold demeanor, my worry for the Count spiked. This deathly silence was not the cheerful man I knew, so since I was feeling a bit better, I got out of bed and came to sit on the floor adjacent to him. He looked so much older in the dim light, so sad and pale with a far-away look in his eyes, and I frowned. "Are you doing alright, Count?"

The Count's sad eyes shifted to mine. "I will be fine."

I frowned at his tone. "We both know that's not true."

He didn't like that, and looking back at the fire, he muttered. "Go back to bed, Miss Kane."

I could tell that he wanted to be alone, but after everything that happened, no one should be alone. His distancing tactic wouldn't work on me, and I knew exactly what to say to get him to converse. "I would like to stay up with you a bit if you'll allow me."

"If you wish…" His voice faded out as if he hadn't really heard what I said, and his gaze slowly drifted back into thought.

My frown turned into a pout. If I had told him weeks ago that I wanted to stay up with him to talk, he'd be beaming with that smile of his. Scratching my head, I gave in against my own good sense to keep the conversation going. "You wanted to know how I did it…" I paused. "I drank holy water."

His eyebrows raised slightly as his attention was redirected to me. "A sacrilegious act. Where did you get it?"

I hung my head and bit my lip. "I was able to take it from a church while Dumitru and I were in Bucharest."

If he had anger from it, he hid it well. Then, he asked me softly. "You have known that long?"

"From before then, I suspected."

A slightly amused grin came over his lips. "You planned to use it on me?"

"Initially, yes, but then I realized you were not the threat I needed to defend myself against." I admitted, but then stopped when he languidly reached forward to stroke my hair. "Count, may I say something?"

His fingers continued to comb my unkempt hair, and the feeling strangely comforted me. "Of course."

I leaned into his hand a bit. "Thank you for saving us."

The Count's fingers stopped, and his frown returned. "I did not do much saving."

"Yes, you did —"

"*I did not,*" he snapped, pointing to my bandage. "This is evidence of that."

I was struck dumb by the resoluteness of his tone. "Petros was about to stomp my head in, but stopped when he heard you coming. So, even if Dumitru would be fine, I would not."

The Count's jaw locked, and he held in a surge of rage, staring intently back into the fire. The vein in his head swelled as he glowered at the words I had said, yet I found myself smiling lopsidedly up at him.

Something in me moved for this tormented man, and I got to my feet and cautiously wrapped my arms around his neck. I drew him close, and although I could feel him tense, I didn't let go. "Thank you, Count, for saving my life."

Suddenly, his arms clasped around my midsection and brought me tightly to him. The Count pressed me hard against his torso and chest, his fingers desperately gripping my sides to keep me there. We stayed like that for the longest time, just holding each other. This was a side of him I had never seen before, and I felt immense pity for this semblance of a man who is more tormented, more broken, than he would ever admit to himself.

He shifted unexpectedly, the tenderness between us passed into something heavier as he laid me softly on the ground. The Count hovered over me, his hair falling past his face, casting shadows on his features from the firelight. I lay beneath him, moving my arms from his neck to touch his face with my fingertips. There was an odd fluttering in my stomach I had never felt before, and I had no fear of him at that moment as he took my bandaged hand and kissed the palm. It amazed me how different he is compared to Petros, in that even his kisses have an air of respect and formality.

A passing realization dawned on me, and it felt like my heart had burst in my chest. "It's true, then?"

He listened to my words, but his mouth continued to kiss down my arm to my shoulder. It was almost frightening but thrilling to me that I was so willing to accept his kisses, knowing full well what he is. Bypassing my neck altogether, he laid his cheek against mine as he whispered. "It is true only if you wish it to be."

His words didn't shock me because I had known it to be true all along. I wanted to ask him why he held these feelings for me, how he developed them, or when he started to feel something more. But that was not the time nor the place to ask him those intimate questions. Knowing the Count as little as I do, I wouldn't be surprised if he didn't answer them at all. I knew in my heart I couldn't deny him as I had come to love him, in spite of what he is. "I wish it to be."

"Hearing that fills me with a warmth I have not felt in many years." The Count pressed his cheek firmly against mine, and a soft vibration danced in the air that sounded like a purr.

My heart surged, but I was still so conflicted. There were so many factors that separated us, but so many still that brought us together. In many ways, we both had been saying 'yes' to each other all this time.

"Look at me." I pleaded, and the Count complied. There was a sadness in his eyes like I had never seen before, and it broke a part of me to see him so pained. "I have never loved another as I love you. It terrifies me because I don't know if I can be all that you need me to be. But I swear I will try as hard as I can if you will have me."

His eyes widened for a split second as he tried to hide his shock. I thought I had ruined our quiet moment, but the Count did not pull away, nor did he condemn me for revealing how I feel. Then his gaze on me softened as he whispered to me as if to tell a secret. "You are too pure-hearted for me. Sometimes I wonder if just touching you will burn me, or if I get too close, I will defile you."

The Count's wordage: 'pure', 'burn', 'defile'… if he had used them before I fully understood what he is, I think I would have been worried for my safety. Now that I know everything as I do, they were essential to understanding the boundaries of our relationship…whatever that really is. Smiling at him, I jested lightly. "It seems we're both corrupting each other."

He hummed in agreement. "Does it really not frighten you? What I am? What I have done?"

I thought for a moment about those unnatural things that I have witnessed him doing, and I knew what my feelings were shouting to me. "The unknown frightened me before, but with time, I grew to understand and accept you as you are. I don't entirely grasp what you are or what you can do, but because it's *you*, I do not fear it."

The Count looked down at my lips, then back up to my eyes. He drew closer, yet hesitated. In his eyes, I could see his self-control waning. My heart was pounding, my neck pulsing with a dull pain, but through it all, I wanted with all my being to kiss him. I was nervous like a schoolgirl wanting to kiss her crush on the cheek, and my face suddenly burst with heat. The Count grinned at my reaction to his intention and closed the distance between us.

Our lips grazed the other as if they were afraid to finally meet, but slowly they accepted the opposite pair. I hadn't been kissed romantically in years, and the sensation was so foreign, so breathtaking. Quickly, he deepened it, and I loved it. I was so overcome by him that I didn't want to stop, and I wanted to be consumed by him completely.

Just as he moved his hands into my hair, there was a sharp stabbing pain in my neck, and all at once the burning spread back into my head and shoulder. The suddenness and intensity of it made me cry out against his lips, and instantly, he was off me. My hand grasped my wound, and I growled through my gritted teeth. "It burns…"

He cooed a lulling shush as the backs of his fingers grazed over my cheek, and I could feel myself grow limp and calm despite the raging pain. The Count pulled back the bandage, and his face fell. "It has already become infected…"

"Is that normal?"

"No…" he frowned. "If done correctly, you should not feel much discomfort, but…Petros was not kind to you."

I muttered profanity as another wrack of needles burned me from within.

Without another word, he burst into action. Leaving me lying on the floor, he went to his herbs that he had left out and began to add this and that into a mortar and then grind away with a pestle. He came back with a foul-smelling paste that he applied directly to the mark and reapplied the bandage. "You ought to rest now."

I melted at the coolness of the soothing balm that began to quench the burning. "Sorry, I ruined the moment."

The Count smiled sadly as he lifted me easily in his arms. "It is not your fault. Sleep."

He must have commanded it, for I don't recall anything else.

Later…

The next thing I recalled was waking past noon, starving. Looking around the room, the Count was not in his chair, and Dumitru was still in his place. Upon examining him closer, his color had returned, and his pulse was strong, which was all we could ask for.

My stomach was calling me to get food, and so gathering my ruined clothes, I made my way up into the main level. I couldn't go about the castle in my nightgown, so I steadily made it to my room. I noticed as I ascended the stairs, the blood splatters and bloodied handprints that dotted the way. It looked like an extended murder scene, and it only got worse when I reached my floor. The door to the library was still open, and an encroaching dread stilled the blood in my veins. I gulped as I passed, not bothering to look inside. I had no time to reminisce about things past with Dumitru still in his state.

I got cleaned up quickly as I could manage, which was so difficult with my injuries. My wrist had swollen, and I could barely move my traumatized neck to either side. In the end, I had to settle for unflattering sweatpants, a t-shirt, and my hair in a ponytail. After that, I went down the kitchen, the pool of Dumitru's blood had been cleaned up, and there was no trace of the previous night's struggle. I stood there staring at the spot, recalling how the blood had slipped through my fingers. My stomach brought me back to the present, and so I just made myself some basic oatmeal and tea. I admit, it was hard to eat.

Afterward, I went swiftly back to the servants' quarters, where I was surprised to see the door open and hear the Count chatting inside. Hastily, I entered, and to a greater astonishment, both he and Dumitru looked over at me. My poor friend's eyes lit up when he saw me.

Then, the Count spoke. "He just awoke."

All the fear I didn't realize that I held on my shoulders for Dumitru lifted, and the Count stepped aside when I rushed to Dumitru, grabbing hold of his cold hand. "Dumitru, how are you feeling? I've been so worried."

He blinked in acknowledgment, but when his eyes caught sight of my bandage, he frowned so deeply. "Petros?"

I nodded but kept a smile on my face. "Yes, but don't you worry about me. You're lucky to be alive."

He looked away. "Yeah…lucky."

For a moment, I wasn't sure what to say. Dumitru's short attitude both hurt and worried me, but I had to remember that he was not himself. "If you need anything at all, I'll be here."

There was a slight nod, although he still didn't look at me.

The Count's hand touched my shoulder. "Come, Miss Kane, I must discuss something with you."

I nodded, still frowning. Squeezing Dumitru's hand before letting go, the Count ushered me out of the room. We walked in silence to the grand entrance before he stopped suddenly and asked. "How are you feeling?"

"Sore, weak, tired." I listed, slouching my shoulders. "The usual."

He gave me a sad smile. "And the bite?"

I felt myself go very silent and tried to think of an answer to lighten the situation. "Better than yesterday. I can hardly turn my head, but I can hold it up."

My attempt to see the silver lining wasn't much appreciated by the Count, for he frowned. I'm sure he knew I was trying to make it not look as bad as it actually was. "After we speak, I will change the bandage."

I nodded. "And how are you feeling?"

"I am fine." The Count commented and began to walk again. "Thank you for asking."

He lied so easily, so convincingly. It made me wonder what else he has lied about to me, but I couldn't tell the difference. As I followed him, I pursed my lips, wondering what to say or do. "Do you remember what I said to you after you told me of your wife?"

The mention of it made him tense. "You told me many things that evening."

"I told you that if you ever needed anything, you should tell me." I reminded him as I cautiously placed a hand on his forearm. "And I know you need something."

The Count eyed me closely. "And what is it that you think I need?"

"Someone to talk to about what happened. You may have grown up in an era where men showed no weakness and never spoke about their feelings, but I know you are greatly troubled. It was written all over your face last night. You can hide it from Dumitru, I understand, but not from me." I clarified, my tone slightly firm but not too much to make it sound like I was chastising him. "I may be only human, but I still have ears to hear and a brain to understand."

He kept his face stern and hard. "It would be a burden to you."

"Was it a burden to admit that you feel for me, then?" I asked him plainly.

The Count's brow knitted, and he looked away, sighing. "Very well. I will tell you only if you tell me all that Petros said and did to you leading up to last night."

How does it seem with him that each time I get the upper hand in a conversation, he swoops in and takes it from me? Needless to say, his trade was a fair one, but I felt a lingering apprehension come over me, and I looked away. My brow furrowed as a part of me revisited those few stray memories that popped up at the mention of it. I had to admit defeat here, again. "It would be a burden to you, too."

"I may be only a creature of the night," he said as he entered the kitchen to collect more herbs for the ointment needed to dress my wound. "But I still have ears to hear and a brain to understand."

Frowning, I glared at him as he used my own words against me. I crossed my arms and pouted, saying grumpily. "You win."

"I always do, my darling." The Count chuckled. After amassing what he needed, he led me to his reception room. I noticed that the room seemed more elegant in the day, with the sunlight picking up more of the vibrant color of the rich tapestries from behind the drawn curtains. Bringing me to a couch, which was in shadow, the Count sat me down with him. "Tell me everything in as much detail as you can remember. Take as long as you need."

I hated doing it, but eventually, I found the courage to begin. So, I told him of Petros' unwarranted advances and his meaningless sensual words, from when he had nibbled so playfully on my ear to beguile me into fornicating with him, to when he had nearly ripped my throat out because I told him 'no' for the final time. The Count sat like a statue, listening to all I had to say with a sorrowful expression on his face. I must have rambled on for 30 minutes before I caught him up to the present, and then we sat in silence.

Finally, after a long pause, the Count asked. "Why had you not told me this before, as you had promised me?"

"I felt I couldn't," I explained, my emotions threatening to surface. "He confused me, made me feel things I didn't want to feel. He said it was a secret, anyway. I'm sure if I told you, he would have retaliated before I had a chance to even come up with a way to defend myself. And if I did tell you, I would have had to admit that I know what you both are, and I feared you'd retaliate against me, too. I knew I could barely fight one by myself..." I stopped talking, biting my tongue. "As I told you last night, I knew I could trust you, but I wasn't sure how far I could take that trust."

"This is one thing I will never understand about you modern women," the Count grumbled and frowned deeply. "You never ask for help because you think you can do everything yourselves. Sometimes asking for help is your only option when you are in over your head."

"Being a woman has nothing to do with it!" I turned back to him, my temper starting to break through. "Yes, I was over my head, but how could I have been certain you'd believe I was telling the truth. Dumitru was right there in the room when Petros openly proposed that I give him a time and place, and he couldn't hear or see anything that would suggest Petros had done anything wrong. It was my word against your old friend's. Who do you think you'd choose?"

His lips went into a thin line. I think he hadn't seen how much the situation had put me between a rock and a hard place. All he saw was Petros' inappropriate actions, and thought we had grown close enough that I would voluntarily tell him things, ordered to or not. "I can see how it placed you in a difficult position, I truly do. But you should have told me nonetheless. It is my duty as lord of this house to protect all who live under this roof. Knowing Petros, I would have taken your side."

I wanted to counter in some way, but had no will within me to argue about things in the past. To signal that I was thoroughly done with the conversation, I stood to leave. "Thank you for understanding. Just the same, I am truly and sincerely sorry for causing such pain to your friend. I never meant to cause either of you such hurt."

"Isadora," he accidentally grabbed my bad wrist as I began to move away, and pain shot into my hand. I inhaled sharply through my teeth at the stabbing sensation, and immediately he let go, but gently took my arm instead to sit me back down. "Forgive me for not being more aware."

"There is no reason to apologize." I let out a long sigh in frustration with myself, not with him. "I'm the one who should be asking for an apology from you and Petros…"

The Count was silent as his arm curled around mine, pulling me to rest against him. I was reluctant, considering the circumstances, but did as he wished. Taking my bandaged hand tenderly in his own, as if to soothe the pain he had just caused, he spoke at length. "For the past few years, I had heard of plans among my kind who wanted to rid themselves of the oldest generation in favor of the newer. Petros, as I was told, had been among those circles but seemed to have no interest in committing any deed against me in particular. So, when he came to visit so unexpectedly after so many years, I knew he could not be trusted. He had this unique ability to sway people's opinion of him with his charm, but knowing he could get nowhere with me, he sought you. Petros knew of my feelings just by using you to provoke me to jealousy, and that is why he would refer to 'smelling' your arousal and touching you."

Thinking back, I wonder what he meant by some people wanting to 'get rid of the oldest generation'. He seems to me to be mid-forties, but if he is considered 'old', how old is he really? I wish I could have asked him what he meant, but at his last sentence, my face blazed hot in such utter embarrassment at those words. Without meaning to, I jumped to my own defense in a snap. "I wasn't aroused!"

"I could smell it too…" He grumbled uncomfortably.

"Oh God," I put my free hand on my face to hide. "What a fool I have made of myself."

"You could not help it. He used your biology and innocence against you. You cannot be ashamed of that." The Count patted my hand again uncomfortably. "That evening when I was called away, he had set that up to be alone with you and set his plan into motion then. But when it failed, he hurriedly chose yesterday evening before I could return to make his move."

My mortification only worsened as I shuddered. "I'm sorry I let him affect me."

"It was not your fault. Any woman or man who did not know him would have had the same reaction. He only did it to instigate me to violence." The Count cleared his throat and changed the subject. "When I returned, I knew something was wrong since he had disappeared. Unfortunately, I arrived too late to protect either you or Dumitru."

I frowned, squeezing his hand gently to urge him to continue.

There was a hint of gratification in his eyes as he spoke. "If you had seen the effect your little trick had on him, you would have been pleased. He had not gotten very far by the time I got to him. He was in quite a state, but still cursed you, so I did not wait long to dispatch him back to Hell. He had overstepped himself farther than he could reach, and he deserved the pain that you gave him, and the end I awarded him."

My eyes widened at his choice of words, which were tainted with malice. I recalled our conversation on forgiveness, and since he was not one to forgive people easily, I made the connection that he does feel a sense of satisfaction for ending Petros…no matter how small. "A part of me wishes I had seen it. He promised to give me satisfaction, and I see he gave you some also."

The Count's eyebrow raised and his head cocked to one side. "You regret causing him pain, yet you still find pleasure in it. A paradox."

Scowling, I glowered under his direct assessment of my contradicting feelings. "Not so pure-hearted now, am I?"

"You said yourself that we are corrupting each other." The Count's face was suddenly close to mine. "But, I like it. It has given me a new respect for you."

My cheeks burned as he drew in, again brushing his lips against mine to test the waters. This time, I initiated full contact, working his lips together with mine almost teasingly before slowly pulling away. The temptation he presented was growing in the pit of my stomach, making me feel tingly all over. "I told him not to underestimate me; you shouldn't either."

He grinned, showing his teeth. "I never will, I promise you."

As he looked at me with those fiery eyes, now being sparked to desire, I stopped breathing. My face burned hotter, and as naturally as I could manage through my other wave of embarrassment, I moved my face away from his. "You said you wanted to change my bandage, Count."

His smile widened, and with one finger, he traced the line of my jaw as he whispered sensually. "Do not underestimate me either, my dearest friend."

Ignoring his insinuating tone, I cleared my throat. "It would be a fatal mistake to do so."

"Fatal, indeed." He jested as he laid a languid kiss on my cheek and took my bandaged hand. After a stare that almost melted my insides, we went and redressed my bandage. The poultice the Count made last night had worked wonders on the wound, but of course, I was still far from a full recovery. It still burned and was terribly swollen from when he dressed it again. He reassured me that I was progressing and that all I needed was a good rest.

Since I was doing far better than Dumitru, who was still going in and out of consciousness, the Count allowed me to stay in my own room that night. I was relieved, but in the morning, I'd have to wake early to care for Dumitru while the Count was away. It was a fair enough exchange, so after a hot bath and a good supper, I settled into bed. In the privacy of my own room, I cried, but my neck hurt too much to sustain my ragged breaths. For that time, I'd have to internalize my feelings until I was well enough to let them out.

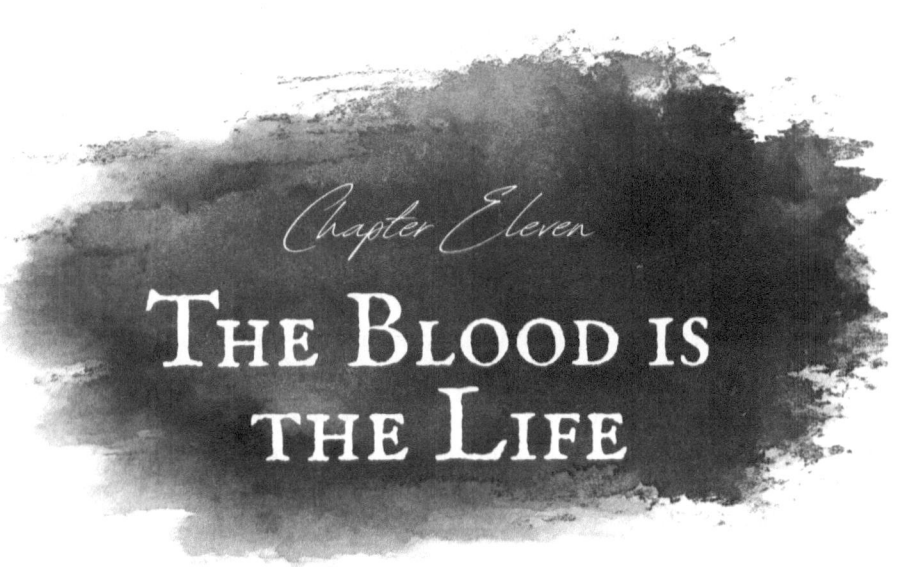

Chapter Eleven

THE BLOOD IS
THE LIFE

*23 June

Morning...

Howevever, sleep was not given to me so graciously as I
thought it would come. At first, I was very optimistic due
to my sheer exhaustion from the day, coupled with my
severe injuries, that I would naturally fall asleep on my own. But, as
the hours ticked by, my pain would come in waves, and my mind
would travel back to that evening in the library. Being it was also that
special time of the month for me, I suffered from more than just
Petros' bite.

I tried to clear my mind, but nothing seemed to work, and my
frustration was wearing my nerves thin. My body, especially my eyes,
was so tired, but my mind would not give them any reprieve from the
torment they intended to bring me. There were times I thought I was
so close to sleep, but then from somewhere, I'd hear a noise that

would frighten me back to reality. Other times, I'd feel like I was being touched by some phantom hands, or think I heard a low growl come from different areas of the room. I couldn't tell if I was imagining things, hallucinating, or if someone was actually there in the darkness.

I wondered if the ghost of Petros had come to torture me. Do creatures such as him have souls that could become trapped on this earth? As I lay there, I couldn't make up an educated answer to settle my tumultuous thoughts. Tears threatened to burst from my eyes, but I withheld them.

At one point, it must have been after midnight, I had finally drifted off to the point where my mind was left to wander into dreams. In that state of half-sleep I found myself in, I began to dream so vividly that if there had been physical evidence of it in the morning, I would have believed everything had actually happened.

I was asleep in bed when I heard a tapping at the barred window, and it woke me. The curtain had been drawn aside to let in the moonlight, but a dark shadow blotted it out as it picked at the lock on the outside. I sat up, and it noticed, with its two red eyes staring wildly at me from the other side of the window pane. Fear seized my chest, and I jumped out of bed to run to the sitting room. There was a sudden crash followed by glass shattering as the creature had ripped off a few bars and broken through the thin glass pane. Before I could react, it had slunk to the door to block my way. I stared in horror as the blackness rematerialized into Petros in his demonic form, his white teeth bared at me.

I wanted to scream, but I had no breath in me. I had enough sense to scramble to the bed and grab the Bible on the nightstand. However, before I had a chance to reach it, Petros snatched my injured hand and wrenched it hard at an odd angle. The bones broke easily, and that was when the scream finally surfaced from my paralyzed lungs. I collapsed in a ball at his feet, holding my hand tight to my chest.

"My flower," Petros snarled as he took my hair and used it to force me to my knees. He bent down at the waist so we met face to face. "You didn't keep our little secret. That was very naughty of you."

I held his stare with one of equal malice and hatred. His face was close enough that when I spat at him, it landed directly into his eye. "You are the scum of your kind. Go back to Hell, devil."

"That's not very nice." Petros wiped the spittle from his eye as his lips curled over his teeth. With his other hand, he ripped the bandage away from my neck and examined his handiwork with an enthusiastic sneer. "Is it comforting to know that you will always have something to remind you of me? Still, it's a shame it'll leave such a nasty scar on that beautiful skin."

To my horror, he leaned in, although I tried to struggle away, Petros held my hair firmly. At first, his teeth grazed over the damaged skin, then his tongue lapped up the crusted blood, breaking the scab to let the blood flow again. I shuddered as he sucked the open wound with his lips, then moved to my ear to bite it again. This time, however, he broke the skin and I whimpered as he sucked there too.

"Please," I breathed out the plea against his ear. "I only defended myself. I didn't want to hurt you."

He laughed at the desperation of my voice. "That's not what I smelled. You wanted me to take you, but you resisted nonetheless...such a very naughty girl."

My nostrils flared as Petros bit into me again, but this time it wasn't as violent as before. These resembled more like literal love bites in that they were quick and numerous. I can't recall how many times he had sunk his teeth into my skin only to withdraw just as the blood began to flow. They reached from under my ear to my shoulder, and when he was finished, a warm wetness had spread into my clothes. I could feel myself fading, my strength dispersing, as he used his tongue to lick up the blood he had drawn. I sagged against him, helpless, but still clenched my broken wrist.

Petros laughed once as he jerked my head back by my hair. "That's better, isn't it? If only you were this complacent before."

I gritted my teeth, a burst of rage spurred through me, and I remembered that feeling I had when I held Dumitru's head in my hands as I heard those approaching footsteps. Something in me snapped. I was about to spout some venomous words when he grabbed my throat, lifting me to my feet. My throat was being crushed as his fingers tightened. "What shall I do with you now, hmm?"

"*V-Vade retro, Satana,*" I growled through my ragged breaths.

Petros grinned, his full teeth sharpened in all their terror. "That's what I thought. I will see you in Hell after Vlady is done with you."

His fingers suddenly dug into my neck. There was a wrenching motion that shook me awake and back into reality.

I cried out and sat up in bed, frantically searching around the room for Petros, but found no one. Everything was as I had left it. The window was intact, my wrist was unbroken, but my neck ached and burned ferociously. My body was covered in sweat, and every muscle quivered in fear from what my mind had concocted for me to suffer. I felt so disorientated, so confused.

Regaining myself, I touched my neck. Reality hit me like a bus when my hand touched something hot and wet. My hand was covered in my blood, and so was my pillow, sheets, and collar of my nightgown. Instantly, I jumped from my bed and rushed to the bathroom to examine myself in the mirror. The sight wasn't pretty.

My face was pale against the redness of the blood that was slowly spreading. I swore loudly as I snatched up the hand towel and pressed it firmly to my reopened wound. My brain told me to go to the Count, but I knew if I were to come to him in such a state, he would insist I tell him everything. I sat on the edge of the tub trying to think of what to do, but as the bleeding would not stop, I had no choice.

I had just made it into the hallway and was halfway down the first flight when I nearly lost my balance. My vision was blurring, but I couldn't tell if it was because of blood loss or shock. My breathing was so ragged that I had to lean against the cold wall to steady myself.

"Isadora," suddenly, appearing out of thin air, the Count was next to me. I jolted back in fright. He just…was there, grabbing my shoulders in alarm. "What happened?"

"It opened again," was all that I could think to say. "In my sleep."

He frowned and took my hand to remove the bloodied towel. I watched him, and I could have sworn for just a split second that I thought I saw his face change. It was like how Petros had been, but it was only a glimmer of the demon within. There was a glint in his eye I had not seen since he had returned from his kill, bloodied and triumphant. This time, however, it was directed at me. I tensed, taking a step back, now fearful that the sight had provoked him.

He grabbed me and took me into his arms. "You must trust me."

In my state, I had no choice but to comply. The Count held me tightly as he rushed back up the stairs, back into my sitting room, and laid me on the settee. Gently, he removed the soaked bandage, his face grimacing when the smell in its entirety flooded the room.

"Is...Is it bad?"

The Count was caught in a war between his instinct and his conscience. I could see it so plainly in his eyes, and it broke my heart. All at once, he grabbed my good hand, his face turning more serious than I had ever seen before. "You *must* trust me."

I clenched my jaw at his repetition, seeing in his face that it was a case of life and death. If I were to survive, I'd have to place all of my trust in him. The cold was starting to seep under my skin again, and I knew I had no choice. So, I resigned my fate. "I trust you."

Again, there was a conflicting look on his face as he lifted my upper half to meet him. His image faded in and out as I struggled to stay awake. The Count's face came closer to mine, and I saw again a glimpse of what lies beneath the surface. "I would never do anything to hurt you, but to save your life, I must do this."

My heart strained to beat harder as the Count's lips touched mine. I was very confused at first as he moved his hands to support my head. I couldn't see how kissing me was going to solve my problem, but the Count pressed harder against my mouth, tilting my head back to open my jaw as he slid his tongue between my teeth. There was this obscure iron taste that accompanied his tongue, and my senses were overwhelmed by the scent of blood. Panicking, I tried to push him away, but he kept his place.

The foreign fluid swelled in my mouth, my shoulders convulsing with disgust as I still tried to spit it out. His lips released me, and he clasped a hand over my mouth. He was breathing raggedly, his eyes still blazing red as a stray drop of blood overran his lips. "Swallow it."

It was a command, for I found myself swallowing his blood without resistance. There was a strange feeling that swept over me as his blood filled every crevice of my being. It was as if a whole new power came into my body, strengthening and repairing it faster than I could comprehend. A tingling sensation appeared in my neck, wrist, and other parts of me which had previously ached...then suddenly didn't.

I was at a loss to understand what had happened to me as the Count removed his hand from my lips. He watched me intently and asked. "How do you feel?"

I didn't hear him at first, for I immediately unwrapped my wrist, moving it in all directions. That was nearly impossible to do before, but now it felt good as new. The small cuts from the rosary's chain were gone too. Then, most carefully, I touched my neck where the wound had been bleeding profusely only seconds earlier. It wasn't completely healed, of course, but had progressed by weeks. Relief swept over me, and I slouched my shoulders.

"Isadora," the Count touched my previously injured hand. "How do you feel?"

"So much better," my voice broke a bit. "I feel so...alive."

He sighed, a frown lifted into a sad smile. "I am relieved."

"It almost feels like a drug," I looked down at my hand to examine the peachy color that had returned to the skin. "Is this what you feel? Remarkable..."

The Count kept his eyes keenly fixed upon me. "You see why I asked you to trust me?"

I gazed up at him and nodded. "Yes...but don't ever do that again."

The Count looked away from me. By giving me the very essence of himself that gave him life, he had, in turn, tainted me with it. I am not of his kind. It is unnatural for me to consume what gives him life, just as it is unnatural for him to eat what sustains me. But, regardless of the natural order, he had provided me with a means of escaping death a second time. The Count knew I would not have accepted if asked outright, so he took it upon himself to force me to live. "I cannot promise you."

I frowned, repressing any opinion I had on the matter for another time. Taking both of his hands in mine, I smiled warmly at him. "Thank you for saving me a second time. I'll have to keep a tally so that I know how much to repay you."

His eyes widened for a moment, but then he closed the distance between us, kissing my forehead amorously. "You may repay me with sweet kisses and your warm presence in my house."

The euphoria of the moment was halted to a standstill with his last words. His eyes were so sincere, his care of me so tangible that

I had to agree to whatever he wished of me. In a half panic, I decided not to answer with words, but only with the kisses he had asked for.

Afternoon…

The Count had gone by daybreak, and although exhausted, after a quick breakfast, I went and stayed with Dumitru. He was still asleep, so I sat quietly in his room thinking over the dream that still tormented my mind. I was surprised that the Count hadn't asked why I was so shaken, but I assumed he thought it was the sequel to my near-death experience that had left me such. There were so many things to think about as the dawn came and went.

I was deep in thought when Dumitru's eyes fluttered open and he stirred.

Careful not to scare him, I took his hand. "Good afternoon."

His eyes shifted to mine. "Isadora…?"

Smiling, I put on the bravest face I could manage. "Yes, it's me, silly. How are you feeling? Are you hungry?"

Slowly, he thought about my question before answering. "I'm sore. And, a bit."

"Thank goodness," I touched his forehead to check for a temperature, just in case. "I'll go make you something, okay? I'm not the best cook in the world, I must warn you."

My small joke didn't affect him. "You seem better than yesterday. He gave you it too, didn't he?"

His quick assessment made me bite my lower lip, but eventually, I nodded. "Yes, against my will, but he did. Although if he hadn't, I wouldn't be here right now."

A frown formed on his lips. "Then, you know?"

"I have known for many weeks." I stood but still held his hand. "I'll be back soon with something."

When I was about to let go, he latched onto my wrist. "He told me you poisoned Petros by drinking holy water you got in București."

"Did you get in trouble for it?" I remembered my guilt as I looked down at his worn features. "I've been meaning to apologize."

"Only stern words…" Dumitru's voice faded out for a moment. "He told me why you did what you did, so I wanted to say I understand why you lied to me. For you, it was a necessary evil, and

I don't hold it against you. Actually, I'm glad you gave that bastard what he deserved."

"Thank you for understanding, Dumitru, but I'm sorry…"

"The Master also said you came to help me even when you thought I was dead, and…" Emotion was breaking his voice, but he continued. "That I was the first thing you mentioned to him when he came to help you."

I chuckled. "You needed my help and I don't give a damn about what the Count orders. You are my closest friend, and if there were any chance, I had to help you. I needed to try."

Dumitru's eyes turned glassy, and he looked away from me. My smile disappeared at the sight, and my heart moved with such care for him that I bent down and gently wrapped my arms around his shoulders. He tensed, but then, slowly, his arms came around my back to hold me there. It touched me that he, the statue who rarely showed a single emotion other than annoyance and anger, had shed a tear in gratitude. "I am in your debt."

"The Count was the one who ultimately saved us both." I caressed his shoulder to soothe him. "We are both in his debt, so there is no need to be in mine. You would have done the same for me, I'm sure."

Dumitru's arms tightened as he hissed. "I'll kill anyone who touches you again, I swear to you."

That anger he kept within him was bubbling to the surface, and I raised myself a bit to look at his face. His eyes were reddened by tears, and his brow was creased in a growing fury. Dumitru's sentiment was something he had told me long ago when I had little trust for the Count. "Don't stress yourself out about it, okay? Besides, the Count will be here for both of us. We'll be safe with him."

His eyes drifted to the fresh bandage that I wore over my healing wound. "Are you so sure?"

My eyebrows knitted. "If the Count didn't care for either of us, we'd both be dead. You should have seen the way he cared for you. In his own way, he must love you because I cannot see him helping others the way he helped you."

"Do you love him?"

The question startled me, but I kept my cool. "I love him just as much as I love you."

A shock came over his face. "You...love me?"

"Of course I do," I wiped a tear away. "Since I got here, you have always been there for me when I needed you the most. You showed me concern when I was feeling completely alone. So, how could I not?"

Through his chest, I could feel his heart racing as his face turned red. "O-Of course..."

"Don't work yourself up," I laid my lips on his hot cheek. Being around the Count so often, I almost forgot how warm others are. "I'll be back soon."

Dumitru's arms held onto me a second more before releasing me. He was obviously flustered. I didn't think that saying I cared for him and barely kissing him on the cheek would reduce him to such a state.

I went to the kitchen to make him something. All the meanwhile I wondered if he had gotten the wrong idea about what I meant when I said I love him. I mean, I love both him and the Count in their own way, but I contemplated whether he thought I was professing some kind of romantic intentions. We were very close when I told him it, and he did get quite red afterward. I had to push the thoughts away and focus on my work, reminding myself how unlikely it was...right?

...

After I had gotten Dumitru settled for the day, I took a break and got to work. Finding an older towel, scrub brush, and a bucket of warm, soapy water, I set to finally wash the bloodstains from the stairwell and floors. With all the recent events, no one had time to think about the castle's upkeep. Since the Count certainly wasn't going to do it and Dumitru physically couldn't, I was the only one. I was grateful I had regained enough strength to lug the bucket up the stairs and begin my scrubbing. It took some time to get the stains from the uneven stone; about two and a half hours just to do two flights of steps.

Cleaning was something that the Count had expressly forbidden me to do because I am a guest. All the same, I wasn't going to live in a place where there were blood splatters so prominently displayed on the walls to remind me of that terrible night. He can punish me if he wants to, but I couldn't stand it any longer.

I thought it would be a good distraction from my current problems, but I ended up just thinking about them more. It was about noon when I got to the bottom, and the bucket, brush, and rag were positively filthy with dirt and blood. I wondered if I shouldn't have cleaned the entire thing and not just parts of it! It was time for a real break, so after I cleaned myself up and disposed of the rancid water, I made Dumitru some more food.

We both ate together, and afterward, we kept each other company. Mostly, I read my Bible for some shred of consolation while he slept on and off.

. . .

When evening came, I left to make dinner early so that the Count wouldn't catch me cooking in the kitchen. It was a good thing, for we both had just finished eating when he returned early. He didn't say anything about the food, and no one brought it up. After I had washed the dishes and set things away for the night, my day-long shift to watch Dumitru was over.

I was very tired as I had very little sleep the previous night. I said goodnight to both of them and headed upstairs. I was nearly on my floor when the Count came up from behind me. "Miss Kane, I would like to ask you something."

"Yes?" I asked puzzledly. Why was I 'Miss Kane' again?

In the semi-darkness of the narrow staircase, I saw him purse his lips. "This may be difficult to ask, but would you be comfortable helping me tidy up the library?"

I shuddered. Certainly, I had no desire to return to that room, but he was right that it needed to be cleaned. Biting my lip, I nodded. "I will help you."

He smiled and took my arm as we ascended the rest of the way and drew near the point of no return. The Count stuck close by me as we entered the untouched library. There was a new stillness to the room that I had never felt before. It was as if the space had been holding its breath since the incident occurred. At our presence, the room's lamps came alight, filling the space with their usual warm glow.

The table and chairs had been thrown into disarray, my papers scattered about the table and floor, and chairs had been overturned in the struggle. I apprehensively drew closer and saw a few blotches of red that stained the beautiful Persian rug. I knew they were all mine: one from where I lay unconscious, and the other few were when Petros had coughed up my 'tainted' blood. I stared down at them, amazed at the sheer amount of it all.

The Count let go of my arm and distracted me from the sight. "Get your things."

I only nodded. I was walking to get my bag when I stepped on something, knowing it was a bead of my rosary. Sighing, I knelt on the floor and began to pick them up one by one. Pieces of the chain were still intact; however, the main bulk of the rosary had been destroyed.

The Count watched me in silence for a moment before he began to tidy up the strewn papers. It was a sad thing for me to pick up the pieces of a very precious item of mine. My parents had given it to me over a decade ago, and now it was unrepairable. Despite that, I was happy it had done all that it could have in that situation. It had been my diversion to let the holy water take effect, so I was grateful.

I gathered as many of the pieces as I could find, then went to search for the rosary's crucifix, which had been thrown from my hand. I found it on the opposite side of the room, unscathed. Holding the pieces venerably in my hands, I placed them in the gilded pouch I had procured from my bag and dumped them in. Then, I meandered to the table where I knew there were remnants of my golden cross, and to my dismay, it was bent and disfigured as though it had gone through a fire. I guess it's a small blessing that the crucifix had not been corrupted by Petros' touch, so thus was salvageable. I placed all of the pieces in my small rosary bag, too.

The Count had moved the table and chairs from the carpet, situating my bag and the water bottle next to each other as he began to roll up the damaged tapestry.

"I'm sorry I ruined your carpet." I half-heartedly tried to joke to lighten the heavy atmosphere as I stowed everything safely within my bag.

"It was not your fault," the Count hoisted the neatly coiled carpet on his shoulder. I was astonished that he could lift it so easily. "I wanted to get a new one anyway."

I nodded solemnly as I picked up my things. However, I stopped and looked at the clear holy water, wondering what I should do with it now that I had revealed my secret.

"Keep it," he said suddenly, and then grinned. "As an insurance policy."

"Are you sure?"

"I am," he readjusted the heavy carpet on his shoulder, which honestly should have taken at least three strong men to carry. "Now, sleep well tonight, my dear friend."

He was about to leave the room when I opened my mouth to speak, but then closed it. I wanted to ask so badly if he could compel me to sleep, but I didn't want to bother him. Perhaps it sounds so silly considering all the other things that he and I have been through the last few days, but I didn't want him to have one more thing to worry about. The Count has enough on his plate already, and my sleep is inconsequential. "Goodnight, Count."

Flashing me a quick smile, he disappeared down the hall. I followed close behind with my things in tow as the oil lamps died out. When I got back to my room, I didn't bother to put them away, but only readied myself for bed. I decided that if I couldn't sleep again, tomorrow I would ask the Count to force it upon me as he had done before...and pray he doesn't ask why.

Chapter Twelve

BITTER PILL

*24 June

Morning, 5:00 am…

I have not slept again. This night was just as bad as the last. Although my mind was much calmer, my body less sore, no part of me would sleep. I'd lie in bed simply existing, listening to everything around me. How many hours passed by, I had no idea, and a part of me didn't care. I tried to use the time productively to think of the numerous events that had occurred, things that had been said, and actions that had been done. Mostly, my thoughts returned to the Count and his actions and words.

As much as I love the man I see daily, who is kind, gentle, understanding, and caring, can I love the monster that is beneath? I told him I love him for all that he is, and I indeed do, but the thing within has committed atrocities I cannot fathom. In essence, the Count, whom I see and do not see, is the same being. I am only shown one face, and the other he hides. Just as before, I must take my time to discern how I feel about the two personalities coexisting within the same body. I mustn't judge because I do not understand, and I mustn't accuse what I do not know.

Once I did sleep, sometime near the morning, I dreamt of Petros again. This time I was lying in bed asleep when I suddenly opened my eyes. In the darkness, he was hovering in the air above me in his demonic form. He hissed lowly and laughed at me, showing his menacing teeth. I went to scream and instead woke myself up. Like a phantom, Petros had disappeared, for above me was only the ceiling. I burst into tears, and my head throbbed until I finally had gotten it all out of my system. Lying there, I stared into nothingness until my alarm went off, then readied myself for the day.

Later...

Dumitru was considerably better than the previous day. He is able to sit up and can feed himself with nearly no assistance. I am so relieved, so grateful, that he is progressing so well. I, too, felt better...at least physically. My monthly time was nearly over, not that it was much of anything because of all the recent stress. I had noticed that once the issue with my neck was corrected, the Count kept his distance from me. I believe it was because now that the blood coming from our wounds has been stopped, the Count's nose is picking up my subtler bleeding. With all of this, I felt sorry for him having to face so much temptation each time he sees us. Dumitru and I are still very weak and vulnerable, and he must view us as two walking-talking enticements.

Oddly enough, I found myself missing him and wishing he were around during the afternoon, but he was off on his business, which I'm certain isn't actually 'business' at all. When he is ready, he will tell me what he wants me to know; until that time, I must wait and keep my head above water.

In the late afternoon, I decided to do more cleaning in the stairwell while Dumitru slept before dinner. This time it was easier to remove the years of dust and dirt, and I completed one flight of the stairs before it was time to start dinner. I was very proud of my work by the end, for it looked almost brand-new.

25 June

It was getting to be well past midnight when I finally put my busy work down and rubbed my burning eyes. I lay on the settee, sulking. Some time passed, and I was dozing off when there was a knock at the door that shocked me back into reality. My head was whirling as I strained to focus my pained eyes. "Y-Yes...yes?"

"Isadora, may I come in?" It was the Count.

Throwing a blanket over my shoulders to hide my pajamas, I called out to him to enter.

The door opened silently, and the Count appeared at the threshold. "Did I wake you?"

"No," I pulled the blanket tighter around me. "Is everything alright? Is Dumitru okay?"

"All is well," he reassured as he entered, coming to me with his inaudible footsteps. "Dumitru is asleep."

"Oh," I watched him as he sat on the couch next to my feet. "Do you need help with something?"

"No, I would only request your company if you would not mind it." His eyes flickered to the blanket, which concealed most of me. "Why are you sleeping out here with the light on?"

I cleaned my throat, trying to come to some kind of response that seemed applicable, but couldn't find one.

His eyebrow raised, and I knew he was on to me. "You seem very tired. Would you prefer I go?"

"Oh, no," I waved at him. "As we say, I'm 'right as rain', 'fit as a fiddle', 'cool as a cucumber'."

I must have sounded like a complete idiot to him. I sure felt like one. Slowly, he reached forward to touch my hand and opened my palm, and examining it, he spoke. "I can hear your heartbeat quicken, you are flushed, shaking, and you cannot look at me. You are lying."

I went quiet, my eyes drifting far away from him. "Am I?"

The Count wove his fingers into mine. "Tell me what is bothering you."

"Nothing," I whispered a bit flatly. "I'm fine."

He went quiet too, pondering my few words. "Dumitru told me that for the last few days you have been very distant and rarely speak to him. I, too, have noticed that since we discussed what happened, you have not spoken to me the same. You are becoming increasingly withdrawn in only three days."

I frowned, taking my hand out of his. "Can we talk about this later? In the morning?"

"I could always force you to tell me," the Count's voice was only mildly threatening, but I knew he'd do it to get what he wished out of me. "But that would not be kind."

"No, it wouldn't," I think I sounded a bit threatening as well, but it wasn't on purpose. "I have a lot on my mind. Forgive me if I have been distant, I didn't realize. I'll be more aware of it."

I went to swing my legs over the side of the settee to stand, but he grabbed them. *"Do not."*

Instantly, I was frozen in place, and my legs went limp against my will, and then the bind he had cast over me was broken. Just that little command sent my head into another whirl, and I found myself collapsing against the pillow. My whole body, even with his control gone, could hardly move. I had to lie there for a while to compose my senses before daring to sit up.

"There is something very wrong if you cannot resist such minor persuasion." The Count eyed me pointedly with a matter-of-fact voice, then it softened, and he asked. "Please, tell me."

I slowly sat up, my eyes feeling heavier than before. "I haven't really slept in four days —"

"Four days?" He repeated exasperatedly.

When I turned to him and saw his creased brow and worried expression. "Every time I close my eyes, I see him. If I sleep, he torments me. Even awake, I think I hear him or see him out of the corner of my eye. It's like I haven't stopped fighting him since that night. You probably think I'm crazy, and I think I'm getting pretty close to being it."

"Why do you tell me nothing?" The Count sounded more hurt than anything else. "Why do you insist on keeping your pain to yourself?"

I scoffed. "Touché."

"Isadora," the Count retook my hand in an iron vice. "You are one of the most hypocritical women I have ever met. You encourage me to tell my feelings, but you insist on keeping yours."

He is right that I am a hypocrite in this. All I have done concerning my feelings is to say one thing but do another. I wondered why I would do that since it wasn't my practice to do it before. "I don't want to be more of a burden than I've already become to you. My own imagination is making me suffer for what I did to Petros. Let me suffer for it."

Suddenly, I was in his arms, being crushed so tightly to his chest that I could hardly breathe. "Isadora, you did nothing wrong. There is no reason for you to suffer for what Petros did to himself."

"Sometimes I tell myself that, but it doesn't help." I cautiously nestled my head into his neck; the closeness of another being was so comforting. "I am sick of fearing shadows, Count. Please, just put me to sleep. Let it be a peaceful one. I don't know how much longer I can live with this."

He tensed so rigidly I thought he became stone. I felt his fists grip the blanket, and it slowly fell from my shoulders. The Count's fingers brushed my left collarbone, near my bandage, then moved to comb through my hair. The Count then kissed the top of my head. "I will never let you go from me. You are mine."

I was shocked by his intensely emotional response, and I gazed up at him. The pain in his eyes was as nothing I had ever seen before from him, and it confused me greatly. All at once, he was kissing me so fiercely I thought he would consume me, his hands groped for me as if I would slip away from him, and his mouth was moving so fervently against my own that I couldn't keep up. My heart felt like it was going to burst, and my lungs were gasping for breath. In my exhausted state, it was as if he were dragging my very soul from me. He released my mouth to kiss sporadically down my jaw and neck. I could barely process the feelings he was giving me. *"Count..."*

"Will you say you love me, then leave me?" He growled, now angrily, through kiss after kiss. "I forbid it, do you hear me? I will not lose you, too."

"Stop," my hands grabbed his face, but he wouldn't remove himself from kissing my collar. The Count pressed further down to a point of no return. An odd feeling formed in the pit of my stomach, something I knew he could smell. *"Count, stop."*

Eventually, he came up to my eye level, his eyes burned like the sunset into me. It was frightening, and although I think he saw my fear, he did not relent. "I will not lose you to yourself, Isadora."

A moment of clarity came to me. Looking back on my words, spoken without true thought, I realized how I had unintentionally asked him to kill me. It had been a misinterpretation on his part, and a miscalculation on mine. A horror seeped into my skin that I said such a thing to such a man whose wife had killed herself. Immediately, I tried to explain myself. "No, Count…that's not —"

"I didn't mean what I said. I wasn't thinking. Please, I'm sorry. I love you. I didn't mean it like that."

The Count's breathing steadied as he laid his head against my chest, probably listening to my racing heart to ensure I was still there with him. The poor man seemed like a whole different person than just a few seconds ago. He had become a threatened animal in the way he held onto me, and his quick, desperate displays of affection were so urgent.

After he took a bit to calm himself, his eyes met mine again, and although they had returned to normal, they still held a deep sadness. The expression struck me so deeply that I leaned in and kissed the Count as passionately as I could and wrapped my arms around his neck. He leaned in and whispered into my ear. "Let me stay with you tonight."

Stay? With me? The room spun at the question, and I felt momentarily lost before I cleared my throat. "What about Dumitru?"

"He will be fine." Gently, his arms were brought around my midsection, and he lifted me with ease. "Will you allow me?"

My face was getting considerably hot at the idea of it. "To stay?"

The Count gave me a boyish smile from my reaction, although his eyes were still so troubled. "You think I will not be a proper gentleman?"

We entered my bedroom, my face growing ablaze. "I trust you, Count. It's just…"

"I am aware." He looked at me knowingly as he laid me between the sheets. "You must not fear me. I will never harm you."

I felt dazed, but I nodded. A gentle rain was falling outside as he climbed between the sheets with me. He was so cool, and I felt so hot. I had never lain next to a man before with this intent behind it. Both of us were completely conscious of what we were doing, as I was willingly lying with Satan's spawn, and allowing him to envelop me in his arms. He did so as if he were cradling a child, and the tenderness of it made my heart flutter like a trapped bird in my ribs. I knew he could hear it, and a part of me wanted him to listen to it closely.

The Count sighed in relief as his face went to rest in my neck, taking in that scent he always seemed to enjoy. "I will protect you from him. Sleep, my dear, and sleep dreamlessly."

Just like that, I fell into unconsciousness. And for once, there was no internal battle, no war to fight in my head, just a quiet tranquility that permeated my soul. Under his watchful eye, I slept more deeply than I had ever slept before. I don't think I moved from my place, nor did I dream or stir, but only slept a lifeless sleep.

Later…

I awoke around 9:30 am after a full eight hours' sleep. When I came to, I was still in his arms, our positions unchanged. The sun was shining through the drawn curtains, and in the distance, I heard the sweet singing of birds. What a heavenly feeling it is to wake up next to the man you hold so deeply in your heart; it was as if nothing I have ever experienced before. All night, we had simply slept next to each other, and neither of us crossed that invisible line.

I hated to stir, but I sat up and looked back at him. The Count was fast asleep with a blanket draped over his eyes. I couldn't help but smile at how peaceful he looked. Rubbing my own eyes, I was about to move the sheets away when his arms came around me to pull me back to him, and he muttered groggily. "Where do you think you are going?"

"I've got to get ready," I tried to wriggle away from him. "I'm late."

"Late for what?" The Count settled himself back into the crook of my neck. "Is it not Sunday? A day of rest for you."

I rolled my eyes, but enjoyed that he desired to remain close to me. "Dumitru, remember?"

The Count groaned as he removed the cover from his eyes and raised himself to sit up. He squinted in the dim, yet quite intense sunlight. It took him quite a while to adjust to the brightness. "I will go."

"But —"

He put his finger to my lips. "It is your day of rest. Use it well."

My brow knitted, and as much as I wanted to tell him I didn't care what day it was, he would keep shutting me down until I conceded. Reluctantly, I nodded and lay back down. "Since it's such a lovely day, may I go outside?"

He looked at me quizzically, and I could see he wanted to say no, but he ended up nodding. "You may if you are careful."

I smiled widely as I took his hand. "I promise I won't go near the wall."

The Count bent down so that our noses touched. "You better not, my dearest one."

The smoothness of his voice made my entire body suddenly burst with heat, and I'm sure my face showed it. He must take such pleasure in tormenting me like that, for he chuckled as he kissed me softly. I felt so breathless when he pulled away, quite proud that he had reduced me to such a state.

I pouted. "Why do you always have to do that?"

"Whatever do you mean?" He chuckled as he left the bed and smoothed out his clothes.

I glared at him, my arms crossing over my chest. I only feigned that I was upset, but as I watched him make his way to the door, I spoke up. "Count?"

He stopped to look back at me. "Yes?"

I turned over on my side. "I'm sorry for what I said last night. I really wasn't thinking about what I was saying. I hope you can forgive me for it."

"All is forgiven." He said after a moment, granting me one last smile before closing the door behind him.

I stared at the empty scene for a long time after he had left, thinking so far back to our debate about forgiveness. The Count had been so adamant that forgiveness is for weak-minded people, and yet he had forgiven me for something that had hurt him so terribly. Had he changed his mind about the subject? There was no way to ask him since surely, he would say his opinion hadn't changed.

Evening…

I had been writing all day outside, enjoying the coolness of the mountains and the warmth of the sun. The landscape around the castle has truly livened up to its full potential under the deep azure sky and puffy white clouds. Today is simply heaven, a wonderful day to recuperate. Even though I wrote about terrible things that haunt my memory, getting them all down has lifted a weight off my chest. I can breathe so much easier now, and a new peace has come into me. I had to forgive myself for all I have done to forgive what others have done to me, so then and there, witnessed by God's creation, I forgave myself. And, in turn, I forgave Petros for the things he had done.

Everything that I have done, both good and bad, has been put to rest in my soul.

I thanked God, as I felt the sun's heat on my skin, that I had someone like the Count to care for me during this time. Even if it isn't the same love I have for him, at least there are mutual good feelings between us. As I thought of it, I found it a little amusing that I would be thanking God that I have a devil in my life.

Time passed so quickly, and the sun was beginning to set, yet I stayed to watch it as I sat on the steps. The colors of the sky were changing to pinks and purples with streaks of blue, and the clouds were afire with redder hues. This scene was paradise to me, even with the chill of the approaching dusk. I felt serene.

"You have been out here all day." The Count was suddenly next to me, sitting on the step.

I hummed as I peered over at him. He looked so tired, so much older, and I frowned. "Are you alright, Count?"

He bobbed his head up and down. "I am fine, only tired. However, you look radiant."

"Thank you." There was a spark of warmth on my cheeks. "I believe I have found a resolution and found peace with myself."

"What resolution is that?" He queried.

It took me a moment to put it into words, but then I asked as I looked up. "When you look up at the sky, Count, what do you see?"

The Count looked up and answered me seriously. "The sky."

I frowned at his unimaginative response. "Yes, you see blue, but behind it is actually space, a void of near-nothingness. Yet in that abyss, there are stars, planets, whole galaxies, and beyond. What I mean is that even though you see one thing that is so normal to you, you have to remember there are things behind it, beyond it, that are just as important as what we see. I can't keep blinding myself by what I see and understand because there are things out there that are so much deeper to be seen."

He looked at me strangely but then nodded. "I see what you mean."

"Yeah," I breathed out. "I know you don't like speaking about forgiveness, but I'm seeing it like that. I was only looking at what was plainly in front of my face instead of searching deeper."

"You have forgiven Petros, then?"

I nodded. "And myself."

A cool wind whisked over the courtyard, howling between the stones. The sun had died for the day but would be reborn in the morning. The Count looked back up as the first glimpses of the stars were just becoming visible through the atmosphere, staring at them long and hard, blinking only a few times before he turned back to me. "Will you show me the light in the dark?"

I sat up to his level and gazed directly into his eyes, glowing in the encroaching night. With my hand, I touched his cheek, and he nuzzled into it like a cat and purred as one, kissing the heel of my hand. His sincerity was the purest thing I have ever felt. Even in all his evil, he was good.

Those eyes of his, like shining rubies, so large and expressive, stared back into mine. The mortal and the immortal, the two opposing forces locked together in balance. The union seems so unlikely, so much against everything in the natural world, yet there we sat, staring into each other's eyes as if all this time we had been searching for something that could be found in them. I don't know what it is, maybe a home? A place of refuge? Whatever it is, it is the most beautiful thing I have ever seen. Nothing in this world seemed more tangible to me at that moment than him and how much he needs me, but also wants me. The perfection of it, the innocence and purity of the devil, that is instead, the fallen angel. All he ever wanted was to reach out to someone who wouldn't see him as what he is, but as the lost soul he became. The perpetual sadness he feels, the fear and regret, I could feel it all from him. All this time, I was seeing the blue of him, and not seeing the empty void beneath.

"I will, Count."

In response, he leaned in to kiss me in his tender fashion, and the sensation of sublime completeness entered me. I knew the answer to my question that I had asked myself during those sleepless nights: could I give up myself to be with him, to show him the way back to the path he had lost? *What did he say was the definition of love,* I thought to myself, *'Love is the quiet surrender of the self, offered without expectation. It is a sacred bond that binds souls together beyond the reach of time or condition.'*

I knew it then. To save him, I would sacrifice anything, because I love him. I ask nothing in return for my sacrifice, only that he finds the person he was and the happiness he deserves.

My heart is pounding as I write this, my eyes brimming with tears. Was this the purpose, O Lord, for which you brought me to him? Am I the one to free him from his corporeal imprisonment by showing him what it means to be human again? Almighty, let me show him the love he lost for you through me.

IN THE FLESH

8 July

Afternoon…

It has been another two weeks since I last wrote. Life has returned to a state of semi-normalcy as it was before Petros' unfortunate arrival. My days are busier than ever now, and I have hardly found time to write the goings-on of the day, for they consist of preparing meals for Dumitru and myself, cleaning, organizing the lesson plans, and other odd jobs. Running a castle by yourself was nothing that I am accustomed to, and I feel very over my head. With Dumitru still unable to do much, I had to learn from him everything in a crash course overnight.

I awake early in the morning to make the meals and see that Dumitru is ready for the day. Some days, I see the Count about to head off to his business by the time I come downstairs, and we exchange the briefest of kisses before we are both forced to go our separate ways. Providing for Dumitru and the castle has given me a new sense of purpose that forces me to get up in the morning. By afternoon, the daily chores are finished, and I stay with Dumitru for a few hours until after tea, then I go and prepare for the Count's lesson.

Dumitru has been doing considerably better. He is able to stand and walk very well, but he gets dizzy easily. Just as I can expect of him, he is very stubborn and hates being cared for. I have to watch him at all times to make sure he stays in bed, or when he's up, that he doesn't fall. It's like babysitting a rambunctious two-year-old who thinks they can do everything an adult can. We often butt heads over it, and I find myself saying things my parents said to me when I wouldn't do as I was told. I think he appreciates the constant company because I sometimes find him staring at me with this odd expression that makes my heart flutter. Of course, once I notice, he immediately looks away, his cheeks dusting pink.

He is eager to begin his work again, although he is most certainly still unable. In response, the Count hired two 'Gypsies', Romani, to help with the more laborious chores I cannot physically do. Both the Count and Dumitru call them 'the Gypsies', but their names are Vasile and Mihai, and they are two very hard-working gentlemen. Both of them speak only Romanian and their Romani tongue, which is no help to me as I speak neither. They understand no English, so I am left with concocting odd sentences using phrases Dumitru taught me. It's not as easy as I thought it would be.

I rely solely on the most basic words and lots of body language to get my point across. Often, I can somehow tell them what I want to be done, but sometimes I'm left at a loss. As a result, they have come up with a name for addressing me: *Doamna* or *Stăpâna*. When I asked Dumitru about the specific meaning, since I thought it meant simply 'lady', he got uncomfortable and said the modern meaning of "*doamna*" does mean 'lady', or also the title of 'Lady'; however, the latter meant 'mistress'. That is, the two men think that I am the lady who runs this residence, and connect me as the wife of the Count, their employer. I am the only female that they have ever seen in the house, and I, evidently, am doing tasks associated with wifely duties. Also, to them, I am above Dumitru in station and am 'worldly and foreign' in their eyes. There was no use trying to explain to them that I am not the Count's wife, and so they continue to call me *Doamna* or *Stăpâna*.

Even if Dumitru had told them otherwise, I doubt they would change their usage of the term. Because they see me as this 'mistress of the house', they hold me in this strange respect that I am not used to. They bow their heads to me when I come near and never smile or speak to me unless they are spoken to. Both of them keep their distance from me, and it depresses me that they won't even try to initiate any sort of communication. But, just seeing and interacting with other human beings has been a slice of solace for me. Sometimes I wish there were another girl to talk to, but I will have to survive with the four men who are constantly around me.

The idea of being associated as the Count's wife is a very strange feeling. I most certainly have no intention of marrying anyone anytime soon, but the mere fact that they believe me to be leaves this unsettling, awkward feeling in the pit of my stomach. As much as I'd love to deny it, the Count does see me as 'his'…like I am one of his many acquisitions, or at least that's how it sounds to me. Sure, it bothers me a bit, but I find my own ways to passively defy him to remind him that I am my own person. He tolerates it, I feel, but for how long, I don't know. Our relationship is so undefined that I don't even know what to call us. We aren't necessarily lovers, but we are very close when we are alone. To term it as a boyfriend-girlfriend relationship seems too much of a teenage fling, and it makes me cringe. Neither of us has formally asked to be the one and only in our lives; it all seems to be an unspoken bond. The bond is not a complicated one, but is rather simple. The only way I can put it is when we are in the same room, we are *together*, but still keep a strict formality between us.

The Count and I have resumed our coursework and have caught up to where we should be. It feels a bit awkward standing up in front of him and lecturing now. I knew it was going to be like that if I started to develop feelings, but now it can't be helped. The show must go on, no matter how much he stares at me. Both of us have been keeping a respectful distance from each other since the night we spent together. That is not to say we haven't been intimate with the other, it just hasn't gotten much farther since that night. And honestly, from what I can see, it hasn't any need to progress any quicker. Ever since I had misspoken so foolishly to him, I have been a bit conscientious to bring up anything that would upset him again. The Count would never admit it, but he is a very emotional and sensitive man behind his rough exterior, and he must be handled carefully.

On my end, my nightmares have nearly ceased. Sometimes I still have some little flashes of terror, but compared to the ones from before, they're so minor that they are almost irrelevant. Sometimes I forget them by the time I awake, and only the fading adrenaline rush is left. I am grateful for it. My neck, too, is practically healed, and to my great relief, it seems the scarring will barely be visible. This is in great part due to the Count's healing blood, which was in its own way a blessing in disguise. So, today I believe that it has healed enough that I have decided not to wear a bandage. A small victory in the face of the evil who placed it there.

All in all, life has returned to its usual peacefulness. With the ever-warming weather and ever-changing landscape, all of our spirits have been high and optimistic to get past the near-tragedy we experienced. I am still feeling the loss of my cross and rosary, but I hope the next time Dumitru and I are allowed to go to Bucharest for supplies, I can buy at least one of the two items. Dumitru is far from being able to drive, so I must wait until then. However, I am sensing that the Count doesn't want either of us in the near future to leave the castle. He hasn't specified as to why, but I have no doubt it has something to do with that group of radicals who want to 'rid themselves' of him. Two weak humans are quite easy targets, so far from the Count's constant protection. Despite this, I am eager to return to Bucharest or anywhere, to see people again, so I pray that I can persuade the Master to let us.

11 July

Afternoon…

For quite a while now, I have been meaning to expand my search of the castle and explore more of its layout. I am only accustomed to my floor, the Count's floor, and certain areas of the ground floor, leaving so much undiscovered. In his tour that he gave so long ago, Dumitru hadn't covered a significant portion of this large and formidable structure, so I thought I'd take it upon myself. The

Count was away, the two Romani were not visiting today, and Dumitru was in bed since he was feeling unwell...leaving me alone. So, because I had some time until dinner and I didn't have much to do otherwise, I decided I'd try to see what I could discover.

The Count had specifically told me that I was at liberty to explore the castle as I wished, but could not go into any rooms that were locked. All my main focus, initially, was to get the layout and not touch anything. I could tell there were at least two or three more floors above mine, and I knew there was also a basement of some kind. I definitely didn't want to explore the cellar, no matter what time of the day, so I took a flashlight from the kitchen and made my way up to the stairwell that ascended up and up. I was quite nervous because I knew I shouldn't be snooping around, but I kept telling myself that the Count had told me I could do this. All the same, I was anxious.

Cautiously, I ascended the dusty steps. As I drew nearer to the third floor, there was an old, musty smell that was circulating in the air, and cobwebs swayed in the corners. There weren't many of them, but enough for me to know that this area hadn't been used in many, many years. My footsteps even left a trail of disturbed dust, which bothered me because it would be easy to identify that I had been snooping. Yet I pressed on, my heart beating hard in my ribs.

When I reached the main corridor of the third floor, I found that it was not as long as the two below. It included a series of windows, heavily dusted with age, that overlooked the deep valley below. The panes were so warped that to see through them was incredibly difficult. On the other side of the hall were doorways, all evenly spaced to the end of the corridor. The golden sunlight was streaming inside and lit up the heavy dust particles that were suspended in the air. As I passed, I disturbed them, bringing up more dust. It was so thick, accompanied by an old, musty smell, that it was difficult to breathe. I put my shirt collar over my nose and mouth as I went further and examined the grand hall.

The stonework was magnificent with its medieval carved dragon heads, eagles, and other beasts associated with the local mythology. There were even some cherubim faces, definitely of Western influence, but they had been smashed away. Other aspects of the hall reminded me of Turkish design. I know that there had been much history between the old kingdoms that made up what is now known as Romania and the Ottomans, and most of it wasn't peaceful. Nonetheless, the symmetrical and finely carved designs were something to behold.

I went to the first door, but it wouldn't budge. Undeterred, I went to the next, and again it was locked. The next door was much grander than the rest, with the slight remnants of gold paint accenting the wooden double doors. Curiosity sparked me, and so with two hands, I tried to push the door open. There was a sharp snap from within the lock, and the doors freely began to part.

The cracked bolt fell to the stone floor. I swore. Panicking, I was about to abort my mission when I caught a glimpse of the inside, and I stopped. Lights of brilliant colors swirled within, and I was awestruck. Something compelled me to open the creaking doors the rest of the way, and finding my resolve, I entered. If I didn't know any better, I'd say I had traveled back in time by stepping over that threshold. Before me, covered in dust and layers of age and decay, was a throne room. At the far end of the room stood a magnificent chair, with imposing pillars leading up to the dais. I could almost see it as it was hundreds of years ago, filled with courtiers and ladies dressed in their finery. Draperies embellished with some ancient family crest would be proudly displayed, and warriors in glittering armor stood at the ready.

Like a veil falling from my eyes, I stepped into the sanctum, my breath escaping me. The air was filled with disturbed dust, but my shirt fell away from my face to expose my gaping mouth. The windows situated on either side of the throne were stained glass and brought in a rainbow of primary colors into the palatial room. From the window, I could see that from the high vantage point, the view encompassed the mountains for miles and miles. Fear and awe gripped me, yet I descended deeper into the cruciform space, drawn to the royal seat that was the main centerpiece. Whoever sat on that throne must have commanded such power and respect.

When I reached the foot of the dais, I almost felt as if I should bow to the chair, so in a moment of infantile play, I curtsied. I didn't dare step onto the raised platform, but only encircled it to look at the wondrous chair. Of course, I'm unfamiliar with medieval furniture, but it looked to me to be wooden, covered in gold leaf and inlaid with semiprecious stones that still gleamed in the colored light. On the feet of the throne were engraved claws that looked sharp enough to cut.

As I encircled the dais, something caught my eye. The transept was decorated with spectacular carvings and painted red and gold to the right of the dais. Situated within an alcove was a large oil painting, definitely hundreds of years old. I strained my eyes in the colored light as I approached, taking out my flashlight to shine it on the aged portrait. It was obviously of a man, and obviously from the same period as the room. It was set in a massive golden frame and displayed in such prominence in the center of the alcove as if it were a shrine to this man.

He was dressed in period clothes, donned with furs and a variety of pearls and other glittering stones. His wavy brown hair, so rich in texture, cascaded to his shoulders. He had a mustache with such large, expressive eyes and an aquiline nose. I recognized the portrait from somewhere, not just the position and colors of the subject, but the man himself. If my eyes had deceived me, they did so flawlessly, for before me was the Count. He was younger, and within him seemed a spark of life that was echoed through the heavy oil strokes.

But as I examined it further, there was something else about it that left me puzzled. I knew the portrait from somewhere *else*. Stepping closer, I could just make out letters at the top under the layer of dust. Of course, I could not read most of it, but I knew all I needed was to find the name of this man in the scrawl. I recognized the old Slavonic, a text with which I am rather familiar. I took my time parsing out what I knew and did not know. Most of it seemed to be abbreviations for titles, but the name was not. I was able to read it clearly, the letters which spelled out 'VLAD AL III DRAKULYA'.

My eyes widened, almost bulging from my skull, as my hands began to shake. Suddenly, things began to make more sense than they had ever before. I knew enough history, enough folklore and legends, to know who was before me. The faded image in my head of where I had seen the portrait before came back to me. It was no mistake when the evidence was so plain before me, hitting me like a bus. The Count was not a count at all, but a prince, and one of the most terrible ones to have ever reigned in Romania's history. I was standing in the throne room of the infamous, most gruesome, Vlad the Impaler, also called

Dracula, or whom I knew as Count Vladislav Negrescu. Even if Dracula was a relative, after 600 years, would he be a spitting image of his hundred-times-great-grandson? Surely the probability of that is astronomical.

Things that the Count has said over my visit came rushing back to me. Things that all of a sudden made sense that never quite did before. When he asked me that evening, when we professed our intentions to each other:

"Does it not frighten you? What I am? What I have done?"

And I had responded that it didn't frighten me. Whatever things he did, whatever he was…it is him: the man I had grown to love. How can I say that any longer? That the man I love is a man who slaughtered thousands in the most abominable fashion, who tortured, imprisoned, pillaged, destroyed, and so much more. Was I wrong to call him a fallen angel when the man who is considered a monster in the eyes of history still walks this earth after six centuries? He is a hellish legend that has come to life before my very eyes. I had kissed the lips of the beast and slept in the same bed as him. He had held me so tightly, so lovingly, in those same arms that had slaughtered enemy and innocent alike.

"…if I get too close, I will defile you."

I found myself backing away from the painting before I turned and ran from the throne room. Slamming the door much harder than I intended, I raced back down the steps to the second floor and the safety of my room, barring myself in my bedroom. My head spun as I collapsed onto the floor, holding my nauseated stomach. Lungs burning, heart hammering, I stared into the carpet's designs as Petros' words surfaced from the recesses of my mind.

"What prestige it is to depose a king? To take his spoils? Supersede his glory?"

Bile was rising in my throat, but I swallowed it down. All the signs had been pointing to this fact that Petros had essentially told me outright. Those hidden secrets are shown in plain sight but are overlooked because they are too obvious…too fantastic. Have I been so attracted to the illusion of goodness that I chose to be blind to the evil? How can I face the Count now, knowing what I know? I cannot tell him that I went against his wishes and broke into a locked room, even by accident, though technically it was on purpose. How can I endure his touch, knowing how truly stained with blood it is? Or even his kiss, knowing it had brought death to countless unnamed victims?

I have been thrown into a pit of turmoil and moral dilemma, and in a few hours, the Count will come. He will see through me as he always does, and then what? Oh God, I dare not even think what will happen. I have crossed that invisible line in the sand by leaps and bounds. I must compose and ready myself for the lesson. I pray I will be here to write the conclusion to this day.

LEAP OF FAITH

Evening…

S oon after tea, dark clouds began to gather in the sky and the
brilliant sun was blotted out. They were truly ominous, the
worst I had ever seen since my arrival here. A heavy wind was
blowing in, and the high currents swirled the color like a calligrapher's
black ink on a moistened page. In the far distance, echoing through
the deep valley and mountains, were the beginnings of the rumblings
of thunder. Shortly after the rain began, at first a drizzle, it soon turned
into a downpour. A great darkness enclosed around the castle so that
when the sun set, one could not see past the raindrops on the window
panes. It was just blackness.

Although I had calmed down and cleared my head to think
intelligibly again, I still sat in the library feeling on edge. I listened to
the raging monsoon hammer against the exterior stone like a deep

roaring moan that never ceased. For hours, I had been mulling over my recent revelation and trying to make sense of how I feel about it. Instead of accurately preparing for the lesson, I found myself staring for the longest time at the other portrait of the man who resembled the Count. Now that I had seen the other one, I could see that the man was definitely him, but it was a different artist and was a bit of a romanticized representation.

He truly had been staring down at me all this time, and I had been none the wiser. As my internal battle about how I should go about this situation was being waged, my mind would return to other things that the Count said to me. These were the kinder aspects of him that I focused on this time. The ones that had made me love him so deeply, even with the knowledge of what and who he is.

"I would never do anything to hurt you…"

"I will never let you go from me. You are mine."

"Will you say you love me, then leave me? I will not lose you, too."

My heart hurt in my chest so much that I had to hold it. Had all those things he said been a lie? The Count is a master of manipulation and shadow, so had I fallen for the puppeteer when I am the puppet? I could hardly make sense of all the mixed feelings that were raging in me like the storm outside, yet my conscious pondered if I should tell him the truth of what I had found out and that I had broken the ancient lock. My parents always told me that honesty is the best policy, and since the Count had been forthright with me, I should be with him. He had chastised me when I didn't tell him of how Petros had acted, and from that, we all were led down a terrible path. The same could be said for this situation: if I tell him I accidentally broke into one of his rooms and I discovered his infamous history, would he still be so understanding? Last time he said he would, but I wasn't so sure.

Eventually, against my better judgment, I decided that it would be best to tell him the whole truth. The only worse thing that could happen as a result is that I would end up in that 'bad place' Dumitru had warned me of when I got here. I said many prayers that I may find the courage to be frank with him, and that he would not be provoked to anger because of it. There was a glimmer of hope I had, and I would reach for it.

Suddenly, I was thrown from my deep thoughts by the faint howl of wolves. I was surprised I could even hear them through the rain, and the pain in me grew. A dull ache began to form in my neck where the bite had been, as a blinding flash of light and thunderous crash bellowed from the outside. Clasping my hand over my throbbing neck, I shrieked and jumped from my seat. A dread settled in me, and all I wanted to do was run from the library and hide in my bed.

"Do storms frighten you?"

I gasped and whirled around, even though I already knew who it was. He stood above me, suddenly, seeming taller and more domineering than before. In the orange cast of the gaslight, the Count's eyes smoldered into my own, and I felt paralyzed by him. "You gave me a heart attack!"

He chuckled. "When frightened, you lose your perception of what is around you, sweet one. Please be more careful."

I gulped, nodding erratically.

The Count took his seat after he softly tousled my hair. "Dumitru tells me you did not eat dinner this evening. Are you feeling unwell?"

"Oh?" I searched my memory, and it was true I had forgotten. The emptiness in my stomach was suddenly noticeable, although I was still not hungry. "I guess I forgot."

The Count raised his eyebrow. I knew he was beginning his analysis to see right through me, and I tensed. "Is there something on your mind?"

There was another flash, and instinctively, I covered my ears just as another boom came from the sky, rattling the portraits on the walls. I could feel the crack resonate through me, and I quivered in my place, trying with all my being to gather my fraying edges. "I guess it can wait until later."

When I looked back at him, his brow was deeply furrowed, a frown forming on his face. "Very well…but you should not fear the thunder."

"I don't fear the thunder itself," I told him simply. "It's the noise that makes me uneasy."

Another flash came, and I slapped my hands over my ears. This one was even worse than the last, and I struggled against myself from slipping into some kind of panic attack. The eerie noise receded as it ricocheted off the mountains. When I opened my eyes again, he was standing next to me.

"Would you prefer we not have a lesson today?" The Count asked as he smoothed my back to calm me.

But it had the opposite effect.

I pulled away before I could think of what I was doing, then immediately regretted it. "I'm sorry, but I guess that would be best."

The Count didn't seem too bothered that I had had such a reaction to him, and he gathered my things before I could say something. "Then let us go to your sitting room, and you can speak about what is bothering you."

So, we moved to my sitting room, and I felt more alone with him there than in the library. I took a seat in my chair before he could ask me to sit close to him on the couch. "You must think it's quite childish to be afraid of something as natural as thunder."

Surprisingly, he shook his head, taking his seat in the opposite chair. "Even I will admit this storm is the worst I have seen in decades, but this castle has stood for centuries, and there is nothing to fear but the noise. The mountains do make it worse."

"I have no doubt —" Just then, the electric lights fizzed out, plunging both of us into complete darkness.

"I hope you are not afraid of the dark either." He tittered when the fireplace burst into flame. I knew it is one of his abilities to control fire, but still, the action was unsettling to me. "So, tell me, what has you troubled? Other than the storm, that is."

Swallowing hard, I looked into the fire. Here we began our game, the dance against which we both competed for the top. Sighing, I tried to find the best place to begin. "You recall how I didn't tell you of what Petros said to me because I was afraid you'd be angry that I knew what you are?"

After a long moment of silence, he answered in a grave tone. "Yes?"

Taking in another breath, I began. "I'm only telling you because you were quite upset that I hadn't been truthful with you the last time. And because of it, it led to things that didn't need to happen…" There was another crack of thunder, and I didn't have the temerity to even look at him. "I went up to the third floor and accidentally broke the lock of the door to the throne hall. I knew I wasn't allowed to, but I went in."

The Count didn't speak for a while, and I didn't dare look at him to judge his expression. I heard him stand and he went behind my chair. "What did you see?"

"A magnificent hall with the most beautiful stained-glass windows I've ever seen in my life." I paused. "And a portrait of you from a different time."

"Of *me*?" He inflected a high tone.

"Why do you feign surprise?" I turned around to him, finally seeing his knowing expression. "Don't you think that before I came to this country that I would read up on its history? I can read, and most of all, I am not blind."

The Count leered. "What did the name say?"

My eyes narrowed. "You know what it says."

"Humor me, Miss Kane," he moved his face closer to mine. "What did it say?"

"No," I shook my head. "I won't say it. I only want you to know that I know. It will take me some time to come to grips with it. That is all."

"You see me differently now, but are willing to become comfortable with this knowledge, still? I would think you would be horrified, disgusted, by things you know that I have committed in the past." The Count stared back at me.

He was testing me, I could feel it from the way he looked and spoke. "I admit, I did feel those things initially. But, I don't pretend to know your history or your motives for things you did, however good or bad they were. I don't expect you to explain yourself because you had your reasons. Who am I to cast judgment? Despite this, it doesn't mean I condone any of it. Besides, I only see from a modern perspective, and you see from one that's from six hundred years ago."

The immortal cocked his head to one side, his eyes turning sad as another crash exploded from the sky. "It is true I have no intention of explaining myself to anyone. But I am surprised that you would not damn me for all these things and wish to leave. How is it that you can stand to be touched by these hands, so soaked with the blood of thousands?"

A surge of torment tightened my chest, and I swallowed my emotions. I looked away from him to hide those feelings in the shadow of the flames. "Because I love you for some damned reason, and it makes my heart hurt all the more. I cannot abandon you for things you did in your past, as much as my brain tells me to. My heart refuses to let me go from you, no matter how many people you have killed. If I am a fool, then I will be a fool."

A finger came under my chin to turn my head back to him. When our eyes met, his seemed glassier than before. The Count studied my face before returning to my eyes, his tone was not cold, but light and so soothing as he grinned. "You would still love me, knowing everything? You are foolish indeed."

A burst of light came from the windows and blotted his visage from me. In that split second of darkness, his two vermilion irises glowed like the firelight, but they didn't frighten me; they fascinated me. "You asked me to show you the light in the dark, remember? I promised you I would. To get to that light, one must first get through the darkness. We both know it won't be easy."

"Yes, I did ask you, my dearest one." His fingertips grazed my jaw as thunder roared, his features flickering from one hidden emotion to another. "My affinity for you has grown quite ardent these past few months. The farther away from you that I am, the less I remember what it is to feel. You have become the sun of my nights, and I know the time will come when you will burn me. I welcome your purifying fire and I wish it to consume me."

I was floored by his confession, so much so that when the next coupling of lightning and thunder shot from the black clouds, I hardly flinched. All I could see was him blurred by the tears that were spilling from my eyes. My heart swelled, and all I could do was place my hand over his so that it was pressed against my cheek. Every part of me knew I should hate this man, but every part of me knew that I could do nothing but *love* this man. "Sir, you do me too much honor."

"Vlad…" He whispered. I looked up at him with widened eyes at the sound of the forbidden name. "That is my name. In private, call me by it."

"Very well," I whispered back as I leaned closer to him. "Vlad."

The Count kissed me then so hungrily as if he had been holding it in for some time. Both his hands held onto my upper arms with this death grip to keep me in place, as if I could even pull away if I wanted. More thunder and lightning flashed and boomed, but I shook for a whole other reason. His tongue slid into my mouth, this time with no surprise attached, and it induced me to moan at the intense sensation. I hated how he didn't even need to work at it to make me swoon, and with it, I had nearly forgotten our conversation. I was lost in him. When he retracted his tongue, his teeth bit my lower lip. Their sharpness just barely caused pain as he dragged them over the sensitive skin until he had released me.

Finally, I was able to breathe again, and my lower lip bloomed with heat from the slight irritation, I'm sure, causing it to become red. It was a bit before I could look at him, still huffing. Without thinking, I muttered. *"Christ..."*

The Count smiled widely at the state to which he had brought me. "To invoke His name at a time like this?"

I scowled through my delirium. "Who else is going to protect me from you?"

"You are right," he inched closer again. "Yet it makes me wonder what other names I can make you sigh so sweetly."

Sense was knocked into me, and my face got hotter. Turning away from him, the thought embarrassed me and gave me images I certainly didn't need. I covered my face. "Why do you have to do that?"

He was laughing now as he came around the chair. "You are easily flustered, and it gives me pleasure to watch you squirm."

I squirmed at the thought of squirming! Now that he has confirmed this power over me, he must have reveled in it. I moved one of my fingers aside to look up at him. "Yeah? Well, it's giving me heart palpitations."

"A heart attack and now heart palpitations? What is next?"

"Cardiac arrest." I pouted and crossed my arms.

The Count shook his head, trying to contain another laugh. "Maybe I should brush up on my, oh, what is the acronym, CPR?"

I mimicked his sentence with a mocking tone and rolled my eyes. However, our conversation was cut short by a near-sonic boom that sounded like it had erupted right outside the windows. I screeched and covered my head with my hands, my eyes shut tightly.

After the reverberation had passed, he laid a gentle hand on my shoulder. "Isadora…"

"That was a bad one," I breathed steadily again. "Sorry…"

"Perhaps you should ready yourself for bed?" His joking tone had been set aside. "It is going to be a long night."

I stood, dreading the idea of suffering through such a restless night. Half-heartedly, thinking he was probably going to say no, I asked him. "Could you make me sleep instead?"

"I could," his hand came up to brush through my hair. I saw him glance, ever so subtly, at my neck before looking back at me. "But if I do that, I will have to stay with you."

The idea of him staying with me another night left me confused as to my feelings. Knowing who he was and what he is, my instinct told me to say no. But, there was that little voice that always grew louder at times like these to tell me to trust him. "Stay, then."

I bet the Count was fully expecting me to reject him, for his eyebrows raised slightly that I had done the opposite. "I shall, just for you."

After giving him a lopsided smile, I moved to go and get ready. The storm was still blowing in all its fury, just as the devil and angel on my shoulders had their war of words. Except their words contradicted their usual roles. It was the angel who told me to remind myself of my compassion and love for him, while it was the devil who told me to condemn the Count for all he is. Shouldn't it be that the angel who would say to remove myself from the evil, and the devil to say I should remain with it? What a paradox, ever so contradicting.

My heart was still torn between my head and my heart, even when I had lain beside him on the bed. He was awfully tense, and his eyes kept flickering around me as he leaned in to rest his head on my shoulder. As I had discovered last time, he preferred that particular place more than any other one. Of course, I knew why, and his closeness made my heart skip. The Count hadn't said a word for the longest time until I broke the silence. "If it's any consolation, I would never have guessed if I hadn't stumbled upon that portrait. With that aspect of your life, you hid it very well."

The Count's arms came around me to bring me closer. "You are the first of my guests I have allowed to get this far. You are lucky I have developed such a fondness for you."

But still, the meaning behind his words struck me, no matter how lighthearted they sounded. I placed my hand on his, which was around my waist. "Would you have punished me otherwise?"

He thought for a long moment before moving his head away from me, and sitting up, he stared intently into my eyes. "I would be left with no choice. I live a very secret life. If someone were to discover it, do you think I could sit by and let the whole world know?"

"I can sympathize," my lips pursed. "Even if someone were to tell, do you think that people would believe them?"

"I suppose not," the Count mused. "But one cannot be too careful."

Frowning, I clenched his hand to show my sincerity. "For what it's worth, I will keep it to myself. I promise you."

The Count lowered his face so that it was inches away from my own and brushed his lips over my cheek. "I will hold you to that promise, sweet one."

His voice was so smooth that I melted into him. I hate and love how he can reduce me with so little, but he had had hundreds upon hundreds of women before and knew exactly what to say and how to say it. He is Don Juan, Casanova, and all the other famous libertines of literature. He is loved and feared, lusted after, yet is revolting, mysterious, but wears his heart on his sleeve. I kissed him longingly. I'm not sure why I did it; it just felt like the natural thing to do. "May I ask you one thing?"

"Just one." He cracked a smile.

I kept my lips close to his skin to keep him enticed. "Shouldn't I be addressing you as 'prince' rather than 'count'. It's a bit beneath you, isn't it?"

He purred, and I could feel his fingers due into the flesh of my hips possessively. Instead of me consuming him, he was consuming me. "It is sufficient enough for this age."

"You are a Prince." My breath hitched at the sensation. "Doesn't that mean anything?"

"That was a long time ago, and many things have changed…" The Count suddenly drifted off, his eyes staring far away. He rested comfortably back into my neck, and I waited for him to continue, and when he did, he had grown very serious, his voice deepening as he explained. "Listen, whatever you have heard of me, I am not the same man as the one who lived then. He died long, long ago, and I am the shell that remains. There is no life in this body, it is only a corpse that houses the damned. I have done many things over the centuries and have come to regret many of those things. Human life is so fragile; in an instant, it can be born into existence, and in an instant, fade from it." He paused. "I hope what you have seen of me has been the man and not the monster."

I thought of his words for a good long while, pondering his last sentence especially. It is true that he had shown me the man and tried to hide from me the monster. But no matter how much he tries to hide it, he is just as much a monster as he is a man and vice versa. No matter how much the Count would wish to banish one from the other, he cannot deny what he had become so long ago, even what he is now. "You seek redemption, then? Is that your light in the dark?"

He didn't answer me.

"Tell me truthfully, Vlad." I rested my head against his, and another flash of lightning alighted the room, then faded. "Tell me what you want. Don't keep it from me, beloved."

Again, he was silent.

I know he was unwilling to admit to anyone what he wanted, but he couldn't keep his intentions from himself forever. "Tell me what it is, and I will help you in any way I can. You know I will. It is the foremost of all the promises I have made to you."

Then, finally, the Count spoke. "I seek it. For the past century, it has crept into my mind. There was a series of events that occurred when I encountered a few zealous men and a woman, who was not so unlike yourself, and they reminded me of the way I was before. They tried to save but also damn me in their own way, but neither came to pass. Since then, I have lived in solitude, wrestling with my past, present, and future. It has only been recently that I have wanted to try again and seek it out a second time."

A burning enveloped my chest, and my eyes grew misty. "I'm fearful that I won't succeed in helping you."

Under the sheets, the Count grabbed my hand tightly. "I would disagree. You cannot see from my eyes the light which radiates from you. It blinds me even in the dark. I can see in people things that others cannot."

I didn't know what to say to that. What does one say? How does one react? "I am not so pure as you think…"

"My eyes are *never* deceived." The Count explained to me with great emphasis on his words. "You cannot deny what you cannot see, Isadora, trust me."

I shut my eyes, my heart shuddering. "Even so, why me? Did you bring me here on purpose? How could you have known any of this would come to pass?"

"You could say I took a leap of faith."

"I thought you don't believe —" I stopped, rethinking my words.

He picked up where I left off. "I do not believe in faith? You forget I was once a warrior of Christ, heralded as a defender of Christendom against the Muslim Turks. I once had faith in God, but it was lost. To say I do not believe in faith is not the same as saying I do not believe in a god. He has given me a gift, your God, a chance for a second chance, by sending you to me. This, I believe."

I froze, and in my mind, I thought back to our conversation under the dusky sky when he had asked me to help him. I knew it then that it was for this purpose that I was sent to him, and for which I find myself moved with compassion for the beast within. I have to give him what he seeks, but how can I? I have no power to grant him his salvation. All I can do is give him my love. Would that be enough? I sat up, his arms falling limply from me. My fingers ran through my hair. "I believe it, too."

The Count sat up with me, his hand touching my lower back. "Then be the answer to my wish, my precious gift."

"I have already promised not just to you, but to myself also." I lay my head on his shoulder. I rested there for a moment, thinking of how this whole thing could come about. "I will do all I am able."

Again, his fingers wrapped around my waist as he purred. The Count kissed my hair and then whispered so softly to me. "Now sleep deeply, and do not wake until the morning. Let no noise disturb you, nor nightmare frighten you, but be at peace and know I am here."

All at once, I felt my mind go blank, and I slept.

THINGS SACRED

12 July

Morning…

In my efforts to aid the Count in his quest for redemption, I have been doing much reading on the subject. At least, doing as much reading as I can find. I don't have many materials from which to draw. It's not like the Count has a treasure trove of spiritually based literature in his library. In fact, I checked, and nothing indeed exists in any language. All I have is my little Bible to gather some ideas on how to go about this. I feel a bit lost and over my head. Often, I find myself staring off into space, trying to find some answer to the trials that plague the Count.

I guess it makes the hours go by quicker, but I know the more time I waste in trying to solve the problem, the less time I will have to set the answer into action. Usually, by the end of the day, I am so exhausted from caring for the castle, even with Dumitru's help, and doing the Count's lessons, that I have found little time for myself. My thoughts have been rather consumed by the subject, and day and night, I think of the options weighed before me.

Never before have the Count and I been so close. When he returns from his business, he follows me like an inseparable shadow. He has come to treat me with such affection that I often worry he will act out in front of Dumitru. As far as I can tell, Dumitru still is not aware of how 'intimate' we have become. To him, we are carrying on as normal, but in private, we are so different. I am certain the Count doesn't want Dumitru to know of this 'love affair' we have, but with only three of us living in this house, the truth has to come to light someday.

This is another dilemma in which I find myself. Dumitru has expressed to me twice that he would kill anyone who touched me, even the Count himself. And as time has gone by, he has opened up to me physically. A few days ago, when I was cleaning, he came up and began to talk to me about something inconsequential. Suddenly, he reached forward and wiped away some stray dirt that was on my cheek. I wasn't quite paying attention at the time, and the unexpected touch made me pull away. Of course, I apologized when I realized his intention, but I think I hurt him by withdrawing. I fear he has developed feelings for me. If he were ever to see the Count and me together alone, I'd hate to see his reaction to it.

19 July

Afternoon…

For the first time today, Dumitru was well enough to take the car out and get supplies. I offered to go with him, but he promptly refused. For nearly two months I have been cooped up in this castle with no view of the outside. It bothered me a lot that I wasn't allowed to go with him, but he returned in only a few hours with a multitude of foodstuffs.

I helped him put them away when suddenly he drew me aside and handed me a small paper bag. "This is for you."

I already knew what it was just by the size, but still, I peeked in. It was a small bottle of brandy. I was shocked that he had remembered my request from so long ago.

"I wanted to." He spoke before I could say anything, his eyes diverted from mine. "We could all use a glass every once in a while."

I couldn't *not* accept the gift from him as he was taking such great pains to acquire the forbidden drink for me. "You shouldn't put yourself in such danger because of me, but all the same, thank you."

"Well, you don't give a damn about what the Master says." He quoted me and smiled with a little nervous laugh.

I hadn't seen him smile or laugh in some time, and although it made me so glad, my heart still sank. I giggled anyway at the directness of his statement, coming from one who used to be so formal with me. "You're right about that. Still, you're too kind, Mitică. If there's anything I can do to repay you, let me know, okay?"

At the use of his nickname, his cheeks turned red, and he struggled to find an answer for me. "Uh, I-I need to scrub the floor to the entryway, you can help with that…if you want to."

"Sure, you know I'd be happy to help." I hugged him lightly. "Thank you for the gift. I'll go put it away before *he* notices."

"Y-Yeah…" He stuttered as he rubbed the back of his head. "I can finish here."

I gave him a big smile before I left. Usually, I am so blind to the ways that men flirt with women, but he flirts so blatantly obvious it hurts. I know he's older than I by a year or two, but if we had met under any other circumstances, I highly doubt that he would have looked my way. Dumitru is a good-looking young man, but he is not of the league of men who would notice me.

I feel like I've said this a hundred times, but this situation has been doomed from the start. I can only hope that, for his own sake, Dumitru will lose all interest in me. I must draw the line somehow before this gets out of hand.

Evening…

In our lessons, the Count's eagerness to learn has not diminished any, and he constantly absorbs all the information he can. That ability to analyze data and commit it to memory is the driving factor in what makes him a true genius. I also believe that it is the way he can so accurately read emotions and body language, and get inside someone's head.

Anyway, we had just concluded the lecture when the Count spoke up. "I have something for you."

I was caught off guard by his sudden transition. "For me?"

From within his satchel, he produced a package and a few other letters and handed them to me. "These came for you. They are from last month, as Dumitru has not had the chance to retrieve the post."

Taking the items in my hand, I immediately recognized my mother's handwriting, as well as the postmark, which read 15 June. I really hadn't expected to hear back from them, and it struck a homesick chord in me that I could feel my heart breaking. The other letters were from my employer, which honestly, were far less important to me than the large manila envelope. I was very curious to know what was inside because it was quite weighty, but there was something in me that couldn't bring myself to open it. All I could do was hold it in my hands.

"Are you not going to open it?" The Count pulled me from my thoughts.

I must have been staring at it for some time. "Later…"

He cocked his eyebrow. "You are not pleased to receive news from your family?"

"It's not that…" My voice faded out. "We're in the middle of work."

"We are finished." The Count put down his pen to focus directly on me. "Do you wish to read them in private?"

"I will," I reassured him with a smile, stashing the effects in my bag. "Later."

He must have been expecting a delighted response to the letters, and I think it quite puzzled him why I had acted so indifferently to them. After giving me one more sideways glance, he resumed finishing his work. I pretended to work on my computer, but my thoughts were distracted by the package. For the life of me, I couldn't understand why I felt so torn about receiving something from my family. I have not spoken for two and a half months. To be honest, I had pushed them from my mind all this time because I could not dwell on things that made me look weak. I had to focus on the issues at hand, which for a large portion of that time was to survive and not fall prey to those I perceived as a threat.

When the lecture was officially over, the Count told me he had to attend to something and would be back in about an hour to have our usual conversation. I knew it was a ploy to give me the privacy to read the letters, but I took it graciously and retired to my sitting room alone. I sat in my chair for a solid ten minutes just looking at the package and letters, trying to decide which one to open first. Eventually, I chose the ones from my employment agency that were from the president of the company. One was in response to the letter I had sent to tell the organization that I had arrived safely, and the other was asking for an update. What an update I could give them!

There was no longer any reason to delay the inevitable after those two, so I opened the other sizable envelope. Within it were numerous letters addressed to me from a multitude of different family members and friends, totaling ten separate envelopes in all. I was shocked that so many people had chosen to write to me, and I felt a frog form in my throat. So slowly, I read each one of the letters, starting with the one from my parents. So many things have happened to them while I have been away, but at the same time, there were many wishes for a speedy return. So many well-wishes for health and safety…if only they knew. At the last letter, I set them all aside to think it all over, once again lost in deep thought.

The Count returned just as he said he would, a bright smile beaming on his face as he sat in his usual chair across from mine. His joyful expression faded when he saw my face. "Bad news?"

I shook my head. "No, all good news."

"Then why do you look so sad?" He frowned. "I thought you would be very happy."

"I'm sorry," I straightened in my chair. "I am, I'm just thinking about it all."

"You must miss them terribly." The Count gazed at me sympathetically. "Are you feeling homesick now?"

"A bit," I had to admit to him. If I didn't, he would have seen right through me. "I didn't expect so many people to write to me. It's only been two months, and there is so much news."

I'm not sure if he inquired because he was genuinely interested or if he wanted to keep engaging me in conversation, but he asked. "If you wish, tell me the news. You never speak of your family, please tell me what they have to say."

"Well," I thought for a moment, trying to pick out the major highlights. "My little sister had a baby boy. Everyone is well and going about their lives, as usual, I guess."

"Then I wish you congratulations, Auntie." The Count beamed again, and he added the title made me smile. "What did your sister name the child?"

"Isaac," I reached inside the letter to show him the photo they had enclosed of the infant. It is a formal photograph of him dressed in a pastel blue bunny onesie. "He's so chubby."

The Count took the photo and examined it thoroughly, his face softening at the sight. If I have learned anything from observing him all this time, it's that when he's experiencing any sort of nostalgia, he becomes very sad. "He is. Your sister must be grateful to have a healthy son."

"Her second healthy son." I clarified as he handed it back to me. "She started early."

"She is very fortunate, indeed." He was impressed by the fact, but then his eyes drifted away. "I regret that you were not there."

I shrugged my shoulders. "I was there last time, and I guess when you see one birth, you've seen them all. Do you have any children, Count?"

At the question, I saw his jaw tense, but he remained composed. "Three...from before."

"Oh..." I immediately regretted the question. I wasn't sure why I used the present tense, as if they would still be alive after all this time. I felt very foolish. "I'm sorry..."

"It was long ago," he cleared his throat, forcing the awkwardness away. "No need to be sorry about it."

"Still," swallowing hard, I hastily put the photo away. "You must miss them very much."

"At times..." He leaned heavily on his elbow, a crease forming over his brow. Eager to get the pressure off of him, he placed it back on me. "And you? Do you wish for children?"

An unsettling and uncomfortable feeling made me look away from him. "Maybe someday if the right opportunity presents itself. If not, I'm alright with that too."

"The right opportunity?" He echoed.

I shrugged again. "Well, if I am in a good place financially and find someone willing to, you know. Those two things are quite hard to come by in today's world. Sometimes you find one but not the other, and it's rare to find the two at the same time and place."

"I can agree that in this modern age, it is difficult. People put more emphasis on love rather than alliances between families. But still, to me it is an odd concept," the Count explained thoughtfully. "In my time, everyone was expected to marry and have children, unless they chose a religious life."

"I suppose it's been that way until only recently." I mused, then said unexpectedly. "Forgive me if this is too bold, but if you had the opportunity, would you marry again?"

He didn't answer at first but stared sharply at me. "Marriage is sacred, and you know I am not."

My brow knitted at his answer. It truly caught me unaware that I hadn't considered that he couldn't enter into a sacred union with him and another person. I cleared my throat to relieve the awkwardness. "I'm sorry…I didn't think of it that way. You told me of your wife, and then a few nights ago, you mentioned another woman you met a century ago. I'm sorry if I've assumed something."

"I had two wives from before, although," he was becoming increasingly troubled, that was obvious from his rigid stature. "The other woman, she was not my wife…in a way, but not."

From the reminiscence of his voice, I could tell he was becoming lost in thought. I hated to let him relive those things alone, so I dared to ask him. "Tell me of her. She must have been a miraculous lady."

A smile flashed so quickly on his lips, but then it was gone. I could see he was reluctant to say anything about her, still, I waited patiently. The clock ticked by in the otherwise dead silence of the room until the Count finally looked at me again. "She was a woman before her time, strong and resourceful, yet she had a gentle and compassionate heart. She was to be married when I first met her, and despite that, I did seek her out. I had planned to make her as myself…" He stopped, swallowing hard. "But it was not brought to fruition, as much as I wished it. It is a very long and complicated story."

"You don't need to explain it to me if it's too painful." Standing, I went to him and sat on the arm of the chair. I hoped the closeness would comfort him, even a little. "What was her name?"

I couldn't see his face, but I could tell he was frowning. "Wilhelmina Harker."

"Harker?" I muttered quietly. I knew the name and laughed to myself. "Funny, my mother's maiden name is Harker. What a coincidence."

He was still as he took my hand. When he spoke, however, his voice was rather flat. "Is it, now?"

"I doubt there's a relation, though." I tried to think of how far I could go back, but I don't even know of anyone from my family tree who was named Wilhelmina. I know Mom will know something more, but I can't ask her, obviously. "There must be thousands of people with that last name. It's quite common."

The Count took his hand out of mine and stood. "Yes, I suppose it is."

His sudden change in demeanor jolted me, and I snapped to attention. "Did I upset you?"

"No, sweet one," he turned and kissed me gently on the forehead. "At my age, memories are painful."

"Regardless, I didn't think to ask would —"

The immortal put a finger to my lips. "Hush, no apologies. You should be getting to bed; it is quite late."

My lips went into a pout that he had shut down the conversation so abruptly. I took his hand and cradled it against my cheek. "Must you go so soon?"

The Count purred as his fingers moved to caress my cheek. "If I stay any longer, my dear, you will have to face the consequences."

"Like what?" I kissed his palm gently. "Staying another night? You know I don't mind. I don't want you to be alone with your thoughts if they're so painful."

"Tempting as that may be," he bent down to my level. "I fear if I stay tonight, I will not be a gentleman. Besides, you must rest."

For some reason, I found his mildly threatening promise amusing. "Your self-control is unrivaled."

"I will let you in on a secret," he was whispering as he moved towards my ear. "The monster in me may be able to resist the temptation you present — but the man cannot."

I gulped at his insinuation and let out a nervous laugh to lighten the mood. "Very well, Count. I'll let you go if you answer one more question."

He huffed once with a slight roll of his eyes. "Yes?"

I took the plunge into that question, which has been weighing heavily on my mind. "That group of people you spoke of, the one with Wilhelmina Harker in it, when you said they 'saved and damned' you. It seems a contradiction that they would do both."

The Count raised his eyebrow quizzically at me, but grew so quiet. A long moment passed before he finally said something, but even then, it was only a whisper. "It was a bit of both. Do you really want to know?"

"If it will help me to help you, yes." Any hints or glimmers of hope would be useful to me. Had they said something to him to make him wish for his redemption? Had they used some holy artifact to drive out the demon, but leave the human soul intact? No matter what it was, I had to know.

"In fairness, I had provoked in them a great hatred of me, and they sought my destruction. In the end, it had been Wilhelmina's husband who cut through my throat, and then an American friend of theirs drove another in my heart." He said it so nonchalantly that I felt myself become paralyzed. The image made my stomach turn, and I released his hand to cover my mouth in disgust. The Count showed no outward emotion to it at all as he continued. "Yet those weapons were made from human hands and did not extinguish me as they thought. The other details of it are unimportant now, but by this unsuccessful act, I remembered the man I was before I became the monster."

Head spinning, I tried to grasp what I just heard. Surely this husband of Wilhelmina must have despised the Count, and I guess rightfully so if he had tried to steal his fiancée away from him. But, I still don't understand how being decapitated 'saved' the Count. Obviously, Mr. Harker and the other man had failed to effectively kill him, so I am left even more confused about it than before.

A tear escaped my eye, and the Count wiped it away. "You asked, darling, but do not let it bother you. All is well. Now, goodnight."

I nodded and managed to bid him a goodnight.

He kissed me once more and then left me.

Needless to say, I have much to think about tonight, but one thing was for certain: even if the Count were to 'die', he would only be reborn again somehow. Although my initiative is not to kill him, there must be some way to do it. His body is dead, his soul trapped within, so how can conventional means of killing affect him? Also, he is not of this world, but of another. It must be the case that a complete destruction of the body is necessary to end the existence of one of these creatures.

The Count often refers to me burning him, too. Does that mean to set his whole being literally or figuratively ablaze? In any case, I shouldn't be focusing on how to end the body, but on saving the soul that is within. I know now that in doing so, the killing of their physical bodies does not equate to salvation for these beings, not that it does for humans either. The Count has been wrestling with himself, as he said, over that very subject of salvation for this past century. Perhaps my job will be easier, in a way, than I thought. This revelation has given me such insight into these creatures.

As much as the Count may shut me down, I must press further into his past to help me understand more of how he feels about the present. By doing such, I believe I can work with him to see what I see. That is, the goodness that he has within him. He does have the potential of being embraced by God again, as long as he freely chooses to humble himself.

Now I see my opening to the darkness that surrounds him. Let it be as it will be.

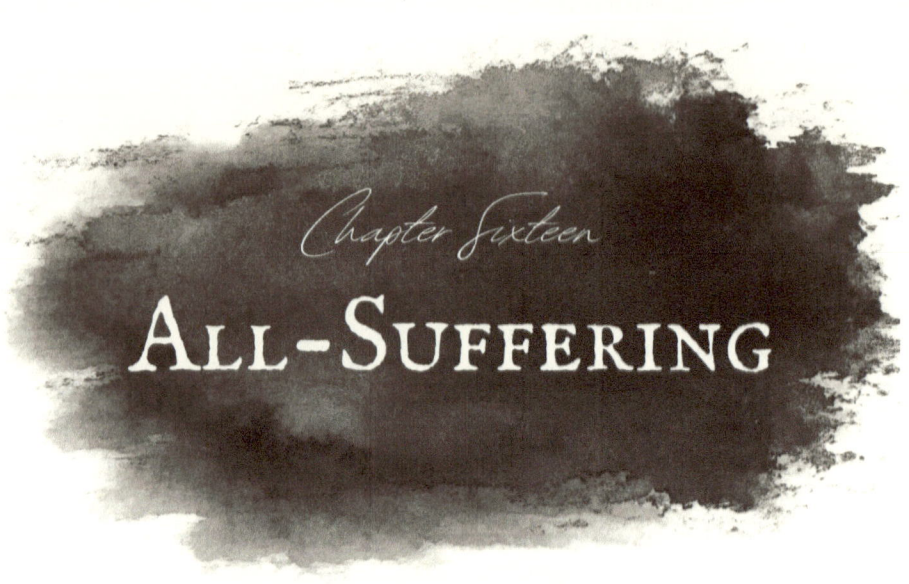

Chapter Sixteen

ALL-SUFFERING

21 July

Morning…

It has been one month since our terrible encounter with Petros. For nostalgia, mostly, I thought I'd make an entry for this date to remember it. So much has changed in one month that it's hard for me to fathom, yet here I write, the living the results of that fateful night. All in this month, I have learned so much about myself, the Count, and Dumitru that I would never have been privy to otherwise. Even though I still look back on it and shudder, there is a part of me that is almost glad it happened. I really found out how much I can endure, and how much in times of struggle, friends need each other more than they realize. Looking back, I am so grateful that each one of us has grown closer to the other. That bond of near-death has cemented us as no other thing could.

In other news, I've been writing responses to each of the letters, and it has been difficult. There is so much that I cannot say to my family and friends, so I am left describing the same pleasantries as in my previous letter. I try to keep any mention of myself out of my letters and focus on the news that they have told me. Also, I mention the weather and beautiful landscape, but I sound like a broken record. If any of them were to read the other's letter, then they would see the blatant repetitive phrases. That can be viewed as suspicious, but in essence, if the supernatural is taken out of this narrative, things seem pretty normal.

Anyway, back to the real issues at hand: since the Count had told me of Wilhelmina Harker and her husband, I have been trying to keep him engaged in conversation about them, but it has been ineffective. Consistently, he has ended my mild interrogations before I could learn anything of use. I've also been trying to ask him about the weaknesses of his kind, but I knew he wouldn't be very cooperative with that either. It seems that asking about his life before…it opens up old wounds that still hurt him. Of course, I don't mean to continually cause him pain, but he denies that he is in any. Despite asking for my help, the Count shuts me out and shuts me down. I must find alternative plans of attack than simply 'asking'. From my last entry, I do have a few in my arsenal, but they are quite risky. They require a gall that I don't think I have. Direct and pin-pointed provocation of the monster within is a more dangerous game that I think I can afford to play. As Petros said, the Count is the king of their kind, and I am only a human poking the beast with a stick.

25 July

Evening…

I damn human frailty to my final breath. As I guess I should have known, I've begun that special 'time' again. As a result, the Count has withdrawn from me completely for a week. Just when I was so damn close, I thought I could reach out and grasp the knowledge I seek from him, I am denied. Now I must wait until I have completed my time to reengage him once again. When he came into the library this evening, I was expecting him to have a bad reaction. Sure enough, his nostrils flared, and he grimaced.

But before he could say something, I interceded. "You don't need to say anything. I'll see you in a week."

The Count winced at my cold tone as he turned away. "Forgive me for this."

Irrationally, an intense frustration made me stand abruptly. "Are you so repulsed by me when I'm like this? Is that why you disappear?"

With his back still to me, he turned his head to the side just enough for me to see his profile. The words he spoke were heavy with remorse. "Trust me, sweet one, it is the opposite."

And then he was gone.

The opposite, huh? I think that answer was even more horrifying to me than it should have been. Is he so attracted by the smell that he must physically remove himself from the temptation? The scent of my blood is tempting to a creature like him, but when he had been confronted face-first with it before, he did not retreat from it. When Dumitru's blood was pooling around us as I held his head, the Count didn't appear to be affected.

I guess I will spend my time cleaning and reading. *Id est*, all the things that I shouldn't be putting so much emphasis upon. My time is short, while he has an eternity to reconcile himself. Perhaps I will try to talk to Dumitru about what he knows of the Count's life and weaknesses. He must know what they are.

27 July

Morning…

The weather has been quite hot and muggy now that we're in the middle of summer. Yet still, here and there, a cool breeze sweeps up from the mountain tops and grants a brief reprieve from the heat. When Dumitru and I go outside for the afternoon, the sun is always shining so brightly. There are clouds, but they don't dampen the warmth as we're up so high. For this past week, the weather has been perfect with just enough sun and rain to bring the surrounding vegetation to full vitality. Just beyond the wall, one can hear so much more wildlife than before, and I still wish I could go out and explore the wondrous teeming life. From the front-facing windows of my bedroom, I can see past the gate, past the natural rock bridge, and into the dense forest that expands farther than the eye can see. Eventually, the road disappears into those trees, and one crest of a hill turns into another and another. Sometimes I forget how truly isolated this place is, and honestly, forgetting is the best.

I have received word from Dumitru this morning that the Count has allowed both of us to go to Câmpulung on Saturday. As it's not terribly far from the castle, Dumitru explained to me at breakfast, and he said that the Count has been hesitant to allow us to go due to our health. In the end, he decided both of us are well enough to venture out into the world again. I found that to be a bit ridiculous, and I know there must be another reason for his reluctance. I recall that the Count told me of a group of creatures out there who wish to depose him, and I wonder if they are the real reason for it.

When I asked Dumitru if those people would be after us once we left the confines of the castle. He shrugged off the possibility, actually, saying there was nothing to worry about. He assured me that the likelihood of someone attacking us was slim to none. According to him, no one would dare raise an open hand against the Count on his own territory, or against his servants or house, after the example that was made of Petros. Still, I am not so sure.

I couldn't help but think that if we were both placed in a situation, could Dumitru and I be able to protect ourselves? As much as he doesn't want to admit it, Dumitru is still recovering, and any serious fight could debilitate him. On my end, I could barely fight one…without using myself as bait.

When I told Dumitru of my reservations, he became very quiet and embraced me tightly. It is a rare occurrence that he would choose to hug me because of something like that, but all the same, he said cheerfully. "Don't let such things worry you. We're going there to have fun, so let's have fun."

That simple sentence really hit home for me. As long as Dumitru is here, I believe that everything will be fine. I mustn't give in to paranoia and fear of the unknown. After all that has happened to me over these three months, how can I still be so fearful of what I don't know? I have friends who will not abandon me, and I have faith that everything will play out in its due course. So, Dumitru is right: I will have fun for my one day of freedom and won't let anything deter me from it.

...

For the rest of the morning, I busied myself polishing the ancient woodwork in the main areas of the castle I noticed were showing their age. It gave me much pride to have the wood's splendid mahogany color resurface after so many years of being hidden under a thick layer of crud and dust. Before I knew it, it was lunchtime. Dumitru and I sat together in the kitchen, chatting about the chores of the day, nothing very exciting to mention. We were alone in the castle, and we had some time before we had to return to our duties, so I decided to press him on some of the questions that had been compiling in my brain.

We were finishing up the dishes when a pause came between us, and I took my chance. "Hey Mitică, I've been wondering something for a while now."

"Yeah?"

"How did you come into the Count's service?" I asked as I handed him a plate to dry.

He froze up for a moment, then took the plate from me. "Why do you want to know?"

"Just curious," I flashed him a bright smile. "You've never told me anything about it."

Dumitru thoughtfully dried the plate before daring to look back at me. "It's a long story."

"Mitică, if you don't want to tell me —"

"No, I do…" He cut me off with a stern tone. "I think it's something you should know since you know what he is."

I remained silent, handing him another dish as I waited for him to continue.

With a steadying breath, he began his tale. "When I was ten years old, my family died, and I lived on the streets. I had to do many bad things to survive. I became a part of a bad group of young people who were…I'm not sure of the English word. We did a lot of stealing from certain people and other crimes for our boss, who paid us nearly nothing for our work. That boss was a very rich and greedy man who wanted to live forever and looked to Romania's old stories to find it. As you know, the Master is one of those stories. I was a part of the group for a few years when he found the Master, and as payment for his immortality, he gave us as gifts to him, and also a lot of money."

"Us?" I gasped.

"Me and the other boys who used to do his work." He stopped to think. "I think it was about fifty of us. We were all brought here and presented to the Master."

Gripped by his story, I leaned on his every word. "And, what did the Count do?"

Dumitru smirked slightly to himself. "You know him, he is disgusted by people such as that man, and likes to deal his own justice. So, my boss did not get his immortality. I know because I saw him dead, impaled to be exact. It wasn't pleasant to see."

I found myself almost grinning. How much like the Count to dispense justice the way he used to, in the most gruesome of fashions, just to prove his point to a dead man. "I'm sure it was…"

"Anyway," he said after a shrug, then continued to explain as he went about his work. "The Master didn't want anything to do with us, so he forced us all to leave and make us forget. But his power didn't work on me, and I hid. Soon, he found me and tried to make me go, but still, it didn't work. He allowed me to stay if I worked for him, so I stayed."

I was positively stunned by him. How terrible that a young boy and all those innocent children should be put up for sacrifice for one man's greed. If it weren't for the Count's mercy, fifty innocents would have been slaughtered just to add one immortal to this earth. "Has he ever…you know…bite you?"

"Not himself," Dumitru set his towel down and leaned against the counter. "Not that he would want to. Another did once and didn't like the taste of my blood. That's why Petros didn't bite me as he did you."

"So, you cannot be compelled or bitten," I scoffed, flabbergasted. "And you're just telling me this now?"

He shrugged again. "There was no reason to tell you. It's the only reason I am valuable to him. I cannot betray him with anyone's will except my own."

With this information he had told me, everything about him started to make sense. Why was he always so angry, so tense, so sharp with words? He had endured far more than I dared even guess about him. My heart moved with such pity for the young man that I touched his hand. "I think you're more valuable to him than you realize. You have your perks, I guess you could call them, but like I told you, he does care for you. Don't minimize your worth."

Dumitru only gazed at me with a sad expression as he sighed. Hesitantly, his fingers came in between mine, a light pink dashing his cheeks. "How do you always know how to say things to make me feel better?"

"I see things from an outsider's perspective, I guess." I squeezed his hand. "Besides, what kind of friend would I be if I wasn't there for you? No matter how much you hated me at the beginning, I think we've become good friends now, don't you think?"

"I didn't hate you." He frowned deeply, ignoring everything else I said. "The Master said I am to keep my distance because it isn't my place."

I frowned too, my heart breaking for him all the more. Cautiously, I wrapped my arms around his shoulders. "You know I don't give a damn about what your Master says. We'll be friends forever. If you need anything, don't be afraid to lean on me, okay?"

Dumitru's arms came around me, but he didn't say anything. This poor man had such little love in his life, only anger and pain to keep him company. The only reason he was dealt a helping hand in life was due to events that were beyond his control, and that he possesses some abnormal quality. Was it a coincidence or a twisted string of fate? Now he finds himself here, in service to a half-millennium-old man, still as alone as he was when he was ten years old.

His grip tightened. "Yes, friends."

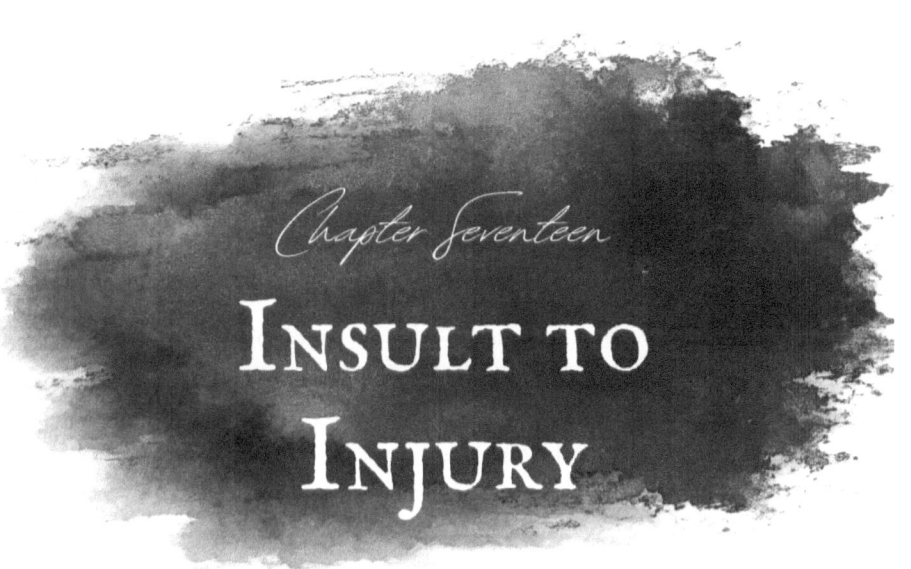

Chapter Seventeen

INSULT TO INJURY

29 July

Morning...

O n Saturday, I awoke a bit earlier than I needed to and completed a few of my chores before breakfast. We left around 7 am for Câmpulung, leaving the Castle Dracula behind us as it melted into the trees. As soon as we were out of sight, I hopped up into the passenger seat, to Dumitru's protest. When the Count isn't around, I am determined not to let these superficial social barriers keep Dumitru and me apart. He grumbled a lot, but I stayed in my place, and eventually, he settled down. I think he appreciated the company more than he let on as we engaged in idle conversation. Soon enough, another silence came between us, and I stared out the window, watching the Romanian landscape roll by.

My mind began to wander, and I recalled the last time Dumitru and I were allowed to go out back in May. How uncertain I had been of myself then, when faced with things so unknown to me, but all through that, I had been thinking of others who needed me more than myself. I am happy that I did not run when the opportunity had presented itself. I could have fled to the American Embassy, to the nearest international airport, and been gone from these men's lives in the blink of an eye, but I stayed. Again, I am presented with a similar chance to flee from them, but now I see that in all the hidden nature of this world, there is no place I belong more than here.

...

What a beautiful and picturesque city Câmpulung is, nestled so perfectly in the bosom of rolling hills and mountains. It's an oasis of charm among the wilds of the green countryside, with its white-washed homes topped with burnt sienna roofs — a mix of medieval and modern, situated so lovely in the valley.

The hours passed too quickly before noon came. Dumitru and I had walked all around the medieval city, which is quite large, to see the sights. Of course, we got our actual shopping done too, which was still as fun as before.

Despite our good time, I found myself always looking over my shoulder. I would examine the faces of everyone around me and pray to God that I would never see them again. Making mental notes as I went along, it was almost exhausting to remember where everything was, but I kept constantly aware of my surroundings. I tried not to make myself too tense about it, but still, I would turn at every noise and be ever aware.

By chance, we came across a religious shop in all our wanderings that happened to sell rosaries. Without even asking Dumitru if he wanted to stop, I went in to examine the multitude of styles and colors. I liked many of them and settled on one with red coral beads. I was feeling much better after being without for so long.

By that time, it was getting close to lunch, so we set out to find ourselves a café. Dumitru brought me to one that he had visited before, and once he ordered for me, we sat in silence.

From the corner of his eye, he stared as the small gift bag that held my rosary. His stoic expression relaying to me that he had an opinion that he wasn't going to vocalize.

I finally spoke. "Just say it."

"What?"

"What you're thinking?"

"You really want to know?" I could feel his frustration seething just beneath the surface, ready to erupt. "I believe that even though you have learned you must rely on others, you are taking things into your own hands again."

I scowled at his words, crossing my arms. "Now you sound like the Count."

"And was he so wrong to tell you that?" Dumitru spouted back just quietly enough not to draw attention to us. "You are planning another scheme in your head, and you don't realize it by buying that rosary."

I leaned forward, my own frustration with him getting to my head, fueled by his use of the word 'scheming' as if I were plotting a *coup d'état*. "Planning ahead isn't scheming."

"No?" He snorted, pointing to the small bag on the floor by my purse. "By buying that, you are proving my point. You don't trust either of us enough to protect you."

I gritted my teeth; those little reminders flickered. "Last time I only had myself —"

"It was partially your own fault that you only had yourself." Dumitru shot back, his angered tone began to turn the heads of our nearest neighbors.

Embarrassed by this growing scene, I steadied myself before giving him a stern warning. "This isn't the place for this discussion."

Dumitru turned around just as the couple behind him looked away as if they hadn't been listening. When he spoke again, his voice was much calmer. "All I'm saying is to trust in someone other than your God for once in your life. The Master protected Europe against the Ottomans in his day. Do you think protecting one woman will be so hard? Besides, there is no threat."

I couldn't look at him. Perhaps he was right, but at the same time, wrong. There are too many radical variables at play that could not determine our safety. This was a perfect situation: being far from the castle, far from the Count, in public, and it didn't matter if it was night or day. I do trust both of them, but what I truly do not trust is myself...nor my ability to protect myself. "I suppose it shouldn't be hard."

"Trust in us," he reached across the table to grasp my hand. "We are here for you."

I could only nod, my emotions and thoughts still brewing nonetheless.

After a moment, Dumitru released me and stood, telling me he had to use the restroom.

And again, I nodded, not watching him disappear from my view. My eyes drifted down to the small bag that held the rosary, and I reached for it.

"Uh, pardon me, but you speak English?"

Startled, I faced the voice. It was a man, perhaps my age or a bit younger, smiling like an idiot with a beer in his hand. He was definitely a tourist. My brow furrowed. "Uh, yes?"

"I'm sorry for eavesdropping, but I haven't heard a native English speaker in quite some time." He laughed nervously, but all the same sounded genuine. "You're American, right?"

"I am," my curiosity piqued. "And from your accent, I can tell you are, too."

"Figured me out already?" The stranger smiled warmly, holding his hand out to shake mine. "My name's Matthew, well, Matt. Damn glad to meet you."

"Louisa," I used my middle name and returned the friendly gesture. "What brings you to the middle of nowhere?"

"I'd like to ask you the same thing," he chatted freely. "I'm taking a few semesters off to do some traveling; you know how it is. I've been in the countryside for so long that to hear an English speaker is few and far between, so I'm sorry if I freaked you out."

I laughed once. "Don't worry about it, I know the feeling. What brings you to Câmpulung, though?"

"Oh, to see the sights, the landscape, the history." Matt grinned wider as he went along. "And you? What brings you out here?"

"I'm on a teaching assignment," I explained vaguely.

"Very cool," the young man began to visibly relax as the conversation took off. As we spoke, I began to notice how handsome he was with his blond hair and blue eyes. He looked more like a college jock to me, the stereotypical lady's man of the campus, so to have him talking to me was nothing short of a miracle. Then, out of nowhere, he asked. "So, was that your boyfriend?"

I felt my face flush at the thought and laughed nervously. "Uh, no, more like a friend. He's just showing me around."

"Well, between you and me," Matt whispered, leaning down a bit. "I can tell he likes you a lot."

"As a friend, I'm sure." I forced a grin.

"Trust me, you —"

As if in slow motion, Matt was suddenly knocked from behind as a group of people wedged passed him. Losing his balance, he toppled half onto me. He caught himself on the table just in time, but I was not so lucky. The full pint of beer, which had been in his hand, came gushing like a waterfall all over my chest and lap. I shrieked as the chilly liquid soaked straight through my clothes.

"Oh my God! I'm so sorry!" Matt exclaimed as he straightened, grabbing the napkins off the table. In his frantic state, he began to blot the beer from my chest.

"It's fine —"

Before I could stand, Dumitru appeared out of nowhere, grabbing Matt by his shirt to yank him away from me. I couldn't see his face, but by my poor American friend's reaction, it was about to go downhill fast. Dumitru growled in a harsh and threatening tone. *"Do not touch her."*

"Listen, man, it was just an accident." Matt put his arms up in surrender.

"Mitică —" I was about to reach for him when he suddenly pulled away.

With blunt force, Dumitru punched Matt hard in the face, and he fell heavily against a table and to the floor. "American pig, go home. We don't want you around here."

Matt was stunned, and the entire café had gone so silent that one could hear a pin drop. All eyes were on us, and I'm sure everyone understood enough English to know what Dumitru had said. I, too, perhaps more than everyone, was shocked by his words that rolled so easily off his tongue. After all this time, I had forgotten his distaste for my homeland, and a deep offense settled in my heart. I stood, my clothes dripping with beer, and I pushed past Dumitru to Matt.

The poor kid was startled, but the realization of Dumitru's words was slowly seeping into his brain. I stepped between the two and extended my hand to help him. We both looked at each other, all too aware of the insult that was pinned on us. Biting his lip in anger, Matt took my hand and got to his feet. "You want to say that again, friend?"

"Don't, please," I whispered to Matt warningly. "I feel it as much as you. Be the bigger man and walk away."

The tall American looked down at me, that desire to lash out in defense so plain on his face. Yet he swallowed, straightening his shirt, Matt forced a smile, too. "Sorry for ruining your clothes."

And with that, he left the restaurant. The entire establishment was still frozen in time, all eyes still upon us. The staff, remembering themselves, bustled to rearrange the table and clean the spill around my chair. I turned back to Dumitru, feeling myself blaze with fury at him. The look on his face, though, was one of regret. But, in my rage, again I blew past him.

"Isa—"

I didn't stop but went straight past him to the restroom and shut the door. In the mirror, I saw the full extent of the damage to my clothes. From the collar of my blouse down to my knees were the remnants of the beer. It had gotten down my shirt and into my bra, and even soaked through my pants to my underwear. There wasn't anything I could do because I had no change of clothes, and it was no simple stain I could work out. For a few seconds, I stood there, unsure of what to do, so I only washed my hands.

I jumped when a woman had suddenly materialized next to me. I don't quite remember what she looked like, but her straight hair was an ashy silver. I blinked, confused as to how she got there and how I hadn't noticed her. I blurted a quick apology and left the restroom, my head spinning.

There was something very strange about how I felt. It reminded me of the dizzying effects of Petros' control, accompanied by an underlying calm that soothed my erratic heartbeat. My neck, too, was feeling the aftereffects of being constricted, as if a hand had been held there for some time, yet I had no memory of anything. My body *knew* something had happened to me, but my mind could not remember it. Everything felt surreal until I was shocked back to reality.

"Isadora?" Dumitru stood before me, holding a bag of food, my purse, and other things. All at once, I remembered the anger I had for him, and snatched my purse, and made a beeline for the door. I made it outside when he came next to me. "Isadora?"

"Don't speak to me if you don't want me here." I snapped, quickening my pace as I dripped beer onto the pavement. "I don't know what your major malfunction is, but until you figure it out, don't bother."

That struck him silent. I was seething as we walked back to the car, and after laying down the extra blanket for me to sit on so I wouldn't ruin the leather, we set off back to the castle early.

All the way was silent, with me sitting in the back. I stared out the window, replaying the events at the café over again, especially Dumitru's part. From day one, I knew he had some issue with Americans, but I never thought he'd take it that far. He told me himself that he didn't hate me at the beginning, but if these are his true feelings, it's far worse than hate.

The trip back up into the mountains seemed much slower than the trip down. My clothes only added to my extreme discomfort, and it felt like I was being marinated in beer, and the pungent smell was making my head dizzy. Every piece of me wanted to rip my clothes off and throw them out the window. So, I sat there, stewing for the entire ride.

Later...

By 3:30 pm, we were in familiar territory, and still neither of us had said anything to each other. My head had cooled a bit, and I was feeling so bad for the words I had said in anger to Dumitru, but I couldn't initiate conversation with him. I needed to be away from him, and I think he did from me, too. What I wanted more than anything was a bath and time to clear my head.

I was still brooding when we got into the castle gates, and I didn't even wait for the car to stop before I opened the door. Dumitru hit the brakes hard, and the whole car jolted to a stop. "What the hell do you think you're doing?!"

"You can bring the groceries in yourself, can't you?" I spat, slamming the door closed.

I heard him yelling something, but it was muffled as I ascended the steps. Once I came close to the smaller door, it opened immediately at my presence. Unfazed, I entered the castle and headed for the stairs.

"Isadora?"

I came to a halt at the Count's voice, again not expecting him to be there so early in the day. I had hoped he would still be out, but I should have known better. I should have been so delighted to see him, but I wanted nothing to do with him. I didn't even make eye contact with him, but I saw him put his hand to his nose.

"What is the meaning of all of this?" He was quite caught off guard by the scene.

"Ask Dumitru." I threw up my hair into a high ponytail as I turned my back fully to him.

I would never act so impertinently toward him, but it's hard to explain how put out I was. Everything was in a blur until I got to my sitting room. I literally ripped the soaked clothes from my body and threw the rest of my things onto my chair. Wasting no time, I went and drew a bath and began to soak my clothes in the sink, but I think they are far from being saved. Not quite thinking, I went to the hiding place where I kept my contraband of brandy and took a few swigs. Instantly, the warmth hit my empty stomach, and only when it spread like fire into my legs and arms was I calmed.

Evening…

It wasn't until 6 pm that I emerged from my bedroom, solely driven by hunger. For the last three hours, I had cooled down considerably and let my head think over my heart. I had reconciled that it was best to apologize to Dumitru for the harsh words I had said to him. On my part, they were terrible things that I should not have said under any circumstances, and the only way to mend them was to admit my wrongdoing. The last time we had gone out together and had a small altercation, we both had kept it to ourselves, knowing the Count would want to have the entire story. This time, I had pinned the entire incident on Dumitru without any explanation, and I was sure that the Count had demanded the story in full. Brainlessly, I had completely abandoned Dumitru to the Master's ire with no backup.

So, I made my way down to the kitchen, where at that time I knew he would be. Sure enough, I found him absentmindedly doing some menial chore as some food was cooking on the stove. Dumitru didn't notice me at first, so I sat down on the steps and waited for him. Yet still he didn't, and a wisp of smoke came into the air. "Your food is burning."

Dumitru jumped up, then turned his attention to the food and cried a curse in Romanian as he took the pan off the fire. He watched me from the corner of his eye as he stirred the contents, asking. "Do you need something?"

I was relieved his tone was not as sharp as it usually is when he's upset, and in kind, I replied softly. "I wanted to say that I apologize for saying those things to you. They were uncalled for, and I immediately regretted them. It was not what a friend says to another friend. I know you may not forgive me, but I just wanted you to know."

He was quiet as he loaded the food, which I saw then to be a stir-fry of a variety of odds and ends, onto two plates. Mitică didn't answer me directly. "Are you hungry?"

"Starving," at the thought of food, my stomach grumbled.

Without saying another word, he handed me the plate and sat down next to me on the step. Dumitru didn't begin to eat, only stared at the wonderful-smelling ensemble. I watched him, seeing in him the will to say something. "I...I had to tell the Master what happened."

I bit my lip. "Was he mad?"

"Furious," Dumitru shrugged and rolled his eyes as he began to eat. "At me, of course."

Sighing inwardly, I kicked myself for having spoken so mindlessly to the Count. "Did he punish you?"

He didn't reply.

My brow furrowed. "I am sorry..."

"For what?" He queried. "I insulted you directly, and by that, had indirectly insulted the Master."

I paused for a moment, then asked. "Do you really think I'm a pig? Do you really want me to leave?"

It took a minute, but he answered me. "You know I don't..."

"Then why did you say it?"

He paused. "Because I forgot...I forgot you are American."

I was astonished. Sitting there with a fork full of food, I stared at him as if he had two heads. Being in this place, I am constantly reminded of the differences between myself and them; from the language they speak in private to the class divide that the Count enforces. Each day, I am confronted with these barriers that separate me from Dumitru, so one would think that he would feel them most of all. "How can you forget something like that?"

"I guess I don't see you as one anymore." He justified it so plainly. "Don't ask me to explain it."

"What do you see me as, then?"

"Don't ask me to explain," Dumitru warned me again and then deflected. "Besides, that guy was assaulting you. It is my duty to defend you when the Master is not near."

I frowned that he had changed the subject, but went along with it. "It was an accident, you know, and he was only trying to help."

"Accident or not," he moved to look directly at me. "He still touched you."

Matt had touched my chest with the napkins, but it wasn't what I considered inappropriate. "You touch me all the time, how is that so different?"

He glared at me, taking some offense at my comment. "I do *not* touch you all the time, and when I do, it's only when you allow it or need it."

"I needed his help then, and I allowed it." I straightened, and glaring back, I pressed him. "So, I ask how it is so different? Tell me, I'm confused. Was it because of the area on which he touched? Was it too close for your comfort?"

Instantly, his face went red, his eyes flashed to my chest and then away, and I knew I was right. "It doesn't matter where."

I rolled my eyes. "Sure it doesn't."

"I told you that if anyone touches you, I'd kill them." Dumitru snapped in his usual harshness. "That means everyone."

I eyed him carefully, reading his face like an open book. His spur to anger was intriguing as it came so quickly after he looked at my chest. Now that Dumitru was on the defense, I dared to ask. "Was it your Master or yourself that put that idea in your head?"

The question, as I had judged, caught him off guard. Dumitru looked back down at his food, his face still pink. "The Master, of course."

He was lying, I knew it. Even if it had initially started as an order, it has grown to be something more personal. The encounter with Petros was the tipping point for him, where he swore not only to me but to himself that he would protect me. Leave it to Dumitru, however, to see anyone who is not him as a threat.

Chapter Eighteen
OPEN VEINS

We spoke further on other things, and in the end, Dumitru and I came to an understanding and apologized to each other. The two of us must have talked for an hour together to come to that point, but the only thing that matters is that it was reached. It relieved my heart that he had accepted my apology, and I felt much better walking out of the kitchen than I did walking in. Although my conscience felt better, my body was heavy from the exhaustion of the day, and it was a struggle to get up the flights of steps.

Knowing I had reached my limit, I was dead set on going to bed early. The Count, whom I was certain wished to hear my side of the story, would have to wait until tomorrow. I had not seen the

Master since this afternoon, and I wondered if he had gone out again. Surely he would be returning soon from wherever he goes, so I was determined to get to sleep to avoid him.

Sneaking into my sitting room, I was halfway to the bedroom before I was stopped dead.

"Going to bed so soon?"

I jumped, turning to face the Count, who sat on the settee. I was so lost in thought that I hadn't even noticed him sitting there, and I placed my hand on my racing heart. "One of these days you're going to scare me to death."

He chuckled, motioning for me to sit beside him. "That dear heart of yours will last longer than you think. Come, sit, I must speak with you."

Of course, I didn't want to, but I went to stand before him. "I'm actually feeling a bit unwell. I know we must speak about what happened, but can it be tomorrow?"

"Unwell?" He repeated, his head tilting to one side. "What ails you?"

Honestly, I didn't have a good enough answer to give him other than that I was only tired. If I lied, he would see it, but I could give him no weak excuse either. "Just a long day that took a lot more out of me than I thought."

The Count nodded once, but took my hands that rested on either side of me. "Then stay for only a moment, we have not been close in many days."

The chill of his large hands warmed my heart with his gentle touch, and I couldn't say no. A few minutes wouldn't hurt, and I had missed him so. Sitting next to the Count, I nestled into his side as his arm came around me. A tension left my body, and I rested my head on his shoulder. "I missed you like this."

His lips, in turn, rested on my hair. "What else did you miss?"

"Your company," I interwove my fingers with his. "And your kisses…"

"I missed them, too." The Count whispered secretly. "Do you think your poor heart can withstand a few of them?"

I hummed, my heart fluttering again as I looked up at him. Those sweet eyes met mine, and I couldn't help but smile. "Perhaps a few, here and there."

He drew me in and kissed me. It had only been under a week, but it felt like an eternity. Welcoming the Count wholeheartedly, I felt myself grow weak as he whisked me away from my internal struggle. It was exhilarating to feel him again so intimately, and I clenched his shirt. The Count's mouth came off mine, but continued to trail down my jaw and throat. Instinctually, I moaned at the sensation, but began to feel something strange. My shaking hands settled, my heartbeat slowed in one skip, and at once I became excessively alert to the change that was shifting my body from a heightened exhilaration to a dizzying calm. Opening my eyes, I began to panic, but my body did not reciprocate in kind.

Then I slipped from all reality, the last thing I remember feeling was his lips generously showering me with kisses. My whole being, my whole existence, was turned off like a flick of a switch.

One second, I was myself, awake and aware, and the next, it was all blackness.

The next thing I remember was opening my eyes, slightly blurred, and feeling came back to my limbs. For some reason, I was lying on the floor, the room spinning, as I fought to regain myself. There was a weight on me, holding me down, and a dull pain radiated from my wrists and hands. As I became more conscious, the pain worsened, driving me from my stupor. My heart burst alive again, suddenly remembering its job to beat, and my vision cleared.

The Count hovered above me, his eyes ablaze in crimson fury as he stared directly into mine. He was the one holding my hands above my head, his lower half pinning me immobile to the floor. A deep terror enveloped me, and I quivered beneath him. I tried to speak, but the words were caught in my throat.

In that moment when his gaze caught mine again, his fury became sorrow. Almost in a defeated motion, his body sank, and he rested his forehead against mine. The Count's extended silence frightened me all the more as I felt him quake in subdued rage.

I tried to wriggle my arms from his grasp. There was this sudden, stabbing pain that made me cry out, and I could feel a sticky wetness between my fingers. A true panic gripped my heart when I smelled the overbearing scent of thick blood, and I pleaded to him. "Vlad, let me go, please."

"I cannot," he choked. "I know you are confused, but answer me truthfully: at any time today, were you alone or separated from Dumitru?"

His question did confuse me, and I struggled to answer. Not only to find that answer but to find the words to relay them. "I think…at a restaurant."

The Count hissed some profanity in Romanian.

It dawned on me, suddenly, as I thought of his words. I felt the strength leave my body as tears welled up in my eyes. Pure helplessness ripped my heart from my body, and the fight in me dissipated. I knew. "My God, what did I do?"

"You did *not* do anything. It was *not* you." He growled more ferocious than I had ever seen, and beneath his lips, his teeth had become those of the demon. "It was *them. They* compelled you."

"I don't remember…" A choking sob escaped me, and the Count gathered me into his arms. My arms had no strength in them, and I couldn't even lift them to embrace him back. I looked down at my left arm and saw a deep gash that stretched from my wrist to halfway up my forearm, where blood flowed so freely from it, like a waterfall, and it transfixed me. My fingers twitched uncontrollably. "I…*can't* remember."

He repositioned me so we faced each other, taking me away from the bloodied sight. "Listen to me, now: you hurt yourself. You must let me help you again."

My voice shook. "I told you not again —"

"*Woman,*" he burst with anger at me as he took his sharp nails to slice open the skin of his neck. The dark blood immediately trickled from the open wound. "Now is not the time for your stubbornness."

And with that, he forced my mouth to the bloody incision and held me there. I tried to struggle against him, but there was no strength of my own to fight. I whimpered at the taste, so revolting as the last time. It filled my mouth, and although I tried not to swallow, it became too much to hold. The foul liquid hit my stomach wave after wave.

Again, an eternity passed before the Count pulled me away, and a tingling set over my entire body. A new strength crept into me, and within seconds, the pain in my arm and hands had gone. The euphoria came, and I raised my arm to look at the remnant blood.

Instantly, I recalled how it had come to be there. Turning behind me, I saw pieces of a decorative crystal vase, broken and dripping with blood. My blood.

I looked back at the Count, his blood slick on my lips. "I see it now."

He nodded slowly. "Remember."

It was a command, and all at once, the recent events that had been hidden from me were reopened thanks to the power of his immortal lifeblood. I relived it all like a dream, both real and unreal. The woman who spoke was not me, but was me. All I could do was stand by as the woman who looked like me used my voice to speak words I never said. And, from the last thing I remembered, the Count's kisses were fluttering around me so lovingly, the scene continued:

She moaned, the woman who wasn't me, as the Count pulled my collar down to kiss deeper into the unknown. Purring, she spoke, the words uttered from her lips didn't sound like my voice, but it was, in fact, mine. Her accent was unexpectedly light and whimsical. "You were always so passionate, Țepeș."

I was horrified that from my mouth she had called him simply 'Impaler'. At the sudden shift, he let me go, returning his eyes to me, a fresh ire manifesting itself in him. "Who are you?"

"Why, I'm Isadora, of course." She jeered.

"You dare to mock me whilst hiding behind another face, coward." He grabbed my upper arms and wrenched me toward him, baring his teeth in their full viciousness. "What do you want?"

She giggled as I felt my bones strain under his strength. "I'm surprised you don't already know."

The Count's eyes flashed like rubies as he roared, nostrils flaring. "You will answer me!"

She smiled, smoothing my hands over his. It was my touch he was feeling, and he growled at the familiarity from such an unfamiliar person. Somehow, by doing that, she had managed to have him unhand me, and she stood and meandered a few paces away. "Don't you worry, I shall be brief."

There was a burst of urgency within him, most likely because whoever this woman was, she was creating distance between him and me. He went to grab me to bring me to him, but somehow, I had managed to dodge his unrivaled quickness and stepped out of his reach.

She laughed as if to mock him. "You know perfectly who we are, Father. For the past century, we have been watching you from afar."

"Finally, you show yourselves to me then, my little group of dissenters." His face was beginning to show the first signs of his hidden feral nature. "Young ones, you know nothing at all."

An anger welled up in my chest, but it wasn't my own. She suppressed it and continued as if the Count had said nothing. "Not only have we been watching you, but also this pretty little toy you have acquired for yourself."

He hissed and stood to tower above me.

"You are weak. A disgrace to all of us. This girl has made you fall farther than you ever have before." She hadn't even flinched at his threatening posture, but she paused, and a feeling of deep and unabating hate came to her. She made me bare my teeth to the Count and hiss menacingly. "She murdered Petros. I demand that you exact justice for his death and end her. I would have done it myself when I had her at my mercy, but I thought her suffering would be too short-lived. If you do not comply with our demands, we will dispense of both of you."

"The only weak one I see here is you." His shadow stretched over me, and a low growl reverberated in the air. "She did not kill Petros, I was the one who ripped him to pieces. He dared to take what is mine. Tell your brothers and sisters to remember upon whom their existence depends, or I will end theirs. Anyone who stands against me will die, and by their deaths, they shall be made examples of to anyone who thinks they can usurp me and my power."

"Always so colorful with your threats," she continued to mock him. "But you have become soft. We have compelled this one to give you this message, knowing you will listen. We, your children, demand you rid yourself of this pet and return to us as you were before. For a century, you have shut yourself away in this crumbling castle, allowing the weakness of human frailty to cloud your true nature. You are the symbol of all we are. If you do not return to your kind, we will have to take matters into our own hands and usurp you."

"You would openly act against me?" The Count spat at her. "The centuries have made you forget to whom you speak. Leave her and be gone. She has done nothing. Your quarrel is with me."

I had never seen the Count so infuriated, but she showed no outward sign of fear. Despite the risk, she turned her back on him and made me walk a few steps away to look out the window. "We will give you time to reconsider and will come again at Michaelmas. Until then, here is a parting gift." Taking a crystal vase from an end table, she smashed it against the stone wall, cutting my hand in *the process. She turned to face the Count, aiming a shard of crystal at him. "Remember who you are, Ţepeş."*

Lifting my left arm, she stabbed the soft flesh underneath my wrist and began to drag it up to the crook of my arm. She was feeling the pain too, and grimaced at the weakness of my human body. Before she could get halfway, the Count was upon her and ripped the implement from my hand. Roughly, he had pushed me to the ground, pinning me beneath him. He grabbed my arms and pulled them over my head, snarling. "You will pay dearly for this!"

She grunted from the pain that she had inflicted upon me and made eye contact with him. "Or you will."

And with that, she had fallen away, disappearing from my mind. She no longer controlled it, and only I remained in the body she had broken.

I shuddered, tears pouring from my eyes. Covering my face, I wept like a child. I hadn't cried so hard in years, and all the meanwhile he held me, soothingly caressing my hair. I cried for so many reasons, some I can't even remember. I was afraid for myself and him, but more for him. What is to become of us now that the enemy is marching to his gates? Will he kill me? All these thoughts broke me inside.

"Isadora," the Count whispered in dulcet tones, his self-inflicted neck wound healing. "Why do you cry?"

"I cry for you, Count." I tried to wipe my soaked cheeks with the back of my hand, but it was too bloody.

"Oh, my sweetest one," he kissed my hair. "Do not feel such sorrow for me."

"But what will you do? They're demanding you…" I stopped, recalling this anonymous woman's words that he should kill me. My mind began to race that he would heed her warning and put me to death. He wouldn't, surely? Doubt seized my heart, and I trembled. I couldn't finish my own sentence.

"You believe that I would kill you to satisfy them?" The Count's jaw rolled, and his eyes flickered to me, the pain in them penetrated my soul. "I told you I would never harm you."

I believed him, but my fear of him only lessened a little. "What will you do, then?"

The ancient Prince didn't say anything at first, but gently stroked my hair. I couldn't tell if his silence was his answer, so I waited, shaking against him. I prayed so hard at that moment that he would not lose faith in me, nor in himself. Then, so quietly, he murmured. "I will protect you from them, sun of my nights."

There was something within him surfacing that I had never seen in him before. This was the part of him he hid from me — the berserker, the monster, the war lord, the Impaler. In his clutches, I was immobile, my eyes fixed upon him in fearful awe.

"You belong to me. No one, man or monster, comes between me and what I desire." There was a resoluteness etched on his face as he spoke. "They will be here by the end of September, when the nights grow longer and the cold begins. You are safe here with me, I promise you."

My throat tightened at his admission and vow. "Vlad…"

With that, the Count let me go, his shoulders slouching and brow creasing as he stood. After taking one last look at me, he then brusquely walked to the bell pull and tugged it to summon Dumitru.

I managed to sit up, my head spinning as nausea rose from the pit of my stomach. The pieces of crystal were strewn about me, and compulsively, I began to gingerly pick up the shards, placing them on an embellished decorative serving tray nearby.

The poor man, who already had so much to weigh his mind down, stood pensively against the wall. The Count stared off at a random fixed point in the room. Already, I could tell he was plotting with that brilliant tactical mind of his. His fury, coupled with a violent mix of sorrow and worry, fueled the fire of his anger. Yet on the exterior, he only looked troubled. I have not known the Count for very long, but even I can see through him when he leaves himself unguarded. In a way, I was honored that he would bare that side in my presence.

I had just finished gathering all the smallest crystal fragments from the carpet when Dumitru appeared, timidly opening the door and entering with his head down. "You called, Master?"

Instantly, the Count began to growl at him in Romanian. From the floor, I peeked over the side of the settee to watch the altercation. The Master pointed over at me a few times, while Dumitru remained quiet, his eyes downcast. It reminded me of a teacher scolding a student for being late, and I cowered at the Master's lingering anger. Then the Count said something, and Dumitru looked up wide-eyed at him, then to me. I looked away, but it was too late.

This time, Dumitru spoke, his words desperate, then he came over to where I was hiding from them. His face went white when he saw my bloodied, disheveled state. He stared for a few seconds, quite defeated, before I stood with the tray. Again, the Count spoke, his words still sharp to his servant.

"Please don't be cross with him," I spoke up to the Count. "It wasn't his fault."

"Don't defend me, *Domnișoară*." Dumitru breathed out.

"Shut your mouth. We both were used in this. It's not your fault what happened." I hissed, then turned to the Count again. "Dumitru has been through enough today, please don't add more to his suffering. Perhaps it's wrong of me to say this, but please, he feels enough remorse already."

"*Domnișoară...*" Dumitru whispered, shaking his head. "Please don't."

"Miss Kane," the Count piped up, coming closer to us. "I admire your willingness to defend Dumitru in this, but no matter whose fault it was, he did not perform his duty."

I wanted to say something more, but I could only think of things that would inflame the situation further. The last thing I wanted was for all the blame to be placed on Dumitru, nor that he felt he was the sole focus of it. Yet, all the same, not only had he failed the Count but his own vow. I could only imagine what he was feeling as he stood there in shame. "If it means anything, Mitică, I do not blame you for anything."

Dumitru remained silent, and he took the tray from me, his fingers grazing over mine as he did. A small gesture of gratitude in a stolen moment under the Count's watchful eye. "Thank you...I will be fine."

"Isadora," the Count cut the moment with a sharp knife. "Clean yourself up and get ready for bed. I will be back momentarily. Come, Dumitru."

My friend gave me one last glance before he gathered himself and left the room, the Count in tow. The door was shut behind them, and I was alone. I stood there for a while to let the sudden events sink in, and another wave of tears came to my eyes, but I swallowed them back. Turning my attention to something other than my emotions, I surveyed the poor Persian rug that had soaked in the blood I had unwillingly shed. My blood stains, this time, were more copious than the last, pooling in large circles into the fine tapestry. With a heavy heart, I pushed the furniture off the smaller area rug, rolled it up, and placed it by the door to be disposed of later. Another ruined rug, another ruined shirt, what else is to become ruined?

As the Count commanded, I mindlessly returned to my bedroom and readied myself for sleep. Once I was finished and had washed the blood from my mouth and arms, I sat on the bed, leaving the door cracked open so that the Count could enter when he returned. Cross-legged, my hands supporting my head, I tried to comprehend the scope of what I had endured and how close I had been to death.

I sat there disassociating for a long time. I'm not sure how long I was like that until a shadow was cast over the light from the doorway, and the Count entered. "How are you feeling?"

"Better," I half lied. I really was not fine at all, not even close. I had been used, forced to try to kill myself, and then forced to live again. "Thanks to you. That's what, the third time you've saved me? I'm going to have to start keeping a tally."

My attempt to make the situation lighter had no effect, and he frowned as he came to sit on the edge of the bed. The Count saw through my mask easily, even in the dark. "You may find issue with my methods, Isadora, but I will not do it again if it means saving your life."

I said nothing in response to that at first, although I wanted to lecture him of the natural order of things. If it was my time to die, it was my time. I cannot *not* keep evading the Angel of Death as he can. Biting my tongue, I sighed. "You know I'm not ungrateful that you saved me yet again. It was very kind of you to help me."

"And I will continue to do so." The Count declared.

His passionate gesture made me crack a sad smile, and I took his hand. "Thank you, Count, for everything."

In return, he gripped my hand back, and a reflective red flashed in his eyes. "I will not allow you to fall prey to them, not when we both have come so far together in such a short time."

My soul warmed at hearing him say that, more than I think he knows. It brought me such comfort to hear that vow from his own lips. "I admire your strength and confidence, beloved. It gives me strength, too."

The Count kissed me, our noses brushing each other as he whispered secretly. "Have faith in me always."

"Always," I confirmed, initiating a second kiss.

Purring, I felt his reluctance to let me go, but the Count withdrew. "If I stay longer, Dumitru will become suspicious."

"I understand...goodnight, Count."

"Goodnight," he went to the door, but stopped and added. "Also, do not fear being subject to the one who compelled you. Their control of you was finite."

He promptly closed the door behind him before I could reply.

Alone in the darkness, I felt for my new rosary that I had hidden in the sheets and clenched it in my fist. Again, too many things had happened today, and from them came too many unknown questions. It was all too much to think of, but with the Count's robust blood within me, I analyzed the day down to the smallest detail. I saw my own actions from a different viewpoint, and it dawned on me how the entire scene at the café had been one big setup. From the appearance of my American friend, the spilling of the beer, Dumitru's predictable reaction, and my escape to the bathroom...all of it had been calculated down to the second. I could not recall those missing minutes in the restroom, no matter how hard I tried, and frustrated with it, I gave up. Whoever it was, they had taken great precautions to keep their identity hidden from me. My only clue is her long silver hair. Eventually, my body and mind gave way, and I slipped into unconsciousness.

Chapter Nineteen

THE NATURE
OF THE BEAST

30 July

Afternoon…

T he weather, compared to yesterday, has grown significantly
hotter. When I awoke from my hazy lethargy, I was sweating,
the sheets were all awry and half off the bed. I think I had
finally fallen asleep past midnight, and when I came to, it was almost
11 am. Thoroughly tangled in the sheets, I had to struggle to break
free and actually fell from the bed, landing with a hard thud onto the
floor. Already I had had enough of this day and schlepped to the
bathroom to wash up. When I saw myself in the mirror, however, I
was taken aback by my unkempt and worn appearance. So, I bathed
and dressed, and I made my way down to the kitchen since Dumitru,
due to my insistence, no longer brings my meals to me. However, I
didn't find him there, which was odd because it was lunchtime.

After I ate a quick sandwich, I went around to the other areas I was sure to find him, but he wasn't there either. By this time, I was getting worried and even stopped by his room, but again, he was nowhere to be found. I wondered if he had gone out for something. I knew the Count wasn't around either, and it suddenly occurred to me that I was alone.

A part of me was beginning to panic when I heard the main door creak open, and I rushed to it. To my relief, it was Mitică, sweating like a pig, and carrying a shovel. He was awfully dirty, with large patches of dirt ground into his clothes. He smelled awful, too, his scent thick with body odor and moist earth. My nose crinkled as I approached. "Mitică, you look terrible."

Dumitru looked up at me and scowled, dusting pieces of soil from his hair. "Thanks."

I giggled at his dirty, pouting face. "What were you doing out there?"

"The Master instructed me to begin fixing the wall." He explained, wiping his dewy brow. "The Gypsies will be here tomorrow to start the heavier work."

I wasn't surprised that the Count was already starting his preparations for enhancing the castle's old fortifications, but his haste in doing so made me anxious. Is he really planning for the worst? "Why does he want to fix the wall? What will that do to stop those...creatures?"

Dumitru set his tools aside and replied. "Appearances."

My brow knitted. "Just so it looks good when they arrive?"

He agreed with a dismissive hum. "I believe the word he used was 'cosmetic'."

A part of me wonders if there is something more to this 'restoration', but I know I couldn't and can't ask Mitică about it. I bit my tongue and changed the subject. "Would you like something to eat?"

"If you wouldn't mind it." He smiled gently at my offer. "I'll wash up."

Nodding, I watched him head towards the servants' quarters, then I went and made his meal. My thoughts were lost in my head about our predicament as I waited for Dumitru to arrive.

When he did, he was all clean again and smelled much better. Sitting down at the servant's table without saying anything to me, he began to eat. I assumed he was already tired from doing so much work outside in this heat, but then suddenly he spoke. "Can I ask you about last night?"

"Of course."

"The Master told me the details, but," Mitică stopped, taking my hand. "Are you alright, really?"

"I'm well enough," I patted his hand, shrugging off his seriousness. "And you? Please tell me all is well between you and the Count? Did he punish you harshly?"

Dumitru was quiet for a moment since I had dodged his question, and his lips pursed. "Don't worry about me, Isadora. You should worry more about yourself. You're the only one of us who can be forced to do their will."

Frowning, I let go of his hand to cross my arms again. The way he phrased it made me feel as if I were the weakest link of this trio, which honestly, I am. All the same, he didn't need to make it so obvious that my presence here is inconsequential. "Even so, you're just as vulnerable as I am."

"Yes and no…" His voice faded out, taking his hand away in return. "When did it happen, anyway?"

Flashes of the incident came to my mind, but they were still muddied by whatever spell the creature who had compelled me used. Sometimes I think I can see her figure standing before me. There are times when I can feel her phantom fingers around my neck, squeezing just enough to make me gasp. "When I was cleaning up in the bathroom. She must have been waiting for me."

"*She?*" Dumitru emphasized, a bit surprised.

I nodded. "I still can't see her face, but she had silver hair and spoke English well."

"The Master would know who she is," he concluded excitedly. "You should tell him. He has been very disturbed by this whole thing. All night he stayed in his study searching through old documents and other things."

The news tugged at my heart.

"He also told me to tell you to rest for the day." Dumitru stood to bring his dishes to the sink. "I am to lock you in your room if you disobey."

I think he was half-joking, but I still tensed. I really hadn't planned much for the day other than the normal chores, but all the same. I remembered the last time the Count had told me to rest on a Sunday. That day, I needed to rest more than I knew, but now was a time for action. Nevertheless, I could not disobey the Count's order when he was in such a state. I don't want to give him more problems than he already has.

I did as the Master wished and returned to my rooms.

Later...

I have quite a few hours before the Count and I usually meet, that is, if he will see me today, so I decided to finish up the letters that I have begun to my family. With some of them, I had no idea how to begin, but in light of recent events, I have suddenly found the wisdom as to how to end them. My heart physically hurt as I wrote of my love for each one of them, that I think of them often, and that I wish I could meet our newest little member. I also asked them to pray for me, although I didn't specify why. The whole thing reduced me to tears as I wrote my possible final goodbye to my loved ones. Perhaps by the time they get this, I may already be dead, so I had to get out all the things that I had left unsaid before I departed for Romania.

Tears forced me to stop frequently so that I didn't accidentally get them on the paper, and thereby betraying my true turmoil through the small droplets and blotted ink. But, somehow, I managed to write all that I think needed to be said before sealing the letters with a kiss. After, I sat there for a long while thinking of their faces and voices, all the happy times and the sad ones too. It made me want to cry all the more. But I know that if I can find the will in me to cry about this, I can find the will in me to do something about it.

Evening...

Sunset came and went with no word from the Count. Usually, he would come and seek me out soon after the wolves would howl, but tonight there were no direct summons to see him. I sat in my sitting room, wondering if I should go seek him out instead, but I couldn't go walking into his rooms unannounced and expect him to be pleased to see me. Besides, I didn't want to disturb him if he was deep in thought with strategy and war on his mind.

As the minutes ticked past 9 pm, I decided it was better for both of us if I didn't go to search for him, so I made myself ready for bed. With the night being so muggy, I chose to wear my new nightgown that I had bought in Câmpulung, which is thin and airy. It is the replacement for the one I ruined that night I reopened my neck wound.

I was just about finished with my nightly rosary when there was a knock at the door, startling me. Dumitru's voice was muffled from the other side, saying I had been summoned by the Master. My heart leapt in my chest that he hadn't forgotten about me, so grabbing my pile of letters, I put my summer robe over me and opened the door. At the sight of me, Mitică looked away, his cheeks turning pink as a mortified expression settled on his face.

"Mitică, what's wrong?"

He cleared his throat. "Aren't you going to get dressed first?"

I looked down at my attire, then back to him. "Do you think he would mind?"

"N-No, it's j-just," Dumitru stuttered, his face growing red. "It's...it's..."

Blinking, I stood there waiting for him to make a coherent sentence. "It's what? You said you liked it when you saw it in the store."

His face was getting so red that smoke was about to come from his ears. He turned away. "N-Never mind, come on."

Shrugging, I followed him down the steps to the Count's floor and into the Master's reception room. In Romanian, Mitică announced me through the door to his Master's office, and there was a reply from within. Opening the door for me, Dumitru stared intently as I passed by, his atypical behavior unsettled me. I shook off his intense gaze and entered the Count's study, which was much smaller than I would have imagined it to be. Perhaps small wasn't the correct word, but more...cozy. Alit by a combination of gas lamps and candles, the semi-circular room was filled with a deep yellow-orange glow. The Master's desk is situated in the center of the room with a large bay window behind him, surrounded by bookcases, full to the brim with books of all ages and subjects. Old oil paintings of past family members were displayed proudly on the walls, but there were also ones of landscapes.

Among these treasured things, the Count sat at his desk, overrun with papers and open books. As I set foot within his private space, he looked up at me, and immediately, I could see the tiredness etched on his face. Still, he smiled, a spark of joy coming alive in him, melting me inside. The door closed behind me, and I bowed my head to the Master. "Good evening, Count."

"Good evening," he greeted in return. "Please forgive the later hour, I lost track of time."

"No worries, I know you're busy," I said as I handed him the letters. "I finally got around to finishing these for my family. If it wouldn't be too much trouble —"

"None at all. I will make sure Dumitru goes out tomorrow to send them." The Count took them from me and set them in a drawer. "I will not be a moment longer, so please, sit."

I thanked him, then sat in a chair on the opposite side of the room, waiting for him to finish whatever he was working on. From a distance, I watched him scratch things vigorously on a piece of paper with a fountain pen, flip through an old book, and scratch some more. Whatever action he did, he did it so intensely that he suddenly said. "Did you get that dressing gown in Câmpulung?"

"Yes," I answered, quite surprised he had noticed my new clothes, but then became self-conscious. "Should I not have worn it?"

The Count grinned, although he didn't look up at me. "Only you would come before me dressed in such and show no fear."

My brow furrowed. "What do you mean?"

"My dear," he rested on his elbows to gaze back at me, his eyes drifting up and down my figure. "Do you recall what I told you? When you entice a man enough, he will act on that temptation."

"You find this tempting?" I laughed at his absurdity. "Don't be ridiculous. It's far from lingerie."

He grinned again, shaking his head. "And only you would laugh at that."

"Forgive me, Count," I tried to settle my laughter. "I just don't see you ever falling for whatever temptation crosses your path. You're better than that."

"Is that so?" Closing the book and setting his papers aside, he came around to the front of his desk and leaned against it. "Come here, sweet one."

The Count's smooth voice made me swallow hard, but I stood and went to stand before him. I kept my distance, not truly believing in my words that he couldn't be tempted.

As I did, he kept his eyes trained on me, watching the folds of the white fabric sway as I approached. "In my day, if a woman willingly presented herself to a man in her nightclothes, it sent a message."

I felt the blood drain from my face. "I am aware of that, but you have seen me dressed like this. It never sent a message before."

"Is that so?" His fingers went to the cord holding my robe and untied it. The action made me step back, but with both hands on the cord, he drew me to him instead. The outer garment slipped from my shoulders to reveal the gown beneath, and he purred. A fire broke out under my skin, and all of me wanted him to go further, then he pulled away. "Forgive me, my dearest one, I crave your company more than I had anticipated."

"Why do you hold yourself back?" I asked in a daze.

"If I did not, I would do things both of us would later regret. Come," he replaced the robe on my shoulders. "Let us sit in the other room."

"How do you know what I would regret?"

"Trust me, young one," he took my hand and kissed it. "Come now, we must speak. Dumitru says you have remembered more of the one who compelled you."

Clearing my throat, I allowed him to lead me to his reception room, where we both sat on the couch. The Count gathered me in his arms so that I rested against him, and he asked me to tell of my recollections. I told him all I knew or thought I knew, and he listened intently, not saying anything for all the while. When I had finished telling of the silver-haired woman, he scoffed and shook his head. "Ah, Imogen, that witch."

I was taken aback by him. "You *know* her?"

"*Of* her, unfortunately," he clenched his jaw, and a vein began to throb in his forehead. "She is originally from Ireland, I believe. I am aware that she is one of the main instigators who believe that I have gone too soft in my old age. The way we creatures operate is dependent on who is alpha, so any sign of perceived weakness is a chance to take power over the others."

"So she wants to take your place?"

The Count thought for a moment. "It appears to be so. She is particularly dangerous, a true daughter of Satan, a prodigy of our kind. I have heard she summoned the Evil One himself, and he gave her his brand. Her gray hair is the result of that."

My blood all but froze in me, and I had to stand up and move away. With my back turned to him, I made the Sign of the Cross with a shaking hand. Nausea rolled in my stomach, and I put the same hand over my mouth. The mere idea that the woman who had held me at her mercy is so in league with the Devil made my skin crawl. To know those same hands that worship the Prince of Lies had held me against my will and used me like a cat's paw was unnerving. My disgust turned to anger, and I clenched my jaw.

"Isadora…" The Count touched my shoulder, making me flinch back to reality. At the sight of me, he asked. "What is it?"

I removed my hand to rest it around my collar. "Have you ever seen Satan?"

The Count's silence was evidence enough, but he still took my face in his hands. "Yes, I have seen him. I am his earthly son."

Of course, the son would have seen his father, the one who held his soul in the tightest grip. Tears welled in my eyes, tears of fear but also pity for whom I love and who had fallen so far. At that moment, I think it was only my love for him that kept me from being repulsed by his touch.

"I know you are frightened," he stroked my cheeks with his thumbs to wipe away the tears. "But never forget this, my dear: I will never let him take hold of you. Besides, he has no power over one so pure-hearted, so devoted, so compassionate as yourself. That is how you hold power over me, why I am so drawn to you, most dear of my heart."

"And you are so sure of this?" I shook my head, withdrawing from his hold. "We're not here to speak about me."

The Prince let me slip from his fingers, a pain entering his heart that resonated in his voice. "You have faith in me and your God, but no faith in yourself."

He was right, but I shook my head. "Never mind about me, I must ask you something that's been weighing heavily on my mind."

He frowned but nodded once. "What is it?"

"I have some understanding of what your kind actually are, but," I explained and then sighed, unable to try and sugar-coat my intent. "I must know what your nature is."

The Count's eyes narrowed. "Our nature?"

"What makes you, you?" I clarified, subconsciously taking a few steps away. "I would not ask if I didn't need to know because I'm sure it's a sensitive topic for you. But if I am to be here when they come, I must understand what you are."

"Evil." The Count answered so plainly, and almost too quickly.

I was startled by his bluntness, and it perturbed me. "Surely that can't just be it?"

"No? I have told you myself I am a son of the Devil, I am the damned father of my cursed children, all of me is evil. My existence is a result of apostasy from God, and if God is goodness, then the Devil is wickedness. Since I am of the Devil, I am sin made into flesh." He stated, making a circular motion with his hand as he spoke, indicating a complete vicious cycle that he is a part of: he began with Satan and ended with Satan.

It hurt me deeply inside to hear him say those things about himself. They were very true and absolute facts of his nature that he lived every day, but a part of me could not see him as the epitome of evil that he claims to be. "If you're so evil, how is it that you are so good? You seek redemption from your situation. There must be good within you to want that."

"It was a long road to get to this point, sweet one." He stopped, taking my hands cautiously so as not to startle me. "In the moments when Wilhelmina's husband and their friend had attempted to destroy me, I truly thought it was the end. Their weapons were ineffective, but they did succeed in destroying a part of me. Still, I realized then that I was not ready to achieve the peace I secretly yearned for. But, I had not completely given myself to either God nor Lucifer, and so again I was brought back to this earthly Purgatory as punishment for my indecision. I saw that light, I had been so close, and yet so very far. I don't know how it happened or why. My body had not changed, but something within me did. It was only then that I began to change this nature to which I am bound."

I looked down at our hands. His encounter with Death was only the first step on his long road that led him to this point. Had he been so terrible before then? I could only assume so. "Is this place so hellish to you?"

The Master inched closer to me, a sad smile forming on his mouth as he quoted what I recognized as *Doctor Faustus.* "'Thinkest thou that I, who saw the face of God and tasted the eternal joys of Heaven, am not tormented with ten thousand hells in being deprived of everlasting bliss?'"

My heart sank further. "To just touch Heaven, and then be denied it, what torture it must be for you."

"Agony," the Count breathed the word out. "If Heaven is Him, and Hell the absence of Him, then this earthly plane is a hell to me. The farther I am from the light, the deeper I am in the darkness. As long as I am in this body, I am an incarnation of all things evil that are contrary to all things good. I still try to remember my humanity and try to be good, although it is not the nature of this body to do so."

Never before had he been so frank with me about himself. He would always evade me, keep me in the dark, but now he was being so truthful and bold. Maybe he thought that, after all this time, and all the things that I had been through, I was ready to hear all that he is and was. Everything made sense then, why he does the things he does, and how far he has come in his journey. It has taken centuries for him to come to terms with himself and the things that he cannot resist. Another tear slipped from my eye. "I'm so proud that you have been trying so hard for so long, despite it being against everything that you are."

"I have still far to go," the Count kissed my forehead. "My sins are many, nearly uncountable in the eyes of man, yet He knows each one of them, and for them, I must atone...someday, somehow."

"I have no doubt you will be shown the way in spite of them," I reassured not just him, but myself of that. There is no way He would turn away from evil who wants to be good. "You have become so good that I cannot see you as anything but good."

"I have hidden much from you," he admitted in a grave tone, resting his forehead against mine. Our eyes met, his glowing a radiant amber. "I am not as good as you believe me to be."

"And I am not so pure as you think I am," I smiled, and softly touched his lips with my own. Lowering my voice, I whispered. "We are both sinners, Vlad, don't forget that."

"Within my kind is manifest all sin." The old immortal's face fell, his eyes drifting from mine. "We are prideful, greedy, wrathful, gluttonous, and envious. Most of all, we are lustful. What we cannot have, we seek to no avail, and we are obsessively possessive of the things we do have. This is why I cannot help but call you mine, for you can be no other's. If someone tried to take you from me, I would show them no mercy. Such is the extent of the sins we carry."

The sadness of his words struck me hard. The Count would protect me not because he is selfless, but because he is selfish. All he does is for his own satisfaction, not for the love or care of others. At least, that's what his nature tells him. I didn't know how to respond to something so profound as that, something that cuts him so deeply.

He continued to speak, explaining. "And from all of this, we cannot love others, not even ourselves. Love is a sacred thing; it is something so pure we cannot attain it."

Slowly, I lifted my head from him, my heart breaking. I always wondered why he never told me in kind that he loves me, although I had never expected it of him. I had figured because of his past trauma, to love another as he had loved Ioana would be nearly impossible. Now I can see how far deeper that fact is. It's just like how he cannot be married again because marriage is sacred, he cannot love because love is sacred. What a torturous existence to be undead and unable to love. "What do you feel for Ioana? For your children you had with her and your other wife?"

His jaw tensed, and his brow became furrowed as he struggled to think of an answer. Shutting his eyes tightly, he grimaced as a low hiss escaped through his teeth. "I love them, I want to say, but in truth, the feeling does not exist. All that is in my heart are painful memories of the love I had while I was still alive. All I can say is that there is a deep fondness for them that will never die."

"I am so sorry to hear that…"

He was quiet for a moment before taking my chin so I would look directly at him. "Do you not wish to know how I feel about you?"

Thinking for a moment and considering all he had told me, I shook my head. "If you cannot love me in return, I understand, just as long as you know that you are loved."

A flicker of red showed in his eyes. "It does matter to you. How long do you think you can last with a monster who cannot love you back? It is a waste of time. You give your whole self to me un-hindered, and I can only give you barely a fraction of that much."

"I don't think it's a waste of time." He had hit the mark, but I said it quietly. "Even if you hate me, I will still love you. Don't ask me to explain why."

"Hate," he spat the word. "How could I hate you after all you give me and ask nothing in return? Without you, I am not a man, I am a monster."

The weight of his words bore down on my shoulders, so I answered. "Just be comforted to know that I will always be here to pick you up when you fall, that I will always follow you in all your wanderings, be your shoulder to lean upon, and be your light in —"

I had not finished when he kissed me violently, and picked me up to lay me out on the settee. Suddenly, I was on my back, his knees parting my legs as he placed himself between them. The sensation was such a shock that I gasped, reflexively trying to close them and push him away. But, of course, he had planted himself there as he desperately kissed me, pushing me into the settee until he hovered over me.

I understood now what he was feeling for me: not love, but lust and greed to possess me as his own. His hands found mine and fastened me down to the cushion, his mouth trying to show me the real emotions he was feeling. I really believe he wanted to show me love so badly, but could only give me frenzied passion. His lips covered every centimeter of my skin on my neck and chest, but he dared not go past my low collar. Between my thighs, his hips remained stationary. I was petrified, not daring to breathe as my head swam at his intimate closeness. His entire being was rigid and then became very, very still.

He had stopped himself, somehow, and a threatening low growl reverberated in the air. He lay to rest on my sternum, between my breasts. The Count strained to speak. "You say I am above temptation, but I am its slave. I want nothing more than to give in. Forgive me."

"There is nothing to forgive." I tried to move my legs, but I was unquestionably immobile beneath him. My breath shuddered out of my lungs when I realized I was unconsciously suffocating myself.

He raised himself a bit to look at me with those burning eyes. "Do you know what it feels like to want something so badly that you cannot have it?"

Honestly, I couldn't, especially at that moment, so I shook my head.

"I cannot have you because I do not love you." The Count hissed between his teeth, frustratingly. "If I did take you, there would be no meaning in it. It would only be taking everything I care about you and throwing it all away for a few minutes of passion. I have too much affection for you to defile you. But God, oh God, how I want to show you the feelings I do have that are more real than anything I know."

I stared at him in awe as his face welled in sudden physical pain that he had pleaded to the Almighty. He grunted, his grip faltering as he shook. The son of the Prince of Darkness, against his very nature that held him bound, had beseeched unto God. My chest surged for the man who was willing to disobey his own instinct, oppose his own kind, just to show and feel love.

Taking my hands from his, I cupped his face as wisps of the demon revealed itself. "I'll make a deal with you. You learn to love again, truly and unconditionally, and I will give you all you desire. You won't be defiling me then, but making us one whole. Do you think you can defy your own nature to do that, not for me, but for yourself?"

The red fire in him burned as he kissed me again. "If I can do that, there would be no nature left to defy."

"Then swear it to me in God's name." I dared to declare. "Make an oath, a vow, to never relent until you overcome all that stands in your way…until you defeat that darkness that lives within you."

The Master's expression hardened as another wracking pain beset him, and he gritted his fangs. The thing within him was holding him back, fighting with him in some internal battle. Another growl, this one setting my hair on end, rumbled between us, yet he breathed out. "I swear in God's name."

Wrapping my arms around his neck, I pressed him to me. His body fell completely limp onto mine, hips included, as he writhed in short bursts of agonizing quakes and quivers. I whispered soft things into his ear to comfort his tortured soul. It was a bit hard to breathe with a large part of his weight on me, but I did not move. Running my fingers through his hair, I held him until his breathing had slowed and he turned his face to rest directly into my neck, his favorite place.

"Stay with me tonight," I whispered into his ear. "Please, Vlad."

There was a long pregnant pause as he debated it back and forth. His lips grazed the skin of my neck as he cooed. "I will stay, sweetest one."

Embracing him tighter one last time, I let him go. The Count rose from me and left my thighs, pulling my gown back down over my knees as he did, his eyes avoiding me. He looked defeated, almost broken, as he sat slouched on the edge of the settee. I sat up too and took his hand. We both stood and I led him from his rooms, and back up the stairs to my floor. We entered my bedroom and lay down together for the first time in quite a while.

I heard the clock chime midnight as we unwound in the other's embrace. We didn't speak a word to each other, and with his arms around me, my head resting on his chest, I cuddled into his side. I should have been able to hear his heart beating, but there was only silence.

VAULT OF GRACE

Chapter Twenty

3 August

Afternoon, 4 pm…

All week, the heat has been unbearable. It feels like someone has dumped an immovable mass of hot air on our heads and refuses to give us any reprieve. The sun has been so intense that I can hardly bear to go outside. The humidity has been the worst part of it, making everything sticky. In my life, I don't think I have taken so many cool baths in a day just to find some relief. Of course, there is no true air conditioning, so one must go into the deepest bowels of the castle to find cool. Unfortunately, most of those areas are closed off…not to mention creepy.

However, I don't have it nearly as bad as those poor boys working on the wall. They have been working four days straight on it, and it has been slow. Structural problems have arisen, along with a whole host of other issues. Dumitru has been quite upset by the slow progress, but honestly, what does he expect from a wall that's over half a millennium old? This whole area is subject to earthquakes anyway.

All the same, I try to do my part to relieve their suffering. I frequently go out with trays of water and small snacks for them, always with a smile on my face. From my perspective, it's the least I can do for them. There are five new Romani in the company, but I am unsure of their names. They all address me as *Doamna* with eyes lowered, and when I draw near, they always take off their hats. It makes me uncomfortable, but I still smile and nod and speak to them in my broken Romanian. They still don't like talking to me all the same.

I've been getting an odd vibe from Mitică when I try to converse with our worker friends. Each time I come out to them, he watches me like a hawk, openly stopping all he's doing just to follow my movements from one man to another. It's off-putting, but this strange behavior all began the evening of the 30th when he had that unusual reaction to my nightgown. He looks at me angrily when he doesn't think I'm looking, but when we're alone, he acts normal. If this goes on any longer, I'll have to confront him about it. I'm very close to having enough of this.

When I am not tending to the boys outside, I mostly remain inside and clean or do lesson work. With our 'guests' coming soon, I almost feel I have a duty to show off the castle in its medieval splendor. For long hours, I have attended to the common areas to which I have access, removing centuries of neglect and restoring them. The place almost looks completely different from when I first arrived here, which has now been four months. The Count seems to be quite impressed by my efforts, despite being so against them in the beginning.

Speaking of the Master, since our discussion from my last entry, we have carried on as normal…somehow. I felt a bit awkward when I awoke that next morning to find he had gone, only leaving a note that he regretted he had to go, but that he would see me at our lecture. I doubted he had someplace pressing that he needed to be. I wondered if he was avoiding me due to the way he acted that previous night when he had, essentially, forced himself on me.

For the rest of the day, I couldn't stop thinking about everything he had said and done that night. Most of all, that he did not truly love me at all, but does feel 'something'…be that fondness or affection. Now that I am of a clear mind and away from him, that knowledge makes me sad. Even though I never expected him to love me in the first place, knowing he does not and cannot, it hurts. At the same time, when I would think of the compromising position in which he had placed me, my core flutters at the thought. To have him, the man I love, so *close*…it felt like a secret dream come true. Through our clothes, I had felt him, and I know he felt me too. Never before had I been placed in that position with the opposite sex, but in that moment when he was inches away…when he could have crossed that line, I felt afraid. Not just the fear of the unknown, but fear of him.

Perhaps I am not ready, perhaps I am too chicken…I don't know. But I promised him that I would consent to it if he does learn to love me. If or when that time comes, sooner or later, I will have to man up to it. An ironic phrasing, I know, but I fear it nonetheless. I will have to get my ducks in a row before that time, that is, if I live to see him get to that point.

Oh God, love sure does make you say strange things, doesn't it?

6 August
The Transfiguration
Afternoon…

For the first day in a week, the castle has been quiet. The 'Gypsies' weren't working because it is Sunday, so Dumitru and I were the only ones here. He has become increasingly worn down by the heavy work, and I still worry for his old head injury. Today, he was tense and complaining about being sore, so I offered to rub his shoulders. He was very reluctant at first, but allowed me to get close to him. The poor boy has more knots in him than a tree, and I tried my best to work them, but he only became more tense as I went along.

When I was just about to move from his shoulders to his mid-back, Dumitru jumped up and shouted angrily that he had had enough. His face was so red that I was sure smoke was about to come from his ears again. Why did he get so angry over it? I was only trying to help. It wasn't like he was in pain. Actually, he was enjoying.

Regardless, I backed off, but was wounded that he would viciously snap at me. I haven't spoken to him since early this afternoon when it happened, and just feel sad about the whole thing.

Later...

I sat in my sitting room for the remainder of the evening hours before night finally came. Partially due to the heat and my issue with Dumitru, I sulked, only listening to the clock tick the hours by. I tried to think of what could be causing my friend's strange outbursts and coldness towards me, but was coming up short. We had made up for our insults and actions we said to each other last Saturday, but suddenly, the next there was another problem.

Reanalyzing my encounter with him on that Sunday evening, when he had been unable to speak a complete sentence, I wondered what could have caused him to react the way he did. This infamous gown I wore is not revealing, just a loose A-line nightgown with a wide neckline. Nothing special, nothing provocative. But his reaction would suggest he had been inflamed by my appearance. Perhaps he was angry that I would go before the Count in my nightclothes? He is unaware of the affair between the Master and me. The thought occurred to me that he may have seen me lead the Count into my room very late that night, but surely the Count would have sensed his presence and acted accordingly. Wouldn't he have? If that is it, then Mitică must see me as some loose woman who lied to him all this time about my relationship with his Master. It's just a theory, but what am I to do now?

...

By the time the Count met up with me in my sitting room, I was feeling better, although still quite melancholy. As expected, the Count noticed as soon as he saw my face when he walked in and asked what was troubling me.

I didn't want to bring up the whole incident, knowing the possible consequences for Dumitru, so I made up a half lie. "I think I've had enough of this heat, that's all, and it's been an exhausting day."

The Count raised his eyebrow, seeing right through me. I half expected him to prod me further on the subject, but he only smiled. "I know something that will cheer you up."

My interest piqued with worry, and frankly, with suspicion.

From his pocket, he pulled out a small, ornately carved box and handed it to me. "For you, my sweet one."

I blinked at the gesture, my eyes flickering from him to the box and back. I froze, unsure whether I should take it from him. He has never given me an actual gift before, and I couldn't think of any occasion for which he would present me with one.

"Are you displeased?" He asked rather worriedly.

"Oh," I breathed out with a pause. "No, I'm just…what's the occasion?"

"Open it." He placed the fine box in my hands.

The thing looked to be hundreds of years old, and I feared it would disintegrate. Swallowing, I unlatched the tiny lock and opened it. Within, padded safely in purple velvet, was a silver crucifix; the immaculate filigree was unrivaled in its craftsmanship. I gasped and gawked at the piece.

"It belonged to my mother." The Count explained solemnly. "She would have approved of you and wanted you to have it."

"I can't accept this, it's a family heirloom."

"That is precisely why I want you to have it." With the back of his hand, he grazed his knuckles over my cheek. "It sends a message."

The Count's words echoed in my head as I looked back down at the beautiful piece. He thinks of me like family, and so wants me to have his *mother's* crucifix? As much as I wanted to say that I couldn't take anything so precious from him, a gift or otherwise, it would be a huge insult to him. Gingerly, I traced my fingers over the delicate silver. "I…"

"There is another reason for you to have it." He added somberly. "Silver burns us, and the crucifix repels us. It will come of great use to you in the coming months. It will protect you far more than that gold cross you had ever could. So, I must insist you take it and wear it always."

Gazing back up at him, I closed the box. "Surely you can't part with this."

The Count shrugged. "What am I to do with it? I cannot wear it. It has only gathered dust all these centuries. She would have wanted it to go to someone who would enjoy it, and yours was…tainted."

I frowned, and setting the box aside, I embraced him tightly. My heart pounded so hard against my ribs as I kissed him over and over again. The gesture he had displayed, the kindness and thought behind it, made me feel warm all over. "I am honored, Count. I will treasure it always."

The Count purred as his fingers traced down my spine. Smiling, he jested. "If I am to have this reaction each time I give you a gift, I should have started months ago."

"*Vlad…*" I scolded him lightly that he would think such a thing, but I still blushed.

He chuckled. "Come now, put it on. I would put it on for you, but…"

The Master didn't need to finish the sentence, and I nodded. Turning from him, I removed the precious crucifix from its resting place and secured it around my neck. I wasn't sure if I should show him, knowing the sight would cause him pain, so I kept my back to him. "It's perfect, Count. Thank you so much."

From behind, he moved my hair away from my neck and kissed me under my ear. The sensation made me quiver, and he wrapped his arms around my waist, securing them in front of me. "It is the Transfiguration in your religious calendar, is it not? Another appropriate reason to give it to you on this day."

I was surprised that he remembered that and hid my surprise. "Why, yes, it is."

"I have another surprise for you," he murmured in my ear after more kisses. "This one, I think, you will like even more."

All of these surprises all of a sudden? Why? I was becoming very suspicious of his gushy behavior, and my brow furrowed. Placing my hands over his, I leaned into him with a purr of my own. "You are too kind to me, Count."

He tittered and whispered jokingly. "My dear, do not ruin my reputation."

At that, he let go of me with all but one hand and led me from my rooms. Down the stairs we went, his hand still holding mine, to the ground floor. We were all alone in the grand entrance, the fires from the candlelight danced on the walls, casting strange shadows. I had never been so disturbed by the main hall before, and it was so dark save for the dim light. For some reason, I felt as though things were watching me from the places I could not see, and I huddled closer to the Master. In the stillness, we were the only two beings that moved side by side. Off to one side of the space, we stood before a grand door that had always remained locked. At the Count's presence, it opened, the old hinges groaning from his command, and we entered the black beyond the threshold.

Instantly, the room we entered came alight, and the door closed behind us. It was another hall, shorter, but heavily gilded with ancient stonework, paintings, and statues. My breath shuddered at its medieval beauty, and my heart burst with wonder at the sight. I thought the room was the surprise, but we kept walking, the Count's face unchanging. A glint of gold caught my eye from the floor before us, and I strained in the faint light to see. I was suddenly aware that beneath our feet were intricate mosaics of finely cut colored tile of all different hues and designs. As we approached the section that glittered and walked over it, I saw to my amazement that the motif was in the shape of a large cross. Beneath the centuries of grime and dirt, I could see the faces of the apostles, haloed in gold, a book with a piece of Scripture on it, and at the center, the image of Christ himself.

I stopped dead in my tracks and stared down at the Messiah, his halo portrayed in gold, white, and red. Mesmerized by the beauty of the piece, I wanted to get on my knees and wipe the dust away to have a better look, but the Count held me firm.

When I gazed back up at him, his face was turned away from me, away from the image. "Come."

He pulled me along, and I stumbled on to follow him.

At the end of the hall, a large window of plain and colored glass stood ominously against the blackness of the night sky behind it. I wanted to stand and admire the twin statues of two saints clad in armor, but he tugged me along as another door opened before us. Again, as on cue, the candles came to life. I peered over the threshold, into the musty-smelling room, my eyes widening in true awe.

The Count remained just outside the door as I went, almost drawn into the room. It was a chapel, small but well decorated in the

Eastern Orthodox style, with traces of the Roman Church. Glittering with faded golden halos of the saints in their spectacular, vibrant robes, the space was peppered with rich hues. In some places, the paint was peeling or had been eroded by moisture and time, but a large portion remained intact. The *templon*, which separates the altar from the nave, seemed to have suffered the most damage over the years, with the icons within being terribly worn away as if someone had tried to sand the paint. Past that, within the holy sanctum, a stone cross was erected just in front of the altar, wonderfully carved in ornate designs that dazzled my eyes. On the domed ceiling stared down the faint image of Jesus, Christ Pantocrator, supported by cherubim and flanked by seraphim.

"Are you pleased?" The Master's voice woke me from my stupor.

I looked back at him, my mouth still agape. "Why did you never tell me of this place?"

He pursed his lips as he took a step into the sanctum.

"Wait —" I had expected him to burst into flames, but he stood there with his hands behind his back, his eyebrow raised. Nothing had happened to him at all. "You didn't —"

"This place is no longer holy," the Count shook his head with a deep frown as he approached me. "Therefore, I can come and go as I please."

"Oh…" I felt stupid. Obviously, in his own house, especially as he is, there would be no place he could not come and go. "Why doesn't the cross bother you?"

His eyes went to it and then back to me, unaffected. "As I said, there is no longer any holiness here. It is only two intersecting pieces of stone to me, nothing more."

"Oh…" I repeated.

"Do you like it?" He asked as he went around me to examine the chapel for himself. "I figured you would like a proper place to pray after being without for so long."

"You would allow me to use this space," Standing straight, I eyed him curiously. To me, it made no sense that he would suddenly give me free rein over *this* part of the castle. "For *religious* purposes?"

"I do not see what else you could use it for." He turned his attention to the paintings above our heads. "Many, many years ago, this was one of my favorite places to come, mostly because of the paintings. But this room now holds many painful memories."

"Painful?" I queried.

"Would you care to know?" He hummed, and I said I would.

He gazed around the room, and I could see in his eyes the reflection of the past within them. It was an agonizing expression, and the Count had to swallow hard before daring to begin. "In my life, there were many 'events' that made me question my faith, be it either things I had done or things done to me. There were many nights I could not sleep and came here to seek those hidden answers to the reasons why they happened. Why did my Father forsake my younger brother and me to the Turks? Why did that once-beloved younger brother betray his country and people? Why had my Father and older brother been so brutally taken from me? Why was my wife of nearly two decades taken from me by her own hand? All these, and many more, I asked God for the answers to…yet no answer was ever provided. I was a faithful man, at least I told myself that, but I am the seed sown among thorns, and was soon choked out by them."

The Count paused to rake his hand through his wavy hair and compose himself. Again, he was leaving himself unguarded and vulnerable in front of me, but I could only stand there and listen to the lament in his voice. Patiently, I waited for him to continue.

"Have you ever wondered how I became as I am?"

Although his tone was soft, the abruptness of the question left me a bit speechless. Of course I have, but how could I ever bring myself to ask him openly about it? Despite our relationship, the personal nature surrounding the incident is taboo, at least to me. Sucking in a breath, I said truthfully. "I have wondered, yes."

"Then I shall tell you, my dear, for it is a thing I believe you should know." The Count's jaw tensed when he came to me and interwove his fingers in mine. With eyes downcast to the floor, averted from me and the Eye of God, he began slowly. "I was on a battlefield near Bucureşti when, in a momentary lapse of judgment, I had been struck down by my own men. It is hard to remember what happened afterward, but the next thing I saw was a man, or at least a figure of a man, standing amongst the snow and blood. I knew I was dying, but instead of feeling the 'peace' one experiences at that time, I was full of hate. The figure of a man spoke to me, and his words were sweet and full of promises. He offered me another life and the power to destroy all my enemies. He offered me the blood of my foes, their heads, their souls, if only I would follow him. I did not want to die, for I knew I was not finished seeking retribution against those who robbed me of my throne, my family…"

He stopped, not that he needed to go on with his story. I understand exactly what happened, and though it frightened me, I wouldn't necessarily blame him for it. "Lucifer offered you a drink from the cup of temptation, and you drank it freely."

The Master shot me a chilling glare at the boldness and truth of my statement, but muttered. "Yes."

I dared further. "Did you achieve all the revenge you sought?"

"That, and much, much more." Looking at me straight in the eyes, I saw a flicker of satisfaction on his face.

"And was it all worth it?"

At that, his face fell, and he showed no emotion but another hard stare. Surely, he knew the real answer to that question, but he did not care to say it. I saw on his face, however, the conflict that was half-hidden there. His nature was saying one thing, his heart another, and no spoken words could convey what the other felt. The Count's eyes drifted away from mine, and he changed the subject. "In this place, one of my sons was christened, where my wife and I stood as we watched the painters create our favorite portraits of holy people. There were moments of great peace in this chapel, but also moments of great sorrow."

Hesitantly, I took hold of his arm, considering what to say. My silence lasted for longer than I had noticed, but all he had revealed to me in those few minutes left me troubled. "Which of those memories have stayed with you longer? The bad or the good?"

"The bad," the Master replied after a moment's thought. "But regardless, I wish for you to use it. However, I cannot guarantee that your God will listen to you from a place such as this."

Frowning, I looked away from him and let go of his arm. "I think He hears more than you realize. But, thank you, I will use it well."

"Perhaps He does hear me, sweet one, but I do not think He listens." The Count put his hand in my hair, stroking it away from my neck. The coolness of his hand against my hot skin made me shiver as his fingers traced close to the silver chain. "Maybe you could convince Him otherwise."

I bit my tongue. "Perhaps you should join me."

He eyed me, an eyebrow cocked. "Join you?"

"Will it harm you?"

The Count's unguarded unwillingness to dare to try was plain on his face. I couldn't tell if it was his nature resisting the idea or if it was something else. For certain, I wouldn't push him to do something he wasn't ready for, but he couldn't sit by and let me do all the work for him. In the end, he would have to do more than I ever could. He, again, couldn't look me in the eye. "I am not quite sure..."

"Well, if only you wish to." Slowly, I moved away from the Count and genuflected before the altar, the stone beneath my knees thoroughly worn from ancient use. Clasping my hands together and closing my eyes, I waited to see if he would actually come and kneel beside me. If he were truly in his resolve to find his peace, to seek his redemption with my help, he would act on his own accord. All I had to do was wait for him to follow behind me.

Quite a bit of time passed before I heard him come to stand behind me, getting to his knees, his breath a little ragged. I could feel that he was not next to me but behind me. As long as he made the effort, the method did not matter. So, we remained there in silence for another length of time, when he whispered to me. "I do not know what to say."

I made the Sign of the Cross. "He knows your heart better than you do. By saying nothing at all, you're saying all you need to say."

The Master made no reply.

I began my Latin prayers, not saying them aloud in case they caused him discomfort. To myself, I prayed for the Count and hoped the Lord would see that I had brought his fallen son before Him. I asked for guidance and patience, but also, I thanked Him for this precious moment. When I closed the prayer, I looked back at the Master, who was still kneeling. Although his face was paler than usual, his irises were red as he stared off into one set spot near the altar. I was a bit frightened by the sight. "Are you alright, Count?"

He was startled by me, jumping slightly as his eyes came to stare into mine. "It is nothing."

Still on my knees, I turned to face him. "May I ask how it hurts you?"

The Count swallowed hard, again struggling to find a reply as his hands balled into fists and his jaw clenched. "My blood boils and I am filled with hate...hate so blinding it is hard to see past. There is more to the feeling, but over time it has become easier."

Taking that balled fist of his, I lifted it to my lips and kissed his knuckles. Almost on contact, his fist relaxed, and his hand opened to cup my cheek. I nuzzled into it. "Thank you for staying here with me, Vlad."

A purr resonated in the air, and all the pain he had just felt vanished as he focused on me. "So, you are pleased with my little gifts?"

Closing my eyes, I took great comfort in his touch. "Yes, thank you so very much."

"Then I am pleased." And with that, he kissed me tenderly.

My heart soared above the clouds, but something still bothers me about tonight. Why the gifts at all and on such a day? Are they his attempts to woo me further, or is he trying to show his ability to be kind? Since the night he told me of his nature, I find myself wondering if his words and actions are as genuine as I want to believe them to be. Did he give me his mother's crucifix to let me know he considers me to be family, or to give me a false sense of security for my situation? It is in his nature to use lies and deceit to bend people to his will without forcing them. Sometimes, just sometimes, I speculate whether he is not using me for some unknown means to an end. If that is the case, am I a blinded pawn being willingly led to my own doom?

At the same time, if the Count is simply wishing to convey to me his affection...I find that hard to believe. He is selfish, though he hides it behind the illusion of selflessness. He cannot love me, and presents me with the delusion of loving me. These conflicting things rip me apart. I hate how I cannot truly see whether he is sincere.

But tonight, by kneeling with me in front of the Almighty despite the pain it caused him, he showed me a sliver of his honest intentions. He has shown me multiple times his wholehearted intent:

by *stopping* himself when he lay upon me, by *showing* me pieces of himself he never reveals to anyone, by *admitting* he wants to find peace, by *admitting* he wants to be redeemed.

The Count explained that he is the incarnation of evil on earth and therefore possesses every instinct that Lucifer does. So how, in all my feeble human wisdom, can I judge whether or not the Count is being truthful to me? Time will reveal all if I'm correct in my judgment of him.

Chapter Twenty-One

IN TENTATIONEM

11 August

Morning...

For the past five days, I have been hard at work cleaning the hall and chapel. The work has been just as slow as the wall, but I have made some progress each day. Both spaces have not been touched by any sort of cleaning agent in centuries, and I frequently have to change out water and replace solutions. It's tedious work with all the little details of the room requiring special care. I haven't even dared to begin the floor just yet, which is the worst of the entire two sections, but I know I will have to tackle it someday soon. Oh, how I am dreading the idea of having to get on my hands and knees and scrub that, but it must be done. I am still very curious to see what that beautiful mosaic cross will look like when it's completely cleared away of dirt and dust.

In the long hours that I have been spending in the space, something still hasn't felt quite right. Ever since the Count introduced me to it, I feel like I am being watched, but there is no one around. All the time I've been there, I have never felt so disturbed by what hides in the shadows. I wondered if I've upset something in this castle by coming so frequently to work and pray there, but I also wonder if it's just my imagination. There are times that I think I see something slink from shadow to shadow out of the corner of my eye, but I can't tell if it was real or not, for by the time I turn to look, it is gone. Knowing that I live in a supernatural place, I am not surprised that there may be things that lurk in the dark, but I am more worried about *what* exactly they may be.

I haven't the nerve to ask Dumitru or the Count of my suspicions about it. Actually, I don't want to know the answer at all. Whatever it is, it can watch all it wants as long as it doesn't bother me. There are plenty of more things to worry about than whether or not there is a lingering spirit in the hall or just passing shadows.

Since the message that I was compelled to relay to the Count, we have heard nothing of Imogen and her faction, at least I haven't been told anything about their movements or whereabouts. I do not doubt that the Count knows everything that's going on in their group, and he won't tell me unless it's necessary. I also have no doubt they know what we are up to as well.

This is the calm before the storm. Michaelmas, which is 29 September, will be here in about seven weeks. To my knowledge, I have no idea if the Count has devised a strategy against them. He has to have something by now. I think I will ask him tonight if I have the opportunity. I have come up with an idea of my own, which may be insane or rather genius. There is a fine line between the definition of those two words. I guess we'll see which one the Count thinks it is.

Evening…

After the lesson, we settled down for our usual discussion. Even after these many months, they have not diminished in their riveting topics and tangents. There is always something to talk about, whether it is about me or him. Although tonight, it was most certainly going to be about him. As we sat in the library, our chairs were close enough to each other that I could reach for his hand. "Count, may I ask you what you plan to do about…" My voice faltered since I was unsure of what exactly to call *them* to him. "Your, uh, children?"

"I have been considering a few things." He didn't look at me and brushed it off. "No need to worry about it, sweet one."

I didn't relent. "Would you mind telling me?"

The Count pursed his lips as his grasp tightened on my hand. "You must forgive me, dear, but in my day, women were not involved with such things. For your own peace of mind, allow me to take care of it. You have faith in me, do you not?"

A part of me had expected an answer similar to this from an old man set in his old ways. I rolled my eyes. "Surely you will let me in on one piece?"

Finally, the Master did look at me, a stroke of annoyance on his face, but still, his voice was calm. "You are too innocent for the things I have in mind, my dear."

Cocking my eyebrow, I leaned forward to whisper with a slight smirk on my face. "So, you *are* planning something devastating?"

"I will not tell you, Isadora." The Count chided me, his irritation flaring.

I went quiet, looking away from him. This was his typical strategy to shut me down before I could even begin to scratch the surface of what he was thinking, but I still asked. "Is it because I could easily be forced to reveal it to them?"

His hand immediately bore down on mine at the thought, and so I knew that was the real cause. "I do not want to say it like that, but yes, that is a partial reason."

"That's fair…" I did agree with him on it. "I would do the same in your situation."

"It is not personal. You understand this?"

"Yes, I understand." I sighed, and after a while of silence that had fallen between the two of us, I added. "I've been thinking of my own strategies. I'm sure they're nothing compared to yours…"

The Count was humored by this. "And how do you plan to fight them, little one?"

"Hear me out." I began, but bit my lip at the boldness of what I was about to say. "You are the lord of deception, are you not? You use smoke and mirrors, mind games, and tricks to get whatever you want. Why not use it here? Show them as you were for a short while until they are satisfied. I do not doubt your ability to paint one picture over another."

The Count grew very serious, and a true scowl came over his face. "That man is long gone. If I were to resurrect him, I do not think I would return the same man that you know now, not when I have come so far to bury him. He is not someone you would want to meet."

I understood the Count's reluctance to be the man he once was, to let it run free again could be a major setback, but at the same time, a bright opportunity. "Perhaps you should not bury him but face him. If Satan rises up against himself, he cannot stand. He is divided, and thereby conquered."

His brow furrowed at my analogy. "What are you implying?"

"Use this opportunity to test yourself. If you are sincere in your fight for your redemption, you must face that demon that lives here." I pointed to his heart. "If you are divided against your demon, you have the chance to conquer it, but only head-on."

Thinking about it for a moment, he shook his head. "That is easier said than done."

"I will be here to remind you of yourself." With both my hands, I grasped his. "If you want this, you're going to have to work for it. You know that God would not give you a burden you cannot bear. You are a genius, Count, and you're the strongest man I know. I have every confidence you can succeed in anything you put your mind to. Besides, there is no need to make any decision now. We still have time."

"All the same," he drew a long sigh. "It is playing with fire."

"Well," I mused after a moment. "You have to play with fire if you want to get burned."

He looked at me, this strange expression on his face. I stared back, straight into his eyes. We both knew what the other was thinking and didn't have to utter a word about it.

So, I continued. "Do not tell me of your strategy, Count. Keep it to yourself. When the time comes, at least let me know a little of what is going on."

"You do realize that what you propose places you and Dumitru in great danger, do you not?" The Count's eyes narrowed, and with a sharp snap, he hissed. "You have never seen my true form, nor have you seen what I can do. If you saw it, you would never look at me the same."

"I've seen bits and pieces, that's how I knew for so long."

He scoffed and mimicked me. "'Bits and pieces' —"

"I saw you crawl down a wall, I've seen you be the mist, the shadow, and when you appear in one place and then another. I've seen your eyes burn red, and your fangs." I retorted, taking my hand from his. "And I may not have seen you in *that* form, but Petros did not withhold it from me. So, yes, I've seen 'bits and pieces' of the things you hide from me. I am not blind."

He blinked, I think not truly seeing the extent to which I had been exposed to all these things. I had not revealed to him that Petros had become the beast in front of me, nor did he ever know that I had seen him that night as he descended the wall like a lizard. I had kept it all to myself for his sake. The Count didn't need to know that I knew all these things and had treated him the same, nonetheless. Sure, it was disturbing, and it took me a long time to accept, but I always strived to see past them.

The Count sighed. "It disappoints me that I have not been able to shield you from those things."

He was lost in thought for the longest time, and I let him lose himself. He was plotting again, I could see it in his eyes. I was a little surprised he would be so willing to contemplate the implications of what I had proposed to him. Though it is very risky, even lethal. If handled correctly, it could be extremely effective in taking care of this problem of ours. He will not tell me what his final motive is. To repel them or to kill them, I mustn't assume anything.

Suddenly, the Master turned back to me, and a spark had ignited on his face. He had something, but all he said was. "I will consider it."

17 August

Today began like any normal day. Being Wednesday, I went about my day as usual. Morning chores, my frequent outings to tend to the Romani, and working on cleaning the corridor to the chapel. In just about a week, I had managed to clean just half of the floor, and today I was beginning the section that involved the masterpiece at its center. I was excited to finally uncover its true beauty. I crave any slice of joy I can find in this time of constant stress. The work has also been keeping my mind off the children, but even still, it remains a persistent thought in the back of my mind.

So, I got to work on the outer edges of the floor and worked my way inwards to the center. It was a particularly hot day, and the air was stagnant and heavy despite the door being open. Often, I would have to leave and get a breath of fresh air before returning to my drudgery. Sweat poured from me, but I was determined to finish the entire section by the evening before the lecture. Because the work was so dirty, I chose not to wear the crucifix the Count had given me and stored it safely away. He wouldn't know I didn't wear it as he instructed, since I planned to have plenty of time to make myself presentable in the evening.

On my hands and knees, I worked tirelessly even when my body ached. I knew I would be sore in the morning, but it was a good exercise, and a little elbow grease never hurt anyone. So, the hours wore on past noon, past tea, to near dinner. Still at my toil, I had just scrubbed the last of the outer tiles and was just getting to the point I had been aiming for all this time.

"Isadora," Dumitru poked his head inside. "The Gypsies have left. Do you want dinner soon?"

"Sure," I grunted with another pass of my scrub brush. "I'll be there in a bit."

After voicing his agreement, I assumed he retreated to wash up from another long, hard day.

With the sun low in the sky, the fading orange and pink of the twilight were coming in from the window, casting the glittering hall in the same hues. The low angle set the gold pieces ablaze, and I scrubbed and scrubbed. I could have sworn I saw that black shadow dart from place to place a few times, but I paid it no mind. From the base of the cross, I revealed the faces of the two Apostles Peter and Paul, and eager to continue, I began to work my way up the cross to its center, where the image of Christ rests.

Time passed so quickly that by the time I reached His image, the sun was about to set. I had no thought in my haze of time, nor that I was starving, nor that I was exhausted, nor that I was close to passing out from suffocating in that musty hall. I pressed myself onwards, sweat dripping into the suds and dirt until finally, I cleared away the centuries to reveal the wonder beneath.

With my worn fingers, I traced the tiny stones so vividly colored in white, red, brown, blue, and gold. Finally, I had reached my goal. A relief washed over me, and in that moment of relaxation, my head began to spin, my vision blurring, and I realized I was suddenly lying on my back. I could feel my chest rising in falling from exertion, my stomach felt so empty, and my limbs so shaky. My muscles had no energy left, no will to move now that I had seen the Savior's face. Exhausted, I willingly closed my eyes, only intending to rest for a moment as the light faded and faded from the sky. The last thing I remember hearing was the door, which was only open slightly, creaking shut. I guess I suppose it was the wind, despite there being no draft, and I slipped from the waking world.

. . .

The next thing I recall was feeling a presence in the room. My head was so muddled that it dozed in and out of sleep, unwilling to wake. My stomach ached with hunger, and it was the sole part of me that screamed for me to get up. I resisted it, not wanting to move. Yet there was something else with me, something close that I couldn't place, like a slight chill in the air that was unnatural in this heat. As I became more aware, my skin prickled at the scent of the pungent odor of rotten eggs. That made me open my eyes. Instantly, I came face to face with two glowing yellow goat eyes; everything else around them was shrouded in black.

If I wasn't awake then, I thought I must've been dreaming. I went to scream, but no air came for me to even put into it. It only came out as nothing at all. The thick smell of brimstone clogged my lungs as the thing above me grinned to show its misshapen yellow teeth, jagged and serrated. In the muddy dark, two horns protruded from its skull and came down on either side of its face. With all the strength left in me, I fought to move out from under it, but a weight like a ton of bricks held me down. Then it spoke, its voice sounding like a thousand voices speaking at once. "Isadora, at last we meet in the flesh."

Every cell in my body shook at the persuasion behind its voice as though I were being pulled into it. *How does it know my name?* I remembered thinking.

"We know many things about you." It replied, a wave of oppressive heat plumed around me. "Even the things you will not admit to yourself."

All I could do was listen to the words said by this creature as I struggled to remain conscious. I could feel another heat well up in my stomach that beckoned me to listen closely to its words. "You are wondering who we are, but you already know. You desire our son, surely you didn't think we would not take notice of your existence."

I was confused by what it meant by 'son', but just then I felt something brush my inner thighs. Instinctually, my hips rose from the ground, and a hot wave rushed from my core. I was petrified, but I listened to the words of a thousand voices being spoken so seductively in my ear. It dawned on me in my adrenaline-induced haze to whom I was speaking, and words cannot describe the terror that burned in my veins. It was Lucifer himself, as Baphomet, who pinned me to the floor and who bade me hang on his every word. At the moment, I couldn't comprehend the scope of this visitation, nor did I ever even consider that Satan would come to me regarding his son. Tremors of fear rippled through me.

"We can give you all things you desire and more if you only worship us." He whispered, those yellow eyes mesmerizing more than just my physical body. "Just imagine an eternity of never-ending passion, eternal youth, eternal pleasure with him at your side. Do us reverence and it can all be yours, and more."

The proposition was more than tempting as I eyed the yellow orbs of the horned mass. Yes, I do want to have the Count all to myself, to covet him as he covets me. I want to give myself to him and have him fill me, but at the same time, he is not mine to have.

I could feel hands, which felt more like claws, slowly gliding over the skin of my ribs as it tore my t-shirt to shreds. "What do you say, Isadora? The answer is easy to say, so say it."

Transfixed as I was by the lure he presented. Yes, the answer was easy to say. Somehow, I managed to regain some air to speak, but it only came out as a half-whisper. *"Vade retro, Satana."*

He cocked his head to one side as he flinched in pain, an amused grin forming over his sharpened teeth. "You are young, impressionable, blinded by the promises of your God. We can tell you for certain that they are empty things that come to nothing. Why spend your time on earth wasting away with age, when you can be as you are forever? Without what we can give you, the man you love will live on while you will turn to dust; so, follow us, join our family."

There was the slightest familiarity in the words that were spoken, but before I had time to ponder them, suddenly the door burst open with a thundering bang. I think I screamed, but I can't be sure. Instinctively, I had covered my ears from the loud noise, but my eyes remained open to watch the horror unfold. In a flash, the black mass was off me as another mass, this one corporeal, took its place. It roared so ferociously that my hands couldn't muffle the sound, its white fangs glinted in the pale and distant moonlight. The face was half-man, half-beast, and unrecognizable in the dark. *Two* of them? I remembered thinking that I would surely die.

The Evil One screeched in a terrible whine and spoke in its thousand voices, but in a language that I didn't understand. Yellow eyes squared off with red, the two growling like rabid dogs bent on the other's destruction. In response, the beast's arms came around me and laid out another vicious barrage of words. I covered my head rather than my ears.

The creature that held me roared again, this one more deafening than I have ever heard in my life. It was laced with blinding rage and malice, a cross between human and monster. The candles burst into tongues of flame, and the blackness cried out in pain as it dissipated into nothing with the light. The room was left in silence, with only me and the other being remaining. Eager now to escape to the open door using that distraction, I began to attempt to pry myself away from the one holding me. This one's strength was of a thousand men, but that didn't stop me from trying.

"He is gone."

It sounded like the Count, but in my state, I didn't know what was real or imagined. I began to thrash again, but these arms held me so tightly I could not break free. "Let me go, demon! You have no power over me!"

"Isadora." A deep growl sounded in my ear, and I could feel it resonate down my spine.

A swirl of haze came before my eyes, and all the fight was gone. I slumped to one side, my eyes growing unbearably heavy. I was maneuvered to meet face to face with my second attacker, and to my dumbfounded brain, I couldn't fathom that I was staring back at the Count. He was a sight for sore eyes, but I couldn't dare to think it, but as I searched his features, I couldn't deny he was there. Tears finally broke as I found the audacity to ask. "Vlad?"

"Yes, sweetest one," the Count moved some stray strands of hair that were plastered with sweat on my face. "I am here with you."

I let out a long sigh of relief, and I rested my head on his chest, my shaky hands coming around him to grip his shirt. He pressed me to him, his strength enveloping me in safety. It took so much out of me just to keep my hands closed into fists, which only shook more violently from the strain. There was so much comfort in his arms, so much strength and support that I needed so badly.

I felt the Count's kisses on my shoulder, gently first, then intensifying. He pulled me away from him, and with an even greater passion, kissed my lips over and over. I could barely return the gesture, making the resulting ones sloppy. O God, how they were an oasis in a desert. They renewed a life in me, brought me back to my senses, and quieted the terror that had my heart in an iron vice. After too many kisses that I could not count, the Master pressed me to him again, and a lulling purr filled the air.

"Was that…" My voice was raspy from screaming.

"Do not make me tell you." If I didn't know any better, I think his voice cracked. "I told you this place is not holy."

I only quaked. "He's been watching me. I saw him —"

"Master," a meek voice came from nearby. "Is she alright?"

I hadn't even noticed Dumitru come into the hall. Inching closer to us, I think he was afraid to approach. I was happy to see him, another sight for sore eyes, and I smiled. However, just as I was about to say something, the Master peeled himself off of me with a grunt and stood to face his servant. With unmatched speed, the Count backhanded Dumitru across the face, sending him hard to the floor. Instead of Romanian, the Count chose to roar at him in English. "You fail me yet again, Dumitru. How many times has it been now?"

I gasped at the malevolence in the Master's voice. "Count —"

"Silence." He spat back at me, and it was a command, so I could not speak. Turning back to Dumitru, who was still on the ground, the Count put his heavy foot on his chest. "Apologize for your failure, grovel for your forgiveness, you useless boy."

Surely the Count's foot was crushing his lungs, but somehow Dumitru managed to speak in short breaths in Romanian. He had only gotten a few words out before the Master pressed more weight down on Dumitru's sternum, making him cry out. I was appalled and tried to call out to either one of them for this to stop, but my voice was simply gone.

"In *English.*" He ordered, accompanied by a low, fearsome growl.

"I'm sorry, *Domnișoară.*" Dumitru's face was contorted as he tried to lift the Count's oppressive boot from his chest. "I failed you again."

With that, the Count kicked him, so he rolled away. "Get out of my sight."

Dumitru looked at me, his eyes pleading for something, then back at the Master. Blood trickled from his mouth, but getting to his feet, he promptly disappeared from the hall. My heart burst as I watched him go, and I let the tears I had been trying to hold back loose. With all my being, I had wanted to defend Mitică, but I was more than helpless in my current state, and I sank to the floor.

The Master's boots were in front of me as he stared down. Still unable to speak, I didn't dare look up at him but quivered at his feet. Was he going to do the same to me as he did to Dumitru? After all I had just been through, I had to expect the worst. When the Count spoke, his malice diminished but was still present. "Why do you not wear the crucifix that I gave you? I told you to wear it always."

The bind that held my voice broke with that direct question, but I couldn't find any words with which to answer him. "I…I'm…."

The Count hissed at me. "I told you never to sleep in any room except your quarters. I told you not to do work such as this that does not befit a lady. I tell you all these things to keep you safe, and you only disobey me."

The words he used made me cower. If I had been feeling well enough, I would have stood up to him and argued back, but I could barely raise my head to protest. It wasn't that he was wrong; I had openly disobeyed him, knowing the consequences of my actions, but…there was no 'but'. I stayed silent and waited.

The Master knelt to my level and lifted my upper half to look at him. In the candlelight, his eyes still burned red, but his voice then sounded more hurt than angry. "What do you have to say, Isadora? Speak."

Taking a few breaths, I gathered enough air in my lungs to let out a complete sentence. But before I could, my body went slack in his arms, and my vision blurred as everything faded away. I think I fainted.

AFFLICTION

18 August

Morning…

Whaen I awoke next, my body felt it was weighed down by a ton of bricks. I groaned, forcing my eyes to open. I was back in my room, and it was daytime, but the curtains were closed tightly to block out the intense sun. Rolling over on my side, which took much effort, I read the time on my little clock as 9 am.

"You have been asleep for nearly thirteen hours."

Looking over to a dark corner of the room, the Count sat there with his legs crossed. Had he been there the entire time? The previous night came rushing back to me when I saw him, and I tensed, ducking down under the sheets a bit so he couldn't see me. I didn't answer him, I couldn't answer him, not after everything I had seen and he had done. I lay there on my side, feeling a depraved hunger as my stomach growled.

"Have you no words for me?" He asked as he came to stand by my bedside.

I didn't look at him but stared blankly at the barred window. There were many things I wanted to say to him, some good, others bad, but at the moment, I wanted to be alone. Although I knew the Count wasn't going to let me have my space, not after thirteen hours of keeping him in the dark.

The Count sat on the edge of the bed as he waited for me to say something. He was patient, but only for so long, and asked quizzically. "Do you hate me now?"

He knew that would cause me to have a reaction, and my eyes went to his. I was a bit surprised at how sad he looked after being so angry last night, but I couldn't look at them for long. In the end, I shook my head solemnly.

"Then why do you not speak to me?" The Count's tone was firm and demanded a direct answer.

I swallowed hard, and finally, I couldn't bear the silence that I kept. "What can I say?"

"Anything at all, my sweet one," he bent to rest his forehead on my shoulder. "I have been so very worried for you."

At his closeness, I felt mixed emotions: one of love, the other of fear. My heartbeat quickened, which I'm sure he heard. "Why?"

"Why?" He looked back up at me as if I were joking with him. He was almost laughing at the absurdity of my question. "Why not? You were confronted by —"

He stopped, his smile fading as he became deathly quiet.

"Say it," I challenged him. "Say the name of your father."

"*I will not.*" His temper flared as he snarled. Then, as if remembering himself, he quieted his ire and reached beneath the blankets to take my hand. "Even I was taken aback that he would reveal himself to you in that form, but please, tell me what…what he said to you."

I remembered the words of that thousand-voiced demon, and my body shuddered. Without realizing it, tears came to my eyes, and I pushed my face into the pillow to hide it from the Count. Quietly, I muttered. "He only tempted me."

In response to his inquiry, the Master closed the distance between us again. Gently, he rubbed the stubble on his cheek against mine to comfort me. "With what, my dearest one?"

"With you." I breathed out. "If I were to worship him, he would give me you."

He tensed, a purr turned into a growl, yet he concluded. "And you did not submit to him."

More tears cascaded down my cheeks and soaked into the pillow. "I almost did…"

"But you did not." His arms wrapped around me, and he kissed the tears on my cheek. "I told you he has no power over you."

I scoffed, my heart filling with shame. "It sure didn't seem like that."

"You are stronger than you think." He whispered, but then changed the subject slightly. "You must forgive me for the way I acted afterward. I was very angry and was not thinking."

"I don't think it's *my* forgiveness that you should be seeking." I replied too frankly.

The Count stared hard back at me, then sat up. "Isadora, I will say this only once more: it is Dumitru's duty to protect you when I am not present. Each time you have been in danger, he has been somewhere else. It is inexcusable."

Again, he wasn't necessarily wrong, but not necessarily right either. "Don't you think that each time it was planned to have us separated? It can't really be his fault?"

"Irrelevant," he dismissed me with a wave of his hand. "It is his duty that he swore to me. However, I feel now he will be more obstinate than before."

"Why?" I asked again.

The Count smiled to himself. "He saw me kiss you."

Closing my eyes, I let out a very long sigh. "It was bound to happen sooner or later."

He hummed in agreement. "I am sure he thinks I forced myself on you in your moment of weakness, but let him think as he wills. It helps him remember who is the Master of this house."

I frowned, my brow furrowing. Was it amusing to him that Dumitru had seen us embracing because it displayed his *dominance*? It irked me, yet that is how the Count operates, so I opened my eyes. "Can I ask one thing?"

"Of course."

"Did you protect me out of concern for me," I observed his reaction carefully. "Or did you have other motives?"

"Truthfully?" He thought for a moment, the wheels in his head spinning. The Master let out a breath with his head hanging. "I felt fear knowing he would take advantage of you, but anger that he would approach you so secretly, as you say, 'under my own nose'. I never thought he would seek you out personally...his tricks evade even me at times."

I squinted at his vague reply, not quite certain what to make of it. "And at the moment you stood against him, face to face, what did you feel?"

"I felt you, trembling in fear." The Count still didn't look at me.

Again, his answer was not one I had expected. Of all the times, when he went toe-to-toe with Satan himself, all he could think of was me? It struck me, and with everything he said, I didn't know what to say.

"I must sleep." He stood, but stopped as he saw the small box that held the crucifix he had given me on my nightstand. Taking it, he placed it in my hand, then bent down to kiss my forehead. "Until tonight, my sweet one."

Then the Count left, and I didn't try to stop him. I dared not try to assume that he had actually been motivated so soon to act not just for his own accord, but for someone else's. There's no way he could be changing that vital spark that is his diabolic nature so quickly. Perhaps he meant something else? I couldn't stop to dwell on it then, for there was work to be done.

I struggled to get out of bed. My muscles were incredibly sore and weary, but I somehow managed to get to my feet. I was still in my work clothes, that is, my shredded shirt and grime-stained capris. It took a lot of effort to get them off, and of course, the shirt was promptly thrown in the trash. What number is that now? Three or four shirts, maybe five that have been destroyed in one fashion or another? Sighing at my diminishing collection of wearable clothes, I examined my abdomen for any sign of claw marks and found none to my relief, but I still broke down into tears. I hated the knowledge that the Prince of Darkness had touched this body of mine. I hated remembering his terrible claws massaging my inner thighs and his full understanding of my weaknesses.

Climbing into a hot bath, I stayed there for an hour before I found the courage to face the world. Putting on my façade and the silver crucifix, I dressed and went down to the kitchen. Despite not having much energy to prepare something to eat, nor actually wanting to eat, I just had a meager bowl of oatmeal with fruit. My stomach was so hungry that it felt nauseous after eating the small amount, so I could just barely finish before I thought I was actually going to throw things up.

When I sought out Dumitru, he was working diligently with the Romani as I watched unseen at the door. Vasile, one of our original workers, eventually noticed me and took his hat off, greeting me in Romanian. I greeted him back, and even being a distance away, Dumitru turned to the sound of my voice. Dropping all he was doing, he came up to me, grabbed my arm, and led me back into the castle. I felt embarrassed that he had done that in front of our Romani friends, as he slammed the smaller door behind us. I thought he was going to yell at me since he seemed quite upset. I was ready for the onslaught, but when he turned his face, I saw the full extent of the injury the Count had inflicted upon him. I gasped in shock.

The whole right side of his face was black, blue, and pinkish, and part of his eye was bloodshot from the trauma, making his gray iris stand out against the red. Dumitru looked like he had gotten a baseball to the face with the swelling lumped around his cheekbone and brow. I felt so guilty that he had been hurt, and I was about to speak to him when, without warning, he embraced me fiercely. So much so that it made my sore muscles ache. Still, I hugged him back, more tears surfacing. "I am so sorry —"

"*Don't,*" he gritted his teeth, resting his uninjured side of his face against mine. "Don't tell me you're sorry. Just tell me you're okay."

Well, I was certainly not 'okay', but I did as he asked. "I'm alive."

Mitică pulled away from me, his arms loosening only a little. "I could have sworn I had heard you go upstairs and tell me you'd be down for dinner. The door to the hall was locked, so I was sure you were finished there, but you never came back down. I thought you were busy with something else, but when I went up to light the lamps, you weren't in the library. Then, when the Master came and you didn't show up for the lesson…you don't know how scared I was."

A tear ran down my cheek. The Prince of Lies had surely pulled the wool over all of our eyes, and poor Dumitru paid the true price for it. His arms, which rested around my low back, felt so warm. After all, he said, I didn't have a clue how to respond. "Oh, Mitică…"

"It was *him*, wasn't it?" He stared so intensely into my soul. "Beelz—"

"*Don't* say the name!" I burst out in anger. "Never say it to me. Never."

Dumitru was shocked by it, and a terrible remorse came over his face. "I'm sorry…"

"No…I'm sorry. I still feel messed up." I don't know why I was so provoked by the name. Perhaps I think that even saying it will summon him again, that he will hear and come. I hated that I had gotten so angry at Mitică, and I took his head in my hands for him to look at me. I'm not sure what possessed me to do this, but I kissed his bruised cheek and eye as softly as I could before wrapping my arms around his neck. "Please, forgive me for everything. I hate that you were hurt for this. Please, tell me what I must do to make this right. I will do *anything* to make this right, my friend."

Mitică tensed at the gesture. I think it was too much emotion, too much physical contact, for him. Yet still, he smoothed my back with his hand to comfort me instead as he whispered sadly. "I should be saying the same to you."

"Shut up and just tell me." My voice cracked a bit.

Mitică was silent for the longest time as his hot breath warmed the cold skin of my neck. Then he pulled away from me and stared at my tear-stained cheeks. With his rough fingers, he wiped them away. From the look in his eyes, there was something he very much wanted to say. "The work on the wall will be completed soon, and I will be finally ready to clean the entrance next week. You can help me if you want."

I sighed in frustration. "Dumitru, that's not what I mean. Besides, I already told you I would help you with it."

"I know," a pink blush began to form on his cheeks, and his voice became low and soft. "What I mean is I want...I want to..." There he went with his stuttering again and became vexed by it. It was easy to see he was flustered, but I couldn't necessarily tell if it was because he was talking about something he wanted, or that he was angry that he couldn't put it into words. "I want to b-be, uh..."

Just then, one of the Romani called to him from the outside.

"I have to go." Mitică put distance between us. "Please take care of yourself, my friend. I'll see you later."

Promptly, he departed from the smaller door, closing it shut without another look or word.

I felt empty that he had left me without saying what he obviously needed to say. His warmth faded from my arms, and the cold seeped back in. "You want to be...what?"

I couldn't even guess at the range of possibilities that could end that sentence. I rubbed my temples to relieve the headache that was growing between them. This day was becoming too much for me, and it had just begun. I stood there wondering what to do next. I would have gone to do my chores, but I didn't think I had the physical strength in me to do any of them. All I wanted to do was to go to bed and not get up until next year, or the next century.

I was just about to ascend the stairs when the door to the chapel caught my eye. Hesitantly, and against my better judgment, I approached. Taking a deep breath, I unlocked the grand door and stepped over the threshold and into the hall. The scene had been unchanged, with my scrub brush and bucket still lying in the same place as I had left them the previous night. Scanning the room for unusual shadows, I tried to spot if any of them moved in unnatural ways against the light as I went deeper. In the midday sunlight, everything was calm and peaceful, as if last night had never occurred.

I went to the cross and stared down at the face of Christ before going to my knees. In the radiant light that came through the large windows at the far end of the room, I could see in more detail the color and precision of the artist's work. The fact that this ancient image managed to survive in such a place for so long must be a miracle, and I felt grateful that I had the chance to see it as it looked centuries prior.

As I sat there, I pondered why Satan had not approached me any time before, but only when I had brought the Count back to kneel before God's altar did he dare to appear. Surely, he must know the Master's feelings and must be so terrified to lose his greatest son that he would bypass him and go straight to me. First to tempt me with my darkest desire, and when that failed, to threaten. How shallow, how pathetic he is? To keep his first son, he would give the Count to me, as long as I vow to stop my efforts and follow the Fallen One. And also, now that I think of it, curse me to eternal damnation and thereby retaining one soul and gaining another.

I know he will be back in one form or another. Due to his close relationship with the witch, called Imogen, she will undoubtedly do his bidding to go against me. This war is being fought all for one man's soul, and I am so afraid I will be ineffective against the children. Slouching, I sat back on my calves. "I don't pretend to know the mysteries of your plan, Lord, and I don't expect you to ever reveal them to me. But, have I fallen so from Your sight that you would allow the one you cast from Heaven to come and tempt me so easily? In the desert, you were tempted by him and resisted him, but I am not you, Lord. I have only so much strength to keep him at bay. I beg you to give me an iota of your fortitude..."

I let out a long, long sigh. What will be, will be. I'm in too deep to back out now. Months that seem years ago, I resigned my fate to this place. So, let it be wonderful, or let it be awful.

Evening...

By accident, I ended up sleeping most of the day, and I dreamt of strange and disturbing things. I'm unsure whether I should include them here because I hate to admit them to myself. I know for certain that they are the result of a mix of my encounter with the Fallen One and those dark fantasies I keep locked so deeply inside. I cannot hide my feelings from myself, no matter how hard I try. So, I shall write them here so that I may face them.

In the dream, I was back in the Count's reception room, wearing the same nightgown I wore that evening he explained his nature. This time, I was alone, and the red setting sun was the only light that illuminated the room. Curious to see the sky, I went to the windows and looked out onto the beautiful mountain range, drenched in so much color. The scene made me lose myself as I gazed from behind the ancient glass panes, my elbows resting on the sill.

There was a familiar purr behind me, and I turned to the source. The Count stood there directly in back of me, smiling, with the sunset's fury reflecting in his eyes. My palms became sweaty, but I smiled back since I was glad to see him. Oddly, we said nothing to each other as he drew nearer to me, his fingers suddenly latching onto my hips and digging into the soft flesh there. My breath caught in my throat as I was about to pull away, when he pulled me back instead to rest my backside against his own hips. Slowly, with those long bat-like fingers of his, the Count brushed them forward over my hips to between my legs. Immediately, heat enveloped me, and I inadvertently pressed against him in response to his prodding. The sensation felt so real as one of his hands dragged its way up to my chest, where it stopped to knead my breasts.

My very soul was at the Master's mercy, and I dared to want to go further. His lips pressed heavily down on the skin of my neck to my shoulder, then he growled like an animal. Whirling me around to face him, he grabbed my midriff and hoisted me onto the stone sill. Again, his mouth was hungrily on my throat, and he opened my legs, his hands sliding the fabric of my dress over my knees. The fear of knowing what was about to happen next squeezed the adrenaline into my veins.

My hazy eyes flashed open. "No, it can't be like this."

The Count didn't seem to hear me as he took my lower half and slid it to meet his. Putting my arms up between us, I tried to push him away as I felt his hand probing into the unknown. Darkness was quickly setting over the scene, and I knew once the sun set, there would be no turning back. I put my fingers into the Count's hair and pulled back as hard as I could. He snarled at the discomfort, but it made him look at me. Instead of those warm eyes that I had expected to see, they had morphed into those of the goat and shone a pale yellow. The blood drained from my face, and any feeling of excitement I had disappeared.

The immortal chuckled at my terror, his voice shifting to that of a thousand as he spoke. "Worship me, Isadora, worship your Master."

Anger and terror sparked through me as I realized whose hips my legs were wrapped around. *He* had dared to take the form of the man I love to entice me to do him reverence in another way. The terror I felt had gone, and only outrage remained. It was a great surprise to me that I felt nothing else, and courage was instilled in my heart as I yanked harder on his hair. "Come out of him, Satan! You can't tempt me with your lies."

He exhaled sharply with a death stare, yet continued to laugh. "But, my sweetest one, this is what you want."

"Don't *you* call me that." I hissed, undeterred by his smooth talk. "Get out, I banish you! In the name of God Almighty, never come to me again in any form, under any pretense!"

He hissed back, his face contorting at the mention of God. His entire body vibrated in fury as he lashed out with those serrated teeth. But before he could touch me, the dream dissolved into reality. I sat up with a quiet shriek, my eyes searching in the dimming light for him. Yet, nothing was there…nothing but stillness. A heaviness rested in my low abdomen, and it ached terribly. I awoke very…hot, bothered, and confused, but most of all, infuriated.

I am not certain if this was a dream of my own imagination or if *he* had come to me a second time to tempt me. If it was him, and so soon, he must be desperate. I wanted to scream in fury, but I held it in, breathing hard. It took me some time to control myself, and by the time I did, it was dinner. After I had splashed some cool water on myself and made myself presentable, I collected myself.

Later…

After dinner with Dumitru, being a man of few words this evening, he told me that the Count had to tend to unexpected business and would not be taking lessons tonight. When I asked about what kind of business, Dumitru said he didn't know. I could smell something was up if the Count just suddenly disappeared with no prior warning on 'business', which was the term he used to cover up all he was up to. I was still very irritated by my dream that I didn't want Dumitru to finish his sentence that he had begun this morning. Thinking I had forgotten, I could tell Mitică was relieved, but I had more important things on my mind.

Since I had a lot of time on my hands until bedtime, I went to the chapel to be alone to think. Being in the room, even if it isn't holy, gave me some comfort for my unsettled soul. The hours wore past, and I was still deep in thought, deep in prayer, deep in misery, when there were footsteps behind me. Not bothering to look back, I remained at my place, although my full attention was focused on the lurking presence.

"Uh, I-Isadora?" Mitică whispered shakily.

"What is it, Dumitru?"

"It's near midnight, shouldn't you be going to bed?" He came closer to stand next to me. "If you're waiting for the Master, he may not be back until the morning."

"I'm not waiting for him." I opened my eyes slightly, and an odd pang of sorrow entered my heart. "I just...needed to be alone."

There was movement to the side of me, and out of the corner of my eye, I saw him sit cross-legged on the cold stone floor. "Do you mind if I sit with you until you're finished?"

I was touched that he wanted to be nearby, but I still wanted to be alone with my thoughts and prayers. "Do you really want to waste your time? I know you're tired."

"I don't mind." He sighed as he settled into his place.

Sighing too, I closed my eyes again. "Very well."

We sat in silence, listening to the wind whistle against the stone. Then, out of nowhere, Dumitru whispered to me without any stutter. "Isadora, I want to be closer to you."

His words rang in my ears as they echoed through the room and into my soul. "What do you mean by 'close'?"

"I mean..." He stopped to think about it, apparently very unsure of what he really meant. "I mean to grow closer to you. To tell me things you wouldn't tell anyone else, to care for you, and to never let you be alone in this world where you don't belong."

My heart physically hurt in my chest, and I had to place my hand over it. What was the definition of all those things that he spoke of? Was it 'friend', or more than that? He had been so angry with me for nearly two weeks, now he wanted to be closer to me than ever before? I looked at Dumitru as he sat there, his eyes pleading and hoping. The black and blue injury now had a purplish hue to it in the candlelight, and it looked more painful than earlier today. Reaching out, I extended my hand. "How can you care for me so much after all you have endured because of me?"

Dumitru took it eagerly with both of his hands, and he looked down at it longingly. "It isn't hard to endure for you, my friend."

Another sharp stab in my chest came as I felt the warmth of his hands, astonished by the heat they produce. How had I forgotten how warm human beings are when they are alive? I gulped at the sensation. My fingers wrapped around his palm, the pain in my chest spreading. "You are and forever will be, my one and true friend in this hell we find ourselves. If you will be those things for me, I promise to be them for you, too."

Mitică smiled the widest smile I had ever seen on his face, his eyes bright with happiness. Getting to his knees, he embraced me, resting his head against mine. Feeling his intense body heat radiate from him, it soaked into me again, replacing the cold there with warmth.

I owe him so much more than I could ever give him. We are only human and find ourselves in a pit of serpents who bide their time to poison and devour us. The snake who deceives and tempts waits just around the next corner to do just that and rid us of our humanity. If there is one thing Dumitru and I must do is ally ourselves together, and remind ourselves what it is to live amongst the dead.

Chapter Twenty-Three

SERVITIUM AMORIS

20 August

Morning, 7 am…

Yesterday came and went, and there was no sign of the Count, and actually, no sign of anyone save Dumitru. The Romani have seemingly vanished from their work like ghosts. There is not a single trace of them having been here. It's like their footprints have been erased. I tried asking Dumitru about where they had gone, and he only confirmed that their services were no longer needed. I accepted the cryptic response.

With the Count missing along with them, however, I was starting to become rather worried. I had no idea where he was or when he'd be back. Considering all the recent events, that is, his father lurking about, I had become a ball of nerves. I had no idea if he was hurt or who knows what! All I could do was sit and wait for him to return, never knowing when he would suddenly pop up.

Last night I had gone to bed a bit late as I was hoping the Count would return to see me. Of course, he had not come by 11 pm, so leaving the barred window open a crack for the cool breeze to be let in, I went to bed. The wafting coolness felt so good after the heatwave we've suffered under for many weeks, so I fell asleep easily and stayed that way until the early morning. I think I dreamt of home and seeing my parents, but all at once, I was awake, sensing something *else* in the room with me. Panic and fury roused my dull senses, and I cursed internally that *he* had come again at this early hour. Out of the corner of my eye, I saw a dark shadow of a man move across the room, and with lightning speed, I reached for my rosary on the nightstand. I almost had it in my grasp when a familiar hand snatched my wrist.

"It is only me."

"*Christ*, Count," I swore loudly as I huffed for breath. "You can't keep doing that."

With a humph, he let go of my wrist. "Figured I was someone else, did you?"

I didn't want to answer that, so I switched the subject. Sitting up in bed and rubbing my spinning head, I asked gently. "Where have you been? I was worried."

His silence made the atmosphere in the room uneasy. "No need to worry yourself about me, sweet one."

"Well, I was worried that…" I watched as the Count came around the other side of the bed and pulled the sheets away. Gulping at his boldness, images of my illicit dreams of him materialized in my mind's eye. "What…what are —"

"I require your company." That was his only explanation. It wasn't a command, but more of a desperate plea masked with a forceful tone. "Lie with me. I must feel you."

His use of those words made my heart skip as he climbed into bed next to me. Was I dreaming again? My palms began to sweat, and that all-too-familiar heaviness manifested in my lower half. I pressed my legs together and bit my lower lip hard, contemplating whether or not I should trust myself with him. I was cut off halfway through my thought process by the Count as he laid me down and set himself on my shoulder. My beloved's arms encircled me, and he purred contentedly. I stroked his hair, feeling all the tension leave his body as I did, and I think we both felt quite content.

However, there was something very wrong with him to suddenly show up in the middle of the night, pleading to be close to me. This whole occurrence was highly irregular and out of character for him. He told me that when he is close to me, he remembers how it feels. What had happened that would make him seek me out so?

Gruffly, the Master warned. "Keep your thoughts in check, Isadora, lest you wish me to act upon them."

My entire face bloomed hot. The dark did not hide from him the erratic beat of my heart, nor did that expert nose miss that scent that came from my budding arousal. The smoothness of his voice made me *want* him to act, and it made me all the more embarrassed. "S-Sorry."

I heard the Count inhale a few times like he was smelling me, a very soft growl reverberating in his throat. I almost couldn't hear the noise, but I could definitely feel the vibrations.

As my lips touched his hair, his earthy scent entering my nose, I asked in a whisper. "What's the matter, Vlad?"

"Nothing." The Count muttered as his cold nose touched my throat. "Go to sleep."

Just as he had said those words, the world fell away, and a deep sleep came over me.

When I awoke around 6 am, just as the sun was beginning to rise, the Count had gone. The only evidence that he had been there was the messy sheets on his side of the bed. I lay there for a long while feeling the emptiness of his side and how I had so wished I could have woken up to him. When I finally began to stir and make the bed, something even stranger caught my eye. On his side, smeared against the white sheets, were splotches of freshly dried blood. Aghast and at a loss as to where they could have come from, I searched all over myself but found no place where I had been cut. If it wasn't me, had he been injured? Was that his blood? Or was it…dare I say it…someone else's?

I swallowed hard at the idea of it and quickly removed the sheets, tossing them in a pile to be washed. This whole thing with him coming to me out of nowhere, staying for a short time, and leaving more than he should behind…it's just so bizarre. If I see him later, should I ask what could have caused the blood stains? Do I really need to know the source? I can only pray that if this were someone else's blood, that they are alive. But, knowing the Count's nature as I do, they most certainly are not.

23 August

Morning…

Things have been strange these past few days, and I can't put my finger on why. Since the night he came to me, the Count has been uncharacteristically silent and moody. He keeps his emotions hidden just beneath the surface, but it is plain enough to see that he is upset about something. Many times I have tried to ask him what is bothering him, but he hasn't admitted to me his feelings.

Since the night he stayed, he has barely touched me, barely even looked at me. No matter how hard I try, I cannot seem to reach him, and it makes my heart break. And most of all, I don't understand why he's acting this way. Dumitru says he hasn't noticed the Count's drastic change in personality, but I guess the Master acts differently when he's around me. I won't relent in my devotion to him but will persist until I have some inkling of what he's hiding from me.

On an even odder note, he seems to me to have grown a little younger. He no longer looks like he's in his 40s, but late 30s now. Am I just imagining it?

I am asking myself that much too often these days.

…

As promised, this afternoon, Dumitru and I began the large undertaking of cleaning the main entrance. Opening up the magnificently grand door to its full capacity, the old, musty air was swiftly removed to let in the freshness of the mountains. It was a lovely day also, not too hot, and with a soft breeze that was to die for. So, within all the buckets we could find, we readied our soapy solutions, scrub brushes, and other cleaning equipment. By mid-morning, we began our daunting task.

In spite of the hard work, I was enjoying being able to let out some stress that had been building in me. As we worked, I kept spotting Dumitru stealing glances in my direction and watching me. I caught him doing it a few times, but I ignored it, thinking that it was just by chance that he happened to look my way. When he wasn't looking, I too would take forbidden peeks at him, regarding his thoroughly masculine features: the defined muscles of his arms and the ones hidden under his shirt. Other than those sneaky eyefuls, I went about my business and kept to myself.

We got a significant amount done by noon, and after a good lunch, we began to scrub the floor again. I was getting quite sore from the repetitive motion and had to stop to take frequent breaks. It was nearing 4 pm, and I was positively exhausted, hot, and sweating like a pig. My back was about to break, and my arms and legs shook from overexertion. Finally, I sat on the wet, sudsy floor to catch my breath and grunted out. "I don't know how much more of this I can do."

"We're almost done." He groaned from the strain and then turned to look at me with a mischievous smile on his face as he quipped. "You're not *that* tired, are you?"

I wasn't amused at that little poke, and I scowled but poked back. "Isn't it obvious? I'm practically dying over here, but you don't look any better than me."

He sat back on his calves, sticking his nose in the air at me to feign offense. "For your information, I'm not tired at all."

"Not tired?" I laughed once. "I think even I could knock you on your butt, and that's saying a lot."

He raised his eyebrows. I was all talk and no action, and he knew it. "I'd like to see you try."

I stuck my tongue out at Mitică. "Why would I want to get near you? You smell terrible."

"I *smell?*" He pouted. "Well, you smell no better."

I could only laugh at his feeble attempt at a jibe and turned away to resume scrubbing the floor. "What kind of insult was that? Go take a bath."

"Maybe you should take yours first."

I was about to retort when suddenly a bucket of cold, soapy water was dumped on my back. I shrieked so loudly I think I could have woken the dead. *"Dumitru!"*

He had buckled over in laughter at my reaction, which only made me spike with anger and irritation. Taking the scrub brush, I whipped it hard at his chest. He caught it before it made contact, still dying of laughter at my expense.

I wanted to go along with the fun, but that was pushing it a bit far. Scowling, I slapped his arms a few times, and then somehow it became a tussle. Not a real fight, of course, Dumitru wasn't putting much effort into it. When he got an opening, Mitică began to tickle my ribs, which brought me immediately and effectively down in fits of squeaky laughter. I hadn't been tickled like that in years, and in my hysterics, my ability to fight back was simply gone. Though whatever breath I was able to take in, I cried that I had surrendered.

He said something that I don't really remember, plus I was laughing so hard I couldn't think straight. But then, out of nowhere, I felt a wet heat on my lips. The sensation was startling, but I didn't need to open my eyes to know what happened. Dumitru had kissed me fervently, roughly, one of his hands going to my hair to press me harder to his mouth. I moaned in a mix of shock and gratification as his other hand went up to squeeze my breast. Instantaneously, my body reacted, growing hot in spite of the cold water. It all happened so quickly that I had no mind at all to act. Mitică was just *there*.

I'm not sure how much time passed, if it was a second or a minute, but reluctantly, he released my mouth. I dared to open my eyes to slits and stare up at him. He was breathing harder than I, his gray eyes so wide. Slowly, he let go completely and turned his back to me. He sat there breathing heavily, a hand brushed through his hair as he stared off to some point in the room.

"What was that?" My voice was barely a whisper. I wasn't mad, I was just...shocked.

"I...I don't know." He muttered back. From the sound of his voice, he was just as confused about it as I was. "I'm...sorry."

"It's...uh, fine." I began to move my limbs again from their paralysis.

"Y-You..." Dumitru cleared his throat, averting his eyes. "Didn't like it, did you?"

The question floored me. How could I answer that when my head was so high in the clouds? In fact, I liked it too much for my own good, but I couldn't tell him that. The Count, in all his affection for me, has never once touched and kissed me so passionately, so fervid, as Mitică had. It was a thing I secretly wanted, something that the Devil himself had tempted me with, and a renewed shame made my heart sink into my stomach.

I guess my silence made him draw his own conclusions. "You love *him*, don't you?"

Having it said out loud like that, by him, made me blush. "I don't know what —"

"Don't lie to me." He snapped viciously. "I saw you liked it when he kissed you."

My heart broke. "Mitică —"

"No," Dumitru hissed, his signature anger boiling to the surface as he turned back to me again. "Don't you see what he is? He is *dracul, Nesuferitu*. How can you love something that cannot love? He will only love you like...like a bee loves a flower. It takes the nectar and the pollen and goes on to the next and the next. But me...I love you like the sun loves a flower. I want to make you warm, give you life, make you grow so beautiful in the daylight. He can give you none of these things. Flowers don't grow in the dark; they die."

I was dumbfounded, again. The one thing that stood out to me in all of that, of course, was that he...loves me? I already knew that he had a fondness for me, not a 'fondness' like the Count has, but one of a deep and caring friendship. At least, I had thought it was.

I was just about to ask him to clarify what he meant when he spoke again. "You don't see what he really is. Please, do not love him. He has only brought you sorrow and pain."

I sighed and feebly responded. "He needs me —"

"For what?" He cut me off abruptly again. For wanting me to explain myself, he wasn't letting me say more than three words. "To feed off of you? That's the only use you really have in his eyes, other than sex."

Mitică's bluntness about it embarrassed me terribly, and I had to chide him. *"Dumitru!"*

"It's true, do you think I would lie to you about it?" He was completely serious, and of course, I knew he wouldn't lie to me about something like this. "I've lived with him for half my life, and I see what he does to women who fall under his spell. It never ends well."

I did not doubt that the Count has had hundreds of women in his day, and I am just one of that number. I had already figured he used them for far more than just a chew toy, but how am I so sure I won't end up like them? I'm not sure at all. "I accepted that long ago."

"Do you hear yourself?" Dumitru grabbed my upper arm, his expression growing more desperate. "Don't throw your life away for something evil that is pretending to be good."

Every word struck me straight to my soul. Is he right? Am I throwing my life away? I sat up and felt the water run from my hair and clothes. I could not for one minute believe that I'm wasting my life to help the Count, but I guess from his perspective, I am. The task that the Count has asked me for help with is a daunting one, like trying to help a blind man to see, a deaf man to hear. But, Dumitru does not know of the Count's sentiments about seeking the peace that has so long been denied him. I was not going to be the one to tell him, so after a long pause, I looked my friend straight in the eye. "Yes, I hear myself loud and clear."

His fingers tightened around my arm. "I can't believe you. Of all the people in the world, you would willingly stand by him after all he has done?"

"If not me, Mitică, then who will?"

Another pain entered his face, into his eyes, and he looked away from me. I think he understood my sentiments, but could not accept or respect them. "You're too good for him, too kind. He doesn't deserve you."

I was just about to say something when suddenly his head popped up, alert to the open door.

"Do you hear that?"

Instantly, the entire room fell silent and still, and we strained to listen to any sound. Faintly, somewhere outside and far away, I heard a woman shouting. My eyes wide, I turned to Dumitru, who turned to me at the same time. The yelling was getting louder by the second, and at once we sprang into action, our conversation dissolving.

We both slid to the door, the wet floor being extremely treacherous, and peered out. Coming over the natural stone bridge was a single woman, screaming like a banshee in Romanian. Confused as I was that a random woman would be storming the castle, I looked over to Dumitru, who was just as confused as me. All we could do was watch her half-hidden as she came up to the main gate and began to rattle on it, spitting slurs at the castle. At closer inspection, she looked like a Romani from her dress.

Despite her shrill bellowing, I could actually understand some of what she was saying. *"Monstru! Dracul!"*

There were other things she said, but I didn't comprehend them from the way she was screaming. Yet, there was one section that I understood clearly than I expected.

She screamed in broken English that her husband had been killed. Her cries were ones of bloody murder, full of rage mixed with despair.

My blood ran cold. Suddenly, it all made sense: the night the Count came to me was the day after the work on the wall had been mysteriously completed. There had been no trace of the Romani at all since. Had the Count been 'cleaning up' the witnesses to his plans? The blood on my sheets that he had left behind wasn't his, but theirs.

I grabbed Dumitru's collar. "They're *dead?!* Did you know about this?"

Mitică turned pale. "Isadora, it's not —"

I didn't want to hear what he had to say. There was no use, so I let go of him and emerged from behind the door. At the sight of me, the woman paused, but then continued her onslaught of vitriol. Again, she cried in English that her husband was dead, as if she knew that I would understand. The Romani workers knew that Romanian isn't my first language.

Dumitru tried to grab hold of me again, but being so slippery wet from soap and water, I slid easily from his grasp. "No, don't go out there!"

I tried to speak to the woman as I dared to descend the steps. I wasn't sure what the hell I was going to say to her, but I would at least try and comfort her. It felt like I was approaching a wounded wild animal.

She pointed directly at me, rage so plain on her face as she screamed in her native tongue that I am a harlot of the Devil.

I stopped dead as the woman shook the heavy metal bars and just stared at her. Her words cut me deeply, so deeply that I couldn't remember how to speak. One accusatory finger was all it took for this woman to hit the target of who I am from her perspective: guilty by association.

Suddenly, Dumitru was coming up beside me, shouting things back at her in Romanian. I'm pretty sure he was telling her not so politely to take a hike, but she did not relent, the poor woman, and began to wail in grief and anger at us. She was out for blood and revenge, and nothing we were going to say or do would stop her.

Just then, a chorus of howls ripped through the air, loud enough that I had to cover my ears. The wolves were so close, just over the ridge, yipping and yapping that they were upon their prey. Fear gripped me with that deathly sound, and every nerve and hair stood on edge as they appeared from the trees. I had never actually seen the pack before, but my God, there were dozens of them, all converging on the stone bridge. Teeth bared and all eyes trained on her, they stalked forward. I wanted to scream for her to run, but there was nowhere for her to go. She was trapped unless she chose to jump.

Distracted as I was by the scene, Dumitru suddenly grabbed me by my waist, manhandling me into his arms. Dragging me like a rag doll behind him, I fought with him to let me go. I barely caught a final glimpse of the woman, this nameless wife so consumed with grief and rage for her husband, as the wolves encircled her. When we got into the castle, Mitică yanked me around the corner, putting his hands over my ears as he pinned me against the wall.

Instead of screams, the chains that held the large doors open were released, closing the fortified defense shut. If she made any sound, I did not hear it, but I knew by the silence she was no more. A few minutes passed, I think, before Dumitru finally released me. We were both still breathing heavily, still dripping wet. He went to speak, but I put my hand up to silence him. Careful of my steps, I returned to my spot on the floor where I was nearly finished and began scrubbing again.

It was the only thing that kept me from bursting into tears, which is something I do a lot nowadays. Taking my anger, I channeled it through the brush and cleaned away the dirt. Dumitru watched me for a long time, not saying anything until he, too, went to his knees and started where he left off. This time, there was no light banter between us; there were only the sounds of the bristles of the brushes moving against the stone and grout work, and our heavy breathing.

When we had finished and had put everything away, I had no intention of eating dinner. I told Dumitru this just as I was about to go upstairs to wash, and he only nodded, then went on to change the subject. "Thank you for helping me today."

"Anytime." I had turned to ascend the stairs when I stopped and bit my lip. "And thank you for saying the things you said. Don't think they have fallen on deaf ears."

Dumitru frowned and said nothing to me.

He was about to turn away when I caught his arm. "One more thing," I couldn't bear to have him look at me like that, not after everything we've been through. "I do love the Count, that is true. I can't tell you much, but what I ask is that you let it run its course no matter what you see, or hear, or feel."

Mitică grimaced like it left a bad taste in his mouth. "And when he kills you, what will you have me do? Nothing?"

Sighing, my hand fell from his arm. "Dumitru…"

"Do my feelings mean nothing to you?" He whispered harshly, possibly afraid that someone might hear due to the late hour.

I was slightly offended that he thought me so heartless. It's because I care too much for some God-awful reason that I'm in this situation in the first place. I shot back in a low whisper. "They mean everything to me. More than you know. Don't blame the Master for this. In a way, he's only human, too."

His brow furrowed at that, so I don't think he really understood what I was saying, though I didn't expect him to. After I embraced him tightly, with a heavy and hurting heart, I ascended the steps. How is it that I'm always crying and my heart is always in so much pain? I feel such guilt, such shame, such worthlessness. Am I such a bad person for wanting to be there for both of them? Oh God, there's too much to think about, and now I must face the Count.

Later…

I remained calm during the lesson, forcing myself to forget about all that had happened today and focus on the task at hand.

After the lecture, which seems only to be a formality now, the Count commented nonchalantly. "You are hiding your emotions well tonight."

Keeping cool, I gave my usual response of faking ignorance, which always invokes men to explain themselves in one way or another. "Whatever do you mean, Count?"

The Master frowned with a tensed jaw. "You know that Dumitru has already told me of the commotion this afternoon."

Commotion. Irked by the insensitivity of the word, I shifted uncomfortably in my chair. I was silent and didn't reply.

The Count took my silence as an answer. He asked plainly. "Do you despise me for what was done to that woman and my Gypsies?"

That was the second time he has asked me if I hate him for something he has done, but I tensed. I gathered he had control of those wolves, that they were sensitive to his will and such, but he honestly must think that each bad thing he does leads people to hate him. I assume the way he ended those men's lives was by taking their blood, which is why he appears more youthful than before.

The way in which he must survive is a direct result of the suffering of others. Of course, I shook my head. "No, you know I don't. But, please, explain it to me."

The Master frowned deeply with a long sigh, then solemnly professed. "If I had not killed them, then they would have been in a far worse situation if Imogen and her group of cowards got their hands on them. They would have been tortured, so I did them an act of kindness by ending their miserable lives. For centuries, I have cared for my Gypsies by doing what is necessary, and their families are well compensated."

*My Gypsies...*I winced at the phrase. He made it sound as if the Romani are his mercenaries, at his command, they live or die. *Compensated...*like lives can be bought and paid for with money or goods. I don't need these moral dilemmas on my plate, but as I looked at him, the faraway sadness in his eyes was growing. There *was* remorse in them.

"I am no pacifist, Vlad, but I think I would have done the same thing in your place." I explained frankly. "It may seem out of character for me, but I understand why you did it. It was a necessary evil, but it shouldn't have to be, and that's what upsets me the most."

The Count lifted his eyebrows in masked surprise but answered. "'All is fair in love and war', as they say."

"Is this why you have been so distant from me?" I dared to tread on that thin ice. "You thought I'd hate you? Your withdrawal from me has been so painful."

The Count definitely didn't want to answer that, but by the immortal's cloaked expression, I knew I was correct. For the first time in quite a few days, I ventured to reach and take his hand, feeling the cool skin beneath my fingertips. He didn't withdraw or push me away, but watched my hands like a hawk as I kissed his palm. His blood-soaked hands, which have ripped men to shreds, were so gentle to me. The Count brushed against my lips with the backs of his fingers, purring softly. "Sweetest one of my heart, I never meant to cause you pain. Forgive me. I only hide things to protect you from them."

There was more he was feeling that he didn't want to reveal to me. I could hear it in his voice, see it in his face. For a man of so many faces, so many masks, even the son of the Prince of Lies cannot lie to himself about the things that hurt him the most. As his fingers passed over my lips to my cheek, I again dared to entreat him. "Moon of my days, kiss me."

I thought he would hesitate, but immediately he was out of his chair, fingers threading through my hair as he covered my mouth with desperate kisses. Those kisses, I could only guess, were the ones he had been withholding from me, fearing I would rebuke him. How I had missed them in their intensity, their ardor, despite only being denied them a few days…

If I am the harlot of the devil, then I am damned by my own devices.

Chapter Twenty-Four

Come, Hell

1 September

Morning…

Again, I write to commemorate the passing of the month. Of course, September has arrived, the dreaded month when the long-awaited ones will come. Time has passed so quickly during my stay here. Wasn't it just last week that I had gone to Bucharest and stolen the holy water? Or even yesterday, when I had discovered the Count's hidden past? Those things were so long ago in the grand scheme of my stay here, yet when I look ahead, I cannot fathom what trials await me in the coming months, or if I will see those months at all. Pessimism sure has become my cruel reality in this house, no matter how tightly I cling to optimism.

Last Monday, as I guess I should have known, the time for the Count and me to part began. I've noticed that I'm becoming later and later with each month, and I can only blame it on stress. As much as I try to relax, I subliminally remain quite anxious, even when I sleep peacefully. It's the looming darkness that shrouds this castle that makes me so. As a result, all last week I kept myself busy finishing up cleaning the floor of the hall, and even that of the chapel too. I felt much pride that I had succeeded in my conquest, and against the Lord of Darkness himself, conquered. Now the full glitter of both rooms can be viewed as they should. The castle is truly changing.

Other than that, I've been helping Dumitru with other things around the castle. I honestly thought that working with him was going to be awkward, but it really hasn't been. I don't quite understand how we are able to work well with each other after the day we — he kissed me. We are shy around each other, but that doesn't detract from our duties. Sometimes when we go out for fresh air, he walks with me arm-in-arm. The sun is still very warm, and with his constant company, it soothes the tension I feel. One day, we were finished eating dinner when suddenly his fingers, so tenderly and willingly, touched mine. I don't know what caused him to do that, but I did not pull away. The look on his face was one of longing. I think it takes a lot of courage for him to even get close to me.

On the other side of the spectrum, the Count has nearly returned to his normal self, although I haven't spoken to him in a few days. I feel such deep emptiness in my chest when we are apart, and that hollowness troubles me much.

5 September

This morning, Dumitru asked me if I would be willing to help him tidy up the main dining hall, and of course, I accepted. I had never been inside the hall before, so I was eager to explore this new part of the castle. I always guessed that somewhere in this house there is an area wear normal people would eat, but I never could find where that room would be. Certain that it had not been used in centuries, I expected the worst. And, when Dumitru led me past the main staircase and down the narrow yet elaborately decorated passage, two large doors opened up into the long banquet hall. Inside was filthy. I have never seen so much dust layered so high in any other part of the castle, with the air so stale and unbreathable.

My heart sank, but I put on a brave face.

In the center of the extended room were three tables, two long ones that ran the length of the room for the guests, and one at the head, which faced the two. These were for the master of the castle and his wife, whose chairs still stand as the main centerpieces of the room. One could almost see them entertaining their multitude of guests with colorful dishes and lively musical performances. But all of that was gone now, and the shell of life that withstood time was a poor monument to those bygone days.

And so, we began to work again, the first stages simply being to remove as much dust as possible from the place before starting the harder work. We went about our business, the hours slowly ticking by as we did. Around 11:30 am, Dumitru stepped out to make lunch while I finished up some extra things.

I was going around the edge of the hall with the broom, bringing in the dust away from the wall. Mindlessly, I did the task, not really paying attention to much else. My drifting daydreams were halted when, as I passed the mantle of a fireplace, my shirt snagged on a tooth of an open-mouthed stone dragon. The snap was what caught my attention first, and I gasped and whirled around. I was sure I had broken something, but instead, a low vibration groaned from the underside of the stone. I scurried away as I thought something was going to collapse, but to my surprise, the back wall of the fireplace let go, and a plume of dust and ancient mortar crumbled around the released opening.

I stood there for a moment, wondering if I should call for Dumitru to tell him what I found. My damned curiosity got the best of me and I cautiously drew nearer to investigate this secret passageway. It felt like something out of a movie as I heaved the thick stone door open only a few inches. Dank, moist air escaped, and it made me gag a little, but I peered into the darkness. It almost reminded me of some sort of dumbwaiter, but those certainly hadn't been invented when this castle was constructed, so why would it be hidden so secretly? Yanking open the door to get my shoulders through and to let more light in, I peeked in farther. There was only a wall and a floor on the other side, and it puzzled me that the space was simply a dead end, and there was absolutely nothing in it. What could have been the purpose of such a small trap door that leads to nowhere?

Puzzled, I slinked my upper half between the door and the inner space to feel if the stone wall was loose. As I reached forward to touch the wall, one hand on the floor to stabilize me, the wall didn't budge, no matter how hard I pushed. Then, without any warning, the floor underneath my supporting hand gave way. One moment I was on my hands and knees, the next I was plunged into darkness. The floor steeped to a sharp decline, and caught off guard as I was, by the time I had slid halfway in, was the time I realized something had happened. There was barely time to scream, for suddenly the rest of me fell headfirst into a tunnel.

As soon as I had fallen completely into blackness, the floor snapped shut behind me just as my feet were clear of the opening. I must have screamed then as I slid down a grimy shaft, my arms and legs desperately trying to grab hold of the slippery stone to catch myself. Of course, it was of no use. There was an abrupt change in the angle of this tunnel, and I hit my left shoulder and scapula hard against the rock wall. Something popped, but I had no chance to scream at that either, for I was unexpectedly in mid-air and was free-falling. I think I gasped just before I was launched by a steep downward trajectory out of the shaft and into water.

My mouth was still open, and all this foul-tasting water entered my nose and throat. In that moment of panicked disorientation, I had no idea what was up or down. When I opened my eyes to see, the water burned them, but everything was blackness anyway. By some grace of God, don't ask me how, my buoyancy bounded me back to the surface. I gasped as air and water felt like they fought for their place in my lungs. I tried to swim, but my shoulder was immobile as it radiated with an intense stabbing pain.

Any sense of bearings I had was lost as I frantically searched for some nearest thing I could hold on to. Luckily, I spotted some stairs that led into the water, and using only three of my extremities, I paddled over to them as quickly as I could. My relief was short-lived when something caught my ankle. It may have been a hand, I'm not sure, and I cried out. As hard as I could muster, I kicked at my own ankle and pulled against the force that was pulling me under. The fingernails of my right hand scraped into the grout of the stonework, locking into place. Yet, my grip was slipping.

Something primal kicked in me when I saw that the situation was growing very grim. I roared in pain and rage, and somehow my other arm managed to grab onto another stair to hoist myself upwards. The hold was weak, of course, but it was just enough to slip from the invisible hand that held my foot. My shoe was sacrificed in the struggle, but by some means, I was able to slither up the stairs to the top landing. Taking off my other shoe, I threw it into the water a distance away to distract whatever lurked beneath the black water. The water went calm as I rested there, poised for another attack, my lungs burning.

I don't think I waited long, for I heaved over and coughed up a significant amount of water and my breakfast before collapsing. Lying as still as I could with my entire body quivering, I felt my shoulder. Blood ran from skid marks as I had grazed across the rough stone, but that wasn't what hurt. There was something internal, something I couldn't pinpoint. It was beginning to swell, and any attempt to move it sent wracks of pain through me.

I didn't want to sit up, I didn't want to move, but by God, I knew I had to. Holding my shoulder using my elbow, I hauled my upper half to sit up, resisting an urge to scream bloody murder. I wasn't completely sure if my shoulder was dislocated or immobile from inflammation, but there was no doubt that something was very wrong with it. The pain was the only thing keeping me from passing out, so with gritted teeth, I shut my eyes tightly to try to calm my breathing. Noises caught my attention, and my eyes shot over to somewhere in the shadows. It sounded like a mix of whispering and growling. Who knows for certain if it was just my imagination, or if something *was* there, but I had to get out of wherever I was.

With shaking legs, I grunted to my bare feet and looked at my surroundings. I was in some kind of subterranean canal, still in the castle, but in the lower levels where I was not allowed. Looking up, I saw the shaft that I had fallen from. It almost seemed to me to be a sort of garbage shoot, though what a strange place for one to be? I had no time to ponder these things as the cavern echoed hauntingly at each drop of water and every ragged breath I would take. The water, black as ebony, danced as slight ripples broke waves over the surface and glimmered in the dim light of scattered torches. Thinking back,

I'm unsure why those torches were even lit since the area was seemingly unused.

The only thing that came to my mind was to go up because I had come down. So, following the stairs up while holding my arm, I forced my feet to keep moving, lest whatever was in the water would come back for seconds. My head spun, and my feet dragged up the stairs that seemed to lead on forever until I reached the top landing. I stumbled to my knees, half hunched over as my eyes struggled to keep focused. I think I had hit my head on something during my fall, though I was only just beginning to feel the low, dull ache and disorientation. Desperately, I cried as loud as I could for Dumitru, but my voice only echoed back to me, desperate, hollow, and empty.

Nostrils flaring, I told myself to press on, and through this imbalance, I made it back to my feet. There was no way to know exactly where I was going. At each door I passed, I tried the lock, but all were shut up tighter than a drum. Each open corridor showed signs of being unused for a significant amount of time. They seemed endless, twisting and turning in all different directions with no real indication of where one part started and another ended. I wandered through them, trying to find any stairs that led up, but could find none with doors that were unlocked.

The halls and corridors were extensive, running this way and that. My only saving grace was the torches that were lit along them, but coupled with my growing confusion, pain, and weariness, I knew I was becoming more lost the deeper I went. Worse yet, I thought the whispers I had heard in the canal were following me. There were many times when I could have sworn something was right behind me, but when I would turn, nothing would be there. In the shadows, I could feel that 'something' was watching me, surely waiting for me to wear myself out and come upon me.

The pain in my arm was growing unbearable, and I searched for something I could use as a sling. The only thing around was a flag-like tapestry, embroidered with a circular gold and crimson dragon, whose tail was brought to wrap around its neck. Strange as the piece was, I hated ruining the priceless cloth, a piece of the Count's ancient history no doubt, but it was the only thing I could find. Tying the sling around my opposite shoulder, it gave me little relief and minor support, but it was enough.

A whisper caught my attention in the corner, and a dark shadow darted from one to another. Frightened, I got up and backed out of the space and drudged on, my footsteps and ragged breaths echoing in the stillness. Surely by now, Dumitru would realize I was missing and come looking for me, but how would he ever think to look down here in this pit? A wave of despair and grief made me choke on my saliva, and I coughed. The violent contractions of my diaphragm made me lose my balance again, and I just managed to catch myself before my bad shoulder collided with the hard wall. Without my other arm's support, it shook uncontrollably from the weakness of the injured muscles and tendons. I yelped in pure agony.

Even in the dim light, I saw a shadow come over me, and when I turned to face it, nothing was there. That time, I was sure I didn't imagine it, so spitting, I growled at the nothingness before me. "Get away from me, demon! I am your Master's! You cannot touch what is his!"

My cry only reverberated down the empty hall and into the darkness. Hastily, I tried to pick myself off the wall, but did so too quickly. Dizziness made my eyes roll back into my head, and I staggered forward. It took a while to compose myself, but when I straightened, before me stood a tall mass. Distinctive horns protruded from the black mist, and those yellow eyes that haunted me glowed.

All the blood in my veins froze, and a renewed dread seeped into my bones. Just as I had seen the apparition, the shadow dissipated. Wildly I looked around, but Satan had gone. Was he ever there in the first place? Terror replaced pain, and somehow, I was able to run a short distance from the scene. However, when I stopped from exhaustion, I realized I had ended up near the entrance to the canal again. I was going in circles. Unceasing, perpetual circles. How did I not notice it? Someone was playing a trick on my senses, be it my own brain or something else. From a distance away, I heard another whisper and then another one that sounded angrier. Sweat dripped from my face, and I swore the air was growing colder around me, and a distinct scent of brimstone and death drifted past my nose.

I backed into a corner, petrified. I was wearing the Count's silver crucifix, and letting go of my injured arm, I gripped it firmly in my hand. "Christ, I beg you, do not forsake me."

There was a growl next to my ear, so close I could feel that hot breath on my face. I screamed this time and then took off running down the hall. Behind me, I heard my name being whispered, then in front of me, to the side, closing in at every angle. I swear I had heard those dreaded voices before, and I was afraid.

Since my body could not run much longer, I had to stop, my knees finally giving out again. I barely had time to recover before wisps of fine black smoke silently encompassed me. And from them, those thousand voices whispered in my ear. "Isadora, why run? You are so weak, so tired, and in so much pain."

I stared down those glinting, menacing eyes. "Begone from me!"

Lucifer chuckled at my feeble command. "Come now, sweet one. We can make you stronger. We can give you all you desire. Only say that you will worship us, and we will deliver you from this place. You and our son will live for eternity together as his consort."

"Oh? The stakes of your game have risen?" I could feel my body growing heavier with his presence so close. "Now you're offering me titles? Power? You disgust me."

"We can offer you more than that." He continued to tempt, his voice penetrating my ears. "We can give you Dumitru, too, since you desire him. Just imagine it: the three of you locked in a passionate embrace. What ecstasy it will bring you."

In my weakness, just for a moment, my mind did consider the idea. Having the two of them inside me was…tempting. But a frog formed in my throat, and anger welled in my chest. "You leave him out of this. This is you and me, bastard. You only dare to come to me when I'm injured and alone. Be gone, Satan, I curse you back to Hell!"

He hissed in my face, similar to the last time, as he bared his jagged teeth, threatening me. "You think yourself so holy, so impervious to us, yet you stand here powerless as your God ignores your pleas. If He does listen, why doesn't He send His angels to defend you? The answer is quite simple: He has no care for you. From the moment you embraced our son, you sold yourself to us."

Then, just as he had appeared, he had gone. All the black mist had dissipated, and only I remained in the semi-darkness. To the deepest reaches of my soul, I felt shaken by those words, which echoed and echoed in my head. Have I sunk so far into Hell? I knew

I couldn't sit around, so I blinked a few times for my vision to clear. Getting to my feet, I had to force my shaking legs to carry me on. As I did, I noticed that I could not feel my arm as it hung limp in the sling. It was completely numb and useless. Pushing my disturbing encounter aside, I concentrated as best I could on how I could get to the surface. There was only one way I knew to go: the opposite direction that I had come.

Strangely, my mind was suddenly clearer, and my breathing steadied. Despite being still beyond terrified at my grim situation, there was a need for action that kicked into gear. If I couldn't find a way to get to the surface from the interior of the castle, I had to find an exterior way. So, I set off down darkened corridors that I knew must end somewhere.

The scene soon began to change as I went along, for the passage became narrow, but there was more evidence of centuries-old human activity. There were the remnants of weapons, covered with a thick layer of dust, that looked as though they had been abandoned and never recovered. I had to be close to some kind of exit, and sure enough, before me opened up and I found myself in a wide room. I stopped.

To one side, there were long, thin slits of light coming through the hewn rock, just enough to see through. There was a door, this one old and unsealed, and light was coming from the other side. Without hesitation, I pulled it open with one jerk of my good arm, and the aged wood around the lock splintered into pieces. On the other side, I was met with a precipice that went hundreds of feet straight down into the valley below. What I thought had been a door was actually a boarded-up lookout post that oversaw the entire river and mountain range. The view stretched for miles, and though I didn't have a fear of heights before, I think I developed one then.

Staring out onto the range, I saw that some amount of time had passed since I had fallen into this hell. The sun was blazing red and was quite low in the sky. As in my dream, I knew when the night came, *he* would come again. In the hours I had been there, I had found no other exit. It was do or die, and as God as my witness, I'd rather have tried and failed than stayed in the bowels of this pit until the Count would come for me…if he would come for me at all.

Stepping out onto the cold stone, my toes instinctively wrapped around the ledge. Clinging to the cracks in the outer stone with one hand, I slowly made my way along the ridge, telling myself not to look down. If I only focused on placing my feet in the right places and gripping the right stones, I would be fine. I rounded a corner, seeing the courtyard off into the distance. I was happy to see it. Praying that my sweaty palm wouldn't cause me to slip, I put one foot in front of the other, remaining as calm as I could be. Strong gusts of wind came running past me, ruffling my now half-dried clothes.

Ahead of me was a small balcony, and I was able to reach it safely by some grace of God. When I looked inside the window, I didn't recognize the room, though it was hard to tell due to the thick cobwebs and dust clouding the glass pane. There was no more ledge past that balcony, so I had no choice but to break the delicate centuries-old glass. I cut my elbow in the process, but I couldn't feel the gash.

I stumbled into the room, nearly falling on my face. When I looked up to see where the hell I was, I was glad that I was certainly not on the lower floors anymore. However, my relief was cut short when I realized that I found myself among dozens of stone sarcophagi. It was the Count's family crypt, and I had disturbed and vandalized it. Worse yet, since I was in the crypt, the door was surely locked.

Cursing, I waded my way through the numerous coffins of the family of the House of Drăculeşti, men and women, even children. They were all filed neatly in rows, their effigies bearing their images. Men wore their brilliant armor, women in their finest dresses, as they rested in dust and ashes. There were so many of them, and all had their special place. It struck me that these were all people that the Count must have known at one time or another, and they were all dead. Generation after generation, all dead, and only he remains to tell their tale. There were faded images of angels flying around heavenly clouds on the walls and ceiling. Normally, I would have been transfixed by them, but I had no time.

As I got closer to the door, I noticed that one sarcophagus appeared different from all the rest. On the wall behind it was written DRACULA, but there were no dates or descriptions to accompany the sarcophagus. Not only did it appear to be of newly hewed stone, but the seal on the lid had been broken. Knowing I shouldn't, I dared to draw closer to investigate. On the surface was the image of a man, dressed in military splendor, holding a sword. Around him was dragon iconography, similar to the symbol that was on my make-shift sling. Many of the men had some sort of dragon emblem engraved on their coffins, but this one was so unusual.

Taking great care, I peered through the crack. The body within wore a purple overcoat, although it was hard to see exactly. Taking a closer look, a familiar smell entered my nose, an earthy musk that I loved. I held my breath as my eyes landed on the face of the man within, except it was not decayed nor corrupted in any fashion, but the recognizable face was very much intact. The Count's eyes were wide open, staring unseeingly into nothingness, and were glazed over in a blackened red. His lips were stained red with blood, his white fangs protruding from them.

Shocked, I gasped in horror.

Then, in response to me, he blinked, his eyes normal again as they turned to me. Terror-stricken that I had been caught, I backed away from the coffin as the lid was pulled back by an invisible force. The Count sat up from his grave, his feral features evaporating. Seeing him like that made me shudder. I was afraid of him, and I backed right into another sarcophagus. I watched him as he looked at me, but instead of being angry, his face contorted in confusion as he examined my disheveled state. "Isadora? What — how did you get in here?"

I don't know what it was, but in my state, I think the sight had frightened me too much. I had forgotten how to speak, and my poor heart felt so worn, I swore at that moment that it stopped beating. With my body feeling thoroughly numb, I sank against the cold stone and was about to faint. Just as I was about it hit the floor, a pair of arms caught me as I was nearing unconsciousness.

"Isadora…" I heard the Count call. "What happened to you? Can you hear me?"

I opened my eyes to slits, my vision blurred and grainy. The only thing I saw was the violet overcoat the Count wore, studded with brilliant amethyst.

I tried to make some protest for him not to touch me, but as his embrace tightened, I could suddenly feel my shoulder again. I cried out in pain, but also anger that he had hurt me. The throbbing brought me back to my senses, although my vision still wasn't very good. My good arm grasped onto the bad, cradling it against me as I whimpered like a wounded animal.

"Isadora, my dearest," the Count continued in an anguished tone, a hand came up to my face to hold it. "Please look at me. Do not go to sleep."

I heard him, but it was hard to comply, so I simply didn't.

At my lack of response to him, he frowned and whispered into my ear. "Feel no pain."

And I didn't. He lifted me most gently in his arms, the crypt's door opening. The sight of the sky was so beautiful that I felt like crying and tried in vain to reach for it. Half in delirium, I rested my head against his jeweled shoulder.

"Dumitru!" He yelled over me, his voice booming loudly into my ears. I wanted to flinch, but I couldn't.

That was the last thing I really remember until suddenly I was being sat on the servant's table in the kitchen. Dumitru was in front of me, holding me upright as I lay heavily against him. The Count was behind me, and I could feel his fingers working my shoulder. "Mitică?"

"Yes, it's me." His voice broke, and I saw that he was crying.

"I called for you," I confessed, our faces so close as I gazed into his eyes, reddened and glassy. "But you didn't hear me."

"Hold her." The Count commanded.

I don't think Dumitru needed to be asked twice, for he held on to me tightly, his cheek pressing against mine. Massive hands held my limp arm and shoulder, and then with one expert pull, a loud pop rang out. I gasped although I felt nothing, and my body jolted in anticipation of pain, although none was manifested. I still whined, digging my face down into Dumitru's neck, finally feeling some semblance of safety. They were talking about something as I went in and out of consciousness, fingers working methodically on stabilizing my arm and treating my wounds. Eventually, I just passed out completely, no longer caring whether I lived or died.

Among Thorns

5/6 September

When I came back to the land of the living, my head was pounding like a hammer on a nail. Groaning, I tried to move but was rather paralyzed. It was a struggle to open my eyes as they fought to remain closed, but when I was finally able to rouse myself, I was in my room. Not for one second had I forgotten in my sleep all that had happened, so wearily I looked to my left shoulder. Well-bandaged and in a real sling, it rested carefully on pillows.

"Sweet one?" A dulcet voice whispered in my right ear.

Straining, I forced my eyes to look over at the Count, who was lying next to me. His face was a blessing to see so clearly. "Vlad…"

"How are you feeling?"

Thinking about how I felt took quite some time. "Like I was hit by a bus."

With his index finger, he traced my cheek. "You might as well have been. Your shoulder was dislocated and you have a severe concussion."

I wasn't surprised by either. I groped for the Master's hand, eager for some contact as I admitted to him. "He came to me again, I think."

"*He?*" The Master repeated, turning to face me with flashing eyes. "You are sure?"

Sighing, I could only shrug with one shoulder. "I think I was hallucinating."

Without any hesitation, he believed every word that I was telling him. Of course, I was skeptical, but my compromised perceptions didn't bother him. "Tell me what he said."

I didn't want to say it because it's far too embarrassing. I think the Count would only be insulted if he knew those forbidden things that I desire. Yet, he was waiting for a truthful answer, and I would rather the Count hear it from me than from his devious father. Clearing my throat, I answered with the 'approximate' truth. "He only told me of the things he would give me if I were to worship him. Of course, I was not impressed."

"This is the second time he has come to you?" The Count questioned, his face betraying his inner concern.

I shook my head slightly. "No, the third…"

"*Third?*" The Master spat. "And you did not tell me?"

His anger made me sink down into the pillows as I cowered. "I wasn't sure if it was him."

"You know if it is him." With his large hand, he laid it on my good shoulder as the Count ordered. "You must tell me what he said."

Remembering the dream made my skin grow hot, and I had to turn away from him. How could I tell the man who sees me as so pure that I wanted something so impure? "Please don't make me."

"How can I help you when you are not truthful with me?" Those eyes bore into my skull, and even without seeing them, I could feel them pressing me to confess.

But I could not, not like this. Not in the dark with him so close. "Some things are better left unsaid."

"Isadora…" He warned in a grave tone. "Do you fear I will judge you for the things with which he has tempted you?"

I didn't answer, but by that, I was just saying yes.

"He tempted me, too, when I was at my lowest. He blinded me by what I wanted the most, so I know." His anger subsided only a little, and he took my chin to turn my face back to his. "I care for you deeply, my darling, do not leave me in the dark about this. How can I protect and save you from repeating my mistakes when you hide from me his temptations?"

How could I say no to something like that? It was a guilt trip, I know, but in my weakened state, I was no match for him. Tears brimmed in my eyes, and my love kissed my cheek and lips to comfort me. The Count rested his forehead against mine and waited. Taking in a deep breath, I bit my lip, and I mentioned vague details about those two incidents, leaving out Dumitru's involvement in the recent one. Still, the Master was quite upset by it all, so I don't think he realized I was telling him only half of the truth. When I explained the sugar-coated version of how his father tried to seduce me in the Count's own form, he growled chillingly. A heaviness weighed the atmosphere as his ire bloomed. I could feel he wanted to grab possessively onto me, but knowing if he did, he would have broken me in two.

"Vlad…" I wasn't going to take any chances of having his anger directed at me, so I comfortingly caressed his clenched hand. "Please don't be angry with me."

"I am not angry with you." The Count dug his face into the pillow to hide from me the demon sprouting from within. "What have you done? Nothing. Nothing but persevere when I have failed you."

Never once did I think he had failed me or let me down. On the contrary, he has been the one who is always there to keep me afloat. "You have never failed me, beloved."

But, no soothing words were going to calm him. "I should have known you were in trouble, but I did not. Time and time again, I have been inhibited in some fashion to get to you, and Dumitru has been consistently useless. No matter what either of us does, it is never enough in the end."

"I'm sorry —"

"Stop apologizing." He growled, raising his head only slightly, and he eyed me sharply. "It is not as if you go out looking for trouble. No matter if you played some fault in it or not, each time you face the sinister alone when it should be me to face it for you. And, despite confronting the root of all evil in this world, you never waver in your loyalty to me. What place do I have alongside you when I cannot even repay a drop of the blood you have shed for me in my service? I cannot even repay the love you have for me. Do you not see the failure this makes me?"

"You are no failure." Again, I had no idea why he felt like that. It was true each time I was confronted with dire situations, somehow, I managed to slip from death's greedy clutches. There was more to his words than just reflecting on his shortcomings in protecting me, but I dared not think what they could be in that archaic mind of his. He is a man who was always expected to excel in all things, to be the victor in all battles, and the supreme defender of those whom he calls his. The Count demands perfection in himself when he is the most imperfect of all beings who roam this earth. I hated that he felt so worthless about this, and I gripped his hand tighter. "And you don't need to repay me for anything. You're the one who always saves my life when I get myself into trouble. I owe you more than I could ever give, could ever repay."

The Count sat up a bit on his elbow and then kissed me, placing his palm against my cheek so that I couldn't pull away. He saw the tears budding around my eyes, and it caused his face to soften despite a knitted brow. "It is because you are the brightest piece of me that I cannot stand by and let you be alone. Your love for me hurts my heart, Isadora, and I will be damned further into Hell if I let you slip from me because of my own inability to watch over you."

Emotion welled in my chest with those words, and since he was so close, I raised my head to catch his lips, forgetting all about my shoulder. I deepened the kiss and daringly slid my tongue between his sharp incisors, finally feeling their deadliness firsthand. At that, he tensed and wanted to pull away, but he quickly gave in to my advances and pressed heavily onto my lips as his tongue danced against mine. I desperately wished I was able to use both hands to weave them into his hair so he couldn't let go of me. But he did, and I whimpered when he pulled away, both of us panting like dogs.

Gazing straight into those glistening crimson orbs, I asked. "Why do I love you too much for my own good? I've never felt this before for anyone. Is that good or bad?"

The Master purred, his eyes focusing suddenly on my neck, then down my chest. He dared to stare so openly, so consciously at me, and it was frightening. When he blinked, his eyes were back on mine as he answered honestly. "I think a bit of both."

I think I agree with him on that, and I grinned although I felt a bit sad. I was very glad to have him beside me through these trials. No matter what he feels he is deficient in, I think he is a pillar of strength for Dumitru and me. He is our Master, but also our provider, protector, and source of lifetimes of wisdom. So, I kissed him again, savoring the feel of him against me and how comforting the chill of death can be before drifting back to sleep.

Sometime later…

When I woke the next time, however, I had taken a turn for the worse. What had woken me was the heat burning my skin from the inside, sweat that made my nightclothes stick to me, and a tremendous swaying nausea forced my dizzy brain to full alertness. The Count was gone, and honestly, I didn't care one way or another. Swearing loudly, I had to use every ounce of my willpower to get to my feet. The ankle that I had kicked relentlessly strained under my own weight, and with it, I knew I wasn't going to make it to the bathroom in time to upchuck my stomach. Dumping the contents of the wastebasket on the floor, I threw up whatever was in my stomach from yesterday. That is, nothing, but my stomach still forced it up.

Instantly, I felt better but was incredibly weak. Somehow, I managed to get to the bathroom and take my temperature, which read near critical. I swore again. As I cleaned myself and the trash bin up, I wondered what could have caused this sudden change. Who knows what variety of bacteria I was exposed to down in that place? The only thing I could think of was when I accidentally swallowed that inky water, or perhaps some other infection.

Muttering obscenities, I tried to think of what to do next, but it was difficult to sort out any plan with the entire room spinning. I wanted to take a shower but lacked one, and two working arms to wash. I was burning up, so I had to choose the bath. However, with only one arm and an immobile shoulder, I couldn't take my clothes off. Finally, I had had enough and got in the tub with just my nightgown on.

It felt like I was going into an ice bath despite the water being lukewarm, but I was too weak to care. So, bandages and all, I stewed in the 'chilly' water, my breathing a bit too raspy. For certain, I wasn't hungry or thirsty, just exhausted as dull pain radiated throughout me. Slowly, I began to feel the cool effects, and my body relaxed. I was only there for a few minutes when I heard a knock at the door, startling me from my stupor.

"Why are you out of bed?"

I could barely turn my head to the door, which was behind me, but I saw the Count's figure there, his eyes averted. I sighed frustratingly, remembering that in my haste, I had forgotten to close the door all the way. My voice faltered when I spoke. "W-What're you doing here?"

"What are you doing *there*? I leave for five minutes, and you make a mess." He countered, his eyes shifting slightly to me. "No matter, your fever is still young, if you are not careful, you could be doing more harm than good."

Groaning, I rested my head against the lip of the tub as I sank further down. There was little energy, little need, to answer him, so I just didn't. Suddenly, he was standing next to the side of the tub, casting a shadow over me. A part of me wanted to chastise him for entering, the other part didn't care at all what he saw. I knew things were pretty bad if I didn't even bother to cover myself, although I was still clothed.

The Count said nothing as he knelt, watching my half-submerged figure shiver. "What is your temperature?"

"Not good," I breathed out hoarsely.

He blinked yet kept quite calm as he reached forward to stroke my knotted hair. "You must drink something."

The thought made my stomach turn over again. Be it water, broth, or blood, whatever he was thinking of, I wanted nothing to do with it. I knew I was only going to vomit it up. "I'm not thirsty."

"I do not care whether you are or are not, sweet one." He kept his voice so sweet, his touch so comforting in spite of my stubbornness. "All creatures must drink to live."

That statement irked me, and I glared at him. Sure, he was right, but I didn't care to be told what to do. If I knew cunning words to throw at him, I would have thrown them, but I just looked away, defeated.

Hesitantly, the Master spoke again. "There is an easier way to end your suffering."

"*No.*" I spat, although it came out as a breathy whisper. "I can deal with this myself."

It was true, it's not like my situation was out of my control…yet. I was not fading away from this world; in fact, I was very much alive in it. All those times before I had been at Death's door, he had brought me back from it, but this I had to work out myself. Sometimes the easy way out isn't the road one should choose, and I wouldn't choose it even if it is my last choice. Not again. Besides, the illness is a result of something natural, and my injuries were caused by accidents. They were not the result of supernatural beings manipulating the clock that counts down to my death.

If I offended the Count, he made no outward display of it, although he looked more disappointed than anything else, as if he wanted to say something to try to sway my opinion. The Count's hand dipped into the water as he sighed. "All I ask is that you depend on me."

The Master was sincere, that was obvious, but I was surprised that he had given up so easily. Has he come to respect my wishes? Doubtful. But oddly, his words reminded me of something Dumitru had said to me so long ago in Câmpulung, as we sat in that café. Something about how I should 'trust in someone other than my God for once in my life', and that the Count and he are here for me always.

"I have always," I had to take in a breath to say each word, and with a shaking hand, grasped his fingers that were dipped into the water. "But how long do you think you can keep giving me your lifeblood before you really defile me?"

His face went static, emotionless. By that, I knew I had hit the mark. I know that he knows I'm right, for how could I be wrong? The blood is the life, and the absence of it is death. If I were to let him give me it to excess, where will those lines in the sand that separate us be? They would be blurred, and I would become as he is to be damned to earthly hell. My purpose here in helping him would have been for naught, and I would become a thing that is evil incarnate. The Master continued to stare at me. "It will never get to that point."

Is he so sure? How can he be when he can't see the future, nor can he predict how my body will react when his blood overruns my own? Without a doubt, he is versed in how to handle these cases, being the father of so many, but that doesn't make it right for me. There was no use arguing over something like this because neither of us will ever submit. So, I stared back at him. "I will hold you to that promise."

13 September

Morning...

I have not written in some time, mostly due to my illness and my inability to stay awake for more than a few hours at a time. Finally, today I feel well enough to get up and write about my experiences this past week. With the fever, I'm having a hard time remembering all of them, but to make very sporadic and nonsensical stories short, the Count has been constantly at my side. At night, when he was awake and I was asleep, I think he rarely left my bedside. Even during the day, he would return frequently to check up on me. Of course, I would be either in between brief periods of consciousness or sleep.

The one person that I haven't seen is Dumitru. All this time that I have been shut away in my room, he has not come to visit me once. Quite frequently I have asked the Count how he is, but he always replies that he is well and busy readying the castle for our 'guests'. I have missed Mitică terribly, and it wounds me that he has not bothered once to ask how I am. When he was in dire straits after Petros attacked him, I was there every day for him. For saying that he 'loves' me...I shouldn't say it. There must be a rational explanation for everything, and I don't want to jump to any conclusions.

Afternoon...

When the Count left to find some rest, I took the opportunity to sneak from my rooms to find Mitică. Prompted mostly by the fact that I couldn't stop thinking about him since I wrote about him this morning, I made my way down to the main floor. Being just after lunch, I knew he would be in the kitchen, and that's where I found him. When I entered, Dumitru was sitting at the servant's table, staring out the small window as the light shined through from the midday sun. There was the thick scent of baking pastry dough in the air. He was lost in thought as he usually is when he cooks, so I sat on one of the steps to watch him. "What are you making? It smells delicious."

Immediately, Dumitru jumped and whirled to face me. His usually emotionless features morphed into one of relieved sadness mixed with joy, and he clamored to his feet. Mitică was on me in a second, his strong arms wrapping around my neck to embrace me. I was shocked at his reaction, although I was glad to see him too. With my good arm, I encircled his shoulder. I guess he did miss me a lot.

He didn't say anything and only rocked back and forth as he held me. Dumitru rested his lips against my cheek and gave me long, drawn-out kisses, which quickly reached my lips. He didn't relent when I feebly tried to separate us. Surely the Count was watching even in his sleep, and as much as I secretly enjoy Mitică's touch, I couldn't let it get both of us in trouble. When I finally caught a breath, I was barely able to protest before he cut me off.

"Let me, please, let me," Mitică pleaded between kisses as he pushed his weight into me. With my shoulder still quite sore, there was no way I could push against him, even if I wanted to. His hands cupped my cheeks as he desperately sought my lips. "I don't care what happens. Let me."

My face was growing hotter with every kiss as I felt the heat of his breath, his lips, and saliva on me. However enticing, I kept pulling away. "Mitică, please stop. He'll see —"

"I don't give a damn," Dumitru growled, those gray eyes red with tears. "I've been in Hell since he took you away from me."

"Dumitru," I begged him. "Stop. He'll see."

"Let him see." His fervor only increased. One thing that I have learned about Mitică during my stay here is that when he feels, his emotions manifest themselves tenfold. "Maybe I want him to see. Maybe I want him to know."

"What good would it do?" I pressed back, my voice was a harsh, hissing whisper.

Dumitru knew exactly what he was doing, I know, but I think he really didn't care. For a week, he had been sitting on these emotions that always had threatened to break the surface of that cool composure. In return, he chastised me. "You don't understand. I had my heart ripped from my chest when he said I couldn't see you. When the food I made was returned uneaten and he would tell me nothing. I deserve to show you how I feel after all I've been through."

My brow knitted as I frowned. "Mit—"

He cut me off with another passionate kiss that sent me for a loop. His lips trailed down my jaw, where he stopped, his eyes returning to mine. Those two gray orbs, which remind me of Athena's from their renowned intensity, were set ablaze. "My lily among thorns, how I missed you, how I love you."

I was utterly dumbfounded, flabbergasted, and that familiar stabbing pain in my heart tore it in two. It burst into a million pieces, and I could only gawk with my mouth open like an idiot at him. I almost forgot how to speak, and if I were standing, my knees would have grown weak. "Mitică..."

His eyes flicked down to my lips again, the desire to kiss me reflected in them. There was a painful yearning that was etched on his face, knowing that he shouldn't continue. Mitică's fingers touched my cheek and, so gently, traced them over my parted lips. He was mesmerized by them and was caught up in an inner struggle to stop himself or prolong this compromising position.

That hidden temptation that the Evil One had offered me came to my mind's eye, and I felt my chest constrict as I watched him. In that fleeting moment, I imagined him subduing me and taking me right there and then, and those forbidden delights made my skin prickle with anticipation. In fear of the repercussions, I sighed a shaky breath and warned him. "Please, he considers me his, and I don't want you to feel his fury. For both of our sakes, Mitică, please, don't do it."

"You tell me to have my feelings, but don't act on them?" He scoffed with a grimace at the pain his own words gave him, but his tone stayed earnest. "Isadora, what I feel is real; what he feels is nothing. What I told you before will remain true, and you will see it one day."

I had to sigh again. "And one day, you will see my reasoning." The sides of Mitică's mouth dipped, and his eyes drifted to my injured arm, then back up to me. I expected him to contort in some way about my bull-headedness, but he didn't. He was silent for quite a while, then changed the subject by the clearing of his throat. Mitică looked very sad when he said, "I'm sorry I didn't hear you call for me."

I was touched that he would apologize, although it wasn't his fault in the slightest. "You wouldn't have heard me anyway. Besides, it was my fault, as it always is. Though, why is there a garbage shoot in the dining hall? Was that customary back then?"

Dumitru went awkwardly quiet for a long second. "It was not just used for garbage…"

I pursed my lips, swallowing hard. The unspoken meaning passed between us, and immediately, I changed the subject. "Anyway, what are you making?"

Once again, he wanted to say something but didn't. So, he stood and began to explain to me that he was making *cornulete cu gem*, a pastry he thought I'd be able to stomach. I was grateful for his consideration and eager to have something sugary. While we waited for the pastries to cool, we sat and talked about this and that. Mostly both sides of the story of what happened the day I went missing. Turns out Dumitru had tried to look for me, but when he couldn't, he sought the Master for help. However, Mitică had been unable to rouse him from his death-like sleep, which was unusual.

I didn't say anything to Dumitru about it, but I know that the Devil must have played a major role in my 'adventure'. The Count said himself that he had no clue something had happened and was surely under some influence that caused him to remain asleep at such a time. If this is the truth, then Old Nick *did* come to tempt me for a third time. Elaborately staged, unnecessarily complicated, it placed me in a delicate position where I was at his mercy. He toyed with my mind, played with me like a puppet, anticipating that I would lose my way in that darkness and give in. What had kept me going when I was down there? Pure survival? Pure adrenaline? For now, I'm not sure of the answer.

Chapter Twenty-Six

LOCUS AMOENUS

19 September

Morning, 11 am...

Ten days. Ten days left until the day of reckoning when the deathless ones will come. I have to admit that I am feeling uneasy, tense, and most of all, anxious. Of course, the Count doesn't tell me of his plans, so I am completely in the dark. What will happen on the 29th when they arrive at this castle? I have no clue. There is no telling what the Master has up his sleeve. I wish I had access to his study so I could see the books he reads, the old papers he pores over, to get some inkling of what is going to happen. Of course, if I did that, I would be putting everyone in danger. Keeping me in the dark is the only solution, although it's terrible for my nerves.

For the past week, with the time approaching, I stare out my windows that overlook the courtyard and watch for movement.

Perhaps I would catch a glimpse of a spy peeking from behind a tree or something out of the ordinary, but obviously, I never see anything. The trees are too dense, and my human eyes are terribly insufficient to see among them. Yet, I'd sit and watch the clouds go by or read some whimsical poetry to take my mind to another place, far from here, where there is no danger. Some land, maybe past a mountain range, where the sun never sets and the grass is always green, the air always sweet. That's where I'd want to be.

But I am here, doomed to be a willful prisoner.

In other news that I ought to report, my shoulder has healed considerably, and I don't have to wear it in a sling anymore. Although I'm still very cautious of using it, it has come back good as new by some miracle. My cuts and bruises have all faded as if they had never existed. I am grateful that in such a short amount of time, I have made a full recovery, although I'm…suspicious of it. It was almost too easy, too quick, and I suspect that the Master has something to do with it. He would deny it if ever accused, but I know he must have given me his blood at some point or another. There can be no other explanation. For now, I will play dumb until I can find more evidence, which is unlikely.

Autumn will be here in a couple of days. The sun will begin to set earlier, and the chill of winter will come upon these mountains. All the life that the sun had brought in spring will die, and the land will be thrown into a deep sleep. There is beauty and life in autumn and winter, but in my case, I don't know if I'll ever see a flower bloom again. Call it melodramatic, pessimistic, but I can't help but wonder. Farewell, summer. To those golden days and ebony nights, *adieu*.

20 September

Afternoon…

Day nine. This morning, I was sitting in the library, going through some old books about this and that, half dozing from boredom. Dumitru was leaving to go into town, and as usual, I was not allowed to accompany him. I hate being excluded from such things, but I understand why: it was far too dangerous for me, especially to leave the confines of the castle walls. As much as I wanted to put my mind off the subject, it still bothers me. Just before he left, Mitică popped his head in to tell me he was leaving. After I had wished him a safe journey, he told me he wouldn't be back for a few hours, so I shouldn't worry. Of course, that wouldn't stop me from worrying, and then he disappeared.

I took in the long and deep sigh as I flipped a yellowed page over. With positively nothing to do, all I could do was sit around. I was half daydreaming about nothing when suddenly the Count was at the door, dressed in outing clothes. "Miss Kane, are you available?"

I was surprised to see him there, dressed as such in the middle of the day. Puzzled by his random appearance and that he had addressed me so formally, I wondered what could be wrong. "Count, is everything alright?"

"All is well, sweet one." The Master approached me as if he floated on air, which by now didn't even make me bat an eye. "I'm simply asking if you are available."

Looking down at my pile of books to read, I had plenty of time to waste since I was just wasting it to begin with. "Well, yes, I'm available. But, shouldn't you be asleep?"

"I should," the Count closed the book which I had been reading. "But I thought you would be interested in a walk."

"A walk?" My brow furrowed.

"Indeed, a walk." He beamed, just like his old self when I first met him. "It is the last day of summer, is it not? I thought it would be good to get some fresh air before we are unable."

I was suspicious of him, breaking his own rules for 'a walk'. At first, he barely allowed me to go outside, but now he wants to go hiking? I was hesitant, thinking this could be some kind of joke. "You're allowing me to go beyond the wall?"

The Count smiled, although he saw my reluctance, those white teeth glistening. "Yes. Dumitru would not approve, and I would never hear the end of it, which is why he is away, and we are...alone."

My cheeks reddened at his insinuation, and I cleared my throat. "And leave the castle? Would that be wise?"

"There is no one for many kilometers who would dare to come near here." His fingers grazed my heated cheeks as they went into my hair. "I will be with you, so please, accept."

Again, the Count made it hard to refuse him, so I didn't bother trying. "I'll change."

He was very pleased with that, and I left to change into my version of outing clothes: that is, jeans and a t-shirt. With my dwindling wardrobe, I didn't really have much else with me that would be appropriate.

Anyway, I met the Count at the stairs and we descended the steps, leaving the castle and the main gate behind us. Today was partly cloudy after yesterday's rain, but the sun shone intermittently. Never before had I been outside the castle on foot, and it was a whole different experience. The Master took my arm, eyeing me under his sunglasses, as we walked over the stone bridge, the wind whipped rather ferociously until we got to the other side. I dared not look down over the edge of the bridge, especially with my new fear of heights, and clutched onto him a bit too much.

Once we entered the wooded area, the wind died down, and a cool breeze wove between the trees and down the road we walked. Before, I had only passed these century-old natural monuments in the car and never got to appreciate their size and majesty. The largest ones stood tall and proud, their lofty canopies swaying gently in the high air currents. The thick scent of earth and foliage wafted past us as we meandered farther and farther into the never-ending forest. The name Transylvania, this region in which we find ourselves, from the Latin meaning 'beyond the forest'. I had never appreciated the meaning until today. It's most appropriate.

"You seem to be enjoying yourself." The Count spoke up, breaking the silence.

"Of course I am," I gave him a wide smile as I leaned into his arm. "But why did you want to bring me out here now?"

"Perhaps I wanted some time alone with you." The Count mused, leaning against me, too.

I scoffed, waving my hand to shoo away his silliness. "You spent nearly two weeks alone with me, yet you want more? Though I admit I wasn't much of a conversationalist."

The Master hummed. "True, however, you were quite busy fighting for your life."

Scoffing again, I shrugged off his seriousness. "I wasn't dying."

"You say so, but I have seen men die from much less."

Saying that made me fall very silent. In his many years, I knew he wasn't lying when he said that. Had I really been so close to death again that he had worried that much about me? I didn't want to think about it.

My speechlessness made him stop, his arm clasping tighter onto mine. "Forgive me if I have upset you."

"You haven't." I lied as I pulled him along to keep walking. "Let's talk about other things."

"Such as?"

"Well, I know you can't tell me much, but —"

"I will not speak to you about *them*." The Master cut me off and shut me down, accurately interpreting my half-spoken question. He wasn't angry or annoyed by it, though, but simply refused to tell me anything about his children's arrival. "It is not your place to know those details, as I have told you, it is for your own safety."

"Right..." I conceded, my head hanging to watch our feet. "Sorry..."

"There is no reason to be sorry." The Count patted my hand to reassure me. "I know your intentions are pure, my dear, but they are...misguided."

So, I let the subject go, and I decided to focus more on my surroundings than the looming future. For once, the song of the birds was *around* me, not far in the distance. Glancing upwards, I saw the little ones dart from tree to tree high above our heads, tweeting their pleasant chimes to each other. The road began to dip and decline the farther we walked along, and over the steep cliff, I saw that the Argeş River was much closer. I knew the road followed the river for many miles in both directions, but I had never seen it long enough to take a good look. Between the trees, I watched it flow steadily along, babbling over rocks and foaming against the shore.

We descended further, and the river rose to meet us. The cliff was not so steep, and it was easily accessible if one were careful. Biting my lip, I asked. "Count, may I go see the river?"

His jaw tensed as he looked down at me. The Count was obviously reluctant to give me an answer, but surprisingly said. "Just for a moment —"

The Master hadn't even finished his sentence before I had let go of his arm and headed into the woods. Lured by the river's gentle sound, I used each tree trunk for balance, hopping, skipping, and jumping down to the bank. No trees grew along the edge for many yards, so it was an easy walk to the waterside. Surveying the area, I watched the sunlight sparkle off the rippling water currents. Parts of it were blinding, but the best part was the clarity of the water. For billions of years, the Argeş must have been cutting through the rock, leaving the impressive split between mountain ridges today. From this angle, they looked so high up, unclimbable and unreachable. On this side, the castle stood out against the patches of azure sky, so small on the outcropping.

The Count came up beside me, putting his arm in mine again. "Are you pleased?"

"I'd say you have prime real estate." I beamed as I turned to face him, but his face was not so happy. So, in my effort to conquer the awkward moment, I kept talking. "You and I should have done this more often during the summer. I think it would have done both of us some good."

"Perhaps." He muttered, then pulled on my arm. "Come, let us continue our walk."

I didn't budge. "Can't we stay just a bit longer?"

"Isadora…"

"Please?"

The Count frowned again, unwilling to allow me. He, after a moment's consideration, conceded. "Just for a moment…"

Instantly, I slid my arm out from his again, and I trotted to the very edge of the water, peering down at my reflection. I bent down to swish the water back and forth before reaching in to pick up a stone. As I did, I glanced back at the Count, who stood just at the edge of the shadows that the trees cast, watching me intently. He was rigid and tense as he stared, which made me uncomfortable. Tossing the stone back into the water, I began to take off my shoes and socks.

"Isadora —"

"Yeah, yeah," I waved him away, then went to roll up my pants. "I know I'll be careful."

"That is not —"

"I said I'll be careful," I began to wade into the freezing water, squeaking from the chill. "It's not even deep."

"Isadora, you will come back this instant!" The Count's voice boomed in a deathly seriousness. He was suddenly at the extreme edge of the bank, but didn't dare to go farther into the water. I was still in arm's reach, but something was stopping him from reaching out to grab me. The Master's eyes darted around the water's surface, watching the running water intensely with reddening eyes. Against the reflective surface, he cast no reflection. No image of his presence was even detectable.

It dawned on me that there was something about the flow of the water that prevented him from reaching me. I obeyed him all the same, and in one step, I got back up onto the shore.

Before I could say anything, he sighed in relief as he grasped onto my forearm. "We can stay here for a while longer, but do not go into the water. It is very dangerous."

Genuinely curious, I inquired. "Why is it dangerous?"

"Do not question me on this, young one," the Count scolded me like a child as his voice deepened. "I know what is under every rock and behind every tree on this land. Trust me."

Living here for centuries, I had no doubt he could go through it blindfolded if he wanted to. I only nodded. "I trust you."

With that, he let me go. "Do not wander too far."

I nodded again and watched him return to his place in the shade to keep an eye on me. Disappointed as I was that I wasn't allowed to go in the water, I knew there were plenty of other things to explore here. Venturing up the bank, I searched for other interesting things, feeling the grass and soil between my toes.

Ahead of me was a patch of those pink, yellow, and purple wildflowers I had spotted farther up the mountain. Picking a variety of them, I returned to sit near the Count under the shade of a large tree whose branches dipped low toward the water. Listening to the flow of the river, we sat in silence as I weaved the stems together to form a chain, which eventually became a colorful crown. I had piles of those wildflowers and pieces of greenery to add in. The Count observed my fingers the entire time as I methodically added one flower at a time. That 'while longer' he had promised, turned into a half hour, then to a full hour. I took my time so that we could stay for as long as possible, and it paid off as I was adding all the finishing touches.

"Who taught you to make those?" The Master finally asked after I had finished.

I laughed nervously. "The Internet…"

He laughed once, leaning forward a bit to examine the completed work. "Put it on."

My eyebrow cocked at his excited insistence, so I undid my high ponytail and placed the crown on my head. "Well, how do I look?"

The Count reached forward to touch my hair, which is almost down to my elbows in length these days. "Like a river nymph…" That distinctive purr rippled in the air as his fingers wound themselves in my tresses. "Perhaps you shall drag me to your watery abode to keep me as your prisoner? Being an immortal goddess, who am I to resist?"

I blushed as I watched his hands. His smooth talk always gets me going. It never ceases to amaze me how he knows exactly what to say and how to say it. "You flatter me, Count."

He hummed, taking off his sunglasses. "Do I?"

Raising my eyebrows, I blushed at his subtle invitation. Slowly, I got to my knees and inched closer to him as he rested against the trunk of a willow tree. Daringly, I swung my leg over his hips to straddle him, bringing my flower-stained fingers to his cheek. As the heel of my hand passed over his mouth, his lips caught it, laying kisses along my wrist. His hands came to my waist to press me against his lower half, and my breath shook in my lungs. Eyelids growing heavy, I planted languid kisses on his cheek. "Moon of my days…"

There wasn't anything more I could say when his mouth found mine, and his hands went to my back to arch me even closer. My arms wrapped around his neck as our mouths danced together, each one seeking another and another. The heart that beats in my chest pounded rhythmically against my ribs, wanting to break free from its prison.

"When they come," he whispered like a secret in my ear as his kisses made it to my jaw. "We cannot show our feelings to each other, for it will be a weakness for them to exploit."

My heart broke as he said that. "I will miss you, beloved."

Hastily, his lips went to my neck and down further still to my collar. "No matter how far away I may seem, sweet one, be mindful of this day and how I touch you now and remember."

"I promise," I leaned back to give him access to go further down my chest, which he gladly accepted. "Vlad, what do you feel for me?"

"What I feel…" The Master tugged on my sleeve to pull it down.

"Normally I wouldn't ask you but…" I instinctively bore my bare shoulder to him. Dew was forming on my skin from the fire burning in my veins. "I hope it isn't too much to tell me."

Another finger pulled the collar of my shirt down to my cleavage, although his lips dared not travel there. "You know you are more precious to me, the sun of my nights, and I wish you could stay in this moment with me for eternity, just as you are."

"Is this what your heart tells you?" Beneath my eyelashes, I watched his reaction.

"If my heart could tell the secrets it whispers about you, they would fill a bottomless ocean, the vastest sky." Another round of kisses pecked the hollow of my throat. "Be comforted, my sweet one, and know my feelings have not waned, but only waxed greater for you."

"Do you think they will wax enough to become a full moon?" I moaned softly when his hand gently caressed my breast. "I fear in the darkness they will only wane, and I will lose sight of you."

His massive, cool palms came to my cheeks, those deep brown eyes radiating warmth into mine. The Count purred again, his thumbs brushing over my cheeks. "Each moment I spend with you is a moment that my chains that bind me become weaker, my heart is freer, my body lighter. A woman with such power over a devil as that is heaven-sent, is she not? How can I ever deny her my love, even when it is against everything that I am to give it?"

I kissed his forehead. He had come so far in just a few months to tell me that much. Or maybe I'm fooling myself and reading too much into those few sentences. I have to take all I can get, so I found whatever small victory I could attain in them. "When the day comes when you are ready to have me, I will not deny you. I could never deny you anything, my love, even if it's my life. It is yours to do with as you will."

The Count brought his hands down my back to have me lie against his chest. "Then use it to live, to stand with me against those who seek our ruin, to fight the darkness that threatens to consume us for daring to dare to love."

"I will." I held onto him so tightly, his sturdy body supporting mine as it always does. He may think he is weak, but to me, he is the strongest man I have ever known. "I will."

The Master let me rest against him for the longest time, to the point where I was almost dozing off. The fresh mountain air had made me so sleepy, but just before I did fade to sleep, he woke me and said we should be going. I wanted to stay there forever against him, but reluctantly got to my feet and put my shoes and socks back on. After I had gotten them on and went to stand, I took the flower crown from my head and laid it gently into the water, and watched it flow away.

...

As the night settled over the land, the Count and I had been sitting in the library conversing about the books I had left out. We had sat there for some time when suddenly he took my hand and told me he had something to show me. Again, suspicious, I stood to follow him. I had no idea where we were going and tried my best to hide my uneasiness. The Master led me to a hidden flight of stairs down the hall, and we ascended them. Up and up he led me, past the third floor, the fourth, and into unknown territory I had never dared to travel before. I was becoming terribly nervous the higher we went, and I wanted to ask him if we could turn back. But holding my hand softly, so tiny in his large ones, he would look back at me, smiling. It was a comfort, but I knew he sensed my apprehensiveness, and so he guided me on.

Without the sunlight, the corridors and stairwells were frightening. Long wispy cobwebs waved as phantoms from the ceiling, and as we went along, he would reach his hand into nothingness to push the webs away. There were times I couldn't see anything, and it took a lot to resist a whimper.

Sometimes there would be a candle or two which would burst into flame as we'd approach, but as soon as we were out of range, it would die away. I clung to his side as he led me onwards in the dark.

"We are almost there, darling." He comforted me when I began to slow my pace. "Trust me, nothing will harm you here."

I swear we must have been at the very top of the castle before we stopped at a heavy door. Taking an ancient key from his pocket, the Count unlocked it, and the thing creaked open. Cool air flooded into the hall, and he whisked me outside. As I had guessed, we were on the roof of the mighty fortress, hundreds of feet up from the valley below. The air currents flowed around us, and it was rather chilly so high up.

There was no moon out, so the space was only lit by the stars that shone so clearly. The clouds of the afternoon had passed, and with no light pollution for miles, the stars could be seen crisper than I had ever seen before. Like paint from a brush, the Milky Way was stretched from one part of the sky to another, the murky grays and pinks were blended to create a heavenly vision of the cosmos.

My mouth dropped open, forgetting all about my previous anxiety. "You are full of surprises for me today, Count. Thank you for showing me this."

He didn't respond but led me to one more area of the roof where he gestured for me to sit on the floor. I did, and he sat next to me so that we both stared up at the night sky in silence. After a moment, the Count drew me to him and laid me against his chest. Due to the slight chill, I huddled into his side, although I received no warmth from him. I felt so comfortable there next to him, that scent of musky earth soothing my senses. I could feel his muscular figure beneath me, so unshakeable. My eyelids were growing heavy the longer we sat there, yet I kept them open to enjoy the view, but also to soak up every second left I had alone with him. The Master's hands went to my hair again, smoothing it back.

A flickering stream of light shot across the sky and was gone as quickly as it came. "Oh, a shooting star! Count, make a wish."

"A wish? For what?"

"For whatever you want." I urged him. "Hurry before it wears off."

Perhaps he didn't care for the childishness of wishing on a shooting star, maybe it was too cliché, but his mouth formed a scowl. Yet, he still took a few seconds to think of something, even if it was just to amuse me. "I wish —"

"Don't say it out loud or else it won't come true." I shushed. "If it ever does come true, you must tell me, okay?"

The Master grinned. "You will be the first to know, sweet one."

I reveled in the Master's closeness, dozing at his side. I find it ironic that if we were as intimate now as we were when I had first come to this place, it would have led down paths of no return. This day had been spent with undemanding caresses, sweet words, and sincere confessions. We had moments where we could have dove into that deep water, but didn't. I think that before, if I had straddled him as I did, he would not have hesitated to go the rest of the way. The Master's progress in understanding, or remembering, what human relations are, has been slow but fruitful.

...

It's nearly midnight now, and Dumitru just got back. I saw him walk in, so at least he is well. If I weren't so tired, I would go down to see him, but surely all can wait until tomorrow.

Chapter Twenty-Seven
FEET TO THE FIRE

21 September
Autumn Equinox
Noon…

Day eight. Being as tired as I was, I slept in a little later than I usually do. Even then, it was hard to get out of bed and face the day. It was raining cats and dogs outside, and a solemn gloom was cast over the entire mountain valley, so different from yesterday. When I stared at the ink-stained sky, I wondered if yesterday had been a dream. At the same time, I knew it was real, but that reality had slapped me back in the middle of my situation to suffer.

When I had gotten ready for the day, I had just finished making the bed when there was an unusual knock at the door. I didn't even have time to answer before Mitică called. "Isadora, come quickly, the Master summons you."

A chill ran through me, and I opened the door, fearing the worst. "What is it?"

"Don't ask me," Dumitru shook his head, although I could see that he was disturbed by something. "Come, it's urgent."

Without hesitation, I followed behind him, my half-sleepy brain struggling to comprehend what was happening. I dared not assume anything, but at the same time, I assumed the worst. Holding my breath, we made it down to the Count's quarters and entered his reception room. As we approached the Count's office, the door was already open, and I could see him pacing back and forth within. At the sight of me, he motioned for me to come in, not saying a word. I did, and the door was closed behind me. Not by Mitică, but by some unknown force.

"What is it?" I asked again, trying to keep my voice calm.

The Master looked worn and tired, that vein on the side of his forehead pulsing. "Yesterday, Dumitru retrieved the post, and you received many letters." He pointed to a pile on his desk. "You must forgive me, I try not to make a habit of opening one's personal correspondence anymore, but this time I found it necessary."

He handed me the very top letter on the pile, and I took it with shaking hands. Nothing about the letter seemed unusual except for the sender's information in the corner: the Romanian Ministry of Administration and Interior, Office of Immigration. I nearly ripped the letter open, despite it being already opened, and read the contents in English. I read it so fast I had to go back and read it again. The world fell away, and I could only see the black and white letters on the page. My hands began to shake as I looked up at him. "This can't be right! I've done nothing to be deported!"

A deep scowl formed on his mouth, his eyes narrowing. "There are also more letters from your company, they say your teaching license has been suspended, and your contract with them has been terminated...not only with me but also your position there."

I stared at him like a deer in the headlights, unable to even begin to fathom what he was saying. The Count handed me the opened letters, and I had to sit down to read them. It was just as he had said: I have been fired for unspecified 'inappropriate conduct', 'violating terms of the contract', and for 'other egregious acts that border on criminal in their nature'. The Romanian government, as I understand it, was contacted to revoke my visa, and I had until 18 September to leave Romania of my own accord. These letters were postmarked 4 September, and I was just receiving them now. I had no idea what to feel or think, and I slumped into the chair as I stared at the pile of letters. I held my ruin in my own hands, and I had to shut off the emotions welling in my chest. "Six years of university, gone in seconds..."

"They do not specify what you did to deserve this." The Master ranted, putting a hand through his hair. "Nothing in any contract was violated."

He went on about something else, but I wasn't paying any attention to him. My denial was sinking in, yet morphed into despair, and I rested my head in my hands. When the room went quiet after his long streams of muddled words, I stood and placed the letters on his desk. Clearing my throat, my voice broke. "I suppose...I should pack."

"You *suppose?*" The Count spat, a snarl laced between his words. "Do you not see what this is? This is Imogen —"

"Don't you think I know?" I cut him off in a fit, my low-lying anger blooming in a flash. "But what can I do now? I'm here illegally, I have no choice but to leave."

Dismissively he waved me away with a scoff. "It matters not to me if you are."

"I can't disobey the law —"

"I am the law," the Count slammed his fist down on his desk, the ancient wood splintering at the hard impact. He was becoming that thing that he hides, I could see it on his face. "And I *forbid* you to leave."

Tensing at the violent act and his thundering anger, I paused before I dared to speak again. Slowly, measuredly, I opposed him. "You were the law, once."

At that, his nostrils flared, and his stare gave me the evil eye. In an instant, he had closed in around me, invading my space as his righteous anger grew. "You think I have no influence in this modern government, young one? Just who do you think I am?"

My emotions dissipated to mostly fright, but I tried to stand my ground. "I have no doubt you do, but surely I will face severe repercussions if I stay here any longer —"

"And when you leave, you will be committing suicide. Those radicals will be upon you like wolves upon their wounded prey. Is that what you want?" The Count cut me off, his face inches away from my own as he growled.

"You know I don't!" I yelled it in frustration at him. Didn't he remember I was there when *they* made me cut myself open to send a message? Sure, the Master has friends in high places, but how can I really depend on what they can do? This is on my permanent record. My reputation is ruined. "Don't you think I know what this means for me? How can I stay? I don't have any options."

"Surely that is better than losing your life!" He barked, his hands going to my shoulders to shake me lightly.

I sighed. Of course, he was right on that: to leave was to give up more than just my livelihood; it would be my life as well. As much as I didn't want to leave, with what choice was I left? "Perhaps, but now my hand is forced for me. My life is ruined, and I must go and pick up the pieces. All I've worked for is gone, Vlad, can't you see that?"

He exhaled sharply as he grimaced. "You would bend at this slight inconvenience?"

"I'm *not* bending," I defended, but I honestly couldn't think of what exactly I *was* doing. Was I giving in just like that? I told the Count I would never leave, but how can I stay in Romania illegally? "I'm...I'm..."

"You *are* bending." He finished the sentence for me in a low voice, more stern than angry. "They are using your modern world's laws against you, knowing you must obey or suffer for the rest of your life. To me, these governments are weak things, easily manipulated when pressured in the right places. Let me apply that pressure, and *they* will bend in the other direction, I promise you this."

I thought about what he said with a furrowed brow. "So, what will you have me do?"

The ancient Prince frowned at my defeat and brushed some stray hair behind my ear. "Become a dual citizen, that will at least allow you to stay. We can worry about your credentials after that."

"But that process takes months," my shoulders slouched at the thought of waiting six or more months just for a piece of paper.

"And they won't accept me when the decision to deport me has already been made."

"They will accept you. You have my word." He said it quite confidently.

My brow furrowed further, and I had to look away. "And what will you use to achieve that? Bribery, extortion, blackmail? I can't condone any of these for my sake."

The Count cupped my cheek. "Then let it not be for your sake, but for mine."

I couldn't let him bear the brunt of this for me; it wasn't right. He had already given me so much already, how could I ask for more? From jewels to sanctuary, from allowing me full access to parts of his castle to saving my life, the Master has given me all without any hesitation. I couldn't bear to ask him to do anymore. "Vlad —"

"Woman," the Count took my chin and forced me to face him one-on-one. "You have no say in this. My word is final."

I didn't have anything to say to that, for what could I say at all to contest him? Lowering my gaze again, I turned from him as those tears I had been holding back surfaced. Swallowing hard to try and quell the raging storm in my chest, I spoke as evenly as I could manage. "Of course, what other choice do I have?"

"None." The Master straightened, his shoulders squaring. From the corner of my eye, he did so with the air of regal bearing as if he were proclaiming an edict. "I will do all that I can. Please, return to your room and take time to compose yourself. There are letters from your family. Find comfort in them."

He handed me the pile, and I took it from him. The ones from my family were unopened, but I had no will in my heart to read them, but still, I held the letters against my chest and thanked him. With that, I left his study.

Dumitru had been waiting in the hall for me, pacing back and forth anxiously. At the sight of the tears streaming down my face, he didn't hesitate to embrace me, and I couldn't help but return the gesture. His warmth against me was more welcome than I knew I needed. Mitică's expression when he pulled away was one of anguish, probably matching my own. We said nothing to each other. He must have already known the situation.

Taking my arm, Dumitru led me back up the stairs to my sitting room. I didn't want him to go because I needed the heat of his human soul to keep me from diving into the pit of cold despair, but there was no way he could stay…not with the Master's eyes always watching. When he sat me down in my chair, he whispered softly, asking if I wanted something to eat. Of course, I wasn't hungry at all and shook my head, but he insisted and said he would return soon. Yet, I couldn't let go of his hand, and I think neither could he let go of mine.

Staring down at the letters on my lap, I set them aside on the table and lay back to try and clear my head. In the gloominess of the day that choked out the light of the sun, I sat crying silently in the murky dark. There was no strength in my lungs, but only raspy breaths between my waves of despair. That despair, mixed with denial, became helpless anger that I could not find a way to express. I sat there, crying and gripping the arms of the chair, staring into nothingness. My body felt nothing but a numbing cold.

When Mitică returned with sweetcakes, he said that the Master bade him go on another round of errands and that he wouldn't be back for a few hours. Even though he didn't say for what purpose those errands were, I have no doubt they are the first stage in the Count's quest to extort the Romanian government to give me dual citizenship. I told him to be careful and to return to me as soon as he could. Just before he left, Dumitru gave me a subtle kiss on my hair that was masked by a hug goodbye.

After he had gone, I couldn't bring myself to eat the food he had brought. Any other time, I would have found it quite appetizing, but now there was no purpose to eat. At a moment of rashness, something that under any normal circumstances I wouldn't do, I went to the hidden place where I keep the brandy. Opening the newest little bottle that Dumitru had smuggled into the castle for me, I shot down a good quarter of it before I stopped. I had no care if the Master saw what I had done through his supernatural sight. Then sat in the chair at my desk, watching the rain fall against the window. I took a few more shots of it straight before I finally replaced the cap and hid it once again.

It's hard to think of what I was feeling then, for the warmth that I so needed spread in me to every corner of my body, and I slouched very ungracefully in the chair, just thinking...and thinking. Another great cosmic shift in seasons, another tragedy of some sort. When the Winter Solstice comes, will it too bring with it sadness and pain? Better yet, will I even live long enough to see it? The future is so unknown. It is impossible to predict the coming minute. All I can do is live in the now, in the present, listening to the rain, as the sky and I weep for the passing of time.

24 September

Day five. For the past few days, it's been hard to sit down and write about anything, although now I have no choice but to recount the days leading up to this one. The Count, as is his fashion, has been a bit distant from me since our tiny spat. He still speaks to me and gives me affection, but there is something that he isn't telling me. He speaks of things that are too general, and even more so, leaves me in the dark to wonder about my fate. I hate being so helpless, so blind to everything, and it is leaving me bitter.

Mitică, on the other hand, has been the greatest source of comfort. When he has free time, he is always at my side, even if we just sit in silence. He has even tried to cheer me up, and although I do feel happier when he is around, once he leaves, I go back to being silent. With these few days of deep reflection, I am feeling much better than I did. I am getting back to my old self, but it's hard with so many other things on my mind.

One of these things, which I must mention here, is that I am...late for my monthly time. I can only attribute it to the stress and distress I am feeling, and I think the Count has noticed. Embarrassing as it is, I've observed that in the evening times he is hesitant to enter a room I am in before he sniffs the air. Of course, finding nothing to be 'repulsed' by, he acts as if nothing is wrong. With the children's approach coming so soon, I pray that I don't have one at all until they leave. And that is, of course, impossible.

But, I digress.

Yesterday, randomly, the Count told me that we were leaving for Bucharest early this morning and that I should dress professionally. I found it very odd that we would be going to the capital on a Sunday when a majority of the businesses would be closed, but I said nothing about it. We left around 6 am, all three of us taking the long trek south into the vast forests. We were silent for the entire ride, and luckily, I had brought a book of Tennyson's poems to keep me company. Many times, I had seen the Count looking at me from under his sunglasses, and I would give him small smiles in return.

When we were about two hours into our trip, the Count suddenly put his hand in mine, our fingers curling together. I was surprised he would openly do this with Mitică nearby, but I squeezed his hand back. He was looking so sad, although it was shrouded by his dark glasses. Frowning, I brought the back of his hand to my lips to kiss it, then mouthed an 'I love you'. The Master placed his other hand on mine.

We got to Bucharest around 10 am, and after some driving around, we drove into a parking lot of a courthouse. I was incredibly confused and asked the Master. "Shouldn't we be going to the Office of Immigration or something?"

"We have business here first." The Count merely answered and got out of the car as Dumitru opened the door for him, and then for me.

Something wasn't right as the Master took my arm and led me to the back entrance, which was already unlocked. Inside, the place was deserted. Of course, I know nothing about the way the Romanian government takes care of its business, but I knew we shouldn't have been there.

Slowing my steps, I hesitated to go in further. "Count?"

"Fear not, Miss Kane." He reassured me with a smile.

Suddenly, from around a corner came a man dressed to the nines in a suit and tie. At the sight of the Count, he spoke jovially in Romanian as he approached and bowed at the waist to us. I was only catching a few words here and there since he spoke so quickly. The Count said something, then gestured to me. The man smiled brightly and bowed his head again, saying something with such enthusiasm that I could only smile and bow my head in return.

The man, whom I could only assume was some official in the court system, motioned us to follow him down a hall. All the meanwhile, he chatted back and forth casually with the Count, which made me only more nervous as to what illegal dealings I was willingly getting myself into.

When we entered his office, which I immediately realized wasn't an office at all but a finely decorated room, my wariness spiked. With the lights off and the blinds shut, the space was cast in an eerie semi-darkness, making its true purpose a mystery to me. The set-up of the room was strange, with only a single desk and chair at its center. There was an open folder with papers in it on that desk, but there was no way that I could read upside-down in the gloom. I shied into the Count's side, wanting to plead with him to leave me out of this. Yet, I knew if I protested in front of this official, it would reflect badly on him.

My heart was pounding as the man got behind the desk and cleared his throat, and asked the Count his name, to which he responded with his alias title. He then turned to me and asked me the same question, which I answered. I was perturbed as to why he would ask both of us our names again, and also why there were no chairs for us to sit.

We stood there in front of him in the dim room as the man then began to rattle off this series of long and formal-sounding sentences that were nearly impossible for me to understand. I was beginning to panic and cursed my lack of proper understanding of the language. Straining to catch those words I did understand, it made it harder for me to focus on the others, and I'd lose my place. I felt the Count squeeze his arm around mine when he saw my anxiety.

I looked up at him, eyes pleading for him to tell me what was going on, but he only responded in reference to a question that the official had asked. *"Da."* Yes.

Then the man said something else to me and waited for me to answer, but I didn't understand him.

"Say 'yes'." The Master prompted.

"Da?"

Then, the official smiled, turning the folder around to present it to us, and he handed a pen to the Count. Without checking what he was signing, the Master placed his signature at the bottom and handed the pen to me. Trying to go with the flow of things, I took it from him and bent down to examine the document. At the very top, it said in fine letters under the Romanian title 'Certificate of Marriage'. I froze, the world spinning away as my eyes pleaded for him to explain. He only reassured me with a nod, encouraging me to sign.

My eyes returned to the document, and I gulped. I didn't understand how this could be, how he could even consider doing this. He told me he could not marry because marriage is sacred, yet on the contract rested his signature. I was so confused, not only about his involvement in this, but also because I was not ready to be married.

"Isadora?" The Count's smooth voice caught me off guard.

I didn't look back at him, and despite my mind racing in panic, I signed my name. Handing the pen back to the official, I turned to face my husband. Before I could say anything, the other man piped up and showered us with a barrage of congratulations. I only stared straight at the Count.

"*Doamnă* Negrescu," the official caught my attention, and I actually turned to him in reference to that strange name. He gave me another folder, which within was my new passport and other identification, all with my new name and title. My nationality said 'Romanian' and I felt my stomach roll over. The two men exchanged some words and even a handshake, but I stared at the girl in the photograph. It was my recent passport photo, but it was not me.

The Count took my arm again and led me from the room, and the door was shut behind us. I was too lost in thought and shock to notice that the official had disappeared.

We were walking to the back exit when suddenly a word came out of my mouth. "Why?"

"Because you may legally stay here." He kept walking with his head held high. "You are Romanian now and, most of all, you are mine."

I tugged on his arm for him to stop. "But you said marriage is sacred."

The Master did stop and peered down at me from his glasses. "Civil wedding services are different. They are not under the law of God, but the law of man."

I scoffed at his lame excuse and tried to pull my hand out of his grasp. "Since when do you care about the law of man?"

"It can be useful…" His voice faded out, but then he cleared his throat. "Come, we must go."

My feet stayed put, anchored in their place. "You…you didn't even ask me."

The Count sighed, his shoulders falling. "You would not have said yes."

"Because you do not love me!" I tugged hard on his arm, but he did not answer. There was no way he couldn't know I was right. My nails dug into his light coat demandingly. "This was only for convenience!"

"If you say to protect you twice over is convenient, then yes. I will go to any lengths to do so." Out of his pocket, he produced a ring, and taking my hand, slid it onto my finger. "For now, under the law, you are bound to me, who is bound to this land, which is now your land. Isadora Kane is dead. Only *Doamna* Isadora Dracula stands before me now, my wife."

I stared at the ancient ring still in denial and could only repeat in a whisper. *"Wife?"*

"And I am your husband." The Count clasped my hand in his and placed it over his heart, which does not beat. "Foremost of all mortal women, deliverer, surely you are not so displeased with this? I have given you myself as a gift, sweetest one."

"But..."

Shushing me lightly, he kissed me. "Please tell me you love me, and never cease in saying it."

"You know I love you," my breath hitched as his lips fluttered down my neck. "But I'm not sure if this was the right thing to do."

In that empty lobby, he pressed me against the wall, his mouth eagerly seeking to taste every inch of skin that was visible on my chest. "Right or not, what is done is done. You will see the benefit of it in time, my beloved, I assure you of this."

My eyebrows knitted together as a hand went to my behind, then dragged down to lift my right knee to his hip. His touches were so different; never before would he dare to do that, especially not in a public place. Struggling to stay afloat and not be drawn in by his sensual touch, I continued. "Tell me one thing, Count."

"Anything." He muttered, going back up my throat.

Taking his face, I forced him to look at me straight on. "For whom did you do this? For me, or you?

The Master kissed me again, his tongue licking my lips. "For us."

For us...

If he had asked me to marry him under any other circumstances, and if he loved me, I would have said yes. I am not ungrateful that he would kindly marry me to keep me safe with him, but the reasons behind that are what troubles me the most. Do I view this as a rash decision? Yes, but it was his decision that I had no real choice but to accept. What if I had flat-out rejected him in front of that government official? It wouldn't have gone well for all three of us. To save my love's face and my own, and in the confusion of that heated moment, I had no choice. I may come to regret it one day, but for now, I must live with what we have done.

On our drive back, I kept thinking about that poor Romani woman who had come to the gates to seek revenge for her husband's death. She was right all along that I am the devil's harlot, even in death, I can hear her scream it, see her point at me. I didn't touch Tennyson's poems on the way back, nor could I look Dumitru in the eye when he stared back knowingly from the rearview mirror. I could only stare at the documents I had been given and study the photo of the woman whose name of Dracula I bear.

Chapter Twenty-Eight
ZERO HOUR

28 September

Afternoon…

Day one. I have been…hesitant to write of anything since we three returned that afternoon from Bucharest. In one day, my life has turned 180 degrees, and I don't know who I am anymore. I've been in a state of limbo for four days, stuck in a constant stream of never-ending thoughts about things that have happened and things to come. Adjusting to this new life, this new identity, will take months for me to become accustomed to. As far as I know, I'm still an American teacher on assignment in Eastern Europe, not a…well, not sure what I am…a Countess? That sounds so weird to say. I don't know for certain. I can only assume that a Count must have a Countess? But the Count isn't really a count. I give up…

That night of the 24th, when night fell, I fully expected the Count to take me to his bed to seal the contract between us. Yet, after we had spent some time together discussing what it meant to be of the House of Drăculeşti, he sent me to my own bed to sleep. As much as I was relieved, it troubled me all the same. I am his wife, whom he half-tricked into marrying him, yet who willingly wrote her name on the contract, and yet who he still treats as 'Miss Kane'...his friend, his beloved one. And for the three days since, he has not forced or coerced me to consummate our marriage. The Master has kept a respectful distance despite showering me with more affection than ever before. The next day, he gave me silk dresses of the traditional boyar and Byzantine style of all different colors and designs, all intricately embroidered with lush beading and brocade. The day after that, fine lace veils with beaded edging, because apparently, I am to cover my hair in the presence of other men.

Yesterday, the Count gave me a multitude of jewels: pearls, sapphires, rubies, opals, emeralds, all set in gold and silver in spectacular arrangements that dazzle the eye. All of the ancient pieces passed down from his ancestors; these family relics from multiple branches, now all bestowed upon me. I didn't want to accept any of these gifts because they are all too beautiful, too expensive for me, but to refuse them is an insult. Overnight, literally, I have become the official mistress of this house and wealthier than I could have ever conceive. For centuries since his fall, and centuries before, he and his family have accumulated wealth from all corners of Europe, Asia, and the Middle East, and now it belongs to both of us. At least, that's what the Count told me.

I don't want any of it, really, but to be his teacher. But that, too, has been nullified since I have no license to teach, so now I must rely on his income...whatever he gives me.

All the same, the worst plight that I have had to endure has been my relationship with Mitică. He has been extremely distant from me, and when he does speak to me, he only calls me by a title. I loathe that he does because I just want to be called by my name, not some title I've never earned...or deserve. A couple of nights ago, I managed to get him alone to talk with him about it, but he shied away from me.

I felt a desperation well in my chest as I pleaded with him. "Whatever happened to 'we don't give a damn about what the Count says'?"

His frown deepened. "It's different now. You're married."

"So? We're still friends —"

"Married women don't have 'friends' who are men...not here." Mitică cut me off and made a greater distance between us.

I snatched his arm and pulled him back, embracing him without any reservations. "This marriage was for convenience, nothing more. Yes, I love him, and he cares for me, but he only did it so I can stay in the country. He had to trick me into it because he knew I wouldn't have accepted. Now I must play the part, especially in front of *them*. I know you must feel very hurt by this, but please know I still need you, Mitică, more than you may realize. Without you, I'm lost —"

"Stop." He hissed angrily as he pushed back. "Don't make this harder for me."

"Don't make this harder for *me*." I wouldn't let go of him, I couldn't let him go like this. "Will you abandon me simply because I signed a piece of paper? Now? When they are coming soon to try and turn this house upside-down?"

He still half-heartedly tried to remove himself from my hold. "It's more than just a piece of paper, and you know it. You both are one now, and who am I to divide one back into two?"

"You think —" I stopped, my face and chest burning. "The Master has not...consummated it."

Dumitru's eyes narrowed quizzically at the unfamiliar word.

"It means..." I bit my lip but put my mouth to his ear to whisper the definition.

Mitică's eyes widened and he looked down at me in bewilderment. *"Never?"*

I nodded. "Not once..."

Brow furrowed, I saw the wheels in his head turn as his eyes drifted off in thought, then snapped back to mine. "The Master has something planned if he has you in his hands, but does not touch you."

"He does..." I confirmed it vaguely. "And I feel he will not for some time. So please, play the part with me, but still be my friend."

Dumitru was reluctant, his jaw tensing as he considered what I said. "You will tell me if things change?"

"You know I will, my dearest friend." I wriggled my way into his arms, and after a second, he finally embraced me.

That conversation happened yesterday afternoon, and it has been a singular comfort. This is all so much for me, in one week, I lost and regained so much, all because of one man. Oh, how my heart aches to go back to those simple days when I had no clue what the Count is. Now things are so complicated, and I have changed more than I dare to admit even to myself.

Evening...

On this last night of our peace, the Count and I sat lounging in my sitting room. I wore a turquoise blue *sarafan*-styled dress with tiny silver-spun rosettes that embroidered the hem, my hair was plaited simply and tied up with a matching blue ribbon. As I read distractedly from my book of Tennyson, my nerves were awry from the anticipation of what is to come tomorrow.

The Count, who sat with his legs crossed next to me on the couch, again eyed me. He moved in to look over my shoulder at the book. "Isa, you have been reading the same page for fifteen minutes."

It was still odd to hear him call me by my nickname, but I still sighed and closed the small gilded book. "Sorry."

"I know you are worried, dear one," his fingertips brushed over my hair. "But all is prepared and set into motion. You are safe here; no one will hurt you."

I frowned all the same and rested my head against his shoulder. "I believe you, but forgive me if I'm rather pessimistic about it."

The Master kissed my temple. "I know a thing that will lighten your spirits. I have another gift for you, and this one is the most precious of them all."

I sighed heavily and rolled my eyes. "Count —"

"You would deny a husband to dote on his wife?" The ancient Prince pouted.

My eyebrows raised at that. "I could hardly bear it when you gave me your mother's cross, and now all these pretty things...and I have nothing to give you."

"Ah, but you have plenty to give me, sweet one," he nuzzled my cheek. "But it is a gift I cannot receive just yet."

I blushed.

"My rosy-cheeked nymph," the Count grinned from ear to ear at my reaction. Taking my hand, we stood and then walked over to the table. The Master told me to close my eyes, which I did, and then to open them. When I did, before me was a centuries-old gilded chest, sealed shut with a heavy iron lock. Where or how he had concealed it from me, I don't know, but it was no illusion. With a wave of his fingers, there was a click, and the bolt was undone, and the curved lid was drawn back to reveal the treasure within: a gold crown, studded with pearls and semi-precious stones, rested on red velvet. This is another national treasure which should be safe in some museum and not being presented to me as a 'gift'.

The sheer stylistic beauty of it made me gasp. "Oh, Count, it's exquisite!"

That smile of his widened. "And it is yours."

"I..." I began, yet the words were hard to find to tell him what I truly feel. "I couldn't..."

"Why?" His brow creased as he searched my face for some explanation, and offense growing on his. "I know it pleases you?"

"Of course it does, but..." I reached forward to touch one of the peaks, on which was set a shining pearl. "Your wives wore this, didn't they?"

The Count frowned, catching my meaning as he replied in a deep tone. "Yes, they did."

"Surely I can't..." I withdrew my hand. "They were born with titles and riches, in great houses and prestigious families, weren't they? They deserved to wear it —"

"You will soon learn that a woman is not born a lady, she becomes one." The Master stopped me and began his lecture. "Because you are of my house, this is your right to wear this, whether or not you believe you deserve it. Both men and women alike, of far lesser morality and dignity, have worn a crown and proclaimed it to be their right. By refusing this, you only prove to me that it is yours to wear."

"But I've done nothing —"

Again, he cut me off by holding up his hand for silence. "Many of your achievements have been the result of hard work and merit, such as your schooling. In my day, my achievements were on the battlefield, but I earned this crown so that you may wear it. Will you deny me my achievements?"

I hadn't thought of it that way. I looked down in shame that I had caused him more offense than I had realized. "Of course not…"

"I saved this crown from the Ottomans and kept it with me for centuries. So, wear it, and remember from whence it came." Taking the magnificent piece from its box, he placed it on my head. It was extremely heavy but rested in perfect balance. The Count's eyes glistened, his face softening at the sight. "You are reminiscent of the old days, my darling girl."

I blushed at his praises as he took my face in his hands and kissed me long and passionately, leaving me gasping for breath. No matter if I believe it should rest there or not, if he believes it, that is all that's important. The crown of the wife of the *voivode*, his ancient title, shall remain firmly planted on my head for his sake.

The Master told me that tomorrow I am to wear it when his children come. I am dreading that final hour because it's so shrouded in the unknown, and I can only pray that something truly awful won't happen. For now, I must attempt to sleep and prepare myself for the rising of the lamentable dawn.

29 September
Michaelmas

I slept little last night and tossed and turned, my mind restless. I wished the Count had offered to make me sleep, but he left me early enough that I didn't know I wasn't going to be tired. A part of me wanted to seek him out, but I was sure he had more important things on his plate than me. So, I lay there half-awake, half-asleep, thinking about my family and my old life. I haven't even touched the bundle of letters they sent me because, even though they are 5,000 miles away, I still cannot face them.

When 5 am came, and the sun hadn't yet begun to rise, I readied myself and went to the chapel to find some comfort for my restless heart. Although I was able to grasp the fading wisps of that tranquility, I was still anxious in this calm before the storm. As long as I have faith in myself and those around me, I keep telling myself, then surely, we cannot fail. Right? If the Lord is with us, who can be against us? But, is He really with us? I can only pray it is so. May St Michael defend us in this battle and be our protection against the Devil. Let all evil spirits who prowl the earth seeking the ruin of souls be thrust into Hell from whence they came.

Evening…

Zero hour. As sunset approached sooner and sooner, I prepared myself both physically and mentally. Changing out of my yellow silk day dress, I donned one that the Count had specifically requested I wear for this evening. This one is a deep crimson red, brocaded with a gold floral design, trimmed in gold. The overcoat, which is ten times heavier than the dress by itself and trails to the floor, is similar in design, embroidered with crystal beads. To set it all off, I wore a lengthy veil that covered my entire face and hair, and thereupon, the crown was placed. Of course, I wore his mother's silver crucifix, carefully concealed beneath the overcoat. The whole ensemble reminded me more of a medieval wedding dress than one for a formal reception.

I felt ridiculous, honestly, although it was very fun to wear such fine clothes. I complained to Mitică, who met me at my door around 7 pm to escort me down to the main floor, that I looked absurd. He said he didn't think so, but I'm sure he was just being nice. Dumitru was dressed quite fancily too, wearing the red velvet livery of a footman. We both looked like idiots, but when our light-hearted joking about our ridiculous clothes had just begun, the wolves howled. Mitică and I froze, the laughter between us snuffed out like a dying flame. Their song sounded so different, so hollow and raw, as if they were both mourning and enraged. It was a strange minute as the fearful dirge echoed off the mountains and the stone of the castle.

I held Mitică's arm, and he gripped me back, I think a bit frightened himself. We both slowly made our way down to the grand entrance, where the Count instructed us to meet him. Soon enough, the sun's red light of dusk faded, and the Count, or perhaps I should call him Voivode, emerged from his death sleep. Clad in his medieval splendor, he appeared from seemingly nowhere, wearing a brilliant golden overcoat with circling dragons around the collar. Upon his head, he wore a diadem of rows of pearls with a large amber stone set at the center, matching the color of his robe. I felt that I should bow or kowtow before him.

Mitică let go of my arm and went up to speak to his Master in hushed tones. I couldn't hear what they were saying, and they were probably speaking in their native tongue, so I put my eyes downcast. I focused on trying to calm my anxiety, but it was not subsiding.

"Sweet one," the Master was next to me, taking my trembling hands. "You are a vision."

"You are the vision, Count." With Dumitru so close, I whispered it for the immortal to hear. "But, why am I wearing this? Why am I here?"

He chuckled. "Fear not, my dear. Trust in me, I have my —" Unexpectedly, he stopped, his head snapping alert to the door, and he growled low. "They are near."

I gulped, a shiver running up my spine. Sporadic yips and yaps of the wolves sounded off close by, just over the stone bridge. Looking at the Master, I tugged on his hands to get his attention and murmured apprehensively. "Vlad…"

"Come," he put his arm in mine and began to lead me away. "Dumitru, you know what to do."

"Yes, Master," Mitică confirmed with a nod.

Do *what?* I wanted to ask, but I knew the Count would not tell me. Trying to keep my breath steady, he ushered me down the narrow passage and into the banquet hall, which had been completely transformed. I hadn't been in there in just under a month, and it looked nothing like the dusty old death trap that I remember. The tables had been moved, but the chairs of the lord and lady remained the focal point of the room. The tapestries had been replaced on the walls, these with golden fire-breathing dragons on blood-red backdrops, and others of the family crest. Was this the place where we would meet *them?* Why not use the throne room floors above us, that was specifically made for receiving audiences? I wanted to ask it but dared not.

The Count brought me to my grand chair that sat to the left of his. We heard the distinctive sound of the massive chains to the door opening, and I tensed. We were just letting them in? No struggle?

No fight? The Master suddenly turned to me, raising my veil over the crown. With those two massive hands, he gripped my forearms, almost lifting me off the ground to him. "Do you love me?"

Shocked by his fervor at such a time, I nodded adamantly. "Of course I do."

The Voivode placed a hard kiss on my mouth, then all at once was gone. "Remember that." Then he drew the veil back over my face and made me sit. "Do not speak, do not move, do not show emotion. Most of all: trust me, sweetest one, trust me."

It was a command, and just as he had demanded of me, I could not speak or move, and all the fright, dread, and weariness I felt were suppressed. I was numb, lifeless, as a doll sitting on a shelf, a fly on the wall, watching the events before me unfold. My husband sat next to me and closed his eyes, taking in a few deep breaths before he reopened them, just as *they* entered.

They emerged from the darkness of the passage, four of them in total, two males, two females. Immediately, my eyes landed on one of the women whose long hair shone a glittering silver in the torchlight. Breath caught in my throat as I recognized her face, her tall stature, her eerily graceful walk. It was Imogen, there was no doubt about it. I could see her face in my mind clearly, when before it was cloudy, and that feeling of her fingers coming around my neck to push me against the café's bathroom wall. Anger flared in me, but I could not show it as long as I was bound by the Count's command.

The other three looked equally menacing in their own right. The other woman has short red hair and is definitely from the British Isles, like Imogen. The two men are very dissimilar in their appearance, one with very dark features, the other quite pale. When their eyes came to me, however, they had a variety of mixed emotions: Imogen openly glowered, one of the males tried to hide his shock, and the other female was confused. It seems they fully expected the Count and I to have bent to their will. It gave me satisfaction that they had not won in that regard.

The head of this pack of dogs, the dark-haired man, bowed his head to the Count and spoke to him in highfalutin Romanian as if he were addressing an emperor. I rolled my eyes, kicking myself as to how, after nearly eight months of studying the language, I still had such an issue understanding it. My gaze drifted to the others of the small party, and when I landed on Imogen, she was staring directly at me. Panicking, my eyes tore away from hers. I was suddenly so grateful for the veil so that they couldn't easily see my face, nor see at whom I was looking.

"I expected there to be more of you." The Count suddenly caught my attention with his English. "Why do the other two of your gang hide like cowards in my forest?"

Without skipping a beat, the same man spoke in English but with a thick Greek accent. "Forgive us, Father, but your tactics are well-known to us."

"Andreas, you insult my hospitality." The Voivode stood from the chair, not wasting any time throwing verbal punches their way. "Let us cut to the chase, shall we? There is no need to continue with pleasantries, as we all know your arrival here is not a cordial one. As each one of you appears to have an issue with how I conduct my own affairs, I ask, what business is it of yours?"

This Andreas grimaced openly and responded to his father's question rather oddly. "It concerns all of us. We see you have not rid yourself of your...plaything."

"You dare to assume the right to tell *me* what I can and cannot have?" The Prince's fury poured from his lips. "All you see here to the horizon is mine, even you and your pathetic existences are mine. Think you that you will deny me one mortal woman, simply because you see her as an inconvenience to you? Pitiful."

"She is more than an inconvenience, Father-King." This time, Imogen spoke, her slight Irish accent made her sound angrier as she stepped forward. "Correct, you may have all that you wish and more upon that, but when your possession possesses you, who is the servant and who is the master?"

The Master had his back to me, and I saw his shoulders roll in laughter, and he waved the question away. "I need not explain my relationship with my possession to any one of you. I am, and always will be, Master of my house and my kind."

"Peace, Father," the red-headed female interceded, causing all to go silent. Her accent was peculiar; Welsh, perhaps? "We didn't come here to argue over the pettiness of our differences, but to plead to you, Father, to exact vengeance on behalf of Petros."

"From whom will you demand recompense when it was I who ended him?" My husband then gestured to me. "Surely not my wife, who bears my name and title, and whom I have made mistress over my domain? A woman has no past wrongs when she goes to the bed of one such as I."

They all became uncharacteristically stiff for being dead and shot each other uncomfortable looks. By their reactions, I believe the word hadn't reached them that we were recently married. I couldn't fathom why he was telling these things that are so private to them…untrue or not. I was nauseous from embarrassment at it all. Glancing over to Mitică, he was obviously tense, and a greater embarrassment made my neck and face grow hot.

"You are fools to believe that a man of my years cares who lives or dies." The Voivode continued. "But all the same, I am the oldest and have little use for squabbling amongst children. I accept the first half of your peace, Georgiana."

The redhead smiled and bowed her head to her ancestral father, although she shouldn't have been so…pleased with that answer. It must have been fake, and she carried on with her carefree charade. "Thank you, Father. Please, let us all not start with angry and hasty words. We have an offering of goodwill procured especially for this occasion."

The Voivode went quiet, then asked redundantly. "An offering?"

"Ah, yes, Father," Andreas nodded to Imogen, who returned the gesture. "And it is one, we believe, in which you will find much pleasure."

He cocked his eyebrow in interest. "Bring it to me."

Imogen's lip curled over her teeth in a vicious smile as she walked into the darkness of the passage. I was confused as to what she was doing or where she had gone, just as an odd chill cut the air and the firelight flickered sporadically. A shrilling cry burst out from the blackness, and I wanted to flinch, but remained still, and watched in horror as she reappeared and produced from the formless black a crying baby. She was holding the naked infant by its leg, and it dangled upside-down, crying in agony. My heart lurched into my throat as I tried desperately to find my voice to call to the Master and tell him to make this stop.

"This infant was born just today, stolen from his own mother's bosom. Maxim had the honor of acquiring it." Andreas explained so casually as he watched the witch approach us, eyes trained on the writhing newborn.

"I procured it myself with you in mind, King, such a delicacy to have one so young." The other male boasted, his Slavic accent was so thick and nearly incomprehensible.

Imogen handed the child over to Dumitru, who then gave it to the Count, who accepted the crying babe with a menacing grin on his face. "A wonderful gift indeed. I am impressed you obtained it so easily, Maxim, you have a unique nose for these things."

"I would have brought you the mother, however," he licked his lips like a wolf. "She gave me a nasty little fight."

I couldn't believe what I was hearing. They all spoke so nonchalantly about leaving this child motherless, so freely about purposefully ending life. It was absolutely diabolical. In this little child, I saw both of my nephews. Despite not being able to show emotion, tears somehow still managed to form in my eyes and flooded over my cheeks.

"No matter," the Count shifted the infant in his arms so that the little one's body was more exposed. "This one will do perfectly."

My eyes were wide with horror. I watched the Count sink his teeth into the little body as he turned his back to me. It cried out in spasms of pain, and I screamed in my head for him to stop. The expressions of the faces of the four demons shone in bloodlust at the scent and sight of the spectacle, tempted to have a taste of this special treat. I pleaded to God to let this stop, and I looked to Mitică for him to do something, anything, but he stood motionless, eyes downcast, and listened to the little one's death throes. Soon enough, the crying stopped, and the Count raised his head, a pleasurable sigh loosened the tension from his shoulders.

"Dispose of this." The Master barked at Dumitru.

Without a word, Mitică stepped forward and took the child from the Master, concealing the tiny corpse in the swaddling blanket and from my view.

I felt like I wanted to die…no, I *did* want to die. If I could have moved, I think I would have shaken with hysterics, wailed, and lamented the murderer of the most innocent of all the earth. Why?

Why would the Count do that? When he looked at that child, did he not see his own when they had first come into the world? That could have been his own descendant, and he snuffed out its existence to suit his pleasure. My tears were unceasing, all the strength in me had gone, and my shoulders slouched ever so slightly from their frozen position.

They were speaking about something else, but I didn't want to hear. Trapped inside the shell of my body, I retreated somewhere deep that I hadn't gone in months. I couldn't hear anything, or see, or feel, and wallowed in the lack of sensation.

What did the Count say I should do? Always remember that I love him? To remember those pleasant memories by the riverside? To trust him? Christ, I didn't want to remember anything, not even my own name.

Some time passed, I'm not sure how much or how little, but I was quite catatonic when suddenly I heard the Master's voice whisper. *"Doamna mea?"*

My body came back to me, and it was so heavy, not just from the weight of the crown or the clothes, but the weight of *me*. Sluggishly, I surveyed the room and saw the four demons were still there, all staring at me. It almost pained me to crane my head up to look at the Count, whose lips were still stained red.

"It is late for you, my wife. You may retire."

I could only nod since my voice was lost. By some miracle, I managed to stand without toppling over, bowed to him, and departed as gracefully as I could. Out of the corner of my eye, I saw the one known as Andreas eye me as we passed. I didn't even notice Dumitru coming up behind me, grabbing my arm, and hurriedly moved me along the corridor.

Once we were a distance from them, Mitică's arm came around my waist when I began to drift to the side. In my ear, he whispered harshly. "Don't faint, I need your help."

I only grunted in reply.

"Upstairs, come on, I can't carry you in this dress." He urged, lugging me up the stairs. I felt so emotionally drained, and by the time we got to my floor, I was huffing for breath. Promptly, Dumitru led me to my sitting room, where he locked the door behind us. Strange as that was, my thoughts were distracted as he rushed to a chair and picked up a small, bloodied heap of blankets. "I've stopped the bleeding, but I've never had to take care of a baby before. You're a woman, you must know what to do."

Without another word, Mitică pushed the unconscious bundle into my arms and brushed past me. "The Master prepared for this, and there are supplies hidden in the pantry. I'll be back soon, make sure he doesn't make noise."

"He?" I asked to thin air as Dumitru had already left, locking the door behind him. I blinked, examining the newborn with glassy eyes. There were only two small pricks in his chubby arm. All the weight that had burdened my heart lifted, and nearly throwing off the crown, veil, and overcoat, I sat and rocked the nameless boy. Oh, how I pity this unfortunate baby who, because he had been born this day, in this corner of the earth, had suffered more in the first few hours of his life than most people do in a lifetime. The child soon roused from the renewed warmth and whimpered in discomfort. My heart broke in two as I tried my best to console him, although I think I wasn't doing much.

Mitică returned with the odds and ends that he obtained, sweat sheen on his brow from the exertion of running up and down the stairs. Giving me a warm bottle of formula, he stopped to catch his breath. "I followed the instructions as best I could. I don't know if it's right."

I was surprised at the intricacy with which the two of them had planned for something like this. My conscience began to nag at me that I had been so quick to jump to conclusions about the two of them. After checking the formula just to be sure, I gave the poor boy probably his first meal, which he sucked down greedily.

Mitică watched for a few minutes, drawing nearer and nearer to observe the small human. Though now that I think about it, I don't think he was actually looking at the baby. "Are you okay?"

"I'll live, Mitică," I tried to give him a reassuring smile, but I doubt it seemed real to him. "Go attend the Master, I'm sure they'll be suspicious as to where you are."

Dumitru nodded once, then sheepishly placed his lips on my hair before quickly departing again.

Since he left, I have kept a watchful eye on the little one. I've made sure he's secure in a chair, and right now he is sleeping. It is near midnight, and I am exhausted, yet I still remain alert. Sometimes I think I hear strange noises echo up through the stone, but I dare not think what they are.

I will end this account for tonight and try to close my eyes.

DANCE WITH THE DEVIL

30 September

Morning, 7 am…

I fell asleep on the floor at the foot of the chair, using a decorative cushion as my pillow and the expensive overcoat as my blanket. Initially, I was just going to get some shut-eye, but I soon drifted off. The baby must not have made any sound or stirred at all during the night because I was not roused by him once. Granted, it had only been a few hours of solid sleep, and in his condition, I wouldn't think he would wake. It wasn't until about 5 am that I was startled by a presence looming over me. Before I even had a chance to open my eyes, the Count's sweet voice whispered my name, his gentle fingers combing through my hair.

Groggily, I opened my eyes, and his blurry figure materialized before me. He was still wearing the same boyar dress as before, however, with no diadem.

313

"What time is it?"

"Almost dawn," the Count explained with a frown, his thumb roughly massaging my cheek. "Did I cause these tears?"

I guess my copious tears must have stained my cheeks. Averting my eyes, I sat up, my back cracking from being so long in one position on the floor. "Never mind about it...tell me what happened."

The Master gave me another frown before joining me on the floor. He explained that, mostly, the rest of the evening had been a chorus of bickering, coupled with peaceful periods of more meaningful speech, although he didn't say expressly what it was about. I couldn't understand why he was playing around with them, toying with them like a cat torments mice. There was no doubt that the Count could have easily ended all four of them as soon as they entered the banquet hall. It could have been a bloodbath, a massacre, yet he chooses to entertain and amuse them. If I dare to contemplate his actions from this past night, it leaves me to wonder if he is pretending to be his old self, as I had suggested to him months ago. Would he really have taken *my* idea into consideration?

I slouched as I let out a long sigh. "I am relieved that it was civil, at least."

The Count smiled softly and placed his face against my neck to rest there. "I hope you were not too offended by what they said about you. I believe it more to be that I am your plaything and you do with me as you please."

His stubble tickled me a bit, and I couldn't help but smile back at him, so I took the opportunity to tease him. "I have come to understand that a lot of what your kind says is all bark and no bite."

"No bite at all?" My husband chuckled, his arms coming around my midsection as he leaned me back, exposing my neck. Eyeing me playfully, he pretended to dive to my throat — straight for the kill, but littered it with kisses instead.

I giggled at the sensation as I feigned death. "So long, cruel world! I have been undone."

"Do not leave me so soon, precious one." The Master teased back, his lips reaching my own. "If you are undone, surely I am too. Then what will I do?"

My heart surged for him, and my arms came up around his neck. Deepening my kisses, I wedged myself closer into him, arching my back. The Count's fingers sank into the flesh of my ribs even through the thick dress and underlayers. I wanted him to kiss more of me, and I began to unbutton the restrictive lace collar.

"Now, now, beloved, there is a child in the room." The Master pulled away yet kept me against him. I pouted that he would stop me, but then he added. "Besides, I must speak with you about something else of a more…sensitive topic."

My brow furrowed as all the fun dissipated. "What is it?"

"Forgive me for saying this, but," he paused, clearing his throat, which only heightened the awkwardness. "You are…late."

So, he had noticed, and I wasn't seeing something that wasn't there. I hung my head, not in shame, but in defeat. "I know…"

Softly, as not to appear as if he had jumped to conclusions, he asked. "What is your reasoning why?"

However, I did jump to conclusions, tensing as I faced him. Searching his visage, I found no anger, which confused me even more. I truly thought he had asked me if I was pregnant, and my thoughts flashed to Dumitru. Distressed that in the first week of our marriage, he would ask me a question like that, I could only defend myself. "I've been faithful —"

"I am *not* saying that." He emphasized, cupping one side of my face. "I could tell if you had, anyway. I am asking if you are affected by this situation more than you care to tell me."

Feeling rather foolish for having assumed, I averted my gaze again. Quite often, I am unwilling to tell him the feelings and worries I have deep inside, even though he sees through me like a pane of glass. Swallowing hard, I only gave vague details, all the same. "Since my little 'adventure' beneath the castle, I have been…stressed."

Resting his forehead against mine, the Count sighed. "I do not blame you, but you see how this presents a problem?"

The scent of earth swirled around me, and I closed my eyes. "I know…I'm sorry."

His lips pressed to mine gently, taking their time to linger there before he spoke. "I will prepare for when the time comes; no need to worry yourself further about it."

Nodding, I thanked the Master for his help. Thinking about all he had said and done last night, it was hard to fathom that I was speaking to the same person. The man who spoke to his children was authoritarian, dominating, and unyielding, but this man is kind, understanding, and so affectionate. That is his power of duplicity, but which one is the real man behind the mask?

Surprisingly, he changed the subject and asked. "How fares the infant?"

"Exhausted, but alive," I commented, my eyes opening to drift to the sleeping bundle on the chair. "I must applaud you for fooling not only me but them as well."

"You understand why I did it?"

"Chicanery, subterfuge, et cetera." Coming out of his hold, I got to my knees to get a better view of the little one, who indeed is so tiny compared to the seat he slept upon. "Nevertheless, it's unfortunate."

"I despise many things in this world, but one of the most despicable is the sacrifice of children for the gains of others." The Count explained, following me up to sit on his calves to watch the babe, too. "When I was a young man, my father had to leave my brother and me in the hands of the Ottomans, and we were hostages for most of our formative years. My father had to prove his loyalty to them, and although I was not as young as this one, it changed me."

Taking his hand, I squeezed it tightly. Times back then were so different from the way they are now. He must have endured so much in his childhood, more than I can conceive. "I can't imagine what that must have been like for you."

"Do not imagine it, sweet one." The Master's jaw tensed, and he placed his other hand over mine. "This afternoon, when the sun is high, Dumitru will take the child back to civilization. Please keep him quiet and content until then."

"You figured out where he came from?"

"With a little persuasion, Maxim will boast to anyone of his conquests." The Count glowered at the thought of this Maxim, like the Slav had left a bad taste in his mouth. "You must be particularly wary of him."

I only nodded thoughtfully.

Taking one last look at the sleeping baby, he planted a kiss on my cheek before he retired to his death sleep. I do feel quite bad for him since he has so much on his shoulders that he keeps to himself. Therefore, I mustn't be a cause of trouble for him any longer. For now, I must keep alert and not fall for the tricks he plays and the lies he spins to dupe them into believing one thing over another. That's all I've gotten so far as to his plan, but to what end he is planning, I am at a loss.

I pray that God will give me a sliver of strength.

Afternoon...

Just around noon, Mitică came up with brunch for me and formula for the baby, who had only roused minutes before. I wasn't very hungry, so I fed the weary infant instead. In the sunlight, I could see what a beautiful boy he is, with his brilliant eyes and tuffs of soft, dark hair. The poor dear was starving again, so I cooed and coddled him as Dumitru and I sat on the couch together. I guess he decided to stick around to watch the baby with me. As we did, I inquired as to what happened after I had been told to go to bed.

I listened attentively as he explained that the children were quite upset that the Master hadn't heeded their wishes to dispose of me. According to them, who are representatives in their own right for this larger group, a multitude of others are unnerved that the Count did not take revenge against me when I killed Petros. They do not believe at all that the Count would kill his beloved friend and that only I was responsible. In essence, they are convinced that the Master is only taking the blame on himself because I have taken advantage of his weaknesses. That is, his newfound humanity, of which I am promoting and exploiting.

This flabbergasts me that I, a mortal, could seduce him. And all of this is because of some ambition I have? In actuality, I believe he was the one in the beginning who seduced me, and I fell for him easily. Also, I never thought of the Count as having any 'weaknesses' that would impede his judgment. Of course, he has the natural limitations of his kind, but I have seen him do amazing things that only leave me in awe. For centuries, he has honed his skills, tested himself past his limitations. How could he be affected so by little old me? In my opinion, he wouldn't be. In all his lifetimes, I am an insignificant girl.

After the little one finished his bottle, it was time for him to go. My heart hurt because I had already become attached to this baby, but it was much too dangerous for him to stay, and his family must be so devastated to have lost him and his mother on the same day. Once he was all set to go, I tucked him snugly in a basket that Dumitru had padded with blankets. I thought then that I should perhaps call him Moses, as I sent him on down the river in a basket to find a better home. Concealing him underneath another blanket, Dumitru took him away from me. I watched from the windows as he drove Moses out of the castle's walls and back out into the living world where he belongs.

...

As ordered by the Count, I was instructed to wear official attire when we would meet the children after sunset. I dreaded getting ready, but eventually found the courage to put on the next heavy set of underthings, dress, and overcoat. These are teal silk with golden brocade, with accented pearl buttons and cufflinks. Just as the previous night, Mitică met me at my door at 7 pm. I discreetly asked him if his errands this afternoon had been successful, to which he replied they had. No details or explanations were needed; only a silent nod relayed all vital information. I was relieved and can only pray that my little Moses was safe and sound.

When Dumitru and I descended the steps, to my alarm, two of the children were already there, whispering to each other in hushed tones. I knew instantly it was Imogen and Andreas, and gave Mitică a concerned stare, although he couldn't see my face well underneath the lacy veil. At the sight of me, they both turned their heads. Narrowed eyes trained on me and pierced through my soul like needles. Swallowing hard, I steeled myself for the approaching confrontation. Without the Count present, Dumitru and I were truly on our own.

"Good evening, wife of Dracula," the Greek Andreas hailed me, breaking away from Imogen as he approached. He reminds me much of Petros in stature and physique, but his eyes are a striking blue. The man's hair is also something otherworldly, with his thick, dark waves and closely trimmed beard. "You appear even lovelier than before. You are well this evening, I trust?"

Why did he address me so cordially and with so much praise? Flattery would not fool me. Besides, I doubt he could even see what I really looked like, and I scowled. The Count didn't tell me if I could speak to them or not, so I bowed my head slightly and trod carefully. "Good evening, sir, I am very well."

Andreas came a bit closer, and Dumitru tensed, taking a step forward to warn him not to come nearer. The Greek halted and glared so deadly at Mitică that I feared a fight was about to break out right in front of me. Just in a flicker, Andreas' eyes were back to me, and all trace of menace had disappeared. "I regret last night that your husband did not present you to us in a less formal setting, as, in a way, you are our mother."

His tone bothered me with its fake formality, and the thought of being their mother made me want to gag. Behind him, Imogen watched the encounter most curiously, I believe, hoping that a clash would develop between Mitică and her 'brother'. "I doubt —"

"For you to accept her as your mother," the Count's voice manifested from all directions as suddenly he was next to me, stepping between the three of us. The robe he wore this evening was of purple and gold and sparkled in the firelight. "I would say you should have to respect her first. From your own mouth, you make a hypocrite of yourself."

The expression on the two children's faces was one of concealed shock. Andreas cleared his throat, not skipping a beat. "Father, you know I respect your property even if I may disagree with it."

Property?! I huffed, but immediately kicked myself for it. Just that little slip had given Andreas all he needed for his next assault.

"I see she doesn't agree," he smirked, speaking of me as if I weren't there. "Modern women lack respect for the superior sex. Do you not agree?"

I cringed and began to seethe, not only for what he said but because I had fallen for his provocation and made the Master look like a fool. Holding my breath, I felt like I was going to burst from my stupidity, and I had to blink furiously to keep tears from overflowing.

The Count watched me out of the corner of his eye. "It is only when they take their place on their backs do they remember who is above them."

His words did bite me this time, and a tear escaped. Desperately, I warred with myself over whether I should say something or not. I could easily dig myself into a deeper hole, or somewhat remedy the situation. Taking in a breath, my voice came out rather flat. "I have displeased you, Master, so please allow me to retire."

Never before have I called him 'Master' to his face, so I hoped it conveyed to him the seriousness of my apology. Yet he turned away from me. "No, wife, you shall stay, no matter how disappointed I am with you."

Another bite, this one sank straight and true into my heart, which tore in two. I felt a hand come to support my elbow and steady my swaying balance. It was Dumitru, his face calm, but his eyes were telling a different story. He was about to erupt, I could see it plainly. Providing me with this small display of assistance was dangerous, but I think Mitică wanted to show his resistance. The last thing I wanted was for him to get punished for helping me, so I subtly pulled away, no matter how comforting this touch was.

"Open the doors, Dumitru." The Master ordered. "Our other guests have arrived."

Quite reluctantly, Mitică did as he was told and went to unbolt the doors. On their own, they swung open, and the brisk night air came flooding in, chilling my hot cheeks. From the darkness, two figures emerged: one male, one female. Eerily, the torches flickered as they stepped inside and plunged the area into spats of light and dark before steadying out again.

The male caught my attention first because he was incredibly tall and massively built. His hard face and sharp features made him look terrifying, and I let out a small gasp that I think the Count heard. He resembles more than anyone else the demon that sleeps beneath the surface. Why I was so affected by his menacing appearance, I don't quite know. His facial features unnerved me, but there was something about his aura that made me tremble.

The female, on the other hand, was considerably smaller, with thick brown curly hair that framed her face. She looks Italian, has these big brown eyes, and is petite compared to the rest of them. She reminds me almost of a cat.

"Ludevit, Cosima," Imogen finally spoke as she went to them, kissing each one on the cheeks. Her amicable behavior, so sisterly, caused my skin a prickle at its unnaturalness. "Please meet your First Father, the Impaler of Tens-of-Thousands."

When they came forward, Imogen leading them, they bowed their heads. Since they had never met the Count before, I assume they must be considerably younger than the others from last night. The Master examined them up and down before asking. "When were you reborn?"

Ludevit answered in a thick accent that almost made it impossible to understand him, saying he died in 1943. And Cosima replied, with a voice that was much higher-pitched than I expected, in 1944. That is so recent compared to the era in which the Master lived as a mortal man, but no less brutal and savage.

The Voivode shifted on his feet, and a deep frown formed on his mouth. "You were reborn from dark days into even darker ones. It is a pity you did not stay dead."

"A pity, Father?" Cosima spoke up, her voice like the dainty chimes of fine china. Coupled with her accent and alluring sable eyes, she drew all of our attention with only those three words. "This world has been dark since the day Beelzebub gave you his blood, and how delightful it has been for those who have benefited from it."

The name shook my soul within me, and I desperately tried to remain composed. Peering over at the Count through my veil, I tried to watch his reaction, but his face stayed emotionless.

A stillness came over us, and the Master let out a breath. "You are not wrong."

The tone of his voice concerned me, but then Andreas butted in. "Great Father, let me propose a second hunt to welcome your new children. Ludevit is renowned for his skill in the chase, and I believe you will be much impressed."

"And I believe Maxim will be much wounded that he is not included." The Count hummed as he thought aloud, and the others smirked. "But I shall see this hunting prowess of yours, Ludevit, if you have not eaten?"

"Not since this afternoon." A thrilled sneer caused Ludevit's features to grow even more horrendous. It was only then that it occurred to me that Maxim and Georgiana weren't present. Where would they have been at this late hour? They couldn't have been asleep still, or out hunting without the rest of their group. My attention was diverted back when Ludevit bowed his head again, beaming that he had been singled out and praised. "I would be honored to hunt beside you, First Father."

"Before we depart," Imogen spoke up and walked in her graceful manner to the nearby table where a large box lay upon it. It glided into her hands, and she returned to the group, her focus now upon me. "Yesterday we did not bestow you, *Doamnă*, with a gift."

I forgot that was me for a second, and my delayed reaction made me stutter. "M-Me?"

Imogen nodded as she drew nearer and held it out to me. "I, personally, would like to present this to you as a gesture of goodwill between us. It is a replacement for the outfit that was ruined when we first met in Câmpulung."

Dead silence fell over us, and all eyes were glued on me. Her phantom fingers returning to my neck again, and my throat tightened. That moment of lost time still haunts me, and as I stood in front of the woman who had forced me to bleed myself dry, I was speechless. Anger welled in my chest that she would so openly bring it up in front of everyone. There was no sincerity in her voice, so I knew she was putting on airs.

Dumitru, who had returned to my side when the younger creatures came forward, burst in a low growl. "Witch, you *dare* —"

"Silence." The Count snapped at his servant so loudly that it echoed about the grand entrance. Before speaking to the silver-haired she-devil, he threateningly bared his sharpened teeth at her. "Imogen, do you believe yourself so bold as to admit you were the one who made my wife commit bodily harm?"

"I simply sent a message, that was all." All the meanwhile, Imogen's eyes remained trained on me, knowing full well the affront that she had provoked. "Isadora was a great help to me that day, and told me many things about you, Father. I am only repaying her for her trouble with a gift of a dress as a peace between us women."

It made me sick to think of what I may have told her and what secrets I had unwittingly divulged. This gift was no true offering of peace, only an opportunity to feign a truce to boast about what she had done to me in front of everyone. It disgusted me, and I could smell her ulterior motives as if they were a perfume she wore. Yet, I decided to play her little game, to dance with this devil, even if it meant betting with my life.

The Count stepped between the two of us, seething in renewed rage. Eyes flaming red, he snapped his teeth at the witch. "This great offense is —"

"A lovely gift," I spoke up, cutting the Master off, which was probably not the best thing to do then. Some new courage stilled my raging heart as he turned back to me, his gaze a plea and a warning. "As a gesture of good faith, I will accept it. Thank you, Imogen."

Dumitru stepped forward to receive it for me, on cue as always.

"I hope to see you wear it one day." She peered around the Count, her distinctive hair falling to one side. "I have a feeling it will suit you quite well."

Bowing my head to her, I bit my tongue from saying something that I shouldn't in retort. I'm not sure if she could see it, but I smiled as I motioned to the door. "Now your hunt awaits you."

"You are kind to let us leave you so soon, *Doamnă*," Andreas cut the conversation between Imogen and me. "May your evening be pleasant."

I bowed my head again as they all rounded themselves up to go into the night. The Count, however, stared down at me with an expression of mixed emotions. On his face, it was so plain that he wanted to say something privately to me, but couldn't. Inconspic-uously, he mingled his fingers in mine, and they brushed together rather sensually. I'm uncertain what he meant by that, but I know I will find out soon enough. Then, he spoke to me formally. "You may retire if you wish, *Doamnă*, for we will be late returning."

I nodded, thanking him and wishing him a good night. Mitică took my arm and led me back up the stairs away from them. Each step was one of relief that I wouldn't be seeing any of them until tomorrow.

Once the door was closed to my sitting room, I went to my chair and laid the box on it, then leaned against it to catch my shaking breath. Dumitru came up behind me and, taking off the crown, he set it on the nearby table. Then, something that I thought was unthinkable for him to do, he removed my veil and let it fall to the floor. Taking my shoulders, I didn't resist as he drew me into a strong embrace. His hands were trembling as he whispered in my ear. "I am so sorry for what they said."

Frowning that he would be so emotional for me, I gripped him back. He smelled of old musk from his clothes. "Mitică...it's alright."

"It's not alright. It will never be alright." He muttered in my neck, but then added somberly after a sigh. "Also, do you realize that by 'hunting' they mean people, not animals?"

My breath caught in my throat, and I felt the air around us grow chill. I foolishly had hoped they meant animals, and I cringed. Shoulders slumping, I sighed, knowing he was right, and a deep anger settled into the pit of my stomach. I glanced down at the box, and disgust came over my face. "Can you light the fireplace for me?"

"Are you cold?" Dumitru pulled away slightly, the pity on his face turning to worry.

I shook my head and asked him again. Without another word, he went to the fireplace and began his work as I opened the garment box that Imogen had given me. Within was a breathtakingly beautiful deep wine-red evening gown, covered with fine appliqué work and beading. Not before long, Mitică had the fire going good enough that he stepped away to wipe his hands. Promptly, I took the dress and threw it into the flames, and it instantly caught ablaze. Being eaten away by the orange tongues, it swiftly turned to black ash. It was a shame that such a pretty dress had been the victim of this night.

Dumitru was stunned as he watched it go up in flames, but said nothing about it. I believe he was pleased that I had done what I did, and we both stood there as the fire popped and cracked. Then a snap rang out from within the flames, and the bodice of the dress began to froth and bubble a yellow substance, and a rancid smell made me cover my nose. In horror, Dumitru and I jumped away as a plume of gray-yellow smoke was sucked up into the chimney. An unsettling weight rested in the pit of my stomach.

"It smells like…acid?" Mitică coughed, and the realization fell over his face as he looked at me. "My God, she poisoned it…"

I could only stare at the rest of the dress as it fizzled out into black, and whatever the solution was, it was burned away to nothing. How interesting it is that Imogen would give me a poisoned gift to make peace between us, so certain my vanity would make me fall for her trick. I may forgive her for trying to kill me twice, but now I see they are willing to get rid of me by any means possible.

The art of war is deception, as it is said, and I will swallow the bait no longer.

Chapter Thirty

SUMMIT OF PAIN

1 October

A ll night I was in a dead sleep, which was surprising since there had been an attempt on my life, but I was so exhausted from the short evening. I don't even think I dreamt at all, either, just slept in that in-between place where one goes to forget the waking world. With the Master gone all night and possibly quite upset with me, I didn't know if he would come to me in the morning. A part of me didn't want him to come at all because I didn't want to face him after the words he said.

It must have been near dawn again when I became suddenly aware of the presence of another hovering over me. Slowly, my brain came awake, but I didn't want to open my eyes since I knew it was him from his familiar scent. The Count was sitting against my hip, both hands on either side of my shoulders as he whispered to me. "Isa, I know you are awake."

Reluctantly I opened my eyes as slits to look up at him, my heart dreading that he had chosen to come. Saying nothing to him, I only stared for a few seconds before my eyes drifted away and I waited for the Master to deal me my punishment.

Bending down, he came close to my face so that his nose grazed my cheek. "Speak to me…"

Another moment of hesitation, and in the quietness, I heard that it was raining outside. There was no way I could look at him, not after last night, but I still found the voice in me. Emotion choked my throat as my eyes edged toward releasing their droplets. "I won't disappoint you again, I promise."

Pain etched on the Count's face as he laid his cheek against mine. "Forgive me for saying things so cruelly to you, but Andreas would have expected it."

My mind was on one track, and although I heard his words, I didn't really believe them. So, I continued my apology as if he had said nothing. "I'm sorry I made you lose face in front of him. I won't be so foolish again."

"Isa, you are *not* foolish, only too…outspoken for the times from which we come." The Master insisted, as his lips sought to comfort me with little kisses. "You are too innocent to know our ways and too stubborn to change yours. I think that if you did not act this way, they would be more suspicious of you."

"Nevertheless, I will be more aware." The tears had grown too numerous for my eyes to hold, and they slid down my cheeks.

The Count's shoulders hunched, and he hung his head when I still wouldn't look at him. With the backs of his fingers, he wiped away the salty streams, then took my chin and moved it to face him. "Say you forgive me, beloved. It pains my heart to see you so wounded."

When I finally brought my eyes to his, I was astonished at the sorrow they held. Did it really cause such grief in him to see me cry? Apparently so, I guess. My heart had already forgiven him for saying those things to me, and I vocalized it as he had asked. "I forgive you."

No sooner had the words left my mouth was he locked upon my lips, his tongue wedging itself in to dance with mine. There was an odd metallic taste, but I still accepted his fevered act of gratitude. When he withdrew, his tongue licked my reddened lips as if to taste the blood that lay just beneath the delicate skin. "I am relieved, beloved."

I was a bit breathless as I watched my husband move away to leave, but I grabbed onto his arm to stop him. "May I ask you something?"

A bit surprised, he returned to my side. "Anything."

Embarrassing as it was to hear it the first time, to say it myself was utterly mortifying. Yet with his feelings revealed, I had to know. "Do you really believe my place is on my back?"

The Master's brow creased, and he closed the distance between us again as he whispered in my ear. "All I know is my place is between your legs, and it matters not to me who is on whose back when I am there."

My face, neck, and chest grew unbearably hot. That was not the answer I was expecting in a hundred years, and I covered my mouth.

Taking advantage of my state, he pressed onward. "So, tell me, where is your place?"

I had a hard time saying the words as the heat spread to other areas of me. I bit my lower lip, which was still plump. "M-My place is...uh, well, when my legs are around you, I guess."

He chuckled. "I do often think of when you mounted me so fearlessly by the river, as bold Alexander daring to tame the wild Bucephalus. Well, my darling girl, you have not tamed this stallion just yet, so when you bestride me a second time, do not expect such a smooth ride."

"*Vlad...*" I hid my face in embarrassment.

Without missing a beat, he took the liberty of continuing his onslaught. "But I believe you will be able to hang on. I know you have endurance, and I have the stamina to ensure it is a...lengthy journey."

"*Vlad!*"

He smiled so widely that his eyes twinkled as he laid another tender kiss on my forehead. "Always remember that you are my wife, and I hold you above all others."

"I shall." Needless to say, I wasn't feeling that heavy shame in my heart anymore after hearing him say that. His tenderness and sincerity touched me. "Dear, I must tell you, though, that the dress Imogen gave me…"

"Dumitru told me…" he breathed out a long sigh, his smile fading, the vein forming on his forehead. "That witch thinks herself so clever, so manipulative."

I frowned at his troubled expression. "What will you do?"

Jaw tensing, he appeared to become quite uncomfortable. "As much as I wish to rip her to pieces, I am not finished with her. Trust me that I wish to make an example of her, but things are not yet in place."

I wasn't sure how I felt about his answer, but I had no say in it, and I had to let it go. I have to place my faith in him. Nodding, I told him simply that I understood, and soon afterward he left.

Since I was up, I took a cool bath to calm down. As I stewed in the chilled water, I took a long and hard look at myself and my relationship with the Master. I wish he would just love me already, because with this temptation that he presents me, some days I don't know if we can stick to that promise we made months ago. As long as in private he treats me as he always has, there is some hope he will continue to open his heart enough to maybe love me. That may be a week from now, or months, or years…I don't know.

8 October

So much has happened in this past week, and I have been so debilitated that I've been nearly unable to write. I will try to go back and skim over the details, which I think are important to write in this account.

On 2 October, I was feeling quite well and reveling in the look of Imogen's face when I saw her the next night, that I wasn't dead. All of them, that is, the four who were present, had this stunned expression that was paralyzing. It was even more satisfying when Imogen asked later that evening if I had tried on the dress to 'see if it fit properly', to which I said I had, and that it was the most exquisite modern dress I own. She blinked numerous times in a row when I described to her in detail how it fit. The Count, who played along in my charade, said he would allow me to wear it in the future. If Imogen saw through us, she said nothing, of course.

However, the morning of 3 October brought an abrupt end to my satisfaction. The Count had come to visit me for a few minutes that early morning, but instead of subtly crawling into bed next to me, he shook me awake. Before I was even able to sit up, the Master retreated to a corner of the room, his hand over his nose and mouth. Like a bus, reality had hit me when I felt the wetness of thick sticky blood between my legs. It was a mess, and I hadn't felt any of it in my sleep. At first, the pain was a dull ache, but once I began to move, it surged like a hot knife had ripped open my innards. I guessed that all the stress that I had been carrying within me was finally too long overdue to be released.

Embarrassed that he had caught me so vulnerable, I pleaded for the Count to go, but he was hesitant. Instead, he sprang into action, ordering me to clean myself up as quickly as I could while he would wake Dumitru. Without much thought, I did as he said. For the life in me, I couldn't understand what suddenly brought my cycle on with no sign or hint of its coming. Once I had gotten myself together, taking perhaps a bit more than the prescribed dosage of pain medication, I ripped off the sheets and threw them into the tub to soak.

By that time, the Count had returned with Dumitru and instructed me to gather some of my essential things, telling me not to ask any questions. Of course, I wanted to ask many questions, but I threw together what I thought was necessary. Just before I was ready, the Master took me aside and kissed me, and told me to never forget the day by the river. At my proximity, I saw the bloodthirstiness in his reddened eyes, obviously affected by my condition, but what he said perturbed me. Promptly, my husband brought me out to my sitting room, where Mitică was waiting, and he handed me over to him with a stern nod.

Dumitru grasped onto me tightly when the Master retreated into my room and closed the door. Not wasting any time, Mitică led me out into the hall and up the stairs. In the dim light of dawn, we went past the third and fourth floors and into that upper floor where the Count had taken me when we went stargazing. By the time we reached the fifth floor, all the energy I had was simply gone, but Dumitru wouldn't stop pressuring me to keep going. All I needed was a minute to catch my breath, but instead, he got quite frustrated and whisked me into his arms as if I weighed nothing.

When we came to a dead-end corridor, Mitică headed toward the very end. An ancient heavy door, which opened itself upon our approach, groaned so loudly it made me cringe. Within was a small room that was well stocked with a small bed and a few other furnishings, even an alcove shrine with a breathtaking mosaic of the Theotokos. Before I could even ask what the place was, Dumitru explained that this was the place the ladies of the house would come when the castle was under attack, and that I would be safe there until I was 'better'. He laid me on the bed, which was more of a well-cushioned cot, and promised he would return soon with my breakfast. Again, I barely got two words out before he fled the room and bolted it shut behind him, locking me in. The bolts on my side slid shut too, securely barring me from ever being able to leave of my own accord.

I was plunged into the semi-darkness of dawn, with only a few candles and a thin, long vertical window for light. Terrified to move, my labored breaths echoed up to the high ceiling. Sure, the place was comfortable enough, but it was so unfamiliar and so far away from other livable parts of the castle. I was isolated by tons upon tons of stone, hidden in a corner, behind a fortified door meant to withstand heavy bombardment. No matter how safe I was, I was alone, separated from my friends, and in pain.

And there I stayed, day after day, in my suffering. My pain only increased, which was extremely abnormal for me, and I lost all appetite for food. I recalled in my semiconscious haze wondering *why* I was so sick. Had I been so stressed about the children's arrival and Imogen's open attempts to kill me that my body had somehow overdone itself? There had to have been another reason why I was reduced to suffering in the fetal position…there had to have been.

As my brain wracked itself, trying to remember the previous days through the waves of what seemed like endless suffering. Just like an old dream, I recalled something.

On that night of 2 October, when I had 'fooled' Imogen into believing I had tried on her poisoned dress, there was something that I had thought strange, but now I see was far worse. That evening, the three females were present along with Maxim. I have observed that they always appear in fours, or they fear everyone being in the same place at the same time. This is because, as Dumitru had explained to me in secret, one of the Master's old tricks was to lure all of his victims together under the pretense of peace before dispensing of them.

Anyway, we had all assembled in the smoking parlor, a room that is just off the main entrance, at the end of a hall. The more intimate setting, I guess, had loosened the formality and separation that I had been determined to keep between me and them. I was sitting next to the Count as they chatted amongst themselves while I sat listening. The air was thick in that room, and with my heavy robes and covered face, I soon became terribly overheated. I feared to indicate my distress to the Master in case I should appear feeble in the children's eyes, so I stewed in sweat. It didn't help that Imogen, Georgiana, and Cosima were all staring at me, while Maxim didn't seem to care about my presence. No doubt their expert senses were picking up on my torment, though they said nothing of it until Imogen broke the flow of their conversation and asked me pointedly if I was well.

The Count smoothly came to my defense, and after a few words that saved my face, he motioned to Dumitru to take me upstairs. As I was ushered from the room on Mitică's strong arm, Imogen still glared at me with unnaturally wide eyes, coupled with a sneer that sent electricity through me. I thought she was just doing it to intimidate me, so I averted my eye contact from her.

"Oh, *Doamnă!*" It was Georgiana who had suddenly sprung up from her seat and glided over to my side. Dumitru stiffened as she approached. Grabbing onto my free hand as if she were a child, her freezing fingers wrapped around my heated ones and squeezed. "Before you go, I just *have* to tell you how lovely you look tonight. What is that delightful scent you are wearing?"

Suddenly, her hands clenched tighter around mine as she leaned in to take a whiff of my light perfume. The gesture struck terror in me, and images of Petros' teeth flashed in my brain as he had sunk them into my skin. I swear I blacked out for a second, but was brought back by the Count's icy voice.

"That is *enough*, Georgiana."

She pulled away and released me at that very second, even stepping aside to let me go by. The brightest smile on her face, she apologized for 'invading my space' and wished me a good night and sweet dreams. Cosima and Maxim snickered at that, mocking me as Dumitru quickly spirited me from the room.

I thought she had done it to frighten me, but could it have been more malicious than it appeared? What had Georgiana done to me? I have no evidence to say she had, or if it had been a distraction for something else. Perhaps Imogen was behind it again, but surely the Count would have seen some sleight of hand and brought a stop to it? Wouldn't he?

In the end, I was determined to believe that the children and their shady, clandestine activities were responsible for my condition.

I lost track of these last few days between 4 to 7 October, being mostly curled up on my cot, unable to move. Mitică could only come and see me a few times per day, and even then, it was dangerous for him to stay in case he had been followed by our unwanted guests. My sweet friend would remain with me only a few minutes when he brought me meals, and of course, I couldn't eat them. He'd sit on the cot, holding my hand through the bouts of pain, and give me tidbits of information about what was going on in the outside world. According to him, my alibi was that I was 'indisposed'; a vague term that could mean whatever anyone wishes it to mean in any host of contexts. Sometimes I couldn't follow what he would tell me, but just Mitică being near was enough. Other times, he would try to feed me the broths he'd make, but the smell was nauseating and the sight repulsive. He became quite angry with me at times, but it was only because he cared.

The times when Dumitru wasn't around and I had a clear head were the worst. Mitică had brought some books for me to read, but I never found the energy to read them. I would lie on the cot that faced the window and watch the murky gray clouds pass by. Now that October has come, the cold has begun. The chilling rains create an everlasting fog between the mountains, so all is gray and brown with the dying vegetation. The trees have become scraggly black dots in the distance, and some are no longer green and full of life. Far below me, the river is concealed by the denseness of low clouds, and I can never see it.

Of course, the countryside is still beautiful, but in a darker, more sinister way. This is the Transylvania as I had read about in books before I came here — a land clouded in literal mystery. A faraway place where supernatural creatures stalk the nights and sleep by day, where no sane human would dare to go out into the woods at night for fear of what prowls within them. No more sunny summer days, and no more warmth.

Yet all during this time, I never saw or heard from the Count once. Usually, he would make some effort to keep in contact, but Mitică never had any messages from him. There were no notes in response to the ones I'd send him, no inquiry as to how I was, no quick visit in the mornings to see me. Only Dumitru saw me, and when I would ask if the Master was well, he'd only say that he was quite well but very busy dealing with the children.

This distance that I endured was the worst yet. Being away from him in general was hard enough on my heart, but this was unbearable. I so yearned to feel his touch and respond to his gentle caresses, to kiss him and let him know how much I love him. With each heartbeat, there was a pang of loneliness, and I wondered if he had forgotten all about me.

There were a few times, I have to admit here, that I dreamt we were by the Argeş again, just as we were that last day of summer. But in this dream, we go further than my conscious mind would ever dare, and I feel every inch of him. These times I knew it was the Master and not some unexpected guest, for when he spoke, his voice settled me, and his embrace enveloped me in safety. They say distance makes the heart grow fonder, and it was surely working its effects on me. When I would wake from the bliss, instinctively I would reach for my husband, to find that beside me was just the emptiness of cold air. To comfort my sadness that I felt from his loss, I'd sit on my bed and face the Theotokos and pray. I would have gotten on my knees, but it was extremely difficult to keep myself upright in that position for long.

More often than not, I prayed for the Count and that he wouldn't forget who he is and how far he has come. It wasn't like I could ask Mitică how the Master was doing in that department, since, of course, my friend was not privy to that sensitive knowledge. I felt this looming dread that things were changing, just like a season of life to approaching death. Something in the air was menacing, and maybe I was overthinking things, but the castle was feeling…different.

If only the stone could whisper to me the secrets that it holds; to see what they see and hear as they hear. I tried to listen as hard as

I could sometimes, so that perhaps I would hear someone talking or simply catch a fleeting sound. Instead, I would hear the perpetual rain.

Yet still, I never stopped praying, never stopped hoping that the Master was safe and sound among those who seek his ruin. Even with Dumitru close by, he is alone. Vlad walks upon the burning coals and lies upon a bed of nails, as from all sides he is tested and tried by them. Playing his mind games, concealing one thing while showing another, the Master Puppeteer works his craft with only Mitică to help him keep up the charade.

And the days wore on to 7 October, when I was finally feeling much better, and I could stand and kneel without any pain whatsoever. Even my appetite was coming back, and I couldn't wait for Dumitru to bring the big lunch I had requested at breakfast. It was something to look forward to. I was in much better spirits that day, even finding some random ballad to sing absentmindedly.

It must have been around 11 am when I heard the sound of approaching footsteps, and my heart leaped in my chest. Dumitru had come a bit early with my meal, and I jumped up to the door and opened up the small viewer to see out into the hallway. But no one was there; the space was completely empty. I could have sworn I had heard someone coming, but there was no scent of food, which usually follows Mitică wherever he goes. Puzzled, I shut the viewer and went to return to my cot when a soft knocking, three times to be exact, was tapped on the other side of the door.

Huffing, I called. "Mitică, is that you? This isn't very funny."

But there was no answer; in fact, it was just silence on the other end until another three taps were ticked against the heavy door. Adrenaline began to pump through me as a chilling electricity shot up my spine, and I knew something was wrong. Frozen, I stared at the door, straining for another knock or any other sound from the other side.

Just as I thought it had passed, there was a whiff of something stale in the air. For certain, it wasn't my imagination anymore. Quietly, I inched to the door again and pulled the viewer back just a crack to see through. Again, nothing.

Just as I was about to close it again, the small handle was ripped from my hand, pulling back all the way with a snap. Gasping, I went to dodge away when there manifested before me a pair of distinctive yellow eyes on the other side of the door. My lungs iced over, and my instinct told me to slam the viewer shut, but I was paralyzed by the spellbinding gaze those eyes held. Wafts of brimstone leaked through the viewer, and the smell burned my nostrils.

I was terrified but more clear-headed than the last time Satan had come to me, so I felt more prepared to defend myself. It was unusual of him to come to me when I had all my faculties, and I steeled myself against Lucifer's tricks. "Have you come to tempt me again? Don't waste my time."

The thousand-voiced one chuckled as tendrils of black mist spread from the viewer, but did not reach me as they strained against an invisible force. "Is that any way to treat your father-in-law, sweet one?"

A gagging sensation formed in my throat, and I cringed at the affectionate title. "Don't flatter yourself."

Completely ignoring my retort, the Devil continued. "Is that any way to speak? We promised you our son, and now he is yours."

Was he implying that the Count's decision to marry me was influenced by him? My brow furrowed, but I ignored the insinuation. It had to be a trick to throw me off course...wasn't it? So, I pressed the more important issues at hand. "The Count is not mine. He is his own person and makes his own decisions. What about your little witch and her gaggle of geese who seek to end him? How does that make you feel that own your children wish to destroy each other?"

I have no doubt he didn't care one way or another, but I wasn't playing on a concern he may have for his spawn. Lucifer took a moment before responding, perhaps to calculate the implications of his next scheme. "If you would only ask us, we could convince Imogen and the others to leave. Finally, you two could be together as husband and wife, even unto eternity if you so wish it. What do you say, sweet Isadora, most noble of mortal women?"

"Don't try to fool me with empty promises," I snapped, although inside I must admit it was a tempting offer. To simply ask and have those six disappear on their own accord...that would be too good to be true. There would be consequences for that, ones I'm sure that I cannot afford. "And don't flatter me, either."

"Empty promises?" He scoffed, the tendrils flaring out from the viewer's opening. "To our own daughter? Come now, wife of our son, you ceased to be a normal soul once you signed your name alongside his. We owe you a wedding gift. Tell us what your heart desires the most, and it will be given to you."

I was treading on thin ice enough these past days, and I couldn't risk falling into the freezing water beneath. When I addressed him, however, my voice sounded rather defeated. "I want nothing from you, Lucifer. Leave me be, and never taunt me again."

"Not a single thing?" He chuckled again, a slim wisp of smoke brushed my cheek, and made me shiver. "Ah, but we know something that your heart desires. What say you to a child of your very own from the loins of your beloved? It is within our power to make it so."

A child with the Master? I had an inclination that he couldn't have children the biological way, but it never bothered me because it was none of my business. Besides, I believe it would be a disservice to the innocent life to throw them into this serpent's pit. Satan must have seen the care I gave little Moses, and it frightened me that Imogen probably knew the Count didn't actually kill the infant.

The thought was unnerving, and I stayed silent for too long, which led Lucifer to chuckle. "You believe we will tell Imogen? You know our services don't come for free. Ah, but you are silent for other reasons as well, daughter. We can see your mind's eye crafting a future with your beloved and his child."

"Stop calling me 'daughter', I'm not *your* daughter. I told you I want nothing from you, so be gone with you! Shall I invoke His name?" I pointed upwards. "Or will you go quietly, and leave me in peace?"

He snorted, and the heat of his breath could be felt even through the door. "Very well, very well. Keep what we offer in mind, darling girl, perhaps you will see its usefulness sooner than you think. Until then, simply call and we will come."

I didn't actually expect him to withdraw, but the black mist dissipated, and in a whispering hiss, Satan had gone. Instantly, I shut the viewer and stumbled back as I fell onto the bed. My heart hammered so wildly in my chest that I had to hold it to catch my breath. Visits from the Devil are never cordial, and I knew something was happening if he would come to me after a month and speak as if we were pals. Disgusting.

I am convinced it's no coincidence that I was well enough to leave the confines of my little prison that evening. As per my request to Mitică when he brought me my lunch, I asked him to beg the Count to meet me before seeing the children. It was more than just his father's sudden reappearance that made me want to see him, but I missed him so that I could hardly bear another night of being away.

Later…

I dressed in fine robes again, these of a deep magenta accented with a leafy-green pattern. It felt good to be back in my old room with the familiar sights and sounds. With the slight chill in the air, Mitică lit the fire for me, and I sat in front of it for about an hour before the sunset, thinking about this and that. The time went quicker than expected, and before I knew it, there was a soft knocking at the door, which opened by itself. I stood immediately as my husband entered, unharmed and looking perfectly well, to my relief. Yet he looked slightly…different, somehow, with his features more angular, the tips of his ears pointy, but I quickly forgot about it as the door closed.

"Count," I went up to him since he didn't approach or say a word to me. Taking his hand, I held it firmly. "My love, I've missed you so much. Thank you for seeing me."

He cocked his head to one side, and then gave me the most insincere smile I had ever seen. "It has been some time, my wife, I trust you are well?"

My brow furrowed slightly at him, realizing something was very wrong. After not seeing me for so long, he usually demands my affection, but his fingers didn't even come around to hold my hand. "I'm well, but are you? Is there something bothering you? You don't seem yourself."

Exhaling sharply, he withdrew his hand from my grasp as if I had offended his royal person and glided further into the room. The Count's back was turned to me as he spoke. "I am better than I have ever been, wife, and you offend me by saying such."

I was left standing there, the coldness of the shoulder he had given me was chilling. There was no tenderness in his touch, and my heart was developing this stabbing pain within it. "Forgive me, Count, I haven't seen you in some time and I have missed you greatly."

"You are forgiven this time." He took a temporary seat on the arm of his chair as he gazed at me sharply after a pause. "If you have nothing else to say, I must be going. My children are waiting."

There was no way I could believe any of the words that were coming from his mouth. Every single utterance was so unlike him that I was left dumbfounded as I scrambled for my own. "Then I will be brief: your father visited me again this afternoon."

There was no spark to anger, only a continuation of that indifferent expression. "And?"

"'*And?*'" I blinked, quickly becoming put out that he would answer it so nonchalantly. "Don't you want to know what he said?"

The Count raised his eyebrows slightly as he shook his head. "Not particularly, no."

I stared at the Master. Who was this man to whom I spoke? He was not the man I know, the man I love. He was someone else wearing his clothing, his face, his skin, and scent. Cautiously, I moved closer to him and asked. "What has happened to you?"

The Count's brow knitted at my blunt question. "Nothing has happened to me."

Still daring to take steps closer, I called him out. "Vlad, you can try to lie —"

"You dare to accuse me of lying? Insolent woman, perhaps I shall cut the tongue from your mouth." In a burst of ire, he snapped at me, baring his teeth. This man was frightening, so easily prone to anger.

Who is this man? Since when was it not alright to call him by his name? This threat chilled me to the bone, and fear of him replaced all else. I dared to approach the beast where he sat upon his chair and fell to my knees before him. I reached for his hand, but he withdrew it each time I would get close, and desperate emotion welled in my chest. "Voivode, beloved, please, tell me what has happened to you. Have they corrupted you so much that you've forgotten —"

"I do not explain myself to anyone, especially my own wife." The Count looked away from me as he made an exasperated sigh. "Woman, you are so easily fooled into believing whatever sad story I tell you. Your longing to assist me was well placed, but is now no longer desired."

"What are you saying?" Astonished, I'm positive that my heart stopped beating. His words made me shake my head in denial. "You no longer seek redemp—"

Seizing me by my hair, the Count lifted me so that he eyed me straight on. I yelped at the sharp, painful pull in my scalp, but he had no sympathy or remorse in his eyes. "Say the word again and I will rip open your throat."

Of course, that made me shut up as tears turned my eyes glassy from the pain. I stared into those red eyes, which before had been so soft when they gazed at me, were now so cruel. I think he would have acted upon his threats if I had pressed further.

Releasing my hair, the Count took my chin and fully exposed my neck. "For the future, if a wife is on her knees before her husband, it is for one reason: to service him. Unless you wish to put that mouth of yours to good use instead of causing me indignation, I suggest you keep it shut and remember your place here." Roughly, he withdrew his hand and stood. "Do not come down this evening."

He had already left, although I hadn't realized it, when I whispered. "Yes, Master."

I sat there on the floor trying to wrap my head around what happened.

How foolish I had been to expect him to hold and touch me, to kiss me and caress me after so long. Instead, he is colder and so distant from me than ever before. Even when we were complete strangers, he treated me with more warmth than that. Is this man the one he was so long ago, or some other being? Soon enough, the tears began, and I've been inconsolable. I can't help thinking that my presence here has backfired. Instead of helping, I have brought him his downfall. Yet a little voice spoke to me from somewhere deep within my mind.

"No matter how far away I may seem, sweet one, be mindful of this day and how I touch you now and remember."

*Be mindful…remember…*what do those words mean anymore?

I will try to remember, but I fear he has forgotten them and me.

PART II

The Man Himself

Vita brevis breviter in brevi finietur
Mors venit velociter quae neminem veretur
Omnia mors perimit et nulli miseretur

Ad Mortem Festinamus
Llibre Vermell de Montserrat
1399

Chapter Thirty-One
VIPER'S NEST

8 October

Morning…

How can any of this be true?

Is it just a bad dream?

It has to be. But it can't be. I know I'm awake, living in the real world. Yet why can't I wrap my mind around any of this? It surely can't be. It cannot.

What happened to the man I love? He's become a monster — someone I no longer recognize. He's no longer the man I fell for, the one who protected me, or the one I married. Is this the monster he once was: the devil he said I should never meet?

Not so long ago, my husband, then my Count and ancient Prince, knelt with me before the altar in his neglected chapel. With Christ Pantocrator looking down upon us from the domed ceiling, my

Count suffered in physical pain to humble and abase himself before the Almighty. This was the antithesis of his existence, and now he has thrown away every scrap of his humanity that he has gained over the last century and has returned to his previous state.

The Count I knew, or thought I knew, is not a man I know anymore.

I am in tears. I've been this way since last night when he cast me aside to be with his 'children'. I know I am in denial. I feel more numb than if I had been immersed in a bath of ice. How can I not be? I am alone in my torment. I cannot tell Dumitru, my sweet and dearest friend, about the master's private matters. I cannot risk verbalizing my worries and concerns lest someone, or something, should be eavesdropping.

My heart is in agony and wants to break free from my chest. I can feel a silence, a bitter cold, creeping into my bones. It feels like the chill of Death; of life fleeting from a living body.

I guess in my own way, I have become undead.

12 October

Evening...

For the last five days, I have suffered in silence, existing someplace between here and there, wherever those two are. This limbo in which I exist, in which I *had* to exist, was a thick fog. Sometimes time would pass slowly, or sometimes too quickly. I have cried an unending stream of tears, enough to fill the ocean that has formed between the Master and me.

As a result, I lost my appetite that night when the Master rebuffed me. Since then, I've eaten very little for the simple reason that I cannot stomach food. Already I feel that my clothes are looser. I know it's unhealthy, but I can't physically help it. I fear I'm developing some kind of eating disorder, but I will not let it get the best of me, not when I've come this far.

Dumitru has noticed, of course, that I have not been eating and has confronted me about it. I cannot explain why because it's been difficult for me to admit, or even verbalize, that the Master and I have fallen out. I know Dumitru — Mitică — knows there is something very wrong, and it frustrates him that I cannot bring myself to speak of it. But by now, I'm certain that Dumitru must have assumed that the Master is the source of my current heartache. My friend has been patient with me, and that is more helpful than anything else.

Rarely in these past few days has the master come to see me in private. When he does have the inclination to do so, it's seemingly on a whim, and once he is bored, he leaves. I have become a kind of tiresome duty he must see every few days before he casts me aside and goes on to the next best thing. When we are alone in those brief few minutes, I try to speak to him about the good times from before. Whether they were fun moments or intimate ones, just to jog his memory and remind him of the promises we made to each other. Either he shuts me down in his usual manner or tries to start an argument about some small thing. So far, no progress has been made, but I won't give up on him just yet.

Recently, I have rejoined him in entertaining our 'guests', yet even then, I am an island surrounded by sharks. To ensure I do not anger the master, I barely say more than two words in one string at a time. Other than that, I nod or make some other gesture. In public, and in private really, he never addresses me as anything other than 'wife'…no more 'sweet one', 'beloved', or even 'sun of my nights'. When I walk among the children, I keep my back straight and my chin up, even when I want to curl into a ball and rot away.

We all gather together in the smoking parlor. The draperies are heavy, and the chairs are plush, creating a laid-back atmosphere that seems to melt the occupants into the furniture and make them a part of the room. And of course, I sit among them, rigid and straight-backed, as they lounge as loafers, engaging in the idlest of conversation or boasting about their conquests. The latter is something they particularly enjoy and retell the graphic details in which they eviscerated their victims in one way or another. I'd rather not recount them, but their stories have only served to prove to me that I live in a house of psychopaths.

Already among them, I have observed who is attracted to whom, and it is very telling of their kind. The Master is constantly fawned over by Georgiana, who jealously seeks his attention, but that is only because Cosima has become the new object of his desire. However, Cosima doesn't seem to care at all that she is receiving the affections of the First Father, but simply sits there and enjoys them, since she doesn't have anything else to do. This makes Georgiana extremely envious, and it makes me cringe to watch her be the third wheel of the two.

Though I have observed that much, it's hard for me to look at the three, for it hurts my heart greatly. Cosima treats the Master's tender touching and sweet-nothings as nothing, and it reminds me of the way he used to...

Well, anyway, all in all, it helps me to realize that he seems to be only interested in the next new thing until he gets bored with it. And, of course, that next new thing is Cosima, the pretty little kitty cat who is the youngest of all of them.

Interestingly, Maxim's affections are spread all throughout the group, men and women alike; however, he seems to gravitate towards Imogen, who seems to have no interest in him. In fact, she doesn't seem to have any care in the world for mingling in that manner among her kind. Of course, she sits among them and is actively engaged, but when it comes to whom she says those sugary words, it is to no one. She is similar to Ludevit, who often sulks with a sour expression on his face like he's going to snap if one were to say a single word to him. He seems to stare at Georgiana and Cosima with disgust, yet when he looks at Maxim, his face is not so harsh.

Of course, not all of them are in one room at the same time, so the fondness displayed by one to another is displaced depending on the day. It creates strange dynamics between these creatures when they are in one room, and it is very entertaining, although painful to watch. It reminds me of toddlers all playing in the same sandbox with only one toy to share amongst themselves.

And in all of these amusing budding relationships, Andreas has taken a particular liking to me. It is disturbing the amount of time he spends near me, speaking to me, even daring to discreetly touch my hand or knee. It is all too reminiscent of Petros, and I so wish he would leave me alone.

According to his features, Andreas was in his early thirties when he died and has this ability to speak so smoothly in that deep voice of his. As much as I don't like him and know his only determination is to end me, I still find him intriguing. When we speak, he is the only one who actually talks, and I listen. Still, I am surprised that his wish to be close to me hasn't provoked some territorial response from the Master. Even though he has tossed me by the wayside, I am still his wife, and Andreas' proximity ought to be making him wary. I wasn't even his wife all those months ago, and he could hardly bear the way Petros had climbed all over me. Now, I see that it doesn't matter to him one way or another since Cosima has captured his attention.

This evening, however, after four evenings of only talking about himself, Andreas turned the conversation and asked me about myself. I didn't want to answer him. I wanted him to know nothing about me, nor did I want to risk the Master's ire. Beneath my thin veil, I bit my tongue as I thought of something to ask him instead. I didn't give a rat's ass to know anything more about his homeland, but I still asked. "You already know about me. Tell me more about Greece?"

"If you wish to know any more about Greece, you will have to go see it for yourself." Andreas leaned in slightly. "And yes, I know you on paper, but not from your own mouth."

"My husband would not appreciate it." These were the most words I had said to him about myself at once, and I hated that I had to say that much. I can see his objective is simply to wedge the master and me further apart or make us lose face in front of the others. Not again would I fall for his infantile tricks.

"And your husband does not seem to appreciate you, *koukla*." Andreas' eyes drifted to the master who had whispered to Cosima something to make her giggle.

I averted my eyes, trembling not just from the sight, but also at his new term for me, meaning 'doll' in his language. Calculatedly, I hissed. "You said yourself that I am his property, so what does it matter?"

He grinned, those sea-blue eyes sparkling. "Even though you are, I would still say there should be some consideration for the other party. Yet, he openly seeks Cosima in front of you."

I felt my chest constrict, but said plainly. "The Master may have any woman he wants."

"For a modern woman to say that, I am surprised." Subtly, Andreas' fingers crawled over my hand that rested on my lap, which was just out of sight of the Master. "*Doamnă*, if I may be so bold as to ask —"

"You may not be so bold." I cut him off, sliding my hand out from under his.

He persisted. "All I wish is to see your face. I've seen it in photographs, from a distance, but never up close."

Shaking my head, I sternly rejected it. "No, my husband wouldn't allow it."

"Very well," his fingers then moved to the hem of the veil to examine the embroidery. "Perhaps another time, then, *koukla.*"

I sincerely didn't expect him to back off without a fight, and I was grateful for it, but I know he will not relent. Andreas' advances concern me greatly because certainly he is taking advantage of my husband's lack of public affection for me. He let the subject go and spoke of other things that I didn't care to hear, and before long, I was sent to bed.

On the way back up to my room, Dumitru whispered to me. "Can't you ask the Master to have Andreas leave you alone? He takes too many liberties."

I was silent for a moment before I answered truthfully. "I don't think I can…"

"Why not? He presses too far for his own good with his wandering eyes and fingers." Mitică stewed and added with revulsion. "It's disgusting."

There was no use in keeping it from him any longer. I didn't care who heard me because it was no longer a secret, so I steeled my broken heart. "I no longer hold the Master's favor…"

Dumitru fell silent, then took my hand, and I received it gladly. "I've seen that he has…changed, and because of it, you have changed as well."

I only nodded at the complex simplicity of those words. "Of course, you understand why I didn't say anything to you about it."

He nodded back, opening my door to my chambers for me. I passed through it, but he didn't let go of my hand. "Forgive me for this, but I have to say it. Perhaps the time has come that he has collected all he wants from you and has moved on to another. Isadora, you know I will never —"

"I know, Mitică," I squeezed his hand tightly. "You don't need to say it."

With another nod, he brought my hand to his mouth and kissed it. Cupping his cheek, I rested it there for just a moment before retreating into my solitary rooms.

As I sit thinking about this night, I can't help but notice something. In my entire life, I never thought that I would be the *other* woman in the eyes of the man I thought had the greatest affection for me. The man who cared enough to marry me, who has said all those kind things, kissed me like I was the only woman in the world. But perhaps that's just it: he never loved me to begin with, so how can I expect him to share that oneness that comes with love? I can't. Now the moon of my days has been hidden by black storm clouds, and I fear I will never see it again.

13 October

Late Afternoon…

To get my mind off my misery, I decided to do some reading in the library this afternoon. It was in the middle of the day, and I didn't expect any unwanted visitors to come snooping about. Plus, when I dared to venture out into the castle during the day before, I never spotted one of them in all my wanderings. I was thoroughly convinced that as long as the sun was up, the likelihood of them showing up was slim, although not too unlikely.

Today I decided to wear my sage green dress with golden daisies embroidered on the bodice to try and lift my spirits. Once I got into the library, I retreated into the stacks with the smell of the musty old books encircling me. I found some other English literature that the Master had from the late 1890s to read, such as old magazines and a concise account of the history of Britain. Wishing to be hidden, I situated a table and chair on the other side of the stacks, between them and the large windows, and settled into losing myself to the life and times of England roughly 120 years ago.

I had successfully wasted away a few hours, dreaming of far-off places, that time slipped by like a gust of wind. My stomach was the one that awoke me from my daydreaming to remind me it was past lunchtime. I was very reluctant to leave my little slice of peace when I was shaken by a jolting shiver running up and down my back.

"Hiding, are we?"

All of the world fell away when I faced Georgiana, but it soon turned into a nightmare when I saw she was not alone. With her two other sisters, the gorgeous women mingled between the stacks as they stalked closer, all eyes on me. Mine darted in every direction, but I was successfully pinned in on all sides. Not only that, but the veil I was wearing was only meant to cover my hair and not my face, so my expressions were perfectly readable to them. I was surprised how naked I felt without it, and a part of me began to panic. Standing from my chair, I kept my face stern and emotionless as I addressed them. "May I help you?"

"Well, we're not here to check out a book." Imogen sneered as she leaned against one of the stacks. "We're here to see you, darling Mother."

She was mocking me already, so I stood taller. "I'm busy, so be brief."

"Are you planning to order from one of these catalogs?" Cosima teased, suddenly having one of the more fashion-oriented Victorian magazines in her hands as she flipped through it. She was so fast, I hadn't even seen her swipe it from the table. "My goodness, this rubbish is older than me."

Georgiana came in beside her to look at the array of clothing designs. "It does seem like you're not doing any work at all, *Doamnă*. You wouldn't be trying to brush us off, would you? Now that we girls are all alone, we have so much to talk about."

My fists clenched as I withheld a biting retort. Being surrounded, I didn't have much choice but to comply. "Talk about what?"

"Oh, so many things," Imogen crept forward, eyeing me up and down like I had a target painted right on my chest. "We women have to stick together, you know."

Them? Women? More like sirens or harpies, I thought. "Say what you must, then."

"Well, first of all," Georgiana spoke up, leaving Cosima and coming too close for comfort. "I want to know how you managed to fool our Father into marrying —"

"Now, Georgie, that's no way to speak to your mother." Imogen interrupted, her insulting tone already egging me on.

"Although I am curious about it. That was one thing we did not expect from *Ţepeş*, knowing him as well as we do."

All three of them looked to me for a response, and I couldn't help but crack a grin that they thought I had been the one to force the master to marry me. Sizing up for the kill, I squared my shoulders and glared straight at Imogen. "You think I had something to do with that? Don't make me laugh. You placed me in this situation, so you can only blame yourselves."

Georgiana growled, but once again, Imogen stayed her hand. "Whatever do you mean, Mother dearest? Are you accusing us of forcing his hand? I am truly pained."

Heat was rising in my chest and neck as I pressed a bit too far, upon further reflection. "If you wanted me to leave as you wish, Imogen, you should have done a better job ensuring that my suicide attempt hadn't been a failure."

Cosima muttered something in Italian I didn't catch, but I'm sure it was no compliment.

"What fire there is in you now," Imogen hissed, her teeth glistening. "That's something I didn't see before."

"I'm glad I'm full of surprises for you." I glared back at the she-devil, almost daring her to pick a fight with me. "Let that be a warning for the future."

"The audacity!" Georgiana was losing control of herself, her beautiful face showing the first signs of the metamorphosis. "You short-lived little whore, you think you can threaten us —"

"Georgiana!" Imogen barked, and immediately her sister went silent and backed off. Turning back to me, the silver-haired witch's eyes were reddening with ire. "You are not so smart nor so cunning as you claim. You fell too easily for the little trap I had laid for you and Dumitru."

She was right. Mitică and I had played right into her hands despite being so vigilant. However, I couldn't admit that, and I quickly jumped to save my face, and I bluffed. "How do you know I didn't willingly fall into it?"

She laughed once. "The look on your face said otherwise."

"Enough of this mindless chatter." Cosima butted in, flinging the delicate catalog over her shoulder without a care, raw malice in her voice. "All I want to know is how you managed to kill Petros."

Imogen's face winced at the directness of the question. It appears she prefers guile and subtlety in her provocation, versus the blunt and overbearing nature of her sisters.

"Do you honestly think I could kill one of you by myself? That's rather unrealistic, don't you think?" My consistent prodding was having some effect on Imogen, whose face was beginning to warp with fury. "Petros was very strong, but you three know the Master is stronger than each one of you combined. So, who do you think really killed him? He deserved everything that he was dealt —"

Imogen was suddenly upon me, swiping all my materials off my table, toppling it over in the process. The heavy crash was startling, but I wasn't quite prepared for when she smacked me square on the right cheekbone. She hit me like an iron club, pain bursting onto the sensitive bone and in my eye. I cried out, but before I could even lose my balance, she had slammed me up against the stone wall with her forearm. My skull whacked against the wall hard, but somehow it didn't crack open.

The witch's eyes were the deepest crimson, flecked with yellow, all too reminiscent of another pair of glowing yellow orbs that I know. So, I guess it's true that she did make some kind of pact with Satan and was marked by him. "Do you take us for fools, little human? We can hear your heartbeat quicken when you lie, and we see the slightest unconscious movements in your face. Without that ridiculous veil that he makes you wear, you are plain for the world to see."

If she had spoken in a thousand voices, she would have sounded exactly like the Devil himself. But, do I really make faces when I lie? The thing is, I'm not really lying about it. I didn't kill Petros, but I got the ball rolling for the Master to finish him. In a way, we're both guilty and both share the noose in the end. "Even if I did, do you think you can do something about it?"

"I can take out your eyes and split your tongue in your mouth, right here…" Then she paused, a sinister thought manifesting on her face. "Or perhaps you can end up like your handsome American friend with the blond hair? Oh, what was his name again?"

My heart sank as I muttered. "Matt…"

"That's right." She jeered, pressing harder against my sternum with a terrible sneer. "He made a tasty lunch after his usefulness was over, and then his organs served as a quality sacrifice to our Greatest Father, Beelzebub."

I could not mask the terror that froze me in place, but there was also an unlikely fury that surged in my chest at the news. I had kind of suspected that my American friend was possibly dead due to the nature of the one who had compelled him against his will. With all my heart, I wanted to believe that he had walked away unscathed from the café, but now I cannot deny that he is dead. Knowing Imogen, she tracked him down and silenced him, all because she wanted to secretly give me a message to relay to the Master. To her, Matt was collateral damage, and that disgusted me. "Then why wait? Do it now. Make it as slow as you like. I can't stop you."

"Tempting," Georgiana spoke up as she came up behind Imogen, revealing her teeth as well. "But maybe we aren't finished with you just yet."

"So, what is the reason you've come to me now?" I growled as I looked at all three of them, demanding some sort of real answer. "To threaten and harass me?"

"A bit of both, yes," Cosima slinked forward and came up next to Georgiana. "But also to warn you not to interfere with our Father. We know you like to put your nose where it doesn't belong, so keep it far from him if you wish to keep it on your face."

"Well, you have made sure of that, Cosima." I spat, letting my anger control me more than I should have. For some reason, I thought it was wise to provoke her further. "Does it satisfy you to know you have stolen him away from me?"

"I don't care whose husband it is." She did respond with little care, giving me a sassy eye roll. "I believe the mere fact that you lost him reflects more on you than him."

I hated the words that I was going to say, but found myself perpetuating Mitică's warning anyway. "Soon enough, he will tire of you and move on to the next new thing."

"We do not operate on the same time as humans." Imogen leaned in to threateningly smell my neck. "You age every day, you are dying with every breath you take, but we are eternal, deathless gods. We could be here for a decade and just scratch the surface of our purpose here. You may be here for a very, very long time before we decide what to do with you."

"And so what is your purpose here?" I tested them further. "Surely one 'little human' is not worth your time, no matter how much of it you have. What have I done to warrant your hatred, other than your accusation that I killed your brother?"

"We are already succeeding in our purpose." Georgiana boasted, reveling in their triumph. "And soon enough, Father will be finished using you. Then you will see your worth in his eyes, and he will lay waste to you and return to how he was before. That is, if we don't get to you first."

Exhaling sharply, I was about to spit some venom back their way when there was the sound of a throat being cleared. Everyone turned to look behind us. Dumitru stood, hands behind his back, as he addressed me like no one else was in the room. "Forgive the intrusion, *Stăpâna mea*, but I must ask you about some things concerning the kitchen if you are available?"

"Of course, Dumitru." Looking at Imogen, she gave me one last death stare before releasing me. I straightened my dress and played along with this obvious charade. "Ladies, thank you for this riveting conversation. I'll see you all this evening."

Promptly, Dumitru and I left the library, leaving the three witches behind us. I was still in a semi-blinded rage that I wasn't really paying much attention to where we were going until Mitică put his arm in mine. The gentle touch snapped me back to reality, and I began to feel the full extent of the soreness burning my cheek and head.

"What did they say?" He whispered lowly in case someone was listening.

"Threats, accusations, the usual." I scoffed after whispering back to him.

My friend frowned, half-disgusted, half-enraged. "Come on, let's get you some ice."

When we reached the kitchen, I sat down at the servant's table, slouching as I gingerly dabbed the tender skin and whimpered. Once Mitică got me the bag of ice wrapped in a cloth, he sat down next to me, resting it on my swelling cheek. The cold weight made me whine, tears forming involuntarily in the affected eye. Placing my head on his shoulder, Mitică's arm came around me, and he let me rest comfortably against him. Dumitru's warmth and support were exactly what I needed to calm my overflowing emotions, and I nestled contentedly into his side.

"Dumitru," the Master was suddenly in the room. We both jumped, but instead of fleeing from each other, Dumitru kept his hold, concealing me from my husband's sight. I feared for both of us, but then the Voivode commanded flatly. "Leave us. Now."

Mitică glanced over at me, a fearful expression in his eyes. Reluctantly, he peeled himself off of me and left the kitchen. The Master and I were alone, and I lowered the bag of ice from my cheek. Surely I was in for it now because there would be no other reason for him to come to me in the middle of the day other than to deal his punishment. News travels faster among the dead than the living, I guess.

The Master came up beside me, taking my chin to move it side to side to examine my developing bruise. Then he asked rhetorically. "Where did you get this?"

I knew he already knew the answer. I dared not look at him to read his face, but I knew I couldn't lie about something like this to him. "Imogen didn't like it when I told her that Petros got what he deserved."

"You are fortunate, wife, that she was only playing with you." The Master let go of my chin to graze his fingers over the swelling flesh, making me wince. "It could have been much worse."

A part of me wished that it had been. I felt myself slouch my shoulders further in defeat and went straight to my own defense and apologized. "I'm sorry I offended you…"

"On the contrary, you showed no fear despite facing all three of them at once." The Master tucked some loose hair behind my ear. "It was too audacious of them to come against you in broad daylight, and you defended yourself well despite it."

I was dumbfounded to hear him praise me, and it felt foreign enough that I wasn't sure how to react. "Thank you, husband."

His fingers suddenly latched around the base of my skull and pulled me to his lips. Again, the sensation was unfamiliar, and I moaned and whined in a mix of fright and shock. To resist him then would have been unwise, so I had to welcome his fevered barrage of kisses. The Master's tongue came into my mouth, and it frightened me that he was suddenly so persistent — then I tasted it. His blood trickled down my throat, and then he abruptly withdrew, leaving me gasping for air. Within just a few seconds, the achy pain on my cheek had vanished, leaving it unblemished. I wanted to scream at him for being so presumptuous that he gave me his healing blood again, but I had to bite my tongue and be grateful.

"Continue to please me, wife, and I will not withhold from you my affections." The Master panted from the exchange with a savage grin, his own blood smeared on his teeth. "If you perform well this evening, perhaps I will come to you before the dawn and make you moan again. What say you?"

Both of my cheeks flared red at his blunt insinuation, and it made him chuckle darkly. Most likely, he meant something far more nefarious, but I didn't want to find out what. Gulping, I moved out of his grasp and bit the bullet to appease him. "You may come to me anytime you wish, husband."

"Good girl," he massaged my newly uninjured cheek, and I quivered. "Imogen and the others will be spoken to, and I will ensure they apologize for their behavior."

Cautiously, I placed my hand over his and looked him straight in the eye. Sliding my fingers between his own, I kissed his palm. "Thank you, my love, for your kindness."

The Master paused, his eyes locked on mine. I swore I heard that distinctive vibration in the air, though it was so slight I can't be sure. But that look that passed between us, it was as if for one second, I was touching the Count, not the Master. Maybe it was just my imagination that I was seeing what I wanted to see, but when he gazed down on me, I swear there was…something. He leaned forward, a glint of red sparking in those eyes. "Perhaps I will see you in the morning, regardless."

Instantly, that moment dissolved when he removed his hand and gave me one last appraising eyeful before turning away. There was a grin on his face; not one of playful intent, but of hidden motive. I watched him ascend the steps and disappear into the corridor, and my shoulders slouched again. Mitică returned immediately after the Master had gone for sure, not asking too many questions when he saw that my injury had faded. By just looking at my face, I think he got all the information he needed and sat down beside me, taking my trembling hands.

Now I am back in my rooms, preparing myself for the trial ahead. Something has me thinking, though. The one thing that has changed more than anything in these few weeks is the amount of time the Master and I have spent together. I remember once the Count said that without me, he is a monster. Back then, I thought it was just a kind of metaphor for him to relate conflicting emotions in a way I would understand, but now I believe that it was much more literal than I had originally perceived. Before the children's arrival, we spent hours in conversation and physical closeness together. Could it be that easy to sway him back to me?

I must give him the interest to stick with me, but how far am I willing to go to ensure that? Knowing them, it will be forcing me out of my comfort zone or placing me in situations where I have to say 'yes'. In my delicate position, I cannot fail, lest I sink deeper into the pit. May God forgive me for the things I must do and forgive them for making me do it.

Chapter Thirty-Two

BANE

14 October

Morning, 10 am…

Yesterday evening, when we all assembled in the smoking parlor, the Master had done what he had promised. In front of the four children present, consisting of Andreas, Imogen, Georgiana, and Ludevit, he strong-armed Imogen and Georgiana into giving me a formal apology, despite Cosima not being there. It was satisfying to see the looks on their faces when the Master gestured for me to sit beside him, and he then thoroughly humiliated them. I have no doubt the three succubi were so confident that the Master wouldn't care what they did to me.

When Andreas and Ludevit heard the Master's reprimand, they both appeared rather surprised. From their reaction, it seems they hadn't been told anything at all about what their sisters had done to me. Does that mean that Imogen is letting her pride muddle their objective here? From what I understand, that objective is removing the Master from power and replacing him with a younger figurehead. I wish I knew more about how these creatures operate.

Anyway, since Cosima was not present, Georgiana was all over the master to passively seek retribution against me. Of course, I said nothing to stop her. It gave my husband something to keep his mind occupied while I focused on Imogen, who was brooding over my little victory. She was stiff in her chair, her eyes sometimes flickering to me, then away. The witch was conniving at something, I could smell it.

Luckily, Andreas also kept his distance from me. This was probably because I was sitting so close to the Master, and his little advances would be noticed. I don't think he wanted to get into more trouble than he was by association with the girls. When I wasn't watching Imogen, I saw him observing me out of the corner of his eye as he would speak either to Ludevit or his First Father.

When the hour struck for me to retire, I stood and addressed a 'good evening' to all of them. To leave, I had to pass by Imogen, who was still brooding, and gave her a death stare from beneath my veil. At the proximity, she saw through the lace and tulle to see my mocking expression. Boldly, Imogen growled loud enough for the others to hear. The undead ones froze, all eyes trained on us, but I kept walking to ignore her little threat despite the chill it caused.

Without any warning, with her lightning speed, she snatched the base of my veil and ripped it clean off my head. The she-devil was in front of me in a flash and was about to spit like a striking cobra when she saw my unblemished cheek. Her brow knitted in shock, and her eyes widened at my uninjured face. This caused her to falter just as she had raised her clawed hand, her talons sharpened, ready to slash into my face and neck. Luckily, her astonishment was stalled just long enough that the Master's body came between ours and pushed me back behind him.

Stunned at his sudden appearance, I could hardly believe that he had come to my defense. The Master had successfully blocked her from me. I couldn't see his face, but I didn't need to see it to know from the sound of the savage roar that he had let the demon within show its visage. "Again, you *dare* to cause such disrespect in my own house?! Imogen, you go too far!"

A chill trickled down my spine, and something told me to turn around. To my utter shock, Andreas was standing close behind. Dumitru, who had been near the door, had leapt at me and pinned me behind him with a quickness I didn't expect. I locked eyes with the Greek, fully expecting Andreas to be the next to pounce, but he did not. Actually, neither Ludevit nor Georgiana had bothered to move a muscle. Instead, the Greek took his attention from Dumitru and placed it on me, cocking his head to one side as he did. The entranced expression on his face made me feel so exposed now that he could see my face unhindered by the veil.

"Listen well, witch," her Father snapped his teeth. "Consistently, you treat my wife with a lack of respect that is unbefitting of her position. While you are in my house, you will treat her as you would treat me. Cross me once more concerning her, and I will not show mercy again. Do we have an understanding?"

From the corner of the room, an annoyed scoff shot into the air from where Ludevit had been sitting unmoved by the spectacle. The nerve of him to show such flippancy, such disrespect, to the master when he was already angered greatly troubled me. He dared to further provoke his Father to a greater ire, but surprisingly, the Master did not show him any care. I thought the Voivode would have lashed out at both of them at once and made some sort of example, yet he did not.

All during this tense silence, Imogen hadn't said a word. She remained rigid, unmoving, as she and the Master stared each other down.

A sudden idea dawned on me, and I softly touched my husband's muscled shoulder. "Master, please show her mercy. I have no place to influence your judgment, but I insulted her pride greatly this afternoon, and she is upset. That is no excuse, but please, show her pity."

Honestly, I could not see him showing her any leniency at all, but to start a fight or kill her then and there would only elicit revenge from the others and more hatred toward me. I know he knew that, but to what extent did he realize it?

The Master turned his head slightly, the demonic side of him melting away. He eyed me intensely but then spoke to Imogen. "Do you understand, Imogen?"

359

Surely her pride wouldn't let her admit defeat, especially since it was her nemesis who pleaded for her life. Nostrils flared, lips quivering in fury, she did not give in but merely abated as she was out-matched and out-numbered. "Yes, Father-King."

No doubt she didn't mean a word, but the promise was made in front of witnesses.

The Master huffed, then turned to me. "Retire for the evening, wife."

Mitică grasped my upper arm to haul me away. As I passed by Imogen, I saw that she was staring right at my cheek, a conflicted confusion on her face. I had almost forgotten all about my trump card and grinned. "Don't let your pride get in the way of underestimating me again."

Before any more trash-talking or fighting could continue, Dumitru dragged me into the hall and away from the scene. I had failed to remember to retrieve my veil, but I couldn't exactly go back to get it. When I got back up to my room, Mitică didn't say much to me, but he looked excessively troubled about the encounter. When I asked him if he thought the Master would be angry with me for asking for mercy, he said he wasn't sure. Needless to say, this evening I am going to bed quite troubled. I have bigger fish to fry if the Master is to come in the morning.

15 October

Waiting for the possibility of the Master's arrival put me on edge, and I didn't sleep very well. I kept waking up every few hours and tossing and turning. About 2 am, I had become rather hot and opened the barred window just a crack to let in some cool air. Being mid-October, the Carpathians are deep in the beginnings of winter, though autumn began just a few weeks ago. Keeping alert, I sat there on the low sill watching the landscape, veiled in night.

I was dozing in and out for some time when I became aware of a mist pouring into the room from the window. I was alarmed for a second, fearing it was Imogen, as I watched the corporeal form rematerialize in the dark, but thanked God it was the Master and not someone else. The window clicked shut on its own as he emerged into the moonlight. "Waiting for me, were you?"

"You could say that." Rubbing my eyes from their sleepiness, I stood. "Firstly, I wanted to apologize. If I said something to —"

"Do not speak of it. Merely thinking about that she-devil makes my blood boil." He interrupted, waving it away. "However, it did remind me that I have much neglected you."

Immediately, I dropped the subject, again thanking God that he wasn't mad at me for speaking out of turn. Yet, that was the thing that made him remember that he had been keeping his distance from me? Frowning, I nodded once, then went to my chair to get my night robe. Despite my tiredness, I played the game while I had his attention. "I'd like to thank you for seeing me this morning, it's very considerate of you."

"Considerate?" He echoed, cocking his head to one side.

"Yes, you are quite busy nowadays." I returned to him and smiled. "It makes me happy to know you'd like to spend time with me."

The Master said nothing as he hooked his finger around the loosely tied belt to bring me closer. He eyed the knot almost quizzically, and then lifted his gaze to mine. "You are thinner than I last remember."

My heart skipped a beat, and for some reason, I felt this frog form in my throat. So, I tried to spin it as a positive, and not for what it really is. "Oh, well, thank you —"

"Dumitru tells me you have eaten very little these past weeks." Again, he cut me off, untying the knot and opening my robe. His hands went to my hips and glided over the satin fabric of my nightgown, my breath hitching as the Master felt my ribs. Those large, cool hands of his, so strong and formidable, I had missed them so much. "Is it on purpose?"

"No, no, of course not." I shook my head, but my heart still soared that he was showing some slice of concern for me. If it was real or not, I didn't care, as long as he said *something* to me. "I just haven't had much of an appetite since my...illness. It's coming back, though."

The Master's fingers met at the small of my back, and his voice lowered. "Dumitru also mentioned you were in great pain."

He was so near to me that I hesitantly rested my hands on his upper arms. I marveled that he was being so gentle after pushing me away. "It was very…unusual, but it's all over now. What about you, husband?"

"I have been…well." That was all he said, his hands sliding down to cup my buttocks and kneading there.

I gasped at the sensation and averted my eyes. Never before had he been so handsy. With his new attitude, anxiety got hold of me, and I began to quake. I could not trust his intentions. "I…I am relieved to hear it."

"Are you afraid of me, my wife?" The Master's fingers began to dig into my flesh, his mouth going to my ear to say softly. "Or do you tremble for…something else?"

"I tremble because I have yearned for your touch for so long." My voice betrayed my desperate feelings. "I have missed you more than I can bear, moon of my days."

At that, he didn't respond but removed his hands from my backside and slipped the night robe from my shoulders. Fingertips grazing down my arms, the Master placed his face at my neck, breathing in deeply. "I have seen Andreas and Dumitru take liberties with you. Do you yearn for them as well?"

What a question! I was floored. Anger rose in me, but I swallowed it back down. I wouldn't let him try to confuse me about my feelings, so I defended myself. "If you have seen Andreas touch me, then you have seen how I rebuke him. And Dumitru, you know he's my friend and I care for him greatly, but he is your servant."

The Master's hands continued past my hips to my upper thighs to latch on there, slowly dragging up my gown. "I have seen in their eyes that they desire you."

This little test was extremely irritating. He knows I don't care, but he was only doing this to egg me to say something I didn't mean. "Well, I am not theirs to have, am I?" I embraced his shoulders, feeling their bull-like strength. "Lie with me, even for just a few minutes, before you leave? That is if you desire me."

Our eyes were only inches apart from each other. His eyes glowed red and stared at me with obvious ulterior motives. Slowly, painfully, he led me to my bed, tensing as he watched me climb in. I daringly pulled him in next to me so that he lay on my side of the bed.

It was a bit awkward at first since he seemed to have forgotten his usual habits, but I burrowed into his side. It felt as if he were holding himself in, so I brought an arm around his broad chest to rest it there. Before, he would have kissed me and brought his arms around my torso, but he lay there motionless. It was as if I were sleeping next to a real corpse, freshly cooled. Nonetheless, I let out a soft sigh, appreciating the few moments that I had that were slipping away like sand through an hourglass.

"Do you recall the first time we had laid together, husband?" I whispered it so softly into his ear as I groped for his hand beneath the sheets. "You held me all night, even to the morning. It made me so happy to wake up next to you."

"I would not remember anything so insignificant." The Master declared, turning his head away from me as he roughly removed his hand from mine. How could he have forgotten something like that? I cannot fathom it at all.

"R-Right," a knife severed my heart in two, a piece of it dying. "Forgive me."

I wanted to cry right there and then, but shut my eyes tightly and clung to his side, holding my breath in. His words might as well have been physical blows from the way they caused me pain.

The Master scoffed lightly, keeping his distance despite being right next to me. "You cannot beguile me, woman."

"Beguile you?" I raised my head, my brow furrowing. "I love you, why would —"

In a flash, the Master had disappeared from my side and was standing, his silhouette carving the moonlight in half. His chest was heaving, and a threatening growl chilled the atmosphere. "You know I have no love for you, I never have, nor ever will. Do not believe you can trap me."

There wasn't anything I could say about that. But, oh, how I wanted to scream at him to never see me again, to never dare to show his face, but my voice was silent. I internalized all that the Master said and sighed. Being that I rely on him for survival, it's only my connection with him that keeps me alive here. What could I say? If I don't cling to the fraying threads of this relationship, what do I have to ensure my safety from the children?

"You hide your offense well, wife." He quoted himself and then vanished.

In ten days, it will be the anniversary of our first month of marriage, but it might as well be that we aren't married at all. It's not funny, but funny that he only showed affection to me for ten days in the beginning before he shut me away in the high tower. I find that I am staring at my wedding ring too often nowadays. Part of me wants to take it off and throw it into the valley below, the other knows if I did that, I would be punished.

I must stop now. I can hardly see through tears.

Later…

I cried for some time. Looking back, I realize that I did so for about another two hours. My face ached, my eyes burned, my head throbbed with a heartbeat that I could hear in my ears. Although I was feeling cold by then, I went to the barred window to let the fresh mountain chill wash over me. It did little to relieve me, for I cried until I felt numb on the inside and out. A prickly frost set itself deep within my chest, and though unending tears ran down my cheeks, I ceased my wailing and grew deathly quiet. I became a statue: cold and still as the stone of this castle and its Master. Eventually, I dozed off.

At first, I wasn't sure if I had felt a shiver pass through me. My mind was someplace that was unknown to me, and it took a long time to become conscious of the fact that time had passed. My skin was an unmalleable sheet of ice that had set my joints in place, and I found it difficult to move them. Just as I had opened my own blurry eyes, two sets of eyes, one glowing amber and the other vermilion, were staring back at me from the other side of the window. I was horrified and threw myself backward as I shrieked.

Just as I did, the other set of eyes forcefully stuck its head as far as it could through the bars of the window. It was Ludevit who gaped at me with shining amber eyes that stood out against his fiendish ashen face. I must have looked terrified because he chuckled. "Did we frighten you?"

"You should not fear us, Mama," by the deep Ukrainian accent, along with his sarcasm, I knew it was Maxim. "We could smell your tears from across the valley."

"Do not fear us, *Doamnă*," Ludevit added with a mocking tone.

My nerves were needles, sticking me with panic as that familiar unsettling calm made my body grow heavy again. They were placing me under their spell, and it took everything in me to look away from them. With all the voice I had in me, I warned in a growl for them to get lost. I thought it would deter them when I said the Master would come if I called, but they just snickered to themselves.

"We just saw your husband, didn't we, Maxim?" Ludevit rattled the bars to frighten me. "He was with Cosima and Georgiana."

"Oh yes," Maxim repressed a chuckle when he scraped his nails against the iron bars. "And he was well occupied with them."

Then they laughed at me and my husband's folly. I held in all of my emotion and swallowed it with eyes screwed shut to keep the tears from pouring back out again. My voice faltered to spit back some vile retort or even an invocation to the Almighty to repel them. Yet shakily, I started to stand when their laughter died down.

"What has happened that makes you cry?" Maxim sniffed the air long and deep as he crawled more into view. "It was our Father, wasn't it? I can tell that he was here not so long ago."

"Did he deny your advances?" Ludevit jumped at the opportunity to shame me as he sniffed the air too. "I can smell the want from between your thighs. How pathetic."

"But how delicious!" In Maxim's rush of euphoria, he pounced hungrily against the bars, causing them to creak under his weight. "If you let me in, *Doamnă*, I certainly wouldn't deny you. You are a feast for the senses!"

I shuddered at the thought as my stomach turned over. They reminded me of monkeys, fighting against their cage for a piece of fruit that was just out of their reach. It disgusted me that they thought it was permissible to conduct themselves this way toward *Stăpâna* of the house. I refused to stand for it. A deep-seated desire to cause them the same indignation that they were causing me took hold of my resolve.

"Let us in," Ludevit's lips curled over his barbed teeth as he rattled the bars harder. He was trying to sway me to do his will, but I set my eyes on another point in the room. "Just say the word."

I couldn't help but grin to myself that those creatures couldn't enter my space because I had not invited them. Fiddling with the silver chain of my crucifix, which was concealed beneath my nightgown, I knew what I should do. Keeping my eyes far from them wasn't helping me to withstand Ludevit's calling, so I summoned up my courage to act. As I plodded forward, I subtly gathered the chain up into my hand. "You mean you cannot enter here? You can become mist and easily get through any small space, so surely bars on a window are nothing to you."

They both chuckled darkly, but Maxim answered. "It is only a courtesy, *Doamnă.*"

What a lie that was. I had reached the window in only a few steps and stood closer to Ludevit's horrifying face, still protruding slightly into the room. "Then I will show you the same courtesy."

As fast as my poor human abilities could muster, I thrust the crucifix that I had held poised in my hand from out of my gown and smacked it hard onto Ludevit's face. He saw it coming, the flash of the silver and image of the crucifixion repelled him, but he had jammed his head so firmly between the iron bars that he was hindered from pulling away. I saw plain as day the face of the demon rise as Ludevit's blood-curdling scream shook the quiet night. The demonic flesh burned hot and boiled against the silver, and I could feel it sizzle. I drove it deeper until he managed to break free from the iron, bending the bars slightly in the process. Instantly, he vanished, his screams fading like an echo.

Maxim had long since fled just as I had produced the silver, so I slammed the window closed, locked it, and drew the curtains. I don't really know why, but I ran to my bed and pulled the covers over my head, as though to pretend I had been asleep should someone come.

There I stayed in petrified stillness until the sun rose.

...

Somehow, I managed to sleep a bit before my alarm went off at 7 am. As much as I wanted to stay in bed and pretend that everything last night had been a nightmare, I forced myself to get up. I rang the bell pull to call for Dumitru, knowing he would already be up and preparing breakfast for me. I readied myself as I waited for him, taking the time to apply more makeup around my eyes to conceal the dark circles and puffiness.

When Mitică arrived, breakfast tray in hand, I had been sitting at my usual place. At the sight of me, he knew something was wrong, and deep anxiety was etched on his face. I wasted no time and told him everything that had happened early this morning. There was no detail that I left out. He listened, his body becoming more rigid when I told him how the Master knows of his desire for me and how I had disfigured Ludevit.

After taking my words in, Mitică sighed and ordered that I should stay in my rooms until the situation died down. He promised he would speak to the master on my behalf to explain that I had defended myself against Ludevit's compulsion. He thinks that the Voivode will not be angry with me because Ludevit had overstepped himself as Imogen had. As for the children, they may laugh at their brother's foolishness for letting his guard down or be infuriated.

I sat there very quietly as I, in turn, listened to him rant about how appalled he was that Maxim and Ludevit sought me out like that. He told me how he wanted to hang them out in the sun to dry like laundry.

Before he left, Dumitru warned me that under no circumstances should I go into the lower levels of the castle. Despite having no intention of ever going into the bowels of the castle again, I still asked why.

"Because that is where they sleep." His eyes grew very narrow in disgust. "Before the Master changed his ways, he told me not to tell you the location because he thought you'd take it upon yourself to move against them."

I laughed once. I think the Master was not too far off in taking that precaution, but all the same, I swore to Dumitru that I would not go down there of my own free will. My friend was satisfied enough with that, and after kissing my hand and telling me to call if I needed anything, he departed.

Chapter Thirty-Three

ICHOR

Evening…

I t took until evening for the repercussions of my actions to catch up with me. Since morning, I had tried to figure out some way I could defend myself against the Master if he were to come at me with the full force of his anger. I had to steel myself for the worst and keep a clear head.

By evening time, I was still shut away in my rooms, unsure if I should get ready to meet *them* or not. No doubt my presence was not desired tonight — not that it ever really is. As a precaution, I wore my underthings beneath my robe in case I was summoned at a moment's notice. And, uncharacteristically, Dumitru waited in my sitting room with me, as though to stand guard. He should have been preparing for the children to awaken, but chose to stay by me for support.

When the clock chimed and the dreadful, empty howl of the wolves sprang forth from the valley far below, Mitică grasped my hand tightly. "You must remember, *Stăpâna mea*, that you were acting in self-defense. Besides, Ludevit got what he deserved."

Swallowing, I only nodded.

From under my robe, I clenched the crucifix that once belonged to the Master's dear mother. It was for the purpose of self-defense that Vlad had given the precious item to me in the first place. The holy image upon it repelled them, and the silver burned their corrupted flesh. There was no better gift to be given to me after what I had endured in Câmpulung. In the past, he had scolded me viciously for not wearing it when I had been attacked by Lucifer. Back then, he would have been relieved to know it had kept me safe from Maxim and Ludevit, but now he might just feed me to them.

I had been lost in thought when the door to my rooms opened and the Master entered without a word. The flames in the fire sputtered and spat out sparks at his presence. He was angry, but he would not show it. His face was too emotionless as he came to where Dumitru and I were sitting.

Mitică stood and bowed to him while I kept my eyes on the Master's boots.

"Dumitru, go attend to the needs of my children and inform them that I will see them soon." The Voivode commanded sternly.

"Master, I will do as you say, but please allow me to speak for *Doamna*." My friend stepped forward boldly, meeting the Master head-on.

I lifted my eyes to watch my husband's reaction.

Sure enough, Dumitru's provocation had made the Master's hidden fury surge to the surface. "Do as I say. My wife has a tongue to explain herself. At least, she has one for now."

I think I stopped breathing when I heard those words. My heart exploded with a new wave of anxiety, and I began to shake. I hated to think what punishment he would deal me.

"Master," Mitică dared to press further. "Ludevit and Maxim intended to harm —"

"Dumitru," I signaled for him to be silent and stood, my knees wobbling. "Thank you, but your Master is right. Please, do as he says."

Mitică pursed his lips, his face reddening as a concoction of emotions swelled within him. I knew he wanted to stay, but he reluctantly obeyed our wishes after a long pause. With a curt nod, he withdrew from the room.

I had just opened my mouth to speak when the Master immediately shut me down.

"*Silence!*" He barked, his fangs showing themselves from behind his lips. "Do you have any idea what sort of dishonor you have brought upon me and this house?!"

His thundering roar made me flinch, but I fired back at him. "I did what I had to do to —"

"To what? Spite me further?" Instantly, he was in front of me, his face inches away from mine. "Of all the things you could have done to cause me indignation, you choose to disfigure Ludevit's face with a holy device!"

I could not believe the words I was hearing. How could I have been 'spiteful' in doing what I did? I did it to protect myself, nothing more. To him, I guess, all I had done was to subvert and humiliate him. Everything was made worse by the fact that now the children know that he has allowed me to keep sacred items that should be forbidden in this house.

When I was still grasping this, the Master carried on. "Even if I should forget your other recent offenses, I *cannot* forget this!"

"What else was I supposed to do?" I snapped after the levee that had held the building fury inside me broke. "Ludevit and Maxim were trying to compel me to let them into my room. We both know what they would have done to me if I had. I had nothing to defend myself but *your mother's* crucifix, which *you* gave me for that very purpose. I had no ulterior motive when I used it against Ludevit, can't you get that through your thick skull?! I only protected myself, not to be spiteful!"

Surprisingly, the Voivode did not spit fire back, but glared at me with such an intense stare that could kill. He looked straight into me, almost through me, his face hard and body rigid. We stared each other down, eyes locked, as we waited for the other to make a move.

I can't recall how long we were stuck like that, but he was the one to look away from me first. Eerily calm, he sat down in his chair, smoothing out his stubble as he did. When he spoke next, the master's tone was softer but still stern and laced with anger. "You are lucky that the other children find what you did to Ludevit to be amusing. Otherwise, they would have made sure that you would not have lived to see the sunrise."

I blinked at his complete change in demeanor. Shocked as I was, I chose to recompose myself, too. "Why would they find it amusing?"

"Ludevit is known for his stealth and ruthlessness in the hunt. For him to be so humiliated by a human is entertaining because he is not well-liked." He spoke like there was a bad taste in his mouth. Then the Voivode stood again, his ire somehow renewed, yet still he would not look at me when he taunted further. "All the same, I cannot allow what you have done to go unpunished. No matter what defense you say you have for your actions, no matter how justified you think it might have been, you still used that vile thing in my house and therefore brought dishonor upon it."

Again, I could not believe what I was hearing. I wanted to fight him, scream at him, but I bit down hard on my tongue. There was absolutely nothing I could ever say to win him over to my side. Crestfallen, I took in a shaky breath. "Then what is your verdict?"

"Ludevit demands an eye for an eye and then your life." The Master paused for a long while, then his gaze finally turned back to meet mine. "Wife, what say you? Should I give him both?"

My palms began to sweat as my mind raced to find an appropriate answer to give him. I knew this was the game the Master liked to play with his victims: to offer them a chance to choose their freedom or death, then twist it to still end up with their death. Of course, I wanted to live, but with my fate hanging by a thread, I growled. "Yes. Then I will be released from this Hell, and everyone will get what they want."

His shock was manifested in a raised brow with a poorly masked expression of alarm. I had caught him off guard by saying that, and it satisfied me. I couldn't regret what I had said, not at that moment when there was no room for weakness. Standing my ground, I waited for him to say something, but the Master remained silent. He observed me strangely, as though he were looking into my soul rather than at my body. Then a grin cracked his cold exterior, revealing his sharpened ivory teeth, and he chuckled. This smile wasn't one of cheer; however, it was one of a sinister nature. "If you believe you live in Hell, then why should I let them send you to Heaven? Keeping you here alive is punishment enough. Do you not think so?"

Like a punch in the gut, all of the air in my lungs escaped. My attempt to throw him had backfired. In case I were to only dig my grave deeper, I kept silent, though I let my face convey all the contempt I felt for those things he said.

"Your face betrays your emotions too easily to me, wife." The Voivode tapped my nose almost playfully with his index finger, causing me to jerk away. "I will tell Ludevit I do not accept his demands and shall say you have been punished according to my will. Do not come down for the next five days to let things blow over."

Before I could say anything more, not that I had much to say anyway, he departed from the room and locked the door from the outside. After I heard his footfalls fade, I nearly collapsed against the chair. The only thing I could think about was that first evening in May when I met the Count. At the end of our cordial and friendly conversation, he locked my door behind him. Back then, there wasn't a thought in my mind that I was a prisoner, and even when I thought I was a prisoner, I hadn't actually been. Now there is no doubt.

25 October

Evening...

I have not written in many days, so tonight I have forced myself to write the current events of my existence...if you can call it one.

I have looked back on my life and see all the things that I did wrong to get to this point. I should never have taken this assignment in Romania, never should have fallen in love with the Master, never should have let him force me to marry him...the list goes on. I thought about my university days and remembered thinking that I thought they were the hardest days of my life. I never had a clue what suffering was until I came to this castle.

Now I am stuck in this lion's den, wasting away my days like an ascetic. The only way I can survive here is if I shun this world. If I don't abstain from all forms of temptation that the children and their Father present, then I will sink deeper into the Pit. I still wear my nice clothes and fine jewels, but every other bit of pleasure I used to get from wearing them is hollow.

My other ascetic-like activities have consisted mostly of meditation and prayer. I pray so hard for strength and deliverance, for the Master, for Dumitru, and even for the children. There are so few things I have left now that console me and take me away from this wretched place. Once I was allowed out of my rooms, every piece of free time I have, I spend in the chapel, on my knees. It goes without saying that I don't know if the Lord can really hear me from this forsaken place, but they say when one is on their knees, they're closer to heaven; and heaven is far, far from here.

In all honesty, being close to Mitică again has been my other saving graces. When we are near each other, I feel as if nothing could ever go wrong in the world. When we are alone, we both dare to give each other the occasional touch, and he even kissed me on my cheek once. Dumitru's warmth keeps my heart alive when it is encased in ice. The more we are in this situation together, the more I see how he was telling the truth when he said that he loves me like the sun loves a flower.

Meanwhile, the bee who has stolen my nectar is still collecting more from Cosima, even some from Georgiana, too. Now they even kiss in my presence and it makes me gag. Once I saw Cosima lay her hand too close for comfort on my husband's inner thigh as she shot me a menacing glare. That is supposed to be *my* place, not hers. I could do nothing but look away. Since the day he left me in my rooms, the Master has not come to see me once. If that means he has fewer opportunities to be disappointed in me, I welcome it. With each passing day, that memory of the day by the river is fading, slipping from my grasp.

Despite all the wrong that the Master has done me, I have not wronged him in any way. He may be constantly displeased with me and shows me no sliver of fondness other than to address me as 'wife', but I still hold that title. Each day, I must remind myself that I am mistress of this castle, and that I demand respect…as a basic human right, I demand it.

Concerning Imogen, she has not tried to make another attempt on my life again. She has been distant, but that doesn't mean for one minute that she has given up on making my life miserable. I've developed the ability, since I have watched her for so long, to notice when she is plotting, and she has not ceased for one instant. We still share moments of conflict and tense words, but never engage. Everyone is biding their time, I can feel it, but for what? I don't know.

As for Ludevit, for good reason, he rarely shows his face anymore at the nightly gatherings. What I did to him was ugly, though I don't regret it. From his eye, which had exploded when it came in contact with the silver, to halfway down his cheek, was scarred. Deep hues of red and purple in the shape of the cross now deform his face. These wounds, according to Andreas, have not healed and probably never will.

To my disgust, Andreas has continued to win my affections. The Master has shown no care to it, since he is preoccupied, strangely enough, I have had to rely on the Greek to protect me from the others when Dumitru cannot approach.

It's perplexing how I have come to like Andreas more than all the rest. I hated him from the beginning, but he has grown on me. Perhaps it's because he is the only one of them who shows me kindness and seems to always be eager to see me in the evenings. When I enter the room, he stands at my presence like a gentleman and is at my side to ask me about my day or how I am.

Tonight, he said something peculiar, which prompted me to write this entry. We were on the settee, which is a little out of earshot from the rest of the group, at least for humans, speaking about his life before he died. We were deep in conversation about it when Andreas stopped, his eyes captured mine beneath the veil. "*Doamnă*, are you not of English heritage?"

I told him that I am struck by the sudden change in topic.

Andreas hummed. "Your mother's maiden name is Harker, if I remember correctly."

Snapping to attention, I flared with rage at the mention of my family coming from his lips. Gritting my teeth, I answered that it was her surname. I recalled the conversation the Master and I had so long ago about the Harker surname, and I felt a sense of foreboding that Andreas had asked so openly about it.

Leaning in, he whispered in my ear low enough for the others not to hear. "Do you know of our Father's story? Of the time when he went to London?"

I had to think about it, but then remembered. "Only that it was not a pleasant trip."

Andreas chuckled. "Then you know of Wilhelmina Murray, wife of Jonathan Harker?"

"The Master did mention her once to me. Apparently, he was in love with her, from what I gathered." I treaded carefully, tiptoeing around that small amount that the Master told me.

"Ah, then you do know some." Andreas beamed in excitement as he eagerly continued his story. "She had our Father wrapped around her finger, if I may say so."

"That was before she was married, I assume?"

"Oh, of course, she was very loyal to her fiancé, but the Master wanted her for himself." The Greek explained before divulging. "Do you know that you look like her?"

With a furrowed brow, I shook my head.

"I have something for you, but you must keep it a secret. If your husband were to find out about this, he'd be very angry." With a wide grin, he produced from his pocket a gold locket, etched with a floral design, and opened it for me. Within it was the gray-toned image of a beautiful woman with dark hair and eyes, dressed in the fashion of the 1890s.

"That's Wilhelmina?" I shrugged at it. "She doesn't resemble me."

"No? Don't think of it as an exact replica, my dear girl, but as a *familial relation*." Andreas stressed the last words, encouraging me to take another look at the photo of the pretty lady.

"I'm not going to fall for your tricks, Andreas." I tried to hand it back to him, but he did not receive it. "Did you edit the image or something?"

"Still don't believe me?" He thought for a moment, stroking his trimmed beard. "Well, I know that Jonathan and Wilhelmina did have a son, Quincey. However, I'm not sure what happened much after that because the Great War began."

I had seen that name before, titled under some old sepia photo in some dusty family album. However, I couldn't admit that much to him. "I think I know my family tree pretty well." I flat-out lied. "There aren't any people named Quincey, Jonathan, much less Wilhelmina."

"Allow me to ask you this," again, he got close to my ear as if to tell me a secret. "Imogen claims that she gave you a nasty bruise on your face when she struck you, and also made you slit your wrists when she compelled you to send that message to our Father. How did you manage to heal yourself from those wounds, life-threatening or not?"

My heart pumped in my ears, and all the blood drained from my face. "What is that supposed to mean?"

Andreas took hold of my forearm and got so close to my veil that he must have seen right through it. "It's because the Master has mingled his blood with yours, am I wrong?"

I shook my head to deny it. "Disgusting, no."

However, he saw through me, even through the veil, and said. "No human could have healed the injuries Imogen caused you in a few hours, or even a few days. Do not be ashamed of it, for our kind to willingly give blood to another is a high honor. But the thing is, to have it enter into you means you become one of us."

"Well, I obviously haven't become one of you, so there's your proof." I tried to pull away.

"I'm not finished." Andreas reeled me back in so that we were face to face. "Wilhelmina did take blood from our Father and did become one of us to a certain degree. Not a full-fledgling, but that degree does not matter in the end. I digress, Jonathan Harker attempted to kill our Father but —"

I had had enough and cut him off. "I know this, but it's obvious the Master is not dead."

"Correct, but your husband did tell me himself that the bond between them had severed, and she became a normal human again when he had passed from this world. But," there was a pregnant pause. "His blood still existed within Wilhelmina until the rest of her days, and in her child and his children."

I scoffed at him, still pulling away. "How are you so sure? It's too farfetched."

"Because you can take his blood and not become one of us." Andreas turned over my wrist to show me my blue veins. "Because, in a way, you are already like us."

"That's ridiculous." I ripped my hand away. "I am not repelled by the image of Christ, I do not sleep by day, nor do I enjoy the sight of blood. I am human."

"In that regard, yes, you aren't like us. I have never heard of a similar case ever, so I don't know what abilities or limitations you do or don't have. Your servant boy is a separate case, if you didn't know. There are many like him out there, but they are a rare commodity. Humans such as him are different in that they can take our blood but do not change or are affected by our compulsion." He grinned, and taking a peek over near the Master to make sure he wasn't looking, he lifted my veil.

My back was to my husband, so he would not have noticed it, and we were separated from the others. We were eye-to-eye.

"Meanwhile, you can be compelled by us." The Greek traced my jaw to my lips, where he dipped one finger in between my slightly parted lips. He pressed against my incisor and raised his eyes to meet mine. The way he looked at me made my breath catch in my chest, and I was transfixed by his beauty. Something in me flipped like a switch, and I mimicked the same stare, my tongue peeking out from behind my teeth to lick the tip of his finger and bite it. I don't know why I did this, but I liked it. The way he eyed me made my insides ache and melt.

Rather than being shocked at my actions, a delicate vibration fluttered between us. He purred, his eyelids growing heavy as he advanced his index finger further into my mouth, where he rubbed it against my tongue.

The Greek was transfixed as well by the spectacle and leaned in. Just low enough for me to hear, he whispered. "Such a beautiful creature you are…"

His words were dulcet, and it caused my heart to race like the wings of a hummingbird. I didn't realize how desperate I was to hear sweet nothings again. I knew what I felt was wrong, but to be noticed by a man, it was something my heart craved.

With his sharp talon, Andreas nicked the inside of my cheek. I was too engrossed in his gorgeous blue eyes to feel if it actually hurt.

Closing the distance between us, he removed his finger and kissed me. A flood gate opened inside me, and I moaned as he deepened it. This time Andreas' tongue entered where his finger had been, and it danced with mine. He tasted me and my blood, only extracting a small amount before retreating from my lips.

I was left in such a state as he withdrew, a purplish red glow shone in his eyes as he swallowed. His purr turned to a wanton growl, and a hand came to grasp my forearm and anchor me in place. Andreas' strength made me weak.

"I wish I could unravel you from all of these layers." He paused, regarding my chest, which heaved up and down. "You are too lovely to be wrapped up as a China doll."

"Andreas, I…" I stopped, unsure what I was even going to say.

Gently, he shushed me. "*Koukla*, the scent of your wanting is going to attract too much attention."

Suddenly embarrassed, my face and chest burned hot. I was painfully aware of myself then and instinctively smushed my legs together.

Andreas released me, taking care to even smooth the area that he had held with his death grip. "Keep the photograph, *koukla*, and think about what I said. Do not tell your husband, for he will be very upset with both of us."

The locket still in my hands, I stuffed it in my pocket.

With that, he stood, taking my hand and kissing it before returning to the group. I sat there shaking, returning my veil to its normal place. I would say that he compelled me, but I wasn't so sure. I had never burned with such desire as that in my entire life. Was I that depraved? I shuddered.

I struggled to clear my head and thought about this Wilhelmina Murray. They have to be all lies. All these creatures tell are lies and deceptions to purposely make others lose their way. I wanted to take the photo out and examine the visage of that lady who once wrapped the Master around her finger, but knew it would only draw the uninvited gazes of others.

Once I was told to retire, I waited until I was in the safety of my bathroom to take the little photograph out of my pocket and examine the visage of Mrs. Wilhelmina Harker. In front of the bathroom mirror, I stood there, going between her image and mine to compare our features. Eventually, I gave up and went to bed. The heaviness in my lower abdomen hadn't lessened. I tried pushing it from my mind, but my imagination ran wild, and I was swept up in the wind.

Chapter Thirty-four

IACTA ALEA EST

30 October

Ever since he revealed to me my 'supposed' ancestry, Andreas and I have become close. After just about five days of considering the possibility that Wilhelmina was my something-times-great-grandmother, I am still unconvinced. Unless there is DNA evidence, I don't believe it for one second. I thought of possibly writing to my Mom and asking her, as I'm sure she has the documents, but I cannot even open the package from my family that the Master gave me a month ago. It still sits in the drawer of my desk, untouched. If I can't do that much, there is no way I can find out for sure.

However, I've been thinking of the implications of the whole thing. It would mean that through Wilhelmina, I am related in some strange fashion to the Master. That being said, does he realize this? The idea that my husband may be my quasi-grandfather makes my stomach form knots. Doesn't that make my entire family related to him by blood and by marriage? Did he look at that picture of my newborn nephew and see his own grandchild? I have to stop thinking about this.

Anyway, so Andreas has become closer to me, though we hadn't revisited that heat that was exchanged between us. Instead, he has even gone so far as to inquire more about my life before I came to Romania. The night before last, he had asked about the subjects that I used to be able to teach and what my field of study was. It was a bit hard to explain to him without visuals, so I brought a textbook with me that I thought would help him understand. He was intrigued, asking about this and that, and I even told him about the papers I co-published with others in my field.

"You know, Wilhelmina had interests in writing and teaching, too." Andreas subtly passed that small detail to entice me. I just rolled my eyes.

We were having a pleasant time chatting, even Maxim joined in for a bit, although he got bored with it very quickly and switched over to where the Master, Cosima, and Georgiana were loafing about. I noticed that Cosima was wearing quite loose clothing that dipped down low to show her cleavage. It seemed to me that each evening she dresses more provocatively, that dusty promiscuous little…

Anyway, it draws everyone's attention.

In turn, Georgiana gets jealous, and the whole thing becomes a childish squabble of who can outdo whom. I've developed the ability to completely ignore them a large amount of the time, but it's those short bursts where they say or do something distracting that makes me want to drink bleach.

Anyhow, so yesterday evening they were all eager to go on a hunt, and the Master ordered that I should retire early. I didn't have any problem with that, so I left with Mitică to go back to my room. When I had crawled into bed, I remembered that I had left my book on the table in the parlor. Since I was already in my nightgown, it wasn't acceptable to walk around the castle to retrieve it. Besides, Imogen and Ludevit were somewhere lurking, and I wouldn't want to be caught in a dark hallway with one of them. So, I resigned to get it in the morning.

I slept very well and awoke an hour before dawn on my own. The Master, to my great relief, had not decided to show up this morning…not that he would anyway. After I dressed, and as the sun was rising, I made my way down to the parlor. In my logic, they should have all been asleep by then, gorged with their fill of blood.

As I was coming down to the first floor, there was no sign of anyone, as it should have been, so I was relieved that I was in the clear. Half asleep as I still was, I wasn't paying much attention as I turned the corner and walked down the hall to where it branched into the parlor. Since it is a common room, there are no doors, and whatever sound that could be heard from within echoed down the stone corridor. I was already halfway down the hall when I heard what sounded like soft moans of pain coming from the parlor, and it sounded exactly like Cosima. Conflicted as to what to do, I froze, but the groaning only intensified. It genuinely sounded like she was in distress, and I tiptoed to the doorway and peered in. What I expected to see was her maybe injured on the floor, but that's not what I saw.

It was only a split-second glimpse, but it was more than I needed to see in an entire lifetime. There, on the chaise, hunched over in the throes of lust, the Master had pinned Cosima beneath him. Her bare legs were tied in a knot around his hips as he made his quick rocking motions, his back arching with each thrust. My vision tunneled, now hearing those moans as explicit rather than painful, I pressed myself against the wall. Without even fully processing what I had seen, my hand came over my mouth to keep in a sob.

I had to get away, and I took off the way I came. As I passed into another hall in a daze, I was suddenly aware that Andreas was standing in the threshold. He stared at me as I approached, my jog slowing to a fast walk as I roughly tried to blot away my tears with my sleeve.

"*Doamnă* —" he tried to begin, but I put my hand up for silence.

I wasn't sure where I was going, but I needed to be alone. I was still in denial and was walking rather blindly through the castle. Somehow, by some miracle, I found my way to the main floor, dashed into the gilded hall with the mosaic floors, and skidded into the chapel.

The image, the motions, the sublime expression on Cosima's face, they all burned into my brain. Falling to my knees halfway to the altar, I sat on my calves, my face dropping to the floor. One after another, the droplets dripped onto the stone from my cheeks, and my nails dug at the grout of the mosaic tiles.

I think a few minutes passed, or it may have been a few seconds, when I heard footsteps coming up behind me. Enraged that someone had disturbed me at such a time, I growled. *"Leave me alone."*

"Isadora…let me come near." It was Andreas, and he had called me by my first name. His voice was that sweet honey that had enticed me before. "I only wish to help you, I promise."

Peering behind me, he stood just at the other side of the threshold, waiting patiently to be allowed to enter. I didn't want him to come near me, but I needed someone…anyone. Perhaps he would kill me, and all my problems would be over. All the pain that I've carried within me would cease, and I would be free. So, I nodded, muttering some kind of compliance to allow him entry.

Andreas came and knelt beside me, a comforting hand soothing my convulsing back as he gently shushed me. "My poor darling, you have been so wronged by so many."

"If you've come to kill me, *do it.*" I spat, the raw emotion in my voice shocked me. "I don't want your worthless pity. I know it isn't real. Don't wear one mask when you hide behind another and do something you actually mean for once in your damned life!"

Andreas halted his hand, and I waited for him to do the deed. Instead of giving me a final blow, he lifted me from my prostrated shape and brought me to him. He did not bite, nor strangle, nor cause any physical pain, but caught me up in his arms. Softly, in his deep voice, Andreas murmured. "I've lost someone in a similar way, so I understand the feeling of that knife in your back. It's a pain that lingers and never really heals."

He was very right about that feeling, and allured by his gentleness, slowly I allowed myself to lean against him. How strange it is that in spite of him reminding me so of Petros, now I clung to him as if he were the only thing keeping me tethered to this earth.

It's amazing how one month has changed so much. I was going to say something about how I was sorry he had felt pain like this, but I hung my head. A few minutes passed, and I slowly removed myself from his embrace. He let me go with no fuss. With the heels of my hands, I wiped the salty tears from my cheeks. "Why are you being so kind to me? I thought you were here to kill me, not to care about what I feel."

"Kill *you*?" Andreas' fingers came up to whisk away some other stray tears, his touch was silken yet so cold like the Master's. "Come now, do you think we're all so bad?"

"What else am I to think?"

Taking my hands in his, he examined their smallness compared to his own. He was contemplating something as he did, smoothing my skin with his thumbs. "Between the both of us, I am not sure I believe what Imogen says." He paused, again the blue sea reflecting in his gaze. "You are too kind to kill, and you would not have lived if you stood against Petros. Also, forgive me for saying it this way, but it's plain to see that you hold no power over your husband."

Swallowing hard, his words cut deep with their truth, and another tear slid down to the stone. "The Master has endured much grief this past century, and Petros took advantage of that. I just happened to be here at the same time. It's true that after that, we grew affectionate toward each other, but when I was threatened, he would not sever his attachment to let me leave. So, here I am."

Andreas frowned. "And now he has you as his own, but has no fondness for you. Even I see that as a tragedy, befitting to be lamented by the old poets. Forgive me for calling you his 'plaything' when you are a prisoner of his house."

I replayed his words over in my head, judging them for their sincerity. Could it really be true that Andreas has had a change of heart and sees me as more of the victim than the perpetrator? I decided to roll with it. "All is forgiven. Although, answer me just this one thing?"

He released my hands and nodded.

"Am I right to assume Imogen is acting on her own accord?" I inquired and watched him shrug once. "You appear to have doubts?"

"She only seeks revenge for the death of Petros, her lover. It matters not to her who was the real killer, but since she could never defeat our Father by herself, she might as well target the one whose death would cause him the most pain." Andreas gestured to me at the very end. "The others want the Impaler to return to his bloodthirsty self. From him, we draw our life. The more he withdraws, the less powerful we are. We are bound to him in this way."

Petros was Imogen's lover? I had to shake off my shock. All of it made so much sense now. They are here not just to seek revenge but to lure the Master back from the edge of his redemption. I swallowed hard and circled back to the Master and distanced the conversation from the purpose of his withdrawal. "My husband would not blink if I died. He feels nothing for me."

His head tilted to one side, perhaps judging my despondent answer. "You are the embodiment of his Wilhelmina, coming from her own blood and thereby his blood. To lose you by one of our hands would be catastrophic to him. You see, since we cannot die naturally, the deaths of those we care the most about are felt a thousand times more."

"You are so sure he feels something for me, when he has told me otherwise." My throat constricted in grief from my own words, and I had to clear it. "I appreciate you trying to give me some hope that he may have a fondness for me again, but it's a false hope."

Andreas rested his hand on my shoulder. "It took him a century to recover after the loss of Wilhelmina, and she was with him a mere handful of days in the months that he was in London. Don't you think the Master would do the same for you, who is his wife, with whom he has been nearly every day for the past six months?"

A fragmented memory came to me of the day by the river, and I could feel in that instant the Count's loving caresses, but the flame was snuffed out. "After what I saw today…" I breathed out a long sigh, glancing up at the altar. "I don't know who he is anymore."

Later…

I have spent the entire day in my room being miserable, dejected, and morose. When Dumitru came up to give me my breakfast soon after my last entry and found me as I was, he held me for the longest time. By then, I thought I had exhausted all my tears, but I still had some fall when I explained to him what I saw. He was surprised that the Master would do an act like that so openly, as he is usually such a private man. Either way, having my true friend close by was all the comfort in the world to me, especially since my world is narrowing and collapsing in on itself.

I decided not to tell Dumitru about all that Andreas had told me. Due to the fact that I am extremely suspicious of the Greek still, he would most likely expect that I would tell Mitică or the Master about the information he revealed. I will keep it to myself and see if any of it really does come about as being true. This is the first time in a very long time that I have withheld vital intelligence such as this from Mitică because I know he will say it to the Master. Also, by doing this, I am trying to make it seem to Andreas that I am starting to completely trust his word above all others, which will come in handy later if he chooses to tell me more of the goings-on of the others.

Although I had no stomach for breakfast, I forced it down as a kind of act of defiance. No more, I resolved, will I let the Master influence my emotions. Next week it will be a month since he became this whole other person, and no longer will I allow him to crush my heart like a grape between his fingers. A month is too long to hope for him to come back to me, no matter how I try. I still care for the man with all my being, and even more now, I pity him that he has fallen from all he has worked so hard to achieve. I am still his wife, and I still love him, but he has made his own bed, and now he will sleep in it.

9 November

Afternoon…

On 4 November, I began my time of the month and knew the drill of what to do. After telling Dumitru the vague details, I gathered my things and schlepped up all the flights of stairs to the high keep. This time, I was much more prepared for my ordeal and brought books that I would actually be interested in reading, along with other things, before locking myself away.

This go-around, it felt almost like a hermit's retreat rather than a brief imprisonment. I spent most of my time gathering myself together from my recent loss, consoling myself with the Good Book and other novels to send me far away. Another plus was that my ordeal was a walk in the park compared to the last one. Sure, I was in pain, but it was far from debilitating and easy to cope with. As usual, the only bummer was the loneliness and the drab scenery outside.

Everything is good and dead now, and we have already had our first spats of snow. The cold that I recall the Master speaking of is beginning to rear its ugly head, with temperatures ranging near freezing because we are so high in the mountains. With winter upon us, I am really trapped here. At least when it was warmer, if I needed to run, I could do it, but with the bitter cold and excessive snow, I wouldn't last a day. With the cold, the wolves will be hungrier and smell me coming from miles away. Not to mention, I could be easily tracked in the snow, and where would I go anyway? The real world is so far away from this one.

When Dumitru came to visit me, he told me of the daily routine and how the Master was. He was 'well', as he always is, and never asked about my condition or anything about me. Now the relationship between Cosima and him has become more formalized. For a man who craves intellect from those around him, I cannot fathom why the Master would choose such a lazy layabout like Cosima. However, she is gorgeous and puts out, and that's all a girl needs to reel in a big catch, right? Unless I am to be replaced, she is only his courtesan and is subject to the fickle whims of the head that is rarely governed by reason.

As usual, the time passed slowly, but it is finished today, and I am back in the land of the undead. Not feeling great to be back, but I am refreshed and have a good appetite. Mitică has noticed my good spirits and is relieved that I am getting back to my old self. Tonight, I will be expected to join the group of devils, and I'm dreading it.

Evening...

When I came down, Andreas was waiting alone at the base of the steps, as Mitică said he had been doing each night since I had been indisposed. I was oddly flattered, but the look on his face was priceless when he saw me. He was staring pensively off into the distance, a scowl on his face, but at the first sound of our footsteps, his head popped up. Smiling, his azure eyes sparkled as he held out his hand for me to take it. "Wife of the Impaler, you are a vision of beauty this evening."

Smiling widely, it had been some time since I had received such a compliment. I took his hand, and he led me away from Dumitru, who was scowling.

We exchanged pleasantries, and he placed his arm in mine, squeezing it firmly against his side as we made our way to the parlor. When Mitică was just out of earshot and we were far from any others, Andreas whispered against my veil. "I have missed you, *koukla mou*, you have occupied my thoughts day and night."

There was an insinuation in his tone that sent shivers down me, and I was about to say something when Georgiana came trotting up next to us and prattled on about me being away. It reeked of her usual fake sentiments, and it irks me that she pretends to be friends. When we three entered the parlor, only Imogen and Maxim were waiting, but the Master was not present. Without greeting them, Andreas and I sat in our usual place, his arm still holding onto mine.

With Georgiana distracting the other two, I took the opportunity to answer him. "I, too, have missed our conversations. I hope you weren't too bored."

He grinned, bringing my hand up to kiss it. "It was agony without you."

I thought he was joking and I went along with it as such with a light chuckle. When I looked at the door to see if Mitică was nearby, I noticed he had disappeared. My brow knitted in worry, and I tensed, becoming conscious of the fact that I was alone with the four of them. My face was already hot, but now I was choking. Instinct told me to get out, and I wasn't going to ignore it.

"What is it?" The Greek asked, glancing in the same direction. "Are you still feeling unwell?"

"Uh, a bit," I lied, but cleared my throat. "Forgive me, I need some air."

I was just about to stand when Mitică returned to the door way and announced that the Master had been called away on business and wished his children a good hunt without him. Georgiana pouted openly, crossing her arms, and huffed like a child.

"You mean busy with Cosima." I heard Maxim mutter under his breath to Imogen, who suppressed a laugh as her eyes flickered to me for a millisecond.

In this instance, I had no idea what 'business' was code for. Had something happened, or was he just preoccupied with Cosima? Standing, I nonchalantly went to my friend and mumbled. "Everything is well, I trust?"

Mitică nodded once. "No worries, *Doamna mea*."

Imogen stood, stretching her limbs as she said to me in a snide tone that they ought to get going. I scowled, and so wanted to tell her to 'not let the door hit her on her ass on the way out' so very badly. The others ignored our brief moment of tension and all began to file out into the hall. Georgiana called back to Andreas, who was still sitting, and asked if he was joining them. He waved them away, muttering uninterestedly that he'd catch up to them later.

Once the three of them disappeared, I whispered to Mitică. "Stay close."

Brow creasing, he nodded once, but then averted his eyes behind me.

I was just about to turn when Andreas spoke. "Shall I accompany you, *Doamnă*?"

Rigidly, I nodded, and he took my arm once more. Exchanging heated glares at Mitică, he led me down the way the other children had gone. We walked for a bit in silence before he stopped by a window and opened it for me. The freezing air blew in, but it was a minor relief from the heat choking my throat. I leaned against the high sill, taking in deep breaths of the fresh air to calm my nerves. Yet the veil was still suffocating me, so throwing caution to the wind, literally, I folded it back over my hair.

"Isadora," Andreas began, taking a half-step nearer to me. "I have something I wish to say to you now that we are in private."

I began to sweat. "What is it?"

"It is forward to say this, but being separated from you made me realize how deeply I feel for you." He was not nervous in the slightest about confessing something like that and was very confident of himself as he placed a hand on mine. "These nights have been so empty without you. I hoped you were warm in your bed, and wished I could join you there."

My face bloomed with heat again, but I grew serious and warned. "That *is* very forward."

"It is," he agreed, his eyes as the wine-dark sea. "But I sense you wished it too."

I couldn't look at him. He was right, there were times I did daydream about him. I felt a great shame overtake me and I removed my hand from underneath his, shaking my head. "Andreas, I'm married…"

"I am very aware of that." He coaxed his touch back upon me, and I allowed it. "But you can't hide behind your marriage when I can read on your face that you feel the same. Wife of the Impaler or not, he does not need to know how we feel."

"He already knows you desire me." I hung my head. "He told me a few weeks ago."

The Greek's brow furrowed, and his eyes narrowed. He was thinking the same thing I was, but only he had the courage to articulate it. "And he does nothing to stop me?"

I could only shrug. "I'm sure he does nothing to you to test my loyalty to him."

"So, I *do* test your loyalty?"

I pursed my lips. "You are kind to me, and that makes me like you. You are handsome, and that does attract me. However, if you do have some care for me, you will not force me to reciprocate."

A melodic purr drifted in the air, so light and delicate. His ego was so inflamed by my meager compliments that it moved him passionately. "If I were to force you, what pleasure would there be to share?"

Shuddering, I hated how he was making me feel one thing and then another. I responded rather annoyed. "What is it you want, exactly? A quick three minutes, is that it?"

"If I wanted that, I would have done it already. Not against your will, of course, I am not so insensitive as the others." Andreas' cool breath whispered in my ear. "In Greece, we take time to appreciate the human form, inside and out. Has your Master ever appreciated your form, or has he only given you a hasty three minutes?"

A hasty zero minutes is more like it, I thought. My stomach seemed to twist in on itself, and I could only respond. "He will kill me if I shame him."

His arms came around to encircle my waist and hug me from behind. "Your fear of him is the only thing that keeps you from me, isn't it? I can protect you from him, *koukla.*"

Was it fear or respect? I think at the beginning it was respect, but it has now turned to fear of him. Frowning, I swallowed hard. "I don't think anything can protect me from him. For your own sake, please, just walk away. I'm not worth losing your life over."

Gently, he turned my back to the wall, pressing me against it with his hips as his hands cupped my cheeks. I placed my hands on his chest to half-heartedly push him away, although it was no use. Bit by bit, he leaned forward, his eyes turning a deep purplish red in the dim light as he tasted my lips as if he were taking sips of wine. I haven't been kissed in so long, and my heart melted again like molten lava into a churning sea. Inadvertently, I was kissing him back, but I couldn't make myself stop, for when his mouth moved one way, mine followed in synchronicity. Andreas was slow, taking his time to extract all my resistance to pull me under his spell, and I loved it.

"*Andreas,*" a voice hissed, making both of us pull away from the other. Dumitru was suddenly behind him, and a menacing glare shone in those gray eyes. "Let go of her."

The Greek's eyes widened with alarm, and he growled. "You're quick, houseboy."

"*Let her go.*" Mitică repeated, never before had I heard such malice drip from his voice.

Without protest, Andreas released me. My senses regained, I slinked from the wall, watching the Greek intently for any sign that he might strike. With my perspective altered as I moved away, I saw that Dumitru had a stake in his hand that he pressed into the Greek's back, just where his heart would be. How my friend had appeared without being detected by the seasoned killer, I didn't know, and I wasn't going to ask any questions.

"*Never* touch what belongs to the Master." Dumitru stressed, digging the tip of the stake in just a bit more, making Andreas grimace. "Your siblings are waiting for you to join them for the hunt. Go find your prey somewhere else."

Scoffing, Andreas turned his head to me. "Think about what I said, darling."

In a flicker of darkness, like a shadow had fallen over our eyes, Andreas had disappeared.

Once a still silence returned to the corridor, Mitică grabbed my arm and began to drag me away. Dumitru said nothing, not that he needed to, before we hurriedly made it up to my room. Mitică told me not to leave until well after sunrise tomorrow.

My lungs were still burning from exertion, but I said that I understood and then asked. "Are you going to tell the Master about it?"

"I have to, regardless of whether he saw it already." Dumitru, who was still holding my arm excruciatingly tight, looked me straight in the eye. "His eyes are everywhere, you know. He sees everything, night or day. Please tell me you didn't say or do anything that would condemn you."

"No…" I sighed after a long moment. "Although it doesn't really matter, does it?"

"He kissed you, not the other way around." Dumitru rested a hand on my shoulder, but then added. "The Master knows you would not betray him, don't worry."

I winced at the last sentence he said, gritting my teeth and sinking my nails into my own skin. Does the Master have so much audacity as to think that no matter how he treats me, I would never go against him? In a way, he is right, but to say it so bluntly to Mitică like that makes me fume. I am not some dog, despite being kicked by his master, still licks his hand and wags his tail. Taking in a deep breath to steady my growing temper, I put my hand over Mitică's. "If you say so."

Chapter Thirty-five

THE DEN

23 November

Morning…

Where to begin these days, which I have suffered near to that of Job, as the companions of Daniel in the fiery furnace — tried and tested, saved and tried again? All the meanwhile in the presence and saving grace of the Almighty, who was the fourth figure in the white-hot fires. Where to start after the three weeks, when so little happened, then everything happened.

*15 November

Since the night that Andreas had confessed his desire for me, I was stuck in a swamp of moral turmoil. Dumitru had told me that the Master had apparently seen the encounter between the two of us, but did not act against Andreas nor spoke in my defense to him.

Actually, Mitică said he was indifferent about it, as if to bring it up was a waste of his precious time. I was becoming convinced that Andreas was just giving me false hopes about the Master, saying that to lose me would be the most painful thing for him, et cetera. Well-intentioned false hopes, perhaps, to lessen the pain of the knife in my back that has not faded.

Despite Dumitru's warning to stay away from me, Andreas did the opposite. His visits became more frequent, even showing up in the middle of the day to see me. Of course, he always appeared when Dumitru wasn't nearby. He would calculate Mitică's comings and goings to the second, but his visitations were always random and never set. I'd always be wary of him, but he had the ability to easily tear down my defenses.

When Andreas would come to me, he was not always so bold as he was that night, but would still make his intentions known. He never hurt me in any way, but would give me the gentlest caresses and softest kisses I had ever received. I didn't want to admit to myself that I was falling for him, not in love, but in lust. Each time he came, it was like a little game to see how far he could press me to give in, which only heightened my moral dilemma. Andreas was sucking me into him, and I kind of wanted it to happen. I hate saying it now, but he was a drop of cool water in the arid desert that I found myself.

I did tell Mitică that the Greek was coming to me during the day, but no matter what my friend did to always stick near me, Andreas would find a way around him. I pleaded for Dumitru to have the Master tell him to stay away, but my husband never threatened him once. And so that was the situation I was in by 15 November: half in desire for Andreas, and half fallen out of love for the Master.

Late Morning...

I was doing some extra work in the kitchen after breakfast, halfheartedly hiding from Andreas, whom I thought wouldn't come near the kitchens since it's Dumitru's main stomping grounds. Sleeves rolled up, wearing a white linen housedress, I washed dishes absentmindedly. I had just rinsed off a plate when a familiar pair of arms came around my torso, causing me to drop the plate back into the sudsy water.

"Is this the work of a lady?" Andreas' whimsical purr lulled in my ear. "Your hands will lose their softness, and what a tragedy that would be."

Rolling my eyes, I reached into the water for the plate. "I don't care if I were a queen, I'd still wash dishes if someone asked me to."

"How domestic of you," Andreas kissed just beneath my jaw, making me shiver to my core. "Do you have a moment to pull yourself away from your labors to come with me? I want to show you something."

My brow knitted as I set the clean plate aside, feeling a strange wave of suspicion tingle up my neck. "What is it?"

"Just something interesting concerning your heritage," He handed me the dishtowel to wipe my hands, and began to untie my apron. "I believe you will find it…stimulating. It will give you a different perspective."

Drying my hands slowly, a small voice reminded me not to trust him. I knew I should tell Mitică, but he had gone to fetch something from upstairs. To leave a note for him in front of Andreas would hint that I don't trust him, so I had to make the decision there and then. "Stimulating, you say? Very well, I have some time."

"You won't be disappointed, I promise you." Excitedly, Andreas took my arm and promptly led me from the kitchen. Leading me a short distance to a usually locked door that is just off to the side of the main stairwell, he opened it. Within were descending stairs, leading down into a dimly lit darkness. The candles that were dotted along the wall burst to life, probably from Andreas' command, lighting the way into the gloom.

He was about to lead me down into it, but I was hesitant to budge; my old horrors resurfaced. "It's…down there?"

"Yes," his eyebrow raised curiously. "Oh, my dear, don't tell me you're afraid of the dark? I will be here to protect you. Come on, I won't leave you for a second, I promise."

"R-Right…" I stuttered, unconvinced of his vow. My feet wouldn't move as I stared blankly down the stone steps, remembering the fear in my heart and the pain in my shoulder.

Blue eyes pierced into mine, and a hand came up to brush my cheek. *"Come."*

Without realizing it, he had compelled me to follow him. And, without another word of protest, I descended with him into the labyrinth that exists beneath this medieval castle, the door closing by itself behind us. Andreas and I walked down some flights of steps, deeper and deeper, the air growing moist with the familiar stench of mold. His command had worn off a little, and I was seeing the horror of my situation, but my head could not make me turn and run back up the stairs.

"*Koukla*, do you remember I told you of Jonathan Harker, the husband of Wilhelmina?" Andreas spoke up, his voice echoing down the winding corridor. I only nodded once, and he continued. "Did you ever wonder how the Impaler came to know of Wilhelmina's existence? Well, it was through her own fiancé, when he came here to this castle just over a hundred years ago."

"Jonathan came here?" My heart grew very troubled for the long-dead man. Oh, what torture he must have endured here under the Master's terrible iron fist. "Whatever for?"

"He was a solicitor, dealing with the drawing up of legal documents, and other such things." Andreas explained, placing his other hand over mine. "He was assigned to come here to help aid the Master in passing over deeds to an estate that he had purchased in London."

The blood in my veins chilled that Jonathan *had* been assigned here as well to do work for the Master, just as I have.

"My Father saw Harker as a friend, even invited him to stay here for a month to teach him English customs. But Harker, very much like you, was too curious for his own good, and learned of the Master's secret of what he is." Andreas stopped at a door, similar to the others, and it opened for him. As we entered, the Greek went on. "Unfortunately, in all his book smarts, Jonathan was not the brightest when it came to negotiating his way out of risky situations. Also, he was rather reckless and easily fooled by the Impaler's deceptions. That combination led him to a dark time when he stayed here."

I felt such immense pity for this Jonathan, ancestor or not. I could relate so much to his trials, yet I wondered what Andreas was actually trying to tell me. When we entered the room, I was distracted by the sight momentarily: it was a bedroom, or at least had the layout of some kind of bedroom. There was a great bay window that looked out over the mountain valley, and the midday sun streamed through the parted heavy curtains. Along one of the long walls, a painted mural showed a wine harvest, the figures diligently picking grapes from the vineyard and taking them to the presses. Returning my attention to him, I asked quite plainly. "Are you comparing me to him?"

"Not at all, my darling girl, you get your resourcefulness from Wilhelmina's side." He took my question as though I had been insulted, instead of correlating Jonathan's and my experiences and tribulations as similar occurrences, both set into motion by the Master. In a way, he had dodged it. Gazing straight into my eyes, he led me to the other end of the room where an excessively embroidered curtain was hung as what I thought was decoration. With a flick of his wrist, it drew itself to the side to reveal a hidden room. "My Father left your grandfather here, in this castle, with his three concubines when he set off for London."

"Left him here?" I echoed as I dared to take a step inside the room. The air was weighted there, heavy with the scent of something I didn't recognize, something sweet and thick. It smelled almost ambrosial and drew me in. An array of pillows and cushioned bedding was laid out on the floor, and draperies of the same color concealed some of the sunlight from pouring in. It astonished me that the style of the décor was hinted with Ottoman influence, especially since I saw an old hookah in the corner of the room. I blinked, and it suddenly hit me that this place was used for more purposes than simply smoking tobacco.

Turning back to Andreas, he was suddenly next to me and stared with a soft gaze that enraptured and ensnared my soul. He was compelling me again, I knew it, and accompanied by that scent in the air, my senses weakened.

"Yes, left him as a plaything for his women. But, you are no plaything, like I said, not to me." The Greek loosened my veil and tossed it to the floor. With his fingers, he untied my braided hair, letting it fall to its full length, and then persuaded me. "Lie down."

My limbs shook as blood rumbled through them. Easing me down onto some pillows, Andreas lay me out, his mouth going to my lips to kiss so deeply, then trailed down to my neck. He hovered over me, one knee between my legs to pin my dress down, and the other to mount over my right leg. I could feel he was already quite aroused, and I remember thinking how much I wanted and didn't want him.

Taking the bodice of the dress, he pulled it down over my chest, his talons slowly shredding the garment as he did, so that it was strewn about my waist in pieces. In doing so, however, Andreas had revealed the Master's silver crucifix that rested between my breasts. In one rapid motion, Andreas ripped it off and threw it somewhere, and I heard it clink on the stone floor far away. He grunted with the effort as the smell of burned flesh lingered in the air. All the meanwhile, everything was slow, methodical, and there was no need to rush what was about to happen.

As his mouth descended my sternum, he hastily rid himself of his shirt, exposing the carved Adonis beneath. At the sight, I shook with a soft gasp, and Andreas purred so loudly that it was almost a growl. "There is more to behold, *koukla*. Trust me, give yourself to me. Only I can give you what you desire."

But before I could answer, I felt this sting above my right breast. Whining, I grabbed onto his hair to try and pull him off, but he released himself of his own accord. Blood dripped from his lips back onto me as he swallowed the mouthful of blood that he had taken. Eyes crimson as my blood, Andreas grinned. "Don't look so frightened, Isadora, you're safe with me."

"Andreas…please —"

"Did you think you would have her all to yourself, brother?" From dark shadows, the two figures of the other brothers manifested themselves, teeth already bared.

I was horrified by their appearance and tried to cover my chest, but Andreas had pinned my arms to the cushions. A renewed fear entered me, and I knew then that it was the end. I had been lured to the same place where my ancestor had suffered, to finish the deed that had begun a century ago.

"So, this is the place where Father used his concubines?" Maxim inhaled deeply as he examined the surroundings, his entire body shaking from euphoria. "How fitting that you should bring her here. Now we all can have a wonderful time, and it's all thanks to *Doamna's* gracious hospitality."

Threateningly, Andreas hunched over me and let out a territorial growl that made the other two take a step back. "Why should I share with you? *Get out.*"

"You can't deny us a taste of her." Ludevit was livid, his eye already shone as a glistening ruby as he crawled toward us. "You may claim her as a prize, but won't you let us enjoy her with you? What great pleasure it would be to cut that pretty skin."

I was beginning to hyperventilate, and I stared up at the Greek, my wrists fighting against his weight. Tears were budding in my eyes, but it was not despair I was feeling the most, but desperate rage. "Andreas, *please...*"

"See, she even wishes it." Maxim groped the muscle of my leg and then addressed me directly. "We'll be gentle, to a point."

"Very well," Andreas considered after a moment and moved off my lower half. "But don't forget whose prize she is, and who is allowed the final drop."

"Trust us, brother." Ludevit knelt next to Maxim, his eye flitting over my exposed figure, and clicked his tongue. A rough hand came to feel up the skin that he so wished to mar. "To hide this under all those clothes; what a shame."

I struggled against Andreas' grip but to no avail, and I cried out a broken portion of the prayer to St. Michael the Archangel, defender against the Devil. All of them hissed as their faces metamorphosed closer to their true forms, their pure malice directed solely at me.

Ludevit's same hand came over my mouth to hold it shut. "We should kill her as Petros intended: slowly and savoring each drop until there's nothing left."

"Agreed," Maxim spoke up and took Andreas' place between my legs, lifting my dress over my knees and to my waist. "We have all the time in the world, *Doamnă.* Try to enjoy yourself, at least while there is still something to enjoy."

With all my might, I tried to kick Maxim in the head, but he caught my leg, and bending it to the side, sank his teeth into the skin of my inner thigh. I cried out, still thrashing my legs as Ludevit grabbed my other one and bit it just above my knee. Both of my legs were subdued, and Maxim's head was too close to my groin for comfort. My only other target was Andreas, who promptly returned to kissing me as if we hadn't been interrupted by anyone. I could taste my blood in his mouth, but soon enough he took my wrist to bite it, then up my arm to bite there again.

And that's what it was. Every minute or so, they would find a new soft spot from which to draw my blood. Only small amounts, as they wanted to make it last, and very quickly, the room began to spin, and I grew so weak.

My attention was suddenly diverted when I heard Maxim gasp. "She's a virgin…"

I was still somewhat clothed, so how he could know something like that was beyond me, but again, terror entered me. The secret was out that the Master never touched me, and now I was at the mercy of three psychopaths with a diabolic need to satiate themselves.

Andreas raised his head from his feeding. "*What?*"

"My nose does not lie." Maxim inhaled again, a crazed excitement made him shout. "What a prize this is! So lovely and untouched! What have we done to deserve this?"

"Give her to me, Andreas." Ludevit lifted his mouth from my ribs, licking them before the excess blood dripped off. "I will repay you dearly if you let me ruin her first. After all she did to me, she deserves something in return."

Andreas ignored him. Facing me, he stared me down with such wickedness. "Why hasn't the Impaler taken you?" I would not speak, so he demanded. "Answer me, woman!"

"Does it matter?" Maxim chuckled after another strong inhale. "Our Father missed out, and now we can have her all to ourselves, but I want to have her first."

"She is *my* prize!" Andreas let go of my arms and took a swipe at Maxim with a clawed hand, who dodged it. "Do not make me regret sharing with you."

Ludevit growled in frustration at the Greek. "I said I will pay you for it!"

"Pay with what?"

Quickly, the creatures descended into a group of bickering roosters, all close to exchanging blows over who could get the first peck. I almost couldn't believe that they were fighting over me like a bunch of school boys. The whole spectacle was so laughable, but I couldn't laugh about it then. Trying to turn over on my side while they were distracted to run for it, I was easily slapped flat on my back again.

Andreas, in a last-ditch effort to really slow me down, bit my neck and took a significant amount of blood. When he finished his ravishing, I had hardly enough strength to hold my head up. Fingers in my hair, he yanked back and was about to scream something in my face when the curtain was drawn aside again. All of them were distracted a second time, and the Greek grew pale.

"Father-King," Andreas hailed, dropping my head with a heavy thud. "Welcome."

My eyes burst open, and I tried to look up to see if the Master was really there, but it was no use. Blood still poured from the fresh wound Andreas had inflicted, and from every other place that they had bitten.

"Your little wife insisted on entertaining us." The Greek went on, blaming me for them being caught red-handed. "You married such a magnanimous lady. To allow such a feast upon her own flesh is truly warrant of praise."

The Master made no reply to any of this, but came up to the bedding, running Andreas off of my top half. Barely able to move my head, I glanced over to the right of me. My vision was blurred, but there was no doubt that the Master was staring down at me, his face appearing cold and emotionless. The heart that still beat in my chest fluttered at the sight of him, hoping that he would deliver me from my doom.

"Do you hear that?" Maxim hushed everyone to silence. "The little lady is happy to see you, Father. Please, join us, there's still a little left. Indulge yourself and let us have our turn with her."

The Master was silent, only staring at me with reddening eyes as Maxim took another bite of my inner thigh. Wincing, a tear escaped my cheek, and I turned away from the Master. My heart plummeted that he would not help me, despite all the emotion that was swelling in my chest, I gave up living. If he would not save me, as his own sons were killing me before his eyes, then my time here was finished. The deep cold began to creep into my lungs, freezing my diaphragm, and my breathing became more labored, and I let it take over.

"Maxim, stop!" I heard Andreas call to him, but things were fading, and more shouting arose. All of them were yelling, screaming at each other, and I thought it was so annoying that they would spend this time fighting amongst themselves, instead of letting me die in peace.

What roused me from sinking deeper was a sudden splash of water on my torso, chest, and face. The sensation made me open my eyes, and I moaned from the burning that encompassed my limbs. Looking down, I saw it was not water but blood that had been splattered all over me. A horror wracked my dying heart, thinking it was my own blood, but as soon as it pooled in the areas of me which were in sunlight, it fizzled and bubbled away.

Confusion awakened other parts of my failing brain, and I looked up at the commotion. The Master and Ludevit lunged at each other, exchanging punches, kicks, and bites, quicker than I could register. Andreas had completely disappeared, so did Maxim, and only the son and his father remained. One would be thrown to the ground, or against the draperies, and instantly be back in the fray, snarling and roaring like tigers in a fight to the death. Bones would crack, skin would be torn, and instantly be repaired by the next blow.

When Ludevit was thrown close to me, he skidded across the fabric, but launched back at the Master, totally ignoring me. In his tumble, he had knocked over with him the severed head of Maxim, badly decayed and burnt. His neck had been torn away from his body, and the ragged pieces of flesh hung like chunks of carbon. My stomach convulsed, but it had no strength to even vomit up its contents. I wondered if Andreas had ended up the same, but there was no sign of his corpse, nor a heap of dust.

A bloodthirsty howl ripped through the air, and by the time my eyes got to the two hell-demons, the Master had ripped out Ludevit's intestines. They spilled out in a soupy mix, but the wounded Ludevit did not relent and struck at the Master's neck with his fangs. The Voivode parried his son's attack with his bare arm, and Ludevit took away a mouthful of flesh. Having had enough, I assume, the Master dug his good arm into Ludevit's chest and clawed out his heart, blood spitting from the ruptured arteries. Then, in one final *coup de grâce*, the immortal Prince sank his fangs into the vermin's neck, separating it from Ludevit's body in one horrendous tear. Skin, tendons, and vertebrae were pried loose from his body, and just with that, Ludevit's headless corpse collapsed to the ground and began to form into a heap of decaying dust.

I fainted from the gruesome sight, my heart giving out at the thought that I was the next one to feel the Master's wrath. I began to drift again, hoping that it was all just a bad dream and that soon I would awake in my bed, safe and sound. But I heard a voice, so far away in the dark, calling my name. Every cell within me was suffocating from the lack of blood in my veins. Drained, depleted, I was exhausted and chose to ignore the voice. I just wanted to be lost and alone and let myself fade into the dark.

I was ready, a strange peace coming into my body, but my mind thought of something that was even stranger to me. I felt regret, but for what exactly? Before I could even take a second to think about what, I had the sensation of the Count's phantom lips on my own. Perhaps it came from a distant memory, but it felt so real even when the rest of my senses were long gone.

Oh, right, I remember thinking, *I loved him, but he never loved me.*

My own last thoughts struck me with such pain. It hurt my lifeless heart that the Count and I never got to fulfill the one most important promise we had made to each other. Did it even matter anymore? The breath in my body had slipped out, and with it, the cold of creeping Death stole me away.

In the stillness, the question was posed to me again: Does it matter? Well, of course, it mattered; it was one of the purposes of my life. The answers came to me with such clarity, then I had been placed on this path for a reason. Every decision I had ever made in my life had led me to this place, to this castle, and its Master. I would be the one to assist him in unshackling the chains of sin and set free this world from the plague of his kind.

I prayed to God that I wouldn't die, and that I would give it one last shot to exist in this body and love him. Maybe it was a hopeless endeavor, but I prayed to be allowed to try one last time, for the Count's sake. That pain, that regret, caused in me this spark which reanimated life in my heart, and the voice grew louder once more.

It was shouting right in my face, right in my ear, and sudden jolts of intense pressure fell on my sternum. The combination of all these things knocked my head back to consciousness, and by some miracle, my eyes opened. I was furious that someone had been screaming so rudely in my face.

"*Isa*," it was the Master's voice. A crushing force pressed me against something cold and hard, and I moaned at the weight. He cried out in anguish. "My God, my God, thank you!"

The world rematerialized around me, and I was right that it was the Master who held me tightly in his arms. He smelled of earth and blood, and was covered in red. "Master…?"

He pulled away slightly so that we stared eye to eye. His face still resembled the demon within, and from his eyes poured bloodied tears. Cradling me as a child against him, he placed a blood-soaked hand on my cheek as his breath shuddered in a quiet but relieved wail. "I am here, my sweet one, my wife."

The list of epithets confused me, as I was so sure he was going to rip my neck open. I'm not sure why I thought that, but I guess I really couldn't believe he was saying kind words to me. Possibly it was my mind playing tricks, and I was hearing what I wanted to hear. "Am I next?"

The Master's demonic face contorted with grief, and he dug his face into my neck, his arms encircling me even tighter. "Please, sleep, dream of happy things in happier times. I will be here when you awake, I promise."

It was a command, and I slumped to one side and slept.

Chapter Thirty-Six

ATONEMENT

*16 November

And when I awoke next, I didn't rouse naturally, but was forced from my death-like stasis by my skin burning. A thousand hot irons, it seemed, were being held against my flesh, or a thousand razors had flayed my skin from the muscle. Every movement I made set a smoldering flame ablaze, and I was certain I was on fire. To the touch, my irritated skin was warm from where teeth had dug into me, but the severed nerves and torn ligaments and muscles registered as fire. Had I died and these were the tongues of the Hell fires, licking away the sinew that held me together? Well, if I were in Hell, I most certainly deserved every sensation.

Amid this hell, something cool touched my hand, and it startled me. I ripped my hand away, which only ignited a chain of stinging needles to stab up my arm, and finally, that made me open my eyes. Surprisingly, my vision returned crystal clear, my hearing too, and all the things I could see and hear overloaded the two senses. I could barely swallow because my throat was so parched. I was in a room that I didn't recognize. It was bare and reminded me a bit of Dumitru's room, but it differed in layout. The walls were a bland, yellowed white plaster, and there was a small window in the center of one wall. This was most certainly the living world, but I didn't remember how I got there. I was in a bit of a panic when the cool thing touched my hand again, and I gasped.

My neck was quite immobile, so I could only move my eyes to the man who sat next to my bed. Of course, I immediately recognized the Master. All trace of the demon's face had disappeared, and only the exterior human man remained. I remembered then that he had promised me, just before I had fallen asleep, that he would be there when I woke. He looked very troubled, and for once in a long while, his eyes expressed an emotion other than disgust or coldness toward me. However, I was in no mood to play his head games, nor be put down when I was in such agony.

"I know you are in pain, but do not move if you can help it." The Master averted his gaze a little when he spoke to me. "You have reopened many of your wounds in your sleep already."

My ragged breath turned to a wailing cry with a surge of fire, and my arms shook uncontrollably. Grunting savagely, I wanted to bear down on something to hold in the pain, but my wrists forbade my hands from closing without adding more to my current predic-ament, until it passed after a few torturous moments.

Initially, I hadn't noticed that the Master had stood, and balancing my head and neck with his hand, lifted me slightly as he brought a glass of cool water to my lips. "Slowly."

The minuscule relief was just enough, but he allowed me to have so little of it before taking it away. I whined to tell him I wanted more, but he did not listen. Whining again, he reconsidered my plea and allowed me to drink just one more sip before releasing my head. The Master sat back down, his hand returning to mine, but he did not look at me. "You have been asleep for just about a day, but there were many times I feared you would not wake at all."

I only listened, examining his well-kept, but most noticeably, healed appearance. I wondered why he 'feared' that I wouldn't wake? Since when? I wasn't going to ask, not then, when he seemed to be in a reasonable mood considering what had happened.

Still, the Master continued, not expecting me to answer him at all, I guess. "I want to apprise you of the situation now, if you are clear-headed enough to hear it."

I bobbed my head up and down slightly, my eyelids drooping a bit as I braced myself.

"You know that Ludevit and Maxim are no more, and Andreas escaped before I had a chance to finish him." My husband paused, sighing deeply. "The women are now demanding that I give you to them as payment for their brothers' and Petros' deaths, so that they may dispense of you as they see fit. It strikes me that they do not see me as the executioner, but only you."

My tired heart sank so deeply at that, and I wondered if I only lived to be handed over to my executioners, who would rip me apart rather than just bleed me dry. I pondered what is worse: a slow death with minimal pain, or a quick, brutal one. I guess I didn't have much of a choice between the two anymore. "When will you? I would like to write —"

"*When will I?!*" He barked, now finally looking at me, the ire in his voice showed in the flashing red of his eyes. "Would I have saved you from the others just to throw you to a different pack of wolves? Perhaps you are not so lucid as I thought, wife."

I froze at his outburst, wincing at the new wrack of agony that coursed through my limbs. Gritting my teeth, I forced out a meager apology to cover my tracks. "Forgive me for offending you, husband. I just thought —"

"You thought what?" The Master snapped rhetorically. "That I have no care for the life of my own wife? Do you honestly think that I would throw you away the first good chance I get? This time you do offend me, greatly."

Turning my head away as far as I could manage, my jaw tensed even harder. There were so many separate incidents that I could cite when he showed no care at all, but I had already insulted him enough for one day in less than four sentences. "I have displeased you. I would leave the room, but I cannot."

His hand came up to my face, but I flinched, pulling away. I thought he was going to strike me, and that caused another burst of pain that made me whimper. The Master stared at me, wide-eyed, his hand stopping several inches from my cheek before pulling away. "I am sorry…"

My brow knitted that he would apologize to me instead, and once my worn nerves subsided, their war on each other, I dared to inquire. "Are you unwell?"

"Yes," the Master's own brow creased as he sank back down into the chair, slouching his shoulders unceremoniously. "I am very unwell."

I wanted to ask why, but I was hesitant in case I would cause him to be angry at me again. Biting my lip, I wondered why he hadn't just left already since I had caused him anger, yet he remained. Why didn't he just go to Cosima if he needed to have his spirits lightened? I'm sure she'd have no qualms, no matter how tense the situation is between them. "Are you hurt?"

"Not physically…" The Master turned away his eyes from me and stared at the floor. Silent as the ancient Prince was, a deep frown appeared over his face, and a hand raked through his hair. "Are you hungry?"

I wasn't at all, but since he had asked, I nodded.

"I will be back momentarily." He confirmed and went to the door, but stopped before opening it. "Not that you could, but do not leave this room. The sisters are still here, and you are an easy target. Do not invite any one of them to enter, is that understood?"

Again, I nodded. "Yes, Master."

Once he left, I ran the two words over and over in my head, recalling his sorrowful face.

"Not physically…"

I felt such sympathy for the man, even though he snapped at me. He killed two of his own children to save me for whatever reason. I wish I had the gall to ask him why, but I feel he wouldn't give me an answer. But his demeanor had changed significantly. In over a month, he had not said a kind word to me, and now he asks how I am, if I'm hungry, and apologizes. He didn't say terribly cruel things to my face, but seemed to lash out only because of my assumption that he didn't care about me, despite saving me. I did feel bad for assuming, but what else was I supposed to assume?

After that, the pain began again, this time much worse.

The Master returned with some broth, which I had to force down each spoonful, but still couldn't finish it. When he had given up trying to make me eat, I passed out from exhaustion. I fully expected the Master to leave, but there were moments when I would wake for brief seconds, and he would be resting his head against my leg and holding my hand.

Not once did he leave during that day, even when Dumitru returned with the various herbs that the Master needed for my wounds. In the evening, however, Mitică stayed for most of the night while the Voivode attended to his children. According to my dearest friend, the Master had been near hysterical when he brought me up from the bowels of the castle, wearing his shirt, and both of us dripping with blood. Mitică said that my lips were turning blue and my skin had a yellowish hue. Soon after I had been stabilized, Mitică told me of how his Master had gone out searching for Andreas in the middle of the day, risking the sun, but the Greek had completely fallen off the face of the earth. He was not in the castle, nor was he in the immediate vicinity of it, so the Master of the house returned empty-handed, but no less enraged. Of course, the three succubi claimed no knowledge of the plans of the three incubi, nor where Andreas had gone.

After a long silence between the two of us, Dumitru whispered in my ear. "I'm sorry that I wasn't there for you when you needed me."

"I went with Andreas of my own accord." I brushed my fingers over the back of his hand, so touched that he cared. "It's my fault, I let this happen, so don't blame yourself."

"That's not what I meant." He responded, resting his lips on my forehead.

I stared at him, and we both exchanged a knowing glance. That hurt my heart a lot more than the stinging that radiated all over my skin and into my bones. It's so dangerous for him to say those things, but they gave me life to hear them. There was so much I wanted to say to Mitică right there and then, but I was afraid that the Master would hear or see. So, I latched onto him as hard as I could, which was very weak, and would not let go. After all these months, not once have I forgotten about those things he said to me that steamy August day that ended so tragically. I want Dumitru to know that I care about him so much, and that it kills me that I cannot reciprocate his feelings in full.

That evening, Mitică waited until I fell asleep before going to bed himself. I dreamt I was back in the den, but none of my attackers were present; there was only the swirling mist of tobacco above my head. I imagined Jonathan strapped beneath the concubines of the Master, sucking him dry as his children did to me. This man, who died decades before my time, stared directly at me as the demon women crawled about him, their sighs drifting in the air. I don't know why I dreamt this, or what passed between my imaginary Jonathan and me, but it was of some unspoken understanding. We both shared this same experience a century apart, and I felt that I had created a bond with him. At least I know that someone before me had stared those demons in the face and survived.

*17 November

That morning, I was in considerably more agony than the previous day. Somehow, I had managed to curl up into a ball in my sleep to hold myself in, which was counterintuitive because it only caused my wounds to throb and ache. The Master had returned from wherever sometime earlier that morning, and actually crawled into the small bed next to me. His cold body was a relief from the burning, and eventually, he had manipulated my limbs gently enough to have me lie against him comfortably. Half out of it as I was, I nearly tore off our clothes to find greater relief for my searing skin.

To my astonishment, the Master obliged, opening his shirt to let me rest the forearm that Andreas had bitten several times against his bare torso. The leg, whose inner thigh Maxim had gorged himself upon, drew itself up to his hips to find alleviation there as well. Essentially, I had climbed all over him, and he had allowed it far past any point we had ever reached before he rejected me. Half-naked and entangled in the other, the Master ran his fingers through my hair to comfort me further, which ultimately led me to finally sleep deeper than I had in nearly two months.

When I came to, it must have been about noon, and the Master had left the bed but was sitting in the chair, brushing my hair and smoothing it out with his fingers. He must have been aware that I was awake, but said nothing for a while as I watched in awe at the sight.

"You were very demanding this morning, my wife," he grinned sadly to himself after a few minutes, yet made no eye contact as he worked. "And somehow I got it all tangled."

Butterflies flitted their delicate wings in my stomach at the gentleness of his words, and I had to smile back. "I'm sorry if I demanded too much."

"Did I refuse you any of it?" Another grin, this one a bit more playful, but then he dropped his handiwork. "I have something for you."

With my eyebrows raised, I was a little wary as to what it might be. From his pocket, he pulled out a velvet box and opened it to reveal the silver crucifix that had been lost to me in the den. "I had Dumitru get it repaired when he was out on his errands. Relieved as I am that you had it on, I regret it did not stay on."

Admittedly, I got a bit emotional, and with much effort, took the box from him and examined the familiar ancient craftsmanship. I was grateful and would have put it on, but my fingers had no strength to manipulate the clasp, and he certainly couldn't help me. "Andreas was the one who broke it, but I am grateful to be receiving it again. Thank you, husband, it is much appreciated."

All this time, he could not look into my eyes, which was unusual for him. Before, he would pride himself on the intimidation or directness that making eye contact brought him, but he was purposefully ignoring my gaze. The Master immediately changed the subject to something else. "I also wanted to propose something to you that you will not like, but I feel is necessary to relay."

"What is it?"

Pursing his lips, the Master leaned against the bed as he spoke softly. "Listen to me, wife, there is no need for you to suffer. You are no longer close to death, so you have a choice: take a month or more to heal or take days."

With the thought of ingesting more blood, my stomach turned over, and I dug my face into the pillow. Although the proposition was very attractive considering the amount of pain I was in, I wasn't sure. "Answer me one thing?"

His jaw clenched, but he gave his reply. "Anything."

When it came down to really asking him, I felt very apprehensive. There must be some reason that he was keeping this information from me, but I had to know now that he was inclined to speak to me about it. "Was Wilhelmina my grandmother?"

"Andreas told you many things…" No eye contact, still. Instantly, he became uncomfortable and took quite a few minutes to think whether he should answer me. Then the Master held out his hand for me to take it, which I did without hesitation. "Yes, she is your third great-grandmother on your mother's side."

That information was a lot to take in, a lot to process. He knew everything and had known everything about my family since the beginning, and I had been none the wiser. There was no reason for him to lie about it, so I took his word, yet, how much of what I was told was actually true? Taking advantage of his silence, I continued. "Then, I am related to you."

The Master sighed. "No, but in a very distant way, you are of my blood through her."

I cringed at that, although to him it may have been another bout of pain, I continued to ask him. "And that's how I don't change?"

"Those are three questions when you asked for one." The Master edged toward annoyance, but still humored me by answering. "But yes, my sweet one, that is why. That does not mean it cannot happen, only that it is difficult."

"Why aren't I affected like you are by certain things?"

"Four questions are enough, Isadora." He chided me as he would a child, removing his hand. Despite being exceedingly more tolerant of me, he still had his limitations, and I cowered back a bit. "Now, give me your answer."

"I —" I cut out when I accidentally nicked one of the bites on my leg as I was shifting my weight. It wasn't even a hard bump, but just enough to irritate it.

Sitting on the edge of the bed, the Master's arms surrounded me and lifted me to him. Stabbing pains coursed in a portion of my ribs from where Ludevit had severed the fibrous tissue that connected them. Just being upright was unbearable, and my torso convulsed. When I was lying down, I was able to take shallow breaths without much discomfort, but in that position, I was suffocating. The Master could only support my broken body so much, so he quickly made a small slit along a prominent vein in his neck and the rich red blood oozed from the opening.

I wanted to turn away from the sight and smell, but he brought my mouth to it, and of my own will, I drank. All the times before, I had resisted, kept strong in the face of whatever injury I had sustained, but this time I caved too easily. Abnormal as it felt to suck blood from another being, all the individual cuts, lacerations, and punctures had begun to tingle away and a euphoria replaced the pain. Strength returned to my arms, and I could breathe again, but no matter how much I consumed, I could not stand the taste. I was not completely healed, and despite the exhilaration, I lifted myself off his neck and rested my head against his collarbone.

For the first time in forever, I heard a steady purr come from him as he peeled away the bandage on my neck from where Andreas had bitten me. "Better, my sweet one. We will continue later, so rest for now."

"Why are you being so kind to me?" It just slipped out, definitely influenced by the renewed vitality which flooded into every cell of my body. "What have I done to please you?"

Where the Master's hands rested on my clothes, they bunched into fists, gathering the fabric in them. I thought I had made him angry for being so bold about it, and I stiffened and tried to retreat, but there was no place I could go. So, I went to apologize for saying it, but he began before me, his mouth right against my ear. "Sleep and dream pleasantly."

As he had commanded, I was sent off to a blissful sleep, his blood to comfort and heal me.

*19 November

After a full two days of taking the Master's blood, I was completely healed. I had cheated Death once again, and it was all thanks to my husband's generosity. My thighs, arms, chest, neck, and torso had been littered with bandages packed with salves that had all been removed. The amount was startling, and I swear I don't remember feeling even a quarter of them, but they had all disappeared with no trace of ever having existed.

Each day, it seemed, he was becoming more affectionate towards me with caresses and sweet words. Yet, all the meanwhile, he never looked me once in the eye. I didn't mind it really, since I was still shy of him when I was fully conscious and feared a sudden reversion to his crueler ways. When I was asleep, however, my subconscious would always beg to be touched by him, and never did he deny me himself once.

In the afternoon of 19 November, I was allowed to return to my room. So, with the Master accompanying me, he carried me up the stairs personally from my hiding place in the servants' quarters. I could walk by myself with no problem, but he had insisted. When we reached my room, I was so glad to be back.

The Master set me down and was about to go when I grabbed the cuff of his sleeve. "Wait, please, I have something that I think is yours."

Eyebrow cocked, he watched me go to my desk and rummage through the back of a drawer where I had hidden the small locket that held Wilhelmina's photograph. Handing it to him, the Master was obviously unsettled when he recognized the piece.

"This belongs to you, I assume." I extended my reach further for him to take the antique. "Andreas told me to keep it secret from you, and I'm sorry that I did, but I was afraid you would be angry at me."

Hesitantly, my husband took the locket of his previous love interest and, without opening it, placed it in his pocket. When he spoke, he wasn't angry, but disappointed. "You feared me so much that you would trust one who wants to kill you over me?"

"Yes," I answered truthfully.

"I...understand..." He looked to the floor, his near inaudible words drifting in the air. But then the Master raised his eyes to my own. "Do you no longer love me?"

The words shook my core, and I had to hold on to the back of the desk chair to balance myself. I was so unprepared for a question like that, and I had to swallow hard to compose my thoughts for a long moment before I could properly respond. "I don't think I could ever stop loving you, husband, but I am, undeniably, no longer the sole object of your affections. I accept this and wish you —"

"*Shut up*," he roared, his eyes suddenly burning. "Shut up, shut up, shut up!" He rushed upon me, pinning me against the wall with a good *thud* that rattled the nearby furniture. It didn't hurt, but startled me, and I recoiled from him as the Master screamed. "You think I give a damn about that lazy whore? Using her was the only thing that kept me from using *you*!"

My entire body shook from the fury he emanated, as his face came within inches of my own as he ranted on. "Yes, I gave in to the darkness and forgot my humanity. Being around you made me feel, and it disgusted me. I wanted to defile you, make you scream my name, and I knew you would let me do it. But even when I came so close, you made me remember that I could not hurt you. Your mere presence repulsed and attracted me, and in those moments where I had to release my frustration, she was the easiest."

Both of his large hands came up to cup my cheeks to force me to look at him. "I failed in what I sought to accomplish. You always had such a high opinion of me as one who could never give in to temptation or could never sink low. Do you not see that I have always been just as bad as they are? I explained to you my nature once before, but you never wanted to see the monster, only the man. You were so confident that I could 'paint one picture over another' for them, but instead I fell the deepest that I have in a century. I am weak. I am the fish who bites the hooked worm with no care if it is a trap, as long as I get the prize in the end."

Shoulders dropping, he closed his eyes and let out a long sigh, that vein on his forehead pulsing. Then the Master wrapped his arms around my neck and brought me to his chest, his fingers tangling themselves in my hair. "All the women I ever cared for have borne the full brunt of my sins. No matter what I do, I can never keep them from you, and you suffer for it."

All during this, I had been too shocked by the words that came out of his mouth to say anything. Cautiously, I brought my arms around his back and rubbed it gently to soothe him. Since October, I had been so sure he had simply not cared for me anymore, and in a way, he had stopped, but had replaced it with a strange combination of thoughtful lust. He still had enough concern for me to stay away when he wanted me, and from the frustration I caused him, he pushed me away because I made him feel lesser about himself. It was an odd dynamic of conflicting emotions that I couldn't quite wrap my head around in the moment. The Master would feel one thing which contradicted another, and another, and so on. He had reverted to his former self; it wasn't some sick act he had put on, which was brought on by the children's overwhelming presence and my absence. I guess in this way, I had played a crucial role in his fall.

"Forgive me for falling, for forsaking everything and becoming as I was, for forsaking you." The Master's voice broke as his emotion came flooding out like a torrent. "I thought I could live two lives: one with you, the other with them. But, I see now that I can only belong to one of these two lives, and not pick somewhere in between. That is what refused me Heaven the last time, and in God's name, I choose this one with you over the other. I hope that, although I have wronged you so, you could still find it in your heart to remain with me, to love me, even if it is not as it was before."

I had been speechless all during his passionate soliloquy, hanging on every word my husband confessed. Having had it explained to me, I understood why he did as he did, but that did not soften the harshness of his rebukes and the insensitivity of his reproaches.

My silence was growing deafening when I wasn't sure of how to answer, and I began to panic. My mind blanked on what I could say to him to not only soften the pain in his heart, but mine too, until finally I said out. "Please, Master, allow me time."

Withdrawing slightly, my husband rested his forehead against mine. From the faraway look in his eyes, I had hurt him greatly by my silence and indecision, but still he whispered. "Take as much as you need, but do not keep me waiting so long that I lose all hope."

And so, I promised the Master that within five days I would have his answer. Perhaps it was too short a time, but if I don't know by then, I never will.

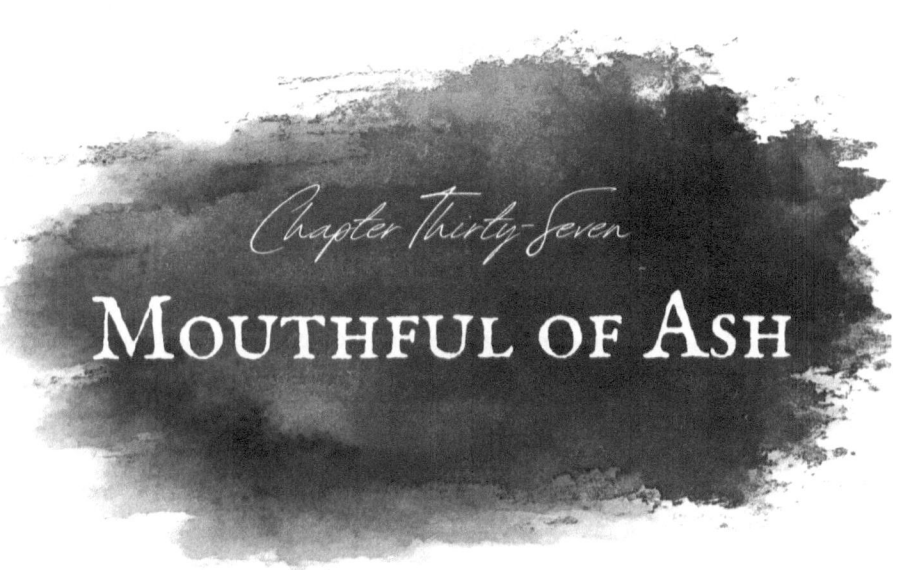

Chapter Thirty-Seven

MOUTHFUL OF ASH

*20 November

That entire night, I could not get the Master's expression out of my head, and slept on and off. A war erupted inside of me, and I spent hours in the darkness of my room just thinking about all that had happened since Michaelmas, and my relationship with the Master. I noticed, suddenly, when referencing him in my head, that I only call him 'Master'. What happened to 'Count'?

'Master', as one who is above me, one whom I serve, and who demands my utmost respect, was the best choice. I had never gotten used to referring to him as 'husband' before this switch occurred, and obviously, I had never referred to him as 'Vlad' since the night he said I was 'insolent' for calling him by his own name.

I guess I had to remember how it felt to be that sole object of his affection. When I tried to remember, it caused my heart a lot of grief. Those precious moments were so fleeting, and I actually got up in the middle of the night to reread some of this account to recall them. I believe that he is sincere, but I am hesitant to let my heart reopen to him. Each instant that he had put me down, I tried with all my being to forgive him, but the pain he caused was great. The final blow was when I had caught him and Cosima together, and no matter the Master's reasons, he still did those deeds.

All day, the Master did not come to me, not that I would expect it since it was during the day, but I found myself missing him all over again. Just having him near makes me love him, I realized, and I couldn't wait to see him that night to speak to him more about what he felt.

Dumitru served me my meals, as usual, and when I asked about the Master's recent temperament, my friend was at a loss concerning the turnaround. He could only boil it down to that the Master had been extremely affected by what his children did to me, since it was only then that he had made his 180-degree change. I had suspected that much, but it was *why* that was the question, not *when*.

To relax my tumultuous mind, I sat myself by the windows in my sitting room that overlooks the Carpathians. At this time of year, their far peaks are layered in thick snow, untouched. The sun still doesn't shine so much, but with the snow, the land has become one endless landscape of stainless white. The evergreen trees are the only color I can see from such a distance, and even then, they are covered in a white glaze. This winter wonderland is so savage and wild outdoors as it is indoors as well. The weather is unpredictable, just as those three harlots of the Devil.

When evening came, I was expected to come down to the parlor to sit among my guests as a good hostess would. I was very apprehensive but dressed myself with quaking hands, and since I was not in the presence of strange men, I only wore a veil to cover my hair and not my whole face. It was a bold move, but I did it to show I had no fear of them. I was ready by 7 pm; however, instead of Mitică meeting me at the door, it was the Master. It was completely unexpected of him, and I became alarmed. "Where is Dumitru?"

"Downstairs already," my husband said, putting his arm out for me to take it. "They are waiting for you, but do not be frightened. They will not harm you while I am here."

I shot him a worried glance as he brought my arm into his. Then, steadily, we began to descend the steps from the private quarters to the common areas.

"Do you expect something to happen?" I whispered just in case someone unexpected overheard our conversation.

"With them, one never knows." He shrugged at it. He was so calm and collected, but then I saw him tense as he inquired. "Have you given any thought to what we spoke of last night?"

I was surprised he would bring it up right then, and it weighed my heart to think it was weighing his down. Subtly, I bit my lip. "I have, very much so. It has been the only thing on my mind."

The Master didn't reply, but I could see that he was relieved that I was at least thinking about him, be it good or bad.

I kept a firm hold on his arm to let him know I was there, and just before we came down into the grand entrance, I reassured his troubled mind. "I am always on your side, husband, please don't ever think otherwise."

Out of the corner of his eye, the Master watched me, a gentle purr accidentally escaping his throat. He was about to bring my hand to his lips to kiss it when two of the succubi emerged from the shadows of the hall. It was Imogen and Georgiana, their eyes already glowing a terrible vermilion as they blended into the firelight. The Master showed no care for them and snubbed his nose at the two sisters as he continued to walk the path they blocked.

"Good evening, First Father," Imogen inclined her head to him in blatant half-respect, then her eyes drifted to mine, her snide tone made me cringe. "Darling Mother, there you are. We have been looking for you."

"We smelled that much of your blood was spilled, yet you appear unharmed." Georgiana's lips twitched into a snarl for a split second as she slinked forward next to Imogen. "Thank goodness you have such a loyal and faithful husband to care for you."

Ouch. It was a direct hit to both of us and was equally effective. My poker face was dead set, and a fake smile concealed my aversion to them. "You are so kind to show concern for my welfare.

It pains me to know your brothers didn't share the same sentiment, and now they rest in pieces."

They did not agree with that as their wrath was thinly veiled. Imogen was the one to finally recover from the further insult to their brothers' memory and answer. "You have endured so much. Come, let us speak before the hunt."

With the two sisters leading us on, I could smell that something was not right. Surely the Master could sense it too, but his face was emotionless, cold, just as it had been before. I felt a sharp pang of panic run through my chest at the sight of that face and had to look away from it. As we rounded the corner to the hall that leads to the parlor, Dumitru was waiting. After we exchanged a warning stare, he followed up the rear without saying a word.

The four of us took our seats in the parlor, and the Master discreetly indicated to me to sit by him. It felt odd to, but I left some space between us. The air was suffocating in the room, but my poker face remained as I situated my skirts around me to appear as if all was normal.

Just as we had all settled, Imogen leaned forward in her chair. "Your husband has told us little of what happened to you, Mother darling, won't you tell us? We three have been very worried for you and your delicate constitution."

I couldn't look to the Master to know if I could speak to them about the details, not that I would wish to indulge them with any of it. The only reason they would be worried is that I might die before they get a chance to get their hands on me. Imogen was leading me into a trap, I knew, so I concocted something vague. "I think both of you know the nature of the assault —"

"An assault?" Georgiana sarcastically gasped, her hand coming to her mouth. "How terrible!"

"Do not pretend, Georgiana," the Master shrugged her off, too, not even bothering to look in her direction. "You are not sincere in your sympathy toward my wife, and neither are you, Imogen. Your asinine pretenses need significant work. If they are to be taken seriously, that is."

I could have burst out laughing and had to purse my lips to keep myself composed.

"Now, Father," Imogen came to Georgiana's defense with a raised finger, her tone light but mildly chastising. "We have only wished to know how fares our little Mother, the poor doll."

I glowered at the witch, and our eyes locked in a cold stare down. A certain rage bubbled up under my skin that she would call me 'doll' just as Andreas did. She might as well have called me *'koukla'* to my face. My tolerance to their false personae was extremely thin, and I struck out at them without much thought to the bite with which I had to back up my bark. "If you think I'm intimidated by you both, don't kid yourselves."

"Intimidated?" Georgiana exaggerated again, her tone feigning disbelief. "Mother, you shouldn't be intimidated by us. No, you should be petrified of us."

The Master growled. *"Georgiana —"*

Imogen stood gracefully, her silver hair shining, as she interjected herself into the scene. "Has your husband told you of our demands in recompense for your crimes?"

"Whatever 'crimes', as you call them," I stood too, readying myself to square off. "That I have committed has been in defense of myself against you devils and your greed to possess what you cannot have."

"But crimes nonetheless," Georgiana joined in again, forgetting the Master's warning. "You have caused the murder of three of our brothers and the weakening of our Father. These are crimes most heinous in our eyes."

At the mention of him, the Master rose, towering above all three of us. "I tore Petros, Maxim, and Ludevit to pieces for having transgressed against me, what do you think I could do to ones such as yourselves?"

"But you agreed to her fault in these things, Father." Imogen came closer to the Master, almost too close. "Don't tell me you've forgotten? You said yourself she should be punished for what she has done to you, and thereby, to us."

I could feel my throat closing, and I struggled to recover from that verbal slap in the face. Did the Master really say that? His silence about the issue was enough proof to me, but who knew at that moment if she was lying? I wasn't going to look to my husband for help either way. Glancing over to Mitică, who was standing near the door, I saw on his face that he was holding himself back.

"Without your strong protector at your side, how silent you become." Georgiana stalked around me, eyes and teeth flashing. "You are all talk."

Not once did I turn to look at the Master, no matter how much I wanted to. If I were only allied with Dumitru in this, then we both were surely dead. There was no way in either Heaven or Hell that I could do anything, so I might as well go down saying what I ought to have said from day one. "Regardless, I am inn—"

"Innocent?" Georgiana laughed as she came up face to face with me. The fire in her eyes seemed inextinguishable as she sneered, her lips coming over her teeth. She was making a keen effort to outdo Imogen in her attempts to trash-talk, and in her strides, she went too far. "We all know you are not so 'innocent', little virgin —"

Georgiana went to pinch my cheek, and I slapped her hand away. "And how would you know if I'm a virgin, Georgiana? Would it be because you have spoken to Andreas? He and my husband are the only two who know this fact."

True, Mitică does know, but that was irrelevant information. The redhead's pale skin grew ashen as the fool realized that she had spilled the metaphorical beans in her haste to be the champion of the hour. I always knew Georgiana was a bit dense, but I didn't really see *how* dense. By admitting that vital piece of information, she had confessed to another attempt to conspire to kill me. No doubt the women had aided the men in their efforts, and now they keep Andreas' whereabouts and the information he had provided a secret from the Master.

"This is true." The Master finally spoke. "How is it that you know, Georgiana?"

"Georgie, you idiot," Imogen hissed out, her aura flaring with a crack of ire.

Georgiana looked back at her sister, shocked and confused, her hot-headedness cooling instantly like an extinguished flame. The expression on her face was almost pitying as she froze.

"Bummer," I caught her attention. "You were so close."

In a flash, she lashed out in a furious rage at me, her beautiful face fully metamorphosed into the demon. Of course, I had no chance to get away, nor did I even get a second to react before she was within centimeters of sinking her teeth into me. I wasn't even able to close my eyes to brace myself before a black shadow descended over us, shrouding Georgiana's encroaching image. There was the thunderous sound of stone cracking and a hard grunt. Just as instantly as the shadow of the Master had come, it had gone. Georgiana came back into my view as she lifted herself from the floor, blood cascading down her blouse from a deep gash on her chest. Her collarbone had been broken, the ragged bone poking through her white skin.

There was another crack, and I saw from the corner of my eye the Master and Imogen make contact with each other. Her silver hair and yellow eyes shone brightly in the firelight, and with her unearthly beauty, she appeared truly terrifying. Another strange chill filled the air, and electricity shot around her as she attacked my husband with razor-sharp talons and jagged teeth.

A heart-stopping shiver tore through my body, and I returned my eyes to Georgiana, whose red gaze fell upon me. She was ready to come at me with a vengeance, and instead of feeling fear at the sight of her devilish face, I felt ready. All of what had happened had come to this point between her and me, and I was prepared to face her. As I was taking off the silver crucifix and winding the chain around my wrist, she had popped the bone back under her skin. Again, she rushed at me, but when I held out the silver crucifix before her, she hissed, stalling her actions. She was extremely affected by the sight, and it only made her angrier.

Dumitru was suddenly at my side, taking my arm to pull me away from the fray. By doing that, it only took my attention away from Georgiana, diverting the angle of the crucifix just slightly so that she could jump at me a second time. Somehow, she managed to claw Mitică's grasp off of me, and in the midst of it, I planted the silver directly on her healing chest. Her blood boiled on contact, and she let out a horrendous scream as we both were sent tumbling to the ground.

The silver chain had loosened itself from around my wrist, and while Georgiana was down, I'm not sure what possessed me to do it, but I looped it around her neck. Holding her down with all my weight, I didn't even need to squeeze the chain tightly to do an effective job. She writhed, her nails cutting the flesh of her neck to try and break the chain, but she was weakening. Her flesh rotted and burned in the line where the chain lay, splitting skin and tendon as it made its way to her bone. I was horrified at what I was doing, but I couldn't stop.

"Imogen!" Georgiana cried hoarsely. "Imogen!"

Before she could make another plea, Dumitru had come down on her hard, a stake of white oak in his hands. He drove it straight into her, like a hot pick through ice. With that, the body that I saw as Georgiana simply faded from existence, blackening and turning to dust. The chain suddenly snapped, and I thought it had broken, but instead saw that it had finished working its way to the bone, severing her charred spine.

I wanted to scream, but it came out so breathy and faint, and I recoiled from the dusty corpse. Mitică grabbed the collar of my dress, hauling me away from the sight. My eyes were drawn to where Imogen and the Master were still squaring off. I expected Imogen to show some care that she had just lost her friend and sister, but there was no emotion in her eyes other than pure hate as she stared the Master down. There were deep claw marks on her stomach and face, which were healing quickly.

As a deathly silence came over the room, Imogen seemed to snap out of it a little as her eyes flickered to each of us. She was outnumbered yet again, and the absent Cosima surely wouldn't have the gall to join her. Cursing, she looked directly at me. "You will suffer for this. You will lose all that you have gained, your victories will become defeats, your God will forsake you, and I will personally drag you to Hell."

"Bold last words, she-devil." The Master began as his claws sharpened.

"You couldn't care less who suffers as long as it's justified in your eyes, Imogen," I yelled between pants of ragged breath. "But, no matter how much you make me suffer, it will not bring Petros back to you."

Her eye twitched.

I continued to curse as I was held back by Dumitru. "Andreas told me a few things about you, too. If you trust him, you're just a much of a fool as I was. But, when you see him next, you tell him of what I did to Georgiana, for the same will be done to him!"

Imogen's brow furrowed in a mix of uncertain emotions, and just before the Master was about to rush her, she stepped into a shadow and utterly vanished from sight. All three of us were left, huffing in the chill which reverberated throughout the parlor.

The Master turned to me, an expression on his face I don't think I've ever seen him give me before. It was almost like, fright? As soon as he did, however, his head lifted as if to hear something in the distance. "I will take care of Cosima. Dumitru, take her to her room."

"No." I growled in protest, not caring if I disobeyed him.

Ignoring me, he gave another nod to Mitică, who swooped me into his arms without any effort. I put up a fight, although I didn't want to hurt my friend, but the Master had already gone by the time Mitică struggled out into the hall with me over his shoulder.

"Mitică, let me go!" I trashed against him. "Put me down!"

"Would you just stop already?!" He shouted angrily. "What do you think you can accomplish now? Just do as you're told!"

He was right, and I wasn't quite sure what I was doing anymore. Unwillingly, I submitted, knowing he was only doing as he was commanded and because he cared. My heart was pounding so loudly in my ears as Dumitru hastily made it to my room, set me down, and locked the door behind us. It was only then that I saw his arm was sliced open from Georgiana's attack, and I felt so bad for being rough with him. Rushing to my bathroom to get a towel, I was stopped on the way there when I heard a *bang* from the outside.

I rushed to the windows that overlooked the courtyard, and there in the dim light of the moon, I saw two figures standing a few yards away from each other. Knowing it had to be the Master and Cosima, I was torn as to keep watching or to get the towel. I didn't need to contemplate my decision for long, for I heard Dumitru's shuddered cry, and I had to pull myself away from the scene. Grabbing a hand towel, I ran back to Mitică and applied pressure to his lacerations, which went deep into the muscle. He winced, the poor dear, trying to hold in the pain as his hands quaked. Gently, I propped him up against me to let him rest before the Master's assured return.

Mitică's chest heaved as he rested his head against my chest. "You were reckless."

"You distracted me." I ran my fingers through his hair.

"No, you distracted *me*." His face dug into my neck as he warned. "Don't do it again."

I scoffed lightly. "Next time, don't get in my way."

Dumitru was about to retort when the door opened and the Master entered my sitting room. Unscathed, the blood splattered on his shirt was not his, as he declared to us with so little sentiment. "Cosima is no more. Come, Dumitru, come, your wounds need tending."

That was too quick, I thought. With a nod, Mitică lifted himself from me, though I still helped him to his feet. Flashing me a quick, sad smile, he sluggishly exited my rooms, the towel's red blooming further.

Once my friend had left, the Master looked to me, his eyes examining me up and down for a second before saying. "I will return."

And with that, he left too, the door closing behind him.

When I was alone, I wasn't sure what to do next. I stood there like an idiot for maybe five minutes before thinking that I should change out of my blood-spattered gown. A bundle of nerves as I was, my head was very clear as I cleaned myself up, the images of the evening replaying in my head. It was difficult to get my thoughts together, and eventually I sat in a plusher chair in my bedroom, staring off into space, the sight of the silver eating through Georgiana's neck was the sole image in my head. I had strangled her with it and had inadvertently decapitated her in the process. For a second time, I had been an active instrument in the death of another, although Mitică had been the one to give the final blow. But this time it felt good, which perplexed me.

A knock at the door startled me from my deep trance. Stuttering, I called out for them to come in.

The Master entered and awkwardly asked. "How are you?"

"I'm fine," a half lie. "How is Dumitru? And you?"

"We both are well." His clothes had been changed, his appearance refreshed; nothing like the terrible one who stood against the others. Slowly, he came up to me. "May we speak?"

"Of course," I went to stand, but he held out a hand to stop me. I watched him grab my desk chair and set it next to mine, but before he said anything, I asked. "What happened with Cosima?"

Sitting himself down, his eyes were far away from mine. "She ended herself."

My eyebrows raised in shock. I couldn't imagine Cosima doing it, but yet again, she knew exactly what would make him revisit some terrible things from his past.

At the sight of my shock, the Master explained. "For a woman of little tenacity as Cosima, when it came to deciding to submit or die, she chose to take out her own heart before I had the chance to take it myself."

I gulped. "I am…sorry."

"For what?" The Master responded flatly.

I knew he was feeling so many raw emotions, but there was no way he would express them in front of me, especially not now. Gently, I spoke, careful not to hurt him further. "Even if you didn't feel anything for her, you two still were…together."

He was still gazing at my hand, his palm turning over to weave our fingers together. "You misunderstand the difference between making love and sex."

His blunt answer struck me dumb. Surely something had passed between them the times they spent together, but I let it go for the sake of not starting a disagreement.

We sat in silence for a long while, just holding each other's hands. My mind drifted far away again, thinking about Georgiana and Cosima's end and where Imogen could have gone. I thought about the words I said to her and her reaction to them. It wasn't really pity I felt, nor sympathy, nor compassion, but maybe a certain amount of empathy.

"Isa," the Master spoke up, adding another hand to the mix. He was hesitant to finish the sentence, but I waited quietly for him. "I want to stay with you tonight, if you will have me."

Stay with me? I was…uncertain. I wanted to be alone, maybe cry a little if I got emotional enough, and I didn't want him to be around to see that. It had been some time since we had spent a night together in full, and I felt a bit uncomfortable and embarrassed to have him so close. After I had seen him and Cosima together, and I began to separate my heart from him to protect myself, to let him in again seemed too soon. Not to mention, I wasn't even sure how I felt about him yet, and particularly Imogen, making it known that he wished to punish me. It all made me unsure of everything.

The Master's massive shoulders straightened, his features hardening when I had given him no answer but did not release my hand. "You do not wish it, then?"

"No, I just…" My voice faded out. How was I going to explain things that my own heart didn't even understand yet? "I'm just confused. I hear one thing, and another is said that contradicts it. I don't know what's true anymore."

"You mean what Imogen said…" My husband frowned, but there was no eye contact when his grasp tightened and he confessed what I feared to be the truth. "I will not lie to you; I said it, and I did mean it at the time."

"Do you still mean —"

"They were just words said without thought!" He snapped, although his defense had no base to stand on, and he knew it. The Master's jaw tensed at his growing frustration with himself. "Another thing for which to ask forgiveness."

"But words spoken, nonetheless," sighing, I stood, but I could not let go of his hand. I wasn't angry, just disappointed that he had been unfaithful to me in more ways than one. I'm sure he was fully expecting me to reject him for this added offense he caused me, but the worst thing for our relationship would be for me to throw him aside. I have to constantly remind myself that it is his nature to do these things. Tolerance and patience were the two things that I need to keep at the forefront of my mind. At that moment, I did my best to cool my temper before I tugged on his hand. "Come to bed."

My husband's whole appearance changed instantaneously from crestfallen to unexpected hope as he looked up at me with wide, shining eyes. "Isa…"

"You are forgiven for saying whatever you said and meant." I kept my head high, firm in my resolve to give the Master forgiveness and show him that I was still willing to work with him as long as he was, too. "I still have things to think about, but all that occurred is behind us, in the past, but that doesn't mean I'll forget about it."

The slightest smile formed on his lips. "I would not want you to, my dear."

"Come," I tugged again. "Unless you want to spend the night on that chair."

Excitedly, he stood and led me to my bed. My heart was hammering in my ribs, and I have no doubt he could hear it loud and clear as we crawled under the sheets. Unlike the last time, where he had lain there like a statue, my husband's arms eagerly drew me to him, purring and snuggling his face against my hair. These earnest affections made me uneasy, but I let the Master have his way. His hand rested on my curved hip, one leg wrapped around mine, and he held me, perhaps grateful to be allowed near.

My husband's closeness was everything my soul needed, and I thanked God that he was beside me again. There was an inner war waging against my head and my heart; one saying that I should be extremely careful, the other wanting him to kiss me a thousand times to make up for the time he had been away. After a long silence, kind of on a whim, I asked. "Why do you never kiss me anymore?"

"I never kissed you until you permitted me, and that you understood what I am." The Master's hand left my hip and slid up to my forearm, where he stroked it softly beneath the sheets. "Now you may have better knowledge of what I am, but you no longer permit me."

Again, he was correct. Shifting, I rolled over so that my body lay flush against his. The arm that he used to caress me came to my lower back and pressed me to him even more so. I gazed up into those big brown eyes, now so warm from when they had been so cold. I was so struck that he remembered that night, so struck that he cared enough to give me space and not kiss me when I was unsure of how I felt. The man who was next to me had to be the one that I married, the one I love above all others, and the one I would walk willingly through Hell to see freed from his bodily prison. I had missed him so much, my Count, and I nestled myself against his chest. Still, he would have to wait just a bit longer to be permitted once again.

And with this slight reprieve we were given from his children's terror, for they are sure to return with vengeance, we rested in each other's embrace the whole night and unto the morning.

THE GIFT

23 November

Late Afternoon...

For the next two days, I have been deep in thought about my feelings. I have been weighing options, considering his transgressions, and rereading my account from those two months. I still have been lost in my decision. Something was missing from this narrative: that vital question of *why*. Not once has the Master explained to me *why* he chose to save me. *Why*, after all those weeks of cruel indifference, did he decide to save me when I was at death's door? He wanted me to be punished for 'making him weak'; why not just let it happen? His sons were exacting their justice for him, and all he had to do was sit back and watch.

It would have been easy to let it happen; I had given up. Only regret made me come back, but if it hadn't, I would have just passed away from this earthly plane with nothing to tether me down. Petros would have been avenged, the Master would have been free to resume his former life, and they would have won. It was just that simple. Yet, the Master chose to oppose them at the very last second. *Why?*

Something had happened to him that he wasn't willing to tell me, and I have been hesitant to ask for fear of his ire. I only have one day left to give him his answer, and I feel conflicted. Each night, he has been insistent on staying with me while I sleep and does not leave until the morning. Although it's considerate of him to do so, his constant presence still leaves me uncomfortable. No matter how much he wishes to be close, I still wait for him to say something to remind me that this is just a dream and that he has not changed at all. Even when the Master would smother me in his protective embrace, I still wonder if he is deceiving me. What if it is all just a tactic he's using to make me put my guard down and let him back in, then end it?

There has to be an answer to this, and perhaps I'm overthinking it. Added to the fact that there has been no sign of Imogen or Andreas, and the Master is uneasy, which makes me uneasy. He never speaks about what bothers him, nor provides any information as to what his plans are, and has not relaxed once during the times that I've seen him. In turn, more stress has been added to my plate, and I must eat it all.

Later...

Shortly after my last entry, I decided that I needed to go to the chapel and find some guidance and solace there. Donning my chapel veil, I went down to the infamous sanctum with a heavy heart and lost in thought. I wasn't quite paying much attention to my surroundings, but when I got to the mosaic hall, I noticed that the door to the chapel was open. I could have sworn that I had closed it the last time I used it, and a recurring fear surfaced in my breast that *someone* had returned. Quietly, I slinked to the door and peered inside. However, within it was not Andreas, but the Master himself. I was in awe as I watched him, his shoulders shaking as pained, raspy breaths echoed to the high ceiling. I was even more dumbfounded that he was on his knees, seemingly praying.

My heart was warmed but hurt at the sight, and I knew I should let him be. I had just turned away when his voice rang from within. "I know you are there, Isadora."

I stopped, kicking myself that I had been caught. "Forgive me for disturbing you. I'll leave you be."

"Come in, if you wish." He beckoned. Hesitantly, I entered and came up to kneel beside him. He looked deathly pale, more than usual, and terribly worn. I assumed it was because he had been put through some discomfort when praying, but I smiled warmly at him. I wasn't going to say anything to him and was about to begin my devotion to ask for guidance, when he commented. "You find this strange, do you not?"

"Strange, and surprising," I admitted, moving my eyes to the cross upon the high altar. I really wished he wasn't there so I could think in peace, but to have him there of his own free will was a miracle in itself. "But it gladdens me very much to see it."

The Master sat back on his calves and turned slightly away from the holy symbol, the discomfort on his face fading as soon as he did. "What brings you here?"

"I am troubled..." I admitted again after swallowing hard. "You?"

Out of the corner of my eye, I saw him nod once. "Troubled...as well..."

"Is it because of me?"

His hand came up to rub the back of his neck, his brow furrowing as he chuckled nervously. "Partially. Are you troubled because of me?"

"Mostly," I smiled sadly, letting out a long sigh. "There is one thing that is keeping me from making any decision concerning you. I want to ask it, but I fear you will be angry with me."

At that, he frowned, the expression on his face displayed emotions of heartbreak that made me immediately regret saying anything. I was about to apologize when he interjected unexpectedly. "You wish to know why I chose to save you?"

"Yes..." I blinked, facing him directly. "How did you know?"

Shoulders slouching, the Master sighed. He wasn't looking at me, nor anywhere near the altar, subconsciously hinting to me that he was feeling something that he wanted to hide. "It is the one thing for which I have given no explanation, but it is because I have been trying to understand why I did it myself."

I was struck by his honesty, and as much as it warmed my heart, I was quite concerned about *what* saving me was troubling him so. "If you're not ready to explain, I can wait."

"No, I want to tell you. I have been trying to find the right words, but I am not sure if I understand it." The Master pursed his lips and mulled something over in his head, then asked. "I will try to explain, if you will be willing to hear."

Of course, I nodded and waited for him to begin.

After a pause to collect his thoughts, he did. "In those days when my brutality was well feared and well used, when the Ottomans invaded Wallachia and were set on doing the same to Transylvania, I was called upon to defend Christendom and my land, and I willingly undertook the task. My Ioana, my wife of many years, mother of my children, was here in these walls, supposedly safe from any enemy.

"The Turks had us nearly surrounded as they had come up the river valley to this fortress: our last stronghold. We were confident that we could withstand the infidels, but we were not as aware of our situation as we thought. A message was sent by an informant in their ranks, and finally, we understood that the Turks were planning an assault that would utterly destroy us. Ioana, realizing her possible fate, jumped from the ramparts and into the river…" His voice faded out, his eyes going downcast. "I just managed to escape before this place was overrun by the Turks, but that time still haunts me. I had failed so many that night, and I felt as though God had failed me, too. In my anger and sorrow that God had stolen her and my lands from me, I strayed far from the righteous path. It was one in a series of events in my life that led me to commit my final apostasy and fall deep into the Pit."

So few times before had he been so truthful with me, and I had such heartache that the Master had felt and lived through things and had fallen so far because of them. Moved with pity for him, I reached out my hand that trembled. Despite everything, good and bad, I couldn't let him be alone.

Seeing the gesture, he hesitated, but took my hand and held it tenderly. "Ioana had given up on life and had admitted defeat to those whom she thought would destroy us that night." He paused again, his grip tightening on my hand. "When you saw me as you lay there, the look on your face was so full of hope despite having so little blood left in you. You were close to death, but your heart still quickened for me. It made me feel guilty for not doing something to help you, and I hated that feeling. Then, when you realized that I would do nothing, I saw so plainly on your face how you gave up and chose to die."

The Master's voice cracked, and he had to take a moment to recompose himself. "It reminded me of Ioana's face, and I relived what I endured when I lost her, and what I have endured since that time. I do not know how I had forgotten, but everything I ever felt came back to me: all my anguish and loneliness, but also my hopes and what you mean to me. I became enraged at what they had done, just as before, and I had to rip them apart."

A crimson tear escaped his eye, and he tried to wipe it away inconspicuously, but I had seen it. I could hardly believe what I was hearing, so I remained silent. It all made sense now, but there was more that he had to say, so I listened.

"So I did, and my revenge distracted me from you as you were dying. You had just slipped away by the time I finished with them." The Master had to stop again to clear his throat before going on. "You cannot comprehend the helplessness and disgust I had for myself when I could hear you had no heartbeat. I had the power to bring you back and give you eternal life, but you would be damned as me. With Ioana, I had no way to help her, but with you, I had a way, though I had no will to…"

"Husband," I interjected because my arms had to hold him. "Please, come here."

The Master's glassy eyes gazed up at mine, and I could see his reluctance. With my own gaze pleading, he caved and came nearer, his arms slid around my back to gently envelope me to his chest. The Master's face came into my neck, his breath shuddering. "I could not let you die there, not like that, not again, but I could not help you in any way. So, all I could do was pray that He would not take you, but give you back to me. I do not think I have ever prayed so hard for one single thing in hundreds of years. I told Him to save you because you have so much to live for, and I only want to live for you. For some reason, He must have heard me and returned to me my gift just when

I was about to throw you back in His face. Why He would ever do that for me, the least of all on this earth, I do not pretend to understand. I have been trying to figure out these things, feeling their shame and guilt, but I cannot seem to pick apart the pieces."

My heart had this strange sensation come to it, something warm, but painful. My fists latched onto him, bringing him to me. I wanted to bare my soul to him and tell the Master how much I still loved him. Recalling the darkness in which I dwelt at near-death, I whispered the secrets of my dying brain in his ear. "When I was lost in the dark, it was you who led me back. I could not leave this earth without having been loved by you."

Instinctually, his grasp on me tightened, and his shoulders shook. The Master lifted his face from my neck and just grazed my lips with his own, afraid to initiate a full kiss.

So, I closed my eyes and kissed my husband as tenderly as I think I ever had. For so long I had been denied his touch, and to have it back removed a weight from my heart that had long oppressed it. Instead of feeling him suck the life from me, it felt more as if he were restoring my very essence with his kiss. I took in all his scent, and it reminded me of a long-lost home that I had returned to after a lengthy journey. "My moon of my days, never leave me again. I have been so cold without you."

"Until the allotted day I never shall," he vowed, kissing me again. Oh, those kisses, which are eternal in their own right, how they sustain me. The Count pulled away from my lips just enough to speak. "My flesh of my flesh, blood of my blood, my best beloved one, my heavenly gift, my wife."

I swooned with happiness and love for him for the first time in so long. Surely, after all the things he had confessed, he has returned to me. How can there be deceit in those words? I wanted to tell him how much I cherish him, but there was one other thing that I had to ask. Choosing my words wisely, I tested. "My love, tell me what you desire above all things on this earth?"

The Count's brown eyes flickered with emotion, and his hands came up to cup my cheeks. I think he knew I was testing him, and just before he brought his lips to mine once again, he expressed the words which he himself had forbidden me to say. "Redemption, absolution, salvation."

I smiled so widely, and a weight fell from my heart and shoulders. The oppression they had felt for so long was lifted when he reaffirmed these things to me, which he had forsaken. "I love you, Vlad, with all my soul. My heart beats for only you, I swear it."

Taking his hand from my cheek, I rested it on my left breast, my pulse accelerating at the intimate touch. The Count rested his forehead against mine, our eyes locking as he felt each thump beneath his palm. "I vow on this heart that beats with my own blood, that I will expel all threats to us by the new year. I promise to give you peace, and one day, maybe even my love if the God on High will permit it to be so."

It startled me that he would make such a statement with such fervor. It worried me more than relieved me, because I knew if he were to do that, my husband would have to leave me again. I do not doubt his abilities, but there was no way I was going to let go of him so easily for a second time. "That is much to promise..."

"It can be done. I have faith it can be." His earnestness was true, but in whom did he place his faith? Himself? Or the Father on High or his Father from below? "Do not forget who I am, young one. I am not weak, and although they are not either, they are no match for me. Please, have faith in me again, and I will do everything in my power to see each one of those things are accomplished."

I was hesitant, of course, but I do believe in him and his power. At least, for now, I would give him that. "I have faith in you, but what will you do now? I don't want you to go away, not when I have you back."

The Master's thumb rubbed my cheek where some stray tears had fallen. "I will finish what I had planned from the beginning, even if that now means we must be separated for a time. The new year will be here in just over a month, so the time will be brief, but I must act now. We still have a few days left, so spend them with me to make up for time lost."

Nodding, I kissed him again and again, refusing to have him be apart from me. In that moment, I loved him too fiercely, too ardently, but my heart could not help it. More than ever, we must not deviate from the other because the real challenge, the real conflict, is only just beginning.

25 November

Evening...
  Life as I remember it before the children's arrival has returned to normal. Naturally, it has only been two days since the Count and I have officially reunified with each other, and I have been in such bliss. Having the three of us together again, a rag-tag trio, has relieved so much of the worry and stress that has shrouded us these past few months. Sure, our doom still hangs above our heads like an executioner's blade, but at the very least, we are together.
  Since his injury, Dumitru's wound has been healing nicely, but he is still unable to do many of the chores. I have stepped in, although the Count constantly reminds me that it isn't my place, I still took over the work. With the situation as it is, who else is going to do the essentials around this place? Besides, doing it helps me take my mind off the ever-looming danger that we still face.
  This evening, the Count summoned both Dumitru and me to his reception room as soon as the sun was down. Of course, that is highly unusual, and we humans both feared the worst. For what purpose would the Master of the house wish to speak to both of us together? He was usually very tactful with his conversations, but I could only guess that it was something very important.
  When we entered, the Master was already waiting for us. The room was dim, and the moonlight illuminated it more than the fireplace. He was sitting on the settee, and didn't smile, nor really acknowledge us save for gesturing to us to come and sit on the opposite seat. As I approached, I greeted him with a 'good evening', and he mumbled a response as if he were lost in thought. He appeared very worn this evening, very stressed, and I would have sat next to him if Mitică hadn't been present. So, I sat next to my friend on the other settee, eyes downcast. It didn't take long for our Master to begin. "I might as well just say it: my sources have found where Andreas and Imogen are hiding —"
  "Where are they?" I interceded, a bit rudely now that I think about it.
  The Count eyed me with a pensive stare and was quiet for a moment before admitting to us only the vaguest of details. "Nearby,

but not in Romania. I must depart soon before they discover that I have found them."

The verb made my heart stop in my chest. Depart? He had told me soon, but so soon? There was a part of me that wanted to put my foot down and forbid him to leave, but I could only choke out defeatedly. "Go…?"

"You will require the boxes, then?" Mitică brought the conversation back to its serious nature, cutting me off. I wasn't sure what he meant by the obscure term 'boxes'.

"Yes," the Count affirmed. "I will hire the Romani since you cannot do it yourself, but you will oversee it and ensure all is in order."

Hire more Romani to pack his bags? Surely that is excessive. Can't the Count pack his own things like a normal person? I wanted to ask, but knew I would only end up looking like an idiot in front of them. My brow furrowed, thinking about it and the fates of the other Romani who had recently worked for the Master. I pray to God they would not be subject to the same treatment, no matter the circumstances we find ourselves in.

"Of course, Master." Dumitru nodded. "When do you leave?"

"The first of December, so you will have plenty of time." He confirmed, and then his eyes drifted away to some fixed point behind us. "I would leave sooner, however, there are certain things I must get in order, and they will take a few days."

"All will be completed by then." Dumitru declared and said something else concerning the business of these mysterious boxes.

My mind soon got lost in thought about what the Count had said, and my head hung so low. December is only six days from now. Six days and I will lose him all over again? I couldn't let that happen despite the cost. Again, that little voice in my head told me to put my foot down, but I couldn't. Now I understand why the Count had brought us both together: with Mitică there, I could not contest him so openly as I would if we were alone. I scowled, and once the room became quiet, I inquired meekly. "Must you go?"

"I must, I have no choice." The Master said it so plainly and then commented. "You know why."

There was little chance of him giving me an answer, but I still asked. "At least tell us where you are going?"

He sighed, I think, knowing that I meant well by asking questions he could never answer, but it would just be the same response as before. "You know I cannot, for your own sakes."

I couldn't let it go, and still pressed him. "And you will not say what you are planning?"

"Indeed, I will not." The Master sensed my growing discontent and frowned. He knew from the day he told me that I would not be so silent about it. In front of everyone, no matter who, I would protest it because his leaving could mean a relapse into his old ways. Away from me, be it hundreds or thousands of miles away, there was that possibility. "You two are staying here. There will be no further discussion about it as all has been arranged."

"Of course, Master," Dumitru reaffirmed, and standing, bowed his head. "I will begin the preparations now."

Giving his servant his blessing, he was dismissed. Once Mitică left the room, a deathly silence fell between my husband and me. Cautiously, I stood and went to sit by him. There was so much I wanted to say, although he promptly came to rest his mouth against my neck. As if the whole previous conversation hadn't even happened, the Count brought me to him and kissed the tender skin. He was hungry for me, I could sense it.

My thoughts turned to disarray when the Count's hands began to caress my hips. I moaned at the sensation, and the Master chuckled as his palms slid down my thighs to part them. I allowed him to touch me so boldly, and we situated ourselves so that he was positioned between my knees as he lay me against the cushion. For a moment, he admired the scene of me beneath him, but then rested his head against my breast.

He purred contentedly, and I combed my fingers through his hair. The Count breathed me in, and I could hear the deep breaths as he lay there enjoying the closeness we shared. He was soothed, while my chest was filling with emotion. I'm sure he could hear my increased heart rate and feel the choppy rising and falling of my diaphragm, but he said nothing.

I indeed have every faith in him that he can do all he sets out to do, but the pain of being physically separated from him is too much to bear for a second time. There was nothing I could do or say but let him know I was there for him and that I love him eternally.

Chapter Thirty-Nine

BLOOD BROTHERS

28 November

Afternoon…

What a long day. Most of it had been spent doing a large portion of Mitică's chores, though the constant work brought my mind no distraction. All during the past two days, I have been trying to think up ways that I could persuade the Count to allow me to go with him or persuade him not to go at all. Sure, I know it's a futile attempt and a waste of time to ponder these things, but I had to try something. So far, however, I haven't thought up any really convincing ones, and that's simply because none exist. For me to accompany him, I will only be a burden.

That fact bothers me considerably, and it makes me feel useless. The Count is doing this for everyone, but mostly for me, and I cannot even offer him any aid except to remind him to remember himself. I've cried about it a few times unexpectedly, which I hate doing. I could be washing the dishes, polishing this or that, and start crying like an idiot. Luckily, I'm able to turn it off and conceal it, or I'm able to hide for a few minutes until the emotions pass. If anyone has noticed, no one has said anything.

The Romani have been here doing some strange work that I haven't been able to figure out. From the windows in my room, I've observed them going into a passageway leading to someplace beneath the castle with shovels and other digging instruments. With them, on horse-drawn sleds, they have large square and rectangular wooden boxes, which they bring below and then bring them out hours later. When they go in, it takes two men to carry a single box, but when they go out, it takes four to six men.

Their work is very peculiar since there are roughly a dozen of these boxes coming and going daily. Since they are obviously digging for something, what are they bringing up from the bowels of this castle that is so valuable to transport? What does the Count need that's so vital to his journey? I wish I could ask, but no doubt he or Dumitru will tell me. I might as well pretend I see and hear nothing, since that will be the answer I receive: nothing. Now there are only two to three days left until the Master leaves for God knows where and for how long, with no answers, no inklings, no hints. This whole thing is maddening.

Evening...

At sunset, I was summoned to the Count's reception room. This, again, was unusual since he customarily prefers to lounge in my sitting room, or the library, or some other place, but rarely his rooms unless there was something afoot. It worried me that I was the only one directed to come alone and told to wear a certain dress. This garment, which was one I haven't ever gotten a chance to wear yet, is violet velvet. The bodice and sleeves are studded with gold spherical beads, and around the hem of the high collar are violets created out of golden thread. I always felt this dress was too good to be worn in the presence of the children in case it should get ruined, so I had kept it aside for Christmas or some other occasion.

Anyway, as I came to the Count's room dressed as he instructed, the door was already slightly open. I thought that was atypical, but I entered anyway. The room was in its usual semi-darkness, with the fire ablaze. Scanning the space, I saw the figure of the Master sitting in a chair with his back to me, facing the fire. I knew he was already aware of my presence, for I saw that his head had turned slightly, so I approached. "Is there something going on? Why did you have me dress up?"

The Master didn't answer me but turned his head to a full profile, which contrasted against the fire, so I could not see his features. I felt a chill that something was not right. For a second, he stood and faced me directly. In the dim light, I thought my eyes were deceiving me, for the man who stood before me nearly resembled the Master, but it was not him. He was just a bit shorter than the man I knew; his hair was not as long and was set in loose curls, which were graying at the temples. Not to mention his facial hair was completely unlike my husband's, although similar enough. His eyes shone like black obsidian as he smiled with teeth as ivory. "Ah, you must be the little bride. What a pleasure it is to meet you."

"Who the hell are you?" I stepped back, adrenaline pushed its way into my veins. It annoyed me that I had been confronted by this strange creature so unexpectedly. He was obviously one of *them*, and an old fear constricted my chest. "How did you get in here?"

Whoever this man was, he seemed quite bewildered by my reaction. Eyebrow cocked, his brow then knitted in great confusion. "Pardon?"

I reached within my bodice to grab the silver crucifix and pulled it out, concealed in my fist.

Suddenly, a large hand slapped over mine, which was about to produce the crucifix to ward off this intruder. The Count himself, who had appeared right next to me, shot me a reassuring glance. "There will be no need for that, Isadora. He is a friend."

"Extraordinary," the stranger emphasized the word as he floated forward to come within a few feet of me, an amused grin wide on his face. I saw then how black his irises are, and they were frightening to stare into. "Same features, same temperament. Your type hasn't changed for centuries, brother."

Brother? Shouldn't he have called him Father? I wasn't going to ask and retreated behind my husband after he lowered my hand. Friend or foe, I would not be fooled by some trick of theirs. I have yet to meet one so good-hearted as the Master, one whom I could call 'friend'. Since his intruder was so close, I could see better how he could almost be a twin brother. It was rather disturbing to see two of the same men standing next to each other.

With a snort in response to the man's bold teasing, the Count spoke, cutting the tension between us. "Isadora, this is my eldest brother, Vlad, the fourth of his name. Well, technically half-brother."

This other Vlad smiled widely, the friendliest I have ever seen a demon smile, I admit, and bowed slightly at the waist. "As I said, it is a pleasure, Madame."

Blinking, I struggled to wrap my head around the concept. I knew the Count had siblings, but I was not familiar with who they were. He had told me of a younger one who was taken hostage by the Turks with him, but this was not that brother. "A pleasure, sir, please forgive me for assuming you had…other intentions. Also, forgive me again, but you mean, like, a real brother? I mean, biological?"

"No offense taken, but you are correct, we share the same father." The other Vlad explained casually, as if it were the most normal thing. Then he commented teasingly to the Count. "I am five years older than my little brother."

The Master frowned at the childish taunting and crossed his arms.

I was astonished that he would allow such prodding, although it was very innocent. Cautiously, I inquired further since this fourth Vlad seemed to be much easier in revealing pieces of the past. "But how are you the fourth, if he is the third? Shouldn't it be the other way around?"

"She's a quick one." The fourth Vlad chuckled. "Our father had his way in his day, if you catch my meaning. I was not born of his wife."

"Oh…" I felt incredibly embarrassed that I had put him on the spot like that. I must have looked foolish for not knowing anything about the family, but there really isn't much that my husband has told me about who they were. "Forgive me, I didn't realize."

"No matter, I was legitimized later, but it is a bit confusing at first glance." He grinned again, a beaming smile similar to the Count's. I was struck that his behaviors, little mannerisms, and quirks were so identical to the ones I was familiar with. But then he grew serious, his voice deepening. "But then again, I guess this family is quite abnormal. I have heard much about this quarrel that has erupted between us and them. It is distressing and unprecedented. I so do regret that you have joined this family, only to be shunned by those who believe their opinion is valid. These young ones have no respect for their elders, and their betters."

It was interesting to me that he used nearly the same language that I had used about the children's disloyalty to their own Father. That impressed me, and I inched out a bit from behind the Count. "That's what I said."

"Great minds think alike." This fourth Vlad complimented, but then his eyes flickered down my frame, and he pouted. He took a step to the side to examine not me, but what I was wearing. His tongue clicked as he chastised his little brother. "Speaking of minds, what are you thinking, brother? This is the twenty-first century, and you're still making her cover her hair and wear these passé dresses? I have heard rumors that you made her cover her face, too. *Tisk tisk*, I condone your attempt to guard her modesty, but your time with the Turks still influences you."

The Count just had about enough of that, and he glowered. My wearing this kind of dress was very important to him, although I don't quite understand why. It wasn't like I minded it really, despite them still making me feel out of place. My husband's eyes narrowed as he warned. "I did not invite you here to criticize my wife's way of dress."

"Of course, of course, my apologies. I have a gift for our new *Doamna*, a wedding present, but also to welcome you into our family. It has been centuries since new blood has entered this ancient house." He held out his hand for me to take it with a genuine smile.

Instinctually, I withdrew, but then remembered myself and cleared my throat. "Sir, you shouldn't have —"

"Oh, nonsense! Please, sister-in-law, I don't bite." The fourth Vlad snickered at his own bad pun and outstretched his hand further, anticipating my compliance.

Hesitant as I was to take it, I had to look up to the Count for reassurance that it was alright. My husband was smiling, his eyes trained so softly on me, but he nodded when he saw my reluctance. So, I took his brother's chilled hand, and he led me to the table, which was situated next to the chair he had been sitting in. It was another gilded box, this one flat, similar to the ones in which the Count had given me many of his family's prized jewels.

Gesturing to the magnificent piece, the other Vlad let go of my hand. "I see my brother has doted greatly upon you already, so I hope this little trinket is enough of a welcome."

I was growing uncomfortable, and with shaking hands, I lifted the lid to the aged box. Within it rested a weighted ruby necklace that resembled a collar, paired with a matching diadem. I was shocked at their brilliance even in the dim firelight, for it seemed they had within them their own luminescence. "This is too much for me to accept —"

"This is too little, believe me." He lifted the crown from its place and rested it on my head, and of course, it fit snugly over my hair and veil. "It suits her well, don't you think?"

His brother had come nearer to witness the exchange. I hated that he kept on cutting me off, and I was growing increasingly apprehensive with the way he was pressing me to accept the gift. It was far too lavish for me, and was no 'trinket', but must have belonged to a wife of his at some point.

Seeing my uneasiness, the Count chimed in. "That certainly is a generous gift, brother. Are you sure you would want to part with it?"

"To whom else would I give it? It should belong to a reigning *Doamnă*, so it's only proper that I should give it to your darling bride." The older brother's eyes were transfixed by the semi-precious stones, but there was something in his eyes that reflected a certain pain. It puzzled me, but there were many things these creatures say and do that puzzle me.

They speak about the past of their family still ruled these lands as lords above the common people. The crown I wear has no power behind it, only the remnants of an ancient title that has no bearing in the modern world, but to them, it appears nothing has changed. I touched the glittering jewels set in gold, and for the sake of decorum, I accepted. "Thank you, sir, I will treasure it always."

My brother-in-law grinned from ear to ear, and a sincere expression of gratitude came over his face. "I have no doubt you will, my sister-in-law." Daintily, he removed the exquisite piece from my head and placed it back into its velvet mold.

The Count quickly moved the subject to other matters, and we sat down and discussed the true meaning of the fourth Vlad's arrival.

It turns out that his brother's visit isn't a quick visit to meet the newest family member, but that in the Master's absence, he will be staying here in his place. What I was able to gather from the things that the Count *wasn't* saying, it seems that the fourth Vlad's presence was only to give the illusion of the Master being here. That's what he explained in a roundabout way, and from what I read between the lines of his lengthy lecture.

"There are very few people on this earth whom I trust, and my brother is one of those few." My husband, who was sitting next to me, held my hand so lovingly, even in the presence of another. "I know you two just met, but I pray that you will come to trust in each other."

"There won't be any issue." Vlad remarked quite confidently. "We will have much to gossip about when you are away, and I will tell her of the time when you were three years old and —"

Quick as lightning, the Count growled at him in a string of Romanian that he should shut his mouth. His brother only rolled his eyes. What a pair these two are. Even in my short encounter with the two of them together, they complement each other. What my Vlad isn't, this Vlad is, and vice versa.

When the hour struck around 11 pm, we had gone deep into the subject of what happened during the children's stay at this castle, and what we all endured. Exhausted, I had begun to lean heavily against the Master's shoulder as I was dozing in and out. I didn't want to go to bed, and wanted to listen to what these two had to say and glean any small amount of information from them as to the real goings on. But, as was to be expected, the Count sent me to bed, and I left without my usual escort.

This will be the first night in almost a week that the Count has not come to bed with me. It feels strangely lonely without him being here, but I am glad he and his brother have a chance to reconnect. All the same, it surprises me that I've grown so accustomed to him being near, just when he is to leave.

29 November

To relieve the overwhelming feeling of dread of the future, I have been desperate for a bit of fun these past few days. We were snowed in this morning, and the Romani couldn't do their work today. The untouched white blanket stretches for miles and miles, and I wanted so badly to go outside and play. I hadn't played in the snow since I was a teenager, but felt compelled to do so. So, early this morning, when my husband was about to go to his own sleep after being with me only a few hours, I begged him to allow Dumitru and me to go outside.

He was quite tired after spending most of the evening with his brother and was reluctant to allow me the privilege. I had to bat my eyelashes at my husband, and persuade him that we would be fine as long as we stayed within the safe confines wall. After a few kisses and innocent caresses, he caved, but made me promise it would only be for a few hours. Of course, I had to promise; besides, I didn't think I could stay outside in that bitter cold for long.

I was so excited to tell Mitică about my plans, but he was not too enthusiastic to learn he had to babysit me again. However, I told him he owed me for doing more than half of his chores for the last week. Grumbling, he submitted as well, and when the sun was at its highest, we emerged into the frozen wasteland. The sun was out, and there were few clouds in the sky, but it was a beautiful near-winter day. There was little heat to be felt from the sun, and it was extremely bright as it reflected off the snow, so that Mitică and I had to wear sunglasses.

The air, which was relatively still after last night's storm, was so cold that it froze my nose instantly. Combined with the fresh air, it was invigorating, and I eagerly hopped down the covered steps and into the snow that went up to my mid-thigh. It was a perfect consistency for snowmen and snowballs, and I grew even more excited to begin my work.

"Aren't you done yet?" Mitică, who still stood at the top landing, groaned. "It's freezing."

"Don't be so dramatic, old man." I lightheartedly chided as I mashed some snow in my hand. "For someone who has lived his entire life in this country, you should be more accustomed to it than I."

"Yeah, but if I don't have to be out here, I won't be." He ducked his reddening nose beneath his scarf and shuddered at a sudden strong gust. "This is childish. If you're bored, there are better ways for you to spend your time."

Scowling, I threw the snowball as hard as I could, and at such a close range, I hit him square in the shoulder.

He frowned, unimpressed at the powdery splat on his coat. "Is that it?"

"You can do better?" I stuck my tongue out at him, gathering another snowball in my hand as I shot him some teasing about being a gimp-boy because of his arm. Harmless banter, but it caused the reaction that I sought. Instantly, Dumitru swooped down, grabbing a handful of snow in his gloves, and was nearly ready to strike when I threw my pre-prepared weapon. He blocked it and threw his that hit my torso.

A full-on war ensued, and relentlessly we attacked the other. Mitică still favored his left arm, which is still healing, but our assaults weren't so violent that he would injure himself again. It was great fun laughing, especially when Dumitru tripped over his half-fallen scarf and he face-planted right into the snow. I fell many times, too, since it was so hard to maneuver, but the fight was enjoyable. I wondered if the Master or his brother were watching from the high windows. From this spectacle, most likely, we are in for a stern lecture about our 'infantile' behavior.

After we were thoroughly breathless, we both sat like heaving plops in the snow. I reclined, and the snow groaned terribly under my weight as I sank even further. Chuckling to myself, I commented to Dumitru. "Hey, that sounds like you."

Still trying to catch his breath, Mitică, who was covered in snow, muttered an echo of my tease and swatted some snow in my direction. The white powder sparkled like tiny diamonds in the sunlight and dazzled against the azure of the sky before it fell all over me. Never before have I realized how pretty it was in the light.

"Hey, can I ask you a personal question?" Mitică asked suddenly, his tone soft but awkward. I told him, of course, he could, but he still hesitated to say it. Turning away from me, he stuttered. "I'm...I'm not sure how to say it, but what you said to Georgiana last week, is it t-true that you're...you're a v-vir—"

"A virgin?" I just said the word, and his face grew red. After all this time, he still can't talk to me about things without getting himself worked up. "I thought you knew this already."

"No..." He shook his head side to side anxiously, eyes averted as he tried to articulate what he wanted to say. "You told me the Master has never...with you. But, I thought you at least had...you know."

"Oh, I didn't realize..." I felt my own face grow hot. It shocked me that Mitică thought otherwise. "Yeah, it's true. Why did you think I wasn't?"

"Uh, I guess I assumed since most people our age have —" he stopped, bringing his scarf higher to cover his ever-reddening face. There was more that he wanted to say, I could tell from his rigid posture, so I waited. Eventually, he looked down at me from the corner of his eye as he muttered. "Don't you want to?"

I felt my cheeks blush at the brazenness of the question, especially considering the feelings we share. "Well, sure I do. I've heard that when you do it with the right person, it's supposed to be one of the most beautiful things on this earth. This doesn't mean I'm inexperienced, you know. I'm not a prude."

My friend shifted uncomfortably, then sighed after he soaked in what I said, his shoulders slouching. "Why does he wait so long? You have been married for two months. It makes no sense to me."

"You know he only married me so that I wouldn't be deported." I couldn't explain to him the real reason why, but I didn't want to lie to him about it either. "Besides, everything he does and doesn't do is a mystery even to me."

"Fair..." His voice drifted off, lost in thought. Another moment of silence came between us before he abruptly spoke again. "You will still tell me when things change, won't you?"

"You know I will."

Dumitru's brow furrowed with a greater conflict growing on his face, as if he didn't say the thing that was on his mind, he would

449

regret it. "Even when they do, I...I want to say again, how much I still —"

"I know," I had to stop him there in case someone was listening. "Me too. But you don't deserve to be in second place, Mitică. You deserve an absolute love, not one that's split."

Eyes narrowing, he scoffed and scolded me instead. "Says the woman who is second place to him. And you know I don't mean that was just when he was with Cosima."

My throat constricted, recalling that morning I had found the two in the other's embrace. Dumitru was not wrong. It is the truth, and a truth I know too well. But still, putting it into words made the cut run deep, and I had to blink away the glassiness from my eyes. "Are you finished?"

Seeing my reaction, his back hunched, and he sighed again. "I'm sorry if I upset you."

"Don't worry about it. I know you only mean well." Sitting back up, I got to my feet and brushed away the snow that clung to my woolen coat. Taking in a breath, I suppressed those inopportune feelings that were rising to my eyes again. "Let's talk of other things, okay?"

At first, Dumitru said nothing, but eventually asked as he stood. "Well, what do you think of the Master's brother?"

That was another tough question. Looking up at the castle, which stood erect, story and stories above our heads, I thought of my first encounter with the fourth Vlad. "It's disturbing how much they resemble each other, but they are completely different."

"I noticed that, too. I had never met him before yesterday, but I knew the Master did have a brother who was still living, more or less." Mitică paused to think, humming to himself. "Historically, he is Vlad Călugărul, the Monk, and was once a ruling Prince of Wallachia, too. All I know about him is that he and the Master are close, but they are opposites in personality. Călugărul is religious, while the Master is not, things like that."

"'Religious'?" My head perked up at the word, and I had to raise the most important question in my mind. "What is his religion?"

"Romanian Orthodox, I assume." Shrugging, he stuffed his hands into his pockets before he motioned for me to follow him. "Come on, we've spent enough time outside."

A Christian...how can that be? I thought as I followed him inside. I guess in some odd way it could be, although I had never considered it a possibility before. It is extremely intriguing to me to think this man held on to his faith even though he is damned, nor did his faith transfer from the One above to the one who is below. Well, if this is the man who is to remain here until who knows when, I'd rather have him than anyone else.

Evening, 6:30 pm...

All the fresh mountain air I received this afternoon wore me out. I am even more exhausted after the warm bath and hot meal I partook of afterwards. I told Dumitru to relay my regrets to the brothers that I would not be joining them this time. Being determined to go to bed by 7 pm, I am quite done with the day and want to forget all that is to come. So, my interest concerning the half-brother will have to wait until another time. Besides, I'm sure they have plenty to speak about that I should not hear before the Master leaves the day after tomorrow.

The day after tomorrow...it's so soon. Tears threaten my eyes at the thought. God, if you still hear me, please help him and be by him always. He is still so lost in his darkness. All I ask is that you lead him wherever he is going and whisper in his ear to remind him of himself. All of this is out of my hands, so I give it all to you, to let your will be done.

SWEET SORROW

30 November
Feast of St. Andrew
Morning…

The Count came to me early this morning to spend some time before he went to his deathly rest. I was dead asleep myself when I suddenly felt his arms come around my midsection as he pulled me to lie against him. Immediately, I clung to the Count, and he reciprocated in kind, planting a kiss on my hair as he held me. With every fiber in my body, I tried to savor every second I had of him next to me, taking in every single sensation so that I will have something to remember him by. God, I sound like he's going off on a suicide mission to never return. As long as I believe and pray that the Master will come back, then I will have some hope to cling to when he is not beside me.

"Vlad," I muttered against his chest. "When do you leave?"

"Tomorrow in the early morning," he whispered back, his hand stroking my arm as he cooed. "Then you will be the sole Mistress of this house, and Dumitru will have to do whatever you say, and Vlad will be here to help and protect you, and all will be well and good until I return."

My fists gathered his shirt, and my heart broke at his attempt to comfort me. "Even if you can't tell me where you're going, please promise me you won't be gone long?"

"I will try, sweet one." Another kiss was pecked on my hair. "It is said that the dead travel fast, so I will be back to you before you know it. But do not fret yourself now about it, and sleep. I will be here until dawn, and then in the evening I will spend all of it with you."

It wasn't a command, but I closed my eyes, and his scent soothed my stormy heart. Eventually, I did fall back to sleep, and when I awoke next, he was gone, and I had been laid gently back in my place. The slight overcast of the sky made the light of the sun fade in and out in the room as I lay there, wondering how I should start the day.

There was nothing I wanted to do but lie there until he came back when the sun set. A radical thought came to me that I should seek him out in his tomb and beg him to let me stay with him until dusk. But that was too much for me, even with Cupid's fatal love-tipped arrow lodged so deeply in my heart for my husband. For his journey, he needed all his rest, and it was selfish of me to demand more of him when he is going out of his way to ensure my safety.

Urging my heavy limbs, I got out of bed and readied myself for the day. After breakfast, I did some of my chores and most of Mitică's before going to the chapel to contemplate things there. I was a bit despondent as I knelt before the dais, staring at the images of the painted saints. I wondered as I sat there what it had been like for Ioana when Vlad left her for battle, and she was uncertain if he would ever return to her. From my life before, I could only imagine those feelings, and now I am experiencing them firsthand. Paranoia was the main voice that spoke, providing me with all these scenarios that all ended up in the worst possible situations. I know if I keep thinking like this, it will drive me mad, so I must keep myself hopeful and preoccupied. They say that idle hands are the Devil's playthings, and in this place, that is a sinister threat.

I prayed in the chapel for quite a while, and then joined Dumitru for lunch. After finishing our work in the kitchen, on a whim, I went up to the library to see if I could perchance find any information about our newest guest. Although I doubted the Count had any material about his family so available, I checked anyway, in case I had overlooked something. In the section where the older books are, meaning books from his era, there were a few actually concerning the history of the region and its famous people. Any ones that were close to what I was searching for were too fragile to look through. I didn't dare open them unless I should accidentally rip them in half, and besides, it was doubtful I could read any of it anyway.

Sitting at one of the tables, I was lost in thought about what to do, my eyes probably glazing over as they stared off into no particular point in the room. I was at my wits' end to figure out what I should do with my time, and I looked about the room for some inspiration. Surprisingly, I found it. Since my first days here, my eyes have always lingered upon the larger-than-life portraits that hang in the library. One was of the Count in his younger years, and the others must be of his father and a few other male relatives whom I do not recognize. The fourth Vlad was not among them, but all these other men did bear striking resemblances to each other.

As I stared at the painting of my ancient Prince, I thought of the other one on the floor above me and recalled that day that I had discovered who he was. That was another lifetime ago, wasn't it? Back then, I was especially naïve. One day, perhaps I'll look back on this day and see how naïve I am now.

I decided then that I would go revisit that room of his past life, when my husband ruled and commanded his tens-of-thousands. By some chance, there I can conceive of some hidden truth to help me relieve my suffering.

...

Ascending the familiar steps, I followed a trail of disturbed dust up to the third floor, and then into the grand hall that I had explored so long ago. The air was significantly colder and was still full of old dust. I could even see my breath in the cold air, but just as before, I had to cover my mouth as I made my way down to the ornate door. I fully expected the lock to have been replaced, but to my surprise, nothing had been done to it. There was no effort whatsoever to open the door, which moaned from its disuse, and I entered the dilapidated Throne Room.

In the low sunlight, the stained glass cast muted shades of color across the room. My faded footsteps, where I had disturbed the layers of ancient dust still remained, and I followed them up to the dais where the two chairs stood aloft in their grandeur. It dawned on me that the smaller chair is now mine, and that left a strange feeling in my stomach. Turning away from it, I noticed something that I hadn't before. Opposite to the alcove which held the Master's old portrait, there was another alcove which held another imposing painting. In the off-colored light from the stained glass, I drew nearer to take a better look at the woman depicted in the timeless strokes. It was Ioana, dressed magnificently in furs and jewels.

As I stared at the face, six hundred years apart, I wished with all my being that I could talk to her about my current plight. We two, although having never known each other, share so many similarities in so many different ways. I wondered what advice, if any, she could give me from beyond the grave. Be it some iota of consolation for my dark days ahead, or a gift of aged wisdom, I would take anything she would give me.

Bowing my head, I closed my eyes tightly to cease the growing pressure in them to release their tears. Brusquely, I dabbed the droplets from my lashes with my sleeve and took in a deep breath as I returned my gaze to the noble lady. I wanted to *be with* her for a while, just to exist with her in her company. So, going back a ways, I brushed the dust from the dais and took a seat. My head resting in my hands, I stared at the medieval princess, a predecessor in title, and pondered what I knew about her. I tried to figure out how I could be more like her, but also to use her misfortunes to help me in the future so that I would not make them myself. Sometimes it felt as if she were whispering in my ear, and I listened to her attentively.

I had gotten so lost in thought for so long that I hadn't really noticed that the sun had dipped just below the horizon, and the wolves' distant howling awoke me from my trance. Sighing, I resigned myself that it was time to face the Master and say my goodbye. Now I dreaded that the time had come, when this morning I could not wait for it.

"I am surprised to find you here, of all places." It was the Count who appeared from the shadows and floated forward to come beside me. The scent of fresh earth lingered around him as he almost impulsively bent down to put his face to my neck. The chill of his lips against the sensitive, heated skin made me shiver, but that was the only reaction that he induced from me. Confused that I had not acted as I normally would have, he withdrew and followed my eyes to where they stared at the portrait of his first wife. "Beloved, why are you here?"

I tried to think of an honest, but logical answer as to the reason why. It didn't make sense when I was trying to put words to it, and when vocalized, it still wasn't rational. "Initially, I came to try and understand you, but instead, she...I don't know how to explain it. I had to sit with her and listen."

The Count's eyes stayed on the portrait as he asked. "What does she say?"

"Nothing, but everything," I said cryptically, and the foolishness of the words which were coming out of my mouth shook me awake. "Sorry, you must think I'm mad, but I'm just troubled. I'm sorry that I came in here without permission again."

"Think nothing of it," the Master wrapped one arm around me and purred, placing his cheek against mine as his gentleness soothed my inner turmoil. "I am pleased you spent time with her. You two would have been great friends if you had both lived at the same time. She had a bright intelligence, a compassionate heart, gentle hands, and not to mention a quick wit; just like you. So, if you are looking to her for guidance, I would suggest instead that you look within yourself. All the same qualities exist there as they did in her."

Brow furrowing, I embraced him back, my head burrowing into his shoulder. "Thank you for saying that, my love, I needed to hear it."

Placing a kiss on my head, he prompted me with a pat on my back. "Come, sweet girl, let us start our night early."

I agreed, and we left the twin portraits alone in the faded multi-spectral sunset and descended back down to my floor. When we entered my room, the smoldering fire crackled to life, sending a burst of heat and light into the chilled space. The door clicked closed by itself, and the bolt slid shut into its place. As soon as it did, the

Count eagerly sought my lips, nearly lifting me off the ground when he wrapped his arms around me.

He was hungry for me again, and I was for him, but I had to separate us once my breath began to run out. "Shall I change into something more…comfortable?" I raised my eyebrows and grinned at the cliché line.

The Count chuckled, lifting my chin to give me another quick kiss, his brown eyes shining. Letting me go, he gently nudged me along. "Be quick, my river nymph, do not keep me waiting too long for you."

My husband's cheerfulness was an answer to a prayer made long ago, and it made my heart so happy to see him this way. While I was changing into a satin nightgown, I wondered what the Count had in mind for this night. He seemed quite enthusiastic about being intimate, as did I, but I feared he wanted to go off the deep end.

I popped my head out of my door and, with my index finger, beckoned him to enter my bedroom. The Master had been leaning against the fireplace, but once he saw my gesture, he did not hesitate to come to me. When he came over the threshold, he closed the door behind him, and the room fell into the semi-darkness of the dim nightlight. Coming to me, his eyes flashing with their nocturnal sight, he grinned. "Excellent choice, beloved. However, before I forget, the letters for your family, do you have them ready? It has been many months since Dumitru has had the chance to go to the post, so I will send them tomorrow."

What a thing to say at such a time. I tensed and had to rub the back of my neck. Perhaps I had misinterpreted his advances, and it all confused me as I stuttered out. "I, uh, don't have anything to send."

His head cocked to one side. "Nothing? Surely all they said was worth a reply."

"I wouldn't know, I never opened them." I said with a sigh. He grew very silent and stern and looked to me for a justified explanation. "Well, at first I didn't have time to write, and then the children came, and I forgot, sort of, and I don't really have anything to say."

The Master frowned. "You were married, is that not enough reason?"

Of course, it was reason enough. I wish with all my heart that my parents and sister would know how happy I am with him, despite all that I have been through. Although doing so would only cause more problems than it would solve. "Don't misunderstand me, but I don't want them to know, not yet. The less, the better."

His hand came up to cup my cheek as he asked most seriously. "Are you ashamed of it?"

The words struck me to the core. Society would frown on this marriage as there are so many aspects of it that are taboo: our significant age difference, our class, our religious views, and even down to our personality. Yet somehow, he has a fondness for me, and I love him. "Of course not, but what would it look like to them? It's better right now for them to think that I've fallen off the face of the earth. I'm sure the American Embassy no longer has records of my existence, so as long as they can't find me, they are safe."

"Still, they must be worried…" Another deep frown came over his mouth as he contemplated whether or not to continue. "It is true that the trail leads nowhere from the American Embassy. I made sure that you no longer exist in their registries. Besides, since you are no longer American, you are no longer under their jurisdiction. Even if your family complained to the Romanian authorities, they cannot touch me, nor do I think they would have the nerve to come out here themselves to look for you because of their own superstition."

Even though I have only had one encounter with the authorities, I saw firsthand the respect and fear with which they treated him…and by association, me as well. I nodded, placing my lips against his palm. One day I will write to them and give some excuse, but that day is far from now.

"Would they have approved of you marrying a Romanian?" The Count asked quizzically after a moment. "I have the blood of Attila in me, and a family name greater and more ancient than those of the Romanovs and Habsburgs combined. Their names have fallen, but mine remains, and now it is yours. Your parents ought to be honored that their daughter is so honored. When Jonathan Harker came here, he did not appreciate the history of my lineage; however, I know that you do."

"I do appreciate it, but I don't think they would necessarily approve." I paused to think of how they would feel if they knew, and

I see them being very dismayed to know the details. "They'd be upset that the decision was made hastily, despite it being of necessity. Also, that it is a civil marriage, but you know that can't be helped."

Bringing me to him, we embraced each other. "If I had the privilege, I would have courted you properly as it was during my time; ask your father's blessing, marry you in a church, and make you a woman that night."

My face grew hot. It was a comforting thing to know that he would not have tricked me if he had been presented with different options. Having said that, Mitică's question came to my mind about why the Master was waiting, and I swallowed hard. "Can't you make me one now?"

He froze, his body growing rigid at the question. His breath shuddering, there was pain in his voice when my husband spoke next, his arms tightening around me. "What kind of husband would I be if I took you for the first time and then left you in the morning? But please, let me take you as far as I can from your troubled thoughts, even for just a while."

Looking up at him, I smiled sadly. He always had my best interests at heart, no matter how painful it was for both of us. "And where will you take me so late at night?"

"Oh, far away, but not too far, lest we lose our way." The Count laid another kiss on me, returning my sad smile with one in kind.

My brow furrowed in confusion at the assumption he made. "What are you proposing?"

"I mean," his voice deepened to a low register as he whispered in my ear sweet words that dripped honey. "Even if we should not, let me touch you before we cannot touch at all."

My cheeks burst with a greater heat.

"I want to feel you, my sweet one, as a reminder of your warmth since I must deprive myself of you." Turning me around, he began to undo my braid and let my hair hang loose behind me. "But, shall I make a promise to you?"

"What is it?"

"Once those who oppose me are…" He made a motion with his hand as of one being swept away. "Then you shall be as Alexander again, and I, Bucephalus, and we shall explore unknown lands, conquer them, and take the spoils. What say you, my sun of my nights?"

My heart leapt in my chest at his use of numerous double entendres that made me giggle, and it amazed me how, in just one sentence, he could make me feel so much better. Yet I still fear he will be like Hannibal, who won many battles before being defeated with his goal in sight. Or as Caesar, to be the greatest of generals, only to be betrayed by his closest friends. Even Bucephalus died in battle, and Alexander, a god among men, was ended by his own human frailty. But I faced him, a playful smile growing on my face. "To be the ruler of the known world? A tempting proposition."

"This I promise," he grinned and kissed my forehead as he began to lead me to the bed. "But for now, if you will be a lady, I will be a gentleman."

"Very well." I squared my shoulders and raised my head high as I placed my finger on the buttons of his dress shirt. "Undo your shirt."

He straightened as he shot me a worrisome glare. "You tread dangerously, fair one."

"Shall I undo them for you, then?" With no hesitation, I began to undo each one, and when I opened them, there was revealed the god beneath. I had only seen him shirtless a handful of times, but I had never gotten to fully appreciate him in the way he had been created. Unable to resist the sight of the body that is mine to touch, I directed him to lie down. Coming in next to him, I kissed down from his collar to his abdomen, doing him homage the only way my mind could devise at that moment.

The Count's chest rose and fell with each leisurely caress of my hands and brush of my lips, and his purr sounded more like a low whine. I took that as he was enjoying himself, and continued my slow work, my fingers running over the muscles of his stomach, chest, and arms. All in me whispered to go further, to undo his belt, but then we would lose our way. So, I forced myself to work my way back up, and put my fingers in his hair as I put my tongue past his deadly teeth. It was a lucky thing that we were going steady, because my tongue would have been cut to shreds from all the times it had accidentally brushed too roughly against his incisors. However, they didn't deter me, and I only withdrew when I needed to catch my breath.

Even after all that I did, my need to feel him was not fulfilled, and I went to kiss under his jaw when the Count put his hand up to stop me, but I cut him off before he got a chance to. "Don't stop me. Just lay there, please, let me have all I can before I can have none at all."

"If you keep doing this and you will have more than you bargained for." His hand came up to brush my plumped lips, which he seemed to become mesmerized by. "So red, like sweetened wine in the heat of mid-summer…"

"Have them," I begged, hastily removing his mother's silver crucifix. "They are yours."

He wasted no time recapturing them, indeed having his way a bit too roughly. When we broke away, I kept kissing his neck. Now that his way was free of silver, he slid the straps of my gown from my shoulders. For the first time, in all the time I've known him, his lips went further down my chest, and I moaned at the foreign sensation. I pressed myself to him and implored him not to stop.

"Isadora, you make this difficult." He wasn't playing around anymore and was most serious, yet he still kissed me. "If you tempt me further…"

"They say virtue is strengthened through temptation…" Another soft sigh escaped me.

"Whoever 'they' are, they have never been tempted by you, it seems." The Master grumbled, moving his way back up my chest to my neck. "Isa, please, you know I could never deny you anything, but calm yourself. This is not the last time we will be together, I promise you."

It was unprecedented that the Count was pleading with me to stop my advances. He always craves every affection I give him, and not once in the months we've been together has he asked me to desist. The realization hit me hard. My brow knitting, I rested my forehead against his. "But I want you…"

"I do as well, my love." The Master's hands came from where he had held my lower back to cup both my cheeks. "Please, sleep. I will wake you before I go."

Nodding solemnly, I lay on his torso and rested my head on his chest, simply holding him. If he had a heartbeat, I would have been listening to it, but his chest was void of all sound. His fingers brushing through my hair, we rested in each other's company, enjoying the closeness we provided each other.

The Count kept awake along with me, but I had grown quite tired, and my eyelids were so heavy. I was falling asleep as the hours wore on, but was so afraid that I would close my eyes just a second, and then open them to find it was morning, and I was alone. But also, I began thinking of a conversation we had long ago about the children, and was urged by my own conscious to speak. "Vlad?"

"Go to sleep, beloved." I heard him whisper, though he hadn't ordered it.

"I told you once that God would not give you a burden you cannot bear, but," my voice cracked a bit, and I had to clear it before I continued. "Are you sure you can bear this burden? Can you face your demons again, and not fall into your old ways? This is my greatest fear."

The Count was silent for a long while as he considered how to respond. "Someone once said that evil comes from within the heart, not without." He wavered for another moment. "I refuse to allow my heart to be swayed again. This is another thing I can assure you. Now, sleep, dearest one. Do not let your own heart be troubled by this fear."

This time it was a command, but in those few seconds before I was forced into unconsciousness, I had comprehended his words. Their profoundness, especially coming from him, was something that was, again, unprecedented. It amazes me how much he has changed from just a few weeks ago when he would do unspeakable things, but now avows that he will not let his devilish nature corrupt him to do evil.

1 December

Afternoon…

The next thing I knew, I was being awoken by a distant voice, so gentle in the darkness, and my eyes fluttered open. The room was still dim, and I was exhausted, but I recognized the cool hand on my cheek and placed my hand over it. Somehow, I had been moved to lie on my back, and the sheets had been drawn over me.

"Isa," a melodic tone whispered, one high, the other low. "Best beloved, it is time."

My head was still swimming, struggling to wake and tell him not to leave me. I said something, and now I'm unsure of what it was, but it was a plea for him to stay. It probably came out as nonsense, but it was the best I could do in half-sleep.

Even through the mist of my mind, I heard him chuckle at my ardent yet incoherent jabber, and he kissed me deeply one final time. The kiss was like a spell, but instead of awakening me as it would like true love's kiss would, it sent me further into sleep. Perhaps that was the end of what actually happened, and I had dreamt the rest, but when he had lifted his lips off mine, I swore I heard him whisper. "Sweetest one, eternity is too short to fill it with all the love I have for you."

My mind shot awake and I sat up and was half through an exasperated, 'What did you say?' when my eyes were blinded by a brightness in the room. It was morning. He had long gone.

Looking at my clock, it read 10 am, and my heart sank deep into my stomach. He had left probably six hours prior, but I could have sworn it was just a second ago. The time loss, coupled with my still-spinning head. He had compelled me to be this way on purpose, I'm sure, so that I would be in a daze until at least noon. My body refused to move once it collapsed back onto the bed. I burst into tears, my heavy arm dragged itself over to rest on his side of the bed, feeling the cool emptiness of it.

Had I just dreamt it all? Had he just found amusement in my ramblings, kissed me to put me back to sleep, and left? Was my mind so cruel to me to let me imagine something like that at such a time as this? I wanted desperately to ask the Count what he said. That anticipation of the answer fell into a pit of helplessness, because now I will not know if he had said anything at all.

Do I dare believe it, or not? Oh God, I don't know what to believe. I have cried so much this morning already, and now the tears are coming back just as I thought I had regained some control over them. For now, I will have to choose to regard that precious sentence as untrue, as much as I want it to be the truest thing on this earth.

Square One

3 December

Advent

Morning…

I have been able to put on a brave face for the last two days, but it has been very difficult to maintain the mask. The castle feels so empty without the presence of the Count. Even the atmosphere is heavy, making it as though the walls of this house are in mourning that he has departure. This weighted pressure is felt especially in the Master's reception room, where the fourth Vlad and I have met each evening for a few hours before I retire.

Having him here makes everything more awkward. His presence emanates the same power and dominance as the Count's, although he is much kinder and gentler than him. This makes me feel confused, and I keep calling him 'Count' by accident. Halfway through the word, I would correct myself, but unfortunately, stopping halfway makes it sound like I'm calling him a 'cow'. It's all very embarrassing, although the Monk finds it amusing and doesn't seem to mind what I call him. He has told me just to call him 'Vlad', which I guess is an easy fix to the problem in a way.

So far, I haven't dared breach the subject of his religion, his kind, or his family, since I want to get to know him better before I ask such personal questions. Conversation with him has still been riveting, and we talk on a variety of subjects which captivate both of us: education, technological development, history, and even politics. We share many things in common, and I have come to like this Vlad, despite the confusion he causes me.

One thing these two brothers share is an ability to enrapture another in conversation and talk and talk until dawn. I don't think it's because they like to hear themselves speak, but that they have so much to say, and so few people to say it to. These two really do crave intellectual discourse, and with anyone who has a brain to comprehend, they will say what they believe and mean it. They don't meander in their topic of choice, but remain firm on it until all of it is discussed. Their centuries of experience have made them especially unique, and when they don't need to withhold that in fear of being exposed, they are a plethora of wisdom.

To have someone to compare the Count to has been an interesting and unexpected experiment. By listening to the opinions of this Vlad, even in the few days I've spoken to him, one can easily sketch out what has remained with them from their era, where they diverged from each other, yet how they stayed together. It's fascinating, really, and I wish I had taken more psychology courses to truly comprehend the scope of what makes these brothers tick.

Anyway, as expected, there is no word or news from the Master. Not that I expect any, but I pray for his safety every time he crosses my mind…which is all the time. Especially during this season, which is supposed to be one of rejoicing and gladness, is now one of foreboding and worry.

Let him be well. Let him not forget.

4 December

Morning, 8 am…

Last night I could not sleep, no matter what I did. Counting, reading, what have you, my mind was tired, but my body would not rest. Each time I would think I was close to sleep, I'd awake and be roused enough that it would take what seemed like hours to fall back to sleep again. And then it would repeat, and repeat. I was growing very frustrated and resolved to go down to the kitchen and get myself something warm to drink. Usually, I would never ever walk the castle alone at night, but I was very fed up by the time the clock chimed 4 am.

Donning my night robe and making myself look semi-presentable, just in case, I went out into my sitting room. I expected to find the room in darkness and the embers of the fire smoldering; however, I found them full ablaze, and the fourth Vlad was sitting in the Master's chair, smoking a pipe and reading a book. I thought I was dreaming, but I certainly was more awake than I would've liked to have been at such an hour.

His eyebrows raised as he looked over at me from beneath his spectacles that were low on his aquiline nose. How does he even need them? "Good morning, Isadora, can't sleep?"

I blinked, my mouth partially agape as I tried to comprehend why he was in my room so early in the morning, lounging about as if my private rooms were public. "Uh, good morning. What are you doing here?"

A lightbulb seemed to flick on over his head. "Oh, I forgot to mention it. My brother asked that I should stay by you at night because you have been having night terrors since those cretins left. He said he didn't suspect you'd have more of them, but have you?"

Night terrors? I don't remember any nightmares or anything of the sort; in fact, I had been sleeping very well since the children were made to leave. I guess it is a bit odd that I wouldn't have some kind of trauma that would be made manifest in sleep, but I hadn't thought of it at all. I guess that was the reason why the Count would insist on staying with me all the nights since the incident in the den: he was compelling me to forget my nightmares, and I had been none the wiser. The idea of him, or anyone, inside my head like that made me shiver.

My shock at his revelation made him purse his lips, and he became quite uncomfortable. "I don't think I was supposed to tell you that. Forgive me, my brother didn't say that you weren't aware of it."

"It's…It's fine," I cleared my throat and pressed the news of the nightmares to the back of my mind to reflect upon them later. "But no, I haven't had any, I only can't sleep. Do you mind if I sit with you for a while?"

"But of course. Please," Vlad beamed a warm smile as he motioned to my chair. "But, please don't tell Vlad that I told you. Also, don't tell him about the pipe. He'd have a cow if he caught me smoking near you."

I chuckled at his colorful phrase as I sat down, promising that I wouldn't tell a soul.

Vlad thanked me for keeping his secrets, yet still took a long, nervous drag on his pipe as he closed his book. "So, what is troubling you, sister?"

"I'm not sure, I suppose I'm just not tired…" I eyed his book, which was quite old and worn, but the name was readable enough in Latin. I was shocked at it, but had to strain in the flickering firelight to make sure. "Pardon, are those the *Letters of St. Augustine*?"

"Y-Yes, they are," he faltered a bit that I had been able to decipher the title of the book, but offered it to me. "Are you familiar?"

"A little, but I've never read them myself." I took the book and thumbed through it. It was in the original Latin and littered with notes written in his ancient native Romanian. "This sure isn't some light reading."

"It certainly isn't." Vlad grinned again when I gave back his book. "Vlad mentioned to me that you are of the Roman Church and are rather astute in matters of theology. That's impressive, especially in this modern age."

It flattered me exceedingly that the Master would give me such a compliment, that is, if it really is a compliment. Overall, it seems my husband has told him quite a bit about me, and I can only hope that it was all good. "I wouldn't call myself astute by any means, but I do know a few things here and there. If I may, can I ask you a question?"

Tilting his head to one side, he raised an eyebrow. "Shoot."

When it came to vocalizing it, I was at a loss for words. I wasn't sure what the most tactful way to say it was, so I just said it. "Is it true that you are a Christian, despite your...condition?"

"Rumors have already begun to fly, eh?" Vlad chuckled to himself, looking back down at the old book as he did. There was something pensive in his gaze as he confessed to me. "I'd like to call myself one, although I don't particularly fit the description."

"Fascinating," thinking back I feel it was a bit rude to have said it so exasperatedly, but I was genuinely interested in his story, views, and theology. If the Monk can read the works of one of the greatest saints in the common era and not be bothered by them, I must know how he does it. I knew there would definitely be something I could glean from him that I could use with the Count, so I eagerly entreated him. "There are many things I wish to ask you, if I may."

Out of the corner of his eye, his gaze shifted to me, a smirk forming on his lips as he took another drag. "You wish to ask me so that you may aid my brother in his salvation, no?"

I froze in the chair, swallowing hard. I was so unsure of how to answer, unsure of how much he knows, unsure of accidentally letting something slip that was meant to be kept a secret. I was at a loss as to how to indirectly answer him without lying.

Vlad became very serious as he sat back in his chair, his black eyes now firmly set on me. "I am aware of his wishes. You needn't keep up his reputation in front of me."

Still, I had a hard time trying to recover, and I stuttered out. "Forgive me, I'm only surprised that you know..."

The Monk certainly saw through my poor attempt at covering my shock, for he eyed me for a second longer before commenting. "I am lucky that my brother has allowed me the privilege to know him as others do not. I believe you and I are the only ones on this earth who know his wishes."

'On earth'...as in there are ones who do not exist on this plane who do know of the Master's intentions. I guess that it was obvious, since I had dealt with one of them face-to-face too many times than I'd care to in one life. That sparked a flicker of worry in my chest concerning the Count and his relationship with his father. I dare not try to guess what is going on between him and Satan. Yet another thing to push back into my mind to think about later. "I am delighted that he has confided in you about this. He might have told you that very recently, he had lost sight of his goal and had fallen back into the way he was before. I constantly worry for him, but I know if he has enough determination, he can accomplish anything he chooses."

"He did mention it to me…" Vlad's voice faded out as he became lost in thought. Staring into the fire, the older Prince solemnly recounted. "When my brother saw heaven and was denied it by his own indecision, he went into a deep depression. He was very angry at himself, angry at the ones who had temporarily robbed him of this castle when they sanctified it, and terribly grieved that the bond between Madame Harker and him was no more. It was only then, when he withdrew from the world, that he developed that goal of which you speak."

I was amazed that the Monk was so willing to provide me with this information that the Count would never allude to. Yet, it tore my heart out that he suffered so terribly at the hands of my own ancestors and suffers still from that experience. Frowning, I hung my head. "The children did say that he had grown weak from being separated from them for so long, and that I added to that weakness."

"Weakness is a matter of perspective, often defined by those who presume their own strength." He reassured, leaning forward to emphasize to me the significance of the next words he spoke. "The only thing that the separation from them did was to remind him of his humanity, and if anything, you being here has only made him stronger. He has a better reason to fight now than he has had in centuries."

His words touched me deeply, and I placed a hand over my pained heart. "You really think so?"

The Monk nodded. "You must understand, when I returned to find out what had happened to him after the quarrel with Mr. Harker, he was in a terrible state, like none I had ever seen him in before." Vlad shook his head as he reminisced. "His encounter with the Divine had changed him beyond recognition, and that change frightened and confused him, but it had not weakened him. You see, although he never did stop believing in Him, my brother had turned his face away from all good things. For so long, he went so deeply into darkness that his very existence choked out any light. Remembering what goodness and compassion are was a shock that took a long time for him to comprehend again."

My brow knitted as I tried to imagine what it must have been like, and I could not. Clearing my throat, I tried to maintain composure. "He told me something similar, although it was just the shell of the matter, I see."

"Be content that he tells you anything at all." The fourth Vlad huffed in sudden frustration. "He hates weakness, especially to be called weak, so to even admit he was ever in such a place at one time is taboo. To him, there is no room for weakness, especially in front of you."

How I wish my Vlad didn't think like that. I want with all my heart for him to show me a hint of emotion that isn't hidden beneath layers that aren't well-checked. My eyes went downcast. "He has these barriers of indifference and secrecy to protect me, as he says."

"In some cases, I agree that there are things that you should be kept from." The Monk paused, but then continued. "But a husband and a wife should bear each other's burdens together, and not keep them secret. My brother has gone through much and has little trust in mortal and immortal alike. It is nothing personal against you that he says so little, but he only fears that your humanity will be used against you, and thereby against him."

"I know…" I had to swallow the frog forming in my throat again. "Imogen used me to send her warning, so I do understand why he does it."

Fidgeting with the pipe, he frowned and inhaled the pungent tobacco. "I don't mean to be so stern, but I simply wish for you to understand. You are very young, a baby to me, and as my own sister, I only want the best for you."

"I do understand…" I was moved that Vlad would already think of me as being so close to him. A little relief eased from my shoulders to know that I have someone else who cares for me, although I am still cautious. Taking advantage of the pause in the conversation, I dared to ask. "Please tell me of what else happened to him…after he was nearly killed."

With a slight grin on his mouth, the Monk nodded once. "I stayed with him a few years, and we grew close again. For once in centuries, he would listen to what I had to say about theology, and that slowly changed him, too. His violence and aggression waned in a few decades, and he even learned to control his hunger. Slowly, but surely, he became more considerate, although he was still very reserved and cold. I left here just before the Second World War, but he chose to stay. Ironically, while the entirety of Europe was falling apart, he was picking up the pieces to become the man you saw when you came here."

I couldn't help but wonder what life was like living with the Master then. It must have been a challenge to help a man whose anger could be easily triggered, especially one who was angry at everyone and everything. "He has come so far…"

"Well, as they say, you gotta hit rock bottom before you can start working your way back up to the top." Vlad chuckled to himself, this time taking a deep inhale and letting the plume of smoke drift to the ceiling. "It was only after the Revolution in 1989, and the reopening of communist Eastern Europe to the rest of the world in the succeeding years, that he reemerged from this place. Shortly after that, from what I understand, Dumitru came into his service. That boy was a good distraction for him and provided my brother with a pseudo-protégé to groom."

I tensed at the last sentence. I had never considered Mitică to be much other than the Count's servant. Granted, he had trained Dumitru well in English, in defense against his kind, and so many other useful trades…but a protégé? As in, an apprentice? A successor? For a moment, I stopped breathing as I considered the word, daring to wonder if that was really the Count's intention or if it was just Vlad's general observation. Regardless, I pushed it to the back of my mind to think about it later.

"Then you came, and I have never seen him happier since the old days when we were still boys, running around as if nothing could ever go wrong in this world." Another smile, this one sad and distant as he thought of the centuries gone by. "He is lucky to have a woman again who sees past the monster to the man, yet loves both equally. Such a gift only comes from the Creator, you see."

My eyes were beginning to water, and I quickly wiped them. "The Count had said something similar to me a few times before. A flattering compliment…"

"'A flattering compliment', you say?" Vlad hummed, gnawing a bit at the end of his fine pipe. "Coming from him, I'd say it's more like he worships the ground you walk upon."

I couldn't suppress the urge to laugh out loud, but caught myself just before I got too carried away. Covering my mouth, I had to clear my throat to recover. "I'm sorry. I agree that he does have a fondness for me, but not so great as you say."

The Monk's brow furrowed for just a second before he averted his eyes back to the fire, muttering. "I've known my brother all his life and death. Do not underestimate how he feels."

Pursing my lips, I felt a sense of shame come over me, and I apologized if I had caused him offense. Throwing me another one of his jovial smiles, the fourth Vlad assured me that I had not, and that he only wanted to help me understand. I still felt bad, even as we kept talking about quite irrelevant things, such as sleep, since the Monk insisted that I try to go to bed.

Around 6 am, the sun wasn't even yet over the horizon when Vlad bade me a goodnight. As much as I wanted to speak to him more about his brother, or even about himself, he was beginning to show signs of the need for his death sleep. I let him go, thanking him numerous times for telling me the hidden parts of the Count's recent past that I would normally not be privy to.

Vlad was just about to leave when he stopped short, his eyes narrowing. Jaw clenched, the Monk seemed to be mulling something over for a second and then turned to me. "Isadora, may I ask you a question?"

I had just stood to leave but felt suddenly paralyzed by the seriousness of his tone. Gulping, I unconsciously drew my robe tighter around me. "Of course you may."

With a rather intense stare, the half-brother stared at me fiercely with those black eyes. "How much do you love my brother?"

What a question to ask just like that...it made me feel so awkward. I wasn't about to spill my inner passions to him, so I simply responded. "With all my heart..."

There was no real reaction to my confession as I expected. Instead, he continued to drill me with another question. "Would you do anything for him?"

"I would give him my last drop of blood if he asked for it." I declared without hesitation.

His own shoulders drooped, and he let out a soft exhale. "Hopefully it won't come to that." Absentmindedly, he went for his pipe again, but not to smoke, but to nibble at the mouthpiece. "Tomorrow evening, if you aren't too tired, meet me in Vlad's private sitting room. I have been considering something, though have yet to weigh the implications. However, I believe it should be done."

My eyebrow cocked at his vagueness. "What is it?"

"You will see if you join me." He promised, then fully turned his back on me and went to the darkness of a shadow near the door. "Pleasant dreams, sister-in-law."

"Pleasant —" I was half through my well-wish when his form faded away in the dark. "Dreams…"

I am at a loss as to what he means by meeting him tonight, but now I am determined more than ever to go.

The sun has been up for a few hours now, and finally, my eyes can no longer stay open. I will think about all the things he said to me later when I have more of a brain to process them.

Evening…

I slept until past noon before I finally got up, coerced by my grumbling stomach. Although I did sleep, it was by no means a restful one, for my mind had so many new things to ponder. I am too tired to write down all my thoughts about it, but I will only say that the Count has some explaining to do when he gets back. At the same time, I wonder what other things have occurred about which I have not even the slightest clue. I hate how much out of the loop I am, yet I'm in the very center of this loop.

Anyway, when I saw Mitică, I didn't tell him about my late-night conversation with the Monk but made up some excuse that I overslept. I'm pretty sure he didn't buy it, for he grumbled, and then went off to make me a big lunch. We did chat a bit, but it wasn't about anything important. After that, I came back upstairs after my chores and prepared myself for my visit with the fourth Vlad since the day was already over.

Before I knew it, the clock struck 7:30 pm, and I went down to the Master's rooms. As Vlad had promised, he was waiting for me.

Even before we acknowledged each other, I noticed a sizable stack of books piled on the table next to him. Just then, he drew my attention away from them, standing and greeting me with a bright salutation. His cheeriness was a wonderful relief from a day of troubled contemplation.

After I had given him a greeting, the Monk gestured to the chair next to his, and we sat. I was feeling even more apprehensive, so without further ado, I asked him straight out. "So, what is that you have been considering?"

Vlad grew very grave, his mouth forming into a thin line as he frowned deeply. Despite the hours he had had to think, he was still indecisive. "I will be frank with you about one thing, and I wish for you to listen and understand not with modern ears, but be open to it, no matter how offensive it may seem."

That wasn't what I would consider a great start to a serious conversation. "I will."

His gleaming ivory teeth bit his red lower lip. He was more nervous about this situation than I was, yet, with a drawn-out breath, the fourth Vlad began. "My brother is a very traditional man, almost so much so that one could consider it a flaw. Being as isolated as he chose to be for so long, he has these archaic views of the way men and women should act that he never grew out of over the centuries. I know that you are aware of this since he makes you wear these clothes, covering your hair, and such. Honestly, I'm surprised he even allows Dumitru to be as close as he is with you, or hasn't gotten you a personal handmaid, but that's beside the point. What I'm trying to say is that he would not approve of what I have to suggest."

I rolled my eyes. When did the Master ever prove anything outside of the box? "Go on."

"Vlad is a firm believer that women have no place in war, no matter if it's on a battlefield, or even nearby. I, too, share this view." Vlad cleared his throat, jaw tensing, and brow creasing. "However, I know that no matter how many people may protect a castle, it only takes one to be the cause of its destruction."

At his brief pause, I felt my stomach twist in on itself. "Me, you mean."

The Monk's brow furrowed so that they almost met in the middle, and a deep regret came over his face. "It's not your fault. Vlad told me himself that he doesn't want you to learn about our kind so that we are out of sight, out of mind, in a way. If you don't see what we are capable of, you won't fear us...or fear him."

I remained silent and fidgeted with the beaded appliqué of my dress. Already, I had grasped what he was trying to say in a roundabout way, and it was troubling me as to how I would reply.

"Unfortunately, he has not been able to do just that." Vlad sighed again, this time with a hint of frustration. "You do fear us; that was evident when we first met, and it is only confirmed by your night terrors. You may put on a mask and say you don't feel this fear, but you cannot hide from our eyes."

My innermost fears, weaknesses, and dread had been laid out on the table, and I felt vulnerable. There was no way I could lie about how I felt. "I have to wear too many masks these days, even to fool myself."

"You are too beautiful to wear masks, little bride." His hand suddenly grasped both of mine. They were so strong and cold, just like the Count's. I was captivated by them and how they resembled the other hands I know so well, but these weren't them. "There is healthy fear, and then there is irrational fear. Your fear is healthy, but I believe it can be significantly lessened if you were to learn what is unknown to you."

My throat was constricting, but my mind and heart raced at the possibility. Yet, I had to remain logical and consider how much the Master would disapprove of it. "I don't think he would appreciate it."

I'm sure Vlad saw my willingness coupled with my indecision, for his hand bore down on mine as he stressed. "My brother has a devotion to you that I don't want to see broken because of his pride. He cannot expect me or Dumitru to defend this entire castle, its treasure, his lands, ourselves, and you at the same time. Even if it was just to learn of ways to repel us, I'd want you to know. Vlad told me of the ways you repelled the one called Petros despite knowing so little. Impressive as the result was, its major shortcoming was that you had to use yourself as bait to kill him."

"I didn't kill him!" I snapped, but immediately regretted my outburst.

"If Vlad hadn't intervened to end him, you would have." The Monk gently responded just as I was about to apologize. "Regardless, imagine how much more effective you could be against us? In this case, knowledge is power. I can see on your face that you do want to learn. That is why I suggest this, so it may be on my head and not yours."

"I am thankful for the offer, but I don't know. I don't want the trust between us to break because I went against his wishes, especially at a time like this." I pursed my lips, my head, and my heart, yelling at each other to say yes and no. "At the same time, I don't want to be the weak link. I want to help him, but I am only a burden. Most of all, if it comes to the worst, I'd like not to die just yet."

The Monk chuckled once at the last bit of my sentence and shook his head. "Then say you will. If not for your sake, then for your family's."

My glassy eyes met his. Could I do it for my family's sake? Of course, the answer was so clear in my mind, and with a defeated sigh, I submitted. "I will."

He smiled widely and kissed both my hands. "For my brother's sake, I sincerely thank you."

Letting go of me, he eagerly took the first book off the stack and handed it to me. On cue, the half-brother began to lecture as if he were a college professor, explaining so many things that I couldn't have conceived of in years. If I had known I was going to class, I would have brought a notebook to record the intricacies of his lesson. Completely caught off guard as I was, I still retain most of what he explained.

He taught for hours, and then we had a discussion about a few topics, considering the foundations of what the Devil and his demons are, and more concerning my husband after he became what he is. I am astounded at the intellect of this man, whose knowledge spans further than just theology, but to the sciences, and even metaphysics. Time went so quickly when we spoke about these things, and before we both knew it, dawn was approaching. We agreed that was enough for one night, and parted. As I think about it, I am finding it a bit ironic how I came here to teach, but instead am being taught.

THE MESSAGE BEARER

Chapter Forty-Two

12 December

Time has gone by so quickly that, before I realized it, a whole week had passed in the blink of an eye. Where to begin? Well, unfortunately, the day after the Monk began teaching me of his demon-kind, I had begun my time of the month. As if it couldn't have come at a worse time! When I discovered this fact, I wasn't sure if I should go up to the high keep again or stay in my rooms. After some thought, I decided it would just be better to have Dumitru send a note to my new teacher to explain that I wouldn't be able to see him for a few days.

As expected, it didn't go over well. That evening, Dumitru was on edge when the sun set, and regardless, the Monk sought me out. My friend was very adamant that Vlad could not see me and stood guard outside my door like an idiot until he came. I listened from the other side of the door to the heated Romanian being thrown between the two, catching bits and pieces of the turbulent conversation. After a few minutes, it had begun to escalate, and I had thrown open the door and chided them for acting like children.

Immediately, the Monk had covered his nose and mouth, but made it look so inconspicuous that it was just as though he had gone to rub his jaw. Mitică went off on a tirade in a long string of English mixed in with fragmented Romanian, but I held up my hand to silence him.

Surprisingly, Dumitru immediately shut his mouth, although begrudgingly. After a few awkward words of explanation, which the Monk didn't need, he explained to me that despite the circumstance, he was not bothered by my condition. The fourth Vlad justified it stating that his nose is not as sensitive as his brother's, but of course, it was hard to believe him. However, since he showed no outward sign of being agitated, I allowed him to sit.

Dumitru was not so convinced and was hesitant to leave me alone with the easily tempted creature. So, he stayed with us that first session, sitting quietly next to me as the fourth Vlad and I spoke more about the previous night's topic. I'm sure Dumitru does not approve of these lessons, but he hasn't said anything against them to me in private. He turns a blind eye and never asks what I have learned, nor indirectly tests me about it.

So, despite my condition, the Monk still made sure he would teach me something new each night. Slowly at first, but he never sugar-coated the reality of what they are. The Master did not lie when he described him and his children as evil incarnate, corporeal demons who suck life from the living to keep themselves alive. Despite their immortality and near-indestructibility, with the correct tools, they can be easily repelled and destroyed.

According to my new teacher, they are repelled by anything that is pure, or holy, or known to possess qualities which offend them; be it from running water to holy items, the name of God to silver, to certain species of wood or garlic. The wood, as I was told, should be white oak and fashioned into a stake, but any kind of wooden stake would be effective. Having been told these things, many of the small events that I have observed over the many months here have become clearer.

During all of this, I have learned a few things about the Monk himself. It turns out that he was quite the world traveler after his 'death' in the 1490s and traversed all around Europe and Asia until he was finally able to go to the New World. Of course, that was quite an undertaking for one of his kind since he had to cross a vast amount of water, but he arrived in my homeland in the 1600s. From what I have been able to deduce, he stayed in the Americas for centuries until he came back to Europe in the mid-1800s. There was some point that I can tell he did come back to the Americas since he uses such dated American slang, but I haven't asked when just yet.

Sometimes he would tell me stories of the frontier and the Old West, of other countries and their bygone eras, and famous people he had seen who have been long dead. Also, he told me of inventions that he considers 'recent events', such as the electrification of entire cities, the capability of flight, and space travel. To me, those things are normal, but to him, they have an air of mysticism around them. Vlad even told me how much he enjoyed the freedom and openness of the New World, where he didn't have to hide his true nature from the teeming millions of Europe and Asia.

I asked him about his brother and if he ever traveled so far, and to my surprise, the fourth Vlad told me that my husband never went anywhere far from Romania. Obviously, he had traveled to numerous places over the centuries, but stayed primarily close to home in the end. He had never gone to the New World, nor as far as the Pacific, to his knowledge. According to him, the Count had to stay close to his homeland, not just because of want, but of need. For so long he had fought for it, and to leave it would be unthinkable. Deciding to go to England as he did a century ago was a major step outside of Romania, and thereby mainland Europe, and it had gone terribly wrong.

To my relief, Vlad has completely consumed my time and energy so that I don't always think about the Count, wherever he is. Dumitru, too, has played a significant part in my distraction, and at least once a day, he reminds me that the holidays are coming. I think he is most excited that he has a reason to celebrate Christmas now that there is someone here who actually participates. It warms my heart when he speaks of what traditions he remembers observing when his family was alive, and how he wants to incorporate mine into the fold. As I am told by my friend, once we get closer to the date, he wants to start making Christmas cookies and preparing other traditional dishes. It's making me excited too, since Mitică is an amazing chef, and to share this time with him and the Monk is a blessing, despite my Vlad not being here.

Speaking of my Vlad, as is expected, there has not been a peep. Is no news, therefore, good news? I can only pray that he is somewhere out there, safe. Recently, I dreamt of him sliding into bed with me in the middle of the night, taking me into his arms, and whispering how he missed me. It felt so real that I was certain that he had come back, and I woke up just to find an empty bed.

Does he know how much I think of him? Does he think of me? I hope he knows and never forgets.

17 December

Since it's Sunday, Vlad and I were not scheduled to have our lessons. With this free time in the later part of the day, Dumitru twisted my arm to bake with him. There was no way I could say no to it, so by late afternoon, we were both hard at work in the kitchen making a variety of Christmas cookies. Like a little factory, we churned out dozens of the sweets of all different shapes and fillings, eating the defective ones right then since we couldn't help ourselves. They all looked so delicious, but I have no idea who is going to eat all of them. I could barely down three pastries in one sitting, and we have made dozens.

All throughout the process, Dumitru was the cheeriest I had ever seen him in many months. He looked like a boy on Christmas morning, and it's sure close enough to Christmas for that to be true. We had a wonderful time together, telling funny stories, cracking jokes, and simply laughing. Laughing is a luxury that is so rare these days. With the fire-heated oven at full blaze and a gentle snow falling outside, it was quite a picturesque scene, if I may say so. All of it seemed to come out of a perfect daydream, but it was all over too soon.

Once our work was finished, I was positively stuffed with sweets, so I bade Mitică a good evening and made my way to the chapel. I was feeling a bit sleepy from my full stomach and the resonating heat of the oven on my cheeks, but wanted to squeeze in some time of contemplation before bed. For once in the weeks since the Master left, I was feeling rather content with this life without him. That's not to say there isn't a large hole in my chest from his absence.

I spent only about 30 minutes in the chapel before heading back to my room. The sun was just about to set, and Vlad would be waking from his sleep soon. There were no plans to see him, and my goals this evening were simply to do some reading and go to bed. But, of course, my plans never seem to come true when I want them to.

I was walking to the steps that ascend to the floors above when I heard Mitică call for me. His voice wasn't coming from the kitchen, however, but over towards the hall that branched off to the parlor. That was a strange place for him to be since he had no reason to be there, so I called back to him to ask what he wanted. For a few seconds, there was no answer, but then again, I heard him call to me. Dumitru didn't sound as though he needed help, but only as though he wanted to show me something. Groaning, I jogged over to the hall and entered it.

With no fires lit and with no creature to light them for me, I entered the semi-darkness of the hall. Since there was no reason for this unused part of the castle to be heated, the air was particularly frigid. The darkness of the shadows, which moved unnaturally in the faint light, made me uneasy. Eager to get out of there, I called out to Dumitru to ask where he was, but my echoed voice was the only reply as it rang back at me from down the stone hallway. When a few seconds passed and there was no answer from him, this electric chill ran up my spine, and instinct told me to get out.

I turned to run back the way I came, but was met with two yellow eyes inches away from my face. Their distinctive pale yellow, as the color of sulfur, shone against the rectangular pupil and surrounding darkness. My vocal folds wanted to scream bloody murder, but I believe they were so paralyzed with fear that they could only gasp weakly. Instantly, the rancid smell of thick brimstone burned my lungs, choking out the oxygen in them. I was so close to

Satan that I could feel the heat of his breath and hide as it radiated off of him and see the ridged curves of his horns.

"We meet again, daughter." A thousand voices whispered the same words a thousand times as the blackened mist that surrounded his body swayed in an unearthly breeze.

An overwhelming dread seeped into every cell of my body as some half-inconceivable realization dawned on me that the Lord of Darkness had come yet again. If he were to show himself to me now, of all times when the Master is away, he certainly hadn't come just to chat. I was at a loss to answer him. My airless lungs had no strength of their own to make another sound, so I opted to say nothing at all.

"You appear much better than last we saw you." A tendril, as a snake, slithered behind my neck as his eyes examined me as if I were naked. "Yet ever such a beauty. A budding flower amongst the deadliest of thorns, with cheeks ever so flushed for your servant boy."

Horror ceased my heart mid-beat and sparked my anger in a mix of embarrassment and fury. The fact that he had seen me baking with Dumitru and had read the deeper, darker temptation of my heart, a temptation that I can't admit to myself, made me sick. I have no doubt he read the disgust on my face. "What do you want?"

"We want many things from you," If I hadn't been held captive by his eyes, I'm sure I would have seen the devilish smirk over his jagged teeth. "But today there is something more important to discuss: there is news about your beloved husband."

My brow furrowed, and my eyes squinted at Satan's strange intonation. Coupled with the brimstone, the fishy smell of his sincerity was unsettling. There was no way he was being honest or sincere. A little voice begged to know what the news was. Steeling myself, I had to shake my head to refocus. "I don't want to hear what you have to say."

Some invisible force grasped onto my hand when I tried to pull away, making it remain limp at my side as his gaze intensified. "This you will want to hear. Best of all, there is no price to pay, we promise you. With news like this, it would be cruel to withhold it from our own daughter, wife of our son." He suddenly broke off, and pain manifested on his goat face as he wailed. "Oh, son! How saddened we are for him! Our own flesh, rotted by his own desires that have led to his destruction."

Destruction... As much as I wanted to ask, have him tell me all, I knew I shouldn't submit to this trick. What would there be to gain from telling me? He has no care for me, nor care for anyone, save himself. No matter how many times I repeated that in my head, that little voice came back and whispered what if it was, and I didn't want to believe him because of my own bias. I had to look away from him and cast my gaze downwards as he continued.

"We mourn his loss and came posthaste to tell you, sweet daughter, who loved him. What sadness there is within us that we could not give you a child through him before his time was finished." The wispy tendrils curled around my cheeks as if Lucifer, of all creatures, was trying to console me. It only left me disturbed, and I cringed as the strangely downy fingers smoothed my hair. "What joys you will never have with him, being departed from you forever."

He was saying things in this way purposefully to cause me to have an emotional response. I wanted to cry, I really did. It was like my emotions believed him, although neither my head nor heart wanted to acknowledge anything he said. After my lengthy silence and building sentiments, I accidentally choked. "He is...dead...then..."

"He is dead, but he cannot die, yet he is no more." Lucifer wailed again, the heat from his partially corporeal form pulsed off him. "He has burned in a fiery torrent, swept away by a stormy sea, fallen into a deep abyss, struck down by his own devices! Oh, daughter, we grieve for you as well, who will never see the face of your beloved husband again."

Everything he said confused me further, although I'm sure that was on purpose. Out of all the things he said, I wasn't certain which one could have been remotely true. Fists clenching, I had been praying to God to deliver me from this, and I think He finally instilled in me some courage and clear-headedness to fire back. "Why should I believe you?"

A puff of rancid sulfur plumed from his nostrils as his feigned grief became a mild anger. "Daughter, you disappoint us. We have come so far to tell you of your husband, and you cannot place a shred of faith in our word? We loved our son from the day he gave himself to us, and you loved him from the moment you laid eyes on him, yet you —"

"If you loved him as you say you do, you would have released him from Hell." I cut him off sharply. "And what proof do you have that can persuade me? You are the Prince of Lies. Why should I believe you're telling me the truth?"

Lucifer snorted, clicked his tongue, and turned away from me. There was a shift in the atmosphere, and the hair stood up on the back of my neck. I thought he meant to leave, but instead began to circle me. "So ungrateful. After all we have done for you, and you still behave like an insolent child. If it is proof you want, we have it, and even that will not cost you a thing."

I scoffed, biting harder on my tongue. Everything has a price to him, so I knew then that if I wasn't to pay for it, it was being paid by someone else. Raising my eyes slightly, I watched as from within the dark mass of his body, he produced a neatly folded dress shirt, white but blotched with bloodstains, with holes and tears. I held the shirt in my hands, staring at the embroidered 'VD' on the inside collar. The worst part about that is that not only was this a shirt I remember him wearing, but it still *smelled* of him.

The blood had been long dried and had turned a crusted black-brown against the whiteness of the fabric, making it stiff. I almost forgot that Satan was standing right before me as I brought the shirt to my chest, holding it against me for dear life. My mind, by this time, had gone a bit blank, and the tears had already begun to fall. There was no way, even if my mind wouldn't believe it, that I could hold back the tempest of emotion I was withholding to save my face. Looking back, I hate myself for showing weakness to the one who is the first to exploit it. "How do I know it's his blood, and not someone else's?"

"You could ask your brother-in-law to confirm it." Lucifer snickered, suddenly reappearing behind me as the shadows dissipated just enough to let some moonlight shine in. "We know you are there, Vlad Călugărul."

A new fear gripped my chest that the Monk had found me in the presence of such company, and I felt ashamed by it. Quicker than I would have liked in that scenario, I was becoming a wreck, with new layers of emotions intensifying the ones beneath. Closing my eyes as tightly as I could, I tried with all my willpower to bury my feelings, to turn them off, to feel nothing…at least just for a little while longer.

My eyes opened again at the familiar voice and figure that manifested from the shadows of the hall. Vlad's irises, like two spheres of churning molten lava, burned with such intense rage as I have never seen from him before. Although I could not see the rest of his face, I knew he was not looking at me, but was trained on the root of all evil. "Isadora, come away from him. He's using your weakness against you; don't let him confuse you."

"Confuse her?" A malice melded with the thousand voices, and I shivered as I felt the hair on his goat-like snout brush lightly against my cheek. I knew I should have jumped away, but he was holding me there by my soul. It seemed that if I moved, it would be ripped right out of my body. "No matter how unappreciative she is of our efforts, she is still our beloved daughter, our sweet one. We may have had disagreements in the past, but we have a new understanding now. Călugărul, you see the blood with your own eyes and smell it with your own nose. You know it is genuine."

"Isadora," the Monk completely ignored him and spoke to me instead, all the meanwhile keeping his eyes on Satan. "Remember the temptation in the desert: rebuke him. Remember the temptation in the garden: do not eat what you know is forbid—"

"Listen to you: spouting Biblical nonsense." Then Satan directed his words at me, his mouth next to my ear, as he whispered seductively. "How will that old drivel help her now? She has lost her husband. How can she possibly live, knowing she will never see him again?"

I was captivated by the words, feeling each of their weights press down in my shoulders. My conscious listened to the whisper, and in a way, I saw the truth in it. How could I live without the Count, the one I love more than my own life? It was simple, really: life wasn't worth living anymore. It had no meaning to me, no purpose. Tears swelled in my eyes, and a deep, empty despair ripped a hole in my heart.

"Isadora," I heard the fourth Vlad call my name somewhere off in the distance, his voice soft yet stern. "You are the lady of this house now. You have a duty *here*. You have people who love you *here*. If you choose to leave, you will only add to their pain, instead of being here to love them back. Do not make the same mistake Ioana made. Remember what happened in the past and don't repeat it."

My downcast eyes lifted to my brother-in-law at the mention of Ioana's name. I could see his features then, so similar to my beloved's, as the moonlight cast upon them from a high window. For just a second, it was as if I was looking at *his* face, and *he* was pleading for me not to leave him. I knew it was the fourth Vlad, but my heart had to believe in that moment that it was *my* Vlad. Whichever Vlad he was, he was right. I have a duty here to the house that I promised to keep watch over while my husband is away, but also to Dumitru, and even to my fourth Vlad. But also, not just to the people here, but to my family I left behind. I could not forsake myself for my own selfishness because a precious person had been taken from me, because there are still precious people here who need me more than I need to die. Of course, living isn't going to be easy; it's not meant to be so. But that is how I believe the pain of death may be conquered: by the living simply living.

I wasn't going to repeat those past mistakes of my prede-cessor, not after the Count has taken so many risks to keep me alive when I had been so close to death. Even when he hated me, he still protected me against Imogen's plots, when he gave me his blood, he was giving me himself so that I may live. He saved me more times than I can count, and to forsake his gifts of life would be a grievous insult to his memory. I have to keep living for the dead, no matter how painful it is.

Lucifer hissed in Vlad's direction when he noticed my changed expression. "Are you listening to him? You know if you come with us, there is a chance you can be reunited with your love. There is nothing left in this world for you, but awaiting you in the next is —"

"*Shut up.*" I growled and stared eye-to-eye with evil. "You have given your message, said what you must, and my answer is no. Go and take your bitterness with you."

The heat of his ire magnified from him, but the air around us became deathly cold. "Imogen, our most faithful one, seeks your head. No matter who takes your life, you or her, it will still be ours in the end. You may always take your life whenever and however you wish, but if you allow her to take it, it will be painfully slow. She is coming for you even now and will be here soon to take what she covets."

"Then let her come and I'll finish what he started." I snapped again; my patience was quite worn thin with him. "If I don't come with you now, I'll be with you later. What's the difference if it's days or months if the end result is the same?" With my hands already so close to my chest, I subtly reached within my bodice to produce the crucifix, which had been hidden. With Lucifer being so close to me, at the sight of the holy instrument, he cried out in a bloody scream and snarled, hurling himself away.

Taking advantage of this distraction, the Monk rushed him with unimaginable speed. I couldn't see what Vlad had done, but a screech erupted and tore through the air, shaking the stone walls. As in a flash, the black mist vanished back to Hell, and the candles burst to life around us. When Vlad turned to me next, his eyes had returned to normal, but his expression was one of horror as we stared at each other, some kind of understanding passing between us.

Not letting a second go to waste, he embraced me tightly. I let the crucifix go and grabbed hold of him instead, my overflow of emotion finally spilling out from my eyes. What happened next, again, I don't quite remember, but my knees lost their ability to hold me up, and we both sank to the floor. Sobbing into his shirt, I wept uncontrollably as the fourth Vlad rocked me back and forth as he would a child, mumbling coos to comfort me the best he could.

Through my sobs, I somehow managed to ask him if the blood on the shirt is the Count's, and Vlad's shoulders slouched. The Monk was reluctant to answer me, but eventually breathed out a crushing 'yes'. A great wave of grief came up from my stomach to my eyes, and I wailed so hard that it came out with no sound. My throat hurt terribly from the stress of the intense weeping, and still hurts even as I write this. I cannot even describe the emotions I was feeling then: one moment it was grief, then on to anger, despair, frustration, and weariness.

Quick and heavy footsteps approached, and Dumitru, his face ashen and confused as he breathed heavily, entered the scene. He probably only realized something had happened when he heard the Devil's departing scream and came running. All the same, I was so happy to see him, and cried even harder on the Monk's shoulder that he had been left unharmed. My poor friend was so stunned that he had apparently forgotten all his English, and frantically asked Vlad in Romanian to explain as he came to kneel beside me. Letting go of the bloodied shirt, I reached for Mitică, and instantly he gripped my hand as if he would never let go.

In a few sentences, the fourth Vlad had told him all in their native tongue. I didn't bother to look at Mitică's face, for I knew it was just as despondent as my own.

He was silent for a long time, then, almost inaudibly, he asked. "The Master…will not be returning, then?"

The Monk smoothed my hair when I whimpered like a wounded animal, and had to clear his throat before speaking. "If he can find a way, he will never rest until he finds his way back here. I don't know how long that will take, but I do know we should not give up hope simply because the Prince of Lies gave us a shirt with his blood on it and said he is no more."

"How can you be so sure?" After all I had heard, I didn't know what to believe; nevertheless, I hated literally playing the Devil's advocate.

"Listen to me, sister," he said, moving me so we met face-to-face. His eyes dripped blood-tears, and his contorted features were so pained and sorrowful, yet his smile was so full of hope. "If Vlad were dust, physically gone from this world, all others would be dust too. If he dies, because he is the first, we who come from him all die. I am still here, so Vlad is not dust. He is still alive, somewhere, I promise you."

I had heard the words he said, but in my state, it was hard to comprehend the scope of them. It did make sense, but I didn't answer as I mulled it over, a small glimmer of hope making my chest feel lighter, though my body was still heavy.

"Just *believe* me." Vlad emphasized, taking my silence as confusion muddled with disbelief. "When Wilhelmina was becoming like us, Vlad was killed by her husband, ending his existence. Her bond with him was still young and fragile, so she became human again. Ours, which had existed for centuries or even decades before that time, did not sever. We all felt him die, but he was resurrected before we met our end. This is how I know."

For some reason, I looked to Mitică as if to seek confirmation from him. When our eyes met, he quickly averted his, but nodded slightly anyway. It bothered me that such a crucial detail concerning the Count had been so purposefully left out of the equation for me.

It added an understanding of the reality of what would happen to him if he were to achieve the salvation he seeks: he would be ending the existence of all the children who have come from him. By breaking his curse, their curse would thereby be broken, and then it dawned on me. "That is why Imogen wants me dead? Because if she kills Vlad, she will be killing herself, and everyone else?"

The Monk nodded too, his head hanging. "This is why they fear, hate, and blame you for everything that he has done. To them, your death is compensation for his transgressions. The exchange is equal in their eyes, since he would repay their loss of something precious by eliminating something precious to him. You are the easy sacrifice to remake Vlad into what he was before he fell back to this earth."

My throat clogged again, but I swallowed the forming frog and wiped away the tears from my cheeks. It moved me so that my husband, even when I fell out of favor with him, had consistently refused to hand me over to them to die. But those feelings had to be saved for a later time, and I pushed another related topic forward. "Imogen could arrive at any time, and if she has trapped him in God knows where, how can we help him get back here before she does?"

"We can't help him ourselves," Mitică finally spoke up after a long silence. "Perhaps Călugărul can send trusted friends to look for him, but even then, we don't know where he is."

"He did tell me his final destination," the fourth Vlad added with a tensing jaw. "However, who knows if he actually got there, or even if that destination had changed before he reached it. Knowing him as I do, he is impossible to track when he doesn't want to be found."

I didn't think my heart could sink so low into my stomach and rise into my throat at the same time, but it did. Helplessness clouded me, and I had to shut my eyes tightly to hold back my next wave of tears. Swiftly, Dumitru lifted me into his arms and stood, saying he would take me to my room to rest. Vlad only nodded and watched as Mitică walked away with me back into the well-lit parts of the castle. Once we were out of sight, I brought my arms around his neck and rested my head against his shoulder. While I could, I savored the permitted closeness I had with him before we were forced to part.

Now, I sit here in semi-darkness, feeling a bit dead inside and so alone. Before I sleep, I will pray for my Vlad's safe return and that we three will be alive to see him come home.

ON FAITH ALONE

21 December
Winter Solstice
Evening…

For quite a few days, I have been thinking long and hard on many things, trying to put all the events thus far into perspective. This account, which I thank my past self for beginning all those months ago, I have reread to help myself come to this understanding. Coupled with a few vital questions answered by the Monk, I will compile here a synopsis for my future reference of how I believe all of this has come to pass. I hope I am not wrong concerning any of this, but I'm sure some amendments will have to be made in time.

Still, it is strange how clearly I can see how the issues at hand began.

…

Thinking back to my first months here, I don't think anyone outside the Count's inner circle cared about my presence and closeness with him. It was only when Petros arrived and tried to play his power move and died because of it that their interest was piqued. By killing Petros to save Dumitru, his house, and me, the Count had inflamed the anger of those who had been previously only discontented with his hermit-like attitude and distance from his kind. In a way, he had lost everything that he symbolized to them: the first great father, most bloodthirsty and ruthless of them all, who reveled in sinning. That monster had become more man than beast by showing kindness and consideration to humankind and wished to be released from his bodily prison after nearly six hundred years.

Of course, Imogen's anger had been specifically provoked by the Count. She was personally wounded by Petros' death and probably already resented the Count for his withdrawn behavior. She knew she could not exact revenge on him by ending his life, so she turned her eyes to me, the Master's most recent interest. Others were upset and unnerved that the Count had killed his friend, their brother, because Petros had hurt the two humans in his care, whose deaths shouldn't have mattered at all. That was when, I believe, Imogen rallied the ones who wished to kill me as recompense and radically reshape the Count back into the image he had been as *Țepeș*.

Since humans are just tools to them, she used me to warn him to change, hoping I would succeed in killing myself by her suggestion. It had not worked, thank God. I have no doubt Imogen's close relationship with Lucifer played a significant role to try and thwart me from falling into darkness. By endeavoring to make me worship him, trying to tempt, seduce, and frighten me, it had been Imogen's hand at work to derail whatever effect I had over the Count. Imogen's last-ditch effort to get me to leave was by getting the Romanian and American governments to list me as some kind of criminal and to have my teaching license revoked. Again, the Master had outsmarted her by ensuring I would not be at her mercy.

When she and the other group of dissenters arrived, she brought forth the baby for the Master to kill, knowing it would upset me. She gave me the poisoned dress to use my vanity against me, but did not suspect that my enmity towards her outweighed that. Yet again, her plans fell through. It makes sense to me now why she was always brooding when I was nearby: I was sitting there, untouched by all her efforts to weaken or kill me. No amount of threats, nor petty gestures of disrespect, would bother me, and it must have infuriated her. Even when she and the others had managed to turn the Count against me, making him hate the sight of me, she could not break the Master down to have me disposed of. Yes, they had made him agree that I should be punished for making him weak, but my husband never acted upon it.

Imogen probably had encouraged Cosima, and to a lesser extent Georgiana, to become sexually involved with the Count, knowing the effect it would have on me. On the other hand, I don't think she really knew what Andreas was up to. It seems he had his own motives in the game he played, especially by telling me about Wilhelmina and Jonathan. By saying he didn't believe I could have been responsible for Petros' death, a lie surely perpetuated by Imogen, Andreas had rebelled from following her agenda to the letter. I'm sure she didn't disapprove of Andreas wiggling his way into my heart to further separate me from the Count. It furthered her cause, even if Andreas had his own plans. Whether or not she had been involved in his scheme to get me alone in the den, one thing is for certain: she was willing to sacrifice her comrades to get me.

And now, knowing the Master would go to settle the score and leave his fortress, she has trapped and wounded him. Undoubtedly, she has done this with the Devil's help, who then relayed it to me. With their relationship growing by the day, Imogen has to be the one paying Satan to be her influential power from afar. He must be letting himself be used, but of course, he has his own motivations. His main goal is to take my soul, and I'm sure working in agreement with Imogen, he goaded me to kill myself to make the past live again for the Count.

Thank God that Vlad the Monk had been there to keep me from slipping into Lucifer's siren-like song. Without question, Satan had whispered into Ioana's ear to kill herself the same way, knowing Vlad would fall because of it.

And so, here I sit, staring at this. If someone had shown it to me at the beginning of my stay here and said this was the way it is to be, I would not have believed them.

...

With all of this in mind, and a long talk with the fourth Vlad concerning it, the nature of our lessons has changed. Before, my teacher had focused on the more academic aspects of topics that concern who and what they are. If that first section was considered 'book smarts', it has now become lessons on 'street smarts'.

After giving me a day to recuperate from my emotional trauma, the fourth Vlad has begun to drill me on the heavier components. Our first night, he taught me what it meant to be compelled against one's will. I recall that he said, "To compel another is simply a form of hypnotism or brainwashing, that may last a few seconds to an entire lifetime. We use all five senses to hypnotize the intended prey and 'cast a spell', in a way, over their senses to repress their emotions and awareness. It may be a suggestive word, a fierce gaze, or a gentle touch, and less commonly, an intoxicating smell or delectable taste. If one learns to be aware of these tricks and trains their mental fortitude against them, it is possible to resist."

The idea of a gentle touch caught my attention. In early October, when I had been brought low by my time of the month, it was Georgiana who had given me a 'gentle touch'. So…it really was she who had been the one to cause me so much pain. The memories made me shiver. It took me a while to refocus on his lecture after that.

In my mental state, I doubt I can resist much of anything, but he assured me I can do this. I was hardly convinced then, and still am not, but I humored him anyway. At first, it was little things: him telling me to pick up a book, walking to the other end of the room, or even to make me say words I don't mean. It has only been a few days since the fourth Vlad has been testing my ability to withstand him, and I have been left mentally exhausted. In my opinion, I have made no progress. I grow quickly frustrated when he releases me from his hold, and I realize I had done a task against my will.

Each night, he has pressed me to my mental limits, and I'm beginning to wonder if this is worth it. If I had an entire year to train myself, to practice night and day, maybe I would stand a chance against someone as powerful as Imogen. According to Vlad, he tells me her physical abilities are actually quite weak, but she makes up for it in cunning tricks and black magic. Also, she has a very powerful 'friend' in a very 'low' place, and that makes up for a great portion of areas in which she is weak.

All the same, I am a peon and stand no chance against any one of these demons. Vlad has too much faith in my mental abilities. Give me a puzzle and I can piece it together, but don't pit me against the puzzle maker, who knows the design of the piece from every angle, and expect me to solve it before he does.

It feels to me that he's preparing me to exact a kind of revenge on Imogen, and as much as a part of me wants to give her pain as she caused me, I know revenge is not the answer. He knows this, too, but it is only through a mentality of vengeance that I can be motivated to stand against them. True, I must know my enemy to defeat it, but this is not *lex talionis*. I have no wish to perpetuate the exchange of hate-for-hate and violence-for-violence with these people simply because that is the only way they show dominance over another. Of course, I am not a pacifist, and I'd like to say not a coward either, but how do I stand when she comes to stand against me?

"Have no sympathy for your prey," Vlad had said to me just last night as he showed me the location of the heart, their weakest point. "Because your prey has none for you."

When I think of Petros and how I had reacted to defend myself, it had been put into motion by a need to survive, but also to retaliate for his unwanted sexual advances. Although the circumstances are different, I don't see a real difference between then and now. Both of them want to end me, while I'd prefer to keep on living. Still, I hope I conquer my inner war before the real one shows up at my doorstep.

25 December
Christmas Day
Evening, 10:45 pm…

Christus natus est! Christ is born. So much, yet so little, has happened these few days. To catch up, I will be brief about the days before Christmas Eve: when something happened that I must write down, although I didn't have the chance yesterday.

There have been minor improvements in my 'training' with the Monk. The other day, to my great astonishment, I had inadvertently resisted a command he had given me. I'm unsure how I actually did it, but I have sneaking suspicions. Perhaps I have been overthinking the whole process this entire time, or perhaps it was simply some kind of Christmas miracle.

Either or, I'm beginning to see the things that Vlad says and does to compel me in a different light. Maybe I have heard him command things so many times that I've gotten used to his black eyes, that some part of me is starting to become almost immune to him? I doubt the immunity now that I think about it, but I know something is changing. I don't know what it is, but I know in the future I will find out all then. I even asked Dumitru how he manages to resist their power. His only answer was that it was completely natural to him, as if they were only speaking to him as any other person would. How utterly unhelpful...

One other thing I think I ought to mention is that there has been no new news about the Count. More often now, I think about his promise to me concerning ending this all by the new year. Well, he has six days.

The Devil has neither come to visit me once since that evening to tempt me nor whisper more lies. I don't really expect him to, since I think for now, he said all he needed to then. All the same, I still wonder if he'll pop up again when I least expect it.

With those two things, I had been thinking about the Count all yesterday morning, and was feeling rather depressed, although I tried not to show it to the others. Dumitru had been so excited for Christmas for weeks, and I wasn't going to rain on his parade. Once I got up, my beloved friend was so happy to start the festivities. While doing chores, we began to prepare a traditional dinner, while sneaking in too many sweets along the way, which made us not hungry for lunch. My blue mood had passed by that time, all thanks to Mitică, who smiled more times that day than I had ever seen before. He was a ray of sunshine in my gloominess.

Not much got finished that afternoon concerning the chores, but we got a lot of food made for dinner that night and the next. During our breaks, we sat and talked of Christmases past, and even of when I first came here. We laughed when we recalled how Mitică had gotten so angry at me for getting close to the wall, and then hauled me up to my room. Such things seemed so silly now, when back then I had been appalled and horrified at the way he had treated me. Even thinking so far back then, despite it being eight months ago, I remember believing the Count was the enemy I needed to save myself from. How time changes things.

When dinner was ready, it was near 4 pm, so we gathered around the servant's table and ate the delicious and colorful displays we had made. It was the best meal both of us had had in years, we both agreed. Before I knew it, I was stuffed, almost to the point of overeating, and was ready for a nap. An amazing meal with great company was all I could have asked for; if only Vlad...that is both Vlads, could have joined us. Granted, they wouldn't find the food as enticing as we did, but just to have them near would have meant the world to me.

As Dumitru and I washed the dishes, I was lost in thought about the Count for the millionth time, wondering where he is and if he is alright. We had just finished putting everything away when Mitică whispered in my ear from behind. "I have a surprise for you."

That did surprise me, and I turned to face him. He had a guilty grin plastered all over his face, those gray eyes shining so brightly when they looked into mine. I felt so embarrassed as my cheeks grew hot. "Mitică, you didn't. We said no presents."

He waved it away and shrugged his shoulders. "I don't need anything anyway, but this I know you will like. It has taken me months, but I think it's perfect now."

That only made me feel worse. "Seriously, you shouldn't —"

"*Shush,*" he abruptly cut me off and sat me back down at the table. "Close your eyes and don't look."

Sighing, I did as I was instructed. I heard him walk into the pantry, and after some rummaging, returned and placed something heavy on the table. I became quite worried at that sound, and when he told me to open my eyes, I only opened one eye initially. Before me was a frosted-glass bottle with a light amber liquid inside, corked with a stopper.

"This is called *țuică,* plum brandy. I made it myself." Dumitru darted to a cabinet to grab two small glasses as he explained further. "It's strong, but since you are Romanian now, I think you can handle it."

"I don't know about that." I laughed nervously as I examined the contents further. Taking out the stopper, the intense smell hit my nose like a train, and I coughed. "But you made *this* without the Master knowing?"

"If he did know, he didn't do anything about it." Dumitru proudly grinned, setting the glasses on the table. "I can be sneaky if I want to be."

"You're very brave." I smiled widely.

He chuckled as he poured the two glasses. "You're not going to tell on me, are you?"

I scoffed, lifting the glass to the light. "Of course I won't. Why would I?"

Again, he shrugged. "Well, I don't think *Doamna* would approve."

"Who's she? Besides, when the Voivode is away, *Doamna* will play...or something like that." I rolled my eyes with a smile to lessen the pain my own words gave me. "Thank you for this. It was sweet of you to make. How much alcohol is in it, anyway?"

"Uh..." He thought for quite a while as he stared at the liquid. "A lot."

"I like it already."

I could barely get it close to my nose before being overcome by the smell, but somehow managed to get down a few sips of the strong stuff before coughing up a lung. Of course, Mitică laughed at me. There was no way I could hold it in with my mouth, esophagus, and stomach burning with such intensity. Swearing, I gasped for breath.

"That means it's good." Dumitru choked out through his bellowing laughter, and then took a sip himself, and choked too.

My eyes were watering so bad from the lingering burn and the sight of him that, when I laughed, it was raspy and hoarse. Despite my unsuccessful first try, I was determined to try again and continued to sip down bits of it at a time until I finally reached the bottom of the small glass. I was already starting to feel the effects of the alcohol itself, although I had been sweating since my first taste.

After his fourth glass, Dumitru was beginning to lose his ability to speak English, though I was only on my third, and I was too. This was the part where I kind of don't remember the series of events, but I know we were both laughing like two idiots at the stupidest things. I don't know what they were, but they were hilarious. Yet through this, there was one part that I recall clearly than the rest, but I'm not sure how it came about. There was a pause from whatever was said, and Mitică took my hand, and most seriously declared in half-Romanian-half-English the equivalent of: "I will wait for you."

Even through my drunken stupor, I understood what he meant, and a great sadness ruined my euphoric happiness that had come with the plum brandy. I averted my gaze and clenched down on his hand in some kind of silent response to him. I'm not sure what it meant in that moment. Had I accepted by doing that? I can only assume that's how he viewed it. However, before either of us could respond either way, a dark shadow loomed over both of us. It was the fourth Vlad, of course. The sun had set, and we hadn't even noticed.

His tone was chiding, sounding more disappointed than angry, although I forgot what he said. After his scolding, he gave us, the Monk must have separated us two, for the next thing I knew, I woke the next morning on the settee in my sitting room.

My headache wasn't so bad that I couldn't function, but it lingered until the late afternoon. Still, I'm glad I didn't drink more than a few glasses. When I saw Mitică later that day, he was hungover and was really confused as to the events of the previous evening. He apparently only remembers pouring the first drink, and then not much after that. I'm not sure I believe him.

Anyway, Vlad had taken away my gift and disposed of it. I don't think he wanted to do it, really, because when we saw him in this early evening, he half-heartedly scolded both of us again for breaking one of his brother's primary rules. He called us 'irresponsible youths' and said that we both should be grateful it was he who had found us plastered and not the Count. Despite his stern lecture and threats, he promised not to tell of this to the Master when he returns because of our youth and foolishness. At that, the whole incident was put behind the three of us, never to be spoken of again.

Vlad's demeanor lessened in its severity after that, and he returned to his lighthearted self. Obviously, he didn't want to end this day on a sour note, so for the rest of the night, he recounted to us the ancient Romanian folktales of his youth. He told of the stories about sprites and fairies, giants and ogres, the tales of fair princesses and charming princes. Dumitru was bored with it, but I was engrossed in them, hanging onto his every word.

Now I am exhausted from eating, and my headache has returned from lack of sleep. I will say goodnight, although I will add that I feel quite lonely.

Merry Christmas, my beloved, wherever you are.

1 January
New Year's Day
11 pm...

Once again, it is a new year; a new beginning, or the beginning of the end. Whatever it may be, I must update the few things that have happened since I last wrote.

My ability to resist the Monk's control has strengthened only minimally, but minimally is better than none. The other day, I was able to oppose his command to cause myself harm, just as Imogen had suggested I do. Remembering the event and all the emotions that came along with it made me able to oppose him more effectively. It still shook me, but in a way, it cleared my mind of those feelings which have been confusing me since Vlad began to teach me these little tricks and tactics. I think I have ironed out the wrinkles of what I must do, but still have much to accomplish in the coming days.

On 29 December, the Monk did something unexpected. It was the middle of the day when he sought me out in the library, where I had been reading some of the books he had given me to study. I was very surprised to see him, especially when he told me to get my coat and boots on. He wouldn't say what was going on, although he assured me nothing was wrong.

I followed him out into the courtyard and then to the gate. Brisk and biting winds ripped past us, and thick clouds brought the sun in and out of sight. My confusion about our situation only increased when he commanded that the front gate lift itself from the icy ground, and taking my arm, he ushered me just to the other side of it. We went no further than that.

"Do not be afraid, sister," Vlad warned as he stared intently at me. "They can smell fear, and it is them you need not fear at all."

"They —?" I didn't even get a chance to intone the question before he let out this high-pitched whistle that reached out into the landscape. The sound didn't even echo back to us before the distinctive howl of wolves sporadically rang up from the rocky outcroppings, the forest, and valley. I felt a chill, that feeling one gets when the primal fear kicks in, and my adrenaline spiked.

"Calm yourself," Vlad warned again, adjusting the hood of his thick wool coat to conceal himself from the sun. "You are their master. They will not harm you."

I shifted on my feet and would have turned to run back to the castle if he hadn't been holding me there. "Still, why call them?"

There was a long pregnant pause as the Monk thought of how to answer. Just as his brother, a crease formed on his brow. "Vlad was supposed to have sent word by now..." The fourth Vlad's jaw tightened. "But none has come. Therefore, I believe it is time for you to meet them."

The sharp knife of reality stabbed into my chest, and I had to look away. I had no time to ponder the weight of his words before he continued.

"You may not be able to control them, but an introduction is long overdue. They guard this place, so that is why I say do not fear them. In a way, they are your children." There was an awkward clearing of his throat, and then he whispered. "At least, Vlad saw them as such."

Swallowing hard, I wasn't sure what to say next. All my time here, I feared those wild dogs, especially when I saw them rip that woman apart. They were the main reason why I could never escape, as they are so numerous and prowl all about this area. I bit my lip. "What if they don't like me?"

"It's not a question of 'like'," Vlad patted my hand, which rested on his muscled forearm. "More of 'respect'."

Gulping this time, I turned my gaze back to the frozen wasteland, and just then, my eyes caught sight of the gray wolves emerging from the barren forest. I thought the whole host of them was going to come, but instead there were only five. I watched intently as they trotted and loped over the snowy ground, tongues dangling from rows of vicious white teeth as their hot breath plumed before them. The color of their fur was mostly tones of gray and black; however there was one of them that was completely white. This one was definitely different from the rest, being larger, and most of all, more graceful than the other four. He is obviously the alpha of the pack, and his expression was almost human-like.

Steeling myself, I tried to calm my erratic heart as Vlad said, but it was hard. I had never seen wolves so close up in the wild before, and every cell in my body said that something was wrong. Yet I stood there as they approached and stopped only a couple of yards away, as if waiting for a signal that it was permissible to come nearer.

"They are curious about you," the Monk let go of my arm and nudged me forward. "Don't be shy."

Slowly, I took two steps forward, and bending down at the waist, I outstretched my hand. Cautiously, the large white one, who was nearly as tall as I was at that level, came to sniff my hand. At that close distance, I could see how pale blue-green his eyes are, like a finely glazed faience or shining blue topaz. I couldn't decide which one was more accurate, and was so captivated by them that it startled me when his freezing wet nose nuzzled into my hand. For a ferocious beast, his fur was softer than I expected, and I smoothed it gently.

Shortly afterward, the others began to creep forward, and I greeted each one the same way. It was quite a thrill to be so close to them, like holding a scorpion in your hand. One of the darker gray ones particularly liked me, I think, for he licked my face and was desperate for me to pet him. It was so strange to see these creatures in a new light, and I wondered why the Count hadn't introduced me to them before.

When I asked Vlad that same question, however, he frowned and didn't really answer it. "They had their master present then, but now they have you."

"But just like you said: I can't control them." I frowned too as I scratched behind the darker gray wolf's ears, a look of pure bliss on his face. "Besides, why should they respect me? I'm just a human, while you are…well, you know. I appreciate all they do for this castle, but wouldn't it be better for them to answer to you?"

I wasn't looking at him, but I could hear the pain that he tried to mask. "It wouldn't be right of me to take what is my brother's. If he didn't have an heir, I would adopt them so that they could remain in the family, but that is not the case."

"An heir?" I queried with a furrowed brow, my hands stopping their work. "You mean Dumitru, right? You did call him a protégé once."

"I meant you, actually." He was quick to correct me, and that only heightened my suspicions. "You are *Stăpâna* of this house, Isadora. Vlad did entrust all of this to you; therefore, it is yours."

My heart sank at the word 'entrust'. How could I be trusted with the Master's house, lands, title, and fortune? I have had so little training in actually running this household, yet he expects me to carry on as if I know what the hell I'm doing. I felt so much weight press down on me then, and I accidentally vented my frustration. "He should have given it to you since you have so much more experience than I could ever have. Not to mention you'll live longer."

"Regardless of whom they answer," the Monk switched the subject back to the wolves. By his tone, I could tell he had had enough of this kind of talk. "The one who rules this house rules them. Vlad would not have given you control of his house if he didn't trust you. If he has faith in you, have faith in yourself."

His light scolding made me hang my head. "I'm sorry…"

"Don't be. This is why I'm here: to help you." It was plain on his face that I had made him uncomfortable by talking like that, and again he switched the subject. "Now they know your face and scent, and if anything should happen, they will do all they are able to help you too."

"Is that what they say?"

He nodded, a sad smile forming on his face. We only visited with the wolves a bit longer before coming back in, and they returned to the wild. I hope I never have to use their services, and if I do, may it be a last resort.

Just now, the clock has struck midnight, and presently, the first day of the new year is over. The Master had promised to me back in November that he would have finished all by this day. Well, this day has come and gone. No one has heard anything from him, and the Monk's allies have not even spotted him, so I am forced to assume the worst. I must face this because whatever has happened to him, he isn't coming back anytime soon. I feel incredibly guilty for not having gone with him, although he would never have allowed it. From this day forth, I am left here. Alone yet not alone, to carry on the fight against the children.

We, a rag-tag trio of a righteous hell-spawn and two humans, must defend this castle and each other. None of us knows when

Imogen will come, but no doubt it will be soon. In the meantime, I can only pray that God will deliver us from whatever may come.

It has been four months since I last wrote to my family. I think, tonight, I will write two letters: one to them, and one to the Count, just in case he should return to find the Devil's promise of my end was served to me.

DEAD OF WINTER

Chapter Forty-four

14 January

Has it been two weeks already? It was just yesterday, I could have sworn, that I had written those two letters I mentioned at the end of my last entry. Surely it was, and everything until now has been one long nightmare.

…

On 3 January, I had begun my time of the month yet again. With everything going on, I had actually completely forgotten about it. With the ever-present looming threat before us, I wondered if I should spend my week in the tower just in case. Eventually, I had decided against it since it was a few days into January and there had been no movement to report. I pondered the possible, yet improbable, fact that Imogen was perhaps not coming at all. It could be that she had taken her revenge on the Count and decided it was enough for her? I doubted that. But maybe the Devil, in his infinite tricks, had actually pulled the wool over my eyes to make me see one thing and not another. It was surely feasible with his track record, so I opted to call his bluff and not seal myself away, foolhardy as it was.

Since the beginning of the month, there had been strange disturbances afoot. The weather had a climatic shift occur that Dumitru could not account for as normal, and all the distant birds and other forest creatures fell silent. Only the wolves, our faithful and fearless first line of defense, stayed behind, but they had become eerily quiet at night. It was as if the land had been holding its breath for something, waiting so patiently for whatever it was to spring up unexpectedly. When the wind blew, it no longer blew in its ferocity as is usual in the Carpathians, but there were mild gusts that barely ruffled the sleeping branches of the trees. A gray sky was all we saw, and the sun and moon hid themselves from us for days. The silence around us made us silent, too, and the castle grew void of all sound save our footsteps.

The fourth Vlad felt this change immediately, and for several days he did not go to his death sleep. He kept awake, always watching quietly out the windows, his obsidian eyes flicking from one place to another. His silence was the most disturbing of all these things; he, who is the most jovial of the three of us, did not laugh or smile, and was almost in a trance until someone would speak to him. We humans felt whatever this was, too. Our senses, despite being dulled, felt the breathless wind. The stillness was maddening.

When I asked my brother-in-law what was happening, it was hard for him to describe. He could only say in not-so-many words that something was coming, but from where or even which direction, he knew not. It was coming from everywhere, yet nowhere.

So, we waited along with nature, holding our breath.

*6 January

It was that evening when all the tension came to a head and erupted like a dormant volcano bursting with spontaneous life to bring death in its wake.

As was my usual regimen, I had just finished my evening prayers in the chapel when the loudest chorus of howls burst forth from all corners of the region. They echoed so that, even though I stood alone in the mosaic hall, it sounded as if the whole pack were in the room with me. The cry was so freakish that all my nerves tingled, and the deepest cold shot through me.

A sudden wind hit the side of the castle hard, and I went to the large window that overlooks the courtyard at the end of the hall to look out. I had barely gotten close when I saw four figures standing in the middle of the yard, and one had long silver hair. Immediately, I threw myself behind the wall to hide, my blood running cold. How had they gotten so close that no one had noticed them until they stood at our front door? I could only guess as my mind began to race and whirl.

Panic hit me like a bus, and I tried to gather my wits and will my body to act. I had prepared for this moment, but when it came so unexpectedly, I was afraid. I had calculated my own hidden motive in the weeks since Lucifer had visited, and once I had come to terms with that inner war I was waging, I knew what I had to do. Yet when I stood there, the only thing that came to my mind was Dumitru. I had to find him.

I don't remember doing it, but gathering my courage, I ran through the double doors to go to the kitchen to find him, yet a large hand caught my arm. It was the Monk, his eyes already ablaze crimson as he held me firm. With a growl, he ordered. "Go to your room, *now*."

That was what he had planned: hiding me in my room while he and Mitică took care of my dirty work. But I was freaking out more than I should have been, and instead responded with. "Where did they come from? How didn't we —"

"Isadora," Vlad spat, stressing each syllable. *"Go to your room."*

I think he had commanded me, but his words had only minor sway. My Vlad would have gotten so angry at my stubbornness, and probably would have called me 'woman' when I said that. "No, I won't leave you two to face them alone —"

"There is no time for this," the Monk swiftly cut me off as his eyes shifted to Dumitru, who had come running from the servant's quarters, his face so pale. Vlad then addressed him instead, literally throwing me at him. "Take her to her room and lock both doors."

"Vlad, please," I begged him, although I knew there would be no way to convince him of letting me stay nearby. However, I had no intention of being set aside as they did all the work. There was nothing more I wanted than to stand side-by-side with them to the very end, but to get there would take some finagling. *"Don't —"*

Before I could say much more, Dumitru hooked his arm around me and hulled me up the stairs, muttering to me about shutting my mouth. Vlad gave both of us one last look before turning away and heading towards the door. My heart sank at the expression on his face, which was one mixed with anger, sadness, but also worry.

Once Mitică had gotten me up to my rooms and set me down, I tried to reason with him, knowing he would expect it. "Mitică, please, let me —"

"Don't be difficult." He scolded as he began to nudge, more like a half-hearted push, me into my bedroom. "We've spoken about this a million times. Just stay here and don't open the door for anyone."

"Please," I grabbed his hand, which had produced the keys. "I'll stay, just don't lock —"

"I'm not stupid, Isadora," he chided in a firm snap, wedging his hand from my grip. "I'll be back for you, I promise."

"That's what the Master said —" the words slipped out, and the trueness of them was a punishment to me. I shut my mouth, biting my lower lip hard.

There was such conflict in his eyes as his brow furrowed. There was something he wanted to say, but something held him back. Just as I was about to ask him, he had pulled me into his arms and kissed my lips so deeply, so longingly. In the months since my marriage to the Count, Mitică had never dared to show me such affection as he had before. The heat of his mouth was shocking, and I accidentally moaned. Then Dumitru released me, and between heavy, shaking breaths, he said to me. "I love you, so I will come for you. Please, stay here until then."

That I had not expected, and I couldn't help but notice that it sounded as if he were saying it for the last time. There was something in his voice that relayed what his heart didn't want to admit. It horrified me, and I went to say something about it, anything, but just like that, Mitică had pushed me into my bedroom, and the door slammed shut. I cried for him, pleaded really, to not shut me away, but the lock bolted from the outside, and his hasty steps faded. I pulled with all my might on the handle, but it wouldn't budge.

Frustrated, I gave up on the door handle and instead crept up to the windows, peeking out through the curtains to see the unfolding scene. Below me, I saw five figures standing in the yard, facing off one another. One, obviously the Monk, and others were Imogen and Andreas, but the other two I didn't recognize. I hadn't predicted that Imogen would bring more back-up with her, but still, only two? Was she so confident that she could easily overcome us? With my plan, however, I was confident not to let it get that far.

Yet still, I watched helplessly from the safe confines of my bedroom, my breath held in my lungs, as they were seemingly having a conversation. There was no way to hear what they were saying, of course, so I watched their body language. Soon enough, Dumitru joined the tense situation, keeping his distance from Vlad. The others didn't appear too pleased by the houseboy's arrival, most likely finding it insulting that he should be present, but my friends stood firm. Surprisingly, there remained a strange peace between the two sides, like neither was willing to make the first move. This made me hold out hope that some truce was being proposed by the fourth Vlad, which he had told me he was considering after Satan's threats. Vlad, a genius orator, I was sure could sway the hearts of the most bloodthirsty to peace, so I waited, in case my plan shouldn't be executed.

I can't quite tell how things fell apart, for they were fine, and then suddenly they weren't. The two underlings suddenly lunged at Vlad and Dumitru while Imogen and Andreas just stood back and watched, uncaring to enter the fray. I'm sure they were waiting to get their hands dirty on me and didn't want to bloody them unnecessarily. I watched from my aerial vantage point, my heart pounding so loud in my ears, tears brimming in my eyes, as the four struggled against one another.

The Monk easily ended the one who had challenged him, whose body turned to blackened dust after Vlad had given him some kind of jerking pull. Out of nowhere, a splash of red was thrown upon the snow from where Dumitru and the other creature fought. My heart went into my throat, and without a doubt, it was my friend who had been wounded. I couldn't let him be hurt because of me. The underling had him in his clutches, no doubt ready for a *coup de grâce*. Vlad froze, most likely persuaded to remain still if he wanted Mitică to live.

There was no time to waste then. Negotiations, if they were negotiations at all, had failed, and I found the courage to pull myself together.

Going to my desk, I pulled out my two letters to my family and the Count, placing them side-by-side. I had spent enough time contemplating my actions in the weeks prior, so taking off my wedding ring and his mother's crucifix, I placed it on the Master's letter. I turned away from both of them. The next thing I sought was the holy water and gulped down a large portion of the liquid.

Having no time to lose, I threw on my wool sweater and retrieved scissors from within my desk. Going to the door, I used the open tool to pry up the pins of the hinges. Being purposefully well-oiled, they were loosened from their places with some force, and within no time, I had successfully shimmied the heavy door ajar. With a sharp tug, the bolt came out of the lock, and I let it fall to the ground with a hefty *smack*. I repeated this on the next door to the hallway that Mitică had locked, and I was free.

So, I rushed as fast as I could down the stairs and to the main entrance, my heart praying to God that I wasn't too late. Without much thought as to anything else, I swung open the smaller door, and a rush of cold air hit my face. It sobered up my shaken senses just a bit, bringing me to the reality that there was no turning back now. Not like it mattered, because I was dead-set on ending what the Master began, no matter the cost. The small door hit the wall with a greater force than I had expected, and I still cried out. *"Enough!"*

Everyone stopped, all eyes coming to me. There was a mixture of shock and awe on their faces, but I didn't bother to look at the rest of them; I only stared at the witch.

Before I was able to utter another syllable, the Monk shouted angrily at me. "Isadora, go back inside!"

"It's alright, Monk," I gave him a glance, seeing the blood sprayed on his shirt and face. He was fearsome, his face contorting in vexation as he tried to make a move towards me. Just as he did, someone uttered a *'tisk-tisk'*, and we both looked to where Mitică was being held by the underling. The horror of what I had seen upstairs was nothing compared to the sight firsthand.

Dumitru was on his knees, the creature standing behind him, holding his white oak stake to my friend's throat. The point was so close to being driven into his jugular, and it took everything in me not to show emotion to it. Blood was trickling gently out of Dumitru's torso, where he had been clawed through his thick coat. Dark bruises were beginning to form on his cheeks and forehead, and blood seeped from a gash near his hairline. His wounds were terrible. Dumitru's eyes showed all the emotion that he couldn't relay in words, and I will never forget them as long as I live. His main expression was that of terror, worry, but also sorrow and anger. All of these things were plastered over his face, which I saw for a split second before turning my eyes back to my prey.

With as much dignity as I could muster, I descended the steps with my head held high. "I'm sick of fighting you, Imogen —"

"Isadora, go back inside!" Vlad repeated with a hiss as his ire flared, but I ignored him.

Not skipping a beat, I reached the bottom of the steps and continued. "There is no need to carry on this useless fighting any longer. You desire my head, don't you? Well, here I am."

Her face was stoic, emotionless, her cold features unmoving as she examined me. Imogen must have immediately thought that it was a trap, knowing we both were playing head games with each other, so she acted the part as I had anticipated. "How very unexpected of you, little Mother," she sneered, her fangs were the color of the snow. "To so easily concede to me. I would have thought you wouldn't give up without a fight. What must have changed to make you so defeated?"

I bit my lip, swallowing the vitriol. She would not get a rise out of me, no matter the provocation. "I will surrender myself to you willingly, only under two conditions: firstly, that you do not harm Vlad the Monk and Dumitru, and let them go free. They are not a part of this and are only under the orders of their Master. And secondly —"

"*Doamnă…*" Mitică's raspy voice tore my heart in half.

It took every ounce of my courage to remain focused, and any feelings I had turned themselves off. "Secondly, to leave this place once all you wish to do is completed."

"Isadora, in *God's* name," the fourth Vlad cried out in a rolling growl. "Stop this now!"

We both didn't listen to either of their pleas, and Imogen raised an eyebrow as she queried. "You would so freely commit yourself to death by my hand?"

"It was predicted, was it not? Why delay what is inevitable?" I tested, a brusque gust whipped through us, my heavy skirts flapping around my legs. The sun was close to setting behind the thick clouds, adorning the sky and clouds afire in hues of red and yellow. These were reflected by the snow, and turned everything to shades of bloody red. "We both have robbed each other of the people we care for the most. Certainly, I cannot defeat you, nor can I escape you. So, do what you will and be done with it."

Imogen's eyes narrowed and her head cocked to one side. The wheels were turning in her brain as she was trying to figure out what I was plotting. After a few seconds of silence, she nodded slowly. "Very well. I agree to your terms."

In a graceful wave of her hand, she dismissed the crony who had been at the ready to end Dumitru. Behind me, I heard a desperate gasp for air as the stake had been removed from against his throat, followed by fits of coughing. My heart melted with relief for that small victory. "Vlad, please take Dumitru inside."

"I will not allow you to kill yourself!" The Monk spat, his tone rising with his anger. He sounded much like the Master then, I have to admit. "Not for our sakes, not for the sake of peace!"

"*Stăpână*, I beg you…" Mitică intervened with a croak. "Don't do this."

"It seems neither of them has any respect for your decision." Imogen's snide grin mocked me for my inability to command them.

Again, I wasn't planning on being goaded to anger, but before I was able to address the Monk, Andreas moved forward to stand beside Imogen. His eyes had been on me the entire time, staring at me intently as I had been ignoring him. "Imogen, who is to say that when your revenge is satiated, these two dogs won't seek retribution? They would rather die than allow her to sacrifice herself."

"They will not be harmed, because they will not seek any kind of revenge," I said to the witch. "Besides, it's three against one now."

Imogen's face scrunched together, her expression perplexed that I was uttering things which were so contrary to my character. "So eager to die, are you?"

"'To be eager' and 'to be resolute' are two different things." It was true, at least in my head, in that moment. I think one is never eager to end life as they know it for the sake of a greater good, but they undertake the burden. "I am determined to end this feud, and I know to do that, I must die."

"*Doamnă...*" I heard Mitică groan, but I stood firm.

"Enough of these heroics," Andreas snarled, and suddenly he was behind me, grabbing my hair. The pain was sharp, and I yelped as he yanked me to him, his other hand latching onto my throat. I felt his talons dig into my skin. I growled, trying to claw at his arm or beat him with my elbows, or even kick him. All had no effect.

Just then, as if some signal had been given that I hadn't seen, the unnamed demon was suddenly upon Dumitru again. Everything happened so quickly that before I knew it, there was another splash of red, and my friend slumped into the snow. I went to scream, but nothing came out as Andreas' claws threatened to rip my neck to shreds if I moved. Honestly, I didn't quite care in the moment, but from where he subdued me, I could not run to help my friend. Although I think I knew by the time I got to him, it would have been too late.

The underling, whoever he was, was faster than anything I had ever seen before. During the previous fight, he must have just been holding back against Dumitru. I thought the Count was the fastest, but he was something extraordinary. Once he had finished off Dumitru, Vlad had already pounced in his direction to try and protect him, of course, being too late. The Monk, just for a millisecond, faltered at the sight and smell of the blood, and gave the demon the chance to dodge his attack. In the blink of an eye, the creature had impaled the brother of the Impaler in the heart through his back and out the other side.

The fourth Vlad fell hard to his knees from the force behind the stake, shock mostly registering on his face. I struggled against Andreas, tears blurring my eyes. To my relief, Vlad did not turn to dust, but merely ceased to function as he sank into the snow and grew still. I knew he was not dead, but that didn't lessen the impact of his incapacitation.

The sight of both of my friends, the ones I love, lying in pools of their own blood in the snow is, again, something I will never forget. I don't even remember what I did next, but I know my knees lost the ability to hold me up, although it seemed Andreas held me in my place. My ears no longer heard anything, and my eyes could not see through my tears. Intense grief and anger came over me and consumed my very being. It was only then that I realized that Imogen had been speaking to me in my ear.

"You caused the deaths of others that I cared for; I might as well give you the same." That was the part I came in on, and she seized my chin to make me look at what was Mitică. "The houseboy had feelings for you, didn't he? We all saw it in the way he would try to protect you from us. He was such a nuisance, and now he's dead, all thanks to you." She paused, reading the expression on my face. "It's amazing, do I detect feelings for him too? What would your husband think if he knew this?" Imogen burst into a girlish giggle. "Ah, but wait, he's dead to this earth, too. And now we have your brother-in-law, although not quite dead yet, he will be dust soon enough. There are uses we have for him, so at least you have one out of three that still live."

After that, I couldn't feel anything. In those moments, all I could think was that I had caused their deaths, and I was determined to follow. I hadn't expected Imogen to keep her word, but I thought she would have been keen on her vengeance before she attacked my friends. I had miscalculated. There was no reason to live then, and I met eye-to-eye with the witch. I was about to spit some heinous slurs when Andreas' hand came over my mouth.

"So, what shall we do with you now? With no one left, I think I have a good idea." Another sinister grin formed on her lips; this time her eyes flashed in their gold-crimson. "Let's have some fun, Andreas. What say you to a hunt?"

My eyes widened as the implications of her words sank into me. Imogen intended to toy with me before finally seeking her revenge, and my blood froze. The playing field had been flipped upside down, and now I was their prey, and she the hunter. I knew I had to have her end my life then, for I couldn't wait much longer.

Once Andreas had agreed to this game, he let me go, and I fell to my hands and knees.

Above me, I heard Imogen say. "This will be the ultimate test of that cunningness you claim. We will give you until midnight for a head start."

"Why exert yourselves?" I think I said something close to that. "I'm right here, and you've defeated me. Just do it."

"Where's the fun in that?" Imogen lifted me by my hair again, and I struggled to my feet. "Go now, run for your life. Don't look back, lest you be turned to salt."

With another hard push, she let go of me, and I was sent back down to the ground. By the time I had recovered, the witch had already turned her back on me and was walking towards the castle. Wrath welled in my chest, and I went to spring to my feet to snatch her hair, but a hand grabbed my arm, and this time I was lifted securely to my feet. I glared menacingly at Andreas, ripping my arm out of his grasp, but his eyes relayed a different emotion. He seemed almost sympathetic, but I still turned away from him, my gaze falling on my friends' motionless bodies.

"Come away," he whispered, taking my arms and nearly dragging me from the scene. I tried to resist his domineering strength by digging my heels into the snow, but he easily hauled me to the gate. By his command, the chain was released, and the gate rose.

Taking one last look behind me, I saw Imogen entering the castle, her loyal henchman following behind her. Something rooted deep in my heart, as if her doing that added another layer of violation. I am *Stăpâna* of the castle, not her, but there she went, usurping my rightful place. This was her *coup d'état*, her revolution, and I was forced to flee in exile and to die by either her hand or exposure.

Andreas let me go, pushing me across the threshold of the gate as it descended back into its place. In another whisper, he said just low enough for me to hear. "Go north, follow the river until you reach the lake. I'll meet you there before midnight."

I felt another emotion come to the surface, and this time it was fury. No doubt it was some kind of trap for his own motives, and I had no intention of following his directions. There were so many things I could have said to him, but I turned away and began to walk over the stone bridge. "Go to Hell."

The sun had dipped just below the horizon, and my long shadow faded as I disappeared into the forest. I hid behind a tree off the main road to stop for a moment to think. Tears were still streaming down my face, and I roughly wiped them from my cheeks. I had to think about the future, not the past, and reformulate my plan. There was no time for the sorrow in my heart to be released, but later I would certainly atone for my actions.

"God, deliver them, deliver me." I prayed as I buttoned my sweater. Looking up to the blackening sky above the sparse canopy, my breath shuddered in the frozen air. "Wait for me, Mitică."

And with that, I headed south, deeper into the forest. My first plan may not have worked, but I prayed my second one would.

Later...

I had no idea what time it was, or even where I was really, but I hadn't stopped moving for hours. Once I had reached the river, which was frozen solid, I was easily able to cross it. Since I knew their kind could not cross the running water, I knew the greater the barriers I placed between us, the better. As I went along, anyplace I found more difficult ground, I took it, going places where they would not expect me to. I went high and low up the side of the mountain, determined to keep moving no matter the cost.

I had lost feeling in my legs and arms, even my face, only about ten minutes into my trek. The bitter cold of this land was seeping into my bones, making it hard to move fluidly, and there were times I would step clumsily and slip. To my luck, I found an old white oak tree mixed in with the evergreens and broke off a sizable branch that I could use as a walking stick and a weapon.

During this time, I kept on having the oddest flashes of memory. Recollections of Dumitru and I playing in the snow before the Count left, him pouring me the *ţuică*, kissing and touching me on the sudsy floor that hot August day when he professed that he loved me like the sun loves a flower. He wanted to give me life then, but in the end, I had only given him death. My heart stung with regret that I never got to tell him how much I cared for him. In the end, I only felt that I had done wrong by the only living man who ever told me he loved me.

Hours passed, and I hadn't encountered a single creature, nor felt the presence of any other being. But if I couldn't even feel my own hands, I'm sure my perception of my surroundings was flawed. I wanted to call out to the wolves, but not knowing the time, I could have been giving away my position. Soon enough, I knew I would have to find a hiding place for the rest of the night and conceal myself from Imogen. As long as I made it to dawn, there was a greater chance I could backtrack to the castle and catch the witch unaware.

The moon faded in and out from behind the clouds, its waning phase shedding so little light before me, but I was grateful for it. When the great celestial body had reached its highest, I knew then that I should find a place to rest. I was exhausted, mentally and physically, but my immediate goal was to see the dawn again, and I would not fail in that. After some time, I found a dense thicket amongst some rocks with low-hanging branches from the nearby trees concealing it. Hoping that nothing already lived there, I crawled into the brush and curled into a ball. I closed my eyes for a moment, and I must have drifted off.

I don't think I had enough time to dream when a hand shook my shoulder. Eyes flashing open, I fought with my dulled senses to focus again, and when they did, Andreas was kneeling next to me beneath the thick, low-lying branches.

"I *told* you to go north." He reprimanded, his blue eyes shining in the dimness. "There isn't much time, we must go. Imogen is looking for you now."

"*We?*" I pushed him away, although he didn't budge. "I'm not going anywhere with you."

The Greek's grip bore down on my shoulder. "Isadora, you have to trust —"

"Why should I trust you?" I spat as I tried to break his hold. "You tried to kill me, you killed my friends, took all that is mine."

"I tried to save you when Maxim was about to bleed you dry, but instead, Imogen whisked me away with her magic. By the time I realized what had happened, I could do nothing. You must believe me, *koukla*." There was a genuine earnestness to his voice as Andreas' other hand cupped my cheek. "I want you to come away with me. There's nothing left for you here."

His touch revolted me, no matter how tender it was. "There is no reason for me to believe any of that."

"Everything I've said to you, did they mean nothing? You can't lie to me and say you felt nothing when we were together." He bent down slightly, his face inches from mine, as if he expected to be allowed to kiss me. "I want to love you, not kill you."

I couldn't stand to hear any of this, and throwing a few Latin prayers his way, he recoiled just enough that I could break free. Swiftly, I escaped the confines of the thicket and was about to take off running when he was suddenly in front of me, barring my way. I held out my staff before me to threaten him. "I told you from the very beginning that if you cared for me, you should leave me alone. My duty is here. I will die before I abandon what my husband entrusted to me."

"Your…*husband?*" Andreas repeated with a sour expression on his face. "Don't you remember what he did to you? All that heartbreak I saw on your face when you saw Cosima and him together, was that nothing?"

"And I remember what you did to me." I countered, stepping around him as I kept the sharp end pointed at him. "If you intend to betray Imogen, I suggest you run for your life before I take both of yours."

"With what do you plan on killing us? That stick?" Andreas ripped it too easily from my hands and flung it a few meters away. "I'm willing to give you a new life, a new existence, with me. I will protect you from Imogen and make you happier than you could ever have been here. Your life in that castle is dead, Isadora, your 'husband' is dead, and your family with him is dead. Have a new life, and come with me."

I said nothing. There was no use in even thinking about a life with him because I wasn't planning to be living that long anyway. Besides, I had promised Dumitru that I would join him, and once I had taken Imogen down, no doubt I wouldn't be far behind. Knowing the Greek as I do, becoming his partner would make me hate myself. If he was sincere, which he seemed to be, I could never forgive myself for forsaking my duty to the Count, no matter if he was dead or alive.

"Come with me, Isadora," Andreas held out his hand, but when I did not take it, his eyes narrowed further and burned red. "Isadora, *come* to me."

He had compelled me, and I could feel my weight shifting to move forward when I realized it. Swallowing hard, I shifted my weight back on my heels, keeping them anchored as I shook my head. Behind me, there was an unexpected ruffling of underbrush, and we both turned. From either side, the rocks seemed to produce pairs of tiny glowing white orbs from the darkness. A chill overcame me as the distinctive malevolent growls of the wolves manifested themselves from the black.

"Isadora," Andreas pleaded in his compulsion, reaching his hand out for me to take it. *"Come to me."*

They were my wolves, but their appearance was petrifying as their teeth dripped with cords of saliva and blood. Whose blood? I couldn't guess. The white one was present, matted with tuffs of blood, as he led the others not toward me, but had their sights trained on the Greek. Turning back to him, I stood my ground as my children came around me, their jaws snapping, as they stalked toward Andreas. Their approach caused him to take a step back. The pack was closing in on him, their backs arching downwards as they prepared to strike. As if on cue, they pounced just as something hit me.

Whatever happened next, I could not say. It felt like I was flying, being clutched in an iron grip as I flew through the air. Then, suddenly, I was let go and hit the snow hard enough to knock the breath out of me. I rolled and slid, but finally came to a stop some distance from where I had been dropped. After that, I can't remember anything.

SILVER LINING

Chapter forty-five

*7 January
Epiphany

When I awoke next, my body was so stiff and my eyes were so heavy that I couldn't open them. I wasn't cold anymore, but my skin had been so numb for so long that I wasn't sure if I could feel at all. In my half-consciousness, all I wanted was to sleep and forget all the bad dreams that I had dreamt, but when cool fingertips touched my cheek, my eyes instinctively fluttered halfway open.

My head was still in a whirlwind from my tumble, but after some time, my head cleared a bit, and I could move again. Groaning, I strained to bring back my sluggish senses, but I couldn't make out the figure who was next to me in the dark. As my vision cleared a little, a ghostly pale face materialized in the gloom, and my heart rose in my throat. "M-Monk?"

"Can you not still tell us apart, sweetest one?"

At first, there was no comprehension that the man before me was my husband. In my logical brain, there was no way he could be sitting there before me. Logic told me it was really a ghost, or a figment of my imagination, or perhaps I had died. My logic was not very sound after all I had endured that day, and I blinked at him. In the night, his nocturnal eyes glowed as he examined me worriedly, and he waited for a response.

I carefully reached out to touch his hand. "Is it you, or a ghost?"

He squeezed down hard as he caught my hand, bringing it to his lips to kiss. Those sensations were too real to be my imagination, and when he whispered. "It is me. I am here with you."

"Oh God," I cried out breathlessly as we closed the distance between us. I embraced the Count so tightly, and wept as with one hand he grabbed my low back to bring us closer together. Ardently we sought each other's lips and I kissed him desperately, my fingers knotting in his already tangled locks. He wholeheartedly reciprocated, and we both exchanged frenzied kisses that I never wanted to end.

I broke from his lips to kiss his jaw and neck.

He purred happily — a sound I never thought I would hear again. "Beloved, I have missed you so."

"I have missed you more." I returned to his lips, remembering their gentleness and the heat they ignite in me. "They told me you weren't coming back, that you were dead but alive. I thought I'd never see you again, but thank God you're here, thank God, thank God."

Those brown eyes of his that I love so much softened as his hand massaged my cheek. His thumb wiped away my salty tears as his brow creased in a new worry. "My beautiful girl, who told you these things?"

"Your father…" I whispered after a pause. "Imogen and Andreas, too."

The Master frowned deeply and then kissed me again, this time tenderly. Keeping his voice just as soft as his eyes, he met my gaze again. "Since you are here, then Imogen has taken my house. Where is my brother and Dumitru?"

"The Monk is incapacitated. Dumitru is —" I choked suddenly, tears bursting from my eyes yet again. I hadn't finished the sentence, and I had been reduced so low.

The Count hanged his head, his eyes shutting tightly. There was pain on his face, but he masked the full extent of it by resting his cheek against mine to hide from me. My husband cooed a series of lulling shushes, stroking my hair as he did.

His efforts did comfort me, but the torment and shame in my chest were far greater. "Forgive me for failing you, for losing everything you entrusted to me —"

"Isa, you did not fail me. You could never fail me." He was adamant about it, but I most certainly had failed him. If I had been some captain under him when he commanded armies, I would have been put to the sword for my defeat. The Count switched the subject, moving his face back to mine. "Why did she not harm you when she took the castle?"

Thinking back on her words made my anger return, but I swallowed it. "Imogen decided to hunt me, to test my cunning."

The Master's jaw tensed and nostrils flared, his eyes flashing red at that answer. He held me possessively and growled. "She will not find you here, and even if she does, she cannot and will not touch you."

Before his anger could flare more, I touched his cheek, and he latched onto my hand, bringing it to his mouth. My blood grew hot when he kissed my palm and wrist so passionately, as if that were his vow to me that it would be so. Slowly, I sat up, and he followed me, unwilling to let go of my hand. "Where are we?"

"In a cave, not too far from the castle," he explained, still fascinated by my palm, perhaps noticing my absent wedding ring. "I used to use these for the storage of military supplies, so it is well hidden. Only I know these exist now."

Ingenious, as always. I went to touch his shoulder to bring him to me, but he abruptly withdrew, and a piercing hiss was shot my way. Just as he had dodged my touch, his face twisted in pain, and he whined like an injured animal. The Master grabbed his left shoulder and gritted his teeth; the razor edge of his canines glinted with an ivory sheen. I was positively shocked.

"Forgive me," he grunted through labored breaths, sounding angrier at himself than at me. He averted his face to conceal his monstrous features that had risen from the pain.

However, that didn't hide the red that blossomed into his light gray shirt, and a dread crushed my heart to a pulp. "What happened to you?"

He didn't answer, turning his face farther away. Whatever did happen, I could only assume it was the reason why he had fallen off the face of the earth and why all his enemies could boast that he had died but was undead. I had to see, so I drew nearer again, not caring if I would be subjected to his ire. His left arm was limp, and the fingers of his good hand trembled to keep hold of it to his side. Cautiously, I unbuttoned his shirt and moved the fabric away. I was surprised he allowed me to touch him again, especially when it was to reveal a weakness.

Beneath was unlike any wound I had ever seen. A rotten black mass stretched from his collarbone, down his chest, and into his shoulder, and feathered blue and gray at the edges. All the veins, which were in the process of being infected, were swollen and rose from his porcelain skin. They knotted in on themselves, appearing purple and varicose. At the very center of this, situated in the middle of the left side of his chest, was a gaping, bloodied hole. It had been clawed numerous times, most likely by his own hand, to try and dig out whatever had infected him. The diseased blood oozed black, mixing with the healthy red in a coagulated mess. Being exposed, it smelled of rotten flesh, and I had to cover my mouth to hide my gag reflex. It wasn't gangrene, I couldn't tell what it was, but I promptly replaced the fabric over the wound.

"I believe it is some kind of mixture of garlic and silver." The Master had almost read my mind as he took in a deep breath, his features returning to normal. "No doubt it has some of Imogen's black magic in it."

Leaning forward, I rested lightly on his opposite shoulder. "What can I do?"

"Nothing," he kissed my hair. "I need to rest —"

"What you *need* is —"

"I know what I need, wife." He chided, adding as he read my mind again. "I will not take any from you."

I wanted to help him in any way that I could, and as I told the fourth Vlad once, I would give him my last drop of blood if he asked for it. In this case, he needed it, and I could not provide it. Raising my eyes, I had to kiss him again.

He wanted to hold me, but when he tried to lift his hand off his arm, he could not. The injured arm began to shake uncontrollably, and the weakness frustrated him.

Wasting no time, I took a section of one of my underskirts off, forming it into a sling and wrapping it from his elbow to shoulder, tying it at one end. He looked funny wearing the frilly muslin garment like that, but it supported his affected shoulder well. A relief came over his face as I prompted him to lie down and placed my sweater under his head as a pillow. His welfare was much more important to me than my own, and I would have done so much more to help him if I could.

"Beloved, you will freeze." He sighed, eyelids half open from pained exhaustion.

"Don't worry about me, husband," I reassured him as I lay next to him on the cold stone. I suppressed a shiver. "Just rest, I won't leave your side."

He gave me a knowing look before resting his head back against the wool and closing his eyes. Soon enough, he became still and calm, although I doubt he was actually sleeping. I kept watch even when my eyes grew heavy and my body sluggish. The damp chill was just enough to keep me awake, but I repressed showing how it was affecting me. Again, I'm not sure how much time passed, but as I expected, I lost all feeling in my hands again, even when they were tucked underneath my arms. After that, I began to fade in and out of consciousness from my own exhaustion.

Hours passed before the Count stirred again, and I felt him get up. The wool of my sweater came around me, and I groaned in protest. I was aware of his movements, but he seemed to disappear for a while when something big and furry came next to me where the Count had been. I opened my eyelids and saw a large black wolf resting in his place. I wasn't frightened because I knew it was him... somehow. He lay right close to me, nearly over my upper half, and rested his head against mine. The fur enveloped me, and when my own warmth returned to my limbs, I fell asleep.

Morning…

The fur was gone when I came to, and daylight was visible at the opening of the cave. Instead of the wolf, the Master lay half over me as he slept like the dead. I was relieved that he was finally resting, so I didn't move to disturb him. It was unexpectedly comforting to have him so close, and I lay my head against his. To have him gone for so long, and then suddenly be there, was a blessing. As I examined him in the dawning light, I noticed he was shirtless, only being covered slightly by the sling. When my eyes moved down, I discovered he was completely nude. He lay flush against me, one of his legs, which he had brought over my hips, hid what lay between his from me. I admired the thick muscle of his thigh, my cheeks warming at the sight.

The Count must have heard my heartbeat increase, for he stirred, moving his injured arm just slightly to bring me tighter to his bare chest. It must have been feeling better since he showed no outward sign of pain. His nose inhaled my scent as it rested in its favorite place, but in due course, he raised his head to look at me. He appeared significantly better than last night; his skin was not so waxen and ghostly, and there was almost a vitality to his face again as he smiled warmly. "My rosy-cheeked nymph, are you well?"

"*Very* well, husband," I reached forward to catch his lips.

He was a bit perplexed at my tone, but then his eyes flickered down both of our figures. When the Count returned to my gaze, his eyebrows had raised in stupefaction at his appearance. "Forgive me…"

"For what?" I then whispered in his ear that if it weren't so cold, I would join him.

"Be careful, young lady," he chuckled with such mirth when he kissed me, and I raised my hips to his, against his heeding. "You would be surprised how passion can drive a man even in a state such as I am."

I was so desperate for him to lie next to me for a few more hours that I whined when he raised himself. Severely wounded as he was, he always had more sense than I. Yet I watched him, his perfection making my heart swoon. As he sat up, however, I caught a glimpse of more than I should have, and my face grew unbearably hot.

The Count straightened, tensing as he noticed my sudden change. He cleared his throat, shifting away from me. "Normally, I would be flattered and would gladly accommodate you, my dear, but we are wasting daylight. We cannot stay here."

I frowned, although I supposed I should have known better. All sense of my usual decorum was out the window, and I knew I had to get over it before it consumed me. "Where will we go?"

"Another cave similar to this one that is even closer to the castle." He explained as he reached for his clothes. "It will be slow-moving, so we have little time. Surely, Imogen is angered that she could not find you last night, so we must keep her guessing, especially since Andreas saw you."

I bit my lip as I sat up, sliding on my sweater. "Well, let's go."

Noon...

About a dozen wolves had been waiting outside, guarding the cave while we slept. They followed us as we started our trek, and to my delight, my dark gray wolf was among them; the white one was present, his fur had the same patches of dried blood crusted to it.

As we walked, my mind kept wandering back to Mitică and my promise I had made to him. With the Count's miraculous homecoming, I was no longer completely alone, but I felt this deepening conflict in my soul that I still had to fulfill my promise. In my letter that I had written to the Master, I told him that he doesn't need me to achieve salvation, but only God. I pondered if I should still go through with my plan to end Imogen by myself.

We all had been moving for some time, walking at a regular pace through the snow as the sun moved to its highest behind the clouds. It was difficult for the Master as the daytime is his weakest period, and being weak as he already was, he struggled. He did his best not to show it, but his labored footsteps were evidence enough.

I had not eaten since noon the previous day, and though I didn't feel hungry, I was feeling faint, which was worsened by the dull ache in my lower abdomen. Never would I admit to him that I was feeling light-headed, but I was forced by my own feebleness to do so when I did faint for just a second. Of course, the Count caught me before I lost my balance and rested me against a tree. With a firm command, he told me to wait there, and before I could say anything, he went behind a tree and disappeared. Some of the wolves had followed him, but my gray buddy and a few others stuck by me.

Minutes passed, and I had begun to doze from my fatigue. The warmth of the gray wolf who lay against my lap and the sun, being just mild enough, brought my weary mind to rest. I had just lost consciousness when the wolves began to growl in unison, and a chill ran down my spine. That sensation is all too familiar to me, and my eyes flashed open.

"Isadora," Andreas stood several feet away from the perimeter that the wolves had established, his hands up in surrender. "Tell them I mean no harm."

My eyes narrowed as a new surge of adrenaline brought me to full wakefulness. It startled me that he would show up in broad daylight, and I unconsciously clung to my gray wolf. "Even if I could tell them, they don't answer to me."

"You know I come in peace," the Greek said, so confident in himself. "And I have brought a gift for you."

Discreetly as I could, I scanned the area for the Master, but he was nowhere to be found. Surely, he wasn't far away, but just far enough not to be detected. "No matter what you give me, it won't change my opinion of you."

He grinned and swallowed my jibe. "This, I believe, you will be most pleased with."

From the underbrush next to him, he bent down and lifted something long and heavy, wrapped in a blanket. From the shape of it, there was no doubt that it was a body, and my breath halted in my lungs. With the utmost caution, Andreas entered the sea of growling wolves, watching them out of the corner of his eye as he approached. They drew back slightly to let him pass, although they still bared their teeth and nipped at his heels.

The gray wolf rose from my lap, his whole body shaking as he hissed and snarled at the Greek. Andreas showed no fear whatsoever to them, and when he came just close enough, he set the body before me as if it were an offering. "I went to great lengths to procure him for you, and I even went so far as to spare a few drops of my blood to ensure he kept his life."

My heart leapt in my chest and burned my veins in frightened anticipation. I wanted to rush to the mass, but knowing to beware of Greeks bearing gifts, I inched my way closer. To my horror, it was Dumitru's corpse that was wrapped so snugly in the blanket, the pallor of his face clashed against the bruises and dried blood. It turned my stomach over. On impulse, I choked and brought my arms around him, but instead of a stiff, lifeless carcass, he was pliable and warm. Andreas wasn't playing some cruel trick on me; Mitică was still alive.

"He was very close to death by the time I got to him." The Greek took a step to test the waters and to come even closer. "We all were sure he was dead, but your friend is too resilient for his own good."

I wanted to cry out in relieved joy, but I was in too much shock to feel anything. Clutching Dumitru tightly as if he would slip away, I raised my unbelieving eyes to Andreas. "Why would you save him when it was you who prompted Imogen to kill them both?"

"Yes, I did persuade her otherwise, but I could see how much his death affected you." He didn't like the words coming out of his own mouth as he openly cringed at them. "I thought that giving him back to you would make you see that I have only your best interests in mind. I have no love for the houseboy, but you do. Therefore, I am willing to help him on your behalf."

I also didn't like the things he said because they contradicted each other, and trying to make sense of them confused me. "If you care so much for me, why did you violate my trust?"

His annoyance that I wasn't giving him the praise he wanted grew. No doubt, he wanted me to be grateful to him so that he could spirit me away and be done with his charade of caring for Dumitru. "Listen, I didn't know Maxim and Ludevit knew where I had taken you, but when they showed up, I could not have denied them. They would have ripped you apart…"

I said nothing in reply.

He paused to inch closer. "Yes, I had planned to take you for myself that day. However, it didn't go as I had hoped." Slowly, Andreas knelt before me to come to my level. "But I still desire you, *koukla mou*, and I will do all I'm able to hinder Imogen."

"Andreas," my shoulders slouched as I sighed exasperatedly. "You know I cannot —"

"Will his ghost care for you?" The blue-eyed Greek snapped. "Can your houseboy give you all that I can?"

All I could do was bite my tongue from biting back at him.

"I admire your sense of duty, I truly do." He reached forward over Mitică's body to brush my cheek with his fingertips. I flinched at his touch, which had haunted me for months. "I know you will need more time to think, but I ask you to leave Imogen be and come with me. The houseboy can come with us too, I promise."

"I…won't leave —"

"Just how long do you think you can last out here?" His frustration at my rejection was boiling to the surface. "Your little wolf friends may help you, but you both will die. They may be able to whisk you away at a moment's notice, but they are only so useful in the end. If you don't die from starvation or exposure, you'll die by Imogen's hand. You can't run from her forever."

He was right to a point, but also very wrong. I wanted to strike a deal with him and say that if he were to kill Imogen, I would go with him with no strings attached. However, with the Count's reappearance, I didn't need to make such a desperate bargain. "Maybe I don't intend on running forever."

Andreas' brow furrowed, and he grasped my chin to pull my face to meet his. "You still will stand against Imogen, knowing you will die?"

After an intense stare, I maneuvered my chin out of his hand. "I am a descendant of the Master. You should know that I don't give up until it's all over."

"You're just as stubborn as him…" He sighed again frustratingly. "I will give you one more day. If she doesn't find you tonight, she will be out here day and night, and you won't be able to move so freely."

I nodded since I didn't want to answer anymore, and turned my attention to my wounded friend. Suddenly, Andreas grabbed the back of my neck with great force and kissed me, sliding his tongue into my mouth. I didn't appreciate his roughness and tried to pull away as he was nearly suffocating me. Even so, with it was relayed a deep longing that confounded me. The wolves lunged forward threateningly, but the Greek only continued to suck out my will to resist. Just when I thought he was going to push me to the ground, Andreas stopped his motions, his eyes flashing open. Awkwardly, he removed his tongue and began to sniff my neck as a dog would sniff something foreign.

"W-What is it?" I stuttered out.

"Nothing…" He muttered after a long moment. "Must be the wolves…"

Not long after that, he bade me a goodbye, his puzzled expression never leaving his face. Taking a few steps into the dark shadiness of a tree, he spontaneously vanished into thin air. After waiting a few seconds, I vigorously wiped my lips and tongue on my sleeve and spat out his saliva.

"It disgusts me how smitten he is with you." The Count's voice, laced with ire, made me jump. He grumbled about how he should have ripped his head in half. Without saying another word to me, he knelt to view the unconscious Mitică. "He is well enough, but now we must hurry. I had planned to carry you, but it seems I must carry him."

With one arm, the Count lifted him over his good shoulder. His anger was fueling him with enough power to carry Dumitru, but the lasting effects of this exertion worried me.

"Come, it is not much farther." He hissed with flaring nostrils. "Our children are masking our scents, so even if Andreas is using Dumitru to track us, he will lose us soon enough."

I nodded again, and keeping close to my gray wolf, I followed behind the Master.

Early evening…

The rest of the trip had been spent in awkward silence. While the Count stewed over Andreas' actions, I fretted over his words. It was hard for me to wrap my mind around the fact that Andreas has greater feelings for me than I had anticipated, but I know for certain that they are not love. He must possess me, and I present him with that challenge. His infatuation with me is the real reason he pursues me. But I still had to wonder if he is more genuine than I thought him to be.

Once we had settled in the new cave, which was much larger than the previous one, the Master set out to find his own nourishment before he would sleep. I was left with the unconscious Mitică for almost an hour until he returned, gorged on blood. His anger had cooled only a little, and he asked me to lie with him a bit before he would rest. I did without protest, but as soon as I had gotten next to him, the Master kissed me and licked my lips. When he drew back, he was grimacing, as if the kiss had left a terrible taste in his mouth. Just as I was about to ask what had upset him, he said to me. "Never kiss him again. Your lips are mine, and I do not want to taste any other man on them."

It was obvious he was still irritated by the liberties Andreas had taken against my consent, but this wording was very reminiscent of his old behavior. He had every right to be aggravated, but did he really have to say it like that? Even though he wasn't chastising me, it left me feeling ill at ease. I nodded, and he kissed me on my forehead and told me to stay near Dumitru for the night in case he should wake. Then, as the sun set, and we were all settled in, the Master slept.

When I had moved over to my friend, I finally had some time to examine my Dumitru's wounds. Just as Andreas had said, Mitică's lacerations on his torso had nearly healed from the blood he was given, although he still had a long way to go. I cleaned off the dried blood on his abdomen and face using a torn piece of my skirt and some snow I had melted. It was the best I could do for him, and afterward I replaced his clothes and wrapped us both in the blanket. As I lay there, I thanked God that two of my loved ones had been restored to me by some miracle. Whatever the reason for it, I didn't ask questions, but gave thanks for the moment.

And with our combined body heat warming us, I had no issue falling asleep at Mitică's side.

*8 January

Early morning, before dawn…

I was startled awake by Dumitru stirring next to me. His movements had been heavy and languid as he had rolled over to rest his head on my shoulder. My friend's eyes were open, though his eyelids drooped as he roused himself from his deep sleep. I never thought I'd ever be so happy to see those gray eyes shine with life. Beneath the blanket, I clenched down on his hand, mine having somehow become interlocked with his in sleep.

Dumitru breathed out each syllable of my name with a perplexed intonation, like he wasn't sure if it was me. I'm not sure why I did, but I kissed his bruised forehead and whispered to him gentle coos to reassure him that he was safe.

"You finally wake, Dumitru." The Count appeared next to me, his features seemed so angular and hard in the dim light.

A deep and uncomfortable awkwardness settled in my stomach that my husband had found me in a compromising position with Mitică. I tried to hide my embarrassment, but no doubt the Count saw through me as he always does.

Dumitru instantly drew back from me, letting go of my hand as he tried to sit up. He was wide awake then and stuttered out. "M-Master, when did you return?"

"The night before last…" The Count's voice drifted off for a moment, and then switched to Romanian to speak to his servant.

I found it quite rude that I was literally between the two of them as they spoke in a language I still don't fully understand, so I sat up with my arms folded. Despite my lacking ability, I caught a large portion of what they were saying, especially when the Count asked Dumitru what had happened when Imogen took the castle. Mitică tensed as he recalled it, and when he looked over at me, we met eye contact. I tried with all my might to relay to him in that gaze not to say a word about what had gone down, but he turned his eyes from me to his Master. Gulping, he went off in quick spurts of dialogue about it, hoping I wasn't going to understand him.

"Shut up," I warned him, but Dumitru kept rattling off everything, so I foolishly tried putting my hand over his mouth. The Master caught my forearm and, with the massive strength of his good arm, lowered it to my lap. So, I was made to forcibly sit there and be ratted out.

Mitică hadn't even finished when the Count's grip bore down excessively on me. "Is this true? Of your own accord, you gave yourself over to Imogen? That is why you drank the holy water again? You wanted to kill her and yourself?"

The Master's wrath always frightened me, but this was laden with a fury that he was trying to keep from erupting. I didn't want to answer, and after shooting Mitică a death stare, I pulled on my husband's grip. "I had no intention of dying —"

"Irrelevant," the Master snapped and yanked on my arm to subdue me. "What were you thinking?"

"Călugărul said that Beelzebub told her to kill herself when he came to inform us of your defeat, Master." Dumitru tried to chime in to defend what he saw as the reason for my actions, but it didn't help. "He said that she would either die by her own hand or Imogen's, but that she would be damned either way."

Eyes burning a bright crimson, my husband was failing to calm his rage. When he spoke, in spite of that, his voice sounded more hurt than angry. "Why did you not tell me?"

"There is no excuse. But in the end, I failed in the attempt only because Andreas wants to keep me alive for his own reasons. It doesn't matter now." Ignoring Mitică's bewildered expression, I looked to the Count. "I thought I was the last one of us left alive after that day was done."

The Master's outrage was becoming a concoction of different emotions, the main one being pain. As the impact of my words sank into his thick skull, his iron vice on my arm lessened as well as did the intense color of his eyes. His jaw still tightly clenched, the Count sighed. "We will rest until the afternoon…" He stood and had turned his back to both of us, but then he spoke, only addressing me. "Never be so reckless again, wife."

I couldn't guarantee that.

We watched as he returned to his corner of the cave and lay down to go to his death sleep just as the dawn came. Mitică and I stared at each other for a long while, both of us wondering the same thing about the Count's behavior. Hidden under his exterior, the berserker was ebbing to the surface. Perhaps he had not realized how close he had come to losing all three of us, or he hadn't seen the full reality of our situation. It was certain to us that when the Master and Imogen would stand face-to-face, there would be no clemency, only blood.

Chapter Forty-Six

WHOM FORTUNE FAVORS

Late afternoon…

When the Count awoke, he didn't say much of anything to us and was eerily quiet. To try and show my support, I helped adjust the sling and check his wound before we left. It was still terrible, though the bleeding hole had healed. It was better than nothing, and I was grateful for that small blessing.

All three of us and the wolf pack were just about to leave when I took the Count aside and attempted to lessen his pent-up rage with a few gentle kisses and whispered sweet nothings. He was rigid when I touched him, but did submit a bit to my advances. When I endeavored to deepen the kiss, though, he bit down on my lower lip hard enough to cause me a sharp twinge of pain, though it wasn't enough to draw blood. I could not pull away since he had brought his arm around me to keep me in place, but also because my lip would have been torn from my face if I tried.

He released me after a few seconds when I whined from the pulsing ache, and the coldness in his gaze sent shivers through me. "That is your punishment for keeping me in the dark yet again. For one who wishes to bring me into the light, the number of times you blind me with darkness is dismaying."

The manner of the Master's tone crushed my soul in guilt, but at the same time, I thought how hypocritical he was in saying that. He always kept me in the dark 'to protect me', so how was I so wrong in doing the same? I was at such a loss to answer him with any reasonable response that I just started to say. "I only want to pro—"

"Protect..." he finished the word, a deep frown forming over his deadly teeth. "If you wish to protect me, you would protect yourself."

Then he released me and walked out of the cave where the wolves and Dumitru were waiting. My lip was swollen and throbbed from the minor trauma it had been dealt, but that pain paled in comparison to the one growing in my chest. Yet again, I had disappointed him. All I had done had been for him and his house, but each time, my methods never pleased him. I remember he once told me that his failure to protect me was a failure of him as a man, and that he would be further damned if he let me slip from him. Could he ever think that it might be the same for me?

I heard Dumitru call to me that it was time to go, and I exited the cave.

Dusk...

It turns out that we had been much closer to the castle than I had realized, at least from the perspective looking up from the valley. The weather of that day had been much gloomier than the previous, and leaving the pack behind, we crossed the frozen Argeş easier than expected, although the Count did have his difficulties. When we reached the other side, we concealed ourselves at the base of the hewn mountain that supported the castle hundreds of feet into the air.

The height was titanic up close, especially from the jagged boulders at the very bottom of the natural structure. We hid ourselves there for a while, plastered against the icy snow that glazed over the stone like a pane of glass.

"Now listen, both of you," the grave seriousness of the Master's voice made me shiver again. "Once we are inside, I will know where they are and how to avoid them. Neither Imogen nor Andreas should see us coming because we have the element of surprise, so neither of you must make any noise, not even your heartbeats."

I rolled my eyes, dreading the impossibility of that, and turned to Mitică who shared the same look as I did. From here on out, I was going to have to grin and bear it, and my body sagged to the side at the thought of having to exert more of my quickly depleting energy.

Dumitru grabbed my arm to steady me. "Master, shouldn't *Doamna* find a safe place to hide? She hasn't eaten in —"

"I am aware," the Count snapped, his patience was paper thin. "Neither have you, but unfortunately, we all must go together."

Because if we don't hang together, we'll surely hang separately, I thought, but kept my pessimism to myself. Giving no further explanation, the Master turned from us and stomped off a few feet away to search for something in the rock face. We both watched him, our spirits daunted by our lack of stamina to even keep ourselves upright. Placing my hand over his, which held my arm, I took in a deep breath. "When I thought you were dead, I came to realize something."

"What is it?"

"I have purposely misled you for a long time with my intentions." I sighed, wishing I had a better time and place to say what I had to. "You say you love me, and I hint that I have affections for you, but then dismiss you in favor of the Master. Please forgive me for being so inconsiderate to you. I never meant to hurt your feelings in any way. All I want is for you to be happy with someone who doesn't see you as second to another. It's not fair to you, and it's not fair to the Master either."

Dumitru blinked at my sudden revelation, and for a few seconds, he was at a loss for words. "W-Why are you telling me this now?"

I frowned. "Just in case."

Pain etched deeply onto my friend's brow, and he went to say something, but was cut off by the Count calling for us to come to him.

Slipping his arm through mine, Mitică whispered that we would finish this conversation later and helped me across the icy rocks to where the Master had revealed an ancient metal door. It groaned terribly, but he eased it open with his massive strength, showing no effort or pain in the process. Then he gestured to us, and when we had filed in, he closed the door.

The air was old and musty, but worst of all, it was pitch black. When I looked to where the Master would be, his eyes glowed a ruddy brown. It was frightening, but the Count put his good arm around my waist and whispered to us. "Stay calm, stay quiet, and follow me."

Being completely blind in this foreign environment was terrifying, and I clung to both of their arms to find my balance as we ascended the stairs. We went up in a winding fashion, sometimes coming to landings, but in the perpetual darkness, it was an eternity of stairs. I tried to keep focused to put one foot in front of the other, but the disorientation was maddening, and my leg muscles burned.

By the grace of the Almighty, after that eternity had passed, we *finally* came to a door. In the air, I could smell the moldiness coming from the other side as well as the hollow echo of a cavern. I knew where we were before the Count even opened the door. Once he had moved it ajar, we both slid through to the opening and into the bowels of the castle. The faint light of a few torches burst brighter at the Master's presence.

Keeping my eyes downcast, I followed the Count's feet so that I didn't have to remember my surroundings. Luckily, he quickly delivered us from it, and after more stairs, the final door opened upon his command, and we entered the main level. I expected Imogen or one of the others to have caught wind of us, but everything seemed deserted, quiet, and still. My husband lifted his nose to the air and his eyes searched for something in the stone, but then he whispered. "Imogen is not here…"

Thoroughly confused, I wanted to ask where he thought she was, but bit my tongue.

Then the Count motioned to Dumitru to take me to the kitchen, and my friend nodded. Without a single word, we three separated, the Master going one way, and Dumitru and I going another. Without a doubt, he had already seen where his brother was being kept and was going to him, but I hated watching him disappear into the dark. My thoughts had to refocus to Mitică, and we descended into the kitchen.

Gesturing to me to keep quiet, Dumitru sat me down at the table and retreated into the pantry. Quickly, he returned with cheese and dried meats, things that would be quiet to eat and filling for the time being. To my dismay, I could barely finish a slice of either before feeling nauseous, but I forced myself to swallow them.

Dumitru noticed my discomfort and moved to sit close to me and bring his arm around my shoulders. It took several minutes before I could dare to try another piece, and by then the sun had fully set and night was upon us. The kitchen had descended into semi-darkness with only the pale light of the waning moon coming from the window for us to see. Just as I was about to reach for another piece of meat, an electrical shock made me freeze, and I immediately straightened. The chill followed, and I got to my feet and searched in the darkness with my inferior senses.

"You sensed me already?" The Greek materialized from a shadow, his blue eyes shining an eerie deep purple. "Your skills improve by the day, it seems."

Mitică stood as well, brimming with a righteous anger. "If you value your life —"

"*My* life? You should be grateful to me, boy, I saved *your* life…unworthy as you are." Andreas slinked closer, his eyes only set on me as he continued before Mitică could fire back. "I gather that because you are here at a time when Imogen is not, that you have come to a decision?"

I had forgotten all about his offer. I would regret it, but improvising was all I had, so I went with it. "Why else would I be here?"

The Greek grinned so satisfyingly to himself and slowly came around the table. He reached out his hand for me to take it, and I would be lying if I didn't say a voice did whisper to take it in earnest. "I'm relieved you came to your senses, *koukla*, for both your sakes."

Dumitru turned to me. *"Doamnă?"*

"It's alright, Mitică." Showing the least amount of hesitation as I could, and steeling my trembling nerves, I took the Greek's hand.

"You will be all that I wish, and more." The triumph on Andreas's face disgusted me, and I felt my already nauseous stomach twist when he kissed my hand. He was so caught up in his victory that I truly believe he saw what he wanted to see in me and not my masked revulsion to his touch.

"Isadora, you…you can't be serious?" My friend stammered exasperatedly.

"She is doing this for your own good, too, houseboy." He barked, but then his mouth came close to my ear and whispered to me in that velvety voice that always compels me. "Come with me, my new wife, we have little time before Imogen realizes we're gone."

I thought I was going to be sick for real, especially when the Greek pecked a soft kiss on my cheek and brought his arms around my waist to lead me away. Just as he had done so, it was as if a switch was flicked, and Andreas' demeanor completely changed, his features morphing into the demon that he hid beneath. Bearing his teeth, the red-blue of his eyes melted into a sanguine red, and his nails turned to claws and dug into the places where he held me.

"My tolerance of your unhealthy obsession with *my* wife has grown thin." It was the Count, his voice laden with a terrifying malice. "You will release her, *now.*"

We both froze, and although I sighed in relief at the sound of the Count's voice, Andreas actually quivered. After a moment's thought, he released me, although begrudgingly. "So, it was you I smelled on her and not the wolves. I knew you would have found some way to escape from that hole, but not so soon. Nevertheless, to use your own wife as bait to catch me is low even for you, Father."

Dumitru caught onto my arm and pulled me away from the two, and put me behind him. From my different vantage point, I saw the Master hold Andreas by the back of the neck, his talons digging into the Greek's skin as if it were soft butter. Behind him, the Monk loomed in the shadows. I was elated to see him, but when I saw my husband's eyes burn hotter than I had seen in a long time, I knew all his self-restraint had left him.

"You intend to betray Imogen. Why?" Behind the two of them, the Monk crept out from the shadows, appearing just as healthy as he did before he had been made low.

Andreas' gaze came to me, and we made eye contact. I have no doubt he really did think that Vlad had used me to capture him, but he only answered in a snide tone. "I have my reasons."

"My wife and your ego are your reasons." The Master drove his nails in deeper, making the Greek flinch. "Prizes of conquest are won by merit, a trait that you lack."

The most savage sneer came over Andreas' face. "You say I lack that merit, then how is it that I pleasured her before you?"

In one swift motion, coupled with a petrifying roar, the Master bashed Andreas' head against the stone wall, causing a terrible crack on its smooth surface. Blood dripped from the jagged edges, and for good measure, the Count gave him a few extra blows against it. "Shall I sever more than just your head?"

Dumitru immediately hid my face from the sight of Andreas' body slumping to the ground with half his skull bashed in. He would heal in time, no doubt. Despite seeing his blood pool on the floor, this overwhelming shame swallowed my soul, and I was left mortified more by his words than the sight of his brains. The lingering feeling of my dirtiness overcame me, and I remembered all the things I regretted doing against my husband.

The Master huffed sharply and threw Andreas to his brother. "You know where to take him. If he resists, be certain to leave him in pieces too small for the birds. You will accompany him, Dumitru."

My friend was obviously reluctant, but we let each other go, and without another word, Andreas was dragged out of the kitchen by the Monk. Suddenly, the place was left depressingly empty with only the Master and me alone there. My emotions decided to take that inopportune moment to overrun my senses, and I collapsed back into my chair.

"Do not let what he says drive a wedge between us." The Master's raw anger was sustained in his voice as it resonated with a growl. "He does it to provoke my anger and make you feel worthless. You are not worthless to me, do you hear?"

I only nodded.

He took a step closer to me, reaching out with his good hand, but retracted it when he remembered that his nails still dripped with Andreas' blood. "I know you were not sincere with him and only said what you did to protect yourself and Dumitru. Do not be ashamed, for I wronged you far worse long before Andreas sought you."

Even if God forgave me for my adultery, I would still feel ashamed. He was about to walk past me when I took his bloodied hand. "Please know that I have never loved him and could never love him the way I love you. I will always be on your side and at your side."

The hardness on his face melted back to his normal self. The Count lifted me to my feet and supported my shaking body against his sturdy one. "Come, beloved, you must sleep and dream sweetly."

Side by side, we walked up the steps to my floor and my rooms. Since we had to keep it dark, I had to fumble around like a fool to find my way. I wanted a hot bath, but I was too exhausted to even draw one. So, to my own disgust, I simply changed out of my torn, dirty, and ragged dress into fresh undergarments and a nightgown. The next thing I wanted to do was at least to brush my hair, but that was too much effort, and I couldn't see what I was doing.

To my astonishment, the Count took my brush from my hand, and bringing me to my desk, set me down for him to work out the tangles in the darkness. I couldn't see well, but I remembered that before me were the two letters, my wedding ring, the silver crucifix, and the bottle of remaining holy water. I said nothing about them, and with my back turned to him, he worked my hair with both his hands, smoothing and detangling with little pain. Together with the soothing rhythm of his hands and my sheer exhaustion, I fell asleep.

*9 January

Around 6 am or so…

The world and all its terrible reality had fallen away with that sleep, and not even I existed inside my own head. I did not dream, nor did any passing thought go through my head that I can recall thinking. Everything was an ignorant bliss, a suspended limbo, and it all came crashing down when I had that instinctual chill shoot up my spine, and my eyes flashed open.

At first, I had no idea where I was because it was so dark, but then I remembered the familiar comfort of my bed and the warmth of my sheets. The Count must have moved me there when I had fallen asleep, but now I was certain this was no dream, and I had been awakened into a living nightmare. I could feel eyes on me, and my eyes shot to the door where a black figure stood, and two iridescent blue eyes shone back at me in the semi-darkness from the doorless threshold. It was Andreas, I saw that immediately, but how he had come to be standing at my doorway when he had presumably been locked up somewhere set a frozen terror over my heart.

"*Koukla*, don't be afraid, it's only me." Andreas whispered in a calming reassurance that only set me further on edge.

"W-What..." I stuttered, my head spinning in a whirlwind. "How did you get in here?"

"I had a bit of help." Andreas admitted as he rubbed the side of his head where it had been slammed against the wall. "Now you must listen to me: my friend has your houseboy and asks that you come with us. Be a good girl and get your coat and shoes on, and don't resist for his sake. This time my friend will kill him, and I'd hate for you to be so wounded again."

I forgot to breathe as I got out of bed and cautiously came into the view of my sitting room. There, in my chair, Dumitru was slouched deep into it. Next to him, however, stood another black figure that I recognized as the underling who had 'killed' my friend and subdued the fourth Vlad. He was standing behind Mitică, holding something to his neck. What struck me the most was how indistinct his form was in the dark, as if he were there, but not there.

Panic gripped me, and I addressed the nameless creature. "What have you done to him?"

"He has done nothing, yet." Andreas spoke instead, moving to block my view of the two. "Please, do as you're told, and no harm will come to either of you."

Swallowing hard, I desperately tried to gather my sleepy wits. I had no clue where the Count and the Monk were, and since I couldn't rely on them, I complied. "Please, just give me a minute."

Andreas nodded back but continued to stare from the doorway at me as I fetched my dirty sweater and put on my shoes. In my haste, I tried to think of what I could discreetly snatch and hide as a weapon, but no doubt the Greek would catch my sleight of hand. I bit my lip as my default weapon came to mind, and my eyes flickered to my water bottle that still stood on my desk. As naturally as I could manage, I picked it up and drank the last of the water. My 'insurance', as the Count had called it, was gone.

Without any other hesitation, I went to Andreas, who held out his hand for me to take. Once I did, he led me past the henchman who had a stake pointed at Dumitru's neck, and I leveled at him a glare that could kill. The creature stared back, his black eyes tracking me as I went by. When we reached my door, the underling released the unconscious Dumitru.

Nothing was said as we three entered the hall, and Andreas moved his hand to place it around my shoulders, and his nose rubbed against my temple as he murmured in my ear. "Your nightgown becomes you, my dear."

I was in no mood to hear his sweet nothings and was about to say something to appease him when Andreas was pushed aside. A hand grasped my forearm and wrenched it behind me, bringing it up to my shoulder as if to break it. The ligaments and bones of my right arm stressed under the oppressive weight, and I cried out in surprise rather than pain. Then another hand came to my throat to squeeze me back against my attacker, locking my shoulder up in a stinging ache. The cold of the touch, so icy and bony, was something that repulsed my soul. It bore down against my esophagus, compressing the air from it. This had happened so quickly that not even Andreas had time to recover and react.

"You said she would not be hurt!" And ranted off about other things that I don't remember. As he did, out of the corner of my eye, I saw it was the underling who held me in his clutches. He smelled of something terribly rancid that made my stomach turn, like smoky rotten eggs and rank body odor.

"You take too much time, Andreas." The underling finally spoke, his voice broken and raspy. His breath was particularly putrid, too, reminding me of decaying meat and formaldehyde. "And we must not keep the lady's appointment waiting."

Not wasting any more of that time, the henchman pushed me along, forcing me into a brisk walk, and left Andreas behind. I wanted to plead for him to help me, but the way my neck was constrained made it impossible. Moving in any fluid manner was difficult, and if I stumbled down the stairs, my arm and neck would bear the brunt of my clumsiness and be strained further. In my awkward position, it was tough to keep my footing, but he pressed me onward, where the great door had been raised open. The cold air and snow had drifted inside, and I feared what was beyond.

My heart thundered in my ears as I was driven out of my castle once again, and the scene before me unfolded. Imogen stood near the steps, her blouse stained with crimson, although she appeared unharmed. She looked up at me as we three entered the courtyard, a satisfied, toothy grin coming over her face when she saw the position in which I was presented to her: bound like a captive slave in chains. On the other side of the yard stood the two Vlads, also battered from fighting.

The underling had brought me halfway down the steps when he hurled me the rest of the way, twisting me so that I landed directly on the shoulder he had strained. The snow cushioned my fall somewhat, but I still cried out and whined from the impact. I had no chance to recover from it when he grabbed my hair, along with the back of my neck, and forced me to my knees before Imogen.

"I was wondering when you were going to show." The witch grumbled with annoyance.

The henchman chuckled to himself. "Good things come to those who wait, daughter. And we deliver her to you so pleasantly wrapped."

Daughter? I felt my heart stop when the realization seeped into my brain. The grave recognition that Satan's prophecy had come and that he had come in person to assure it, I knew I was in bigger trouble than I fathomed. My doomsday had finally arrived, and Imogen was the pale horse. Holding my aggravated shoulder, I turned to meet the gazes of the two Vlads to plead to them to do something. With my hair awry and eyes glassy, their images were blurred, though I couldn't look upon them long.

Imogen grabbed the collar of my sweater to hoist me to my feet. "You did, lord, and now we have an esteemed audience to add. You indulge me too much."

"Now you can say that we fulfilled our contract with you with interest." He was quite amused with himself, but then warned more seriously. "End her soon, and do not be so assured of your victory lest our first sons find their resolve."

"Imogen!" The Count cried out from yards away, and the three demons went deathly silent. "You are a coward if you kill the most innocent of any of us here to simply take revenge on me. Petros deserved his punishment, and you are a fool to think I will let you harm her, too. If you so much as let a drop of her blood be spilled, I

will hang you upside down from a tree and bleed you dry like a slaughtered pig!"

"And what position are you in to say such things?" The she-devil cackled as if she held no stock in his threat at all. "Do you recall what I told you the first day your little wife and I met all those months ago? I warned you to rid yourself of her and return to us, but you refused. You chose to save their lives and kill Petros, my love and your son, and because you hold your withered humanity over the race which you bore, you have chosen her fate."

"Insolent witch —!"

"Traitor! You are unworthy to lead us if you are not like us! You are weak and inept, but we can't simply end you for these things. Therefore, we will end the one who holds your humanity." She shouted those things over him, her face slowly becoming the demon. Imogen's eyes, which were so close to mine, took on the pale yellow of the Devil's. "You can only blame him for what must be done to you."

"I could never blame him for your pride, Imogen. I only pity that you can't see that there's another who has really betrayed you." I paused as her eyes sparked ablaze. "May God forgive you for all the lives you have ruined just to ruin his."

With a firm yank, she pulled my hair and head back to expose my neck. Gritting my teeth for impact, I cried out with the only defense I had left: my words. *"Crux sacra sit mihi lux, non draco sit mihi dux. Vade retro, Satana!"*

At my words, they both recoiled. Taking my opportunity, I continued my onslaught. The underling quickly made distance between us with a horrendous shriek of pain. Imogen faltered, her grip lessening only a little.

To shut me up, Imogen drove her teeth into the left side of my neck. The familiar burn exploded from my skin, and as I felt my life being sucked from me, my vision blackened. She must have taken so much of my blood in just the first few seconds, the next thing I remembered was I being dropped into the snow, the cold shocking my senses alive again. The pain in my neck reminded me I was still alive, and I moved my eyes to see Imogen. It was then I heard something in the distance, like the fearsome roar of a bear, but it was so loud that it sounded like it was coming from right in my ear.

Looking at Imogen's transformed face, her yellow eyes were wide and nearly bulged out of her skull. This expression of the purest terror and panic encompassed her, similar to that of Petros' when he had been given a lethal dose of his own medicine. She began to shake and dropped to her knees, and held her stomach in. Andreas came next to me to hold my upper half and support me. He was yelling about something, his words indistinct but frantic as he placed a hand over my dripping wound. Immediately, he cried out in pain as my blood burned him, his face showing the demon as he dropped me and withdrew.

Andreas growled as he held his burned hand to his chest. "Imogen, what is this magic?"

At that, I laughed, although it was choked through lumps of blood clotting my airway. Coughing up spurts of it, I still managed to mock Imogen when our eyes met and laughed in her face.

From within her, a violent contraction of her stomach vomited up my blood all over the snow. Like a wave, it spread out, and more followed as she quaked and trembled, the blood vessels of Imogen's eyes bursting from the burning pressure. It was a struggle for her to remain on all fours, and her clawed hands dug into the snow to keep from screaming out in pain. I took no pleasure in watching her suffer as she was, but there was satiation in it.

A great snarl ripped through the air to the other side of me, and I shifted my eyes just enough and saw that the two Vlads had come significantly closer but had been blocked by whatever corporal form Lucifer was in as they fought. He was easily hindering the two's approach while they fought like beasts. The Prince of Lies bellowed out in a maniacal laughter, seemingly enjoying his rampage, and inhibited the Count each time he tried to break away to get to me.

With great effort, I got to my elbows, heaving my weight to my legs, but dizziness spun my head around, and I sank back down in the snow. The redness of the blood that had leaked from my wound was startling against the white underneath me, and I wondered if Imogen had nicked an artery. I had to escape, but my strength and heart were failing.

"*Andreas,*" Imogen hissed out as she had collapsed into the pool of my toxic blood. It burned her pallid face, turning it black. "*Do it!*"

He grabbed onto me, and there was no use fighting against him since I could hardly raise my head. Cradling my face in his large palm, Andreas and I met eye to eye. With my breathing labored and sight failing, I was going to bleed out soon, and he knew it just as well as I. "She means for me to turn..." He couldn't finish the sentence, so he began a new one. "Please, this will save you."

The meaning of his words dawned on me. The fact that Imogen meant to use him to turn me was abominable. Had that been her goal all along? To bleed me dry, and refill me with their damned blood to guarantee that I would be reborn as one of them? Thereby, she would have successfully killed and condemned me at the same time. She knew of the Greek's feelings for me and how to use them to her advantage. Imogen probably had no intention of letting me remain undead for long.

It struck me that Andreas understood that I was fading away, but didn't want to change me because of Imogen's orders, but because that was his version of *saving* me, not *harming* me.

Andreas slit his wrist with his fangs, his own blood trickled onto my gown. For a moment in time, the world fell away and only Andreas and I remained. A look of desperation, and maybe some hesitation, came over him as he brought his bloodied wrist over my lips, and I felt the droplets splash on my tongue.

I was about to tell him to let me die in peace when Andreas growled, and his eyes darted from mine. "Houseboy, you keep your distance if you want to keep your head."

Andreas had turned slightly from me, distracted by Dumitru's well-timed arrival. From the look on Andreas' face, my houseboy didn't keep his distance. Setting me back down, Andreas bore his fangs and poised to strike. The Greek ignored me just enough that I managed to lift my hand to grab a fistful of snow that I had bloodied and fling it the short distance into his eyes. He cried out in pain and temporary blindness. It created the needed distraction, and the next thing I saw was Mitică taking a fist full of the hissing Andreas' hair and driving a stake beneath his jaw and up through his head. Then, another was plunged into his heart, and the Greek slumped to the ground.

Without a word, Dumitru picked me up in his arms to whisk me away, but just when he had taken his first steps to run, his footing was yanked out from underneath him. Mitică lost his hold of me, and I was dropped, the ligaments of my neck bursting in agony. Of course, it was Imogen, half undead and half dead, her skin bloodied and charred, but teeth ever so white, and irises yellow. Her death would be slow, I know, but I didn't think it would be so slow that she still had the determination to come after me.

Like a snake, Imogen slithered on the slick snow, coming directly for me. Dumitru tried to kick at her, but that did little. Probably using the last bit of strength left in her, the speed at which she came at me with her arm outstretched and clawed hand was unbelievable. She was aiming for my chest, no doubt to rip out my heart, and I was about to spit out some more Latin when something blocked my view of her, and her blood-soaked hand went right through it, hurling bits of gore on me.

Silence came over the entire courtyard, at least I think it did, but my ears were ringing. The Master had protected me from her yet again, and grunted as Imogen tried to rip her arm out of his torso, but it would not budge. It was thoroughly wedged in place, and she was finally at his mercy. Desperately, she pleaded to Lucifer to help her, but he did not come. He did nothing for her and only focused on his battle with the Monk.

Between heaving breaths, the Count addressed her. "Imogen, you once told me to remember that I am a monster, but I remember that I am a man. I give you your punishment. May God have mercy on your soul, because I have none left for you."

She whined as her arm strained to break free, but slowly the Count's hand went into her chest, his flesh sizzling along with hers as he relieved her of her heart, and then her head. Her body sagged downward, and what was Imogen crumpled to dust in the third Vlad's fingers. At that same moment, Lucifer's bodily frame vanished as smoke, and we four were left in a sea of snowy blood and ash.

After a long pause, my husband turned his head slightly to look back at me. His ghostly, waxen face was sprinkled red, which bubbled as it burned his flesh. As the gaping hole in his abdomen began knitting itself shut, the Count had little breath to say. "It is finished…"

Then, he collapsed to the side and was still.

Chapter Forty-Seven

ONE FLESH

14 January

It has been almost a week since the Count lost consciousness, and since then, he has not woken up. From what I have seen and what the Monk has told me, he has gone into a deep death sleep and will not awake until he has regained his power. The earth in which he is buried is essential in this process, being the source of his strength, and as long as he is given fresh blood daily, he will recuperate in his own time. The fourth Vlad reassures me often that the Count will be well and that even supernatural beings have their limits.

Needless to say, I was incapacitated for half of the time the Master has been asleep, fighting to keep my head above water. My wound, although not as bad as what Petros had dealt me, was still debilitating. Imogen had cut through a part of my carotid artery and into my esophagus, severing several of my fine muscles and ligaments.

It was only due to the fourth Vlad's quick thinking that I didn't bleed out or suffocate on my own blood, and so I owe my life to the other Son of the Dragon yet again. My recovery has been very slow and painful, but once I had made enough of my own blood again, the Monk administered to me small doses of his to help me.

Thank God Dumitru had been here to stay by me, even when we said nothing at all, every moment with him was a haven. And when I could speak again without major pain, I asked Mitică and the Monk's forgiveness for my foolishness when I had taken matters into my own hands, causing both of them to be harmed. By some miracle, they both granted me their forgiveness for it, although I still feel remorseful.

Since the time I have been able to stand and walk, I have spent the majority of my hours in the family crypt to stay by my husband's side, waiting in case he awakens. When he wasn't doing much else, Mitică would come and sit with me and the Master, but I believe he did it to watch me and not the Count. All the same, the company was appreciated. And when he wasn't around, I'd sit curled up in a thick blanket and think.

My thoughts, however, are never my friends. They visit me like phantoms of my past enemies come to haunt me even in death. Sometimes out of nowhere, I'd think of Imogen's yellow eyes when I'd see a similar color, or even the turning of pages as I would read would remind me of the sound of her arm going straight through the Count's torso. Other times, I would replay the scenes of that day in my head, wondering if I could have done something differently to help Imogen. I can't help it, really. Would she have taken my hand if I had held it out to her? Probably not...

One evening, when I had been lost in thought about this very subject, the Monk had awoken to find me still there when I usually would have gone to bed. Like the great mentor and confidant that he is with his quirky dated expressions, he asked me about my problems and counseled me on my inner thoughts. About Imogen, he doubted she would ever have taken a hand extended out of kindness or compassion, even to save her own life. What tragedies did she endure to become so prideful and so brokenhearted?

The topic upsets me, I don't want to write about it anymore...

Concerning Andreas, since that day, I haven't seen him. No doubt he's somewhere in the castle, still incapacitated with the stake in his heart. I haven't asked Vlad where he is, but I can guess it's somewhere under the castle, where he knows I won't go. Often, my thoughts do turn to the Greek, and I wonder about him too, but I am afraid to confront him. I wish I had never met him, that I hadn't allowed him to wiggle his way into my heart. But what's done is done, and I can't change any of it.

I hope that the Almighty hears my prayers for the souls of Petros, Imogen, Maxim, Ludevit, Cosima, and Georgiana, and that one day He will save them from Hell. Even if that day won't be until the real Doomsday, I hope, perhaps against all hope.

It's very late now, and my neck and hand are sore. Let these six who sought to destroy me be put to rest here with the conclusion of this entry.

16 January

Morning…

This morning, I got some unexpected news from the Monk concerning the Count. According to him, yesterday, when night fell, the Master awoke and was conscious for a few minutes before slipping back into sleep. I wish someone had called me, but Vlad said my husband did ask about me and was relieved when he heard I was recovering. Other than that, the Monk only told me that the Count was lethargic, but still very much alive.

At least this is good news, and now I am off to see him. I doubt he'll wake during the day, but at least he may know I am there with him.

18 January

Dawn…

The Count hadn't awoken the last two nights, to my dismay, and my small hope to speak to him was dashed. Vlad saw it on my face each night when the sun had set, but my husband didn't stir, and he reminded me to have faith in God to help him, since the Devil and he were no longer on good terms. I could assume that the Count drew much of his strength from Satan, and without his father to fuel his recovery, he is left to his own abilities. It strikes me, however, how for so long he was away and I could never speak to him, and now he is here, and I still can't speak to him.

When I'm not visiting the Master, Dumitru and I try to carry on as normal, but it's difficult. We never did finish our conversation from that day. I told him how I hold much guilt for the way I've treated him, but I don't think he wants to finish it. He doesn't want to hear what I have to say, and honestly, neither do I.

In addition, one thing that has puzzled me these last couple of days: the letters which were on my desk have disappeared. The last time I had seen both of them was when the Count was brushing my hair, and with the events of that next morning, I hadn't noticed they were gone. I wonder if the Master took and read them, or if it wasn't him, maybe Dumitru had when I was unconscious or out of my room. Either way, if my husband did read them at some time, I'm worried about what he thinks. To put it plainly, they were my suicide letters, and the Master and suicide do not mix. But, I have put my wedding ring and crucifix back in their rightful places, and as long as I am *Doamna*, I will never take them off again.

...

In the evening, I decided to take a hot bath to help soothe the ache in my heart from all the things that still haunt me. So, hair piled on top of my head, I settled into the steamy bath. I had been lost in thought for so long, humming sad songs that popped into my head and then faded like the vapor as it rose from the water. The relaxation in my muscles, still sore from a week ago, turned to Jell-O in the heat, and I found some relief from the soreness in my heart.

I closed my eyes and drifted off a bit until I felt freezing fingertips combing through my hair and my eyes flashed open. The sensation had startled me, but when my eyes went to the source, I almost couldn't believe them. The Count, who was kneeling at the side of the tub, had been watching over me as I had dozed off. At first, I wondered if it was him, or if the steamy mist had created some illusion for me, but when he smiled and his chilled hand came to caress my cheek, I knew he was real.

As if on cue, tears cascaded from my eyes, and I embraced him, not caring if I had drenched him with soapy water or that I was completely nude. His smell was thick of earth and musk, and it overwhelmed me. My husband chuckled as his arms, so terribly cold against my heated skin, came around my midsection to pull me to him, lifting me a little out of the water. I was flush against him as I hastily caught his lips and muttered incoherently how much I thank God he was alright.

"My rosy-cheeked nymph, did you miss me?" The Count was his old self again, purring and beaming with joy at the sight of me like he always used to before summer ended.

"More than you could ever imagine." I cupped his face, the brown of his eyes and softness of his mouth making me swoon. "I have prayed every minute of every day for you, husband, and now my prayers have been answered."

Landing another tender kiss on my lips, he rested his nose in my neck and kissed there too. "Precious girl, I have also prayed for you. Vlad tells me your recovery has been slow, but that you are very sad."

My heart broke at his tone, and bringing my hands into his hair, I held him tighter. "You know me, I think too much and worry too much. But you're here now, and I am so blessed to have everyone I love safe after all that's happened."

The Count didn't respond immediately to that but dug his face further into my clavicle. "Does she haunt you?"

I weaved my fingers into the waves of his hair and frowned. "Admittedly, yes."

"Do not think of her anymore, and do not let her preoccupy your thoughts as Petros had. Neither of them deserves your pity…" He made his grip firmer around my low back. "After what I did to her, no one will dare oppose me, so we must pick up the pieces. Let us only focus on *us* and not others."

Brow knitting, I kissed his head. "Do you remember the evenings we would spend together? They seem like an eternity ago. We should start them again, and maybe invite your brother to join?"

"We will die of boredom if we do that." My husband scoffed in a lighthearted jest, but then let it fall as he raised his head so that his nose traced my jaw. "No, just us, and no one else. For too long I have withheld myself from you, and I shall not anymore."

I brought his face to meet mine and read his commitment all over it. Heartwarming and exciting as it was, I felt more troubled than I had expected, and I knew why. I sank a bit to rest my head on his chest.

My reaction frightened him, I think, for he tried to mask the hurt in his voice when he asked. "You...you are unwilling, my love?"

"It's not that, Vlad..." I bit my lip, trying to find the words to say what I needed to say without actually saying it. "I want to ask you about something, but I fear the answer."

"Ask me, please." He leaned in to peck my forehead and waited. I guess I took too long in trying to formulate the query in my head, and the Count became agitated. "Is this about Cosima?"

"No, Count," I sighed in frustration at his immediate assumption. "It's something I heard that I don't know is true. I could have been dreaming for all I know, but I don't want to put you on the spot for having to answer. Maybe I shouldn't ask...forget I said anything."

"Ask me," his voice became much deeper at my deflection. "Ask me anything, no matter how much you think it may offend me, and I will answer it."

Such a rare occasion as that was, there was a whole host of questions I could have asked in that moment. Yet, I had to know the answer to the one thing that had been bothering me for over a month, so I took a deep breath. "The night you left to find them..." My voice faded out, and I felt a subtle shift in the tension of anticipation in his body. "I-I thought I heard you say something to me. Did you say anything then? Other than that, it was time for you to go."

He released the breath that he had been holding in, and he whispered in my ear as if it were a secret. "You mean when I said that I have love for you? Yes, I said it. Was that it, or something else?"

At first, I wondered if I had misheard or misunderstood him somehow, but there was no doubt in my mind about the words he had spoken. I raised my eyes to his, taking in the moment despite feeling I was a deer in the headlights. Had he really achieved the impossible for his kind, and learned to love? I tried to keep my composure. "No, that was it. Does that mean —?"

"That I love you?" The Count finished my sentence as he grinned from ear to ear. Bringing a hand to my cheek, his thumb grazed over the sensitive skin of my lips as he declared dreamily. "Yes, my Isadora, I love you."

I sat there dumbfounded and unsure of what to say. My thoughts went back to the time he had told me of his nature and how he cannot love because love is sacred. It's something that is so against what he is, something that I was skeptical that he could achieve, but I had no doubt he had the drive within him to achieve it. I never thought this day would come so soon, especially with recent events, and I was hesitant to believe him. "Are you sure? Since when?"

"I am more sure of this than anything." The Master laid a gentle kiss on me before he explained. "Since the day we spent by the river, you wore your flower crown, and straddled me so boldly, called me the moon of your days, and kissed me like I was the only man on this earth, I knew."

Back then? And I hadn't noticed? Where had I been? I frowned, although everything he was saying was putting me on cloud nine. "You never told me."

"I was afraid to tell you how I felt because it was frightening to me, and then you had asked me how I felt." To admit he had been frightened by it was quite something coming from him. Still, no wonder he chose to marry me so shortly afterwards: he was scared of me being taken from him just as he had learned to love again. "I tried to say it differently, but I did say I could not deny you my love, despite it being against my nature."

"I remember…"

"Much has happened since then, so I understand if you are hesitant." The Count rested his forehead against mine, but his mouth turned downwards at the sides, and he averted his eyes. "You know that I forgot, but I did regain my fondness for you. Still, a part of me was not certain if it was true until recently."

I saw how he was still ashamed of it, but I asked. "Then how are you so sure now?"

"You know I never act without thought, and to do something so thoughtless is, well, unthinkable for me." He whispered again in a secretive tone, but paused as his eyes began to redden, not in anger, but from tears. "But when Imogen went to rip your heart out, I had acted before I knew what I had done. In that second, I did not think of anything except that I would not let her take your heart that you gave to me, and that if it meant she would take my heart instead of yours, I would have let her have mine without question. Luckily, she had poor aim."

My mouth partially agape, I stared at him wide-eyed. He had been willing to sacrifice himself for me with no qualms, no demand for compensation for it? Not that he would ever have me pay for anything he has given me, but that he expected *nothing* in return for his actions. I recalled when he said to me, all those months ago, when I asked him what his definition of love is, and he said it was sacrificing one's self and asking nothing in return. That unshakable bond between two people: is that what we have now? Tears had fallen down my face, and I quickly wiped them away. "You have come so far, beloved. I am so happy, so proud of you for having defied what you are. I thank God that He has helped you succeed in what you swore you would never relent in achieving."

"It was only because of you that I managed this." My husband brought me into another embrace as his fingers sensually bore into the flesh of my ribs. "I love you, and I wish we could go back to that day by the river when I first felt that pang of love and tell you how much I love you."

"Perhaps it was best that you hadn't said it then, because I think my life here would have been unbearable to know that and be kept from you. But, if all we endured has brought us to this point, I don't regret a single day of it and would bear it all again with you, for you." A frog had formed in my throat, and I had a hard time swallowing it. "Thank you for saying you love me, and for all you have given me, and done for me. For saving my life a billion times over, and for so many other things."

I could feel him tense again, and a hand moved to trace along my spine as he thought of something to say. His gentle touch was enticing me, and a heavy weight grew in the pit of my stomach. The Master sensed it immediately and whispered. "Say you love me."

I didn't need to think twice. "I love you, Vlad."

The Count purred, this time dragging both of his hands up from my low back to my shoulder blades. "Let me make love to you then, sweetest one."

The question was so straightforward that a deep heat came over my face, and I became painfully aware of my nakedness. My face grew hotter than the surface of the sun. The heaviness in my core released its gates, and I submitted to him with a kiss. "From the first night you ever came to me and you told me I am yours, I wanted you."

"Isa…" His voice deepened as his eyes became lost in mine.

I brought my hands to cup his cheeks as we stared eye-to-eye. "I love you, and I want to show you how much I do. So, make love to me, moon of my days, make me yours."

No sooner had I said that did he lifted me out of the tub, careful to be slow, although by doing so made me drip sudsy water all over him and the floor. With both of us on our feet, our noses intermingled as my hands meandered down to his shirt and began to unbutton it. I was a bit too slow for him, and he helped me finish the rest of the way, then the fabric slid from his shoulders. I had expected his wound to be gone, and though it was much smaller, it was still well bandaged. It didn't seem to pain him so much, so I kissed it as his hands went to my hair and took out the pins, a purr and soft whimper escaping him when my hands moved down to his trousers. My heart was hammering so hard in my chest as I undid them.

Soon enough, his clothes were pools on my bathroom floor, and for the first time, we both beheld each other as we had been created. The Master kissed me deeply and reached to take my hand to lead me from the bathroom. Without any words, not that we needed them, we crawled onto my bed, and the Count drew nearer to hover over me. Bringing his face down to mine, he began to kiss from my lips down to my chest before moving my legs apart so that he came between them. His skin touched mine in places none had touched before, and it was exhilarating.

The Count was slow in his design to edge me closer so I would be fully prepared for him. The way he used his mouth to adorn my skin with the most tender kisses, and his hands to caress me, my blood was maddened with desire for him. It was a drawn-out thrill, and he did such reverence to my body that I forgot about everything except him. From me, he extracted sounds which I never thought I could make; some of them were strangely whimsical, while others were beastly.

When that time had come when he could no longer restrain himself, he whispered and said he would never intentionally hurt me, and that I should tell him if he did. I promised I would and held onto him because I felt if I let go, I would lose myself. And just like that, we fit together like jigsaw puzzle pieces, irregular but perfect. It did hurt, but the Count made every effort to comfort me, bringing me back from the brink with kisses as drops of the sweetest honey.

Trusting him completely, I did my best to conform and not hinder his movements as he began. He panted softly, and I could hear how his breath shook with each thrust. The sound he made receiving pleasure from me made my heart rapt in love for him. I had to kiss him then and had to keep kissing him as he turned my insides to pulp.

I was nestled beneath him like a rock being beaten by the gentle waves of the sea as they came in and out, being directed by the moon's constant orbit. It was the most natural feeling to be like that, and even when those waves grew more turbulent, I weathered them. They encompassed me, made me feel so full to the brim, and even when they let out, they came right back to fill me again. The oneness, the completeness, the expression on his face when he saw I was delighting in him…it was the most imperfect perfection. So many times, I was brought to my highest by him, and when I thought I couldn't go higher, he brought me to heaven.

Even though the time stood still between us, our breaths soon became ragged in our exertion. I was sweating as if there was this raging fire in my body that no amount of water could quench, but though he was cool to the touch, I saw in his eyes the same fire. He raised his upper half from me, but I couldn't let him go, so I locked my ankles around his hips. The Master growled, not at me, but at the waves which were becoming choppy from the approaching storm. I reached for him and called his name, pleading to him for something that I *wanted* but *needed.* I was imploring him, and he knew what I was begging for.

He had been teetering at the edge, but then finally he submitted, making his release. Eyelids hooded in ecstasy, I had never heard him make such noises as those as his body, especially his hips, quivered. When his breath had steadied and the tide had gone out, he fell upon me, fingers entangling themselves in my hair. The Count's tongue came between my lips to mingle with my own, and it overwhelmed me that I was being permeated by him.

When my husband released my mouth, the reality of what had happened hit me. The fog had cleared in my mind, and when I examined his blissful features, I had to smile.

The Count grinned back as he moved some of the hair he had disheveled from my face. "How do you feel, sweet one?"

My smile widened. "Hungry. You?"

The mirth of his laugh warmed my heart, and he shook his head at my silliness. "The greatest I have felt in a very long time."

It made me happy to know that.

When he slid out of me, I felt so hollow without him there. Between my hips ached, and although I actually was hungry, I just wanted to sleep. Still eager to be touched by him, I huddled into his side and rested my head beneath his neck. "Moon of my days…"

"Sun of my nights," he kissed the top of my head again. "You do not know how long I have waited for you to smell only of me."

I searched for his hand, and our fingers wove together. "Since the day I came here, right?"

"Since the second you came here." The Master corrected, bringing my hand to his lips to kiss it. "My dear, do you recall that night you told me I should wish on a shooting star?"

I hummed to him, saying that I remembered the idyllic scene.

His voice became soft, like a whisper. "When that wish came true, I said I would tell you."

I opened my eyes to look up at him. "It has? What was it?"

He cocked his head to one side a bit as he studied me, a small smile on his mouth. "Just this," he revealed with a little kiss. "Just as we are."

A warmth overcame my chest and spread all over me when our eyes locked. I hated that I had been so blind to his feelings for so long, even when he had forgotten them. It made me want to cry for the trillionth time, but instead I squeezed his hand. "I love you, husband, so much more than you could ever know."

The Count swallowed hard, and his eyes drifted away. I thought I had offended him somehow by the conflicted expression on his face, but then he asked. "Isadora, will you marry me?"

I was shocked and confused by his seriousness, and a nervous laugh escaped me. "Silly, we've been married —"

"I mean in a church," he said seriously. "In the sight of God."

For a long while, I was silent. "Is it even possible?"

"If this is possible, then all things are possible." He reassured me, although I don't think he is so sure of it. Even though he has achieved a miracle, his body is still a demon, no matter how good his heart is. I hate being so pessimistic about it, but that is the reality of his situation.

Regardless of all of that, I had only one answer. "Yes, Vlad, son of Vlad the Dragon, I will marry you."

The Count purred in satisfaction and brought me back to rest on his shoulder. So, I listened to each slow breath he made, his purr lulling me to sleep.

I firmly believe that the Impaler, the demon he faced in himself, died the day he ripped out Imogen's heart. She, who to him represented the hate that made him evil, the pride that held him back, had taken with her those things, thereby setting him free. Vlad is his own man, and with this, there is only one step left now that all of his enemies are dust.

Chapter Forty-Eight
UNDONE

19 January

I fell asleep sometime that previous night, and when I awoke, the first rays of the sun were streaming through the drawn curtains. My body was heavier than a brick, my hips were so sore, and I felt very messy. When I tried to move, I was thoroughly subdued by the Count, in whom I was entangled. The sheets were awry, and our limbs were jumbled in them and entwined with each other. In the chaos, he was lying on my hair, and one arm was wrapped around me. I couldn't move at all, not that I really wanted to, but I needed another bath pronto. Yet he appeared so peaceful as he slept, with his skin a pale peachy color that made him almost look alive. I managed to free one of my arms, and caressing his muscular pectorals, I kissed his chest.

The Count purred when he opened his eyes to gaze down at me, that dreamy look still fresh in his eyes. "Sweet one, how are you?"

"Wonderful," I winced at the throbbing ache that unexpectedly blossomed in my hips when I tried to move them. "But sore."

He chuckled, a devilish smile manifesting on his face. Raising himself, he placed me so that I lay beneath him again and hovered over me. "Shall I kiss it to make it better?"

My cheeks blazed with heat from his innuendo, and it flustered me greatly.

The Master's smile widened at my reaction, and he kissed me deeply. I was subdued once again by his passion and immediately caved to him. His hunger for me had grown, and I whined as he pecked *petits bisous* down my neck and chest. In the faint daylight, I could see so much more of him, and I reveled at the spectacle above me. My Count's mouth descended my abdomen as he observed from between my thighs the involuntary reaction I had to the delight that his tongue provided me. Once again, my body strained to keep up with him. Although I was exhausted, he elicited from me wave after wave of ecstasy. The thrill of his touch made me moan and cry out, perhaps louder than I should have.

After my love had his fill of me and achieved his own bliss, he collapsed next to me. Possessively, he brought me to rest at his side, his loud purr was muffled out by my labored breaths. We looked at each other from beneath heavy eyelids, assessing the satisfaction etched on our faces.

Brushing his nose against my cheek, he whispered. "Does it feel better now?"

Before I could reply, the Count nibbled my ear playfully. His deadly teeth tickled my skin, and I giggled. "You always know how to make me feel better. Do your talents know no end?"

"Believe me, my love, you have only had a taste of me." And once again, Vlad brought me to his lips to kiss him. "I will come to you again tonight. Be ready for me."

The thought made my head spin, and I blushed more.

He stayed with me until late in the morning, by the time Vlad *finally* decided to dress, I was positively starved. He had lingered for quite a while, using every excuse he could to stick around for just a bit longer. Before he departed, he said that he would have Dumitru bring up my breakfast, and although I protested, he insisted. I didn't want Mitică to even have a hint of what had happened until I could speak with him. Would the Count be one to kiss and tell? The idea mortified me.

Once my husband left, I rolled out of bed with much effort and got to my feet, taking the sheets with me. I was trying to plan how I could go about being discreet with the messy sheets. I rolled them into a bundle and went to the bathroom to run another bath. Yet when I came into the fluorescent light, I saw the true extent of my injuries. I had been bruised around my hips where he had held me in his death grip, and also a few places on my arms and legs. They are a light purple and are rather sensitive to the touch. I didn't think he had held me so firmly, for they hadn't hurt at the time.

It took me longer than expected to make myself presentable, but just as I had left the stained areas of the sheets to soak in some soapy water, I heard Dumitru come in with my breakfast. Steeling my nerves, I went out to greet him. He was quite grumpy about something when I gave him a 'good morning', and I feared he had already discovered my secret. "Mitică, what's wrong?"

"Nothing," he didn't look at me as he put the dishes on the table. "You know that the Master has awoken?"

My eyes narrowed in confusion at his tone, and I knew then what the issue was. So, I dodged it slightly. "Yes, he came and saw me last night for a bit. I am very relieved to see him feeling and doing so well. For a while, I thought he wasn't going to wake up."

"Yeah…" He muttered with a curt nod, and still refused to look at me.

His behavior was so strange, and it reminded me of when I first came here. My friend was just about to leave without a word when I grabbed onto his arm. "What's the matter, really? Are you mad you had to bring me breakfast? I would have come down myself —"

"I'm not mad about that." He snapped with a glowering pout. "I'm not mad about anything, so eat your breakfast."

"You're obviously mad about something." I kept my voice soft as I took his hand to show him my earnestness. "You can always talk to me, Mitică. We're best friends, remember?"

Dumitru didn't pull away from me, but I had a feeling he wanted to. He wanted to say what was on his mind, but as always, what he had to say was too bold for his own good. The amount of honesty I received, however, was more than I expected. He whispered just low enough for me to hear. "I didn't want him to wake up, I didn't want him to come back. I wanted…I hoped he would be lost, not dead, but just lost."

I couldn't believe the words that had come out of his mouth. No matter what, Dumitru had always been loyal to him, and I feared his reasoning for this change. "Why? He is our Master, and he saved us both. We would be dead if it weren't for him."

"I know that too well," he sulked with a deep frown. "But you will be with him again."

A lead weight suddenly formed in my chest, and I remembered that feeling of guilt I had when I thought my Mitică had died. I hate these feelings I have, and I wish they would go away. "Please don't say anything more. You know I care for you deeply, but for God's sake and for your own safety, say no more." I placed my other hand on his shoulder and stared directly into his eyes. "He has given you a home when he didn't need to give you anything and so much more. Don't throw that all away because of me, especially when he relies on you and loves you so."

He huffed at that last bit, but he did pause to think about what I had said. I tried to read his face as he thought, but the main emotion was his predictable anger. "Each time I think I'm so close, he takes you away from me."

"Dumitru, he's my —" My own frustration began to flare, but I stopped, taking in a deep breath. "Think about what you're saying."

Dumitru blinked as he let my words sink in, and he looked away when a growing expression of distress furrowed his brow. He knew I was right, but his feelings were stronger than his reason, and he hung his head. "I hate this…"

With all that pained emotion, I had to embrace him. The warmth of his arms when they came around me and pressed me to him was a stark contrast to the Count's, and I leaned into him.

There was another pause as his grip tightened around me, and I had to hold in a whine from my tender injuries. I bore it for only a few seconds more before trying to pull away from him.

He stiffened. "Where did you get those bruises?"

"What bruises?" I tried my best to act aloof, but Dumitru hooked his finger around my collar to pull it down. There, the discolorations in my skin were visible, and I made up some excuse. "Oh, I must have done those in my sleep. I've been restless."

He wasn't convinced, and grabbing my forearm, he hiked up my sleeve before I could resist or pull away. Mitică's face darkened with a tensed jaw as a new anger sparked in him, and he leveled his eyes to mine with the most intense glare. "He did this."

"What? No," I tried to take my arm away, but he held it firm. "Like I said, I've been restless, bad dreams and such. You know the Master wouldn't hurt me."

"Then how is that you developed all of these the same night he awoke?" My friend released my arm, and I quickly covered up. "What did he do to you? Tell me."

"He didn't do anything." I retorted, but knew that answer wouldn't satisfy him and repeated. "You know he wouldn't hurt me."

We stared at each other knowingly. He knew I was lying, and I was trying to keep that bluff on my face. Turning away from him, I signaled that the conversation was finished and sat down at the table to eat my breakfast. However, in the heat of the moment, I had forgotten all about my sore hips and landed too hard into the chair. The pain was a sharp stab that shot straight up into my abdomen, and I visibly winced. The pain had startled me more than it actually hurt.

"Isa—" I heard Dumitru begin, but he stopped. When I raised my eyes to him, his face had turned from hurt to disgust mixed with betrayal. Trying to recover, I forced myself to straighten through the pain, but he had already seen where my hands had instinctively gone to clutch, and then all emotion fell away from his face.

Like a flick of a switch, he became the stoic driver I had met those months ago, cold and distant, and he backed a step away from me. Dumitru didn't speak but stared with this expression of incomprehensible denial that made him appear almost catatonic. Without saying anything, my body had revealed its secrets against my will to him, and he had read them. The Count and I had done the deed that Mitică had promised would be the end of our friendship.

I saw in his eyes how he judged as he looked down, literally, at me. To him, the Count is *dracul*. Those eyes condemned me, and it was as if I wore the scarlet 'A' on my breast. It made me think of that

565

Romani wife who called me the 'harlot of the devil' with her accusatory finger pointing at me from beyond the grave. Dumitru's frown deepened. "I dreaded this day, but it was to be expected."

I tried to stand, to hold onto him in fear that he was going to slip away. "Mitică…"

"It's not proper to call me that. It implies we're friends." He said so coldly as his hand bore down on my shoulder to keep me seated. His gray eyes pierced my soul with a disappointment so pure that it haunts me.

Panic set into my brain, and it scattered a million different directions to think of ways to convince him otherwise. "Mitică, don't be ridiculous! We'll always be friends no matter what."

His brow twitched, revealing the anguish he felt just before covering it back up. "I told you after this, we cannot be friends. Your contract is legal now, and like I said, here no woman has male friends after she is married. Besides, no man would want to be your friend if he knows who your husband is…"

That last sentence hurt my heart terribly, and the ache will linger for a very long time.

From my lack of response and despondent expression, Dumitru added. "I didn't make these rules, I only follow them."

My friend, or whatever one wishes to call him, turned and began to walk out of the room. Abruptly, I stood and searched for something to say to him, though I knew he would not bend in this. Ordering him to stay as his *Doamna* would only prove his point, and even if I got him to do so, he would never be so open with me about what he thinks and feels again. A great ocean opened up between us when he walked out my door. Sinking back down into the chair, I wept.

Evening…

When the Count arrived, I was ready for him. I changed my dress to one with a high neck and long sleeves to fully cover any indication of my bruises and applied some makeup to conceal the puffiness around my eyes. I really hadn't left my sitting room all day due to my extreme fatigue from both my late-night escapade and my excessive tears. I knew the Master would see right through me and knew something was wrong.

At the allotted time, my husband appeared from a shadow. Eagerly, he kissed me and wasted no time divulging to me his want. He acted as though he were starved, like these few hours apart had been simply unbearable. My husband weaved his hands into my hair, removing the pins and letting my tresses fall loose.

He released my lips and peeled himself from me, the pure joy in his face made me smile. "My sweetest wife, I pray you are feeling better. All day I have dreamt of you, your lips, and the things I shall do to you."

I blushed, though it touched me that he was so happy to see me. Being so spurned by Dumitru, his words set me on fire for him. I felt my smile weaken a bit at the thought when I replied. "I'm better, my love."

His brow ceased when he detected my true feelings. The back of his fingertips brushed my cheeks, the concern in his eyes so tender and heartwarming. "What is the matter? Why have you been crying?"

I frowned and resisted a sob. Ashamed as I was that I was showing my emotions too plainly on my sleeve, I knew I couldn't hide why I was feeling this way. Though I couldn't answer then lest my voice betray my raw emotion, and I swallowed hard.

The Count was shaken by my dejected expression, and he embraced me tightly. "My beautiful girl, please, tell me what has you so upset."

I buried my face in his shirt and held him closely. No matter how much Dumitru hurt me with his words, I could not tattle on him to his Master. Lost in thought, I only breathed in his scent.

"Isa?" My husband smoothed my back and implored me. "My love, please speak to me. Tell me what is the matter?"

So, I bent the truth slightly, explaining how Dumitru had seen my bruises and put two-and-two together, and I was embarrassed that he discovered our actions.

The Master listened as I professed my humiliation, and once I had finished, let out a long sigh. "I understand, however, the servants of a household inadvertently know much of the comings and goings of the lord and lady's bedroom. It is unavoidable, but there is nothing to be ashamed of."

I lowered my eyes from him. His words brought me no comfort, nor did it concern him that the whole house knew about our relations within minutes of Dumitru leaving my room. There is no real way we can hide what we do, and honestly, we shouldn't have to. We are married, we love one another, and our relations were consensual. Dumitru's knowledge of how intimate the Master and I are could never be easily hidden.

"Tell me how I may make this better for you, and I shall do it." He proclaimed when I hadn't answered him.

I shook my head. "There's nothing for you to do, only love me."

"I will do that and more, beloved." He took my chin and kissed me once, then brushed his nose against my cheek. "Before I whisk you away, there is another thing I wish to discuss."

"What is it?"

After a pregnant pause, the Count sighed. "I have decided Andreas' fate and I would like you to be there when I wake him. I hate to have you present, but it will keep him calm and level-headed, and he will listen to what is said. It appears he only listens when you are near."

I nodded. "May I ask what you intend to do with him?"

He sighed again, this time with more frustration than the last. "I have considered many things, but I must ask if you wish him dead."

I shook my head at his candidness. "No, I didn't even wish Imogen dead, nor any of the others. But they were dead in more than one way long before they came here. Do you want him dead?"

"Most definitely, yes." He shifted uncomfortably as that vein in his forehead pulsed. "If I were my old self, the right thing to do would be to impale him and let him burn in the sun, starved and in agony as an example to others. His manhood would be relieved from him, possibly his hands as well, if I felt particularly inspired that day. That would be a satisfying end..."

"But...?"

"But I wonder what is worse for him: to live knowing he lost his prize and his manhood, or to die most terribly but then not have to live with any of it at all." He mused as he studied our hands, which had locked together. "I find myself thinking of our conversation about forgiveness so long ago, and I am conflicted."

I was flabbergasted and had to blink a few times to comprehend his meaning. "You think you may forgive him despite everything you just said and everything he did?"

"Unless you do not wish for him to be forgiven?"

"Don't forgive on my account, forgive him on your own." I smiled sadly, even though I was so proud of him for considering leniency, and kissed his cheek. "I leave the decision to you, beloved, do with him as would a father."

The Master purred softly in my ear and requested that we go to bed. We retired to my room together, and he told me that he had asked the Monk to be the officiant over our marriage ceremony. The fourth Vlad is hesitant, as he is not ordained and does not have any sort of authority, but he is concerned about the effect it will have on his little brother. It took some persuading, but the Count said Vlad agreed to preside over it. I'm relieved, I wouldn't want anyone else.

Chapter Forty-Nine

REMAIN IN ME

21 January

After only taking a day to think things over, the Count decided his final plans concerning Andreas' fate. Last night, after he had made love to me significantly gentler than the previous times, but no less passionate, he revealed to me his intentions for the Greek. All he had told me in those few minutes before I had fallen asleep was that his judgment would happen the next day in the afternoon. This way it wouldn't be their natural time to be awake, and Andreas would be disoriented after his long coma-like sleep. Other than that, my husband told me no more. I had said I understood and then had fallen asleep.

So this afternoon, with the Count and the Monk at my side, and Dumitru following behind, I was led back down into the depths of the castle. Once we descended another staircase and passed through a heavy iron door, it was as if we had gone through some sort of portal into a real-life Hell. Once the Master of the castle entered the pitch blackness, the well-used torches burst into flame to reveal the scene.

The walls were roughly hewn by ancient chisel marks, which were sharp enough that one could cut themselves against the stone. Water gently trickled down them in some places, or dripped in others, and it echoed all around us. Being down there, it was almost like being buried alive, and I grabbed onto the Count's arm. He sensed my apprehension and rested his hand over mine in an attempt to reassure me. Instead of smiling back, my eyes were drawn to a series of doors that appeared in the dark. They were peculiar in construction in that their only feature was a bolted lock on the outside. Tarnished silver coated the exterior of the doors.

We three stepped aside, and Dumitru approached one of these doors and produced a set of keys. The hinges of this door were oiled, making little sound as it was opened. The other side revealed a well-polished sheet of brilliant silver. Both of the brothers had to avert their eyes and cover their noses from the pungent whiff of garlic that followed.

The design of this cell was ingenious to hold their kind indefinitely. In an environment where the only way out was through a door he could not touch, being deep underground provided no crack for him to slip out of, and the air which surrounded him was poisoned and burned his skin.

I watched as Dumitru entered the cell and lit a smaller lamp on one wall that barely shed any actual light in the chamber, but it was enough to see inside. On the bare floor, Andres lay motionless, the two stakes were still firmly planted in his head and chest. Dumitru then went to him, and in two swift motions, pulled out those stakes, and we all waited. Within seconds, there was a loud, painful gasp, and Andreas jerked awake. He coughed and wheezed as the tainted air entered him, choking him further while he rolled on the floor.

"Welcome back to the land of the living, Greek." The Count said once he stepped over the threshold of the cell, leaving me with his brother. From a few feet away, I could hear his own breathing turning raspy from the dried garlic that was hanging from the ceiling. "Did you have a pleasant sleep?"

Andreas' eyes shone as red orbs in the semi-darkness, and through his fits of panting, he hissed at the Master. The white of his deadly teeth flashed in the faint light, and in response, the Count dealt him an immediate and hard kick to the face. Andreas was sent back down to the floor, groaning in pain and subdued rage.

"One of these days, you will learn to heel, dog." The Master spat and kicked Andreas again in the gut. The Greek moaned and wheezed some more as he tried to recover, and at the sight of him, I did feel some pity. The Count crouched down to watch him suffer. "Such bestial behavior, especially in the presence of a lady."

At that, Andreas' head perked up, and his eyes strained to look toward the open door. He had to squint and blink, not sure if I was there. The garlic must have dulled his sense of smell, but after taking another whiff, there was relief that registered on his face, and his shoulders slumped.

"I thought that she would get your attention." The Count grabbed his collar to force him to sit upright. "Now behave, because she is the only one keeping you alive."

Pure hatred shone in the Greek's eyes toward his father, but he kept silent.

"Good boy." The Master mocked him, and even went so far as to pat him on the head as he would a dog. "Now hear me, son of mine, and listen well. Your little sister, that she-devil, has returned to the dust of this earth. Her revolution is dead along with her, and you are the only one left alive."

Finally, the Greek spoke with a hoarse voice. "If you think I care that she is dead, you're mistaken."

"Either way, it matters not." His First Father dismissed him flippantly with a wave of his hand. "You have no one left to help you, I know this for a fact."

Andreas' eyes narrowed to slits of glowing vermilion as he glared at the Master. "No doubt you have some other use for me, then. I wouldn't be alive otherwise, even if she wished me to be."

"You are correct, I do have another use for you." He admitted, although I know it wasn't all true from what the Count had said before about the Greek. "I want you to return to your den of vipers and relay to them the events here, accompanied by a warning that if anyone else tries to oppose me again, their fate shall be ten times worse than Imogen's. That is simple enough for you, is it not?"

Withholding his rage to lash out, Andreas snapped. "I am *not* your servant."

"Actually, you are. I am king to all my kind, even if some are degenerates like yourself." The Count clicked his tongue to chastise Andreas as a naughty child. "Of course, when you return, you may lose respect in the eyes of some others. I believe that is a small price to pay for freedom versus your death."

The Greek growled and his nostrils flared as the two of them stared each other down. "Even through this foul air, I can smell you rotting from the inside. You are weakening from the wound Imogen gave you, and soon enough, you will be a husk of your former self."

His outburst rattled me, and the Monk placed a hand on my shoulder to remind me to be calm.

Andreas then snapped his teeth. "Do what you will to me, but I will not be your lackey."

Little emotion showed on my husband's face other than annoyance. "You can send the message and live, or die. You choose."

The Greek chuckled and coughed in response. "I will leave and do all you say, *if* you give me Isadora."

"Master!" I cried out as the Count had brought his hand down, claws at the ready to slash through Andreas's neck.

He halted immediately, mere inches from his target.

"Please, let me speak to him in private."

It took him a moment to see through blinded rage, and when he had cleared his head, his voice was low and chiding. "You speak out of turn, my wife."

"Please, just a few minutes," I begged, and the weight of the fourth Vlad's hand bore down on my shoulder as he was warning me to shut my mouth.

After considering my plea for a few seconds more, the Count dropped his hand and straightened himself. He didn't want to leave me alone with one so diabolical as Andreas, but my husband knew the Greek wouldn't actually harm me in the end. Jaw tensed and forehead creased, the Master nodded. "Very well…"

I was astonished that he conceded to me and watched him wide-eyed as he and Dumitru exited the cell. Mitică shot me a terrible glare as he did, definitely to warn me that I was making a poor decision. I looked away from him to Andreas, as if I hadn't seen his signal for me to reconsider.

The Monk must have seen my reaction, for he whispered to me. "The Devil has many voices and many forms. Do not fall for what you know is deceit."

As always, he was right, and I nodded to him before entering the dank cell. The door remained open, though the faint glimmer of the small flame cast frightening shadows on the walls. Despite my friends being just feet away, I felt completely isolated with Andreas so close to me. He stared at me in wonder, his eyes flickering around my frame in awe.

"Koukla…" Andreas outstretched his arms for me to come to him, but I kept my distance. His smile turned to a straight line at my rejection, although he didn't lose the softness of his tone toward me. "I'm relieved that you're alright, I thought I was going to lose you."

"Andreas, I beg you to reconsider." I ignored his comment, which made me shiver, and focused. "He is willing to let you go, so take your freedom and run. All you need to do is tell the others what happened and live your life as you want to live it. What's so terrible about that?"

"It's more than *just* that." He wanted to reach for me, but retracted his hand. "I want to take you with me, away from him. Come with me, and I'll leave here and do all that he asks."

"Enough." I started to scold him, but remembered my temper in time. "Stop this charade. I have no reason to trust you after all you've done."

"After all *I've* done?" He scoffed, which caused him to cough a bit. "At least while I have been with you, I haven't been sleeping with other women. Not to mention, I never lied to you."

His words were cutting deep under my skin, and I retorted sharply. "We've never slept together in the first place, you idiot!"

"We almost did." The Greek had a faraway look in his eyes, like he was reminiscing about what he had done to me that day in the den. "He is a fool to deny you."

Looking back, I know he was baiting me to lash out, and unfortunately, I fell for it. "He doesn't deny me *anything*. If I asked for your head, he would give it to me."

The intonation of my voice caused him to pause, and his eyes darkened. "You said yourself that you don't want me dead. Frankly, my love, we both know you still desire what we have."

"Don't flatter yourself." I turned away from him, but stopped when my conscious reminded me to remember that things said in anger are often regretted. "You're correct that I don't want you dead. Even after all you've done to me, I have no grudge against you. Take the Master's offer and relay the news, and go in peace."

"I will not leave without you."

I shook my head with an exasperated sigh. "You only see me as your war prize, but this is a war you did not win."

"*Have* we lost?"

"Don't think you can trick me. Not now." After the spectacle that the Master had made of those who had opposed him, from ripping Petros to pieces to turning Imogen to dust, who could deny that he had emerged victorious in this fight? Andreas only wanted to plant doubts in my ear. I didn't look back at him and went to move toward the door. "I will ask the Master to give you time to reconsider his offer. Take it and move on with your life."

"He's dying, you know," he revealed, knowing it would make me halt in my tracks. "At least, he's decomposing. He may try to stop it, but whatever concoction Imogen used won't cease until it has consumed him. He's just delaying the inevitable, but one day it will spread to his heart, and from there, to the rest of him. He will be forced to go to sleep and be dead to the world forever, and you will be without him, and die without him."

I said nothing but felt my throat tighten. Shaking my head, I moved to leave, but was stopped again.

"*Koukla,*" Andreas' tone implored me to stop. "You know I'm telling you the truth. Help me escape, and I will take you far from here where you'll be free from this prison."

Swallowing hard, I shook my head again. The conversation was going nowhere, so with another long sigh, I said what needed to be said. "Andreas, there was never anything between us. You know that, I know you do, so don't make it out to be something that it wasn't. Spending time with you was an error in my judgment, and you preyed upon me. I consistently told you to leave me alone for your own sake. Your luck is running out, and I suggest you return to your life and leave mine. Have your answer by tomorrow."

The Greek continued to call out to me even as I had exited and closed the fortified door behind me. The three of my friends were standing there with their arms crossed with perturbed and disturbed expressions on their faces. My conversation with Andreas was easily overheard, and they had heard all of it.

"Will you allow him the day to reconsider?" I asked the Count as I approached him.

"Because you wish it, I will allow it." He affirmed over Andreas' muffled cries for me. The Master's jaw tensed again when the Greek's shrieking turned to slurs thrown at him, which were so terrible that I won't recount them here. Patting my shoulder, my husband told me to go to my room, and that he would see me shortly. I nodded and looked to the Monk and Mitică to gesture to them a goodbye. Dumitru was the only one who wouldn't make eye contact with me when I passed by them.

I was halfway up the final flight of stairs to the first floor when I heard a faint blood-curdling scream come from the depths. It echoed off each slab of stone and disrupted the hollow stillness. Without a doubt, it was Andreas' scream, and no doubt it was the Master relieving him of his manhood, just as he promised. So, I turned a blind eye to the scream and left the darkness behind.

24 January

Since the Greek had left a day ago, the feeling in the house has shifted back to the way it was before the children came to this castle. There is a lightness to the atmosphere inside and out, as if the sun has remembered to shine. The warmth that everything emanates is so life-giving, though it's midwinter, and it permeates all things in this place. The birds have returned and chirp in the snowy branches of the evergreen trees, and the other animals have come back to the valley. All the unnatural death has passed away, and a new earthly winter paradise has taken its place.

My husband's mood has changed with this passing, and he is the happiest I have seen him. With all the negativity that has been expelled from his life, he deemed that today, on the fifth-month anniversary of our marriage, we were to be married again. It would take place in the old family chapel, as that is the only sacred place that he and his brother could stand to be in.

This was a test of their faith and bodily strength for both of them. I feared especially for my husband, still weak from his shoulder wound, which has not healed. I feared that his existence would be terminated if this should push him to the extreme edge of his limits. Due to this, I spent the greater part of yesterday praying that the Almighty would show him mercy.

In the morning hours, I prepared myself alone for the ceremony. I wasn't sure exactly what to wear for this occasion since white was no longer appropriate for me. Luckily, I had a few hours to fret over the issue, and finally I decided to go with an ivory satin dress, which harkened back to the Byzantine fashion, embroidered with pearls. The veil was also ivory with gold threading woven around the edges, and to accent these, I decided to wear the rubies that the fourth Vlad had given me as a wedding gift, as well as the silver crucifix. I was so caught up in the haste to make sure everything was perfect that when I finally got to sit down and breathe before Dumitru was assigned to come and get me, I forgot to think about the bigger picture.

I sat there in my sitting room in my finery, staring into the fire, thinking about how I should be surrounded by my mother, my grandmothers, my sister, and my other female friends, but I was all alone. My father did not come to wish me well, nor was there any laughing or reminiscing about stories, nor last-minute advice. I was dressed in the most beautiful clothes, most precious jewels, but I felt empty without my family. May God forgive me for keeping them so far from me, even if it is for their own protection.

Luckily, before I got too glassy-eyed, there was a soft knock at the door, and it opened. Dumitru did not enter but remained at the doorway as he announced to me that I was summoned by the Master. When I went to him, he kept his eyes far away and would not even peep in my direction. Despite our tense relationship, I had hoped he would be just a little happy to see me, and it crushed my already broken heart.

Following slowly behind him, I could feel my emotions welling up in my eyes again.

When I sniffled, it caught his attention. He almost raised his eyes to me, but then suddenly remembered and lowered them. "What's wrong?"

I took in a steadying breath and tried to blink the tears away. Still, his eyes were off in the distance, his face emotionless, and I had to ask. "Why can't you look at me?"

"It's not my place anymore, *Doamnă*. Besides, if I don't look at you, I won't see you marry him." He pursed his lips and turned completely away from me, but put his arm through mine. "Come, the brothers are waiting for you."

I was startled by his gesture, but although I was hesitant, I gladly accepted it. Touching him again, feeling his warmth through his splendid clothes, it was a depressing reminder of how far away he is from me, and was about to be farther still. We walked side by side down to the chapel where the two Vlads had been waiting for us. The mosaic hall and the chapel were just as they had always been, except the musty smell had been replaced with the freshness of myrrh. It smelled like a church, and I took in a very deep breath as Dumitru released my arm.

The Count had been waiting for me at the side entrance, dressed in his traditional princely garbs, glittering gold with sapphires and pearls. When I approached, his eyes came to mine, and on cue, we both smiled at each other. He reached out his large hand and I took it, feeling with renewed senses the coarseness of his skin, but the gentleness with which he held my hand.

"You look so handsome, my love." I whispered in awe.

He purred and brought the back of my hand to his lips to kiss it. Just as he was to reply, Dumitru announced our presence to Vlad the Monk, who bade us to enter. With a squeeze of my hand, the Count led me up to the altar where the eldest Son of the Dragon was waiting patiently.

He wore nearly the same kind of robes as his brother, except his were a light silvery gray. Greeting us warmly, he wasted no time speaking. "I would like it to be stated for the record that I have no right to conduct this marriage under any law or jurisdiction, nor in any country or province. I am not an ordained priest in any Church, East or West, but I have studied for centuries the Word and the implementation of it. I know the words to say, but in this unprecedented case, it is between you two and God to fully undertake this union in His sight. Do you two understand?"

We both declared that we did, and with a nod of his head, the fourth Vlad turned to the altar and began to chant in Romanian. I watched in wonderment how effortlessly the Monk recited the words without pain or stumbling. His sublime, deep singing voice reverberated around us, filling the chapel with a sacred, ethereal beauty.

Instantly, the Count tensed, his body jerking slightly. He bore down on my hand, and using all my strength, I leaned into him to keep him steady. From the red sparking in his eyes and the quivering of his limbs, the pain began to roll like black storm clouds into him. Sometimes his brother would say something that offended the Master's body, and like a strike of lightning, he would jerk a little one way or another. While his body was trying to flee, he stood firm, leaning into me for support.

After a while of chanting, from the altar, the Monk lifted a crown, different from any of the other ones I had seen before. It was beautiful, much larger than its counterpart, which remained on the altar, and glittered gold. He went to his suffering brother, and after making the Sign of the Cross, placed the crown upon his head. Then he repeated the same thing to me, chanting in Romanian, and placed the sister crown on my head. At the proximity, I saw the sweat dripping down the Monk's forehead and how his irises would flash back and forth between red and their normal black.

Halfway through the ceremony, the Count was beginning to slouch as he breathed heavily. His weight was becoming too much for me to keep him straight, but on cue, Dumitru had already come forward. Shifting the Master off of me, my friend bore the burden that I could not, still keeping his eyes downcast.

Worry was etched in the Master's elder brother's face when he turned back around to see how pale his little brother had become. He eyed me nervously and was afraid to continue. In response, the Count snapped at him sharply in their native tongue to continue, and with a deep frown, the Monk wrapped a long section of embroidered cloth around our interwoven hands.

Slowly, the fourth Vlad continued, and I heard our names mentioned as he made another Sign of the Cross over his brother. The Master let out a low whine of pain, and his eyes had become completely red. I dread to even fathom what he was feeling, as he had once described it as his blood boils and he's blinded with hate. It must have been a thousand times worse for him, and my heart moved with such pity for my beloved.

Then the Monk came to me, and repeating the same Sign of the Cross, he said in English. "The servant of God, Isadora Louisa, is now betrothed to the servant of God, Vlad the Third Dracula, of the House of Drăculeşti, in the Name of the Father, the Son, and the Holy Spirit. Amen."

I was barely finished saying 'Amen' before the Count cried out in a burst of pain and lost his balance. Dumitru could not hold him, and we three dropped to our knees to keep him from falling. Fear overtook me, and I grabbed onto the Master's face for him to keep his head up.

"Vlad," I called his name over and over, but he was transfixed in some half-conscious state. "Vlad, look at me!"

"Brother, take deep breaths." The fourth Vlad instructed, and we all waited.

A few seconds passed before the Count blinked and refocused back into reality. My husband's eyes faded to brown and shifted slightly to my own, and just as before, his breathing steadied, and a peace came over his face. Relief flooded me, and I lightly kissed his lips and smoothed his dewy, waxen skin.

Our crowns were removed, and the Monk's hands replaced them. "Lord, your servants deigned to come before you against all odds to seek your blessing to be joined in your Name. They have heard the Word, and through Grace, you have made it possible. As it was said, 'remain in me, and I in you', and now they have become one flesh from two. Vlad, Isadora, you have done a thing no others have done, and now there is greater hope than ever before."

Taking his hand out of mine, my husband brought it to rest against my cheek, and I held it there. When he spoke, his voice was so weak. "Wife…"

"Husband…" I kissed his palm as the tears began to stream down my face. "You did it."

"We did it." He corrected me with a soft smile. "I promised you we would."

Not caring who saw us, my heart burst with love for this man who is my husband by heavenly and earthly law, and I kissed him deeply. My love had regained enough of his strength to be stabilized on his own, and he wrapped his arms around my back. When our lips broke from each other, we embraced tightly.

The Monk lifted his hands off our heads and, I heard him say. "And so, the past reflects itself in the present, and they become one endless, unbroken circle…"

And with that, our marriage ceremony was completed, and the Count had survived.

It's afternoon now, and just as a precaution, the Count has gone to sleep to recover from his trauma. His brother is staying to watch over him and insisted that I rest as well. Thank God for good men.

At sunset, my husband said he would come, so until then, I wait for him.

Later…

The Monk had dropped by after lunchtime to tell me that the Count was resting peacefully and that he was in no pain. Of course, I was relieved to hear that, but then my brother-in-law spoke candidly to me concerning his current situation. He relayed to me his sense of uneasiness that he had been feeling toward his brother over the last few days since he awoke, and had a suspicion that something wasn't right. Apparently, when he was helping the Count to undress from his garments, the Monk had seen that his brother's shoulder wound had grown exponentially since the previous time he had seen it.

When he asked if I had noticed that he had been concealing the wound from me, it dawned on me that he had been. Each night when he would come to me, he always had a loose shirt on which he would not remove, even when we became intimate. I hadn't really thought anything of it, and he had shown no outward signs of pain or discomfort. In fact, the Master had acted normally, as if nothing was ever wrong at all.

Vlad said he tried to say something about it to his younger brother, but he insisted that he was fine and that he was remedying it with herbs. Even if he was doing his best to cure his malady, it wasn't working. The copious amounts of herbs, blood, and sleep he had been using and consuming weren't enough.

"What do you suggest we do?" I had asked, fearing the answer he was to give.

"If what Andreas said is true, that he had never lied to you, then he certainly wasn't lying about what he said is happening to Vlad." He paused, raking a hand through his hair. "I don't know much about Imogen's skilled witchcraft, but I know she was very talented in her ability. Any cure died with her."

"There's nothing that can be done?"

"I can make some inquiries, but I don't think anyone will know how to help." He bit his lip, and without a doubt, he wanted to chew on his pipe to take the edge off his anxiety. "He is the first. He should be above this, but we all know he isn't."

Falling silent, the truth of what the Monk said settled in my stomach, making me nauseous. There was no use denying the facts, and I braced myself. "Will it be years or months?"

Vlad let out a long sigh, his head dropping when he admitted to me. "If he hadn't chosen to undergo today's ceremony, I'd say he would have years until it would have presented a problem. But, after what I saw this afternoon, he has months. If he continues to progress spiritually, I guess that he won't see summer."

That was a hard blow to bear, and I had to shut my eyes tightly. Frustration and despair welled up in my chest, and I choked out. "I just don't understand it. How did this even happen to him in the first place? What did Imogen do to him?"

The Monk's hand came to rest on my shoulder to comfort me. After a few moments of thought, he whispered. "Vlad confided in me to never tell you, but I shall: she lured him to the place she knew he would never return to and poisoned him with her black magic, then imprisoned him."

I raised my teary eyes to him. "Where?"

Vlad bit his lip again. "The land of the Ottoman Turks, our enemy for centuries."

The wind was knocked from me, and I sank into a chair, placing my head in my hands. Realizing the weight of all that the Count had endured, plus the added insult that Imogen had placed upon him, I could not fathom how he must have felt. What hell he must have suffered there, imprisoned just as he was when he was a young man? What tortured memories did he remember of how his father had been forced to give him and his younger brother up for the sake of Christian peace? And that little brother of his, how he had betrayed Vlad and his countrymen in the end and sided with the Turks.

All the things that had tormented him during his old life came back to haunt him. But, somehow, he had broken free from his chains and returned to his home to defend it yet again.

Oh God, I beg, ease his suffering of body and mind.

...

I had been replaying that over and over in my head for hours. After all the Count and I had been through, just as we got to a point where we are happy, Imogen steps in from beyond the grave to keep us apart. But this time, there would be no way to fight against her.

When it came time that he would come at night, I knew I had to see the extent to which his wound had grown. The only way to do that, however, was to make him want to remove his clothes, which I could easily entice him to do. After the sun set on the horizon, my husband came to my bedroom to see me, and I was waiting for him, wearing nothing under my night robe.

"I am relieved you have not gone to —" the Count stopped upon seeing my lack of clothing, and was immediately inspired by it. Slowly, he came to kneel at the foot of the chair, close to my knees, and purred as he kissed my hand. "You are bold this evening; I like it."

"I figured you would." I judged his appearance, and despite today, his complexion was rather peachy instead of the translucent porcelain it was earlier. "How are you?"

He nestled into my hand when I laid it against his cheek. "Very well, but a little tired. However, I would not pass up being with you tonight."

"I wouldn't either," I grinned, but then it faded. Leaning forward, I looked straight into his eyes, which shimmered in the dying light. "You did frighten me, though. I thought I was going to lose you."

"I am not so easy to get rid of." He reached behind me to pull my hips forward to the edge of the chair, and he came between my knees. "Thank you, though, for bringing me back when I had lost myself."

My body tensed at his wanting. Letting my muscles loosen against his unyielding hold, I allowed the robe to fall open for him to see me. "And thank you for what you've done for me, especially the things you didn't have to do."

"I would do them a thousand times over again for you, my precious one." He mumbled between hasty kisses as he made his way up my inner thigh and beyond.

In the course of our relations, I had managed to sneak peeks of the growing black wound. The Count had, to my relief, let me remove his shirt at my insistence, but he had bandaged it to cover the expanse of the area. He tried to keep my mind distracted from his upper half, but my eyes still lingered on the wrappings that covered his chest and over his shoulder to his back. There was a faint smell to it, but with his usual earthly scent, it was indistinct. Still, it confirmed what the Monk had told me, and what Andreas had warned.

When my mind cleared from its euphoric haze, it was near midnight. We were both on the floor, exhausted from our rounds. I was positively a mess, sweating even though my skin felt cool, and my muscles ached from my repeated exertion. My head felt heavy when I had regained my breath and had looked at him, who was already looking at me. The moonlight from the barred window cast over him, and until the end of my days, I will never forget how beautiful he appeared to me at that moment. "May I ask you something?"

Seeing my strange emotional reaction, the Count rolled over to me and nodded.

I had to hold onto his hand to find the courage to ask it. "If it were even possible, would you let me have your children?"

The Count's lips parted slightly in surprise, and he squeezed my hand tightly in return. "You need to ask such? We would have at least ten, and they would all look like you, pretty one."

"Ten?" I laughed once. "I can't even think up ten names."

The smile on his face diminished unexpectedly, and his eyes drifted to my lower abdomen. The atmosphere between us fell silent, and it turned my stomach to knots. With a knitted brow, I watched as he moved down my form to rest his head there, and he whispered to me. "Someday, even if it is not mine, some little one will find life in here. When they grow up, I hope they know the wonders their mother worked by creating life in the dead."

Emotion immediately burst from my eyes at those two sentences, and I choked.

He cooed softly, shushing me to soothe my pained heart. "Do not be troubled, my love. All that is meant to be, will be."

Without any hesitation, I gathered him to me, and we held each other. He purred in my ear as I cried silently. If I could wish for one thing, it would be that I could return to that moment and never leave it. Perhaps someday God will let us go there to bask in the pale moonlight together, the living and undead, for eternity.

Chapter Fifty

ARS MORIENDI

27 January

Afternoon...

For the last few days, despite the perpetual dread that seems to follow the Master of this house, things have been status quo. Nothing has gotten better, nor gotten worse. Perhaps instead of calling it a 'status quo', one should call it a limbo between neither here nor there. Whatever this go-between is, its weight presses down on my shoulders.

Along with that same weight, we all feel the constricting noose around the Count's neck, and we smile and carry on as if it is all well and good. When he leaves, it will be the third time I will lose him, and it will be for the last time. I try not to think about it, but it's all that haunts me. To prevent myself from going stir crazy, I have begun to do extra chores again to wear myself down. Then, when the

Count comes to me at twilight, I never deny him, and he never denies me. It is those times when I feel the most tormented. When I'm with him, I'm the happiest, but I know the end is coming near. I know we all are hastening to our deaths with every breath we take, and those breaths are ones we can never get back. My Vlad, with each breath I take, is slipping from me.

Today, I was at my unending scrubbing in the kitchen when Dumitru came in unexpectedly. I had tried to time it so that I could finish the floor before he came in to start lunch, but he had caught me in the act. Dumitru didn't look at me and stared down at the wet floor. "You shouldn't be on your hands and knees, *Doamnă*, it's not proper."

I scoffed at him and kept on scrubbing. "Since when have I ever been proper?"

"The Master does not approve of this." He came and took the bucket away from me, not batting an eye at my protests. "You shouldn't lower yourself to do my work. Besides, I was hoping we could talk for a moment."

I was confused by his sudden transition. All the same, I had to jump at any chance of talking since he had been ignoring me for a week, so I nodded. "I'm listening."

"I've been thinking if I should say this, but I know I must," Dumitru mumbled after a long pause. "I would like to apologize to you for not believing that you love the Master, and that the Master doesn't love you. I didn't see it until I saw what you did for him at your ceremony, and how he endured the pain for you."

I was utterly shocked by him that, being still on the floor, I had inadvertently sat in a pool of sudsy water. I blinked at him until finally I pulled my wits together to reply. "In fairness, he didn't fully love me until recently, so you haven't been wrong all this time. We have been very private about it, so I don't blame you for being skeptical. I know you were only concerned for me."

He frowned, his eyes going farther away. "Do you accept my apology?"

"Of course I do," I tried to sound cheerful despite his distant expression. "Though, you shouldn't regret doing something you thought was right."

Nodding once, he walked out of the kitchen, taking my bucket with him. Just like he had come, silently, he had gone. Like he had done when I first arrived, he put up this barrier to keep me away, and now it has returned to stay. Each day that goes by, I feel Mitică becoming colder, and nothing I can say or do will make him warm again.

16 February

It has been nearly a month since I last wrote, and although I have no desire to write at all, I must for the sake of this record. I've been putting this off as I couldn't bring myself to write, as this record would have just ended up being a medical log of a patient's slow and painful decline. Only today, out of necessity, must I write again and record an overview of what has occurred before this date.

Oh God, let me be emotionless when I say these things because I can already feel the frog forming in my throat to burst into tears. I wish I could turn off feeling and be numb.

Now I don't know how to begin this. Where to start?

At first, it was the little things: small twinges of pain, weakened muscular strength, and mild irritability when the wound would ache. I grew to notice a pattern of events as the days went by, as to *when* the Count had these small occurrences turn into bigger problems. When he slept his death sleep, and drank the lifeblood that sustains him, his condition would neither better nor worsen, but remain steady. It was only when he was with me that he was caused such agony, but each night he would eagerly seek me out. It was when he would be face-to-face with the object of all that is against what he is, that the disease would sicken him further.

There was an occurrence once, when we were in the heat of passion, one second he was sending an endless current of satisfaction through me, the next he had cried out in a howling pain to the point that the demon revealed himself. He had completely transformed: his face deformed, fangs dripping with his own blood from where he had bit his lip, and the entirety of his eyes glowed in a mad red haze. Collapsing on top of me, his full deadweight pushed the air from my lungs.

At my closeness to his shoulder, I saw with my own eyes the black infection eat its way out from underneath the bandages that hid it, the veins throbbing as the blood began to flow in the opposite direction. He was still conscious but somewhat delirious, as his shoulder twitched, and he held in a cry. It took my poor beloved a long time to calm the demon and find the strength to raise himself from me. Since that time, he has had to wear a sling, and it has made him miserable.

When I asked him what he thought caused it, I could tell he used an excuse and said he had placed too much pressure on the joint. It was a lie; there was another reason. I speculate that, as the fourth Vlad had said, as long as he is advancing spiritually, he will only worsen. I believe he was feeling something then that was contrary to his nature, probably love or such, and with his demonic side weakening, whatever power he uses to keep the wound at bay is weakened as well. Before his injury, he could balance the combination of good and evil in him, but now they wage a constant power war, pitting his mind against his body. The Master chooses this path; however, he could decide to revert to his old diabolical ways. It makes me so proud of him, but so very brokenhearted.

In order to curb his advancing condition, I suggested to him that we should spend some time with his brother for a change of scenery. He grumbled about it, warning that it would be boring, but eventually agreed. So, we began using a portion of our evenings visiting the Monk and partaking in conversation. At times, I could see on my husband's face how much he would rather be playing around with me than wasting time listening to all the old family stories for the millionth time. Of course, I was enthralled by my brother-in-law's breadth of knowledge, experience, and wealth of stories told in dated American vernacular. But, like Andreas had said, I was only delaying the inevitable by doing this.

To try and add something positive to this list of negatives, a week ago, the brothers and I went on a walk one cloudy afternoon to try and lighten the Count's moodiness. The snow had melted significantly from January's deluge to where there was barely an inch on the ground. It was easy walking, and the fresh air and change of scenery were doing all of us some good. We were having a pleasant time, my arm in the Count's good arm as we meandered along, and chatted about what the land used to look like centuries prior.

The Monk was explaining something about the topography when a dark gray wolf suddenly emerged from the denseness of the underbrush and loped toward me. I was hoping to see my buddy, and I had lost all interest in the fourth Vlad's geography lesson when my wolf came up and licked my hand. I bent down to his level to greet him, and his slobbering tongue drenched my cheek with licks. Just then, a dark shadow was cast over us, and the wolf retreated a few steps, head brought low. Of course, it was the Master, and I rolled my eyes and pet my wolf anyway.

My husband glowered over us, very annoyed that I was showering my four-legged friend with affection. I ignored him, and the fourth Vlad made some teasing remark that his brother had been replaced by another man. That only served to rub him the wrong way, although it was enjoyable watching the Count stew over it.

On a whim, I asked him if I could name the gray wolf, and he grumbled back that I could, so I took my opportunity. "I think I'll name him Wolfgang, because he's a wolf and he's a part of a gang, get it?"

Vlad the Monk laughed once. "For that reason, I approve."

The other Vlad didn't see the humor in it, for he answered me seriously. "I do not believe that is what the name means."

I chuckled at the Master and smoothed my wolf's fur. "Either way, my quota of bad jokes has been filled for the year. But I'll keep the name."

After shaking his head, the Count finally conceded that the name was a good one, and we began to meander back to the castle, Wolfgang in tow. That was the only true time I had been distracted enough to forget about things, and when I remembered seconds afterward, it devastated my heart all over again.

...

So, this evening, Dumitru and I were summoned to the Master's study. I thought the brothers had gone to sleep for the day, but when I entered the room, the number of papers that were piled on his desk made me uneasy. It seemed they had been working for hours finalizing whatever they had been doing, and if Dumitru had

had the gall to look at me, we would have exchanged worried glances at the sight.

Upon the Count's insistence, we sat in the two chairs that had been placed next to each other in front of his desk, then waited in silence for someone to say something. My heart was pounding, and I tried to look to my husband for any indication as to why we were summoned, but he wouldn't look my way either.

"As you know…" He had begun, but paused and glanced down at his tensely folded hands. "My body, to put it as the Greek explained, is decomposing. However, instead of submitting to the sleep to which I am to be condemned, I wish to use this opportunity to die as I have desired for some time. With that, I agree with my brother's diagnosis that it will not be long now."

I felt a sob surge in my chest, and I quickly placed my hand over my mouth to hold it in. They all saw my reaction, but it was Dumitru who reached over to place his hand gently on my arm to comfort me. It was surprising that, after all his rebuke, he would perform such a gesture in front of his Master. I was touched and gratefully accepted it, placing my hand over his. That was the first time I had felt his warmth in many long weeks.

"I never thought I would have to do this so soon, but with my brother's help, I have made my last will. In it, since there are few mortals in whom I have placed my trust, both of you are the sole inheritors of all I have accumulated these centuries." With his good arm, the Count lifted a leather portfolio. "When it became apparent my children were to go against me, I understood that there was a possibility of my death occurring suddenly. Therefore, I had already planned ahead these things that I am about to tell you. They are all planned in your best interests, and I wish for you two to follow what I am to say, for it is my final will."

"I will do it, Master," Dumitru confirmed with a bow of his head.

I was anxious about what he meant to say, but I affirmed. "As will I, husband."

The Count nodded and gestured to his brother to take the portfolio in his hand. "I am glad to have young people as loyal as both of you."

The fourth Vlad took it, opened to the first page, and began to read in Romanian the legal jargon at the beginning. I listened the best I could, but my mind was so far away that it couldn't fully comprehend the highly technical words. As the Monk droned on, I saw Dumitru perk his head up, eyes wide, and he blinked in alarm. Of course, since I really hadn't been listening, I began to panic when he squeezed down hard on my hand.

Vlad the Monk had reached the end of a certain part, and sighing, looked at me. "Your Master has decreed that upon his death, this house and its property will be bestowed upon Dumitru for his years of devoted service to him. And, upon the Master's passing, Dumitru will assume his current alias of Count Vladislav Negrescu."

Even in English, my head could not comprehend the scope of what was said. My shoulders slumped, and out of the corner of my eye, I saw Dumitru go white as a sheet. I guess he hadn't expected this from his stupefied expression. Thinking back, I recalled the Monk saying he thought that the Count had been grooming him to become his protégé, his successor, and I suppose he had been right all along. It felt right to me that he should have this place after all his labors, and I smiled.

"Master, I couldn't…" Dumitru stammered as he held onto me.

"All has been decided." The Count said, and then motioned for his brother to continue.

At this, the fourth Vlad paused, shifting uncomfortably on his feet. "With this, Dumitru also receives the whole of the Master's holdings and other investments, under the condition that, upon assuming his legal identity, he signs a contract swearing that he will care for, provide, and protect *Doamna* Isadora. That is, because you are becoming the Master legally upon his death, you will be married to *Doamna* by law as she had been married to your Master."

The whole world fell away. I felt like I was spiraling down into some deep pit, and with the earth closing in around me, I couldn't breathe. My lungs were seizing in my chest, and I had to get away. Everything I heard wasn't real; it couldn't be.

"I could not…" I heard Dumitru whisper softly again before recovering some of his composure and correcting himself. "I should not…"

"You can, Dumitru, and you will. Many people who have had dealings with me have worked through you and have never seen my face. By taking on my name and this house, nothing would change in the eyes of the outside world." The Master's tone cut through the tension in the air. "I understand that this is unconventional, but such are the consequences of taking another's name. All I ask is that you be married for a time until other accommodations can be arranged if you do not desire each other's company. You may divorce or do whatever you wish, but only until you, Dumitru, can ensure that *Doamna* wants for nothing for the rest of her days. However, I would prefer that you two stay together in this house indefinitely."

We were both speechless, dumbfounded, because of this. So, Dumitru would rule over everything that is the Master's, including me. A part of me wanted to stand up and refuse, but I didn't know how to make words out of the war of emotions in my chest. I was still suffocating, drowning in feeling, and I hung my head.

"I will," Dumitru said, putting his fingers between mine, smoothing my shaking hand. "I promise you, Master."

I had had enough of being spoken about as if I wasn't in the room, and have decisions made for me as if I couldn't care for myself. I was furious that I was being traded off to another man as if I were an accessory to this castle. All the same, I knew the Count had chosen this to keep the castle together, and that I would not have to want anything in his permanent absence, but everything about it angered me. It shouldn't have to be this way in the first place, and just before my emotions overran my dignity, I promptly pried my hand out of Dumitru's. "I need air."

Hastily, I left the Master's office, accidentally slamming the door hard behind me. I didn't know where I would go, or what I was doing, so I went to the windows overlooking the mountain valley and opened one. The sharp chill of the winter air, in turn, opened up my lungs.

"Isa," the Count's dulcet voice came from behind me as his arm wrapped around my waist. "Sweet one, I know you are upset, but please, try to see it from my perspective. Dumitru has run this house under me for over a decade, and Vlad told me that you dreaded being in control while I was away. I do not wish this to be a burden to you."

I shook my head and roughly wiped my wet cheeks. "It's not that. I agree after all he has done that he deserves this, and he's the only one suitable to run this place. But, no offense to Dumitru, but taking your place doesn't make him you."

"You are correct that it does not make him me, but you two have a fondness for each other. To act as though you two would never get along is untrue." Dainty kisses started from my shoulder and were pecked up my neck to my ear.

Despite how frustrated I was, my neck had exposed itself for his mouth, and I wanted him to take me away from my torment.

With his lips close to my ear, he whispered. "You have a life and a family outside these walls. I do not want you to be tied down to this place, but I also want you to always be comfortable and protected when I cannot provide for you. This is the best way, beloved, you know I would not be hasty in something like this."

"I know…" Another tear accidentally fell from my eye, and I turned to face him directly to say. "But he is not you."

"My girl, such a gift you are to me." He littered my cheeks with slow kisses and brought me to his chest, which I wrapped my arms around. "I simply hope that you both will stay together and remain being good friends as you always have."

Slouching more as I was becoming increasingly crestfallen, I sighed. "We are not friends, at least, not anymore."

Brow furrowed, the Count eyed me strangely. "When did this happen?"

"A while ago, Master," Dumitru cleared his throat. He had come from the office and had been standing there watching us, completely unbeknownst to me. "It was no longer appropriate."

I felt the need to clarify further when the Master's expression fell in disappointment. "That's not to say we don't care for each other, and wish the best, but we no longer share a friendship."

"Master," Dumitru began when a silence fell between us three. "May I speak to *Doamna* in private?"

Eyeing me, I nodded once that it would be alright, and he released me. "Of course…"

I didn't watch as my husband returned to his office and closed the door to give us that privacy, but they most certainly could hear through the wall. Ignoring Mitică, I stared back out over the mountains, waiting for him to say what he wanted to say, and be done with it.

Dumitru dared to approach a few steps but stopped a few feet away. "Are you upset about what I am given or upset about what the Master has arranged for us?"

I sighed, keeping my back to him when I responded. "I don't have an issue with what he has given you. You may have this house and all that is yours with my blessing; you deserve it."

"It's me, then…" I heard the pain in his voice, and I felt so horrid inside. "You don't want to be married to me even for the convenience of it, even for a short time?"

"You aren't the issue. I just hate that this has to be…" I finally looked back at him, and he had this terrible expression of hurt on his face, and I knew I had caused it. He wasn't looking at me as I continued. "Besides, you shouldn't have to step in to provide for me when I *can* provide for myself. He's doing this to try to make things as painless as possible, but I cannot help but feel the pain every second of every day."

He winced at that, raising his eyes just enough not to look at me directly. "We both agreed to follow his last will, no matter what it would be."

"I didn't say I wouldn't follow it. If he wishes this, I will do it." I paused, hating the words coming out of my mouth. Pursing my lips, I sank into the chaise situated near the window. "But after he passes, what then?"

"You would stay here, of course, this place is your home just as much as it is mine." Dumitru took another step forward in my direction, again stopping short. "Unless…you want to leave?"

I simply shrugged, then mulled the possibility over. "I still have my flight scheduled to leave May first from Bucharest. Perhaps something can be arranged by then."

Mitică's brow knitted as a slight panic came over his features. "Must you go so soon?"

I shrugged again. "If the Master has passed before that time, it's a possibility. I don't want to be a burden to you any more than I need to be."

"But you aren't —" he burst out in bits of anxious sentences. "I w-want you to stay…"

"And when it comes time when you may wish to get married for real, what then?" I tried my best to convey that with enough sensitivity that he would understand my seriousness, and then added. "It's true that I care about you very much, I want you to be happy, but your commitment to me shouldn't stand in the way of that."

Dumitru frowned deeply, his hand raked through his hair as he tried to decide whether to say something that he knew he shouldn't. Just as he looked as though he was about to explode, he hurriedly sat beside me and whispered almost inaudibly in my ear. "I knew of his plans to have you married so you could stay in Romania. At first, he didn't know to whom, if anyone, so he asked my opinion about it. I…I said I would marry you, and he was jealous. If he weren't so possessive, you would have married me. At least I'm human, I'm your age, and I have a heart that *actually* beats —" He stopped himself short when he noticed his voice and emotions were rising. "If you can't bring yourself to marry me, I won't make you, but now you must if only for a while."

I was shocked that he had known about the Master's intentions for so long, but had said nothing to me. It must have eaten him up inside to know that he was so close to being with me, and yet so far. I wondered why he had been so silent that day we three went to Bucharest, but anyway, my heart moved for him who has endured so much because of my existence here.

"For his sake…" I repeated it to myself, then sighed heavily. "Listen to me when I say that I don't want to be alone when he leaves me, but by replacing you with him…it's just like you're in second place. I've told you I can't do that to you, it's not fair. You deserve to be first."

He had been keeping his distance from me even at his proximity, but then reached forward to grab my upper arm. "I don't want to be alone in this place, knowing you could be here with me, but you aren't because you think it's unfair. When, finally, we have a chance to start over, be what we dared, and you reject me for what reason? *You're* the one being unfair."

Was I being unfair? I thought I was being honest and forthright with my feelings, but unfair? What was the reason why I didn't want to stay here? It was obvious: I could not replace my husband with another man at the end of his fleeting breath, and be 'okay' with it. And this other man, no matter how much he loves me, is still just that: the other man. If I am being unfair to him, I can't see it.

So, I gave him the answer, which was tertiary in my mind. "You rejected me first. All I can think about is the look on your face the day you walked out my door and said we were no longer friends. How disgusted you were…" There was a pang in my heart when I remembered it, causing me to falter. "I accept that our friendship is over, and that all you have said to me is no longer true. Even if you did say I am still in your heart, that can mean anything. It confuses me that, knowing how sickened you are by me, you'd want me to reside here."

It was only then that he finally looked at me, our eyes locking, and the gray of his irises glistened like a brilliant silver as they turned glassy. Slowly, he released my arm, his eyes drifting downcast again. "I was not wrong to say it because it was the right thing to do, but every day since then, I have hated myself for it."

A frog developed in my throat, and I tried to swallow it to no avail.

"Isadora…" He breathed out my name, the first time in so long, and took both of my hands. Getting down on his knees, he implored me. "I beg you to stay with me after he passes. I will take care of you, and you won't need anything. I'll give you all the time you need to mourn for him, I'll wait years if I must, but stay here in this house with me and never leave."

The manner in which he said it shook my core. I have heard him sound desperate, but this was greater than that. He was pleading for me to remain, and the last time I had heard him beg me, he was at the mercy of his executioner's blade. How his eyes gazed at me was so heartfelt, but I didn't know if I could believe it. "You would be willing to be with me, even after everything?"

"I am willing to be much more to you, *especially* after everything." Again, that expression fell over his face that he wanted to say something he shouldn't, but he stated. "Please, let me do this for both of you as my last duty under his instruction, and for my love of you."

I tensed, fearing the Master had heard his confession, even if it was exactly what he wanted to hear. Looking down at Dumitru, he held his breath and waited in the void silence for me to answer him. *To be much more to me...*I gulped, tears blurring my vision as my heart was ripped to pieces. It was the Master's will, and I didn't have the heart anymore to deny either of them their wishes. "If you change your mind about it, you will tell me?"

Dumitru began to breathe again and ardently declared. "I won't change it, I swear."

I believe that he won't, and I resigned myself. "It is the Master's will, so I shall do it, for both your sakes."

He kissed both my hands that were clenched tightly in his own, and then helped me to my feet. Upon returning to the office, the brothers acted as if they had heard nothing. A contract was presented to Dumitru, as well as another affirming our union. In the sight of my husband and brother-in-law as witnesses, I signed my name next to Dumitru's, and with the Count's seal added at the bottom, all was concluded. The portfolio was closed, and the deal was done.

Later, evening...

I had been silent for many hours, sitting on the chair in my bedroom, staring out onto the vast forests, thinking about everything and nothing. I felt so many things, and they crowded in on each other into a muddled mess of emotion. It became so oppressive that I ended up sitting there feeling nothing. There was no sound other than the ticking of the clock, the whistling of the winter wind, and an occasional howl down in the valley. When dinner came, I had no stomach for food, and to my dismay, Dumitru had made some of my favorite side dishes. No doubt he made them to make me feel better, so I felt obligated to eat them, so I tried my best to swallow each bite and ignore my stomach's revulsion.

It took a very long time to finish eating. I was staring off into space when the choral howling of the wolves harkened the Count's awakening, and it snapped me from my stupor. I had just finished gathering the plates and utensils together when the Master arrived to see me. Before he could utter a word, I muttered. "I've been thinking about what you're doing, and it's an abomination to our vow to each other."

He was mildly put out by that, and his voice became bass. "It is a necessary evil to guarantee my legacy has not been in vain, that all

I have worked for is not left to follow me in becoming dust." He came to me, his face inches away from mine. "You are young and have only seen the changing of one century, while I have seen six. I have seen with my own eyes men's accomplishments become lost to time in under a generation. You, who are my descendant, will ensure I still live on through you and through the little ones whom you will bear. This dynasty will not pass away with me, which is why I place it in your capable hands."

I bit my lip, tears resurfacing. I knew he was right, I truly understood that, but I couldn't accept it. "But I only want the little ones to come from you —"

"Your blood is of my own, therefore they are already of me by you." The Count's tone was sharp with frustration. "That is a miracle by itself, Isadora. Do not waste it. Dumitru will perform his duty to the fullest, and you must as well."

My stomach twisted that those words were coming out of his mouth, and I snapped. "Vlad, this is an abomination."

"Isadora, I am dying and I love you." He took my arm to bring me to face him when I had turned away, I couldn't hear it, not ever. "If our roles were reversed, you would do the same."

I shook my head, though I agreed with him. "Abomination."

He furrowed his brow, and of course, he saw right through the feelings I couldn't grasp. "I can sense you are not angry with me, yet you feign it. Why?"

"Do I have to spell it out for you?!" I lashed out at him. "No matter how right it is, it's still wrong!"

The Master stared me down in silence. I couldn't tell if he was angered or was taking my outburst into account, but then he shook his head. "Do not make this harder for me. You are the only thing left on this earth to which I am bound, and if I know you will find happiness in another, be safe and well cared for in my house by a trusted friend, what have I left here to hold me? I ask you to remember that."

"Forgive me…" My fury dissipated in a flash, and I looked down, feeling ashamed for putting so much emphasis on myself. I wasn't the only one suffering because of this decision, and I hated that I had forgotten him. "I am making this harder. Do you think I'm being unfair? Selfish, too? All I want is for you to accomplish your goal, even if that means losing you. I don't care what becomes of me after, I'll figure it out."

"But I care, that is why I have done all these things." The Count kissed my forehead and brought his arms around my shoulders to hold me close. "And I believe that your distress comes from the fact that you do not want to admit to me, nor yourself, that you would be happy here with Dumitru. You want to be all he wants you to be, but to do so would mean leaving me behind, which I know you do not wish."

I tensed. Was that the reason? I have admitted to myself in the past that I have not had the purest thoughts about my friend. Lucifer had picked up on those and used them against me. Have I been training myself to suppress them, knowing they were a liability to my husband and me? It was a piece of myself that I haven't been so keen on recording here, nor showing to others, in case it would be used against us. "Forgive me for all of my unfaithfulness to you, body and mind…"

"I was unfaithful to you first in far worse ways." He began to stroke my hair to soothe me and rested his cheek against mine. "Do not be ashamed of how you have felt long before we were married. Once you came to me, you two did nothing immoral together."

"But with Andreas —"

"He used your love of me against you. He compelled you to make it seem like you were acting of your own free will." My husband placed his hand on my cheek, using his thumb to wipe the wetness on it away. Then, staring me straight in the eyes, the Count frowned. "Isa, I am not afraid of death because I have died before. I have seen what awaits me there, and I am determined to go as soon as I am able. I have given my material possessions away, and I remember that my steadfastness will lead me from this earth. I'm trying to die the good death, the selfless one, the one that professes I am only a man in the body of a monster, but a man all the same."

It was hard for me to fathom that all the time I have known him, he has always been dead, but not dead. He died centuries before I was born; he has seen Heaven and Hell, seen the coming of life and the going of death, and now it is his turn. Grief overwhelmed me, and I pressed my hand over his to hold him there, feeling the coolness of his dead flesh against my steamy cheek. "I will do all you ask of me, I promise, until that time when we meet again in a better place."

His eyes softened, and he leaned his forehead against mine as he searched for something in my eyes. I don't know what it was, but I kissed him and took his hand off my cheek to place it on my chest where my heart beats. The Count purred contentedly against my mouth but released it slightly to say. "You are still mine for now, sun of my nights, and I will give you my love each night until I am unable."

"I am yours, and you are mine." I brought my lips to his again, desperately seeking him. I had to have him, all of him, and I would not stop until I had consumed all of him.

Those are the precious moments with him of which I will not and cannot waste a second of. I cannot bear to think that within the coming weeks that my beloved one will cease to be, but because I love him so, I must let him go.

Chapter Fifty-One

LOVE AND DUTY

9 March

O nce again, I have been unable to write, unable to sleep. If I could list the number of things troubling me, the list would be longer than my arm, maybe even longer than me. I won't bother with most of them because they are insignificant. For now, I'll recount the key parts of my life in this castle for the last three weeks.

I forgot to mention it in my last entry because it seemed so irrelevant to me at the time, but Dumitru was not left the complete inheritor of all the Master's things. As my portion, which is a considerable amount, I am to receive the entirety of my husband's physical assets that relate to everything from jewelry to real estate, as well as art. I have been given accounts in Switzerland and Dubai, and properties in Bucharest, Braşov, Târgovişte, and Sighişoara, where the

Count was born. Outside of Romania, there are estates in Vienna and London.

With this in mind, I possess everything regardless of whether I decide to keep my side of the contract. Meanwhile, Dumitru is held accountable for his side, and if he fails in providing for me, his losses are far greater than mine. One would think this is unjust, but in the end, it oddly equals out. He owns the house, but I own what's inside it. He owns the external assets, while I own the internal ones. It's two halves that roughly make up an equal amount. Not that money means anything. In the end, it has no value to me.

All during these weeks, as was predicted and expected, the Count has been becoming progressively worse. The blackness has spread past his shoulder and halfway down his upper arm and is slowly creeping its way into his ribs. I fear that when it enters his heart, that will be the finishing blow, but it has grown in the opposite direction. I am thankful, but it only prolongs my love's suffering. I hate seeing him decline, even aging in the process. He appears in his early fifties now, with graying temples and a tired face, he becomes wearier by the day from the amount of pain he is in. The Master sleeps for a large portion of his nights and days to regain enough strength to function for a few hours, and then goes back to sleep. Despite this, he is still himself, smiling when he looks at me, and never ceases in his affections.

With his absence, I have been spending more of my time with the fourth Vlad and Dumitru. There is not much to do around the castle these days because of the efficiency with which everything is finished by the afternoon, so my friend and 'fiancé' keep me company. During this expanse of time, I've come to terms with my pseudo-engagement with him, and just being with another person is a comfort to me, so I welcomed his camaraderie. He still keeps his distance, though.

By the time the sun would set, and the fourth Vlad would wake, but my Vlad would not, we three would congregate in the parlor to chat. It was an interesting setting, since without the looming threat of the children's arrival, nor anyone threatening us in general, our topics turned to more personal matters. I learned many things about the Monk that I hadn't been privileged to before, such as that he's actually a professor of theology in some prestigious college in New England, and holds doctorates in numerous subjects.

On the other side of this spectrum, we talk about the darker parts of his life, such as how he has been ready to die since he had died the first time. He expressed to us that he has seen many things, gone to many places, and has had a full life, but is glad his brother has made this decision and hopes to be with his wives and children very soon. I've come to love my brother-in-law very much, and to live without him, or his brother, is unfathomable.

Other than these times, I pray for the Count and the rest of us. I pray his pain won't be so great when his hour arrives, that his brother will follow him in his salvation, and that Dumitru will have the strength to follow in his Master's footsteps. In the end, all I can do is hope, pray, love, and support my family in any way I can.

15 March
Ides of March
Dawn…

I feared the coming of this day, knowing its renowned past reputation. Sure enough, when knocks were being hammered on my door early this morning, I burst awake. My husband had not come to me last night, so I was the only one disturbed by the rude awakening.

Instantly, I sprang to the door, not caring that my hair was a complete mess, nor that I was only in my nightgown. My heart was in my mouth when I opened it, fearing the worst. The fourth Vlad stood on the other side and told me that the Count's wound was spreading; it was forcing him into sleep, and my husband had something to tell me. Fear entered me, and I had barely enough time to process his words when the Monk hoisted me into his arms, and the next thing I knew, it felt like I was flying. When the world stopped spinning around me, I was in the darkness of the family crypt. Vlad let me down and quickly went to his brother's open grave, motioning me to approach quickly. "Vlad, she's here."

"Isa…" The Count's hand came out of the stone to search for me, and I didn't hesitate to grab it. When my husband came into view, his appearance shocked me: he was shirtless, yet in the dimness I could see, to my horror, the wound as it was spreading deeper into his ribs. His breathing was hoarse, his skin was so ashen that it seemed translucent, and a faint red shone from his eyes in the dark.

My emotion overcame me, and I went to reach down into the flesh-eating stone, but the Monk put his hand up to stop me, warning. "Don't get too close. He hungers."

The seriousness of his tone was frightening, so I nodded, gripping tighter onto my husband's hand. "I'm here, my beloved, my moon of my days."

His gaze drifted around me as though he couldn't focus on my face, nor anything else for that matter. Once he found me in the haze of his vision, his speech was slightly slurred when he whispered. "Forgive me for not seeing you tonight…"

"Don't worry, you know I need time to recover from you." I tried to jest lightly, knowing it would cause him to chuckle.

However, he only made the smallest smile at it. "My girl, sweetest girl, how I adore you."

Pain erupted through him, which had been caused by the feelings associated with his statement. The Count gritted his teeth and squeezed down on my hand, his tremendous strength evading him, making that squeeze feel like nothing more than that of a normal man.

Tears did come to my eyes, and I kissed his knuckles, wishing I could kiss more of him to relay the same sentiment back. "This can't be the end, not yet, not like this."

"Not yet…" The Monk reassured me, but in his tone was a deep despair. Coming around me, he then bent down to recapture his brother's attention before he slipped into delirium. "You said you needed to talk to her about her commitment before you sleep again, do you remember?"

"Oh yes…" He breathed out, wincing at the wound. "How could I forget?"

I smoothed his hand, which had gone limp. "Please, husband, tell me. I'll do anything."

Blinking, he placed his eyes back onto me, a frown forming over his mouth. "I do not think I can keep awake much longer, so I will have to sleep. I will not awake for a few days, but before I go, I want to say something to you that I have been thinking about." He paused, the muscles in his hand flexing slightly to indicate to come closer. I did, going as far as the Monk would allow me. "My wife, the very second I am gone from this earth, your commitment to me is over. Your vow is only to the name, but it is a name you will share with Dumitru."

Tears overran my eyes, and I put his hand against my wet cheek, kissing his palm. My heart was breaking as I understood perfectly what he meant. All the same, despite being too hard to bear, I nodded. "I promise that I will never give up the name you gave me and my vow to it."

The Count's face relaxed, so I assume he was content with my answer. Then he moaned, his eyes rolling every which way. "I must sleep…"

"Keep the faith, little brother." The Monk reminded him before he removed the Master's hand from my face. I didn't want to let him go, but the elder brother's strength outmatched us both, and we were separated. I just managed to kiss his hand one last time before it was taken from me, and then the lid of his sarcophagus closed itself shut.

My head hanging, I leaned heavily against the lid's carved effigy, the cold of the stone seeping under my skin, cooling my blood. Finally, I could withhold it no more, and I wept because of how far he has declined in such a short amount of time.

The Monk's arm came around my shoulders, and he led me away from the scene. "Sister, I must say one more thing that's upsetting."

Shoulders drooping, I dreaded what other thing could upset me more.

"Forgive me for saying this, but for his health and your safety, you two should not be intimate anymore." It was an awkward topic, and he pursed his lips. "The exertion would only weaken him, and as he is already weak, it will tempt him to feed. He is not of the right mind to make rational decisions. I know he has not the strength in him to stand, let alone the deed."

Frowning, I found that I wasn't so upset about it that he thought I was. My carnal gratification is the very first item on my list of things I've set aside, not like I've been in the mood at all while my love has been suffering. "The deed means little to me when it comes to his welfare. It's a small sacrifice in the end."

"For you, perhaps, but having you means much more to him than you realize." The Monk frowned too as we left the cemetery behind, his eyes going downcast. "Stay near him, be always at his side, but at a distance."

"I will…" I promised him, then brought my arm around his back. "Thank you so much for taking care of him. I wouldn't know the first thing to do."

He smiled warmly. "I will do all I can for him. He will not fail, not after coming this far."

There is no doubt in my mind that my dear brother-in-law will not cease until his brother finds salvation. I believe both of them, not just my Vlad, have far exceeded others' expectations. With those two working together, anything can be accomplished. Both of them are tired of existing for so many centuries, and they both want freedom from this mortal coil.

24 March

Existence has been a drudgery. I thought that during those days when the Master rebuked me were the worst days of my life, but I almost wish I could go back to them. At least then he was physically well and strong, although very unwell and weak in other areas of his life. He awoke two days ago, in no better condition than he was when he went to sleep, perhaps in worse shape. The blackness had spread further, and today it entered into his chest cavity. There is no doubt that his heart was infected and is spreading the infection through him. I have been with him since he awoke, and it's obvious that his mind has been affected too.

The Count's short-term memory is becoming flawed, so that he becomes distracted trying to think about one thing and forgetting another. When he's been lucid enough, I talk to him about his aspiration to help remind him of it. I know he listens to me and ponders what I have to say, even though he may forget it the next day. His pain is on his mind constantly, and I hope that I'm providing him a little diversion from it. When the Monk isn't around, I dare to get very close to my husband and whisper to him the sweetest of nothings. I kiss him, and I know he wishes he could reciprocate, though his weakened immobility restrains him.

While the Monk has been my spiritual and moral support, Dumitru has been my physical one, always keeping by me when my brother-in-law sleeps. Rarely do I have minutes to myself, for where I am, Mitică is. If I move to the library to read, he makes up some excuse that he must dust something there. If I go to the chapel, he asks if he can join me. It's sweet of him, but I know he doesn't do it for my sake, but for his own.

Today, we were both in the kitchen cleaning up after dinner, and I was lost in thought about the Count. I hadn't paid attention to what I was doing and dropped a priceless china plate on the floor, shattering it. The funny thing was that I didn't notice the plate slip from my fingers, but it was the crash that jolted me back into reality. Swearing, I bent down to pick up the pieces, but with my dexterity being so shaken as of late, I accidentally cut my hands in a few places. They bled terribly, and that shocked me also. I remembered how my blood had poured like a stream when Imogen had bit me, and I was captivated by how it dripped so freely.

Dumitru cursed, and was suddenly kneeling beside me, driving a clean dish cloth into my hands. With his strength, he bore down on them to stop the bleeding, his expression distressed when we locked eyes. "Are you okay?"

"Yeah, I'm sorry, I wasn't thinking…" I lost my train of thought as I saw my blood be soaked up through the white cloth, and resembled the blossoms of red chrysanthemums.

"Isadora, if you're not strong for yourself, you can't be strong for him." Dumitru said after he had covered the sight from my eyes. With it blocked, my wandering mind returned to me, and my throat constricted as I wanted to cry for the millionth time, but he reeled me back from the edge of my despair. "Besides, I need you to remind me to be strong, too. Having you here reassures me that there will be a future after they are gone."

I felt terrible that I hadn't taken more of his feelings into account, rather than just focusing on my own. Nevertheless, his words touched me so deeply inside my broken heart, and they restored in me a small courage. "Forgive me for being selfish about it. I am in so much pain that I forget everyone else is too…"

"You're not selfish. You're human, just like me." He smiled sadly, then brought me to him, his voice lowered into a whisper. "You, of all people, know how important you are to me. So please be careful, my lily, and be strong."

Our faces were so close that I could see the individual flecks of gray shine in his eyes underneath his dark lashes. Cautiously, I leaned into him more, placing my head under his chin. "I don't know what I would do without you, my dearest friend. Thank you for reminding me."

I felt his lips on my hair as his hand stroked my back, and we stayed there for a bit. His being there was exactly what I needed, and I didn't even know I needed him. I had forgotten his warmth, or at least it had been so far from me, that I thought it was unattainable.

Perhaps there is hope for that imminent future without the Count in my life, and Dumitru has been the answer to it all along.

29 March

Late afternoon…

Sweet Jesus, grant me fortitude. I can't remember the last time I've slept. My body is exhausted and heavy, but my mind refuses to surrender to sleep. I have been by my husband for days, unwilling to leave him for a second. There is little time left, and I will not waste any of it.

Please forgive the choppiness of my sentences, because for once I don't care about their grammar or structure. All the same, I'll try to be concise and recall all I can. Let me think back, although I can't remember on which day happened what. Well, I'll try.

Since the Count was prone to an erratic need to feed, the Monk had given me a few drops of his blood to heal me. Knowing that the sight of my cut-up hands was sure to invoke the demon to the surface, we had to take every precaution to keep him calm and in control of himself. This was especially important since he would go between waves of intense hunger to no need at all. It did the trick, and the lacerations disappeared as if they had never existed.

In my last entry I had mentioned how my love was beginning to lose his recollection of the little things, but that was just the tip of the iceberg. The infection certainly did affect his memory, and the decline was quick, seemingly happening overnight. He started by forgetting English words, and the word would elude him like it was lost in a fog. Soon enough, he had forgotten structure altogether, and then me. It was as if his memory was regressing a century or two at a time, for soon he didn't recognize Dumitru either.

There were times my husband would look at me bewildered, other times he'd smile and call me Wilhelmina, and mix Romanian and English together. I'd play along, engaging in idle conversation in English as he could understand me, but couldn't answer in the same language. As the days dragged on and he grew worse, he'd call out for Ioana, sometimes his mother, and ask where his sons were. Sometimes he'd think I was Ioana, other times he'd ask me where she had gone. It was a painful thing to watch. Very rarely did he have moments of clarity. There were a few times he'd recognize me and say my name, but they didn't last long.

Each day, it was becoming more and more apparent that it wasn't a question of weeks, but of days. The Monk decided to bring in a group of Romani to help move him up to the chapel so that he could be reminded of his promise to himself. It did help, I think, for the familiarity of one of his favorite places helped him to relax. We made him as comfortable as we could, and now we wait for the end.

It was this day, around noontime, that a miracle of sorts occurred. Vlad the Monk was asleep, and Dumitru had gone to do some chores after staying with me for the morning. I was at my Count's side, holding his hand, dozing in and out of consciousness. It took all my endurance to keep my eyes open to watch him in case something should happen, but I guess I must have nearly drifted off when I heard a melodic, "Isa…"

My eyes fluttered open, and they met his, and I saw in them that he recognized me. Immediately, I sat up and drew as close as I dared. "Vlad, do you know me? Are you alright?"

"Of course I know you, my Isadora." He smiled weakly, even lifting his good hand to touch my face. Suddenly, his expression turned to confusion, and he muttered in perplexity. "I cannot feel the pain anymore."

I was shaken by his tone and that he was speaking English as if he had never forgotten it, but most especially that his fingers felt warm to me. There was a significant chill in the air, but was my skin that cold? Latching onto his hand, I kissed it over and over, so grateful to have a sliver of him back. I'm sure his loss of feeling was nothing to rejoice in, but at least his affliction had been lessened. "I'm so glad to hear it."

"Kiss me, sweet one." He begged me, and I didn't deny him, though I was careful of his teeth. His lips were chilled against mine, but his breath was tepid. Something was happening to him, there was no doubt, and my heart broke in my chest. Gently, I lay my upper half on his and pecked kisses on his cheeks, nose, eyes, and forehead. Vlad moaned softly, indicating to me that he was enjoying my affections, and remarked. "I had a dream that felt real."

I brought my fingers through his hair, then returned his gaze. "Tell me about it."

"I saw my father and my mother right here..." He gestured with his eyes over to a part of the chapel and paused, lost in thought for a moment before continuing. "And they were young, like when I was a boy. I thought I had forgotten what they looked like. They were happy, too, and they spoke to me, saying they missed Vlad and me. They want me to be with them soon."

Swallowing my tears, I had to force my composure. "That sounds like a beautiful dream."

"It was..." the Count grinned just a little, his eyes still locked on the places where the ghosts of his parents lingered. "Then Ioana was there, and she was young and happy too."

"Did...did she say anything?" My voice cracked terribly.

"She said, if I wanted, I could renounce my apostasy and be with her again. I said for her, I would do anything, but..." He hesitated again, those brown irises coming back to me. "Then she reminded me that if I did, I would have to leave you."

There was no way I couldn't withhold my tears after that. "What did you say?"

"That you do not want me to leave, and there is a part of me that does not want to depart from you." With his fingertips, he traced my facial features and tears as they fell. "But you are so strong; stronger in faith and fortitude than I could ever be. You would let me go if I wanted to leave this life."

"You've been too long without them, my beloved, and you shouldn't be kept from them any longer." I bit my lip to keep control of a sob and was compelled to kiss his lips again. "But no, I don't want you to leave me, but I love you so much that I want you to go.

After all you have done to get this far, you deserve it. Besides, remember, Dumitru will be here for me in your place, and I promised you I will stay with him."

A great sorrow came over him, and somewhere he found the strength to lift his head to take my lips in his own. My husband brought his hand behind my neck, forcing my head down harder to his mouth, where his tongue slid between my teeth. Heart soaring, I moaned against him, wishing we could join as one flesh one more time before he was to go. The Count surely sensed this, and he broke from our embrace, and our foreheads rested together. "You are the greatest gift to me. What did I ever do to deserve you?"

"You deserve me." Smiling, I cupped his face and was shocked at how warm his cheeks were that I flinched. On a double-take, I could have sworn it looked as though he was blushing or flushed, and it unnerved me. "Vlad, you're…you're really warm."

My husband hummed as if he didn't mind it, and that was frightening. He didn't seem to care that something inside of him was changing his dead form. "It is a strange feeling to be warm again. I had forgotten it…but I told you that you would burn me, did I not?"

Breath caught in my lungs as I remembered all those months ago when we had professed our fondness for each other. It was like a lifetime ago that we had been brought together by common enemies we didn't even know we had. Clearing my throat, I asked the Count. "And did you 'defile' me in the end as you thought you would?"

"Some would say I did…" He whispered after a moment's thought, as if it were a secret. "But I would say that my love for you is pure, and therefore it was not defilement."

Again, I was overcome, and my tears fell onto his cheeks. "Oh God, how I love you."

"And I love you most ardently." He kissed me and my salty tears. "Thank you for all you have done for me. Thank you for being the rock upon which I rebuilt myself."

"And I would do it all again for you." That is true. We walked through Hell together and were purified by the fire instead of being consumed by it. "Remember me when you are in Paradise."

The Count nodded as a tear overflowed his eye. This one wasn't bloody, but clear. "I promise you."

We held each other for hours, listening to each other's breathing, each one going in and out as time continued to fly. Its wings beat steadily as the ticking of a clock. It is certain, now, that he is to leave me at dawn. At the rising of one light, another will go out, and life will go on in kind as if nothing had happened. I had a strange thought then, when that entered my mind: even for immortals, time is too short in the end. There is never enough of it, no matter how much of it one has. It slips through fingers before one can grasp it and vanishes like a ghost before one can catch sight of it. It is eternal and ephemeral, a beginning and an end in an instant.

The Monk and Dumitru have arrived, and I have informed them of what is to come. The Master sleeps, and now that we know the time, we sit and watch pitiless Death draw near.

30 March
Good Friday

Before dawn, I went up to my room and quickly changed my day-old clothes into new ones. Exhausted as I was, I tried my best to appear presentable so that his last image of me would be a good one. I donned a deep blue dress of the Byzantine fashion. I braided my hair, situating my veil upon it, and I was ready. I stared at myself in the mirror for a few minutes, lost in my own reflection. Soon, this woman who was staring back at me, *Stăpâna* of the Castle Dracula, would be dead along with the man who had given her that title. I had never wanted to become this woman, but now I cannot imagine *not* being her. But, I accepted her death, I bade her a farewell, and turned away from my own likeness.

Returning to the ancient chapel, nothing had changed since my brief departure, and I went back to my husband's side. The Monk and Dumitru had been sitting on the floor to one side of the Master and stared at me since I entered. Dumitru, especially, gazed upon me with such intensity in his tear-filled eyes, but when I looked at him, he pretended not to have been.

"You are lovely, sister. He will be much pleased." Vlad the Monk smiled slightly, reaching forward to take my hand and kiss it. The gesture touched my heart, and I didn't let go of my brother-in-law's hand.

"I already am much pleased." The Count's eyelids then fluttered open to look up at me. It shocked me to see him awake, and a great dread entered my heart that it would be the last time I would see him open his eyes from sleep. My husband saw my sad expression and frowned. Weakly, he lifted his hand to take hold of mine, which was still being held by the Monk. "Lovely one, one as beautiful as you should never be so sad."

That only made me sadder, and I smoothed the skin of his large hand. "Forgive me, beloved, I never thought I would hate the coming of a dawn."

"Isadora, do not say things you will regret." The Monk chastised me with a hard stare that made me freeze. To everyone else, it seemed like a curious thing to chide me for saying, but I understood. Now, at the moment when the Count's hardest trial had begun, I shouldn't say anything that would jeopardize his success. I was the reason he had prolonged his stay here for a few more hours, and I shouldn't say something that would make him feel guilty for fulfilling his dream.

Slowly, I nodded, acknowledging my wrong.

Suddenly, the Count's face changed to one of breathless shock, and his chest surged upward. My shame was immediately forgotten as a strange wind rustled through the enclosed space. My Vlad breathed heavily and rasped. "The time draws nearer..."

Vlad the Monk shook too, feeling something we mortals could not. Dumitru came to support him instantly when his hand clenched his chest and he hunched over. "My heart..." But then the Monk's eyes widened, and he gulped. "My God, the curse..."

Frantically, I laid my ear against the Count's chest. I listened, and sure enough, a sound came from within it. I thought it was my heart at first, but the sound was steady while mine was pounding. I don't think my eyes had ever gotten so wide to hear that within his chest, a heart was beating. I could say nothing, being dumbfounded, but all that needed to be said was said through our eyes when we exchanged that knowing glance.

"It won't be long now." The Monk solemnly took his brother's other hand. "I must go."

Panic set in me at his words, and I exclaimed. "Go? Go where?"

"I must return to my grave for the last time and wait to be called." He responded calmly. "Little brother, let your heart no longer be at war, but at peace. I pray I will see you very soon."

My husband frowned, but then smiled and nodded once. "Until then, brother."

"Pride could not define how overjoyed I am to see you come so far. Not just you, Vlad, but you young ones as well." Grasping his brother's hand one last time, the Monk released him and stood. He was about to turn away when he stopped, turning his eyes to us instead. "Dumitru, remember my advice to you. And, sister-in-law, let your heart be at peace."

With those words, Dumitru and I watched as the Monk made the Sign of the Cross to the altar and left the chapel, each of his footsteps dying away. I wanted to run after him, knowing that I would never see him again in this life. A little voice spoke in my head then, and told me to take courage, so I remained in my place.

"Young ones," the Count caught our attention. "Help me up."

On our shoulders, Dumitru and I supported the Count's weight as he got to his knees.

The effort had left him breathless, and sweat dripped from his brow as he strained to remain upward. Facing the altar as well, he took in a deep breath. "Listen to me. When I had reached my end that day, I had fallen upon the battlefield, I had willingly drunk from the cup of death and suffering, thinking I did not need goodness to achieve all I sought. In my revenge and hate, I had fallen from grace, and I became a thing most abhorrent to the very people I had sought to avenge. I thought I hated everyone who was against me, but I only hated myself for my weakness." He had been looking down when he paused. I thought he had been speaking to us, but instead he was speaking to someone else, and then he raised his eyes. "My heart misplaced my anger and hatred and forgot the lessons my loved ones taught me. I forgot the faith that kept me steady when I was held by the Turks: the faith my younger brother forsook in his weakness, and the faith I did forsake for my own.

"I have fallen so far, never thinking I could be raised again. It took so long, and a taste to remind me of what I could have, before I could finally take a first step to turn back on the path I had so long strayed upon." My husband eyed me with a small smile. "And now, I wish to renew the vow I had broken."

There are no words to describe how I felt then, but I had no time to feel, only act. I understood what he wanted me to do, and so I asked him most candidly. "Vlad, I ask you, do you reject Satan and all his empty works and promises?"

"I do —" It was then that he cried out in great agony, and I expected the beast to emerge to fight against its death throes, but it did not. The chill in the air grew, and an eerie wind swirled from nowhere. I saw the pain begin to show on his face again, yet in the shadows of the fleeing night, I saw things move. I knew who it was even before the silhouette of horns manifested against the stone.

Wasting no more time, I asked. "I ask you, do you believe in God and the faith in which you were born, and which you fought to uphold against those who sought to destroy it?"

"I do!" He cried through tormented wails that sounded exactly like the wind, which howled like wolves before all went quiet. A dead stillness came over us when Lucifer had gone, rejected and cast out by his own son, and the Master's body heaved itself forward. His body was becoming unmistakably warm to the point where it seemed as though he were burning within from an intense heat. Groaning, he barely came back to his senses. "Let me rest."

Once we had returned him to his bedding, I saw definitively the full effect that his reversed apostasy had on him. He was flushed, his skin a true peach color, and his teeth no longer had their characteristic sharpness. Those eyes, which always appeared red when he was under stress, were simply brown. I could not believe my eyes that he was, in fact, human. The monster, the devil that he had been, had passed away, and he had defeated it.

My beloved peered up at me through hooded lids and smiled. "We did it."

"Yes, we did it." I tried to be happy, but all I felt was despair. "But now you must go."

He frowned, realizing that now his duty to himself and his kind had come. He examined his hands for a minute, and then, with a yank, removed his wedding ring and enclosed my hand around the gold piece. "Isa, give this to Dumitru."

I didn't want to do it; everything in my body said it was wrong, but I had made a promise. Taking Mitică's shaking hand, I slid the ring onto his finger. *Doamna* Dracula was no more.

While our hands were still together, the Master put his over ours and told us both. "Your services to me have ended, be faithful to each other, and love each other as I have loved and cared for both of you since you came to me, but far better than I ever could. Dumitru, you have been like a son to me. Forgive me for any wrongs I have done to you, I hope that I have righted them by this end."

Dumitru choked. "There is nothing to forgive, Master. Thank you for everything you have done for me."

The Master smiled and held our hands as he stared upwards to the brilliantly painted ceiling. His expression changed again, this one to panic as he whispered. "I grow cold again…"

From the windows, I saw the very first light of morning stream through the glass. My heart sank, and I bent down and kissed his warm lips. I had to say all I could before it was too late. "I love you so, moon of my days."

There were tears in his eyes, but he smiled at me again as his breathing grew strained. "Where I will go, I will prepare a place for you. When your turn comes, I will come to you. On that day, I will take you to where I am. I am with you always, until then."

Nodding, I caressed his cheek as the Count's breath was being choked from his lungs. His heart was probably the organ that failed in the end, and I watched as the life he had just renewed leave him. The sun broke over the horizon, and the rays of light shot in between the window panes. The sight, coupled with the softness of the morning, was morbidly beautiful. His face was peaceful as his muscles relaxed and let go of our hands. Just like Lazarus coming out of his opened tomb, from the darkness of death and into the light of life, he departed.

I sat back and looked up at the ceiling, and the faded faces of the saints almost seemed to shine anew in this new dawn. The spectacle was enchanting, but I abased myself next to the body that once held the soul of my love and pleaded to the Almighty. "Gather him to yourself, oh Lord, shelter him under your wing, and give him the true eternal life which exists only in you. Cast off from him Satan, and lead him back to yourself to rest for everlasting unto everlasting. Amen."

"Amen…" Dumitru echoed, and then I felt him touch my back. "Isadora, we must bury him quickly. His body is ancient and won't last in the open air."

I nodded once. "Do what you must."

So Dumitru disappeared, and I was left alone for a final few minutes with his body. It just appeared as if he were sleeping. I expected him to reanimate, or his eyes would flutter open again, and he would smile at me. All of that was just a cruel joke I was telling myself as I held onto his still-warm fingers.

Then Dumitru returned with a few Romani men and a wooden coffin that was obviously made of white oak. It was filled with garlic, and I looked away from it. I did not move when the faithful pallbearers lifted the body using one of the blankets he lay upon, and our fingers slipped from each other as he was placed within the box. It was nailed shut, and without a word, he was taken away from me. I impulsively wanted to stand up and follow him, but Dumitru helped me to my feet, which were awfully unsteady, and he led me up to my bedroom in silence. He helped me undo my cumbersome dress, and then he said he would be back after checking with the Romani. I only nodded and watched him leave.

Again, a quiet void came over the room. I was about to go to undo my hair when I saw a book open on my desk. I thought it peculiar because I never leave things out and open, and when I came closer, I saw it was the old book of Tennyson's poetry that I had put back in the library some time ago. I hadn't touched it in months. It was open to a certain page, and a few stanzas were marked off in pencil with a note that read.

In memory of our love and duty.

VD

When I read the three stanzas, I finally broke down and wept as a child would for the loss of my beloved husband. I am grateful that he, who endured insurmountable hate to love again, found it in the end.

Epilogue

ARS VIVENDI

1 May
Name Day
Noon…

I t has been just over a month since I have written here last. I had expected to put an end to this record with my beloved's death, but with this being the date that I arrived here one year and one day ago, I will update it to this day, and then never again.

    After taking a day to recover a little from my sorrow, I finally opened the letters my family had sent me back in September. There were other stacks that they had sent, about seven in total for each month that I hadn't responded. There were letters from the Romanian and American governments, and other family friends. Mostly they included what I had suspected: questions as to what had happened to me, the more personal ones asking if I was alive.

For the ones to family and friends, I used the excuse that in autumn there were very heavy rains which flooded the river, blocking the road to the closest city. Then, in winter, the same rains were replaced by a terrible snow, again blocking all routes to civilization. I ensured them that I was very well, and that in our isolation, 'the Count' and I had developed a 'close relationship'. Not so much of a lie, but little untruths that made up a truth.

Concerning the letters from the authorities, to my surprise, the issues about my unspecified criminal acts were resolved by some miracle. They were postmarked in mid-January, so I wonder if Imogen's death had something to do with it. She could have been compelling a few officials, but upon her demise, they were released from her control. They explained that there was some misunderstanding between government agencies, and I had been unlawfully accused for things which they had no grounds to prove.

A few times since my husband's passing from death to life I have dreamt of the Master. The first one I dreamt I was asleep in my bed when he crawled in beside me and caressed my cheek and hair as he watched me sleep. I stirred, reaching out to pull him to me, but when I did and opened my eyes, I was alone in my room. My arms were outstretched to empty air as if they were searching for him in the paleness of the moonlight. Heart crushed, I wept until morning. There were others such as that, but also during my waking hours sometimes I'd feel a chill and turn to expect him to be standing behind me. Every cell in my body could swear he was near, but if he was, my sight was too inferior to see him. I knew I couldn't be imagining these things, but if I am, they are sweet reminders that he is still watching over me.

During the day, I go and visit him and my brother-in-law often. Sometimes I'd talk to them about what I was feeling or problems that I had, and it was nice to think that they were listening. And at night, when I couldn't sleep, I'd go to see them. Perhaps that was excessive, but it was a comfort to my grieving soul to have him be near.

Spring had come ten days before he left, and now that it's May, and vivacity has fully returned to these mountains, life has also returned to this castle. I had never thought it possible, but now weeds grow within the walls, and one can bring flowers onto these grounds without having them wilt and die unnaturally. The birds fly near and perch themselves on the high battlements, and they sing. With regard to the wolves, they no longer howl at dusk to herald in their Master's awakening and have returned to their wild state. They still stick around, but I believe they don't recognize me anymore, not even Wolfgang. But that is how it should be, that is their wild nature.

To verify that the Master was successful in conquering his own nature, Dumitru used his newfound influence to send out a few Romani to places where his children were known to dwell and assemble. Sure enough, they were told by unsuspecting neighbors or acquaintances that he or she had died unexpectedly of what looked like a voracious flesh-eating disease. When the bodies were found, apparently, they had decayed to a skeletal state within a day or so. No one knew what to make of it, and with no family to contact, they were simply buried by the authorities. This same kind of story was repeated no matter how far Dumitru inquired: all of them had been brought low when the Count broke his curse. It is a bittersweet victory.

I know Andreas was among those numbers whose undead existences ended.

On the other side of the spectrum of these things is the relationship that Dumitru and I have developed this past month. It has been difficult for both of us, but as the Count had wished, I am giving us a chance to rekindle what we lost. We have been supporting each other, but Mitică has gone above and beyond for me. That late morning when he returned from ensuring 'the Gypsies' were properly compensated, he found me rather catatonic from my intense grieving. I know it frightened him immensely to see me like that, but I couldn't help it. I had been fine up to when I had read Tennyson's poem that the Count had left me. It had hit where it hurt the most.

According to him I was frozen to the touch, so he had lit the fireplace in my sitting room and carried me out there to sit close to it. I didn't feel cold, but the fire did warm me. Wrapped in blankets, Dumitru and I sat on the floor in front of the fire as he held me. I remember that he was exceptionally warm, and I felt his heat more so than the fire's, and it revived me by some miracle. As time passed, we eventually laid down, embracing each other in silence, listening to the crackle of the fire and each other's breaths. There, we grieved with no tears.

I recall staring at Mitică's hand, which bears the Master's wedding ring, I guess one could say it was really *his* ring now, and how it fit him quite well. But, to me, it didn't belong there. Since then, he has moved up from his quarters into the Master's private rooms, and although he deserves it, I feel they don't belong to him. Yet, over the weeks of closeness we have shared by healing with each other, we have been coming to terms with our new situation. I apologized to him for all the times when I had pushed him away, lied to him about this or that, or betrayed him in whatever way. He had, of course, said there was nothing about which to apologize because all that had happened here during these past months had been out of our human control.

In response to that, he revealed to me as he wrapped his arms around my waist. "So many times, I thought you were crazy to want to be with him, knowing what he is and what he could do to you. It frustrated me, but you were the final piece of his puzzle to salvation, and I had tried to come between you two. Can you forgive me for that, Isa?"

My heart melted when he called me by my nickname. "Like I told you before, you shouldn't feel guilty for things you thought were right. I wanted to tell you about his wish, but it wasn't my place..."

"I understand why..." After a brief pause, his arms were brought fully around my midsection, and he slowly pulled me to him. "Do you still want to leave?"

Staring into his eyes, I felt the anguish his voice resonated, and it hurt my heart more than I thought it would. "I promised the Master —"

He shook his head solemnly. "No, I...I mean, now that he's gone, do you still want to leave and divorce?"

I grew deathly silent, his words weighing heavily on my shoulders. He must have been wondering if I would make that move, despite our promise to each other and my vow to the Count. I hated that I had said and done those things to him when the Master told us his will, making it seem as if I didn't want to be around him. Despite having promised Dumitru that I would stay, he obviously hadn't believed it, so I hugged his neck. "My place is here. The castle has become my home, and to go back to the States, well, I don't think I would ever be happy if I were so far away from here."

"What about the other part?" He dug his face into my neck, bracing himself for the worst.

"The same goes for you, Mitică." I ran my fingers through his soft hair to soothe his torment, and then cautiously pecked a kiss on his temple. "I couldn't be happy somewhere else with anyone else. I promised you, too, don't you remember?"

"I just want to know that you're doing this because you want to, not because he said so. Not because of a contract or a promise, but because of the feelings we share. Maybe it's too soon to say these things, but by God, I want to be by you always. I-I want to sleep in the same bed and wake up next to you." His voice suddenly dropped, and a fervor spiked in him, making him lose his stutter. "My blood sets me on fire when you're near me. My mind wanders, and I want you, I want to worship you —"

"Mitică," I interrupted gently, laying my lips against his cheek. "You know that I love you so."

"I know, and I love you..." He breathed out, but then he raised his head to say in my ear. "And I know it's been only three weeks, but please, I need you. I only ask that I can be next to you, if only for a few hours. Please, Isa, my nights have never felt so empty."

I related to his feeling of emptiness too well, especially the nights when I would dream of the Count. Secretly, I had been wanting to seek Dumitru out all those nights, but hadn't the courage. Yet it struck me that he had been feeling the same way, but just like me, knew it was too soon to move on. A small, painful memory came to me of something the Master said to me once: something about how I couldn't admit that I would be happy here with Mitică. So, I whispered back to him. "Then I will stay with you for as long as you like tonight."

When night came, I went to his new room. We both were nervous, but I climbed into the grand bed anyway. I had never been in the Count's old bedchamber before, though I hadn't had much time to examine my surroundings before Dumitru had blown out the light. We lay there for a while until, drawn in by the heat of his body, I moved into his side. He had been waiting for me to come near and enveloped me in his arms. Surrounded by him and the blankets, my entire body unwound itself from all the stress it had held on to for weeks.

Quite a while passed, but he hadn't made any gesture to me to leave. He had specifically stated he wanted to do this for a few hours, but that time was far exceeded. I was quite comfortable and didn't want to go, but I still asked. "When do you want me to leave?"

"Never," Mitică muttered sleepily as he brought one leg around my knee.

My heart surged with emotion at that answer, so I took his hand beneath the sheets. I looked up at him, and our gaze met in the darkness. Slowly, gently, our lips met, and the ember between us reignited. We had never kissed each other in this way before, never had we sought each other's embrace without any hindrance. His lips were so warm as he kissed me places that only one other has kissed before. I stayed with him that entire night.

Since then, which was just about a week ago, we have dared to come closer together, spending even longer hours wrapped up in each other. However, I noticed in Dumitru a slight change as the date of my 'planned' departure approached. I believe he was becoming paranoid that I would leave, no matter how many times I swore to him I would not. I couldn't really blame him for being skeptical.

Last night, I was just finishing up some irrelevant things when he opened my door, which was slightly ajar, without knocking. It was unprecedented that he would come to me instead of vice versa, and that he was already in his bed clothes. Promptly, he got into my bed, on the Master's side. I followed him there, and with my arms encircling him, I pulled him to my chest so that he lay his head against me.

We fell asleep like that, taking comfort in one another's presence. Then, sometime last night, I was awoken by a chill. The moon was shining brightly through the windows when my eyes suddenly opened. I swear I had felt the Count near, but no one else was there except Mitică. Heart sinking, I turned my attention to my sleeping husband, whose face was nestled against my shoulder as he breathed softly. There was a slice of perfection in that moment as I watched him sleep so contentedly in my arms. I felt a love pang in my heart for him, and I kissed his hair. In response, he sighed and smiled in his sleep.

I haven't been able to sleep since then, so I snuck from his embrace and am writing this at my desk. Dumitru is still sleeping peacefully, and outside, the dawn is approaching. As I think about it, this past year I have had so many things taken away from me, but in return, I have been given so many gifts. I am grateful for the time I spent with the Count and the Monk while I could, and now I'm grateful for the time I will have with Dumitru. I love and have been loved, who can ask for any more than that? Now the sun has come, and with it, I end this account.

Julianna Mechowska

FINIS

"...

The slow sweet hours that bring us all things good,
The slow sad hours that bring us all things ill,
And all good things from evil, brought the night
In which we sat together and alone.
And to the want, that hollow'd all the heart,
Gave utterance by the yearning of an eye,
That burn'd upon its object thro' such tears
As flow but once a life.
      The trance gave way
To those caresses, when a hundred times
In that last kiss, which never was the last,
Farewell, like endless welcome, lived and died.
Then follow'd counsel, comfort, and the words
That make a man feel strong in speaking truth ;
Till now the dark was worn, and overhead
The lights of sunset and of sunrise to mix'd
In that brief night ; the summer night, that paused
Among her stars to hear us ; stars that hung
Love-charm'd to listen : all the wheels of Time
Spun round in station, but the end had come.
      O then like those, who clench their nerves to rush
Upon their dissolution, we two rose,
There — closing like an individual life —
In one blind cry of passion and of pain,
Like bitter accusation ev'n to death,
Caught up the whole of love and utter'd it,
And bade adieu for ever."
...

     Love and Duty
     Alfred, Lord Tennyson

AUTHOR'S NOTE

In February 2018, a much younger me was bored one weekend. I was in university then and had some downtime, so I decided to hop onto Netflix to see what was new to watch. On a whim, *Bram Stoker's Dracula* (1992) popped up on my "For You" list, and after some scrolling through, I decided to give it a try.

My generation of the late 1990s grew up with a plethora of vampire novels and movies inspired by them. I, of course, was no exception. The gothic classics always held a special place in my heart, and I loved to see different adaptations of the same stories come to life on paper and the silver screen.

The 1992 film had left me in a chokehold unlike anything I had ever experienced before. The Dracula of this adaptation was alluring, sexual, and dark, but throughout this film, I couldn't help but notice how spiritual he had been represented. It presented me with an idea, one that I couldn't shake: could the character that is Dracula seek his redemption? Would what is symbolically evil supplicate to God for their salvation?

For the next week or so, I couldn't get the story out of my head, so I read the original novel to see how the two compared. I was inspired then to put this novel to paper.

I finished writing this book in only six months. Through my finals, graduating from university, and starting a new job, I worked tirelessly on this story. Then, when it was done, I sat on it for months. A few of my friends were gracious enough to read it and give me feedback. I wondered if it would be good enough to publish, so I attempted it through the normal channels. Unfortunately, publishers were not interested in pursuing this work, and I was left feeling rather frustrated. It was at that point, with the 2020 Pandemic approaching in only a few short months, unbeknownst to the world, that I decided that this story was not meant to be read by anyone other than me. It would be for my eyes only.

Years passed. I met a wonderful young man, and he asked me to marry him. I hadn't told him much about my novel while we were dating. Not that it was a failure that I was ashamed of, but more that I was never one to discuss or share my interests with others. My then-boyfriend suggested that I try to publish it again, but I refused, saying it wasn't worth the time. I had mused about self-publishing this work in mid-2024, but as I was pregnant with our first child, it was very low on my list of priorities.

In December 2024, however, things changed.

I was eight months pregnant with our daughter when I was hospitalized with severe preeclampsia, a pregnancy complication that can cause death to both mother and baby. I was in the hospital for nearly the entire month of December on bed rest, and then in and out of the hospital during January.

I had a lot of time to think during those two months as I would stare at the four walls of my hospital room, or stare out the window over the university where I had graduated eight years prior. It was then that I thought about returning to this novel, but I was so ill that my heart couldn't bear the stress of lying in a hospital bed, let alone reading. My mortality was staring back at me, and there were times I thought that I wasn't going to make it. Twice, I had been in severe danger of becoming eclamptic without medical supervision. Those brushes with the fragility of human life made me think about what I would leave behind on this earth.

After I had finally given birth at the end of January, I knew I was not the same person. Physically, mentally, and spiritually, I had changed. There was a nagging little voice in the back of my mind that it was time to pick up the pieces of this book and put it to print. It didn't have to be perfect; it just had to be on paper. After what I had endured, all those nights when I lay awake wondering if I was going to live to see my child born, I owed this to myself. This is my magnum opus, and it deserves to be put to print.

And so, it is.

Julianna

30 May 2025

SELECT BIBLIOGRAPHY

McNally, Raymond T. and Florescu, Radu. *In Search of Dracula: The History of Dracula and Vampires Completely Revised.* Houghton Mifflin Company, 1994.

Stoker, Bram. *Dracula.* Introduction and Notes by Brooke Allen, Barnes & Noble Classics, 2003.

Stoker, Bram. *The New Annotated Dracula.* Edited by Leslie S. Klinger, introduction by Neil Gaiman. W. W. Norton & Company, 2008.

ACKNOWLEDGEMENTS

T his novel would not have been possible without the support of my mother, Diane, and my friends, Mindy S, Berenice S, Polina T, and Christinia B. Thank you for giving me the motivation in those early days to keep writing, providing amazing feedback, and for being so enthusiastic about this story. From asking when the next chapter would be out, to graciously filling out a questionnaire once this story was completed, you all sustained me when I thought I should have given up. Thank you to fellow author S.E. Fisher for your guidance in finalizing the printing and publishing of this work. Lastly, to my husband, thank you for planting the seed in my brain to revisit this novel and publish it. I dedicate this to you.

ABOUT THE AUTHOR

Julianna Mechowska is from Upstate New York and spent her formative years pursuing her interests in history and language. While attending college in New York, she studied English literature and French. She continued to obtain a bachelor's degree in linguistics with a minor in multicultural studies from the University of Missouri. There, she studied Latin, Russian, as well as Eastern and Western religions, the history of the English language, and classical antiquity. It was during her final semester there that this novel was written, when she was 23 years old. As a hobby, she studies Egyptology as well as fashion history and historical costuming. Along with this, she restores vintage Singer sewing machines and enjoys a quiet life with her husband and brand-new baby girl in the Midwest.

www.ingramcontent.com/pod-product-compliance
Lightning Source LLC
Chambersburg PA
CBHW021832010726

47493CB00005B/1356